The Complete
Virtues and Valor Series

by

HALLEE
BRIDGEMAN

Published by

Olivia Kimbrell Press™

Olivia Kimbrell Press™

COPYRIGHT NOTICE

Virtues and Valor Series Books 1 to 8

> Temperance's Trial, Virtues and Valor series part 1
> Homeland's Hope, Virtues and Valor series part 2
> Charity's Code, Virtues and Valor series part 3
> A Parcel for Prudence, Virtues and Valor series part 4
> Grace's Ground War, Virtues and Valor series part 5
> Mission of Mercy, Virtues and Valor series part 6
> Flight of Faith, Virtues and Valor series part 7
> Valor's Vigil, Virtues and Valor series part 8

PUBLISHED BY: Olivia Kimbrell Press™*, P.O. Box 470, Fort Knox, KY 40121-0470
The *Olivia Kimbrell Press*™ colophon and open book logo are trademarks of Olivia Kimbrell Press™.

Olivia Kimbrell Press™ is a publisher offering true to life, meaningful fiction from a Christian worldview intended to uplift the heart and engage the mind.

Some scripture quotations courtesy of the King James Version of the Holy Bible. Some scripture quotations courtesy of the New King James Version of the Holy Bible, Copyright © 1979, 1980, 1982 by Thomas-Nelson, Inc. Used by permission. All rights reserved.

Original Cover Art and Graphics by Amanda Gail Smith (amandagailstudio.com)

Library Cataloging Data
U. S. Library of Congress Control Number: 2015916471

Bridgeman, Hallee (Hallee A. Bridgeman) 1972-

Complete Virtues and Valor Series/ Hallee Bridgeman

598p. 23cm x 15cm (9in x 6 in.)

Summary: A team of women from diverse backgrounds but with a shared faith embark on a dangerous mission to help overthrow the Third Reich in Occupied France.

IDENTIFIERS: ISBN: 978-1-68190-023-0 (trade perfect) | 978-1-68190-085-8 (hard cover) | 978-1-68190-024-7 (POD)

1. Christian fiction 2. World War II 3. war stories 4. spies 5. historical fiction 6. espionage
PS3568.B7534 T941 2015
[Fic.] 813.6 (DDC 23)

Table of Contents

The Complete Virtues and Valor Series_____1

    Copyright Notice_____2

    Table of Contents_____3

    Dedication_____8

    Virtues and Valor Series_____9

Book 1

Temperance's Trail_____11

    Copyright Notice_____12

    Dedication_____13

Prologue_____14

Chapter 1_____18

Chapter 2_____23

Chapter 3_____33

Chapter 4_____45

Chapter 5_____53

Chapter 6_____60

Inspired by Real Events_____65

Reader's Guide: Suggested Discussion Questions_____70

Book 2

Homeland's Hope_____73

    Copyright Notice_____74

    Dedication_____75

Prologue _____76

Chapter 1 _____80

Chapter 2 _____86

Chapter 3 _____95

Chapter 4 _____99

Chapter 5 _____104

Chapter 6 _____110

Chapter 7 _____118

Inspired by Real Events _____123

Reader's Guide: Suggested Discussion Questions _____127

Book 3

Charity's Code _____131

    Copyright Notice _____132

    Dedication _____133

Prologue _____134

Chapter 1 _____137

Chapter 2 _____140

Chapter 3 _____146

Chapter 4 _____151

Chapter 5 _____161

Chapter 6 _____168

Chapter 7 _____172

Chapter 8 _____176

Inspired by Real Events _____181

Reader's Guide: Suggested Discussion Questions _____191

Book 4

A Parcel for Prudence _____195

    Copyright Notice _____196

    Dedication _____197

Prologue _____198

Chapter 1 _____201

Chapter 2 _____208

Chapter 3 _____216

Chapter 4_____222

Chapter 5_____230

Chapter 6_____236

Chapter 7_____241

Chapter 8_____245

Inspired by Real Events_____252

Reader's Guide: Suggested Discussion Questions_____256

Book 5

Grace's Ground War_____259

    Copyright Notice_____260

    Dedication_____261

Prologue_____262

Chapter 1_____268

Chapter 2_____277

Chapter 3_____282

Chapter 4_____287

Chapter 5_____296

Chapter 6_____303

Chapter 7_____310

Chapter 8_____313

Chapter 9_____319

Inspired by Real Events_____324

Reader's Guide: Suggested Discussion Questions_____330

Book 6

Mission of Mercy_____333

    Copyright Notice_____334

    Dedication_____335

Prologue_____336

Chapter 1_____340

Chapter 2_____344

Chapter 3_____349

Chapter 4_____353

Chapter 5_____360

Chapter 6_____368

Chapter 7_____376

Chapter 8_____380

Chapter 9_____384

Inspired by Real Events_____396

Reader's Guide: Suggested Discussion Questions_____404

Book 7

Flight of Faith_____409

    Copyright Notice_____410

    Dedication_____411

Prologue_____412

Chapter 1_____419

Chapter 2_____425

Chapter 3_____431

Chapter 4_____439

Chapter 5_____446

Chapter 6_____450

Chapter 7_____458

Chapter 8_____467

Epilogue_____473

Inspired by Real Events_____481

Reader's Guide: Suggested Discussion Questions_____487

Book 8

Valor's Vigil_____491

    Copyright Notice_____492

    Dedication_____493

Prologue_____494

Chapter 1_____500

Chapter 2_____514

Chapter 3_____522

Chapter 4_____532

Chapter 5_____539

Chapter 6_____545

Chapter 7_____549
Chapter 8_____558
Chapter 9_____565
Inspired by Real Events_____571
Reader's Guide: Suggested Discussion Questions_____574

References

Translation Key_____577
Cast of Characters_____591
About the Author_____593
   Personal Note_____594
   More Books by Hallee Bridgeman_____595
Hallee Online_____597
   Newsletter_____598

For Those Who Served...

THIS series is dedicated to the amazing women who have worked, planned, strategized, served, led, and fought alongside men throughout human history. Each novella is specifically dedicated to actual individuals who served heroically and at great cost. To read more about these true heroines, read the "Inspired by Real Events" section at the end of each story.

VIRTUES AND VALOR SERIES

Virtues and Valor series

DON'T MISS A SINGLE EXCITING STORY

SEVEN women from different backgrounds and social classes come together on the common ground of a shared faith during the second World War. Each will earn a code name of a heavenly virtue. Each will risk discovery and persevere in the face of terrible odds. One will be called upon to make the ultimate sacrifice.

Part 1   Temperance's Trial

Part 2   Homeland's Hope

Part 3   Charity's Code

Part 4   A Parcel for Prudence

Part 5   Grace's Ground War

Part 6   Mission of Mercy

Part 7   Flight of Faith

Part 8   Valor's Vigil

INSPIRED by real events, these are stories of VIRTUES & VALOR.

Temperance's Trial

HALLEE BRIDGEMAN

Virtues And Valor Series

Temperance's Trial

Virtues and Valor Series Part 1

a Novella by

HALLEE BRIDGEMAN

Published by

Olivia Kimbrell Press™

Olivia Kimbrell Press™

COPYRIGHT NOTICE

Library Cataloging Data
U. S. Library of Congress Control Number: 2014949655

Bridgeman, Hallee (Hallee A. Bridgeman) 1972-
  Temperance's Trial; Virtues and Valor part 1 / Hallee Bridgeman
    80 p. 23cm x 15cm (9in x 6 in.)
      Summary: The Third Reich Seeks to Extract the Information She Alone Knows

      ISBN: 978-1-939603-45-6 (ebook)

1. Christian fiction 2. World War II 3. war stories 4. spies 5. historical fiction 6. espionage

PS3568.B7534 T941 2014
[Fic.] 813.6 (DDC 23)

For Those Who Served...

THIS novella is specifically dedicated to Eileen Mary "Didi" Nearne and Florence Violet McKenzie OBE, aka "Mrs. Mac." To read more about these true heroines, read the "Inspired by Real Events" section at the end of Temperance's story.

Le Chambon-sur-Lignon, France, 1941

THE small but ancient church where the reverend André Trocmé preached his Sunday sermons lay dark and quiet in the middle of the peaceful French night. The light of a three quarter moon painted the still countryside silver and black and nearly every home had extinguished their candles and gaslights. Even the electric lights in the town square had been darkened shortly after sunset. To all appearances, the night would pass quietly and without incident.

Marie Gilbert woke with a start at the sound. She could hear the pounding on the front door from up in her room. She rushed out of bed urgently. Without turning on the lamp, she threw off her nightgown and quickly slipped her dress over her head. As she buttoned the top button, her bedroom door flew open and her brother, Edward, ran inside, going straight to the window and looking out into the back garden.

"Go!" their father ordered from the doorway. "Don't look back."

"Papa!" Marie cried as Edward put an arm over her shoulders and guided her to the window. "Come with us."

Her father adjusted his coat and buttoned it at the waist. His spoke directly to her brother, his tone ignoring her pleas completely. "Take her to Switzerland. Don't look back."

He straightened her bed and flipped her pillow over in case the authorities felt it. He didn't want to risk them detecting her body heat. He picked her nightgown up off of the floor and shoved it into the top drawer of her bureau before he left the room, shutting the door behind him.

Edward looked out the window again. Marie felt her stomach knot in fear. "Edward, how can we leave him?"

"Because he said we must," he answered almost impatiently before he pushed the window open and looked all around. The cool evening breeze filled the room and made Marie shiver. Whispering now he asked, "Can you make it to the tree limb?"

Marie looked at the branch that nearly brushed her window, remembering all the times as a child she and Edward had jumped from her window to the limb. The last time their father had caught them, he'd threatened to have the tree cut down if they ever did it again. "I haven't in years. I'm a grown woman now. I don't know –"

Edward held out his hand. "No time to waste. We'll go through the trees until we're in the Philipe's yard. Ready?"

Marie took a deep breath, and slipped a leg over the window sill. She looked down into the yard two stories below. Without hesitation – well, maybe with a little bit of hesitation – she reached her hands out and leapt forward.

The trees on the estates had occupied this land far longer than the houses they presently shaded. Their stout branches actually entwined. Marie and Edward moved carefully and as quietly as possible through the branches. In the dark, whiplike twigs scratched at her face and pulled at her hair, but she kept silent. Hearing a ruckus below, she paused just at the fence line and looked below and behind her, seeing the Vichy police officers and the Nazi Security Forces haul her father out of their home.

Biting back a cry, she met Edward's eyes. His face looked grim, but he didn't say a word. He just pressed his lips together and gave a harsh shake of his head, silently urging her onward.

They didn't climb down out of the trees until they arrived on the far side of Philipe's yard. Marie rubbed her burning palms against the sides of her dress. Silently, they dashed across the grass and over the fence into the garden of Edward's friend, Andre. In the far back corner, next to the stone fence, Edward knelt at the ground and removed a stone from the bottom of the pillar. He reached inside and pulled out a packet, quickly opening it and inspecting the contents.

"Here, take this," he said, handing her identification papers and a small cloth bag. They identified her as Andre's sister, Muriel, despite Muriel's age being closer to 30 than Marie's own 20. Inside the bag she found a blonde wig to cover her brown curls. With the wig on, the picture would match well enough, and at a glance the papers looked good.

"Do I call you Andre now?" she asked as he quickly pasted a mustache onto his clean shaven face.

"Yes, for now." He counted a stack of francs and shoved them into his jacket pocket. "I have a car waiting in Tence. We'll drive to Firminy then take the train to Geneva from there. Hopefully, it will be far enough away that they won't look for us."

They tried to leave no trace. Over fences, under cattle gates, and through the wilderness, they ran and hid until they reached Tence. In a barn on a farm on the outskirts of town, they recovered the car Edward had secured. The keys lay under the third nest from the right in the chicken coup. They pushed the car out of the barn and down the lane before starting the engine.

As they drove along the dark roads, Marie thought of her father. Tears burned in her eyes while she considered what might happen to him. But, she knew it was all in God's hands.

Their family had worked with many families in their town in sheltering Jewish children from the Germans. It wasn't something that brought her any shame or that she wished she hadn't done. Rather, it was something she wished she hadn't had to do. The evil treatment of the Jews ate at her soul and she felt proud that she could play some small part in saving some lives.

Still, they all knew the risk. Edward had spent months planning escape routes, hiding identification papers, storing money, securing a vehicle in case something like this happened. He knew one day the Nazis would come for them.

"He should have come with us," she said, leaning her head against the window.

Edward remained silent until Marie started to feel unsure whether he even intended to speak. Finally, he said, "You know we only escaped because he didn't."

"I'm just glad we didn't have any children in the house last night," she said, weary. She blinked against her burning eyes. "Now it's all just accusation without any substantial proof."

"God is good. Maybe they won't detain him since no children were there." He gestured with his chin. "There should be a canteen in the back seat."

"I just worry about who else might have been arrested," Marie said. She rolled her head on her neck then gasped. "Do I have any terrible scratches on my face? I don't want to stand out at the train station."

Edward looked away from the road long enough to look at her face.

"Nothing terrible," he said.

"Thanks." Reaching behind her, she grabbed the canteen. "Where will we go?"

"London." Edward reached over and squeezed her shoulder. "With Papa being English, maybe we can stay there."

"I'd rather be where he is."

"Of course you would. But, you must put that aside for now." Putting both hands back on the wheel, he said, "We both must."

CHAPTER 1

Chapter One

TEMPERANCE - Prohibition, moderation, or self-restraint, (especially in eating and drinking). Constant mindfulness of others and one's surroundings; practicing constant self-control, abstention, and moderation. Sobriety.

Outside of Milton Keynes, England, 1942

"TELL me what scares you the most," The cocoa skinned woman with the code name Hope insisted. Hope sat sideways in the pew inside the chapel on the training grounds so that she could face Marie directly. She kept her legs crossed at the ankles and her spine perfectly straight up to her long curved neck.

"Seeing my brother and somehow placing him in danger," Marie immediately replied. This group only knew her as Temperance.

Marie looked into the striking jade eyes of the famous musician and entertainer, Virginia Benoit. Like everyone else, she pretended she didn't recognize the beautiful black singer.

The seven women assembled in the room called this space The Chapel though the British engineers who had assembled the temporary building called it a multipurpose building. Still, this is where the women came to worship together three times a week. Twice weekly with a chaplain and the times like these when they gathered together to read scripture, pray for each other, sing a few hymns, and steal a few hours just talking in fellowship.

The room sported small plain glass windows, a pine wood floor, and simple whitewashed walls. To the women sitting on the rough hewn and very functional benches which they referred to as pews without fail, the tiny building may as well have been Chartres Cathedral.

The American female pilot code named Faith, who looked no older than sixteen but could outfly any pilot Maria had ever seen, laughed. "Seriously? You're about to go to France and transmit radio signals with coded messages, receive radio signals with coded messages, all the while getting tracked down by an army of Nazi soldiers determined to capture you, torture you while they interrogate you, take no care whatsoever for your virtue, and eventually kill you, and your biggest concern is your big brother?"

Marie chuckled. "When you say it like that," she said, rubbing her arms, "I can't help but think of a number of things I am more afraid of now."

"Listen," The physician code-named Mercy interjected, gesturing with her delicate surgeon's hands and speaking with a very slight Scottish accent, "eventually, almost all of us will be there. Even if we can't openly look out for each other, we can hope to be able to."

"We can't know they'll send us to France," the rail thin aristocrat assigned the code name Prudence observed.

"Of course they will. All of you speak French as if you're natives. That's one of the main reasons you were chosen," Faith said. "They ain't teaching you Dutch, that's for sure."

The chapel door opened and all heads turned to watch Major Charlene Radden enter the sanctuary. She looked sharp and authoritative in her forest green skirt and jacket, with medals and rank pinned to her chest and lapels. Her blonde hair had gray streaks running through it and fell in a straight line to her chin, giving her a regal look.

"Thought I might find you ladies and lasses malingering about in here," she announced. She had recruited all of them, working with each woman on specific skill sets, communicating with families on their behalf as needed and establishing cover stories, teaching and molding them under the rules of military intelligence. "I suppose my constant warning concerning you girls knowing too much information about each other continues to fall on deaf ears. One wonders if that deliberate deafness will logically lead to dead ears in the field."

"We need sisters on the ground, Charlene. I think you know that." Prudence had somehow discovered Charlene's espionage background and knew something about her actions as a teenage girl in the first great war.

"Stuff and nonsense. You pose a risk for yourself and your 'sisters'," Charlene announced, purposefully stressing the word, "by ignoring the suggestion to keep your distance from one another other during training."

"All due respect, but until it becomes an order and not a suggestion, I for one will not refrain from this kind of fellowship." Hope spread her arms out. "It's what keeps me going, personally, knowing these girls have my back and I have theirs, that they pray for me and I for them."

A murmur of agreement spread through the small room. Charlene nodded. "That I understand, Hope, and I heartily approve of your relationships. I just wanted to make sure you Virtues understand why we say not to get too involved."

"So that under torture we couldn't reveal too many personal details about each other." The brilliant military strategist who had been code named Grace shrugged. She had olive skin, dark green eyes, and curly black hair. Her English wasn't perfect though her accent wasn't French, either. Something else. So far, no one dared ask. "I don't think you can scare us any more than we're already scared."

Charlene tapped her chin with a manicured finger. "Yet you're all still here just chatting away like it's high tea. Very well. Remember that. Admire that about each other. Take pride in yourselves. And know that we will be doing everything we can for you here on our end. There is a briefing in twenty minutes in the situation room. Do try your very best to arrive promptly."

"That doesn't sound promising," the woman code named Charity offered with a smile. She was a British housewife who had sent her three small children to the countryside to stay with in-laws until the bombings subsided. Charity could decode encrypted messages in her head nearly as fast as they could be written down.

Temperance felt her stomach tie into knots. She held her arms out. "Come. Let us pray together before the briefing."

They formed a circle, a bond of women, different ethnicities, different backgrounds, different nationalities, but sisters in Christ who came together under a common cause – to do the best they could do to help end this war.

⚜ ⚜ ⚜ ⚜

MARIE pressed the earphones tighter against her head and wrote the code currently transmitting at a rapid pace as quickly as her pencil would scratch the paper. Her instructor stood over her shoulder, making her nervous, but she continued working and tried to ignore her. Outside the thin walls of the temporary structure, she could hear a formation of trainees run by, but did not let the sounds distract her from translating the codes beeping in her ears.

"Stop!" The instructor said, hitting a button on her stopwatch. She looked at the numbers. "Absolutely brilliant," she said with an approving smile. "I think you nearly broke a record, Temperance."

Marie held up her pencil. "I think I nearly broke my lead, too."

"I'm certain," the instructor replied. She put a hand on Marie's shoulder. "You're the best I've ever trained."

"Thank you." She pulled the earphones off the top of her head.

"Charlene wanted to see you when you were done," she said. "I'll ring her up and tell her what your time was this round. She'll be impressed."

They trained on the estate of an earl. Temporary barracks housed the intelligence trainees and the manor home proper held the administration offices. Her radio training always took place in an unpainted Quonset hut that backed up to an improvised loading dock. Their communications gear, even the training rigs, resided in a steel safe on the back of what her instructor called a "lorry" whenever class was not in session. Stern faced soldiers solemnly guarded the safe day and night and the instructor had to sign for every part of a rig whenever it entered or exited the safe. Marie knew with a cold certainty that anyone trying to get at the gear without authorization could be shot dead without too many questions.

After returning her rig, she made her way across the training grounds' campus, around a beautiful fountain in the front of the home, and into the main hall that led to the administrative offices. She wore a dark olive-green wool jacket and skirt with a heavy brown leather belt on the waist of the jacket. Her khaki brown tie was the exact same color as her stiffly starched shirt. Her otherwise utterly unadorned uniform wasn't too much different from what the men wore , aside from the skirt of course.

Up two flights of stairs and down a hall to the third door on the right. With a quick rap-rap of her knuckles, Charlene bade her enter.

"You asked to see me, Major?"

"Yes, Temperance. Please, come in and have a seat."

She'd been in Charlene's office before, but the very masculine decor compared to the ultra feminine Charlene continued to surprise her. Heavy furniture, dark colors, absolutely no decoration – if Marie had just met her on the street, she would have assumed the older woman surrounded herself with fine china and delicate flowers. It made her wonder if the earl had prohibited certain decor changes to his home.

Marie sat in the heavy wood chair in front of Charlene's desk. Charlene rested her forearms on the wood surface and laced her fingers together. "I'll get right to it. It's time, Temperance."

Her heart immediately started beating a little bit faster. She licked her lips and tried to breathe steady. "Oh? So soon?"

"We've lost contact with the last wireless operator in area three. It's been a few weeks. It's time to send someone new. I know it's early but let's be frank. You're the best we've got and you're ready."

Cold sweat beaded her brow, but she nodded. "Okay. Okay. I can do this."

"Well of course you can. I have every confidence in you." She slid an envelope toward her. "Here are your cover documents. You are a seamstress named Marie Perrin. Memorize everything. You won't be taking it with you. In fact, it will be burned before you leave this office so take as long as you like." She gestured at the clock on the wall. "Faith will fly you into France tonight. Report to the north hangar at twenty-one hundred hours."

After thirty minutes, they burned the documents and then Charlene stood and held out her hand. "I cannot tell you the level of joy it has been watching you train, Temperance. With all my heart, I wish you godspeed."

"Thank you," Marie said, heart pounding furiously. "I hope to see you again."

CHAPTER 2

Chapter Two

MARIE brushed at her skirt and shifted her suitcase to her other hand. Inside her leather bag, her wireless machine sat hidden under her seamstress materials in a secret compartment. Stern faced and silent solders wearing white leather belts, white ascots, and deadly sidearms stared at her with cold eyes. She had never before even touched a wireless rig outside of the training Quonset hut.

The hanger felt balmy, humid. The seasonal rain had let up only about a quarter hour earlier and the night felt very warm. Shallow puddles covered the tarmac and the sky looked more gray than red with the setting sun. She checked the time for the fourth time in the last few minutes and tried very hard not to tap her foot impatiently. She longed to talk to someone, burn off some of this adrenaline, but the guards clearly had no inclination to make chit chat. Rather they looked as if they hoped she might try to remove the wireless rig from the hanger. Then they could just shoot her and go to bed.

With her wireless, she would hide in plain sight of the Germans who had taken up residence in Occupied France. She would receive information and transmit information, all the time having her location triangulated by German soldiers.

Speed was her weapon. The faster she could transmit, the faster she could decode, the less time they had to find her.

She'd made the clothes she wore by hand. In order to keep a cover as a seamstress, which would give her the ability and excuse to travel. She'd had to not only learn code, she'd also had to learn how to sew. She'd had a small base for it, but most things she'd learned from scratch. Personally, it had been easier for her to learn the code and how to operate the machine than how to master patterns, stitches, and fine knots.

She and Edward had arrived safely on English soil after a nightmare three-day journey. They hadn't even found a hotel to stay in first, but had gone straight to the British Intelligence offices in London. Edward had explained his background, his training in the police forces before the beginning of the war, their father's lineage, and his skills. He had only offered himself as a recruit, but Charlene had been there attending a high-level meeting and pulled Marie aside to question her.

Edward had protested, rather vehemently, but Marie lifted her chin and insisted that she could fight for her country, too. After two days of them arguing about it, her older brother finally, finally relented. He had pulled her into his arms and, with tears she pretended she didn't see, begged her to be smart, to be careful, and to stay alive.

They'd returned to the offices together, him taken in one direction by a uniformed man, her the other. Surprisingly, they'd encountered each other rather regularly during training, but they did not ever give away that they knew each other. Any personal information, if extracted from the right interrogator, could be a danger to them. It could also be a danger to their father, if he happened to still be alive and well.

Edward hadn't required the same level of training as she. He already knew ships from his time sailing during school, so they gave him a cover as a worker in a dock yard. She didn't know more than that. She didn't know what dock yard on what body of water in what city. Apparently, it was important that she not know. She only knew that in the chapel on the training grounds, in the first hymnal on the first pew, he'd left a leaf from a bush near his barracks. That had been their agreed upon symbol when one or the other of them left the premises.

He'd been gone for over a month now, and she longed to know if he was okay, if he was alive, if he'd discovered anything about their father. Of course, there was no way to glean that information, nor would she dare if she could.

Now she stood in a hangar waiting to board an airplane that would fly her into enemy occupied territory so that she could practice espionage against the evil giant spider that had cast an inescapable web over Europe and claimed it as its own.

"Well, Temperance. All set to go, then?" Charlene asked, coming from a side door in the hangar.

"I imagine I'm as ready as one can be," Marie confirmed, fingering a button on her blouse.

Faith walked next to Charlene, a jaunty lift to her step as always happened in the moments before she took the pilot's seat.

"You'll do great," Faith offered with her Texas drawl. She patted the side of a well maintained North American Na-16. The nose of the plane bore a painting of a large diamond in the center of a map of the state of Texas colored in the same red white and blue of the lone star state flag. Faith had named her airplane *Texas Diamond*. "Not enough seats to fly you tonight, old girl. Have to fly that fat girl over there. She's an Avro Anson 652 and just a tad younger but don't be jealous, now. I'll be back before you know it." She looked at Temperance and winked. "I'm going to do my preflight checklist."

Charlene watched Faith stroll jauntily across the hangar and said, "Now we're just waiting on Prudence. She's going tonight as well." As if on cue, the door opened, and Prudence came into the hangar carrying her own leather suitcase. "Ah, there she is now. I suppose I shall not have to dispatch the troops to hunt her down after all."

Charlene accepted a box from Prudence and spoke to her in low tones, then gestured to a table near a wall and said louder, "Please place your cases on this table, ladies. We want to ensure that nothing in there would accidentally give you away."

"You mean other than my wireless?" Marie weakly joked as she set her case on the table.

"Indeed," Charlene said with a smile. She made eye contact with the armed guards. "I think that will be all for now, lads. Perhaps you can wait for me in the smoking area out front."

The senior sergeant saluted crisply and his gravely voice pronounced a respectful, "Marm!" She returned the salute and they marched out of the hanger.

Charlene opened their luggage and looked through the clothes, ensuring that the bags contained no uniquely British items. She checked labels on clothes Prudence had packed and made sure nothing seemed out of sort.

While she did her work, Marie looked at her friend. She wondered, again, why someone of Prudence's obvious aristocratic background would even consider this type of service. Of course, she would never ask such a question. Instead, she took the woman's hand.

"I am glad we're going in together," Marie said.

"As am I." Prudence squeezed her hand. "I am somehow very much less anxious knowing we'll be in the same area."

"Everything looks good. Spit spot," Charlene announced, snapping the latch on Prudence's bag. "When Faith lands you must disembark very quickly. She'll come in with no lights, but the sound of the motor is something we can't disguise. If it wasn't for your wireless, Temperance, you'd parachute in. The equipment is too delicate to risk a bad landing." She pulled the bags off of the table and returned them to the women.

Temperance grinned. "Right. So, if I were to die parachuting in, you could get a new girl, but wireless rigs are important."

Charlene raised an eyebrow and with a single nod said, "Bob's your uncle. Now, your contact will meet you at the air strip. Assuming they received the message transmitted in code on the radio programme. If not, then you will be baptised by fire, as they say."

"Do you want me to signal when we arrive?" Marie asked.

"Your contact will take you to Praetorian, the director of that region, provided he hasn't been compromised at the same time as the wireless operator you're replacing. Praetorian doesn't know to expect you. He's flying blind at the moment. Without any communication we can't hide in radio programmes he may or may not be hearing, that is. Once you're there, accept any communiqué he needs to send, then go secure yourself and transmit all at one time." Charlene handed them each their identification cards. "These should withstand the most rigorous inspection."

Faith came from around the plane and shot them a thumb's up. "She's a fat girl so I'll eat up some runway getting airborne, especially with the wet out there. She has a lot of wing so I'm guessing she'll fly about like driving a boat. And I'm not terribly happy with the shape of that back tire but it's in spec. Barely. So, I guess we're all set, Major. Prudence? Temperance? Grab your saddle bags and climb aboard." She grinned. "Let's get this show off the ground."

"Ladies, be smart and be safe. Always. Godspeed."

Marie held out her hand and Charlene took it. "Thank you for believing in us."

"You've no idea," Charlene said, warmly squeezing Marie's hand. "I look forward to your return."

❦ ❦ ❦ ❦

THE twin engine Avro Anson 652 aircraft looked new inside though it apparently rolled off the line the year before. This aircraft had not been modified for combat. It had been intended for reconnaissance and courier work mainly on this side of the channel and had only recently been painted

OD Green. However, the interior remained bright factory yellow and smelled clean. They didn't feel cramped inside and they each spread out a bit after Faith got them airborne.

Marie looked at her friend Prudence, who sat on the uncomfortable flight seat, strapped in tight. She had her head turned away, obviously deep in thought. Occasionally, she rubbed the empty space on her left ring finger, as if remembering a ring that once adorned it.

Clearly, Prudence had no intention of chatting the flight away even if she felt inclined to shout over the sound of the engines. Knowing how scared Marie personally felt, she didn't blame her. She wished she could escape inward and get lost in some thoughts. Whenever she did, though, all she could think about was the night they had left her father behind.

"Hey ya'll!" Faith shouted over her shoulder. "We're getting our feet wet!" Marie knew they had just crossed the shoreline and now flew over the English channel toward Occupied France. "When we get our feet dry again, we might meet some Archie." When they crossed into France, they might become the target of some antiaircraft artillery fire. "Might want to go ahead and make sure you have your parachutes handy now. Though at this altitude, they wouldn't do much good anyhow. Still, never know."

The parachutes were useless below 500 feet. Even given the best of chances, the canopies would likely never get full should they have to bail out. Somehow, none of this worried Marie. Somehow, she knew God had put her exactly where she needed to be for now.

One of the worse parts about this mission would be the inability to check on him. She could only do her part to see to a swift end to this awful war. Then she and Edward could go home. Thoughts of her family kept her occupied until Faith's cry of "Feet dry!" nearly startled her.

By some miracle, they never came under antiaircraft artillery fire and no fighter aircraft chased them down. The light above switched from red to yellow. Faith started bringing them in for a landing. They'd have to disembark very quickly. The longer Faith kept the plane on the ground, the more likely they would be found out and the mission would be over before it began.

She clenched her hands together and bowed her head. "Please God," she whispered, but nothing else came out. *Please keep me safe, please keep me from being detected, please make me smarter and wiser and faster than them.* All of those thoughts collided in her mind until all she could manage was a mumbled, "Please," praying that God would hear what her heart cried out rather than what her mouth did not.

As the plane began descending, she looked up and caught Prudence staring at her. As soon as their eyes met, her blonde friend said, "I'm beginning to wonder if this was a wise decision after all. Do you suppose it's too late to change my mind?"

With the bark of a laugh, Marie said, "I think I know what you mean. The worse part is the unknown. If I only knew what waited for us..." The plane shuddered and Marie gripped the side of her seat. "Of course, we may not have to worry about it."

The plane shuddered again and suddenly hit the ground hard. Then, it rose off the ground, and hit again, staying down this time. They heard Faith shouting, "Graceful as a bull in a china shop!"

Marie felt her body strain against the restraints as Faith hit the brakes and brought the metal beast to a stop. The second there was no more forward momentum, Marie and Prudence both unbuckled from the canvas straps. They grabbed their bags just as the copilot rushed from the cockpit area to the door. He pushed it open to the nighttime of countryside in occupied France.

As Marie walked past the cockpit, Faith turned her head and yelled, "God be with you two."

Marie shot Faith a thumbs up then climbed out of the plane, followed closely by Prudence. Before Prudence even had both feet fully on the ground, the copilot had secured the door and Faith started taxiing away.

Marie looked around her, peering into the darkness, but didn't see anyone among the trees bordering the open field. "Come on," she whispered, "lets get away from the noise of the plane."

Holding their bags, they ran toward the tree line. Faith's plane flew safely out of range and the silence of the night settled around them. Marie leaned against a tree and listened, waiting.

"I wonder where we should go," Prudence said, looking around.

"I think we ought to give it just a minute," Marie said. Just as she said that, she heard the snap of a twig. Heart beating furiously, she turned toward the sound, the wireless in her hand suddenly feeling like it weighed five hundred pounds.

From behind the trees, three men appeared. They dressed simply, overalls and cotton shirts, looking like farmers. *Où avez-vous de deux venez?* The tallest in the group spoke in French, asking where the two of them had come from.

Marie licked her lips. "Avalanche," she replied in French, using the code word given to them by Charlene.

The man raised an eyebrow. "Seriously? Two women?"

Prudence stepped forward. "What is the return word?"

One of the other answered. "Pigeon."

Prudence nodded. "Very well, then. Kindly take us to Praetorian."

"Things must be going pretty badly out there if they're sending us two girls," the tall one spoke again.

Marie stepped toward him, until the toe of her leather shoe hit his boot. "It can and will go badly right now if you don't get us away from this field. Now, like Prudence here said, we need to talk to the Red Wolf."

He clearly didn't like it, but he didn't argue anymore. His companion reached for Marie's suitcase, but she pulled it back. "I can pull my own weight," she said. "How far to where we're going?"

"Thirteen kilometers. We'll stick to the woods until we just can't anymore. The further we are away from the noise of the British airplane, the better." The third man spoke for the first time. "Best step quickly. I want to get there within three hours and we have to get the pig."

He turned and started walking. Marie fell into step immediately behind him, with Prudence right behind her, and the two other men bringing up the rear. Marie had never been briefed on anyone with a code name of Pig and so she felt complete astonishment when the three men came to a halt and produced an actual pig on a leash. The pig grunted and snorted and the shortest man took the leash in hand and resumed his march.

They walked through the woods for at least four kilometers, maybe more. The lead man walked with confidence, as if he maneuvered through the French woods in the dead of night all the time. Every once in a while, the pig would root in the soft soil near the roots of a tree and the men would stop and look all around.

The third such stop, Marie asked, "Why are we waiting for your pig?"

The tallest man peered at her with a look of stark astonishment. "He is finding truffles!"

Of course. If the Nazis caught them in the woods in the dead of night, they could explain that they were hunting for truffles. Likely they even had a few truffles hidden away in their clothes to bribe their way out of any sticky situation.

Marie expected to feel tired after the first hour, but she didn't. Her nerves spurred her energy, and she had to hold herself back to keep from running past the man and encouraging him to go faster. If she were completely honest, the short breaks while the pig rooted around also helped. She saw Prudence appeared to be in as good of a shape as she.

When they finally stepped out of the woods, they walked along a dirt lane. The night was silent around them. Marie trotted ahead to catch up with the man who led them. "What happened to the last wireless?" She couldn't help but ask.

"At first, we didn't know. Information still came and went through normal channels. Someone on the inside got a message to us that they had him in the prison. We still don't know how long they were impersonating him before that." He looked her up and down. "I imagine it's smart to bring in a girl. Be a while before they reckon you're the new operator."

With a wry smile she said, "I suppose that's the plan."

He pushed his hat a little further back on his head. "Wouldn't want to be you when they catch you, though." He held his hand up as a signal to stop. The group immediately complied, and Marie and Prudence followed the lead of the men and stepped off the lane and into the dark wood line.

As they crouched behind the bushes lining the trees, a Zundapp KS750 motorcycle complete with sidecar and two German soldiers in it rambled by. As soon as it was all the way gone and all returned to quiet, the man who led them spit on the ground and shook his fist in the direction the Nazis had gone. Then he waved them forward and they kept walking.

Hours later, as the sun began to lighten the night sky, they turned down a lane that led to an obscure farm house. A younger man, maybe mid to late thirties, emerged through the screen door and onto the porch. He leaned against the porch railing and watched the group approaching.

He did not call out to them, nor did he speak until they all stood in the yard. He looked at Marie and Prudence with serious, tired gray eyes. "Names?"

Marie knew he only wanted code names. "I'm Temperance and that's Prudence over there."

He nodded. "Wireless?"

"That's me."

With his chin, he gestured at Prudence. "You?"

"Courier." She set her suitcase on the porch and shook her hand as if to work out a cramp. "And you are …?"

"Praetorian." With a sharp gesture he pointed to the door. "I have coffee and some eggs. I can make some tea if you prefer." He opened the door and let them precede him inside. The cottage made Marie think of her mother's parents' home – a very simple farm cottage with simple wooden furniture and threadbare carpets on the floor. He led the way into the kitchen, where a coffee pot sat on top of a wood stove. Pointing at the table, he said to them, "Sit. Rest a moment."

To the men he said, "Find any truffles?"

The tallest man nodded. "Three. You need anything?"

Praetorian shook his head. "I got a shipment lined up. Thank you. Your help is more than generous."

"Happy to help, Praetorian. Get us a message if you need anything else." The tall man tipped his hat at the women. "Good luck, girls."

He almost said it mockingly, but Marie refused to bristle. "And to you as well," she said with a sweet smile.

He likely intended his grimace to pass as a smile. He and his friends took their pig and left, leaving the two of them alone with Praetorian. He set two metal mugs on the table and poured each of them some coffee. In English, he said, "I am relieved to see replacements come in. We're in the process of planning a massive operation, and without communication with London, I didn't know we'd still be able to pull it off."

"Will I stay here?" Prudence asked.

"You will. I'll sleep in the barn. You will take messages from me and leave them in the hymnal closest to the aisle on the second row in the church in town. Temperance will retrieve the messages and leave any she has for me from London." He opened a cupboard and removed a heel of bread. "Rationing is tight. I apologize for the scarcity of food but as I said I have some eggs."

"No need to apologize." Prudence tore a small piece off of the heel of the bread and offered some to Marie. She followed her friend's lead and only took a small amount.

"Where will I say?" Marie asked.

"You are single?" he asked. He stared at her like he could see all the way through her, and she fought the impulse to fidget under his look. She wondered how someone so young could look so old.

"I am."

He nodded slightly. "There's a boarding house for single women in town. What is your cover?"

"Seamstress."

He nodded again and sat quietly for several breaths. "I believe that will be perfect. There is a good population in town that would require your services." He bent down and pulled a tray out from under the stove. Using a small stick he pulled out of the wood box, he drew a rough map in the ashes on the tray. "There's a bicycle in the barn. Take that and go this way." He drew and talked, telling her landmarks and directions. "It is eighteen kilometers. Let me see your identification."

She handed him the ID and he opened it and looked at it, looked at her, and looked back at it. "Shouldn't give you any trouble." He handed it back to her. "I'm going to give you a message to transmit. Once you're in your location, it will be up to you to secure places where you can use your wireless. There's a farmer on the way to town who is friendly to our side. He will likely let you use his property sometimes. Stop there on your way and let them know you arrived. Tell them Operation Marquee is still on." He sketched landmarks to get to the farm in the ashes.

Marie stood, understanding that Praetorian had just dismissed her. "Marquee. Got it."

"Also let them know that as far as we know, it's been 27 days since capture and to disregard any information received in that time frame."

Marie sucked in a breath, knowing that London thought it had only been 21 days. "Understood."

"Do not ever come back here for any reason."

Marie nodded. "I understand."

"I mean it. I don't care who is chasing you or what is going on. Do not ever come back here." He held out his hand and she put her hand in his. "Godspeed, Temperance."

"You, too, Praetorian." She turned to Prudence and put her arms around her. "Be safe. I hope to see you again."

He did not walk her to the barn. She left him and Prudence in the kitchen and went out on her own. She found the bike where he told her to find it and secured her suitcase to the back of it. As she pedaled off, leaving that farm house behind her, it occurred to her that she'd never felt so alone in her life.

Then she remembered – she was never alone. Whispering to God as she pedaled, she thanked Him for safe arrival and prayed for continued protection.

Chapter Three

MARIE thanked her new landlady and warmly wished her a good night. She carefully set her bag on the little bed and then looked all around the room performing a little inventory. Everything had been carefully prearranged. She had a chair, a bed, a small bedside table, a sewing machine table, two lamps and an electric light. Black out curtains covered the windows. A privacy screen leaned against the wall next to the window, folded up behind the sewing machine table. She had a small cast iron wood or coal burning stove she could use in the wintertime. The stovepipe unpretentiously ran directly up from the stove and out through the roof.

The building was old, perhaps two or three hundred years old. The room was clean and had been painted within the last three or four years. She set the single chair in the center of the room beneath the electric light and stood on it to inspect the hiding place in the ceiling. It was simple but quite well hidden. The electric light shone in the eyes of anyone looking up. She could store her wireless rig in the space with little effort.

Marie went back to the bed and opened the antenna for the wireless machine and set everything up to transmit. Transmitting from her room came with enormous risk, but she had never done it from that location and would make it very quick. She simply had to transmit a quick missive to London from Praetorian about the upcoming mission. She didn't need more than a few seconds. Simple enough to do it without having to pull out the complicated code book.

She dashed out the missive, then waited, getting a response almost immediately. As soon as the last tone sounded in her ear, she disassembled the equipment, boxed it all up neatly, and climbed on a wooden chair to reach the ceiling. Carefully moving the wooden beams out of her way, she slipped the box into the ceiling, then secured the beams again.

She hopped down and set the chair back in its spot. Looking closely at the floor, she inspected it to make sure that the chair hadn't left any scrapes that might give an indication that she'd had the chair in the middle of the room like that, giving a clue to anyone searching her room to look up.

Everything looked in order so she spread new material out on her bed and started pinning the thin papered pattern to the material. She listened to the street sounds coming through her open window to her third floor room and considered how perfectly normal everything sounded. The noises outside could have come from any French village on any regular day. Then she heard the sound of a medium duty military Opel *Blitz* truck roll by and the harsh German language of the soldiers riding in the back. It made her neck muscles tighten.

How would this all end, this war? Sometimes, she didn't see how it could possibly end. But no war could go on forever. There would be a victor. Only, which side this time?

Marie's father had served in the first great war. That's how he'd met her mother. He'd fallen in love and never returned home to England. If he still lived, he was doing his part to battle the Germans once more. Even though they dragged him out of his home in the middle of the night, if they had released him he would have gone back to his normal anti-Nazi activities. He would have secured Jewish children, hidden them in his home until he could get them out of the country or into other homes with passable identification. The threat of punishment or imprisonment, even death, would never stop her father from doing what he knew was the right thing.

Thinking of her father led her mind to her brother. She whispered a prayer as she worked, praying he was alive and well, wondering where they'd sent him to operate, and in what types of missions he participated. She caught herself praying for his safety, but she knew none of them would be safe until the Nazis were gone for good.

⛯ ⛯ ⛯ ⛯

THE pounding on the door surprised Marie and she let out a startled cry. The pounding came again, even louder and more insistent, and the scissors she held in her hand clattered to the table as she covered her heart with her hand. Her mind could not avoid taking her back to the very night she and Edward had fled from their home in the dead of night.

She looked around the little room. She had neatly made her single bed when she first woke. The trifold screen in the corner had no undergarments draped over the top of it. Her sewing machine in the center of the room stood ready. Most importantly, the ceiling beams above the screen were in place and did not look like they had been moved at all.

The visual inspection took place instantly and concluded within seconds. She quickly reminded herself not to answer to Marie Gilbert, but rather Marie Perrin. Since accepting that code name and her mission, nothing in her life was exactly as it appeared.

Running suddenly damp palms over her skirt, she went to the door and opened it. The sight of a German officer, a Second Lieutenant, made her heart freeze in her chest. Had they finally discovered her?

"You are the seamstress, are you not?" he demanded by way of introduction. He stood tall, a couple inches over six feet, and looked young for an officer. He had hair the color of straw and piercing dark blue eyes – the very caricature of an Arian leader in Hitler's army. His French accent sounded different than the accent she had heard from other Germans, though she couldn't place the discrepancy.

Trying not to sound as nervous as she felt, Marie answered, "Yes, *Leutnant*. I am a seamstress." She looked him up and down. "Perhaps you need a dress?"

He opened his mouth, closed it, then barked a laughed. "A dress? I like that, *Fräulein*. Very amusing." The smile completely transformed his face and made him look less formidable. Putting a hand over his heart, he gave her a stiff and short bow. "I am *Leutnant* Leopold Schäfer and I have an emergency."

"What kind of emergency?"

"An unexpected uniform malfunction. It seems I have lost a button." As his face flooded with color, he gestured toward the fly of his trousers.

Looking over his shoulder and seeing he was alone, she said, "Well, I can't sew it on while you're still wearing your pants. Bring them back anytime today. It won't take a minute to mend."

"No time for that. I have my promotion ceremony to *Oberleutnant* in twenty minutes. I cannot go to that ceremony with a button missing from my fly." He put his hands together like a child begging for a cookie. "Please, *Fräulein*. I am at your mercy. I beg you to help me. I am a desperate man."

Torn, not wanting to offend a Nazi officer but very much not wanting to help Germany either, she looked around again. "I'm very sorry, *Leutnant*, but men aren't allowed into my room."

"I am aware. I sought and obtained permission from your landlady before knocking on your door."

Marie raised an eyebrow. "How did you manage that?"

He smirked. "Must you ask?"

Of course. This man was a Nazi officer, a conqueror. He represented the military might of the entire Third Reich, of Adolf Hitler himself. Her landlady was merely a lowly French woman, a commoner. If she didn't want any trouble, she couldn't refuse. Likewise, how could Marie refuse to sew on his button right this very instant?

Fresh anger surged through her heart, but she did not let it show on her face. Instead, she stepped back. "Please come in, *Leutnant* Schäfer. Leave the door open, if you please."

He raised an eyebrow but pushed the door back fully open instead of shutting it behind him as he had automatically begun to do. Marie continued. "There is a dressing screen just there. Remove your trousers and pass them over to me but do not come out from behind the screen in a state of undress."

With the door wide open and the privacy screen in place, she could hope for some decency or humility in this situation. Not that any kind of modesty would protect her from a German officer who might have other intentions. Nonetheless, nearly two decades of social etiquette drilled into her by her father could not go ignored, even in a war zone.

While the German went behind the screen and began to disrobe, Marie looked through her jar of buttons and found a few that should work on his uniform. In a matter of seconds, he flipped his pants over the top of the dressing screen. As she reached for them, she couldn't help but glance up at the ceiling. Almost directly above the German's head, the case containing her wireless lay hidden in the ceiling.

"I am very happy you were in this afternoon," he announced from behind the screen.

"I'm sure you would have been resourceful if I hadn't been," Marie answered, threading a needle with dark gray thread.

"Are you curious to know how I lost a button on my trousers?"

"Dare I ask?" Uninvited images raced through her imagination.

He laughed. "I wish I knew myself. I left my room this morning in a perfect state of dress. Now, right before this important ceremony, I find myself out of uniform."

"One hopes this is the only time you lose your fly button before a military ceremony. I'm not going to be around all the time after all," Marie said, deftly sewing on the button that most closely matched the others on his uniform. He laughed again while she sewed. It took her less than a minute. With small scissors, she snipped the thread and lay the trousers over the screen again. "All done. Here you go, *Leutnant*."

"*Danke*," he said enthusiastically.

"Please, don't mention it." She crossed her arms over her chest and waited, listening to the rustle of clothing as he put the trousers back on. When he came from around the screen, he carried his highly polished boots. She gestured toward the chair facing her sewing machine.

"I will be out of your hair in just a moment," he said, sitting down. "I can't be late, after all."

"Of course. After he made the trains run on time, I imagine the *Führer* looks down on any officers who are less than punctual." Her voice remained very monotone.

He looked up at her sharply, staring at her with very serious eyes for a moment, his jaw set to speak something in anger before he apparently reconsidered and quietly said, "Yes, I imagine he does." He finished fastening his boot strap and stood. "How much do I owe you, *Fräulein*?"

Marie waved her hand dismissively. "Nothing. I'm happy to help, *Leutnant*."

"As a matter of principle I insist on paying you for your work."

"I'm afraid I must insist on accepting nothing from you, *Leutnant*." She walked to the open door and gripped the handle. "Congratulations on your promotion, *First* Lieutenant. I hope I have not delayed you too long and that you make it to your ceremony on time."

He stopped at the door and looked down at her. "Very well. At least accept my gratitude. Thank you, *Fräulein*, from the bottom of my heart."

She felt her cheeks flush with color as he rushed from the room. When she was certain he was gone, she shut the door and locked it, pressing a shaking hand to her suddenly nauseated stomach. She stared at the ceiling, where the wireless machine sat hidden.

"Dear God," she prayed in a whisper, thankful for whatever protection He'd just granted her. "Thank You, God. Thank You."

MARIE pushed the headphones tighter against her ears. "Come on," she whispered urgently. After several seconds of silence, she retransmitted the message and waited. A bead of perspiration trickled down her forehead and she closed her eyes and prayed. It was taking so long.

The longer she transmitted, the more time the Germans had to do the arithmetic. They would intercept her signal, intersect her frequency, triangulate the origin from more than one angle, and resect her exact location. The computations could be made within minutes. Say what you wanted about the German Army but no one could criticize their math skills.

The barn was dusty. The debris of four or five generations of farming this land occupied two stalls and livestock occupied three others. The stall she used appeared to be Marcel's hay loft. The smell of the hay always made Marie's nose itch. She had been here too long. When she had arrived on her bicycle the roosters were still crowing. It had to be late morning already.

Suddenly, a reply sounded in her ear. "That a girl," she uttered, guessing the identity of the operator on the other end.

Marie wrote as fast as she could then quickly dashed off a confirmation. With nimble fingers, she packed everything up into the bag, hid the equipment in the false bottom, then stacked seamstress supplies on top of everything.

When she stood, her stomach rumbled and she looked at the barn next to her, wondering if Marcel, the owner of the farm, would mind much if she just took an egg or two. Before she could even devise a way to ask him, his wife, Armelle, came around the corner.

"I don't want you here," she said without preamble. "You are placing my husband and I in danger."

"Marcel said ..."

With the wave of her hand, the older, stockier woman cut her off. "I do not care what that man said, *Mademoiselle*. It was fine when it was another man. We could easily pass him off as a farm hand or a neighbor come by to help. But you have no business here. Do I look like someone wanting a new dress or some socks darned?"

Marie pressed her lips together, and kept from replying that a new dress might make her feel better. She understood the woman's point. "Very well, *Madame*. After today, I won't come back."

"See that you don't."

Armelle glared at her while she strapped her bag to her bike and got on it. She could feel the stare right in the middle of her shoulder blades as she pedaled down the lane.

♙ ♙ ♙ ♙

NERVES danced in her stomach. She hated confrontation. She hated anger. Suppose the farmer's wife decided to turn her in to the *Gestapo*. Would they simply show up out of the blue in the dead of night in the company of the Vichy police? Would they pull her out of her bed as they had so many others in her hometown of Le Chambon-sur-Lignon? She had read in the paper that Pastor André Trocmé and Reverend Edouard Theis had both been brought in for questioning but she had no news at all about her father.

How had it all come to this? How had she ended up back in France exactly where her father didn't want her to be? She missed Edward and she very much missed her father. She missed worshipping with the other Virtues. She just wanted to go home. She wanted this war over and the Nazis gone so she could just go back home.

She pedaled along the country road and scooted closer to the road's edge when she heard the sound of a motor behind her. Instead of passing her, though, the vehicle pulled carefully up alongside her.

"Excuse me, *Fräulein!*"

Startled, she looked over and saw an armored *Kübelwagen* driven by First Lieutenant Schäfer. Her heart started pounding frantically in her chest and the front tire of her bike wobbled. She hit the brakes and put both feet on the ground, unconsciously laying a hand over her heart. She darted a glance all around, fearfully searching every dark corner and copse for Vichy, German soldiers, or *Gestapo* laying in wait, but it appeared they were alone on the road. "You startled me, *Oberleutnant*."

He stopped the *Kübelwagen*, killing the engine and setting the parking brakes in the same motion. He hopped out and jogged around the front of it to where she stood straddling the bike. He moved in a very precise manner, efficiently and with a total economy of motion. It was as if all of his movements were staged and well scripted in advance or he had rehearsed them for hours before executing them.

"I am so sorry to startle you, *Fräulein* Perrin." His voice rang out in the cool air, confident and baritone, and a little bit self-satisfied.

A man so precise was bound to notice any mistake. All she could think of was the wireless in the bag strapped to the back of the bike. Her hands went cold and she felt perspiration bead on her upper lip. "How do you know my name, *Oberleutnant?*"

His smile was handsome, despite his German Army uniform. Marie couldn't believe she even entertained the thought. "I made an inquiry of your landlady. She was generous to give me your name."

What was she supposed to do? Shake his hand? She needed him not to ask her any questions about her recent whereabouts or ask for an explanation of why she might be on this country road just now. Had they triangulated the position of her last broadcast? Was he just a decoy until a larger arrest unit arrived? How did she handle this?

"Well, it's nice to see you again, *Oberleutnant*," she said, trying to appear calm. "Did you make it to your ceremony on time last week?"

He held his hand out, and she felt inclined to take it. His palm felt warm, his fingers strong. "Yes, thanks to you." He smiled with even white teeth, his eyes crinkling up with laugh lines. "You are very beautiful, *Fräulein* Perrin."

Despite her circumstance, she felt her cheeks fuse with color. She felt her fingers tighten against his grip. "*Oberleutnant* Schäfer, I hardly think that is appropriate."

He finally released her hand and bowed stiffly. "You are correct, *Fräulein*. I apologize."

She gave him a slight nod but suddenly felt afraid that she'd offended him. Him, a German officer. "Thank you. I hope you don't –"

He cut off her panicked apology. "Of course not. I should have kept that thought to myself even though it is a fact."

He stood close enough that she could smell the earthy wool smell of his uniform. Marie felt her eyes lower as her cheeks grew hot. She noticed the mirror-bright shine on his boots before she heard her heartbeat thundering in her ears. Was this fear or something else?

He cleared his throat. "I have been searching for you, *Fräulein*."

Marie tasted bitter bile in the back of her throat and kept her gaze downcast. Had she gone too far taunting him about Hitler in their first meeting? Had a careless glance revealed the hiding place of her wireless? Had he sent a team of *Gestapo* to search her quarters while she had been away? Had she transmitted too long and been discovered? She relied upon her training and forced her voice to remain even as she prompted, "You've been searching for me?"

"Yes. I want to ask you. Would you like to go see a show with me?"

Was this some new euphemism for imprisonment and torture? Confused, she raised an eyebrow. "A show?"

"Yes. In a few weeks, Virginia Benoit will be here to perform for our *Oberst*, our Colonel. *Herr Oberst* is her biggest fan and we are all invited to see the show ... to lift the morale of the troops, you see. Tell me, *Fräulein*, do you know Virginia Benoit?"

Marie swallowed. Hard. How was she supposed to handle this situation? Never, in all of her training, was this brought up. "Of course I have heard of her," *and laughed with her and prayed with her*, though she kept that part to herself.

"She is from America, like me," he proclaimed, almost proudly.

She knew his accent had sounded wrong somehow. "American? Why are you here in France, then?"

He gestured in the air. "The call of the Fatherland I'm afraid. My father insisted I return a few years ago."

With wide eyes, she let that digest. "Do you know Virginia Benoit?"

"No." He chuckled, perhaps at her *naïveté*. "America is enormous. She's from a state called Louisiana in the deep south near the Gulf coast. I'm from Oregon a few thousand kilometers away on the north of the Pacific coast. Also, I understand the lady is a Negro. Perhaps you've heard that Negros and Arians hardly ever socialize in America. Still, it will be nice to hear an American accent again, I think."

His casual remark establishing his racial beliefs disgusted Marie and she tried very hard to conceal her loathing. She knew with an unshakable faith that God had made all men and all nations of just one blood. Every living person on earth was a son or daughter of Adam and Eve. The bloody Nazi campaign of terror relied on faith in a lie – a form of Darwinism establishing entirely separate races coupled with the notion Friedrich Nietzsche proposed, that some races were inferior while other races were superior. Hitler aimed to create a "master race," a race of supermen, by practicing enforced eugenics that either sterilized or eliminated the races Hitler deemed inferior.

In practically the same breath, Schäfer had mentioned his father. Thoughts of her own father rushed through her mind, and she once more remembered that First Lieutenant Schäfer was her sworn enemy. How had she forgotten that for even half a second? She could not let her thoughts travel too far down that road or else her expression would betray her. She had to lighten the conversation somehow. "I imagine you must feel very homesick at times, *Oberleutnant*."

"I am homesick." He put a hand to his heart. "It would do me a great deal of good to attend the performance with the most beautiful woman in the village on my arm."

"*Oberleutnant* Schäfer, I don't think —"

He held up a hand to halt her speech. "Please, don't say no, *Fräulein*. At least let me have a little hope by telling me you'll consider the offer. Besides, I still owe you for sewing on my button."

She would have to clear any action with headquarters. It was possible that she could collect valuable intelligence by accompanying the junior German officer. It was even possible that Marie, code named Temperance, could pass intelligence to Virginia Benoit, code named Hope, in person. Pressing her lips together, desperate to find a way to end this conversation, she nodded. "Very well, *Oberleutnant*. As you say, I will think about it."

His eyebrow cocked, "You give me your word?"

After perhaps a half second of hesitation, she nodded. "You have my word."

He clicked his heels again. "*Wunderbar*! I will seek you out in two days time to learn your final decision." He leaned closer and whispered as if conspiring with her. She could smell his musky aftershave. "I hope you say yes."

Then he took her hand again and kissed the backs of her fingers. She struggled not to snatch her hand back from his grasp before his lips touched her skin. He smiled and said, "I look forward to speaking with you again, *Fräulein* Perrin."

"Good day, *Oberleutnant* Schäfer." She stayed put while he got back into his *Kübelwagen* and drove away. As soon as he was out of sight, Marie let the shaking overwhelm her. Carefully lying her bike on its side, she sat down on the side of the road and wrapped her arms around her knees while tremors shook her entire body. Out of nowhere, she felt very sick and crawled into the grass.

While heaves clutched her body, tears raced down her face. Spent and terrified, she lay back and covered her eyes with her hands. She felt so afraid all the time. What did she think she was doing here?

She silently prayed, desperate for God to reach out to her and physically reassure her that He hadn't abandoned her. Of course, He did not, and she eventually remembered not to test her Creator. In His infinite wisdom, He had given her all the skills and tools she needed to make it through. She simply needed to rely more on Him.

Rolling to her feet, she stumbled to her bike and climbed back on. Her legs felt so weak that she wobbled a bit while she pedaled back to town, but eventually her strength returned.

8 8 8 8

ABOUT forty minutes later, Marie secured her wireless in the hiding place in the ceiling of her room, rearranged her bag so that an examination wouldn't reveal an empty false bottom, and laid out the fabric she intended to use to make Mrs. Chevalier a dress for her mother-in-law's birthday.

For three months she'd maintained her cover as a seamstress and each time she took a needle and thread to hand it only further emphasized that she absolutely did not want to be a seamstress for the rest of her life. Chuckling to herself, knowing she complained more about the sewing than she did the code transmitting, she pulled out her scissors and carefully cut the fabric

Marie also did not enjoy the solitude that came with her job. At least Prudence had someone else in whom she could confide on that farm. Here, Marie lived completely alone in the middle of town. She had to maintain her cover at all times and the strain of that had not previously occurred to her during training. She had no one with whom she could talk or laugh.

If it weren't for occasional work measuring an uppity French housewife or German camp follower for a new dress she probably didn't need, she would have almost no human contact at all. It made her think of her father, who made a good living as a solicitor in her home town, but who always, always, pressed that helping others and giving to those in need should come before new dresses or shoes.

Seeing how other people actually spent money, especially with so much want, need, and despair all around them, made her heart ache. But, the work provided her cover, and she felt thankful for it.

The person she did not know how to handle was one *Oberleutnant* Schäfer and this apparent and exceedingly unwelcome attraction he had for her. Marie knew that this exact type of unwanted attraction on the part of the enemy amounted to one of the main reasons Charlene had met with such resistance when forming this team of women.

Marie didn't think she had a choice in whether she must accompany him and see Virginia Benoit, code named Hope, perform for the German soldiers. After all, one simply did not deny a German officer in the Occupied Zone Doing so would surely just bring her additional unwanted scrutiny.

Still, she supposed she had no choice but to tell him no, unless headquarters countermanded that. She just prayed that Schäfer would understand she had absolutely no interest in him whatsoever. Also, she prayed that he was actually as kind in his personal life as he came across, because she didn't relish having an angry, rejected Nazi officer peering through her windows.

8 8 8 8

Chapter Four

MARIE rolled her neck on her shoulders and pushed away from her sewing table. She'd spend the earlier part of the day attempting to find a secure location from which to transmit and had pedaled her bike for miles and miles. She'd finally transmitted, received a reply, then had to come all the way back to her room and immediately work on the dress she'd started the week before. Her customer expected it tomorrow. Marie had no excuse she could give for not finishing it.

"I'm sorry, *Madame*, but I had to update London on the status of the labor camp being built twenty-three kilometers outside of town. Please give me a few extra days on the dress. I'm very tired from my work as a spy, you see."

She chuckled at the thought of actually saying that out loud as she filled her kettle with water and lit the single burner stove. While she waited for the water to boil, she went to the basin and splashed clean, cold water into the bowl then used that to wash her face. Her eyes burned from lack of sleep for the last week as her work for the resistance grew more and more demanding and the need to maintain a good cover more important than ever.

The loud whistle of the kettle broke her out of her thoughts with a start. Had she just dozed for a few moments while standing up? She poured tea leaves into the pot and covered them with hot water. While it brewed, she extinguished her lights and removed the blackout curtain so that she could open her window. Within minutes, she poured herself a cup, wishing she had even just a little bit of sugar or honey to go into it.

She took her tea to the window and leaned against the frame, enjoying listening to the sounds of the night coming through the open window. A baby cried down the street and the sound of the mother softly singing a lullaby somehow made it her way as well. She could hear the sound of an engine, but without lights she couldn't see it. From somewhere not far away, a woman's laughter floated in with the breeze.

Marie smiled and took a sip of her tea. The world might be at war, she thought to herself, but life still, somehow, went on.

Relaxing for the first time in days, she contemplated turning in for the night and waking very early to finish the dress. The idea appealed to her, but she knew it would be better to finish it now and sleep in than the other way around. Resigned, she turned away from the window to set her cup on the little table by the bed.

She saw the light of the explosion and felt it shake her whole building a half second before she heard the sound. A giant pillar of fire very briefly lit up the sky, casting eerie orange framed shadows all around. When it dimmed, it took a minute for Marie to see clearly again.

She could hear sirens, shouts, engines. Below her window, she heard booted feet, dozens of them, running toward the river where the explosion originated. Marie wondered what was happening. Was it possible that this was merely the precursor to a larger invasion? That France was being liberated? Could the end finally be here?

On the street below, she witnessed chaos as an amphibious Trippel SG-6 *Schwimkraftwagen* and an Opel *Blitz* truck, both working without headlights and both loaded down with German troops, ran head-on into each other. Men yelled in harsh German. Engines hissed. The smell of bitter smoke began to creep into the air though Marie could not be certain if it came from the crash below her window or the explosion. Marie felt certain she could still feel the rumble of the explosion somewhere down inside of her chest and the fire it had caused began to light the night sky in the horizon.

She stared down at the scene below, as an ambulance arrived and medics removed soldiers from the scene on stretchers. Sirens still rang through the night sky, and in the horizon toward the river, the faint glow of a fire grew brighter every minute.

However, no British tanks rolled through their town. No airplanes delivering paratroopers arrived in the night sky. Only the sound of men's voices and truck engines broke up the steady wailing of the alarms.

When she felt like she'd seen enough she shut her window, replaced the blackout curtain, and turned the lights back on in her room. She looked from the dress at the sewing machine to her bed and decided that despite the lost time as an onlooker to the scene below, she still needed to finish that dress before morning. With a sigh, she finished off her tea, cracked her knuckles, and sat before the machine.

¤ ¤ ¤ ¤

"IT was quite awful, let me tell you," *Madame* Bardes said, standing on the footstool while Marie knelt on the floor next to her, stick pins held between her lips as she measured the hem. "We were at the party at the dock manager's place and the explosion happened right next to me." She shifted as she put her hands to her face and gasped. "I declare my ears are still ringing!"

Her companion, Marie did not know her name but had nicknamed her *Madame* Peacock due to her outrageous hat, put a hand to her heart. "I imagine it must have been terrifying, *Madame* Bardes."

The rather plush home of *Madame* Bardes sat not too far from the bridge which members of the resistance had destroyed the night before. Some of the debris from the explosion had even landed on her roof and in her courtyard. Marie had found navigating here somewhat challenging this morning since so many Nazi soldiers crowded the area near the bridge.

The three women used *Madame* Bardes' den for this appointment. Marie had spread her tools out and asked her client to stand atop a low stool while she worked. Once she crouched down to finalize the fittings for the dress, the two women began to speak to one another as if Marie simply were not present.

Madame Bardes was speaking. "… such a loud noise! I was dancing with that *Oberst* who runs the prison. What is his name? Müller? *Oberst* Müller. *Oui, c'est si.* When the explosion happened he stopped right in his tracks and his face turned white as a sheet. I think he thought perhaps we were next to blow up. The more he looked like that, the more frightened I became!"

Madame Peacock clucked her tongue before taking another sip of her tea. "I heard the entire bridge is completely gone and that a train was on it when it happened."

"Terrible! We were waiting for some ranking dignitaries to arrive on that train. The whole town is in an uproar. What exactly were the people who did this thinking?" Marie moved to the other side of the stool and kept working while *Madame* Bardes kept speaking. "Of course, the party was ruined after that. Half of the people left right away!"

"I wish I had been at that party last night, too. But, my Sébastian will not allow it." *Madame* Peacock sniffed as if offended.

Madame Burdes tightened her lips. "Your husband should listen to my Arnaud. He knows that the only way to thrive right now is to make friends."

"You and I both know that. That's why you're standing there and I'm sitting here." Marie watched *Madame* Peacock eye the silk of the dress longingly. "But he would rather be loyal to what he thinks France was than what it is surely to become. He also remembers the women who were dubbed *collaborators* being pulled into the street in the dead of night after the Armistice. "

Madame Burdes scolded, "Sébastian could not possibly be old enough to remember."

Peacock nodded. "It's true that he was quite young but he clearly remembers the mob shaving the heads of all those women then marching them through the streets naked for the entire village to see. My late father-in-law made certain that my husband witnessed every minute."

Marie felt her eyes widen. She had heard such stories but never a first hand account.

Madame Burdes waved her hand in a dismissive gesture. "No matter. There will be no eleventh hour treaties signed this time around. The Third Reich is the future of France, I'm afraid. I fear those who don't already understand this will be the ones left naked and hungry."

Marie sat back and looked up at *Madame* Bardes. "Ready, *Madame*."

She stood and held her hand out so that *Madame* Bardes could safely step down off of the stool.

"You'll have this for tomorrow I hope?"

"*Mai non, Madame.* All that's left is the hem. I can have it to you today."

Madame Bardes clapped. *"Chic alors!"* She rushed to the dressing screen in the corner of her large dressing room. "I will pay you an extra five *Reichsmark* if you can get it to me in the next two hours."

The thought of having to accept Nazi currency sickened Marie though she did not let any sign of her disgust show in her smile. As surreptitiously as she could, Marie watched Peacock adjust her shawl over her shoulders and wondered if the woman would ever eventually convince her husband to conform to the Nazi lovers all around him. Instead of making eye contact, Marie just kept her eyes averted and used the time waiting for her exit to straighten her supplies and pack up her bag.

Long minutes later, *Madame* Bardes came out from behind the screen, back in her red house dress, the silk dress laying over her arm. "I look forward to seeing you again this afternoon," she said as she handed Marie the dress.

"I'll return just as soon as it's done." As she left, she nodded her good-byes to the two women, already so engrossed in yet another story about the explosion the night before that neither paid any attention to the lowly seamstress.

⚜ ⚜ ⚜ ⚜

MARIE sat in the second pew from the very front of the only cathedral in the village. As a child, she had attended the small church led by Pastor Trocmé and often also enjoyed sermons by Reverend Edouard Theis. As a student, she had joined the French Protestant student organization Cimade, which had supported the efforts of her father and Pastor Trocmé along with numerous other believers such as the Salvation Army, the Quakers, even the American Congregational Church. Therefore, Marie was not Catholic but had also never really respected such denominational lines.

She had heard disturbing rumors about all manner of collusion between the current Catholic Pope and the Fascist regimes. It only made sense. The Vatican sat in the center of Italy, after all, and Prime Minister Mussolini had already shown that he was not above all kinds of coercion. Marie chose to believe that her brothers and sisters in Christ such as the local priests and nuns in this village were above such political motivations.

Besides, the small cathedral was the closest house of worship to her apartment. That made it her church according to her cover. She stared at the crucifix hanging on the front wall beneath the small Rosetta window. If she actually lived here in this village by choice, she would very likely worship here. The building was well over five hundred years old. The woodwork and the stained glass inside was frankly beautiful, the congregation even more so.

Sitting in the quiet house of worship, she briefly wondered what God thought of the humans waging this war on the face of His creation. She wondered, as always, how it would end, and knew God already knew. But what did He *think* of it?

Shaking her head at her fanciful thoughts, she reached for the hymnal and opened it to the appropriate page, but found nothing there. With a frown, she looked at the pages before and after, but still could find nothing.

Curious. Prudence had never missed a scheduled drop before. Not ever. A worried frown marred her brow as she set the hymnal back in place. Then she felt someone sit in the pew beside her.

Her heart skipped in fright and she turned her head to look, relieved to see Prudence.

"Hi," her friend whispered. "Thought I'd come in person this time."

"You gave me a fright," Marie whispered back. "I thought we'd been compromised somehow."

Prudence looked around and noticed the single old woman three rows back, her head bowed in prayer. She gestured with her head and the two escaped the dim church into the bright light of day.

Not wanting to draw undue attention to themselves, Marie didn't grab Prudence by the neck and hug her even though she wanted to do just that. What a blessing to see her for the first time in months.

Prudence looked a little wane. She'd lost some weight, and had a rough edge about her. Strangely, it appeared as if she had dyed her blonde hair a dark chestnut. "How are things at the farm?" Marie asked.

"If you can't tell by the missives, it's been very … engaging."

Marie smiled at the sarcasm and looked around to ensure their privacy. "Indeed. I even witnessed some of the after affects," she said, referencing the explosion. "Well, will it slow down after the big operation next month?"

"I'm sure that will just pave the way for another, and another. It would be nice to see an end to this war very soon."

She gestured at Prudence's hair. "The dark hair is a bit of a change."

"It's been a month and I am still not fully used to it. Every time I look in the mirror, I have a bit of a shock."

They walked into the town and stopped at the park in the town square. Marie gestured at her favorite bench. "I can't bear to be indoors. Let's sit here."

"Have you been keeping busy making dresses?" Prudence asked, keeping the conversation simple in case someone overheard them.

"More than I care to, that's for sure," Marie said with a smile. "But, the business is good. You hear a lot bent over someone pinning their skirt. It's funny how they think you don't have ears because you're in service of some sort."

Prudence nodded in understanding. "I know. It's how they're raised." Marie watched her friend's thumb go over her ring finger in the habit she'd gotten used to. "So, do you think you may know who most of the unhappy wives are?"

"Exactly. And how they're seeking out happiness." Marie looked up and groaned. "Oh no. Here he comes."

"He who?" Prudence asked and started to look behind her.

"No! Don't look!" She leaned forward and whispered, "A German officer has taken a shine to me."

Prudence's eyes widened and she grabbed Marie's hand. "Oh no, Temperance. That's awful."

"Tell me about it," Marie said through gritted teeth, but smiled at the young officer's approach. "Hello, *Oberleutnant* Schäfer. How are you on this beautiful autumn day?"

"*Fräulein* Perrin," the blond young man greeted. He looked at Prudence. "Who is your friend?"

Prudence giggled and held out a hand. "I'm Murielle St. Pierre, *Oberleutnant*." She emphasized his rank as if promoting him to General. Then she looked at Marie and stage whispered, "He really *is* handsome, Marie. You weren't exaggerating."

Marie gasped. "Murielle!"

The young officer's ears turned a bit red. "I am pleased to hear you think that of me, *Fräulein*." One of the men in the group of soldiers near a truck across the street barked in their direction. "I must go. We have to go arrest a farmer who has been helping the resistance. I hope to see you again soon. I am still waiting on your answer! I only hope you don't make me wait much longer, *Fräulein*."

He held his hat against his head as he trotted back to the group. Marie looked at her friend. "What was that about?"

"Survival, my friend. He had to believe we were talking about something girlish." She gave Marie a very serious look. "What answer is he seeking?"

"He wants to take me to see Hope perform. I guess she's going to be here in a few weeks." She pursed her lips. "It would be so amazing to see her. I've only heard rumors of her performances."

"But at what risk?" Prudence asked.

"Tremendous risk. There are times I have to remind myself that we have a mission and are at war. I get so caught up in dress patterns and such." Suddenly, she put a hand to her forehead. "Oh my goodness. He's going to go arrest Marcel Bernard!"

"Why do you think that?"

"Because the last time I was on his farm, it took so long to hear back from London. But, with the operation about to go down, I couldn't stop. I had to have a reply. I bet they were able to triangulate the signal enough to narrow it down to the vicinity of his farm."

"Will he give you up?" Prudence whispered, looking around them.

"No." Marie swallowed in a suddenly dry mouth. "But his wife certainly will."

Prudence abruptly stood and brushed at her skirt. "We may need to pull you out, if you've been compromised. Let me go check with Praetorian. I'll leave you a message at the church." Her eyes darted all around. "Talking in public was dangerous for both of us. I'm sorry I risked it."

"I'm sorry, too."

"Go. Hurry. I will be praying for you!"

Marie rushed to her room in the boarding house and grabbed the wireless. Removing the false bottom from her bag, she put it and the code book inside. Then she wrapped several yards of cloth around her waist, covered it with her shirt, refilled the bag with sewing implements, and rushed out of the room.

She rode her bike to the cemetery on the edge of town. Thankfully, it sat behind a hedgerow and it didn't look like anyone was there at this time of day. She rushed through the gate and found the tomb with the broken door. She slipped inside and worked in the dark, removing the wireless, the code book, her earphones, and the antenna and stashed them in the farthest corner of the tomb. Then she unwound the fabric from her waist, folded it as well as she could in the dark, and placed it in the bag where the machine had been.

She looked all around before leaving the tomb and running back to her bike. Looking around again, because if the Nazis caught her here she had no ready excuse for her presence in a cemetery. She secured the bag to the back of her bike and pedaled as fast as she could back to town.

Anxious, worried, every sense heightened, she pedaled through town, forcing herself to pedal at a normal pace. When she finally reached her boarding house, she secured her bike and walked instead of running up the stairs to her room. Once inside, she bolted the door with shaking fingers then leaned against it, sliding down the door and drawing her knees up to her chest.

Silent tears falling from her eyes soaked the material stretched over her knees. She started praying then, for help, for wisdom, for protection.

¥ ¥ ¥ ¥

Chapter Five

MARIE spent three days looking over her shoulder. When she felt certain that her impending arrest might not actually happen, she ventured out in the predawn hour and went to the church.

No one occupied the pews within the dim church interior. She made her way to the appropriate pew and found the hymnal. Inside, on the correct page, she found a slip of a note. Marie decoded the hymn lyrics and read:

Cover blown.

Transmit immediate evac request.

Coordinate with HQ

She didn't know whether to laugh or cry. She folded the note into a little tiny ball, then put it in her mouth and swallowed it.

After she left the church, she went to the cemetery. When she arrived at the tomb where she had hidden her wireless, she rushed inside and felt around in the dark. Once her seeking fingers found and secured her equipment, she felt an enormous amount of relief. As far as she could tell, it hadn't been tampered with and was exactly as she'd left it. Not wanting to risk the code book falling into the German's hands, she left it behind. She should be able to code the missive from memory.

She packed her bag carefully and exited the tomb to find no one in the church graveyard. Securing her bag to the back of her bike, she pedaled back to town, back to her boarding house.

The bag felt incredibly heavy to her, and she felt like everyone looking at her knew what it contained. Every glance in her direction transformed into an accusing glare. Anxious, nervous, paranoid, she rushed up the stairs to her room, securing the door behind her.

It took no time at all for her to set up the antenna and hook everything up. Checking over her shoulder in her empty bedroom, she slipped the earphones on her head and started transmitting, using code.

TEMPERANCE COMPROMISED.
NEED IMMED –

The pounding on her door interrupted her transmission.

Unable to do anything but shove the equipment under her bed, she straightened her dress and rushed to the door. On the other side stood a German Sergeant and four men. She felt her eyebrows knot.

"May I help you?" she asked.

He was a large man, with round features and a big nose. He glared at her but did not speak to her. "*Durchsuchen den raum,*" he barked out.

She knew he'd given the order to his men to search the space, just as she knew they would quickly find the wireless equipment.

"Sergeant," she put her hand up in a halting gesture. "Men are forbidden from entering this room. It is improper."

The sergeant grinned. It was not a look of happiness. "Papers, *Fräulein*?" he asked in coarse French and extended his gloved right hand. With his gloved left hand, he gestured impatiently at his men. "*Mache schnell! Suche das Zimmer. Suche überall.*"

Hurry up, he urged. *Search the room. Search everywhere.*

While the soldiers tore through her closet and bureau, she pulled her identification papers from her pocket and handed it to the sergeant.

He opened the leather cover, nodded once as if confirming something, then looked at her. "*Fräulein* Marie Perrin?"

"Yes," she said, crossing her arms as one of the men got on his knees to look under the bed. Before the sergeant could say anything else, the soldier made an exclamation and pulled the machine out from under the bed.

"You are under arrest, *Fräulein* Perrin." Then, with a balled fist, he punched her in the cheek with his leather gloved hand. The impact felt as if he had something metal inside his gloves. Her world turned a nauseatingly dark gray before it went completely black.

☷ ☷ ☷ ☷

MARIE lay on a cot in the corner of a cage. She remembered to pretend she was still unconscious this time. The longer they left her unmolested, the longer she could rest, recuperate, save her energy for what lay ahead.

Every part of her seemed to hurt in one way or another. Her face felt like a giant burning blister from the vicious punch and the dozens of backhanded slaps that followed. Her teeth felt loose in her jaw and she tasted blood every time she swallowed. Her back had deep burning welts from a beating with some kind of whip or riding crop a few hours earlier. But the worst part was the cold. Her damp skin felt freezing cold and she could get no relief from the chill because they had only left her with her light undergarments and a thin cotton slip with which to cover herself.

The first thing they had done when they had taken her into the interrogation room was to manacle her hands far above her head so that she had to stand on the very tips of her toes just to keep her wrists from bleeding. Then they had used a razor sharp bayonet and taken turns cutting her clothes from her body and laughing with each rag of fabric they removed.

One of the soldiers had painfully sawed off a hank of her hair and lewdly inhaled it, making his companions guffaw. Her skin crawled at the memory of the feeling of the cold steel gently caressing the bare skin of her arms, legs, and stomach.

She kept her eyes closed and tried not to groan in pain or shiver too visibly. Her cage had no walls, only bars. It sat in the center of a large room with guards all around her. She had no privacy, no escape from the constant stares of the guards. Not that she spent much time in the cell. They had her out and interrogated her almost constantly. As far as she could tell, she'd been there for fifteen waking hours. She had no idea how long she'd been unconscious or how often. It could have been seconds or hours. Time meant nothing at this point – nothing but a continual state of misery.

She wanted to dab at her cheek, but didn't want any of her watching guards to see. She was certain the sergeant had broken her cheekbone. Her eye had long since swollen shut. She knew she had at least two broken ribs, along with her pinkie finger on her left hand.

Once they'd finished cutting her dress completely off of her body, they had mercifully left her in her cotton slip, barefoot. The bed had neither sheets nor a blanket and she had no shoes. Every time she started to fall asleep, someone took a water hose and doused her, which meant that the mattress was soaking wet. The only time they let her be was when they were certain she was unconscious.

A shudder of cold went through her body and she knew if she had no relief from the constant wet, she would soon get sick. Whether they would nurse her back to health remained a giant question mark.

They wanted the code book which she'd left in the tomb. If they got the code book, they'd be able to decipher the transmissions they had intercepted for the past several months. At the very least, they would find out about the mission Praetorian and his team had been planning. That would not only endanger their lives, it would hurt the war effort. She could never give them that information, even if it cost her life.

Instead, she refused to talk. They almost broke her. Fracturing her pinkie nearly did her in, but the interrogator did not continue the conversation. He had her removed to her cell, where she could think about whether or not she wanted to continue holding back. She knew it was to reset her brain, which was starting to go into shock, making his interrogation tactics useless.

She started to drift inside herself, then. If it were possible to will herself to die, she would have died three hours ago. But maybe she could sleep through the next blast of hose.

※ ※ ※ ※

OBERLEUTNANT Leopold Schäfer stormed into the office of the head interrogator. "What is the meaning of this?" he spat out.

"Meaning of what, sir?" Sergeant Marco Hans asked, warily.

"Is it not obvious you incompetent fool? What is the meaning of your treatment of the female prisoner?" Schäfer spat. "The prisoner who was arrested without my orders and without my permission or foreknowledge."

"*Oberleutnant*, I am only doing my job," the older man said with disinterest. "What is it to you?" He had resented the young Schäfer's placement as head of the prison since his promotion, but Schäfer had pretty much left him alone. Until now.

"Where did you get your training, Sergeant? Let me guess. The gulags of our friends to the east?" Though, recently, the political landscape had changed, the Soviets had partnered with Germany for many years. Until very recently, Stalin had provided Hitler's Nazi party with safe ports for his U-boats, training, weapons, fuel, raw materials, even rations. He waited for the Sergeant to offer a slight nod of confirmation before slamming his fist on the man's desk. "Idiot! That is not how you interrogate a French woman. You will get nothing from her using these tactics."

"What are you talking about?"

"You are treating her just like a male prisoner and your actions have cost us at least a week, if not two, of work for me. Have her removed to a private cell, and get her some dry clothes. See that her wounds are treated. Do it immediately."

"*Oberleutnant* Schäfer, I must protest. I personally trained with the *Schutzstaffel* in the Ukraine in 1939 and these tactics were very effective with the local women we interrogated there."

Reaching for patience, Schäfer explained, "Sergeant, when your SS friends beat and tortured a female villager to death without getting the information they needed, what did they do next?" He paused while the noncommissioned officer reflected. "What did they do, Sergeant? Did they simply take another woman into custody? How many women did they kill before they obtained the information they desired."

The sergeant shrugged.

"Fifty? A hundred? Let me speak plainly. Was it more than one? Because, Sergeant, we only have this single prisoner. Just the one. We do not have the luxury of every village in all of the Ukraine we can raid in the middle of the night. You understand?"

The Sergeant looked suddenly resentful, "Exactly what is your training, sir? How many interrogations did you perform in America, *Oberleutnant*? Who are you to tell me –"

Schäfer put his nose to the other man's. "I assure you there are less desirable duty stations than France, Sergeant. Perhaps you would like to go back and visit some of your Soviet friends in Stalingrad? Who am I? I am your commanding officer, and if you don't follow my orders immediately, I can only assure you that you will regret it for the rest of your time in uniform."

The man came to sharp attention. "Yes, sir." He saluted and said, "*Heil* Hitler."

Schäfer casually returned the salute without even raising his hand above shoulder height. "*Seig heil.*"

He left the man behind, knowing his orders would be followed exactly, and stormed through the halls of the prison offices. When he reached his own office, he was surprised to find *Kapitän* Neumann waiting behind his desk. He immediately came to attention.

"*Oberleutnant* Schäfer," the captain said, standing, "congratulations on the arrest."

"It was premature. We had her under surveillance and I did not know she was arrested until an hour ago."

The captain raised an eyebrow. "Do you need to be replaced as head of this facility?"

"Not at all, sir. I just need competent sergeants who don't act on their own accord without orders."

The captain froze and murmured, "Without orders?" The man began to pace around the office. Schäfer had not been told to stand at ease and thus had not moved from his position of attention. Therefore, he did not turn his head and visually track his commander as the captain paced around the room. Instead, he stared straight ahead.

"Why did your sergeant arrest her prematurely and without orders?" He asked, looking at a portrait print of his beloved Führer on the wall.

"I had to go to Paris for a meeting. While I was gone, he acted. I think he wanted some glory. Instead, I think he's getting some prison time."

"Just have him beaten and be done with it." The captain waved a hand toward him then realized that the junior officer still stood in a stiff brace. Schäfer noted that his commander very carefully asked no questions about his Paris meeting. "At ease. What have you been able to glean from her so far? Anything?"

"Nothing. She's been beaten until she can't sit up by men twice her size. I suspect her jaw is broken. I don't know why they expected to get anything from her."

The captain met his eyes. "Did they violate the girl?"

Schäfer shrugged. "I do not yet know, sir, but I think not."

His captain said, "Does the girl have family?"

The question had plenty of depth. Did the girl have political connections? Would her rape while in custody prove an embarrassment? Is it possible they were mistaken about their quarry?

"None, here, sir. She is from the south of France originally."

The captain nodded then waved a hand. "If any of the men violated her, have them publically hanged. Best to set an example early on before the camp is built. Can't have any of the men sullying themselves with any of the filthy Jews we bring to the camp. We must keep the bloodlines pure for the glory of the Fatherland. If they think it's acceptable here with any female prisoner, they're going to continue to think it's acceptable there with those hairless apes."

Schäfer nodded. "It will be done, sir. I'm not sure her interrogation can be salvaged."

The captain raised an eyebrow. "You have ideas of a different method?"

"Of course. She's a woman. Like all women she'll respond better to silk than to steel."

Neumann narrowed his eyes. "Rather American thinking. I suppose I should have expected no less."

Schäfer felt his cheeks burn, silently cursing his complexion that allowed the captain to see his visceral reaction even though he attempted to hide it from his expression. "I cannot change where my father raised me, *Kapitän.* Besides, many great minds have come from America and been embraced by the likes of the *Führer* himself. Effinger, Pelley, Ezra Pound to name a few. Even now, Robert Henry Best is winning countless Americans to the great Nazi cause over the radio."

"Indeed." Neumann cocked his head and looked at Schäfer as if studying a laboratory rat. "I read your file, *Oberleutnant,* as I do with every officer under my command. I know that William Dudley Pelley and the Friends of New Germany endorsed your commission and I know that none other than Rudolph Hess himself personally pinned on your rank. Very politically expedient, I'm sure. I am only observing that your thinking is very different than most european Arians."

Schäfer wisely kept his mouth shut.

"I will give you three weeks to break her with your silky American kindness. Then, *Oberleutnant,* and I say this with all sincerity, *I* will make her talk using the steel."

"Impossible. I need at least four weeks, sir. The girl has been beaten to within an inch of her life."

The captain retrieved his cap from the top of the desk. On his way out of the room, he stopped at Schäfer's shoulder. "Three. I have a schedule to keep."

"Understood sir." He clicked his heels together and saluted. "*Seig heil.*"

"Yes, yes. *Heil* Hitler," the captain answered tiredly as he walked out of the room.

Chapter Six

OBERLEUTNANT Schäfer sat at his desk across from his clerk. He signed papers, made notations in logs and records, and issued orders. Under a stack of supply requests, he found four unsealed envelopes with hand written letters inside.

"*Was ist das?*" he barked. What is this?

"The weekly letters allowed out from the ranking officers held here. Three are British officers and an Australian. *Herr Kapitän* felt your ability to read English so fluently might help the censors in this case."

Schäfer nodded. Everything in order, then. He quickly thumbed through the envelopes and read the addresses on them. Then he opened each letter and skimmed the contents striking through anything that might be of strategic value to their enemy. Mostly, the letters related to past shared events and encouragement that the prisoners were being treated well by their captors. Nothing dangerous. Senior officers knew better. When he finished, he stuffed the letters back inside their respective envelopes and handed them to the clerk. "Go ahead and post them to the censors immediately with my endorsement. See that they are posted as soon as possible. I assume I will also have the pleasure of reading mail that arrives for our special guests?"

"Yes, sir," the clerk said, taking the envelopes from him. "But the censors from both sides will have already gone through them."

Schäfer felt his eyes tighten. "Very well. That will be all for now I think."

The clerk stood and saluted, then left the room. Schäfer leaned his chair back and closed his eyes. He felt so much anger that Marie Perrin had been arrested. He hadn't wanted her arrested until it couldn't possibly be helped. Now, with all the evidence against her, he had no choice but to keep her behind bars. He could not even secure her release and, even if he were somehow able to, they had no guarantee she would resume her activities.

He felt fortunate that he had maintained command of the prison. Admitting that the sergeant had acted without his orders or consent could easily have cost him his new rank and responsibility. At least they hadn't replaced him. Fortunately, *Herr Kapitän* had political aspirations and didn't want to risk offending any high ranking officials that might be looking out for his newest *Oberleutnant*. Maintaining his position as the commander of the prison garrison gave him more control over what Marie would have to endure.

Of course, his motives were not purely to the betterment of the Fatherland. Not purely. He had other motives.

He sat up and turned back to his desk. He had too much to do in a short day to sit kicked back and thinking about the fate of a beautiful spy who was, after all, an enemy of the Third Reich. The important thing in the next few weeks would be for her to come to trust him. If she didn't trust him, then he didn't know what might happen to her.

☙❧

MARIE warily sat up and scooted painfully to the corner of her cot, carefully placing her tattered back into the corner of the cell. She could only open one eye, and her cheek throbbed in a painful rhythm with her heart.

The small cell contained a single cot and a bucket. The stone walls looked damp, and she could smell a musty smell, could hear water dripping somewhere beyond her room. A heavy wood door with a barred window provided the only aperture. Through it, she could hear sounds from beyond her cell. A single bulb hung above her cot, the light dim and barely penetrating the shadows in the corners.

Some hours ago, she'd woken with vague memories of being removed from the central cage and placed in this cell. She'd woken up dry, with her ribs tightly wrapped and her finger set, splinted, and wrapped. She wore a thick cotton slip, under which she could feel the wrap that bound her aching ribs. On the corner of the cot, neatly folded, lay a clean gray cotton dress and thick wool socks.

Her captors had kept her cold and wet for so many hours she'd forgotten what dry felt like. As she dressed, she'd had a hard time even securing the buttons on her dress because her hands shook so badly and her finger hurt with every movement of her hands.

After dressing, she tried to shut out the throbbing in her cheek, torso, and back and dozed off, but the sounds in and around the prison made it nearly impossible to actually sleep. Thirst unlike anything she'd ever felt in her life consumed her, and the gnawing hunger in her stomach hurt almost as much as her cheek. The thirst, hunger, discomfort, the banging of metal on metal as doors opened and closed, the sound of heels clicking along stone floors, the whispered conversations of some prisoners and the anguished cries of others – those sounds kept her from truly relaxing into a deep sleep.

Now her cell door slowly opened and she feared what she would face next. More beatings? More ripping off of her clothes? More razor sharp ice cold blades against her skin or riding crops across her back? Did they put her in here, dry and nursed, merely to strip her bare and terrify her even more deeply?

In the midst of her reverie, First Lieutenant Leopold Schäfer, perhaps the last person on earth she expected to see here, walked into her cell. He entered carrying a tray with some broth, a heel of dark bread, and a chunk of cheese.

She turned her body so that her feet touched the floor, but she did not stand. Nor did she speak first.

He set the tray on the corner of the cot and stared down at her, appearing to inspect her bandages and her clothes. She tried to read his expression, but the hunger overwhelmed her and she could do nothing but watch her hand snake out, grab the bread, and bring it to her watering mouth for a quick bite. She dipped the remainder into the soup, and shoved another bite into her mouth. It tasted better than any meal she could remember.

It hurt her cheek to chew, but she ignored the pain. On the side of her swollen cheek, she felt a loose tooth, so she shifted the food to the other side of her mouth. As she slowly chewed around the mouth full of bread, the tall blond man just watched her. He did not speak until she swallowed.

"*Fräulein* Perrin, I must apologize for the treatment you've received here. I promise you that there will be no repeat of such treatment. You understand?"

Marie lifted the eyebrow of her good eye and picked up the cheese. "I beg your pardon?"

He nodded stiffly. "This is my prison. But, I was away. I did not even know they'd arrested you. Had I known –" He knelt next to her and put a hand over the bandaged hand she kept cradled in her lap. She tried not to stiffen away from his touch, but could not help the instinctive reaction. He ignored it and looked her in the eye with very serious blue eyes. "If I had known I never would have allowed any of this to happen."

Searching his face, wondering at his game, not trusting what came across as sincere, she said, "I don't believe you."

The smile briefly crossed his face but didn't touch his eyes. "You don't?"

"No. I don't." She didn't tell him that she thought he was being nice hoping that she would confide in him.

"Ah. Well, I shall simply avoid asking you any questions. Then maybe you'll start to trust my sincerity. I don't want to see you hurt, Marie." The use of her Christian name sounded strange coming from him. "You will be safe here. My men are under orders not to come near you. I will provide for your care."

"You?" She narrowed her eyes at him. "What do you get out of that?"

"Only the knowledge that a woman under my care isn't being tortured or … otherwise mistreated." He gracefully stood. "There is no right way to do the wrong thing. There are some things that are simply wrong even in a time of war."

He clicked his heels and stiffly nodded. "I pray that your injuries don't hurt you too much and that you heal quickly." While she contemplated his use of the word 'pray' as if it naturally and normally came out of his mouth, he slipped his hand into the inside of his jacket and pulled out a small French translation of the King James Bible. "Please keep this hidden. I know it will bring you comfort, but if any guard sees it, they will take it and it may compromise me."

She did not take it from him. After a heartbeat or two, he set it on the cot next to the tray. "Good day, *Fräulein* Perrin."

She stared at the door for long minutes after he left. Her stomach gave a painful turn and broke her out of her trance. Taking a small bite of cheese, she slowly chewed and reached out to run her fingers over the Bible, knowing that giving it to her amounted to nothing more than a ploy. He must have seen the Bible she kept in her room that day she had mended the button on his trousers. From behind the screen, he would have been able to examine the area by her bedside table completely unobserved. Her worn Bible sat on the nightstand. He would have guessed at her Christian faith.

Regardless of his ploy, she brought the Bible up to her cheek and closed her eyes as a tear slipped out of her eye. "What He brings me to, He will see me through," she whispered to herself. She thought of a verse in the hymn "In the Hour of Trial". *When my last hour cometh, fraught with strife and pain, When my dust returneth to the dust again; On thy truth relying, Through that mortal strife, Jesus take me dying, To eternal life.*

Peace settled around her like a mantle. She slipped the Bible under her thin pillow and took a sip of soup, ate some more cheese, and contemplated the visit from Lieutenant Leopold Schäfer.

She polished off the small meal. No longer ravenously hungry, no longer wet, no longer cold, she felt incredibly sleepy. She stood on weak and shaky legs and carried the tray over to the cell door and set it on the ground. Half stumbling, she went back to her cot and lay down, feeling the haze of sleep taking over her brain.

As she drifted off, she thought of the missive she'd started to send to London. No matter what happened to her, London knew any new missive did not come from her. If nothing else, her last thought was voiced in a short whispered prayer of thanksgiving that she'd started to send that transmission to headquarters. At least they would know the Nazis had captured her.

They would not continue to send transmissions thinking she waited on this side of the channel. The German soldiers who had possession of her wireless, and even now pretended to be her, could have thrown a serious wrench into their plans. With the big mission coming up, and with Praetorian needing the already staged support from London, the knowledge of her capture could play a key role.

Willing her mind to stop thinking about her circumstances or worrying about her future, she closed her eyes and let sleep finally overtake her.

The End

INSPIRED BY REAL EVENTS

WHILE the story of the special team of operators I named The Virtues is entirely fictional, set in a fictional town, and comprised of fictional characters who form a fictional military division, every single one of my fictional heavenly heroines was inspired by a real World War II heroine and the story was inspired by real events.

The hometown of fictional Marie Gilbert and her brother Edward, *Le Chambon-sur-Lignon*, is an actual place and the great and honored reverend Pastor André Trocmé as well as Pastor Edouard Theis were actual people. These men of God inspired the entire town to smuggle uncounted Jewish children and their parents, possibly as many as five thousand or more, out of the country and to safety. Those children who could not be safely evacuated were taken in and "adopted" by families who informed the Nazis that the children were visiting relatives or war orphans.

When the *Gestapo* or the corrupt and collaborates Vichy police would raid the town, the citizens would routinely risk their lives by hiding children and parents anywhere they could and using elaborate schemes to signal when the coast was clear. Many residents were eventually arrested by the *Gestapo*. Sadly, the Reverand Trocmé's own cousin, Daniel Trocmé, was sent to *Maidanek* concentration camp and tortured to death.

It may be significant to note that the townspeople received contributions from the Quakers, the Salvation Army, the American Congregational Church, as well as other Jewish and Christian ecumenical groups, the French Protestant student organization *Cimade*, and the Swiss Help to Children. All of these organizations helped to ensure that the Jewish refugees were housed and fed and could travel in relative safety to Switzerland or other safe havens.

In 1990, the entire town became the only French town and one of only two towns on earth to be recognized as "Righteous Among the Nations" for their humanitarianism and bravery under extreme danger during the Second World War.

Marie Gilbert, code named Temperance, was inspired by the incredible Eileen Mary "Didi" Nearne who served as a wireless operator in the Spiritualist Network in Occupied France under the code named "Rose."

Like Temperance, Didi Nearne, her brother Francis, and her sister Jacqueline fled the Nazis as the German war machine rolled into France. They eventually made their way to Great Britain via Spain.

All three of the Nearnes entered service with the British Special Operations Executive, or SOE, which was called "Churchill's secret army." A group within the SOE was called the F Section Networks. These networks were established in France to transmit and receive coded messages just like Temperance does in Temperance's Trial. Due to the ease of detection and the German's determination to track down these operators, it was one of the most dangerous duties assigned to agents within the SOE.

While Didi's sister, Jacqueline, was sent to France to act as a courier (much like Temperance's friend, Prudence), Didi stayed in England as a signals operator and received the encoded messages coming from France. After some time, she volunteered to go to France and act as a wireless operator for the F Section.

On March 2, 1944, Didi became one of only 39 women to parachute into Occupied France. She used the aliases *Mademoiselle* du Tort, Jacqueline Duterte, and Alice Wood – and went by the code name "Rose". She worked as part of Operation Mitchel, which organized finances for the resistance. During her first five months in France, she transmitted an astonishing 105 messages.

After many, many narrow escapes, including a time on a train when a Nazi soldier offered to carry the suitcase containing her wireless radio, Didi was finally arrested. While in Paris, she had sent a coded transmission from her room, much like my character Temperance. Within minutes, the *Gestapo* arrived and found her in possession of her wireless rig.

According to wartime records, Nearne "survived, in silence, the full revolting treatment of the *baignoire*" in the torture chamber of the Paris headquarters of the *Gestapo* on the banks of the *Rue des Saussaies*.

She nearly died from the torture. They beat her, stripped her, and repeatedly submerged her in a bath of ice cold water until she started to black out. Yet, she did not break. She stuck to her story of being an innocent French girl who had been duped into helping someone by sending messages she didn't understand in return for money to buy eggs and bread.

She never once revealed her true identity. She never told of the other agents with whom she worked. Despite days of endless torture, she never gave up any information of planned operations.

At the time, Eileen Mary "Didi" Nearne was only 23 years old.

On August 15, 1944, she was sent to the infamous *Ravensbrück* concentration camp near Berlin, and from there was sent through several forced labor camps. She refused to work in any of the camps, even under threat of being shot. Instead, she defied her captors to shoot her, and ended up being transferred each time instead.

Eventually, she ended up in a camp in Silesia. There Didi finally realized that the only way she would survive this experience would be to give in and work otherwise she would starve. During the bitter cold winter in December of 1944, the Nazis moved Didi to the *Markleberg* camp, near Leipzig, where she worked on a road-repair gang for 12 hours a day.

On April 13, 1945, while being transferred to yet another camp, along with two French girls from a work gang, Didi escaped. The trio evaded their pursuers by hiding in the forest. Astonishingly, they were apprehended by the SS in *Markkleeberg*, but she used her French language skills to fool her captors into letting them go. In Leipzig, a Catholic priest hid her until the arrival of the United States troops.

Sadly, American intelligence officers initially identified her as a Nazi collaborator and held her at a detention center alongside captured SS personnel. Once London verified her identity as a secret agent, the Americans finally released her.

After the war, Eileen Mary "Didi" Nearne was awarded the *Croix de Guerre* by the French government, that nation's highest award given to foreigners, and was appointed a Member of the Order of the British Empire (MBE) by King George VI for services rendered in France during the enemy occupation.

Given what she underwent at the hands of her captors for years and years, her very survival is remarkable. When asked how she kept going, she replied, "The will to live. Willpower. That's the most important. You should not let yourself go. It seemed that the end would never come, but I always believed in destiny, and I had a hope."

Didi lived with her sister Jacqueline until her sister's death in 1982. Afterward, she lived alone, a total recluse, haunted by her experiences as a captive of the *Gestapo*.

When Eileen Mary "Didi" Nearne died alone on September 2, 2010, it was several days before her death was discovered. It wasn't until officials looking through her belongings hoping to find a relative whom they could contact that they discovered her true identity. Once they realized her incredible bravery and service, the entire community of Torbay, France, came together and gave her a funeral worthy of such an amazing war heroine with full military honors.

Unsurprisingly, there are very few actual photographs of Didi from the war and none of her operating a wireless rig. For the cover of this book, another suitable individual was selected. Pictured on the cover in place of "Temperance" and operating a wireless radio is none other than Mrs. Mac.

Mrs. Florence Violet McKenzie OBE (nee Wallace), aka "Mrs Mac" (1890-1982) was Australia's first female electrical engineer, first female amateur radio operator, and the founder of the now international organization, the Electrical Association for Women. Mrs Mac is best known, however, for her work during the Second World War.

Having founded the Women's Emergency Signalling Corps in 1939, she then successfully campaigned to have some of her female trainees accepted into the Royal Australian Navy, thereby originating the Women's Royal

Australian Naval Service. As the head instructor for the military, it is estimated that during the war some 12,000 servicemen from nearly every Allied nation passed through her Morse code training school in Australia.

🎖🎖🎖🎖

SUGGESTED questions for a discussion group surrounding *Temperance's Trial*, part 1 of the *Virtues and Valor* series.

While the characters and situations in the *Virtues and Valor* series are fictional, I pray that these extended parables can help readers come to a better understanding of truth. Please prayerfully consider the questions that follow, consult scripture, and pray upon your conclusions. May the Lord of the universe richly bless you.

☸ ☸ ☸ ☸

The fictional character, Marie Gilbert, her brother, and their father, live in Le Chambon-sur-Lignon, France. In real life, in this town, the people came together as followers of Christ and helped to save THOUSANDS of Jewish children from the hands of the Nazis. They did this as a community under the threat of arrest and death.

1. Would it be easy for you to be convinced to help children in such dire need of rescue?

2. If helping children put your actual life at risk, but not helping children would put their actual lives at risk, then do you think you'd still do it?

☸ ☸ ☸ ☸

In a very black and white world, the Bible is very clear in the words,

You shall not steal, nor deal falsely, nor lie to one another. Leviticus 19:11. However, this is a series that deals entirely with people who are basically lying as a means of survival. And God Himself directed Moses to send spies into Canaan in Numbers 13.

3. As Christians, is there ever a time in our lives when lying might be acceptable?

4. Do you think Marie Gilbert and her companions are 'sinning' in the purest sense of the word by covertly battling the enemy?

§ § § §

Marie is a deeply spiritual person who relies on prayer in all avenues of her life. She continually prays for protection while in Occupied France; however, she's arrested, beaten, interrogated, and humiliated.

5. Do you think God did not hear her prayers?

6. Why do you think God doesn't always come to the 'rescue' of Christians even when their very well being is at stake?

§ § § §

Homeland's Hope

the Virtues and Valor Series part 2

a Novella by

HALLEE BRIDGEMAN

Published by

Olivia Kimbrell Press™

Olivia Kimbrell Press™

Library Cataloging Data
U. S. Library of Congress Control Number: 2014953676

Bridgeman, Hallee (Hallee A. Bridgeman) 1972-
  Homeland's Hope, Virtues and Valor series part 2 / Hallee Bridgeman
    102 p. 23cm x 15cm (9in x 6 in.)
      Summary: Star of stage and screen turns her God given skills to the cause of the Allies in Occupied France during World War II.

      ISBN: 978-1-939603-46-3 (ebook)

1. Christian fiction 2. World War II 3. war stories 4. spies 5. historical fiction 6. espionage

PS3568.B7534 T941 2014
[Fic.] 813.6 (DDC 23)

For all the Josphine Bakers...

THIS novella is specifically dedicated to Josephine Baker. To read more about this true heroine, read the "Inspired by Real Events" section at the end of Hope's story.

Paris, France: 1939

VIRGINIA Benoit leaned closer to the mirror so she could apply the final coat of bright red lipstick onto her full lips. As she rubbed her lips together to help even it out, she could hear the sound of the late evening crowd.

She stood and ran her hands along the sides of her gold sequined gown. The shimmering gold perfectly complimented her mocha colored skin. Satisfied with the fit of the gown, she opened a small box on her dressing table and poured several of the gold sequins that matched those on her gown into the palm of her hand. Using hair grease, she applied the sequins to the corners of her eyes, swirling them out from the corners of her eyes toward her hairline and making a spiral design. It gave her an exotic look that left her male fans wanting to know more about her.

It didn't seem to matter to the crowd here in Paris that her grandfather had been a slave on the Creole plantation that her grandmother's parents owned, or that her grandmother gave birth to her mother, alone and ostracized, in a shack in the poorest section of New Orleans. All that seemed to matter to them was that she seduced them with her voice, giving them a hint of a promise that made them come back again and again, seeking more.

As she selected a flower from the vase next to her dressing table, she thought of how her grandmother and mother had come back to Paris to the welcoming arms of their French family when their Creole family in the United States had disowned them. Her grandmother's cousin had embraced her, welcomed her into his home, and her mother grew up lacking nothing. At twenty she married the French musician, Alsander Benoit, and the two traveled back to her original home. Finding no welcome in New Orleans, they settled in St. Louis, Missouri. There, Virginia was born and grew up listening to her mother sing and her father play trombone in the clubs all over the musical city.

When Virginia had followed in her parents' footsteps, she'd received a moderately warm welcome within the Negro clubs, but she was kept at arm's length due to the whiteness in her blood. When she tried to play in the white clubs, she hadn't had good experiences all around. Her father encouraged her to go to Paris and sing her heart out, knowing the Parisians would embrace her. And so she did.

Five years later, she filled the club nightly. Hundreds of people came just to hear her sing. She headlined shows all over Europe and her growing notoriety resulted in several film roles. She starred in French films, mostly, though she had a few cameos in English speaking films as well. She had a special case built in her country chateau to hold all of her honors and accolades. Of course, America began to beg her to come back to the land of her birth.

Now that her beloved France had officially declared war on Germany, she thought maybe she'd give her home country another chance.

She stepped back from her dressing table and looked at her full body in the mirror. Her dress fit tightly everywhere it mattered, molding to her athletic shape. Though her arms and shoulders remained bare, the golden neckline rose up and hugged her neck, with a collar poking out all around her head, giving her the appearance of a golden flower. She looked royal, exotic, dangerous, and the crowd would love it.

"*Mademoiselle* Benoit!" A rap of knuckles on her dressing room door followed the call. "Five minutes, *Mademoiselle!*"

A minute later, her personal maid, Cyllia, rushed through the door. Her dark eyes stood out from her pale skin. Black ringlets framed her narrow face, and her petite body and narrow frame made her look like a child. "He's out there, Virginia. Paulo at the bar saw him."

Virginia cringed. The last thing she wanted to do was to entertain a Nazi General with a serious schoolboy crush on her. She'd met him years ago in Africa, but he had started coming to her shows in Paris about two years before while he visited with his daughter at the university. Despite the constraints of war, he had somehow traveled to Paris with French papers to see her about once a month. Since it had been well over three months since last he'd visited, she'd hoped that the tensions between their two countries had risen too high for him to keep coming back. Apparently, that wasn't the case.

"Not much we can do about it, is there, Cyllia?"

"I reckon we could call the police on him. I bet not everyone knows he's a Nazi." Her smooth southern voice made Virginia long for the streets of New Orleans.

She walked gracefully over to Cyllia and put her palm against the young girl's cheek. Her hand looked even darker against the very pale white of Cyllia's skin. "It's better to have friends among the enemy right now. We don't know what will happen in the future."

"God does say to love your enemies," the young maid said. "Oh, but it's so scary knowing he's out there."

Virginia nodded, then swished her floor-length skirts and turned. A diamond shape cut in the back exposed her skin all the way to her hips, and just below her hips, lay a bow. "Please check my bow. It's time."

The audience surged to their feet as she took the stage. She smiled and waved, taking the stage with such grace it appeared her legs never even moved. Rather, she appeared to glide to the microphone on the shimmering golden cloud of her dress. When she sang, the entire building fell silent at the sound of her voice. She danced. She sang. She fed their souls with her music.

Forty minutes later, she left the stage and sashayed her way to the bar. Paulo waited with a tall glass of iced tea with a wedge of lemon, sweetened southern style just as she liked it. She figured she was the only woman in Paris who drank sweet iced tea, but she had Creole blood, and the Creoles were known for going against societal norms.

She took a long pull from her glass just as she felt Lars Schmid lay a gentle hand on the small of her back as he slipped into the seat next to her. "Beautiful, Virginia Benoit," he said in perfect French, no trace of a German accent coating his voice anymore. "It has been far too long."

"Gen –" At his raised eyebrow, she grinned a conspiratorial half grin and corrected what she'd been about to call him. "*Monsieur* Schmid. I had worried I might never see you again." She used a napkin to dab at the tiny beads of perspiration that began to form at her temple. She could blame the stage lights if necessary. "It is always a pleasure, sir," she said in her richest, warmest voice.

"The pleasure, *Mademoiselle*, is all mine, I can assure you," Schmid said, taking her hand and kissing three knuckles. His lips felt dry and a bit cold against her skin. "Would you kindly do me the honor of sharing a late supper with me?"

Resisting the urge to wipe her hand clean after the touch of his lips, she faked a gleaming smile and gestured with her hand. "I must confess I am very tired, but I would love the pleasure of your company if we can steal a few moments over a meal. Lead the way."

❂❂❂❂

CHAPTER 1

HOPE - optimistic attitude of mind based on an expectation of positive outcomes, often without evidence that events can or will end well.

¤ ¤ ¤ ¤

London, England: 1941

VIRGINIA sat in a wooden chair set against a concrete wall in a hallway that smelled of freshly applied industrial paint. All down the long hallway, empty wooden benches or lonely ladder-backed chairs sat outside wooden doors with frosted glass windows. The mint green walls bore posters from the Ministry of Health Evacuation urging parents to remove their children from London and other urban centers, posters calling for Victory, posters reminding people not to talk about their work for the Ministry of War. Regularly, people passed her in the hall; some in uniform, some in civilian clothes, always rushing.

Everyone studied her as they rushed by, often with their eyebrows knotting in confusion. Perhaps they thought her, a woman of dark skin, extremely overdressed to perform typical maid or janitorial duties. She could always tell when someone recognized her. The curiosity at seeing a woman of color sitting outside the door of the Special Operations Executive changed to joy when the person realized this particular woman was THE Virginia Benoit, stage and motion picture sensation, and the darling of France.

Her journey to this wooden chair in this mint green hallway had taken nearly a year. When the Nazi's marched into Paris, she'd fled her home city by rail to Spain. From there she'd boarded an ocean liner to northern Africa, eventually ending up in free French controlled Casablanca. There, she'd performed for several weeks before getting very sick and finding herself hospitalized. While recuperating, she spent time praying and strategizing. By the time she left the hospital, she had already made plans to travel to London.

Her name and fame opened doors and within days she had a planned meeting with Charlene Radden, head of a unique Special Operations division. As Virginia sat outside her office, she thought about what she would say and how she would explain her plan. Before she could decide on a good conversation starter, the heavy wooden door across the hall from her opened and a young male clerk in a crisp British military uniform waved in her direction, gesturing her inside.

She stood and ran a casual hand down the skirt of her blue silk suit, then shifted her hand to the hat perched at a daring angle on the side of her head. By touch, her appearance felt right. With a dazzling smile, she stepped forward and followed the clerk into the office.

Empty bookshelves sat behind a scarred desk. Nothing personal adorned any surface at all. Two posters with the 'V' for victory hung haphazardly on two of the walls. An older woman wearing a crisp white cotton shirt and black skirt sat at a table by a window. Her blonde hair, cut in a bob to her chin, had gray streaks running through it. When she spotted Virginia, she stood and came toward her.

"Miss Benoit," the older woman greeted warmly while very precisely and correctly pronouncing her name, "it is a very real pleasure to meet you. I am Charlene Radden."

She extended both of her hands, and Virginia placed her fingertips in them, returning the squeeze. "I am so thankful you agreed to see me," Virginia said in English, her voice betraying a Louisiana accent developed during her childhood on the banks of Lake Pontchartrain.

"How could one refuse to consider such an intriguing offer?" She gestured toward the table. "Come and sit down and let's talk."

Virginia perched on the end of a wooden chair across from Charlene but did not settle back and relax. Years of stage training showed through as she sat bolt upright on the edge of the seat with her body turned at a very slight angle to the room's best light. Her knees bent and her ankles crossed and she folded her hands neatly on the scratched wooden tabletop before she spoke. "There is a Nazi General named Schmid who has confessed that he is madly in love with me."

Charlene lowered herself into her chair and looked at Virginia with wide eyes. Then she blinked and her face cleared. "Well," she said in her cultured British voice, "I must say I don't hear claims like that every day."

Virginia smiled. "I imagine not. Especially when you consider that I am not of the Aryan race. Far from it, in fact." She gestured at her trim and athletic dancer's body. "In 1932, Schmid saw me perform in Morocco. He has been enamored with my stage presence ever since and arranged private meetings with me on more than one occasion."

Charlene raised an eyebrow. "I can think of a dozen ways that can help us. What I can't think of is how. After all, you're French with an American heritage. Strictly speaking, neither country is a friend of Berlin at the moment. The news is full of all the American Nazi sympathizers: Rockefeller, Hearst, Mellon, Lindbergh..."

"Well," Virginia said on a drawn out breath, "I think I have an idea."

"Oh?"

"America has been begging me to come back. I think I can use the racial tension there to generate some really bad press that will make everyone think I'd rather be in Europe."

Charlene sat back a bit. "I'm not sure what you mean. There are no worse racists on this planet than the Nazis. I'm sure you've seen the newsreels of the Olympics a few years back."

The memory of Jesse Owens taking the gold medal right before the very eyes of the infuriated *Führer* in the very heart of his capital city brought an involuntary if dazzling smile to Virgina's lips. "It was a very proud moment for me, actually."

Charlene allowed herself a mean little grin. "For me as well. Now do tell me, in your mind, how does your plan play out?"

Virginia unfolded her hands and placed them in her lap. She didn't want even a slight tremor to affect this woman's judgment about her competence or ability to pull off a dangerous mission. "There is a very well-known broadcaster in America who is vocally against the Nazi movement there in the United States and abroad. He insults Hitler throughout his show and it is the most listened to and widely heard Radio show in ..." She considered her next words. "In the history of the world, I suppose."

Charlene nodded. "I'm familiar … and a bit of a fan. Do you know him personally?"

Virginia nodded. "I do. I think I can convince him to play along. He and I can stage a very public disagreement which would make me look sympathetic to Hitler's Berlin."

Charlene pursed her lips and sat back in her chair. "That may destroy any hope you have of a career in America. Or in England after the war, for that matter. Certainly wouldn't make you popular in France, either."

Virginia leaned forward and placed her palm on the table. "Mrs. Radden …"

"It's Major, actually," Charlene corrected with a long-suffering smile. "I just don't wear the uniform when I'm in London. Loose lips and whatnot."

"My apologies. Major Radden, everything I hold dear has been destroyed by the Fascist war machine. I've lost my home. I've lost my work. I've lost many, many friends. Win or lose, I'm afraid the world will never be the same."

Without actually moving in the chair, she appeared to settle back into her seat, then casually brushed at the upswept hair at her crown. As if weighing her words carefully, she added, "I am entirely unfamiliar with your religious beliefs, Major Radden, but speaking for myself, I feel very strongly that God has called me to do this. In light of that, I feel my reputation is a small price to pay. I am determined. If I can arrive in occupied France at the invitation of and as a trusted – *friend* – of General Schmid, and if I can perform for him, then I can observe all kinds of things and report to you what I see. I feel I will be ideally placed for exactly the kind of 'on the ground' reconnaissance you require. Additionally, I may have access to sensitive information the General may inadvertently disclose because he ignorantly believes the illiterate Negro girl on his arm doesn't know any better."

"It may very well cost you more than your reputation," Charlene said. She leaned back in her chair and braced her elbows on the arms, steepling her fingers. "Racial tension speaks nothing to what's brewing in the Nazi controlled territories. Our intelligence has uncovered reliable reports of the utter destruction of lives, of arrests for nothing more than the color of one's skin, and of the slow deaths of thousands by means of starvation and deprivation in the forced labor camps Hitler is building as quickly as he can fill them."

Despite the flutter of nerves, Virginia pulled strength from her core and spoke without hesitation. "General Schmid is a man of very high power and influence within the party."

Charlene nodded. "Miss Benoit, I know exactly who Schmid is and the scope of his responsibilities. Rest assured, I understand the value of the proposed target." She brought her steepled fingers to her lips and pursed them, clearly considering every angle. After several long moments, she finally spoke again. "Schmid will only be permitted to consort with you for so long before it becomes a political problem for him. No matter how much power he may wield, it will be no match against the combined hatred of the High Command. The very second the tide begins to turn, your life will be in grave danger."

Virginia lifted her chin. "Major, I'm aware of that. I'm willing to risk my life, or even sacrifice my life. I would not be here otherwise. I am willing to put my life on the line exactly as so many others are doing right now while you and I sit here safe and sound carrying on this hypothetical conversation."

"I see." After a few more breaths and a decisive nod, without leaving her chair Charlene reached back slightly behind her and pulled open a file cabinet drawer. From within it, she withdrew a thick file and set it on the tabletop.

"I'm recruiting members for a special team. I still need a few more members with particular specialties, but I'm looking for exceptional women who can all work with or for each other. Traditionally, this hasn't sorted out well because of what the higher ups refer to as petty jealousies, infighting, and generally catty behavior. Therefore, this team is under a great deal of scrutiny. It will require a special type of woman. I believe you to be such a woman.

"You mentioned your faith. I think women working together in a team who have a shared sense of purpose and shared faith will be incredibly useful." She opened the file and Virginia caught a glimpse of a photograph of a very serene and proper looking blonde woman. "You can imagine there are countless missions needing to come off very quickly and immeasurable intelligence needing to be gathered if we're to actually win this war."

"Of course."

"Be honest. Do you feel Schmid might warn you if he were ordered to arrest you?"

Virginia considered the man, examined his actions and words in her mind. "I do believe he would warn me, but I don't believe he would risk completely ruining his career for me. He certainly wouldn't aid or abet my fleeing the country, for example."

"Miss Benoit, we are not completely absent of resources. If we had sufficient warning, we would have no need of any German aid or assistance."

Charlene closed the file and stood. "Very well. Let's make contact with our counterparts in America and see what we must do to set this rather gigantic ball rolling. In the meantime, we'll send you to our exclusive training ground outside of Milton Keynes where you may begin your training in how we do things, and meet your counterparts of course."

Virginia stood. "Thank you, Major. I hope you won't regret this."

As Charlene walked with her toward the door, she smiled very warmly. "Somehow, I am beyond certain that I will not regret this, Miss Benoit. I've learned in my career to listen to those God sends, and I believe you are such a person. Speaking of hope, you have certainly inspired a sense of hope in me today; hope for the war and hope for my homeland. For that, I thank you most sincerely."

❚ ❚ ❚ ❚

CHAPTER 2

Chapter Two

Outside of Milton Keynes, England: 1942

VIRGINIA used the fountain pen to carefully inscribe the coded message on the back of a sheet of staff paper. The front contained the sheet music and lyrics for one of her songs. It was difficult to do because she could only see the message until it dried, and with the busyness of the music on the other side, it eventually made her eyes want to cross.

The department had worked with her to develop a code based on music she could easily remember. It wouldn't stand up to any serious scrutiny by enemy crypto-analysts, but it was what they could do without actually giving her a code book that might, despite caution, become compromised once detected. A code book would certainly give her away.

Virginia worked closely with Aaron Turlington, the chemist at the Special Operations Directorate, to create an invisible ink that could be carried with her while she traveled and performed, yet not stand out as suspicious if someone searched her belongings. They developed a compressed cobalt salt that looked like blue eye shadow. He taught her how to break down some of the compressed chemical, how to mix it with her light perfume, which was mostly alcohol, to catalyze the ink and make it liquid, and how to use it.

As she finished the last page, she sat back and rolled her head on her shoulders. All this training made her antsy to return to France and put the skills she'd learned over the last several months to good use.

"Beautiful," Aaron said in his Scottish brogue, scooping the paper up from in front of her. "You have truly mastered this technique."

"Thank you. You've been an amazing teacher." Virginia stood and moved out from behind the table. She wore a dark olive green wool suit, with a tan shirt and tan tie, a thick brown belt sat tight around her waist. She tugged at the hem of the jacket and straightened the material. It was certainly a far cry and well removed from gold sequins and high heels. She wore her hair twisted into a tight bun and no makeup. She barely recognized herself in the mirror in the mornings.

Aaron waved the paper and let the last of the ink dry. He was a small man, probably just a few inches taller than five feet, with thinning brown hair and pale brown eyes. He also had a brilliant chemist's mind. Virginia had learned so much from him in such a short amount of time, surprising herself at her love of chemicals and reactions. For weeks, she'd read every book they would lend her on the subject of chemistry and her fascination just continued to grow. She and Aaron had formed a strong bond of mentor and starry-eyed student that she absolutely loved and hoped to always have.

The door opened, and the woman known to Virginia only by her code name, Prudence, came in. She stood average height with a thin build and blonde hair. She spoke, walked, and moved like a member of the aristocracy. Like most women there, Virginia wondered what her real story was. Of course, they couldn't ask. The fewer details they knew about each other, the safer all of them would be in France.

"Well, Hope," she greeted, using Virginia's code name even though everyone knew her real name, "it's official. I am now the new piano instructor who will travel between Montoire-sur-le-Loir and Paris." She smirked and wiggled her fingers, granting an exceedingly rare glimpse into her prewar life. "Who knew all those hours and hours my governess forced me to practice would actually be of use to anyone at all?"

With a sigh she continued, "Good thing she didn't allow me to learn to ride steeplechase as I'd have strongly preferred, else who knows *what* Major Radden might have me doing over there. Mucking stalls, no doubt."

Virginia giggled. It sounded like a little sneeze. "You'd be jumping fences and riding away from Germans like an American cowboy."

"Or toward them with my six-shooter blazing, like as not, if this experience has been any indication."

"Exactly. Just like Ginger Rogers." Virginia scooped up a sheet of staff paper. "See anything here?"

Prudence took the paper from her and examined it, front and back. She held it up to the light. "No, absolutely nothing. Not even marks from the pen."

"Wonderful!" Virginia said. "I think Aaron's going to show you how to reveal the ink now."

"I will, yes. And we're going to find a way to keep the supplies simple so that anyone inspecting your residence won't find it odd that you have them." He wagged a thin finger in her direction. "Destroy them every time you read a missive. Do not keep them. All of them will be Hope's personal music sheets and will be traceable back to her."

"Of course, yes," Prudence said. "I'm aware of the risks."

Virginia took her hand and squeezed it. "For both of us." She looked at the clock on the wall. "I need to rush. I have another code writing class."

"If you see Temperance, remind her of the Bible study tonight. I don't know if she got the notice that we've changed the time."

"I will." Virginia looked at Aaron. "Thank you for your patience in working with me all of these weeks."

"I've greatly enjoyed it, Hope. Godspeed to you."

Virginia left the small room in the wood framed structure and stepped outside. Their organization trained on the estate of an earl. Temporary buildings and barracks filled the once beautiful lawn, and uniformed men and women, horses, cars, and trucks created roads and paths all over the grounds. Virginia imagined the estate was an amazing sight to behold in its glory days before the war.

She thought of her own little chateau in Royan in the southern part of France. Her property overlooked the ocean and she'd spent many, many nights in her gardens extending hospitality to friends and colleagues in the entertainment industry. She tried to always keep her fully staffed home open to guests. She rarely had a breakfast without a friend sharing the table with her.

A part of her wondered what would return to normal when this war ended. Wondering about the state of her home in France, she considered this family which had so willingly given up their home for the war effort and the sacrifices they made to have their personal space so thoroughly invaded.

She crossed the east side of the estate and entered a long, low building that housed the dozens of men and women training at row after row of tables filled with wireless machines. In no time, she spotted her friend, Temperance, sitting at a machine, earphones over her dark curls, head bent as she listened to the tones coming through the speakers on her ears. She transcribed quickly onto a scrap of paper with a dull pencil while two men stood over her shoulders watching. A few more scribbles on the paper and she tossed her pencil down and straightened. She glanced over each shoulder and looked surprised that the men stood there.

"Brilliant," said the one on her right. He had tucked his uniform cap under his right arm and reached out to pick up the paper with his left hand. "I've never seen anyone transcribe so quickly."

Temperance tapped her temple. "You should have had women doing this before." She smiled. "Maybe it's the female brain that's so brilliant." She stood when she saw Virginia. "Vvv … Hope!"

Virginia moved around two tables before she reached her. "I don't mean to interrupt," Virginia drawled. "I just wanted to make sure you knew about tonight's time change."

"Yes! Eight. Grace has something she's doing."

"A night jump from a balloon, if I'm not mistaken," Virginia said. The war had taken a toll on aircraft and fuel. Hot air balloons exactly like the Barrage Balloons employed for air raid defense over London's factories with the addition of large baskets strung beneath, now trained parachutists over empty pastures. Hot air balloons were far more inexpensive to fabricate and operate than the propeller driven aircraft that were desperately needed elsewhere. Virginia considered what it must be like to step out into a thousand foot drop in complete silence and the thought made her shudder. "I'm so glad they aren't sticking me in a parachute."

"I can't believe you didn't have to learn like the rest of us," Temperance laughed.

"I'm not going in secret," Virginia said. "I'll be arriving back in Paris with cameras rolling and lights flashing. No need for me to risk injury that could delay the mission by leaping out of a perfectly good airplane."

The field telephone in the corner of the room rang. One of the men who had observed Temperance transcribe answered it, then looked at Hope. "Major Radden wishes to see you in her office," he said as he hung up the phone.

Virginia nodded and smiled at Temperance. See you tonight." She looked at the man who had answered the phone. "You and I have a transcribing class."

He waved in her direction. "Charlene first. If you still have time, come back after."

Virginia hurried out the door and across the grounds. She passed by the beautiful fountain that stood sentry in front of the home of the earl, through the large front doors, and into the main hall that led to the administrative offices. She went up two flights of stairs and down the hall to Charlene's office door.

She tapped lightly on the door and almost immediately Charlene's voice bade her enter. As she came into the room, she stopped, surprised to see her business manager, Benson Dubois, there in a chair in front of the desk. He stood as she entered and approached with his arms open. "My dear," he said in French, kissing both of her cheeks, "I have missed you so much."

He stood perhaps three inches taller than she. A dark gray suit, tailor made, fit him perfectly, accentuating his boxer's body that received a daily workout in his brother's gym. A silk burgundy vest covered most of his white shirt and she could see the gold chain of his trademark pocket watch hanging out of the vest pocket. She recognized the familiar smell of his favorite hair pomade and the peppermint on his breath.

Homesickness swamped her eyes filled with tears. "And I you." She squeezed his hands as she moved to sit in a chair in front of Charlene's desk. "What are you doing here?"

"We have accomplished our mission," Charlene interjected, leaning back in the chair. "Your double performed perfectly thanks in large part to Mr. Dubois. I confess I had my doubts and I am overjoyed to have been incorrect in my assessment of our chances. She got into a very public racial fight with some prominent media personnel in a night club. America has collectively withdrawn any desire for Virginia Benoit to perform there, and many newspapers have bid you to return to France and good riddance." She paused and looked Virginia in the eye.

"They were not kind. I know it must be hurtful. This nation and France are so grateful for the sacrifice you have made. I believe America is at a tipping point and will soon be forced to choose sides as well. I personally believe they will come to our aid as they did in the last Great War. When that happens, this conflict will get very bloody and more's the shame. But as soon as this wretched war is over, we shall come clean with as much about you as we are able. You have my solemn word."

Virginia always dreamed of achieving the kind of success that would allow her return to America with love and acceptance despite any ill conceived prejudices about skin color. She knew the damage today would be hard to undo, even with full disclosure after the fact.

Sadness swept through her at the thought of the destruction of one of her dreams. But she realized, as she sat there internally feeling sorry for herself, that her friends and loved ones currently lived under the brutal jack boot heel of Nazi rule. How could her sacrifice measure up against that? If her professional reputation was the price of aiding to bring an end to the Nazi reign, so be it.

She cleared her throat. "I'm happy it worked. What's next?"

Charlene raised an eyebrow, her eyes giving away the respect she clearly felt for Virginia. "Now we get you back to Casablanca. As far as anyone is concerned, you're on a ship bound for the South of France, with a port call in Casablanca. We'll sneak you on board."

Virginia nodded. "Very well. When will that be?"

"Tonight."

Her heart felt like it fell to her chest. "Tonight?"

"Right-o. Spit-spot. No time to waste. Go collect the checklist we created last week and get packing. Aaron should have made your chemicals to look like makeup items by now. Drop in on him first and collect those things."

Virginia knew she was being dismissed. She stood and held a hand out to Benson. "I cannot thank you enough, Benson. As with so many things you have helped me with since the day we first met, I couldn't have done this without you."

He stood and took her by her shoulders, looking her up and down, inspecting the olive green wool suit. "I will not be able to live with myself if I don't say this. Hope. Please reconsider. It's not too late to back out. We can spend the war in Switzerland. You can nurse the wounded and play for hospital camps in relative safety and freedom."

She framed his face with her hands. "I shall not."

Benson shook his head. "This isn't our war, Virginia."

"Tut tut!" Major Radden corrected.

"Hope, I mean." Benson conceded.

Virginia smiled at him. In her memory she had never seen him so flustered. She found his concern touching. "But God hath made of one blood all nations of men that dwell upon all the face of the earth, and hath determined the times before appointed, and the bounds of their habitation. One blood, Benson. We are all sons of Adam and daughters of Eve." She had paraphrased the verse from Acts so many times, it spilled off her tongue like a poem.

Benson digested her words and she added, "Pray for me, my friend. I will see you as soon as this is over," she said it warmly, meaning it. She would not be defeated.

"I am going to hold you to that. I have a big comeback tour already planned for the hero of France. We'll get someone to write your memoirs. Forrester or Williams, perhaps. Then Broadway and Hollywood for the rest of your days."

She touched his cheek. "I'll keep my promise, Benson. Count on it."

Determined, she left the room and went to her barracks to pack.

8 8 8 8

VIRGINIA pulled the cotton burka over her clothes and placed the thin obi veil on her head, pulling the edge of it over her face and fastening it so that only her eyes could be seen. She slipped the door open and stepped out into the busy alley.

In her attire, she blended in perfectly and no one spared her a second glance. She had always traveled to Morocco in style, with drivers and guides and status. On the ground, in a burka, just woman among a sea of other humans, she experienced an entirely different Casablanca. The heat of the African sun beat down on her head and baked everything around her. The smell of the alleys and ditches rose up and mingled with the stench of unwashed bodies, making her thankful for the veil that covered her mouth and nose. No one appeared to care whether they knocked into her or tried to walk through her. After a few seconds of getting knocked about, she turned aggressor and pushed her way through the busy streets. Five minutes later than she should have, she made her way to the docks and found the rendezvous point on the edge of the proper dock. As soon as she bent to check her sandal, the directed tell for her contact, she felt someone stop next to her. She looked up and met his eyes.

He gestured to the stack of crates filled with pomegranates. As he picked one up and put it on his shoulder, he watched to make sure she did the same. Struggling against the heavy skirt and confining head piece, Virginia picked up the crate and hefted it onto her shoulder, then followed him down the dock, holding the crate steady with one hand and holding her skirts up with the other so that she wouldn't trip.

They boarded the ship and followed a deckhand to the galley storage area. There, Virginia set the crate down as her double came out from behind a stack of boxes. The man spoke in English, "Change clothes. I'll wait outside."

As he shut the door behind him, Virginia unclipped the veil covering her face. "This thing is heavy in that heat out there."

It shocked her how much the other woman resembled her. She thought that surely they must share common relatives for the likeness to be so strong. Of course, much of it had to do with the careful application of makeup. And, Virginia was at least an inch taller. Despite that, it was shocking.

"Hopefully, I won't be in it long," the double replied. "I'm going from here to the airport."

They switched clothes. Virginia slipped on the blue silk dress and blue heels. She settled the hat with the peacock feathers on it on her head while her double fastened the veil. The shoes pinched her toes, and she hoped that some of her real clothes and shoes waited for her in her cabin.

"You're in cabin 72. Cyllia is waiting for you there."

"What?" Incredulity raced through her. "What is she doing here?"

"We did everything in our power to keep her from joining us, but she absolutely insisted. She said you'd want her here."

"I sent her to you to keep her safe."

They spoke in harsh whispers. "She gained permission from your superiors to join you, saying that it would look wrong if she was not with you. Apparently, they agreed."

Clenching her teeth to keep from screaming in frustration, Virginia ripped open the door. The man waiting looked from one to the other, but she barely spared him a glance. She looked behind her and lifted her hand in a salute before she turned the corner and found the stairs. As she put her hand on the railing, someone spoke from behind her.

"Can I help you?"

The man spoke in French and wore the uniform of a waiter. Virginia smiled her warmest smile and replied. "I certainly hope you can, young man. I was looking for the kitchen to ask for a snack and something cool to drink. This heat will be the death of me! I'm afraid I've just gotten so turned around."

When he saw her face, he clearly recognized her. The star struck gaze filled his eyes and his cheeks flushed bright red. "Of course, *Mademoiselle* Benoit. What is your cabin number, if I may? I will show you to your room."

"You are too kind," she said, scooting next to him and looping her arm through his. "I don't know why I didn't just ring the kitchen."

"I'll get you to your room and bring something back for you. What would you like?"

"Just some fruit and lemonade would be wonderful. Perhaps some coffee for later?" She patted his arm and batted her eyes. "Thank you. I was so fortunate to run into you."

He walked her through the narrow hallways. As they approached her first class cabin door, she cooed and thanked him and he gave a stiff bow. "I will return immediately with fruit and coffee, *Mademoiselle* Benoit."

As she slipped into her cabin, she saw Cyllia folding clothes and packing them into a suitcase. As soon as her maid saw her, she rushed toward her, tears in her eyes. "I have missed you!"

Virginia hugged her tightly then released her. "What are you doing here?"

"You wouldn't travel without your maid. Schmid knows that."

With a sigh, Virginia took off the hat. "I know. But I wanted to keep you safe. I was going to hire a maid."

"France is my home, too. I can't sit in America while you do this. I need to be with you and help you." She put her hands on her hips. "A hired maid would find you out. You'll have more freedom of motion with me."

Defeated, she sat on the edge of the bed. "You're right." In the familiar luxurious surroundings of her favorite ship line, in the presence of her dearest and most trusted friend, she felt exhaustion suddenly swamp her. Holding back a yawn, she kicked off the tight shoes. "When do we arrive in France?"

"Not until tomorrow night."

"I'm going to rest. A waiter is bringing a snack. Enjoy it." She slipped off the dress, and clad in only a slip, crawled under the covers. "Her shoes are too small for me."

"I have a trunk of your clothes. I'll take care of it."

"Thank you," she acknowledged, almost slurring as she closed her eyes and let sleep overtake her.

§ § § §

Chapter Three

VIRGINIA sat, posed, in the winged back chair in the living room of her hotel suite. She wore a flowing gown of peach chiffon that gathered together in the front at a diamond-shaped cluster of rhinestones. Silver high heels studded with matching rhinestones adorned her feet, and multiple silver bracelets clinked on one arm whenever she moved.

She expected General Schmid at any time.

When she heard the knock on her door, she nodded her head to Cyllia who opened the door for General Schmid. He held his hat under his arm and rushed into the room, making a beeline for Virginia and ignoring Cyllia entirely. "*Mademoiselle* Benoit," he said enthusiastically, "how I have missed our rendezvous."

Virginia held a hand up to him to take. "General. It is a pleasure to see you again. Thank you for the papers allowing my passage back into Paris."

"I am sorry that your home is not available. High ranking officials have taken up residence in every home on your street."

"I appreciate the hotel room. I'm very grateful. I'm sure it was hard to come by."

"Not for me. You may stay here as long as I am in Paris." He finally released her hand and she gracefully laid it in her lap. "Your offer to entertain the troops in France has been approved. I am already making plans."

"Wonderful! I think I would go mad if I had to continue not performing."

"You have not performed this entire time?" The General lowered himself until he sat, perched on the edge of the couch. He set his hat on the cushion next to him and angled his body toward her.

Virginia waved a hand in a dismissive gesture. "I have not performed in weeks. I have no desire to perform for the Americans." She said the last word as if it tasted bad on her tongue, despite her true and genuine love of the country of her birth. "I knew I would come home."

Cyllia hurried into the room carrying a tea tray. Virginia motioned toward the low coffee table and watched as the younger woman gracefully set it down. "Tea, General?"

"No, I really must be going. I have to leave for a few days. My clerk will contact you soon with details of our tour." He scooped up his hat as he stood and nodded. "I am so pleased to see you. I hope that you will do me the honor of having a meal with me when I return next week."

Virginia moved her arm just so the bracelets would jingle. "Of course, General. I look forward to it."

"Not nearly as much as I do." He turned toward the door and reached it just as Cyllia opened it. He did not even spare her a glance as he left the room.

Virginia sat and waited until she counted to one hundred, not wanting to make any major moves until she was certain he would not return. Once she felt comfortable that the coast was clear, she stood and rushed to her room. She grabbed a folder off the top of her dresser and took out a sheet of music for *La Grâce du Ciel,* the French translation of *Amazing Grace.*

She went to her dressing table and opened a container of pressed eye shadow with three shades of blue. Using a small metal file, she scraped some of the blue from the center section into a little glass bowl. Going through the process taught to her by her instructors, she added a squirt of this and a drop of that and stirred it all together.

Then she took a small, thin lipstick brush, and dipped it into the blue liquid. Using the brush, she dashed off a note in between the lines of music on the sheet.

TOUR APPROVED. WILL FORWARD SCHEDULE WHEN I HAVE IT. ALL IS WELL. HOPE.

She waved the paper so that the liquid would dry. Once it was completely dry, Virginia examined it. She could see no sign of the markings.

She slipped the sheet of music into her portfolio, grabbed her hat and her bag, and slipped out of the town house, telling Cyllia only that she would return soon. Her young maid had an infinite amount of loyalty, but absolutely no training. She knew nothing about Virginia's specific mission nor her methods, only the covert nature of their presence there. Virginia intended to keep it that way.

As casually and confidently as possible, Virginia strolled to the little church on the corner of the street catty-corner to her favorite bakery. She glanced around as she entered the church. At three in the afternoon on a Tuesday, the building was relatively empty. She entered the sanctuary and moved quickly down the aisle. She placed the sheet music at the organ under the stained glass window.

Moving back to the first row, she turned the first hymnal book around so that the back faced out. This was the signal that she'd left a message.

Once she'd completed her duty, she pulled out a prayer bench and slipped to her knees. She didn't feel fear or apprehension, but she knew she needed strength and endurance to get through the next several weeks. She prayed that the mission would go smoothly and for her friends' safety and protection. And, as always, she prayed for an end to the Nazi Regime and the wisdom to know what she could do to help hurry that along.

In a way it surprised her that Schmid had managed to arrange her tour dates. The Nazi high command did not look kindly on people different from the so-called Aryan race. She wondered what strings he'd pulled to maneuver it. Perhaps her stardom offered her some respite from the typical racism.

Either way, she'd need to move quickly when the time came to leave. She had a feeling that the acceptance of Miss Virginia Benoit was merely temporary.

𝄞 𝄞 𝄞 𝄞

VIRGINIA closed her eyes as she sang, giving the appearance of soulful emotion when all she did was give her eyes a break from the glare of the burning hot lights. She gripped the microphone stand and finished the song, opening her eyes and raising her arms above her head. The feathers attached to the white silk of her sleeves and the lights shining off of her golden skull cap gave her the appearance of an angel.

The German soldiers filling the audience surged to their feet in one accord. Their applause, whistles, and yells almost made the walls in the little club shake. Virginia posed, a hand on her hip and one foot jutted out, knowing that the lights reflected off of the gold sequins sewn throughout the gold lamé skirt. The slit was cut to her thigh, and on her feet she wore gold and silver heels. Light reflected off of the sequins and metal, adding to stunning appearance.

She'd swept her hair up and tucked it under the gold cap. Hoops dangled from her ears, gold tassels hung from her hat, rhinestones glittered around her neck, and wore silver and gold gloves that ended at her elbows. All in all, she knew she looked remarkable and that she dazzled those soldiers out there.

With a sly smile, she sashayed off of the stage, stopping at the curtain to turn and blow a kiss to the audience. She ignored the feelings of disgust at the thought of her performance, both off and on stage. With absolute certainty, she knew she was doing the right thing. Nothing else mattered.

Forty minutes later, she stood in the ballroom of a mansion, holding a glass of champagne in one hand and the back of a wing backed chair in the other. Two generals and a colonel stood around her, all of them talking over each other to get her attention. While they talked, she took note of names, faces, and as much information as she could glean from conversations around her, doing her best to memorize it all.

"*Mademoiselle* Benoit," General Schmid announced, putting an unwelcome and all too familiar hand on her waist, clearly staking claim, a movement not lost on the other officers in their corner. "You were stunning tonight."

"Thank you," she said with a slow smile. "I'm so glad you enjoyed the show."

"It was everything I had hoped it to be," he said sincerely.

She set her still full glass on the tray held by a passing waiter and disengaged herself from the General's hand. "It felt good to perform again after so long." With a smile at the men, she said, "Would you excuse me, gentlemen? I'm afraid that General Schmid has a tough schedule outlined for the next few weeks, and I need to finish packing."

As they murmured their good-byes to her, she turned and faced Schmid. "General, thank you again for the honor of performing."

"I will see you bright and early, *Mademoiselle* Benoit," he said, taking her gloved hand and pressing a kiss to her knuckles. He held up a hand and waved at a young uniformed man who stood by the doorway. As the man approached he said, "See *Mademoiselle* home, *Oberleutnant*."

Virginia gave the young blond man her brightest smile. "Thank you, sir."

"My pleasure, *Mademoiselle*."

Chapter Four

VIRGINIA stepped out of the truck, taking the hand of the large white haired man with the thick black framed glasses. "Thank you, Colonel Müller," she said, stepping up onto the walk in front of the building that housed the prisoners. "I am so appreciative of you taking the time to show me around." She glanced at the predawn sky. She knew it wasn't quite six. Her conversation with Abiel had happened less than five hours ago. When she returned to the hotel room, she had scrambled to arrange this meeting. Thankfully, Müller typically arrived to work by five, which gave her time to make official arrangements.

She'd dressed carefully in a yellow wool suit. She'd added thick wooden beads painted a deep orange around her neck, matching bracelets, and red shoes. Her hat perched at an angle on her head, sported red, orange, and yellow feathers. She intended to look like a morning sunrise. The look of appreciation on the Colonel's face told her she had more than accomplished her intent.

"Well, General Schmid was generous to share your company," he said, offering his arm, clearly buying her lie that Schmid had suggested the prison tour to her. "I was surprised to hear that you wanted a tour of the facility, especially so early in the morning."

"I am determined to see as much as I can at each of our stops. I know that the German army is very skilled in … dealing … with prisoners. I admit I'm curious. And, with my schedule, this is truly late at night for me. I would typically be going to bed soon and rising for the day in the mid to late afternoon. Your secretary assured my assistant that you would be available."

"Of course. I am an early riser. I hope you don't mind that I took the liberties of having a breakfast meal prepared." He cleared his throat and paused with his hand on the door. "I'm afraid that some things in here would be shocking to a lady. If you'd rather just go enjoy breakfast –"

"Colonel," she said with her coyest smile, "I was raised in the nightclub scene in St. Louis, Missouri. I can assure you, little would shock me."

He laughed as if he understood what she meant, even though he couldn't possibly know. Instead, he opened the door. "I will begin your tour, then."

He took her through a guard gate and into the inner sanctum of the building. Her heels clicked on the tile floor. Along the walls, propaganda posters shared space with posters of rules and regulations written in both French and German. As they passed soldiers and guards, they came to attention and stared straight ahead. The colonel did not acknowledge anyone in the halls.

"The first two floors are simply administrative. They really have nothing to do with the prison." As they walked along the hall, he pointed out some of the rooms, explained some of the duties, but left some rooms ignored. They reached a large staircase and he gestured for her to go up. While they climbed, he talked about the past.

"My wife and I saw you perform in Paris about six years ago," he said. "We loved it so much that we went back the next night. You are a very talented performer."

"Thank you," Virginia said, smiling. "Where is your wife now?"

He frowned. "She died at the hands of a British bombing raid." They reached the landing. "We lost her parents on the same day."

Virginia gasped. "That's awful. I'm so sorry."

With a nod, he said, "Those are the horrors of war." He gestured to keep climbing. "The second floor is where confidential duties are performed. I'm afraid we'll need to continue up." They went up another flight of stairs. At the landing, he opened a door and they stepped into a room almost the size as the footprint of the building.

He waved his hand toward a cage in the center of the room. "I'm sorry you have to see this. We have a new prisoner who has just come in yesterday afternoon. A spy. I'm afraid it's not a pretty sight."

As she looked up, she prepared herself to show no outward reaction. Instead, she forced a look of stoicism onto her face as she looked at the beaten and battered body of one of her best friends. Temperance wore only a thin slip and stood in the corner of the cage, her back to the soldier who currently shot her with a strong stream of water. Their eyes met, and for a moment, she didn't think Temperance recognized her. When she did, Virginia could see the change in the look of her eyes, but she gave nothing away. Instead, she lowered her eyes and reached forward, gripping the bar of the cage with one hand, holding her other hand cradled against her chest.

Colonel Müller barked an order from beside her and the deluge of water ended. The guards tossed the hose aside. As Virginia looked on, Temperance did not move from her position. But she watched as her friend's body shuddered against the cold.

Virginia looked away before she lost her composure. "That method has proven to be effective?" As she spoke, she swallowed the bile that had rushed to the back of her throat.

"Keeps them awake and miserable. Soon, she'll do anything and say anything to be warm and dry again." He gestured with his hand. "This way, *Mademoiselle*."

They toured the third floor and Virginia met several officers with various titles and duties she did her best to remember. Most of the floor was reserved for administrative offices, but there was a long hallway of prison cells. She saw prisoners with every luxury imaginable in a prison, and some that looked like they were on the verge of death in bare cells that contained nothing but a mattress and a bucket. There didn't appear to be a rhyme or reason for the difference in treatment. She wondered if that was also an interrogation tactic.

They went up to the fourth floor, which was basically comprised of two large cells with a wide aisle running between the two. One of the cells was empty, the other full of too many men for the few beds available.

"We are constructing a prisoner of war camp about twenty kilometers outside of town," Müller said. "This side just left for their shift in building the prison. In another month, we will transport all of these prisoners to live there." One of the prisoners in the crowded cell, a tall black-haired man, approached the bars. "This is British Captain Ewing. He is the resident leader for Block B."

"Virginia Benoit," the Captain said in a British accent. Virginia felt a tug in her heart, missing her sisters in arms and the months she spent training in England. "I never imagined that I'd meet you under these circumstances, but I confess I always held onto a slim hope I could meet you someday." His smile was very charming.

He said hope. He must be the contact. She had to insert yes into her reply so that he'd know she'd seen Temperance. Virginia raised an eyebrow. "Yes. Indeed."

He winked and leaned a shoulder up against the bars. "Very few people can –" he looked her up and down very pointedly, "–carry a tune like you."

Virginia allowed heat to flood her cheeks and gasped out loud. "Such impudence from a man behind bars!" She turned toward her host. "Colonel Müller, I believe I am ready for that breakfast you promised me."

"Of course! Please, this way," he said, holding an arm out for her to take. Without a backward glance, she strolled from the room, but not before she heard Colonel Müller ordering the guard to have Captain Ewing whipped. She felt her heart leap to her throat and wanted to turn back around and beg him not to do such a thing, but she knew she could not. Instead, she kept walking and started praying.

♫ ♫ ♫ ♫

VIRGINIA wrote with her special chemicals as quickly as she could.

TEMPERANCE ALIVE. HARSH INTERROGATION

She didn't know what else to say. She wasn't sure if she should mention the man who made contact with her at the prison or not.

As she glanced at her watch, she saw that it was already nine in the morning. She had no idea how long it had been since Temperance's capture. Maybe fifteen or sixteen hours?

Shaking off the fatigue of being awake all night, she rushed to grab her cloak. The chemicals were almost dry. She slipped the sheet music into the inside pocket of her cloak and rushed out of the hotel room. No one intercepted her as she exited the building, and she quickly walked down the street to the designated church.

When she went inside, she saw two women lighting candles so she went to the front of the church and sat in the front pew, bowing her head. As soon as she heard the door close behind them, she turned to look and saw no one else there. She rushed to the organ, placed the music on the music stand, then went back to the first row and flipped the appropriate hymnal over.

Not wanting to take any more time, she went ahead and left the church. She rushed back down the street, but as she approached the hotel, she slowed her walk to a stroll, lifting her head high and casually sauntering into the lobby.

Nodding to the people who caught her eye, she went to the lift. When she stepped inside, she said, "Four, please," to the elevator operator.

It wasn't until she was safely inside her room, her mission accomplished, that she felt emotions bubble to the surface.

She went to the bathroom and turned on the faucet to run water for a bath. While the tub filled with hot water, she fell to the floor and leaned against the porcelain tub. Putting a hand over her mouth to stifle any sounds, she wept, feeling like some of the sobs could possibly rip her in half.

The sight of Temperance, what those monsters had done to her; knowing she was lying on some soaking wet cot while Virginia dined on caviar and pastries at six in the morning made her hate herself. Having been through the fortress of that building, she couldn't imagine how they could possibly help her friend.

Fear, foreboding, and helplessness spurred the despair she felt. But, after a few minutes, she brushed her hair back and gracefully stood. That would be the last emotional outburst she'd allow herself. Any more would be too dangerous and would risk exposure. Another time, in another place, she could afford to surrender to her emotions. For now she had to be cool, sexy, and angry enough at America to want to be performing for the Nazis. No matter how ill it made her.

Shoulders squared back, she stripped her clothes off, determined to soak out the horrors of the prison and wash the tears away.

CHAPTER 5

♫ ♫ ♫ ♫

VIRGINIA sat up in her bed. She knew she'd heard something. Listening as intently as possible, she heard no other sound, but suddenly a hand covered her mouth.

"Shh," a voice whispered in her ear. "It's me."

His hand still covering her mouth, she turned her head to see Abiel. As soon as the panic left her chest, he released her mouth, clearly watching her face for signs of her intent to scream.

Virginia looked around the empty room, thinking of her assistant and maid in the other rooms somewhere. She looked at the clock on the nightstand and saw that it was four in the afternoon. She'd come in to lie down and rest before the night's performance.

"What are you doing here?"

He sat on the edge of her bed. In the afternoon light she could see that he had brown curly hair and green eyes. He looked somehow familiar to her, but she could not place him. He spoke with a fluent French accent. "Your missive was incomplete. Did you get a message to the prisoner who had your verse?"

"Yes. I told him I saw her."

He nodded. "Good. Right now he is our only communication with London. He'll inform them that she's still alive and, hopefully, receive information on our instructions."

Virginia's heart twisted painfully in her chest. "What can I do?"

"Tell me everything you saw. Draw me a picture if you can." He looked at her, his dark eyes serious. "See if you can reschedule your prison performance for one week from Thursday. Can you do that? Do you think you can arrange that?"

"I don't know. General Schmid arranges the performances. I don't even know where we're supposed to be next."

He reached over and took her hand. "You must convince him to allow you to come back. Understand?"

"How?"

His smile transformed his face from cold and serious to warm and friendly. "Come now, Virginia. You and I both know you have much in the way of the power of persuasion."

As sweat beaded her upper lip, she nodded. "Very well. I shall endeavor to try."

"You will do more than try. You will succeed. Because we have a fortress to break through to save Temperance, and every single person doing his or her part is the only way our plan will work."

Virginia raised an eyebrow. "Then I will succeed."

"One week from Thursday."

"I understand."

♌ ♌ ♌ ♌

"GENERAL," Virginia said, leaning against his arm as they stood in the drawing room of the home that the local commander had secured for his residence.

"Yes, Miss Benoit?" The General took a sip of his Schnapps as he turned to face her.

"Surely you can call me Virginia by now," she said coyly.

"Of course, Virginia." He reached for her gloved hand and placed a kiss across the knuckles.

"By now I'm sure you know that I had breakfast this morning with Colonel Müller in the prison in the center of the town." She looked around the room at all of the uniformed officers. There were very few women present, and those that were there did not look like wives. They looked too young and too French. Virginia wondered about their situations and whether or not they were here by choice.

He nodded. "I heard. If you had waited for a more reasonable hour, I would have accompanied you."

With a small laugh and a hand to her chest, she said, "I would never have dreamed of disturbing you so early. I was restless and could not sleep. He had extended the invitation through the post with my secretary, so I just took him up on the offer. I pray that I did nothing wrong."

"Of course not, Virginia."

"Well, I was wondering if we could reschedule my performance for the prison workers. Colonel Müller requested it." She put a hand next to her mouth as if to whisper conspiratorially. "He claims he is my biggest fan, but I think both of us know that's not true."

His eyes flared with indignation as his cheeks fused with color. "We are on a schedule. That is impossible."

"Oh come now. It's not like we would be rescheduling for paid ticket holders. We can just shift everything around as needed, could we not? The Colonel informed me that a week from tomorrow, he has a personal friend of Hitler coming to tour the prisons in the area. He has confessed that he would love to impress him with a concert."

"Why would you presume to think it would be that easy?"

She lifted her chin. "Because I have been performing since I was five and I know how the business works. I am Virginia Benoit. Men will wait to see me perform, if they must."

He narrowed his eyes. "Or what?"

She contemplated all of her options. Seduction, manipulation, tears. None of it felt as effective as strength. What Nazi General wouldn't react to strength? "Or maybe I'll get a sore throat for a week or two."

"Is that a threat?"

"A simple request." She waved a waiter over and set her untouched champagne on his tray. "Good evening, sir." She started to walk away. Three feet away, he called her name.

"Virginia!" She paused, but did not turn. "Very well. I will try to reschedule the show here. I will contact Colonel Müller and find out when this official is coming and make the adjustments and arrangements."

Rather than run back to him and thank him, as he likely wanted, she kept her back to him, but regally inclined her head to affirm that she'd heard him, then continued walking.

§ § § §

VIRGINIA carefully painted a map of what she had seen in the prison. She hoped that whoever read it would be able to make sense out of the notes and markings. It was hard enough to write with the chemicals, much less draw detail.

She worked steadily for hours, listing references and details, using the skills for memorization and recollection she'd acquired in training. She included the locations of the prisoners she'd seen, the sounds she heard, the location of the guards that moved and did not move, the extreme number of administrative personnel who were there so early. She marked the rooms Müller ignored when he gave her the tour. When it was all finished, it was as thorough as she could make it.

Around five in the morning, she finished the last of it and set it out to dry. She went into her adjoining bathroom and washed her face and prepared to get some sleep. During this tour, she would have some accommodations as private and comfortable as this one, and some that would be harsh at best. It was her intent to get as much rest as she could while she had this level of luxury to enjoy.

When she went back into her room, she stopped short when she saw Abiel sitting in the armchair next to her fireplace. She pulled the cream silk robe closer around her, gripping it at her throat.

"What are you doing here?"

"What do you have?"

"Did you know that every time you come into my room, you run the risk of exposing us both?" She shifted, uncomfortable with her lack of clothes.

"I don't have time to play cat and mouse with hymns." He stood in a fluid movement and approached her. She realized he was about three inches taller than her, a strange phenomenon for a woman of her height.

"You're right." She moved to the corner of the room, where she'd laid the pages out individually on the floor so that they'd dry. As she gestured to the papers, she turned to face him and realized he'd followed her across the room. "That's everything I could think of, and probably more that you don't need. I gave details of the rooms and the personnel I saw. But, remember, it was early morning. I don't know anything about what would be there in the middle of the night."

"No. But it's something. It's been forty-eight hours since capture. We will soon run out of time."

"How do you know she hasn't been broken yet?"

His eyes were intense when he looked at her. "I don't." In a nearly desperate voice he said, "Did you see her?"

Images assaulted the forefront of Virginia's mind. "I did." Her voice barely came out in a whisper. "They have her in a cage in the middle of the second floor. They were shooting her with a water hose."

"Keeping her awake." He put his hands on her shoulders. "I think that's a good sign of her not breaking yet. We'll hold onto that."

"Hold onto that?" She couldn't help but raise her voice, then immediately regretted it, praying she hadn't woken anyone. She continued in a harsh whisper, "My friend –"

He gave her a small shake. "There is no time for friendship now. That is what the Major tried to drill into you and your little prayer group. Right now, your feelings for Temperance are putting her at risk."

Virginia lifted her chin. "I can work beyond my feelings. And my friendship with her is what is driving me forward, not hindering my ability to work." It suddenly dawned on her what he said. "Wait. Our little prayer group? Who are you?"

He gave a tight shake of his head. "I was just there at the same time as you, is all. I remember seeing your group and thinking that forging bonds that close could only hurt you in the end." He released her and took a step back.

"I thought you looked familiar." She bent and picked up one of the sheets of paper. "The ink isn't quite dry."

"Will it smear?"

"No, but if you're caught with it, an inspection would show that something was written on the back of the music. I would hate for our cover to be blown because you couldn't wait an hour."

He barked a short laugh. "I'll take my chances. I'm meeting Grace at dawn. We have to create a plan."

"I've made arrangements for the show to happen one week from Thursday. Perhaps the preparation and attendance of the show will make everyone a little less diligent, maybe make the prison a little less staffed."

"That would certainly be a vital part of our working plan. I'm sorry that you've been placed in this situation." He knelt down and started stacking the sheet music carefully.

"No need to apologize. We are all here for the same purpose."

He gathered it all into a neat stack then stood straight. "I'm sorry to startle you. Hopefully, I won't have reason to break into your room ever again."

He said it with a smile, and Virginia couldn't help but return it. "Godspeed, Abiel. Please leave me word if there's anything else you need from me."

"Just keep those Jerries' attention while we act. Thank you for what you've done."

Virginia watched him go to the window and step out onto the balcony. He turned and saluted her before going over the side of the railing.

8 8 8 8

CHAPTER 6

Chapter Six

VIRGINIA glanced up at her window as she walked to the hotel and saw the curtains tied together with a red handkerchief. That was her signal to Abiel that she needed to speak to him. She hadn't tied them. What did that mean?

She paused and contemplated before going into the hotel, thankful that Cyllia was at the dressmaker picking up a gown she'd had repaired. As she walked into the hotel, she nodded greetings to the desk clerk and the elevator operator. The ride up to her floor felt like it took forever, and she couldn't help but feel a cold sweat of anticipation.

She approached her door with caution. After the slightest hesitation, she unlocked the door and stepped into the outer room. Nothing appeared out of place. Carefully setting her purse down onto a little side table, she reached into the hidden compartment and pulled out her double barreled .22 caliber Derringer. The tiny weapon fit perfectly in the palm of her feminine hand. As she walked toward the bedroom doorway, she held it at ready, finger on the trigger.

Before she could open the door, it opened and Abiel walked out, followed by another man with dark hair and dark brown eyes. Virginia gasped and put a hand to her chest. "I almost shot you."

Abiel raised an eyebrow. "I think not." He gestured behind him. "This is Matthew."

Virginia held out her hand and shook his. "Hope." She looked at Abiel. "You're lucky I didn't have my maid with me."

"Your maid is currently flirting with a very attractive French boy over a chocolate pastry." Matthew spoke French flawlessly. He moved through the room and sat on the couch. "We have a few minutes."

Virginia pursed her lips. "What do you need?"

Abiel walked over to the window and removed the red handkerchief before responding. "Did you secure a dressing room inside the prison?"

"Yes. Muller got me a supply closet with a connecting bathroom on the first floor." She lowered herself into the wing backed chair and gracefully waved a hand toward him. "I am at your disposal."

His grin transformed his face, softening hard lines, giving him an almost boyish quality. "If only, *Mademoiselle.*" After he winked and she smiled in return, he sobered up again, his face showing the wear of the war on his heart. "Tomorrow I am going to hide in a steamer trunk that you'll have carried into your room."

"I don't think I have –"

Matthew interrupted. "We'll use my trunk. It has a false bottom for my explosives."

Virginia gasped and stared at Abiel. "You're going to ride in the same trunk as your explosives?"

Matthew smiled and she suddenly saw Grace's face. Her eyes widened as she recognized him as one of Grace's brothers. "If something happens and those bombs go off, it won't matter if he's in the same trunk or the next room." He looked at his watch. "What time are you scheduled to arrive at the prison?"

"The show is at twenty-one hundred. I usually arrive two hours before to dress and prepare. Where will the trunk be?"

Abiel slipped his hands into his pockets and leaned a shoulder against the fireplace mantle. "It will be delivered tonight. You need to prepare your items to go into it, in case anyone wants to inspect it. Matthew will come here in the evening and load up the explosives. I'll be with him."

Virginia nodded. "Anything else?"

"We feel like it's getting too dangerous for you here. Word is coming down that the high command does not approve. We feel like this should be your last performance."

Restless, she surged to her feet and paced the length of the room. "I've felt the same way. I would have asked to be removed before now if it wasn't for Temperance."

She stopped in front of him, enjoying the feeling of security at having these two warriors in the room with her. He put a comforting hand on her shoulder. "We have a cafe down by the docks. You go there and tell the waitress, 'Grace and peace abound.' She'll secure you for removal."

She nodded, understanding what he said but not wanting to speak, worried that if she did, he would grab his hat and go, and that would be the last time she saw him. He seemed to understand, because he ran his hand down her arm and took her hand in his. As he opened his mouth to speak, Matthew cleared his throat.

"I hate to interrupt," he said, "but we've been here too long already."

Virginia felt heat flood her cheeks and stepped back, breaking contact. "I'll see you tomorrow, then."

Abiel winked. "God willing."

The two men left the room so silently that she didn't even hear the door close behind them.

8 8 8 8

VIRGINIA rushed into the room designated as her dressing room. "I'm running so late!" She kicked off her shoes and pulled the pin out of her hat at the same time. "I had to go by the church –"

She paused at the look on Cyllia's face. Her normally pale skin looked ashen, and fear pooled in her eyes. Every sense suddenly alert, she glanced around the room and saw the polished toe of a man's boot sticking out from around the corner. Her eyes flew back to Cyllia, who stood with her back to Virginia's dressing table, hands behind her back, panting in fear.

"May I help you?" Virginia inquired as she finished taking off her hat.

The boot moved and a man wearing the black and silver uniform of the *Schutzstaffel* complete with a red and white armband sporting a *swastika* and the distinctive *SS-Totenkopfverbände* death's head emblems on his hat and uniform stepped around the corner. The SS officer had pasty smooth skin broken up only by thin lips and an equally thin white mustache below ice cold blue eyes.

"You are causing quite a stir among the high command, *Fraulein*," the man announced. She spared a glance at his rank and identified him as a Colonel.

"I tend to cause a stir wherever I go, *Herr Oberst,*" Virginia said coyly. "It comes with the job."

"I also have a job," he said, walking toward her. From behind him and around the corner, another uniformed SS trooper appeared. She didn't spare him enough of a glance to figure out the complexities of his rank. The identifying SS symbols were all she needed to know – and to fear.

"Oh?"

"My job is to ensure that the vision the *Führer* has for the superior race meets with no resistance. When those of you from the inferior races claim leadership or power over a superior race, it upsets the balance." Cyllia cried out as the other man grabbed her and held her in front of him, gripping both her arms in a vice-like grip. "That is when I have to do my job. I have to step in and restore balance."

Virginia considered her options. At the moment, she had very few. Her Derringer lay hidden away in her makeup box on her dressing table and she had no other armaments close at hand. Instinctively, she knew she could not call upon any of the German officers from the *Wehrmacht* to come to her aid. She assumed the SS Colonel had the authority to do whatever he had in mind and to whomever he had a mind to do it without interference from the regular German Army corps, even a general who outranked him. She decided to bide her time and see what this visit would involve. It was possible the SS simply wanted her to stop making a stir.

He marched over to Cyllia. "When we reclaim territories like this, we understand there is a learning curve. After all, the local population has been without guidance and discipline for far too long. The locals often require reeducation to understand the will of the *Führer* and the great vision of the Third Reich which will stand for a thousand years. For instance, you would never have been allowed to perform on any stage in the Fatherland. And yet, here you are, seducing German soldiers with your primitive witchcraft and bending them to your will."

"No witchcraft involved, *Herr Oberst*," she replied, lifting her chin. Eyes darting between Cyllia and the Colonel, she felt her hands grow cold and had a hard time catching her breath. "Only God given talent."

He took two steps in her direction and reached forward and slapped her face with a black leather gloved hand. "Silence, *schvartze*. You have no authority to speak to me."

She saw flashes of light brighter than any stage lights when his palm made contact with her cheekbone just below her eye. The pain shocked her and she immediately felt involuntary tears sting her eyes.

Without hesitation, he then spun, returned to his position near Cyllia, and reached out and gripped the young woman's chin with the same gloved hand. He squeezed his hand as he lifted her head, moving her face from side to side, and examined her like a horse at the market. "Filthy little Jew acting as nursemaid to an ape?"

Cyllia gasped, "I'm Catholic."

The SS Colonel shook his head and clicked his tongue in disapproval. "Not possible. Only a filthy Jew would act as servant to a monkey." His gloved fingers caressed the side of her cheek. Rhetorically, he asked his partner, "Interesting how close to real humans they look, no?"

The SS soldier holding Cyllia very still in his iron grip spoke for the first time. "I remember that American monkey at the Berlin Olympics. One could quite easily see the apelike bone structure as he loped along."

"*Ja.* Owens," the Colonel mused. Virginia heard her maid start to cry, but could do nothing except wait to see how this played out. She might have been able to fend off one of the soldiers even without her pistol. As a young child, she had fought her way out of the Saint Louis race riots after all. But she didn't know if she could take on two trained soldiers, at least not without a weapon. His hand began to slide down Cyllia's face and down along her neck. Cyllia's eyes widened in terror and Virginia knew with an ice cold feeling in her chest what the Colonel intended to happen next.

"Leave her alone!" Virgina ordered. Out of the corner of her eye, she saw the lid of the steamer trunk open.

The Colonel released Cyllia's face and turned back toward Virginia. He leapt and with a balled fist, he punched her in the stomach, causing her to bend over as the breath completely escaped her body. He had aimed the blow perfectly, just as he had been trained. She lost the ability to breathe in even one more breath. Gasping, gagging, light headed, she closed her eyes and thought about what to do while she tried to drown out the sound of Cyllia's sobs.

The second she could catch her breath again, she opened her eyes in time to see the Colonel reaching for her, a murderous look in his eyes. Just as his hands grabbed the front of her dress, they heard the sound a body fall to the floor. They both stopped and turned. The Colonel's companion lay there, his eyes wide open in shock, blood gushing from his neck.

The Colonel straightened and turned just in time to block Abiel's stabbing blow with the hunting knife. He gripped Abiel's wrist, then twisted, hard, and the knife flew across the room. As the two men engaged in hand-to-hand combat – fists flying, grappling, kneeing, punching – Cyllia retreated to the corner of the room with her back to the wall and covered her ears with her hands. Gasping to catch her breath, Virginia rushed and retrieved the knife, holding it in one hand as she turned back toward the struggling men.

The SS Colonel had the upper hand in the fight. He had pinned Abiel against the wall and with one hand pushed against Abiel's face, forced him to expose his Adam's apple. In his other hand, he clutched his long ceremonial SS dagger and pressed to sink it into the man's throat.

Virginia didn't hesitate to run toward them. Without a second thought, she plunged the hunting knife she held into the Nazi's back, right between his shoulder blades. The knife was very sharp and it surprised her how easily it slid into the man's flesh, fitting into the man's upper torso by sliding between two ribs.

Abiel reached up and covered the man's mouth as he tried to scream. With his other hand, Abiel forced the man's own ceremonial dagger down, a job made easier by the Nazi Colonel's suddenly weakened condition. The point oriented downward and Abiel slowly and ruthlessly slid it into the Nazi's chest and directly into the man's heart.

As the Colonel fell to the ground, his eyes rolled up into his head and his breath leaked out as if from a flattened Barrage Balloon. Virginia put a hand to her heart as a sob welled up in her throat. Before she could release it, Abiel had her securely against his chest, his arms wrapped around her.

"Beautiful Virginia," he said, stepping back enough to frame her face with his hands. "Brilliant job."

She didn't realize she was crying until she felt the tears streaming down her cheeks. "I – he – I –"

He pulled her to him again and she gasped, struggling to steady her breathing. He led her to the chair in front of her dressing table and helped her sit down, then knelt beside her.

"If you hadn't been here –" she started to say, but he shushed her.

"Then God would have found a different way to protect you." He looked at his watch and looked at Cyllia. "I have no time." It surprised her when he put a hand on her cheek. "Are you okay?"

Taking a shaky, deep breath, she nodded. "The show must go on," she said in a very weak voice.

His smile completely transformed his face and made her heart leap in her chest. He pushed away and stood. "I think I will borrow the uniform from the sergeant here. He won't be needing it." As he started unlacing the boots, he looked at Cyllia. "Can you help me?"

"Yes, sir," the maid whispered, rushing forward. "Where did you come from?"

He winked at her as he stripped the jacket off of the man. "The trunk, of course." When he looked at Virginia, the serious expression had returned to his face. "Finish this up. I'll move the Colonel."

While Virginia and Cyllia undressed the sergeant, Abiel dragged the body of the Colonel to the back. He was gone for several minutes, then returned wearing a white T-shirt and carrying the Colonel's blood-soaked shirt. At Virginia's questioning look, he gestured at the pile of clothes next to the man on the floor. "He has blood on his collar."

She watched the look of distaste on his face as he started to slip his arm into the shirt. "Wait," Cyllia said. She jumped up and dug through a drawer in the table, pulling out a long pair of scissors and a spool of thread. With skill, she cut the collar off of both shirts and quickly and sloppily stitched the Colonel's collar onto the sergeant's shirt.

While she worked, Abiel and Virginia lifted the body of the sergeant and propped him against the wall, then arranged the dressing screen around him to hide him.

"You have to leave immediately after everything starts tonight," Abiel said.

"I will."

He took her shoulders in both of his hands and squeezed. "Listen to me. You must leave. The second they find these bodies and the trunk, they'll know. You have to be far away from here. Don't come back for anything."

"Abiel —"

"Edward."

"What?"

He looked at Cyllia across the room and spoke softly. "I know your name, it's only fair you know mine. Edward."

"Will I ever see you again?"

He pulled her to him and for the second time, his arms wrapped around her. She closed her eyes, pulling strength and courage from the embrace.

"All done," Cyllia said a little too loudly.

Embarrassed, Virginia kept her head ducked as Edward slipped the mocked up shirt on. When he put the jacket of the sergeant over the shirt, she could hardly tell the collar had been so hastily sewn into place. He grabbed the rest of the uniform and disappeared into the back.

Virginia looked at the clock. Her show began in less than thirty minutes. "Go!" she ordered Cyllia. "Go to the cafe I told you about. Tell the waitress the code phrase, 'Grace and peace abound.' Do it calmly. They'll help."

"What about you?" Cyllia cried.

"I have to go out there and sing. If I can possibly extract myself from Schmid and Müller, I will follow you. Take a change of clothes for me. Don't forget shoes." She went to the coat rack and found Cyllia's wrap, placing it over her shoulders.

"I can't leave you," the maid sobbed. "Please come with me."

Virginia reached out and gripped her face with her hands. "Listen to me. I have to do this right now. There's a plan in place to save my friend and this show is part of it. I don't need your help to get dressed. You go and tell them the code phrase. When it's safe, tell them what happened. They'll send someone for me."

"I d-d-don't kn-kn-know —" Tears streaked down Cyllia's face and her teeth started chattering. Moving her hands from her face to her shoulders, Virginia gave her a harsh shake.

"Don't risk our lives by breaking down now, child. Snap out of it."

Cyllia closed her eyes and took a deep, shaky breath. When she opened them again, there was less panic and more reason reflecting back at Virginia. "Okay. I will see you soon."

"Don't panic when you leave this room. Just keep your eyes down and go to the cafe."

As Cyllia left, Edward came out of the back room, fully dressed as the SS sergeant. As he secured the hat on his head, he looked at her. "Can you still perform?"

She raised her chin. "Of course."

He nodded and opened his mouth as if to speak, but closed it again.

"Godspeed, Edward. I will be praying."

Without a promise of a reunion, without another word, he walked to the door. He stopped and looked behind him, but not at her — instead he surveyed the room. He clearly had his mind on the job now and left without speaking.

CHAPTER 7

Chapter Seven

VIRGINIA stripped out of her rumpled clothes and grabbed her performance outfit for the night. She tossed her clothes over the top of the dressing screen as if she'd undressed back there.

Dressed in the red gown, she sat in a chair in front of a portable mirror and attached a rhinestone to her temple with some Spirit Gum. A tremor shook her hand, making her drop the rhinestone three times before she finally got it attached. With a delayed reaction, fear clawed at her chest and threatened to strangle her. She closed her eyes and took a deep, cleansing breath. Then another, and another.

Calmer, she sat back and looked at her reflection. When someone knocked on her door, she gave an audible yelp. Heart hammering, pulse pounding, she turned in her chair.

"Yes?" She called loudly.

The door opened and a German officer marched into her dressing room. Terror squeezed her chest. As she stood, she gripped the table behind her, calculating how quickly she could retrieve her Derringer pistol. "How may I help you, sir?"

He stood tall, with blond hair the color of straw, and perceptive blue eyes that examined her clinically. "I am *Oberleutnant* Leopold Schäfer. This is my prison."

Keeping up appearances, Virginia raised her eyebrows. "I was under the impression that this prison is Colonel Müller's responsibility."

"You are correct. *Herr Oberst* Müller is responsible for four prisons in this sector and I report to him. This prison is under my command." He stepped closer to her but did not shut the door behind him. Virginia's senses were heightened and she felt her vision start to gray. "I did not know that your show had been moved up. When *Herr* General Schmid's men arrived yesterday to construct your stage, it was the first I had heard of your rescheduled performance. I do not like arrangements like this being made without my knowledge or consent."

Virginia licked her incredibly dry lips. "I apologize. I do not have any experience in the politics of your military. I just have a General and a Colonel telling me when to be where."

He cocked his head and looked at her. "As do I," he said with a laugh. She could recognize the American accent in his French.

"You're American. Where are you from?" She asked in perfect southern-accented English.

He raised both eyebrows. In plain English, he answered, "Oregon."

Continuing in English, Virginia answered, "I'm from St. Louis by way of New Orleans."

"I know exactly who you are." Her stomach fell at his words, but then he smiled and said, "Even if I hadn't, I thought I heard a twang in your French."

"You heard no such thing." She shifted her long red skirts so that her feet would not trip on them and cross the room to the tea service Cyllia had left for her long before they'd been accosted by SS soldiers. The dress fit so tightly on her waist and bodice that when she bent, she almost gasped out loud from the pain in her midriff where the Colonel had punched her. Instead, she did her best to bend over with grace. "Would you care for some tea?"

"No, thank you." She could feel his eyes as he watched her pour a cup and she swished her skirts as she turned back to face him.

"I do hope you will enjoy the performance, even if you didn't get to approve it," she said with a flirtatious smile as she took a sip of the long cooled tea.

"I hope so, too," he said. "I confess I have been looking forward to meeting you. I will return in a moment." He clicked the heels of his highly shined jack boots and left the room, shutting the door behind him.

As soon as the door shut behind him, her tea cup clattered to the table and she raced to the bathroom, suddenly very sick to her stomach. As she ran cold water on a cloth and dabbed at her forehead, trying not to disrupt the makeup she had so carefully applied, she wished she knew what would happen next. She knew they had a plan, that it involved explosives, but she had no idea what it could be. She just prayed the information she'd given Abiel – Edward – about the interior of the building would help.

Knuckles rapped harshly on her closed door. She nearly cried out in startled fear, but put a fist to her mouth instead. The knocking was just a routine signal to alert her of the remaining time for her curtain call.

The young German Officer entered the room once more. The fact that he carefully pretended not to notice her nervousness told Virginia that he had certainly noticed and had tucked the observation away for later analysis. She said, "No matter how big or small the venue, I always get a little jumpy right before a show."

She could tell he didn't believe her. "I find that astonishing, Miss Benoit, given your credentials and years of experience."

Virginia took a deep breath and let out an exaggerated sigh. "It's true. Please don't let on. Underneath the glamorous gowns and the makeup, I'm still just a southern girl from small town America."

Oberleutnant Schäfer's expression didn't change which made reading his thoughts difficult. His blue eyes stared at her coldly as he shook his head. "I would not be overly concerned about this crowd if I were you. The men are in such need of distraction after months of boredom, a monkey grinding a hand organ would surely entertain them at this point."

Virginia tried very hard not to react to the words which were so similar to what the SS Colonel had used. *Oberleutnant* Schäfer had apparently spoken them in an awkward attempt to ease her nervousness. He had no knowledge of what she had been through less than an hour before. Instead of reacting, she smiled a toothless smile and said nothing.

The officer's eyes took in the room. Before he could study the dressing screen behind her too closely, she asked, "Have you seen me perform before?"

He shook his head. "I'm afraid not. But I am very much looking forward to it."

Virginia stood, placing herself between the officer and the dressing screen, hoping to keep his all too perceptive cold blue eyes on her and her formfitting dress instead of the room. She prayed that no blood was seeping out onto a visible part of the floor or that no other tell-tale sign had been left where this young Nazi officer could see it. "It's only a bit early. Would you escort me to the stage, sir? We could continue our conversation until it's time to perform."

"It will be my honor. And I hope it isn't forward of me to propose that we speak together more before you must depart, Miss Benoit. My English has suffered greatly in the last few months since my arrival."

She smiled her most practiced dazzling smile and nodded, "An opportunity to speak more with a handsome young officer in Hitler's mighty Army? What kind of red blooded woman could refuse such an offer?"

§ § § §

RIGHT on time, Virginia sashayed onto the stage amidst the catcalls and applause of about two hundred men. She knew she looked good. Her bright crimson gown was formfitting, with long full skirts falling to the ground, then gathered up on her right hip, exposing most of her right leg. It was cut low in the back, all the way to the curve of her hips, and her dark skin shone in the lights. She knew she looked exotic, alluring, and sexy. She also knew the effect she had on the men.

She stood on an outdoor stage near the prison. Bright lights broke the night, giving the entire area the appearance of day. Some of the audience sat on folded chairs, and some sat on the ground. She imagined who sat where just depended on rank and position. Scattered throughout the audience of uniformed soldiers she saw several civilians – both men and women.

Winking slowly and seductively at a group of prison guards sitting on the ground near the stage, she wiggled her hips just so, eliciting a series of cheers and catcalls. When she reached the microphone, she clutched it with both hands before her crystal clear voice called out, "*Danke. Danke schön!*"

When the cheers and applause died down, one final wolf whistle echoed from somewhere in the back. She allowed herself a giggle and then winked before layering her reply of "*Ich danke Ihnen,*" with additional nuance. The crowd broke into bawdy laughter.

Slowly, almost quietly, Virginia set into an *a cappella* version of *Das Lied der Deutschen*, though singing the German national anthem at this moment in history secretly disgusted her. Still, her strategy worked perfectly. By the second verse of the first stanza, every German present had risen to his feet and sang along. She chose to add their patriotic song to her lineup with the intent to pull the crowd in, in hopes that they would see her as a trusted comrade. It worked.

The sight of so many rigid right arms in a stiff armed salute filled her heart with growing dread. Fortunately, clutching the microphone in both hands afforded her an excuse not to render her own *Seig heil* offering to Hitler.

While she performed, in the back of her mind she wondered, what was happening right now inside the prison? Would they get Temperance out? Was the plan even happening by now? Was someone even now searching her dressing room? Had they discovered the corpses of the two SS troopers?

She sashayed to the end of the stage and leaned down toward General Schmid and Colonel Müller. They sat next to a visiting dignitary who sat stone-faced, cheeks flushed. He sat next to an empty chair, which she guessed had been reserved for the dead SS Colonel stashed in her dressing room. She imagined, as she smiled and sang, that the politician probably hadn't realized the color of her skin until she stepped out onto that stage. She guessed, by the uncomfortable glances Müller gave him and the bright red that flushed his cheekbones that perhaps things would not go well for the general and colonel tonight despite the enthusiasm of the crowd.

She gave none of those thoughts or assumptions away. Instead, she gave a smile that made each man in the audience feel like she performed exclusively for him - a slow and seductive smile that kept the audience's eyes on her and their minds on nothing but the sound of her voice and the sparkle of her sequins.

Just as she hit a particularly high note, the world beneath her feet violently shifted. An explosion from somewhere inside the prison blew out the window above her. She screamed as she covered her head with her hands. She felt the concussions of the following three explosions within every cell of her body.

Terror ran with adrenaline through her veins. The music stopped suddenly, and after a moment of ear ringing silence, the roar of men's voices washed over her though their words were muffled and unintelligible. The entire world started moving in slow motion.

Within seconds, Schmid appeared at her side, covering her with his jacket, yelling to the people around them in German as he escorted her from the stage. Virginia swiped at a wetness on her face and was shocked when her hand came away covered in blood. As her stomach rolled at the sight of the blood on her hands, she felt her world gray and she stumbled. As she fell, the stage rolled up to meet her. But, before it made an impact, her world went completely black.

The End

WHILE the story of the special team of operators I named The Virtues is entirely fictional, set in a fictional town, and comprised of fictional characters who form a fictional military division, every single one of my fictional heavenly heroines was inspired by a real World War II heroine and the story was inspired by real events.

While the actual person Jesse Owens is mentioned more than once, the fictional character Virginia Benoit is inspired by the very real heroine Josephine Baker.

James Cleveland "Jesse" Owens was born on September 12, 1913 in Oakville, Alabama and passed away in Tuscan, Arizona on March 31, 1980 at the age of 66. According to his obituary which ran in the New York Times, during his lifetime, Jesse was recognized as "perhaps the greatest and most famous athlete in track and field history." His achievement of setting three world records and tying a fourth in less than an hour at the 1935 Big Ten track meet has been called "the greatest 45 minutes ever in sport," and has never been equaled since.

It is well known that while competing at the 1936 Summer Olympics in Berlin, Germany, while then Chancellor Adolf Hitler looked on in disgust, Jesse Owens won international fame along with four Olympic Gold medals for the 100 meters, the 200 meters, the long jump, and the 4 x100 meter relay. Jesse Owens was the most successful individual athlete at the games that year. His victory flew in the face of the Nazi's stated supreme "master race" theories.

Josephine Baker's heroic actions during the second World War are less well known even to this day. Born into poverty in St. Louis, Missouri in 1906 as Freda Josephine McDonald, she would later be known to the world as Josephine Baker. Despite her dire circumstances as a child, she loved dancing and learned how by watching and mimicking the dancers at the famous Booker T. Washington Theater. At the age of 10, she won a dance competition and decided on the spot that she wanted to be a dancer when she grew up.

In 1917 she witnessed the St. Louis race riots and the "black exodus" that followed. A sea of people fleeing the murderous riot behind them as they crossed the St. Louis Bridge toward her was forever etched in her mind. What she saw in those days spurred her heart to spend much of her adult life confronting and fighting racism.

In 1925, after spending much of her career dancing in New York City, Josephine went to Paris to perform in *La Revue Nègre* at the *Théâtre des Champs-Elysées*. Paris loved Josephine Baker, and she loved Paris. Soon, she was among the highest paid entertainers in France of any race, a stage and movie sensation. She came to be known in various circles as the "Black Pearl," the "Bronze Venus" and even the "Creole Goddess."

In 1928, Josephine went on a European tour and witnessed how racist much of Europe was becoming. Nazi run newspapers condemned her for performing on the same stage as "Aryan" performers, and some places even threw ammonia bombs at her. After that, Josephine rather correctly equated racism with Nazism.

In 1934, Josephine took the starring role in a French film, *Zuzu*, a great success in Paris. The name Zuzu comes from Zuzana, a Czech/Slovak form of Susana, but for whatever reason it stuck and Josephine's close friends often called her Zuzu in private and in letters after the film's release.

In 1936, the same year Jesse Owens won four Olympic gold medals in Berlin, Josephine returned to America to perform, but was treated with open racism and general hostility. She returned to France, heartbroken by the way her home country had treated her. When she returned to Paris, she married Jean Lion and became a French citizen.

On November 9, 1938, Nazis in Germany destroyed Jewish homes, synagogues, and businesses in what is today called *Kristallnacht* (Night of Broken Glass). After that night, Josephine joined the International League against Racism and Anti-Semitism.

An organization in France called *Deuzieme Bureau* was looking for undercover agents who could afford to work without pay and who could travel without suspicion. They approached Josephine and asked her to be an agent for them. Without hesitation, Josephine embraced the opportunity. After several weeks of training in weapons, self-defense, and memory, she was given her first mission: attending parties at the Italian embassy and reporting the information she overheard.

Her chateau, which was a large rural home in southern France she had named *Les Milandes*, became a stopping-point for Resistance workers, a safe house for refugees, and occasionally was used to store weapons. Eventually, the Germans grew suspicious and started watching her home, and she left. She traveled through Spain, Portugal, and North Africa, performing, attending parties, and listening. Just like the fictional Virginia Benoit, the real Josephine Baker used invisible ink and wrote what she saw and heard in the margins of her sheet music.

In June 1941, she became very ill and was hospitalized in Casablanca until December 1942. When she was finally released and strong enough to perform, she performed for the Allied troops, insisting that the audience, which was traditionally seated with white soldiers up front and black soldiers in the back, be desegregated before she performed.

After the war, Josephine received the Legion of Honour with the rosette of the Resistance, and became the first American born woman to receive the Croix de Guerre. These are two of France's highest military honors.

When the war ended, Josephine returned to her chateau, *Les Milandes*. In 1947, she married again, this time to French orchestra leader Jo Bouillon. She adopted 12 children, all of different nationalities, which she referred to as her "rainbow tribe". Her intent was to impress upon the outside world that people of different colors and ethnicities could live together as a family.

The "incident" with the radio personality which fictional characters Radden and Benoit stage is based on an actual event which occurred in New York's Stork Club on the night of October 16, 1951. To set the record straight more than half a century later, by all accounts the radio personality, Walter Winchell, was utterly innocent of any wrong-doing. He was simply also present when the incident occurred. The blame for the mistreatment Josephine Baker suffered should have fallen squarely and fairly upon the shoulders of Stork Club owner, Sherman Billingsley. The problem was that no one had ever heard of Billingsley while absolutely every "Mr. and Mrs. America and all the ships at sea" knew the name of Walter Winchell in 1951.

Josephine continued to perform her own show at the Roxy to sold-out crowds throughout the remainder of the season, though the Stork Club incident continued to haunt her career in the United States from that day forward. Despite bad press, Baker took several trips back and forth to America in the 1950s and 1960s to help with the growing Civil Rights Movement.

On August 28, 1963, two separate parades were held for male and female civil rights leaders during the famous March on Washington. The men marched down Pennsylvania Avenue. The women–including Josephine Baker, Daisy Bates, and Rosa Parks–marched down Independence Avenue. When the groups met at the Mall, on the platform, Josephine stood right beside Martin Luther King, Jr., and was the only female speaker at the march, preceding the famous "I Have a Dream" speech by Reverend King.

Whenever she performed in America, she insisted on a nonsegregation clause in her contracts. Most places honored them, causing a desegregation in clubs that never would have happened otherwise. The NAACP eventually named May 20th "Josephine Baker Day" in honor of her lifelong efforts to end racism.

In 1973, Josephine performed at Carnegie Hall and was received with a standing ovation. Two years later, she performed at the Bobino Theater in Paris to celebrate the 50th anniversary of her Paris debut. Celebrities in attendance included Sophia Loren and Princess Grace of Monaco. Just days later, on April 12, 1975, Josephine Baker died in her sleep. She was 69 years old.

At her wake, an estimated 20,000 people lined the streets for her funeral procession. For her service during the war, Josephine Baker became the first American in history to receive full military honors in a French funeral.

SUGGESTED questions for a discussion group surrounding *Homeland's Hope*, part 2 of the *Virtues and Valor* series.

While the characters and situations in the *Virtues and Valor* series are fictional, I pray that these extended parables can help readers come to a better understanding of truth. Please prayerfully consider the questions that follow, consult scripture, and pray upon your conclusions. May the Lord of the universe richly bless you.

Virginia Benoit stages a racial fight with a prominent media personality in the United States in order to add validity to her desire to sing for the Nazis. When she does this, she knows it harms any chance for a career in the United States even if Great Britain comes clean with the plan after the war.

> 1. How realistic do you think this scenario is if you consider racial tensions in the United States in the 1940's and 1950's?

> 2. Why do you – or do you not – believe this set up would harm her in the future even if Great Brittain came clean about it being a fake staged event?

In a very black and white world, the Bible is very clear in the words, *You shall not steal, nor deal falsely, nor lie to one another.* Leviticus 19:11. However, this is a series that deals entirely with people who are basically lying as a means of survival – and God Himself directed Moses to send spies into Canaan in Numbers 13.

3. As Christians, is there ever a time in our lives when lying might be acceptable?

4. Do you think Virginia Benoit and her companions are 'sinning' in the purest sense of the word by covertly battling the evil enemy employing lies and deception as weapons?

§ § § §

Virginia Benoit is battling racism in a time period in history when racism was rampant throughout the world. Yet, the Bible is clear in Acts 17:26 that, "He has made from one blood every nation of men to dwell on all the face of the earth, and has determined their preappointed times and the boundaries of their dwellings…" The true heroine, Josephine Baker, upon whom this fictional character is based, spent nearly her entire life engaged in a war against racism.

5. What can we as Christians do to battle the racism that is still prevalent in our society today?

6. The Nazis would not even allow people of color to perform on the same stage as those they consider "Aryan", and executed millions of people based on nothing more than their skin color or religion/heritage. Do you think that we as a society could be threatened to repeat the past, or are hearts and minds of men changing for the better with every passing year?

7. Josephine Baker and Jesse Owens both stood up to the Nazis amid the lights and cameras of the world. Do you think they can be considered heroes for nothing more than their fight against racism and the hardness of men's hearts?

Charity's Code

3

HALLEE
BRIDGEMAN

Virtues And Valor Series

Charity's Code

the Virtues and Valor Series part 3

a Novella by

HALLEE BRIDGEMAN

Published by

Olivia Kimbrell Press™

Olivia Kimbrell Press™

COPYRIGHT NOTICE

Library Cataloging Data
U. S. Library of Congress Control Number: 2014953677

Bridgeman, Hallee (Hallee A. Bridgeman) 1972-
   Charity's Code, Virtues and Valor series part 2 / Hallee Bridgeman
   100 p. 23cm x 15cm (9in x 6 in.)
      Summary: Dorothy Ewing, code name Charity, works to decode messages from Occupied France in support of the Virtues team.

      ISBN: 978-1-939603-47-0 (ebook)

1. Christian fiction 2. World War II 3. war stories 4. spies 5. historical fiction 6. espionage

PS3568.B7534 T470 2014
[Fic.] 813.6 (DDC 23)

Dedication

For all those who kept the home fires burning...

THIS series is dedicated to the amazing women who worked, planned, strategized, served, led, and fought alongside men throughout human history. This novella is specifically dedicated to Dodo Barry. To read more about this true heroine, read the "Inspired by Real Events" section at the end of Charity's story.

London, England: 1932

DOROTHY Ewing moved her eyes over the paper as quickly as her brain could compute. Question, answer, scribe, and repeat. Her pencil tip broke, but she just tossed it behind her and picked a new one up from the five perfectly sharpened spare pencils beside her. Her hand moved quickly, filling in the letters, completing the acrostic as a tiny bead of sweat trickled down her temple.

Finally, she reached the end. Last question, last answer, final input into the intricately interlaced cipher of interdependent code words, forming a perfectly clever pattern on the page. She tossed her pencil down and announced, "Done!"

The crowd around her erupted into applause while she glanced across the table at Sir Percy Montrose, reigning crossword puzzle champion. Well, at this moment in time, immediate former crossword puzzle champion. Dorothy could now proudly claim that title.

Coming from a long line of British aristocracy, Percy Montrose had a height, build, and coloring that very much resembled the American film star, Clark Gable. He went to some small lengths to increase the resemblance from the pomade he used on his thick dark hair to his always perfectly trimmed pencil thin mustache. Despite his knighthood and his apparent wealth, he considered Dorothy's husband, Thomas, his dearest and closest friend.

Her husband, Thomas Ewing, could not look much more different than his longtime friend. Thomas stood a towering 6 feet and 3 inches and supported his height with a stout, 240 pounds, muscular frame. He had started balding at the very tip of his black haired crown, though very few people were tall enough to spot it. He sported an enormous mustache with curled up tips and had green eyes that peered out from a lightly freckled face, looking jolly and keenly intelligent. His smile confessed that he clearly enjoyed the fact that his long time best friend had just suffered a defeat at the hands of his beloved bride.

Percy, with only one more line to complete, one more question to answer, had clearly been beaten. He raised his glass and tipped it in Dorothy's direction. "Well done, old girl. I didn't believe anyone could beat me, much less a housewife from East Ham. I yield to the better man who is, in this case, a woman. Bravo and huzzah."

Dorothy tried to maintain her composure. In her mind, the outcome of the contest had never been in doubt. She wondered what Percy saw as he raised his glass in her direction. She had glorious red hair, courtesy of her island blood. No one would ever dare to describe her as "ginger," at least not in her husband's presence. She normally had a slight build, though now her belly swelled with their first child, coming to her husband's chest when she stood next to him. She did not have many freckles, rather she had a porcelain complexion that looked like ivory against her favored, if somewhat daring, red lipstick and hint of blush.

At Percy's informal salute, she smiled, revealing perhaps her best feature, her perfect white teeth. Her smile reflected her sincere joy at this competition and her deep respect for her opponent. "Thank you, Sir Percy. I'm quite sure it was simply my day and equally certain we shall meet on the field again and again."

Percy covered his heart in mock agony, his eyebrows falling in consternation and making him look comically like the American movie star. "And suffer further ignominious defeats at your hands, madam? Nay! Nay, I say. I yield to your clearly superior prowess once and for all."

His announcement spurred some jolly laughter and light applause from the gathered crowd. Before the echoes of adoration had even faded, Tom Ewing's strong arm fell gently over Dorothy's shoulders. "What'd I tell you, Percy? My wife takes the biscuit, she does!" He kissed her enthusiastically and Dorothy laughed as soon as she could come up for air.

Tom turned to the small crowd and led a final impromptu cheer with a roaring, "Hip, hip!"

"Huzzah!" They answered. Everyone proceeded to cheer her victory the traditional three times, Sir Percy possibly the most enthusiastic of all.

They reveled for perhaps another hour, though Dorothy declined the offer of any strong drinks. Such offers, to her chagrin, her husband and Sir

Percy never once declined. The men were in rather "high spirits" by the time they left the party. Dorothy took the wheel of their little automobile and they began to make their way home.

Thomas chuckled and gave her a sly look, "Well done, you. About time Percy ate some crow. I do believe he thought he had you when your pencil gave out, but his look went all pear shaped when you announced 'Done!' Ah, Dotty, that was just bonnie. Simply brilliant!"

After a moment, her eyes on the bumpy road ahead, she answered, "High skills, solving crossword puzzles." She wondered if he heard the hint of sarcasm in her dry remark. "After today's sound victory, I'm certain employers shall fall over themselves and soon be beating down our door with offers of vocation."

She pulled their car into the slim parkway in front of their modest home and exited the vehicle before he could answer. By the time she made it around the vehicle, her husband's large frame blocked her from entering their home.

Tom pulled her to him and placed a hand over her stomach. "No more employers for you, Dotty my bonnie lass," he promised. She could feel their first child kick against his fingers. "Not for many years ahead, my love. You have to take care of our home, now. I'll win the bread by the sweat of my brow. You'll keep me fat with your puddings, no doubt. I can barely wait to call the midwife in a few wee short months."

Dorothy looked into her husband's green eyes and smiled, feeling the tug of love in her heart. "We have a while yet before our *daughter* arrives."

"Don't be too sure. Our *son* may be in a bit of a rush to meet his lovely *màthair.*"

She enjoyed this contest nearly as much as she enjoyed her husband's unfailing adoration. But looking up into his loving eyes, Dorothy decided she had experienced enough victories today. She would let him win this one for now. "Aye, my love. Little Tommy might just be in a hurry like his da'."

CHAPTER 1

♥ ♥ ♥ ♥

CHARITY – benevolent goodwill toward or love of humanity: generosity and helpfulness, philanthropy, especially toward the poor, ill, or helpless, the needy or suffering; aid or donations given to those in need or in disfavor; leniency in judging others; forbearance; Christian love; agape (Greek).

London, England: 1940

DOROTHY stood on the platform at the train station as close as she could to her husband who looked like a recruiting poster in his RAF Officer's uniform. He easily pulled her out of the way to avoid an unintended jostling by a group of soldiers running to hop aboard a departing train. His touch, as always, felt astonishingly gentle for a man of his enormous size as he guided her to safety.

Feet back on the ground and needing to do something with her hands, she straightened Tom's tie and swallowed, trying to disguise her distress and trying very hard not to cry. She was determined that his last memory of her before he left would not be of womanly tears. "There you go, Captain Ewing. I believe you'll be the most handsome pilot in the RAF, though I confess I am still a bit astounded they make aircraft large enough to lift you from the earth."

He cupped her cheek and brushed a thick thumb beneath her eye, capturing the moisture threatening to fall down her cheeks. "Only in your eyes, love. But I shall certainly be the most courageous. That I vow. I will protect you and our children with every shred of courage my heart and body can muster." He kissed her so softly that the breath hitched in the back of her throat.

Their lips parted and his deep voice echoed in her chest as he said, "You mind after the *bairns*. Remind Tommy he's the man of the house now and must help you with his sisters."

"I think the lad understands," she said with a smile. "Even at eight, he grasps the enormity of our present circumstances."

"He's brilliant, that laddie … Just like his *màthair*." Tom's occasional Gaelic brogue never failed to turn her knees to water.

"And stout and clever just like his da'," she responded.

Suddenly his arms went around her, strong and tight, comforting her as only he could. "You'll stay in my heart and in my prayers, *bhean chéile*. Pray for me, my darling, my bonnie Dotty."

"I never stop, *mo ghraigh*." Their lips met as naturally and as comfortably as taking the next step when walking or the next breath when breathing. They came together in a kiss exactly as they had perhaps tens of thousands of times before over the course of their courtship and marriage. His hands rested on her hips. Her fingers caressed his smoothly shaved cheeks as his waxed mustache tips tickled the backs of her hands.

She kissed him soundly. But despite the triviality of its beginnings, this kiss felt somehow important. It felt bittersweet and frighteningly final. Her heart thundered in her ears and she suddenly wanted to just kiss him and kiss him and kiss him… and never stop. She desperately wanted all the clocks to stop ticking. She wanted all the trains to rust onto their tracks and stop moving. She urgently wanted this wretched war to end in the very next second so that she could just kiss her husband and pour every ounce of love she kept in her heart into him.

A shrieking train whistle startled her back to the present moment in which clocks still ticked, trains still rolled, and soldiers still made their way to the front lines. She opened her eyes as their lips parted and beheld the present reality, a reality in which wives still remained behind minding children, keeping busy, staying useful, and fearing every moment that the last time they had seen their husbands alive would be the very last time.

After seconds that passed like hours, her heartbeat faded to distant thunder in her ears instead of deafening nearby cannon fire. Knowing one of them had to be the first to break away, she stepped back, slipped her gloves back on, then brushed a hand down her wool coat. "Go on, then. Don't miss your train. I imagine even kind old King George would frown on tardiness as a result of dallying with your wife on the platform."

"Well, his majesty has never met *my* wife. Had he done, I'd wager he might understand." His eyes looked down into hers, dark with passion and promise. She realized in that heartbeat that this image of him would be the one she carried with her in her mind's eye throughout the coming days and carried to sleep with her each night.

"Oh, Thomas, you are quite the charmer. Always have done."

He hopped up onto the step of the train, surprisingly agile as always, and turned to blow her a kiss. "I love you, Mrs. Ewing, with all my heart."

"And I, you, Captain Ewing."

A hand slapped Tom's shoulder from behind, almost knocking him off of the step. "Let's go, old boy. Off to see the elephant and whatnot," Sir Percy announced. He glanced over Tom's shoulder. "Send me some of those wonderful biscuits in the post when little Tommy isn't looking, Dorothy."

She laughed and waved as the train's whistle blew again. When she knew they could hear her again, she said, "Assuming I can get sugar rations, I'll send just as many cookies as they'll allow. But you must promise me to watch out for my husband, Sir Percy."

"Madam, Captain Ewing just shot to the very tip-top of my priority list," he promised with a wink.

Dorothy did not chase the train. The platform was far too crowded and she chose not to make a spectacle of herself or her husband. Instead, she waved, and Tom waved back until she simply could not see him anymore.

Her gloved fingers brushed her swollen lips where she still tasted him. Her lips tingled, still feeling his lingering kiss as if feeling the sensation of an amputated limb. Dejected, she turned and walked away slowly, completely alone, back down the platform, back to their old car, so that she could collect her children from her neighbor Beatrice in time to prepare dinner. She tried very, very hard not to burst into tears.

Chapter Two

London, England: 1941

DOROTHY wrapped the crocheted blanket tighter around her shoulders and watched the mother across from her rocking and shushing her infant. Sirens continued to go off despite the hours they'd spent down in the crowded shelter. Her eyes burned from lack of sleep.

A rumble around them caused dust to fall from the ceiling. Weeks ago, that would have caused alarm and a round of concerned murmurs throughout the crowd. Unfortunately, it no longer alarmed. Now, it merely annoyed. The continual bombing raids and nightly destruction of their fair city had become a major annoyance to the populace. As one member of the House of Commons had wryly observed, war was so awfully inconvenient.

Blitzkrieg, the Nazis called it. Lightning war. Despite the *inconvenience*, these endless nights spent in shelters had become old hat to the London population. They *inconveniently* hovered together in the underground tunnels and designated cellars and shelters. Many prepared during the day for the *inconvenient* nightly bombings. Every evening they brought some creature comforts with them such as Victrolas or Gramophones. Many brought decks of cards and engaged in highly contested rounds of Old Maid or Go Fish between sirens and bombs.

A blackout warden, wearing his rounded helmet and black coat, moved through the crowd, assisting as needed, encouraging where required. No room for panic in the tube tunnel. Can't have that. Stiff upper lip and whatnot.

Some Londoners had simply taken up residence in the tubes. Perhaps their homes had been flattened during the infamous raid on November 14 when Hitler had sent five hundred bombers against them in a single night. Perhaps they had simply given up on the *inconvenience* of having their sleep interrupted each night and making their way into the shelters with their remaining valuables. Regardless, she nearly always found familiar faces in the tubes, many of whom intended to stay there until the unpleasantness of the current *inconvenience* had moved on to greener pastures. Some of them had even volunteered as blackout wardens. But this particular tunnel was new to her, close to the train station from where she'd come, intending to spend the weekend at home. The air raid sirens had started going off as soon as she exited the station and she followed the crowd to the safety of the underground.

Dorothy closed her eyes. Grit under her eyelids scratched and burned. Her mother's last letter pleaded with her to come to the relative safety of York, to join her children who had been there since the first bomb landed in London. Her reply had been the same: she had work in London and that couldn't be promised in York.

What she couldn't tell her mother – or anyone at all for that matter – was that right now, she spent her days at Bletchley Park, working with other women like herself as crypto-analysts. The project was classified above Most Secret and she understood that even speaking of it could result in her execution for treason.

Feeling blue after driving her three children to her parents' home, she'd responded to an ad in the *Telegraph* about a crossword puzzle competition. Six hours later, after a timed crossword puzzle test, she'd signed an agreement under the Official Secrets Act and moved into a dormitory she shared with three other girls.

By day, she provided administrative support to the mathematicians who worked on breaking the Nazi's enigma cipher. By night, she lay curled in her bed, aching deep in her heart to be reunited with her husband and their children.

On her days off, she took the train to London and visited with her neighbor and best friend, Beatrice. When she sat in Beatrice's kitchen, enjoying a cup of tea and her homemade scones, catching up on neighborhood news – and occasional gossip – she could almost pretend that the children would be home from school any moment or that Tom would be home in time for supper.

Tom. Her breath caught in her throat and a tear leaked out from behind her closed lashes. Three weeks ago, Dorothy Ewing had received word that her husband had been shot down over France and captured by the *Wehrmacht*. The absolute terror she felt at receiving that news had taken her breath away. What must he be enduring right now? Was he warm? Was he fed? Was he hurt in any way?

She couldn't dwell on that. It would make her crazy. No room for panic when your husband was a prisoner of war in the hands of the Third Reich. Can't have that. Stiff upper lip and whatnot. Instead, she would do her part in this war effort to bring an end to the Nazi war machine.

When the 'all-clear' sounded, Dorothy stood with the rest of the people occupying this particular shelter and half stumbled her way out of the underground structure. The dazzling early morning light nearly blinded her. She squinted her eyes against the glare.

The smell of burned cordite and TNT almost overwhelmed her. She put a perfumed handkerchief to her mouth and nose and started picking her way among the rubble. She didn't think she'd ever get used to the dazed looks on people's faces as they examined the new ruins after a night of bombing.

When she turned onto her street, her stomach fell. She rushed toward her building and tripped over a chunk of concrete. Her knees and hands hit the ground hard, sharp shards of brick and cement cutting into the palms of her hands and ripping the knees of her stockings. Brushing it off, she regained her footing and continued forward, more carefully placing her steps this time, absently rubbing her burning palms, until she reached Beatrice's house – or, rather, what once was Beatrice's house.

A giant crater greeted her vision right where their weekly tea chats took place. Next door, the entire side of Dorothy's home had been blown away, but the rest of the structure stood solid and steady. She looked everywhere for Beatrice and her husband, but saw no one.

The irony of having to use a key to open her front door when most of one wall no longer existed did not escape her keen mind. She gathered the mail that had come through the mail slot in the door during the week off of the floor and took it with her to the kitchen where morning daylight spilled into the room from the gaping hole in the wall.

"Blast it!" she uttered to no one in particular.

She went upstairs and grabbed pillow cases, using them to pack whatever she could find. Boxes would be easier to pack, but clumsy on the train. She wished she could just load her car, but she'd left it at her parents' with the children, knowing how prohibitive gas rations made driving in London.

She'd take the next train to York bring what she could carry to her parents' house before she had to report back to work in two days.

It took her a couple of hours to pack her pictures, the children's baby clothes, her own wedding gown, and various other bric-a-brac that held mainly sentimental value. While she worked, she prayed for her dear friend, Beatrice, and for John, Beatrice's husband. She prayed that they had spent the night safely in a shelter as she had done, knowing how much John loathed hunkering down in the bomb shelters.

Carrying what she could, she walked back outside. Relief flooded her heart when she saw Beatrice sitting on a pile of rubble near where her house used to be, sipping a cup of tea. She placed the cup atop her knee and tugged at the gray sweater draped lightly over her shoulders. Dorothy could see a neighbor walking down the street, pulling a wagon with a tea pot and cups in it, serving the neighbors working on clearing the debris.

She set her bags on the ground and crawled up the rubble pile to sit next to her friend. She set her mail in her lap and waited for Beatrice to speak first.

Beatrice grinned and offered, "Sixes and sevens, what?"

Obviously, things were indeed in a terrible mess, topsy-turvy and completely haywire. Beatrice had summed it up nicely. "Stroppy, Bea?"

"John didn't want to go last night. We'd just gotten to bed and he was so tired from the day." She gestured with her chin to her husband, who stood, looking lost as he gazed down into the crater. "Glad I nagged until he finally got up and went just so I'd belt up."

"There, there. You've got a lotta bottle, you and your John."

Beatrice grinned, sipped her tea, then whispered, "Codswollop."

Dorothy reached for her friend's hand. Despite the calm look on her face, she gripped her fingers so hard that Dorothy tried not to wince. "What can I do?"

"We had nothing dear inside, but we got nothing left," she said fiercely. She gracefully raised her cup. "'Cept for a cuppa. Still got that."

"I can use the flat at my job. You're more than welcome to stay in my house." She pointed at the near perfect cut out of her home. "John can mend the wall, you suppose?"

As a tear slipped out of Beatrice's eye and made a streak in the dust on her face, she nodded. "I reckon he can make a bodge of it. Thank you, my friend." Beatrice used the sleeve of her sweater to dab at her eyes. As she glanced down, she gasped. "Is that a letter from your Tom?"

Immediately, Dorothy's heart started racing as she glanced at the return address on the letter in her lap. "It is!"

She recognized his boxy precise handwriting. For some reason, it was crooked on the front of the envelope so that it slanted up toward the upper right corner. She wondered if he had written it in darkness or at an uncomfortable angle. Tom's writing was normally smallish and square with perfectly dressed corners like a well made bed. Her husband, an engineer by trade, was very meticulous about everything and well used to annotating fine diagrams in even finer print. So, why was the address crooked?

She dreaded the next thought. Could it mean that his mind or body was somehow broken?

With shaking hands, she carefully opened the envelope. She pulled out the two-page letter and started reading. After less than a minute, she shook her head and started back over, certain that if it weren't for the fact that she'd know Tom's handwriting better than her own, this letter had arrived inside this envelope by mistake.

My Darling,

I take it you are well and I think about you daily. Writing a simple letter to you is such a treat. I await yours to me in reply with much anticipation.

You likely heard Colonel Stafford passed last week due to injuries he sustained during his capture. He was a young man and I mourn his loss. I am no saint, but I find I am now senior officer among the allied prisoners. I would rather James had that honor but he is junior to me by many months.

Memories of our street and home are never far from my mind. I hope you to remember me fondly.

Do not ever let them say I won't return home to you. I will not sign a parole so I must remain here until the end, I'm afraid.

My kite took 13 hits before she fell out from under me. I did what officers must do. I stayed aloft 42 or 45 seconds, perhaps after Jerry got the best of me. I say, their enlisted pilots are quite as good at shooting us down as their officers. Another 3 or 4 of our boys escorting us likely wouldn't have mattered. On the ground, civilians rounded us up rather quickly. I am well. Never doubt it.

I hope you send me some of your biscuits, as does Percy. If you ask, instructions for packaging and sending them to me can be obtained from the Red Cross.

My darling Dotty, never ever ignore the fact that I love you. I will never stop loving you. I am continuously praying for you and our children. I'll send a message to you as often as I can. When the war ends, we will never speak of this terrible time.

I dream of watching you with our young children each morning after we rise. I miss you most terribly. You are an angel what with having our four children to raise all alone. Aunt Mildred should let you visit them this Christmas. Uncle Rory said as much when last we spoke. Perhaps you could all go to the lake house in Wales as we did the month before my departure. What a grand time we had there! I see no sign of this endless war concluding by the Holy Days.

Be brave and courageous. Let no one stop you in what you must do. I am counting on you, darling Dotty.

Yours forever,

Tom

Dorothy looked through the letter again. What was he talking about? There was no Uncle Rory, no Aunt Mildred, and Tom knew their three children were at her parents' home in the country, hopefully and prayerfully protected against the bombings. What did she need to see? They had never visited Wales in her lifetime and Tom would not consider such a surely boggy trip any kind of vacation. He had misspelled 'too,' which he could never do in his right mind. She looked again at the envelope and back at the letter.

"Well?" Beatrice demanded. "All right, then?"

What did it mean? "Suppose so," Dorothy replied. Something bothered her. Something nagged at her subconscious mind. "It's rather short."

"If you can write him back, be sure to send our love and prayers." She drained the cup and carefully stood. "I love you, friend. I look forward to the end of this war. Sorry to be such a whinge."

Dorothy stood and hugged Beatrice. "Not at all. I'm headed to mum's to drop off these things, then it's back to work with me. I'll send you the address so you can forward my mail." She looked at the man who had not moved from his spot. "If he can't fix the wall, maybe someone else can do it for him. I have money in a savings."

"You don't worry about a thing, dear," Beatrice said, pulling her sweater straight. "We'll take care of it and we'll mind it until you and Tom and the kids return safely. You go on now. Don't miss your train. Pip pip."

AN hour later, Dorothy sat on a bench at the station waiting for the train to York. She stared at the letter from Tom. She had finally realized that he'd attempted to communicate with her in some kind of a code. But what?

She lifted the envelope to the window and looked at it through the light. He'd written the address at an angle, angling up toward the stamp. What if –?

Looking around her, thinking people would surely consider her mad, she dipped her finger into the teacup next to her on the bench and used the tea to dampen the area around the stamp. The edges of it loosened up and she did it again and again until she could completely remove the stamp.

And there it was, beneath the stamp. Tom had written in a tiny, tiny print, the number four. He'd also said four when talking about their children, not three.

Brows knitted in concentration, Dorothy counted the fourth word of every sentence and formed the crypto quote.

```
take letter to Colonel young saint James
street   to   let   sign   13   officers   42
enlisted  4  civilians  send  instructions
never stop praying message ends
```

The rest was gibberish. Excitement made her fingers tingle. She picked up her bags and rushed out of the station. Forty minutes later, she sat outside of an inner office in the building on St. James Street that was camouflaged with a "To Let" sign in what appeared to be an empty window. A uniformed woman sat at a desk across from her, furiously typing and studiously ignoring her. Dorothy tried not to fidget and forced herself to look calm and collected. Internally she was a mess of nerves and anticipation.

When the door opened, she almost jumped out of her skin. Seconds later, a large man with salt and pepper hair and a thin mustache approached her, holding out his hand. "Mrs. Ewing? I'm Colonel Young. Please, come in."

Dorothy gathered her pillow cases of belongings and followed him into the office, noting the wooden paneling and the heavy desk. A thin blanket of smoke hovered over the room, and she detected an unpleasant combination of cigar, cigarette, and pipe tobaccos.

He gestured to the chair in front of the desk and waited for her to sit before he took his chair. "How may I help you?"

As she pulled the letter out of her purse she began her explanation. "My husband is a prisoner in France. He is Captain Ewing of the RAF." She waited to see if there was any hint of recognition in her husband's name, but there was nothing so she continued. "I received a letter from him today but the letter was wrong. Nothing made sense until I figured out it was a code and then deciphered it. It simply said to bring it to you and offered a count of his fellow prisoners."

He looked at the letter in her hand and back at her face. "You figured out there was a code?"

She stopped from shrugging, knowing it would make her look defensive. "Naturally. Clearly, Thomas did not intend this letter for me. I simply had to suss out the intended recipient. Once I decoded it, I came here straight away."

Without a word to Dorothy, he reached forward and picked up his phone. "Patty, be a good girl and get me Major Radden. Immediately." Apparently without waiting for a response, the Colonel returned the handset to its cradle before he surged to his feet. "May I see the letter?"

Dorothy held it out to him. "Our home address was angled toward the postage stamp. The number four was written on the underside of the stamp in tiny writing. I could barely make it out. Then I counted the fourth word in every sentence."

Inside the envelope, she'd placed the stamp and the letter. Colonel Young inspected each in silence for several minutes. Before he spoke, there was the sound of a brisk knock on his door. "Enter!" he shouted, neither turning nor returning the letter.

Dorothy turned toward the door and watched an older but still quite beautiful blonde woman in a navy suit enter the room. She had frosted hair cut to her chin in a bob and very subtle makeup that gave her a rather unapproachable and stern look.

"You gave us a bell, Colonel?" The woman's accent was vague, but sounded somewhat cultured, upper class.

"Charlene, this is Mrs. Dorothy Ewing, whose husband, Captain Thomas Ewing of His Majesty's Royal Air Forces, is presently enjoying the hospitality of the *Wehrmacht* in a POW *Stalag*. Dorothy, meet Major Charlene Radden. Mrs. Ewing here received an obscure letter from her imprisoned husband and deciphered it, discovering instructions to bring it to me."

Charlene raised an eyebrow. "Indeed? May I see the letter?"

As Colonel Young handed it over he said, "It may interest you to know that Mrs. Ewing is presently employed at Bletchley House where, I am told, she is serving admirably."

The fact that the Colonel knew about her actual vocation surprised her, though perhaps it shouldn't have. Major Charlene Radden's eyebrows raised up a fraction, but her expression didn't change in any way. She rhetorically asked, "Indeed?"

"Indeed." Dorothy spoke up. "The work we are doing is of utmost importance."

Colonel Young and Charlene stopped and looked at her.

"Mind if we have a bit of a chin wag as to how you went about securing your employment with the Bletchley Circle?" Charlene asked, sounding very nonchalant for a question of such weight.

The Major had referred to the project name itself, Bletchley Circle, not House or Park, but Circle. It informed Dorothy that she knew of the work. She cleared her throat, still wondering how much she could say under the Secrets Act. "I won a crossword puzzle competition."

"And are you actually working on encrypted messages?"

Dorothy stared back and forth between the Major and the Colonel. Finally, the Colonel chuffed and said, "Good girl. I assure you we both have the clearance to have this conversation with you."

Dorothy nodded and decided to take the Colonel at his word. "For now I'm doing administrative work. But, my supervisor gave me some simple encryption last week and was impressed with what I could suss. So, my prayer is that they'll let me take on more soon." She let the sentence fade away as she finished speaking, not understanding the looks on their faces.

"Colonel Young, if you'll pardon me for a tick, I'll be right back," Charlene announced, setting down the letter and hastening out of the office.

Colonel Young leaned back in his chair. "Just so you know, Major Radden is assembling a unit of talented lasses who will be an integral part of the war effort. Her ideas are unparalleled. I think you are in a position to be a valuable member of her team, though I defer to the Major's good judgment. Tell me, did you participate in crossword puzzle contests before the war?"

"Only for a lark." She smiled, remembering the fun nights, racing Percy or his friends. "My husband's dear friend, Sir Percy Montrose, was the reigning champion, though I could beat him nearly every time."

Colonel Young raised an eyebrow. "Sir Montrose? I know him, actually. Been to state dinners and had a chance to chat him up from time to time. Brilliant chap, I'd say. Rather posh. Rather a sharp dresser as well. Very *debonair* as our friends across the Channel would say."

"Indeed." She shifted in her chair. "He is captive alongside my husband."

Colonel Young pursed his lips. "That could very well work in our favor."

"How so?" Dorothy asked, confused.

Before he answered, Charlene came back into the room. As Dorothy turned around to look at her, she saw her nod to Colonel Young. "I would like for you to join my team," she said without preamble. "I need people skilled at deciphering. You clearly fit that definition and your superior at Bletchley agrees, though he'd rather not lose you. I'm afraid I had to insist, Colonel, with your kind permission."

The colonel made a brushing gesture with his hand as if brushing away the suggestion that it would present a problem. "Mrs. Ewing's reassignment to your unit ought not throw a spanner into the works at Bletchley. Plenty of bright folks at their disposal."

Dorothy shook her head. "It was a simple code. The fourth word of every sentence. Anyone could have figured it out."

"I beg to differ, Mrs. Ewing," Charlene said. "Few women would have understood a code. Fewer women would have discovered the key to the code, and even fewer women still would have had the courage to follow the simple instruction. Once they reached this building, what with how it appears empty with a 'To Let' sign in the window, they more than likely would have turned away, thinking that they'd made some embarrassing mistake. Yet you came inside and pushed forward, from clerk to agent to clerk, until you found yourself seated in the office of none other than Colonel Young himself. Now, tell me, why do you think that was simple?"

Listening to it spelled out like that caused an excited flutter in Dorothy's heart. "Very well. What must I do as a member of your team, Major Radden?"

"I'd say the very first thing you and I will do is reply to your husband with instructions for how to get hold of a much safer code." Charlene looked at the note. "You have children?"

"Yes, but not four. Three, actually. They've been at my parents' home in York since the bombing began."

"And where are your things? At Bletchley House?"

Dorothy nodded.

"Right. Then it would simply be a matter of you coming with me. When we are at our destination, I can explain a lot more and introduce you to some pretty amazing women. We'll have your things brought along directly."

It took Dorothy about three seconds and the quickest prayer for guidance she'd ever prayed, to respond with a nod. "I think I am very interested, Major."

Charlene smiled, and the smile transformed her face, warmed it. "Wonderful! Meet me here tomorrow morning at seven. Settle your home. You won't be back right away or any time soon, I'd wager."

Dorothy gestured toward the stuffed pillow cases at her feet. "My home was destroyed in last night's bombing."

Charlene sighed. "That must be a terrible inconvenience. But, the silver lining is that you can come with me immediately. Shall we go?" With that, Major Radden plucked one of the pillow cases from the floor with one hand, leaving the other two for Dorothy to retrieve, and gestured toward the door with her free hand. Dorothy rose to her feet and plucked up the remaining pillow cases. "Colonel, thank you again."

Colonel Young nodded. "No need, Major. Seemed up your alley and so forth. Get her sorted and I'll continue to keep my ear to the ground." He reached forward and picked up his phone once more. "Patty, have some of the lads drive the Major and Mrs. Ewing to their destination. And see if you can scare up some proper luggage for Mrs. Ewing's belongings. There's a good girl."

He, again, abruptly hung up the phone without awaiting any kind of response from Patty. "I'll have a lorry sent with a detail to escort you in case there's any trouble. Please don't leave without some of the lads close at hand. Always a pleasure, Major." With that, Colonel Young looked back at the stack of work on his desk, clearly dismissing the women.

CHAPTER 4

Chapter Four

Outside of Milton Keynes, England: 1941

DOROTHY pressed the headphones tighter against her head. The faint signal barely sounded through the static. As she listened, she copied what she heard as fast as she could, until her hand ached and her pencil was dull. Then the signal stopped.

She sent her own message, confirming the end of the transmission and receipt, then pulled the headphones off of her ears. Using the key, she translated the message. In an effort to confirm what she read, she went over it one more time, then sat up and tossed the pencil onto the table.

"Brilliant, Charity!" Her instructor, Martin Watson, looked at his stopwatch. "You and Temperance are just about neck and neck in speed."

Dorothy grinned. She liked the code name given to her as part of the Virtues squad. Charity was a virtue for which she strove in life, something she and her husband focused on when the world wasn't in such a state of turmoil.

"Temperance does a lot more in her head than I do," she said as she shook out her aching right hand and pushed the chair back from the wooden desk. "If you gave us each new keys, I bet I could decipher faster."

"She said exactly the same thing about you." Martin looked at the clock on the wall. "You have a meeting with Charlene in an hour. And, as Temperance left earlier, she asked me to tell you to meet her in the canteen when you were done here."

"Thank you." She grabbed her dark green wool jacket off of the back of her chair and tossed Martin a wave. "I'll see you this evening." As she moved through the crowded room, full of equipment and students, she buttoned her jacket and ran her hands over the side of her hair to make sure none of it had come loose during the tense moments of decoding and ciphering.

Certain her appearance was in order, she left the clapboard building and stepped out into the busy campus. The facility was housed on the estate of an earl, and all around the once beautiful gardens, temporary structures were built for barracks, training rooms, and various clandestine activities. In the main house, administrative offices took up most of the first and second floors, leaving the earl and his wife to live in a small cottage intended for the dowager on an outer part of the estate.

Dorothy skirted around the fountain in the center of the long drive and turned left, rushing to the student canteen. She stepped up into the long wooden structure. As her eyes adjusted to the dim interior, she saw Temperance at a table with Hope and Grace. Dorothy waved at them, but went to the counter and got herself a cup of tea before joining the little party.

"Hello, ladies," she said as she set her cup and saucer down and slipped into a chair.

"How'd it go?" Temperance bit into a biscuit and made a face at it before setting it on the table next to her cup. Temperance had long dark hair she wore pinned up in rolls in a style that complimented the green wool hat on her head perfectly. She had dark brown eyes set in a beautiful face with high cheekbones and full lips. She honestly looked like a picture on a poster put out by the ministry office.

"He said I was, and I quote, brilliant." She took a sip of the tea and closed her eyes for a moment to savor the warmth in her mouth.

"We all knew that," Grace said with a smile. She had dark curly hair and dark almond-shaped eyes. She spoke English with an odd accent that made Dorothy want to question her about where she was from, which was against just about every rule in their organization.

"Well, I think God was just gifting me for this time in our lives," she said with sincere modesty. "What good does it do anyone to be able to solve a crossword in record time? Not the least bit useful, really. However, if that very skill can be translated into something like this, then I'll happily accept it."

Hope, who still used a code-name despite the fact that everyone at the facility knew her as the famous singer Virginia Benoit, and despite the fact that everyone felt a bit star struck by her presence, smiled. "They tried to teach me code, but I'm afraid I was incapable of learning it." When she smiled, her white teeth glowed against her dark skin. She spoke with a southern American accent that flowed around them like warm honey. Like Grace, her French was nearly perfect.

"It doesn't much matter whether you're writing in code, anyway, right?" Grace clarified. "You're going to be spying then writing down information they already know. Yours is not to hide what you're writing, but the fact that you're writing. The chemicals and disappearing ink and all that you're learning about is more important than any code they could teach you."

"This is true," Hope said with a grin. "But they simplified a code for me anyway. Chemicals are so much easier to learn."

"So you say," Temperance said with a shudder, causing the women to laugh.

The door to the canteen opened, and Dorothy automatically looked up. She was surprised to see Charlene, a senior staff member, enter the student canteen. A woman followed her who appeared so young that Dorothy was sure she was a teenager. She had short brown hair that curled haphazardly around her face. Even more unusual, she wore blue pants and a brown goatskin flight jacket.

Charlene led her straight to their table. "Here are most of my Virtues now," she said. "Ladies, I'd like you to meet the seventh and final member of your team. This is Faith. Faith, please meet Hope, Temperance, Grace and Charity. Prudence and Mercy will be in the chapel tonight for their weekly Bible study, I'm sure."

Faith's cheeks flushed and she nodded. "Pleased to meet y'all."

Hope raised one perfectly sculpted eyebrow. "You're American. And bless my soul, from the South, too."

When Faith looked directly at Hope, her eyes widened. "And you're in America."

The star grinned and gracefully stood. "Well, obviously."

"I saw you perform in Dallas less than a week ago. Even met you backstage."

"I'm sure we had a wonderful conversation, though I can't say I remember it." She picked up her empty cup. "I have a class in five minutes." She placed a hand on Faith's shoulder as she walked by. "Welcome to our group, child. I'm thrilled to have you."

Dorothy looked Faith up and down, from the toes of her butter soft riding boots to the top of her brown curls. "You're a pilot!"

"I sure am. How did you –?"

Charlene laughed. "I think you'll find that Charity is a master at solving all sorts of puzzles." She gestured toward a chair and Faith perched on the edge of it. "Faith is not just any pilot. Faith is your pilot. You'll learn more about that later." She looked at her watch. "For now, I have a meeting and then one with you," she looked up and met Dorothy's eyes, "in forty-five minutes."

"Yes, Martin gave me the message."

"Very well. See you then."

As she left the building, Dorothy turned to Faith. "Charlene had said we had another team member coming. Welcome to the group."

"Thank you. I've been here a few days, but she just now assigned me to your team."

Temperance snorted. "She catch you praying or something?"

"Something like that." Faith appeared to relax as she leaned back in her chair. "After I refueled in Iceland I had fuel to make it here so I flew straight through then landed down this a'way. I figure I must have slept for a good day or two."

Dorothy had to make certain she understood what she was hearing. "You flew all the way here from America?"

"Well, heck, yeah. Me and the *Texas Diamond* on a wing and a prayer. Daddy gave her to me for my sweet sixteen. She's a North American NA-16 so he thought that was cute. She's just the prettiest thing you ever did see."

"That's brilliant. How long have you been flying?"

"Got my license at twelve but I been flying the oil fields since I was ten. No, nine. Just runnin' errands and stuff, ya' know."

"That's simply aces." Dorothy wondered how old this young woman might be. She certainly couldn't be much older than sixteen. "How does your father feel about you being here what with the bombings and, well I suppose I should just say it, the *Messerschmitts*?"

"Didn't ask him. Daddy supports my decisions. And he's sure no fan of Hitler." Faith sat back and stretched her legs before crossing one straight leg over the other. It looked like something a gymnast or a ballerina might do to stretch out a cramped hamstring. "Charlene said she knew exactly where I would fit in best."

"Charlene knows us well. The strong faith in our group excites her." Dorothy took a sip of her now cooled tea. "It's what gave her the idea for our code names."

Grace, always the direct one, asked the question on Dorothy's mind. "How old are you, Faith?"

Faith's smile was genuine. "Almost twenty, though I know I look much younger. You should see the looks on the men's faces when I climb out of my plane. They all think I'm a little girl."

"We've encountered very little resistance from the men here," Dorothy said. "Most are even supportive of what we're doing."

"No offense, but y'all aren't flying with 'em." Faith frowned. "It's like they're threatened by my sex. Have they never heard of Amelia Earhart for goodness' sakes?"

Temperance shook her head. "You flying missions for us frees one of them up to fly in combat. What's threatening about that?"

Faith laughed. "Maybe the ones complaining don't want to fly combat missions. They're scared they'll get shot down."

Temperance shot a look at Dorothy, who immediately felt her heart twist with pain and fear for her husband. "She doesn't know, love," Temperance said, reaching over and taking her hand. It surprised Dorothy how much comfort she found in that touch.

"I realize that. All's well." Dorothy stood and picked up her cup and saucer. "I'm going to go so I have time to freshen up before my meeting with Charlene. It was a pleasure to meet you, Faith."

As she set her cup and saucer in the bin near the counter, she glanced back and saw Temperance and Grace whispering to Faith. So, now the young American knew about her husband, the engineer turned pilot shot down over Occupied France.

Tears burned the back of her eyes as she stepped out into the bright sunlight. She missed her husband. She missed her children. She just wanted this awful war over and life to return to normal. She started praying for Tom's safety and for the safety of her children as she walked to the barracks.

8 8 8 8

"YOUR husband included a private note for you in his latest missive," Charlene said. She handed a worn piece of paper over to Dorothy. As Dorothy scanned the words, the tears that threatened earlier slipped out of her eyes.

> QUIT WORRYING I'M WELL. MISS YOU PROUD OF
> YOU. KEEP FIGHTING KEEP PRAYING FOR ME MIND
> THE KIDS BRILLIANT DOTTY BE HOME SOON.

"Thank you," she whispered, brushing a finger over the words on the paper.

"Of course. Thank you. This country owes your family a huge debt of gratitude. The information trade back and forth with your husband and now the other prisoners is paramount to the operations we're performing where he is being held." Charlene handed her a file folder with the word "MOST SECRET" stamped across the front. "Here is the information to be contained in a new letter to him. We need it to go out immediately, so if you can spend tonight coding it, I would appreciate it."

"Of course."

"I'm finalizing the details with Command, so it will be after the supper hour." Charlene narrowed her eyes at her. "What's wrong?"

Dorothy shrugged. "He's such a good man. It's just hard to see him trying to lift my spirits. I can't even imagine what he's going through."

Charlene nodded. "I see."

Dorothy didn't know what made her continue. Perhaps it was the fact that she knew she could trust this woman, Major Radden, her superior officer, with anything she said. Perhaps it was the privacy they presently enjoyed in her office. Perhaps she still just felt raw after the unintended remarks about getting shot down by the young American pilot. For whatever reason, she continued.

"I just don't know what I would do if I never see him again. How would the children handle it if the worst were to happen? I had a great uncle come back from the Black Forrest missing an arm. What if he comes back but he's not well? I think about these things and it is quite distracting. And I know I am far from alone but I miss him. I just miss his big strong body and the way he looks at me with such pride and joy and the way he tussles with our son and teases our daughters. I pray and pray and pray and I don't hear God answering any of my prayers. And I am terrified of what he is going through in that awful place. The very idea of his conditions appalls me yet here he takes the time to try to cheer me up!"

Quite suddenly, she fell silent, feeling a bit embarrassed at her outburst.

"I see." Charlene repeated. "Well, would you like to intellectually understand what he's going through? Or what he's been through? Or do you just need to have a good cry then get back to work?"

She felt her chin rise, despite her mind telling her that Charlene intentionally set it up so that she'd get angry and get her mind off of feeling sorry for herself. "I'm sure I know he was tortured for information. You don't need to pretend. I also know that you've been sending him packages hidden in Red Cross supplies to help sustain him and his mates. I don't need any intellectual knowledge."

Charlene raised an eyebrow. "Indeed. Well, then, back to work, is it?"

Dorothy stood. "Why must you be so unfeeling?"

Something flashed in Charlene's eyes - a hidden, understood pain that vanished just as quickly as it had appeared. It left Dorothy to wonder if she had imagined it. Then, surprisingly, she stood and leaned over her desk until they were nearly nose-to-nose. "Because this is war. And it's not the first one in my lifetime. I can only pray it will be the last." She straightened and tugged on the hem of her jacket.

Dorothy let out a breath of air she didn't realized she held. "My apologies."

"It's not an easy time. But we must keep our wits about us, or we'll lose this war. As you said, you are far from alone. Many wives are having to get on in exactly the same position you find yourselves in and several, as you know, will never see their husbands again. If we should lose this war, Charity, then the simple fact is that none of us can ever get back to normal." Charlene sat in her chair. "No one wants that."

"I –"

"You have a letter to write." Her commander picked up a pen. "And I have work to do."

Contrite, Dorothy left the office. As the door closed behind her, she heard Charlene say, "I'll see you this evening after your meal."

Though Charlene clearly couldn't see her, she nodded her reply and walked down the large staircase. As she reached the bottom, she spotted Mercy coming out of the drawing room. If anyone's hair was more gloriously red than her own, it was this brilliant and befreckled Scot. Her friend carried a gray dress draped over her arm and glared at Dorothy. "This just brings it all home, does it not? D'ya see this dunderheaded thing?"

"What's the row?" But the dress and the white apron draped over her friend's arm hinted at the issue.

"Apparently, I'm to be a nurse," she whispered, looking around her. Her Scottish brogue rolled the 'r' in the word nurse. "D'ya ken how many years of medical school and training I have endured in my lifetime so that I can go undercover and pretend I'm now a nurse? That's just magic, that is. A dafty nurse!"

She said the word as if it left a bad taste in her mouth. Dorothy couldn't help but giggle as she slipped an arm over her friend's shoulder. "At least you get to be a doctor in private, right? You get to treat the underground."

"Evidently, I would present – and this is a direct quote, mind – 'too high profile' were I to actually go in as a doctor. Which I am! An' I've been told," she spat, "that I'm lucky to be going into anything medical at all." She held up the apron and glared at it, then draped it back over her arm. "Bah!"

"Come on, my friend. Let's go find us some tea and cry into it."

Mercy sighed. "Sounds delightful. Let me go put up my magic nurse's uniform," she said, as if the word 'nurse' hurt her tongue, "and I will meet you there."

Twenty minutes later, they held paper cups of tea and sat in the room that Mercy and Faith shared. Like Dorothy's room it contained two twin beds covered with hand crocheted woolen blankets donated by a local women's group. A small nightstand sat between the two beds and held a lamp with a faded flower pattern on the shade. The only other furniture in the room was a single dresser and an armoire.

Worn Bibles sat on each bed. On the foot of Mercy's bed sat a large black bag that contained her doctor supplies with the initials "RWB" in a silver plate on the front of it.

Dorothy took a sip of the cooling tea and looked at Mercy's face. "Who was he?"

For a moment, a startled look crossed her face, then she smiled a wry smile. "Am I to be your puzzle now, brilliant Charity?"

"No. Well, everyone is since we're so very, very secret. But, the initials are engraved in a very masculine style. I would imagine you would have selected a bit of scroll with your name."

Mercy reached over and ran a slim finger over the silver plate. "He was mine for a wee bit," she nearly whispered, "and now he's gone until I go to meet him one day." She cleared her throat and lifted her cup in a toast. "But his earthly absence leaves me free to go fight this battle in a nurse's uniform."

"Temperance would say, 'At least you didn't have to learn to sew.'"

Mercy let loose a loud laugh. "You are absolutely right!" She drained her tea and crushed the cup. "I am thankful that I will at least still get to work on patients. The hard part will be in restraining myself from performing surgery."

Dorothy stood. "Just keep the faith, sister, and you'll be fine." She gestured at the door. "I have a letter to write before the dinner hour."

"Your strength amazes me," Mercy said out of the blue. "I think if I were separated from a husband and children as you are, I would be insane by now."

The tightly contained control almost slipped, but with an unsteady grasp, she shoved it back in place. She kept so much buried deep inside. Nothing would be solved by letting all the fear and anxiety rise to the surface.

"My children are in the safest place possible and this job gives me almost constant contact with my Thomas. I am more fortunate than so very many wives." She ran her fingers over the black handle of Mercy's bag. "I'm sorry for your loss."

"It will be better when we win the war."

"Aye."

8 8 8 8

DOROTHY sat on the hard packed ground and leaned her back against the chain linked fence surrounding the airfield. A cool breeze blew wisps of hair against her forehead, tickling her. In the warm sunshine, she knitted winter stockings for her youngest daughter, Beatrice, named for her best friend and neighbor of so many years. Wee Bea, as they affectionately called her, would be five in a month. She couldn't imagine how the time had gone so quickly. It felt like she'd just been born yesterday, and now she planned to start school next year. Her last letter had been penned in her own hand, and not that of Dorothy's mum. She'd talked about gathering eggs and cutting squares for a quilt, giving Dorothy a longing for the farm where she'd grown up and the smell of her mum's kitchen.

While her hands worked the knitting needles, she looked up in the sky and saw the plane approaching. Right as it approached overhead, five people jumped out of it, one immediately after the other. Knowing Temperance and Prudence were third and fourth in line, she held her breath and her hands momentarily paused their task until their parachutes opened.

The women had jumped from barrage balloons six times in preparation for this jump from a fixed wing aircraft but Dorothy had never seen any of the parachute jumps. The descent occurred much faster than what she had imagined. Rather than a gradual weightless fall, it looked, from her perspective, like a controlled plummet.

In her mind, she automatically calculated rate of decent, variables with the wind and atmosphere, and projected landing locations. She performed the calculations without thinking about it. Simultaneously, she counted stitches in the gray wool, feeling a small bit of victory as each of the jumpers landed almost exactly where she'd calculated they would.

Several minutes later, she stood as her friends approached, holding their helmets under their arms. "Well done!"

Prudence grinned, clearly enjoying the rush of adrenaline. "That was fantastic," she said in her cultured voice. "I very much want to do it again!"

"You're insane," Temperance replied. She collapsed on the ground next to the fence. "Sweet ground," she said, closing her eyes and patting the hard surface next to her. "I have never appreciated the earth enough."

"Silly to feel upset afterward," Grace said from behind them. "You did fine. Looks like you executed the landing perfectly."

Dorothy looked at Grace and smiled. "There you are! I waited for you for a bit."

"*Oui.* I offered to help Faith black her windows. She's flying blind this afternoon."

"She's so brave." Dorothy packed up her knitting and held a hand out to Temperance to help her stand.

"We're all brave." Grace never minced words. Dorothy had come to count on that. "Even when we feel fear, we still act," she said, looking directly at Temperance. "Fear is normal. Don't let it discourage you."

Temperance paused, then took a shaking breath and nodded. "Thank you."

A rare smile lit up Grace's face. "Welcome." She glanced at the watch strapped to her right wrist. "I'm ready for that back room at the pub and some pie. What about you?"

to normal. She started praying for Tom's safety and for the safety of her children as she walked to the barracks.

8 8 8 8

Chapter Five

DOROTHY'S eyes watered as she yawned wide enough to feel her jaw pop. Fatigue seeped through her, making her neck ache and her limbs heavy. She rested her elbows on the table and placed her chin in her palms, then used the tips of her fingers to gently rub her eyes.

"Long night?"

Startled, she lowered her hands and looked at Grace. "Been a while since I pulled an all-nighter."

Grace raised a questioning eyebrow. "What did you do that had you working all night before?"

"My middle, Daisy, was a doozy. She'd wail on and on. I used to sit and just cry with her. First time she slept through the night, I couldn't sleep because I'd keep checking on her to make sure she was still alive." Realizing she'd started babbling, she blushed. "Sorry."

Grace's normally stern face gentled as she smiled. "No need. You're tired."

"Aye."

"And you miss your babies."

With a hot sting of tears in her eyes, she took a sip of her tea. "More than I can say."

Grace sat back and shifted so that she could prop her foot on the chair next to her. She balanced her cup and saucer on her knee and rested her forearm and the palm of her hand on the table. She wore a white cotton shirt and pants. She looked very relaxed, but Dorothy saw through the facade to the hum of nerves bubbling under the surface.

"You're doing the right thing."

Dorothy nodded. "I realize that. What about you?" They'd shared a room since Grace arrived at the training camp, but they worked such long hours that they mainly used the room for sleeping. Often when Dorothy would come into the room, Grace would already be asleep, and when Dorothy woke, she would be gone.

With a half-smile, Grace asked, "Family? No. I am a soldier." She looked behind her and examined the still empty canteen before redirecting her gaze to Dorothy. "My father knew this war would come. My brothers and I were trained from when we were – how do you say it? *Yalahdeem?*" Grace held her hand perhaps three feet above the floor and closed her eyes in concentration. When she opened them again she said, "Children. Since we were children." She sighed and took a sip of her tea. "I have always struggled with English. I was too old when we started learning it."

Dorothy wanted to ask this woman a million questions, starting with her native language – of which she believed she had just overheard a single word – and ending with her training as a small child. But she couldn't. Rules. Secrecy. Regulations. Instead, she put her together like a group of puzzle pieces; a solitary person, more comfortable around men than women, well skilled in everything she did here at the camp, anxious to begin her mission.

"It's enough for me to understand my husband's occasional Gaelic. I never sought to learn owt else."

Grace tapped the side of her temple with her finger. "You have the brain. You wouldn't have any problem learning languages. You'd just have to look at it like a puzzle."

"Speaking of puzzles," Dorothy said, "why are you up? It's barely six in the morning."

"I don't like sleep and rarely do it. I decided to get dressed early and get my exercise before the rest of the camp gets busy. I learned early on the men here don't like it when I use their facilities and they're working out, too. Apparently I distract them. It's less of a problem when I exercise after hours."

Dorothy raised an eyebrow. "Does the attitude bother you?"

With a smooth shrug, Grace replied, "I don't much understand the thinking that men and women are so different but I know my father raised us rather counter to the popular culture. It never occurred to me to place such restrictions on women."

Dorothy laughed. "Yes. I met my husband while I pursued a degree in engineering. The restrictions are not just on the gymnasium equipment."

"That is certainly a traditionally masculine field. But with your intelligence, I can see that being a good career for you."

"I thought I would love it. But, I didn't. I think I enjoyed learning about it, but implementing it only bored me horribly. Far too easy."

Grace drained her cup and stood. "You are perfectly suited for this job, then, so? No boredom here!"

"Not a jot." Dorothy rolled her head on her shoulders and stood much slower than Grace. "I think I'll go nap for a bit before getting back to work."

Grace lifted her arms above her head and stretched. "Think I'll go for a run before breakfast. Have a good nap. Meeting at the pub tonight?"

"Right. Half eight."

"If I don't see you before, I'll see you then."

Dorothy walked back to her room, feeling tired, achy, and gloomy. Talking about her Daisy as an infant brought to mind the years she spent in perfect contentment, raising her babies. She loved teaching them, hugging them, holding them, singing to them.

Her breath hitched and she rushed to her room. With the door firmly shut behind her, she fell to her knees by her bed as hot tears slid in silent rivers down her cheeks. Body shaking, throat burning, she grabbed her pillow and buried her face into it so that no possible sound could escape.

Would Wee Bea even remember what she looked like? Did Little Tommy resent the abandonment of his parents? Did Daisy hate the dirt on the farm as much as she hated grass stains on her favorite dresses? What kind of emotional suffering were they enduring?

With a fist, she hit the mattress and her hand sprang right back up again, like a ball bouncing. Any other time, that would have amused her. This morning, it infuriated her. She hit it again and again, until the muscles in her hand ached from clenching them so tightly.

When she felt like she'd exhausted the tears at least temporarily, she crawled onto the bed and hugged the damp pillow to her. "Tom," she whispered as she closed her eyes. What would he think of this show of emotion? *Rein it all in. Stiff upper lip and whatnot. Don't let the Jerries get you down. That's a good girl.*

She closed her eyes and thought of him, of his bravery, of his embrace. Aching for his touch, she drifted off to sleep.

※ ※ ※ ※

DOROTHY ducked her head as she entered the low door of the pub. She waved hello to the locals she'd met and briefly spoke to the woman behind the bar. "Can I just get some chips?"

"Not hungry tonight, love? We have stew and pudding." Bonnie wiped her hands on her flowered apron.

"I took early supper. Working a late shift."

The locals knew *something* happened at the estate, but they had also been trained by enough vague answers not to inquire as to what or how or when. "I'll get it to you." She slid a teapot across the bar. "Mind you take that back on your way? I'll start another lot going for your group."

Dorothy picked up the pot and walked through the room, stepping carefully on the sloped wooden floors. This particular pub had just celebrated its 300th birthday. Over time, owners had upgraded electricity and plumbing, but much of the original structure remained the same. Heavy wood beams above, dark wooden floors below, and wooden furniture made the rooms dark.

She walked through an arched doorway and stepped into the back room. Since they weren't meeting for another thirty minutes, seeing Hope at the table with papers spread out in front of her surprised her.

She set the teapot near Hope's elbow and took the chair next to her. "What are you swotting?" She picked up one of the papers and looked over the formula, recognizing the symbols and abbreviations from when she was in school.

"I have learned so much since I've been here. Including the fact that I LOVE chemistry. How have I lived over thirty years and not known that?" Hope reached down to the seat beside her and lifted a thick chemistry book, plopping it down on the table. "Love it. I'm borrowing this book, but I must find one for myself after the war."

Dorothy shifted to the side while the waitress placed her dinner plate in front of her. Once the waitress stepped out of earshot, she observed, "Isn't it strange how we each have these sort of niche gifts that have formed such a strong team?"

"Not strange at all," Hope said, looking up from the paper in front of her. "Don't you think God has equipped us all perfectly for this work?"

With a nod, she sought to further explain. "I do believe that. It's just that the perfection of it all, when I consider it, rather surprises me."

"Us with our simple human thinking," Hope agreed. She started gathering her paperwork. "I feel so honored that He has opened such doors and given us such gifts." As she neatly stacked the papers and placed them in her bag she said, "Though I'll confess to being frightened. The Nazi party is so racist. I saw a taste of it when I was a just child in St. Louis, the city where my parents worked in America. There was a horrible race riot and so many people were killed and made homeless. To think that an entire nation teaches such hatred and seeks to spread that hate throughout the world is just horrifying."

Dorothy popped a twice fried potato wedge into her mouth before she reached over and took Hope's hand. After she swallowed she said, "I know in my heart that one day race won't be an issue."

With a wry smile, Hope said, "Something will always be an issue. The enemy is a master of deceit and spinning hate and discontent, and when it's not race, it will be something else: social status, wealth, lineage." She squeezed Dorothy's hand before she lifted the teapot and poured each of them a cup of the brew.

"You say that so casually."

"I've had a few eye-opening moments in my life when I've faced pure hate. It tends to lead to revelation."

Dorothy ate another chip and washed it down with the strong tea. "Will you be safe?"

"I will be as safe as I can be for a short time. Then it will no longer be good for me to be there. Charlene will have ears on the ground so we'll know when I must be evacuated."

"I can't believe this is all happening already," she said rather wistfully. "I mean, I know we've been here training for weeks, but to think that the time is drawing near for you all to leave." She felt her breath hitch in her throat, surprised by the force of emotion that swamped her. "I will go a bit crazy thinking of you all on the ground."

Hope slipped an arm over her shoulders. "And we'll have you over here – listening for us, praying for us." She squeezed tight before releasing her and snagging one of her potatoes. "Don't you wish you were coming with us?"

"Oh, heavens no," Dorothy said with a shudder, "not on your life. I'm thrilled to be here. Waiting. Holding down the fort, so to speak." She smiled as she looked up and saw Prudence come into the room. "Hello there!"

Prudence slipped her jacket off her shoulders and shook it. "Beastly weather out there. Dogs and cats." She draped her coat over the back of a chair and poured a cup of tea. "Bonnie's brewing another pot."

"What with this weather, I reckon we'll drink it," Dorothy replied.

Prudence sat across from her and Hope. "I have it on good authority that Mercy's *en route*. She had a personal errand to run." She looked at the book in front of Hope. "What's this, then?"

Hope smiled. "Chemistry. Who knew my singer's brain would fall so readily in love?"

Prudence didn't move her head but her eyes shot toward every corner before she spoke, as if looking for spies hiding beneath the tables. Then she nodded and asked, "Invisible ink?"

"Yes. It's so much more complicated than I ever realized."

"You should see the camera they trained me on today," Prudence said as she brushed her fingers through her damp blonde hair. "It fit inside my palm with room to spare!"

"Today's technology is incredible." Hope shook her head in amazement. "We'll wonder how we ever did without some of this stuff soon."

Grace stepped into the room, ducking under the low doorway, moving with a fluid grace that made her look almost as if she glided across the floor. "This weather!" She exclaimed, brushing the raindrops out of her short black curls. "I can't believe how quickly it turned from the sunny day."

"Going to be rather a soggy trek back, I fear," Prudence complained.

"No worries," Grace replied, "I stole a truck."

For a moment, silence fell over the room as the other ladies stared at Grace with open mouths. Then Hope started laughing, and soon they all laughed. "You stole it?"

With a smooth shrug, Grace slipped into a chair and poured a cup of tea. "I was told to improve my skills. I'm going to claim it was practice."

"Better to beg forgiveness than permission, eh?" Prudence laughed.

With a wink, Grace said, "Something like that."

Dorothy hopped up when Bonnie came into the room, balancing a big platter of lamb stew in one hand and another teapot in the other. "Here we are, ladies," she announced as Dorothy took the platter from her. "Be wanting more tea, I reckon."

"Perhaps one more," Dorothy said with a smile.

"Kettle's already on. I'll bring it in when it's brewed."

"You're a dear," Dorothy said. She set the platter in the center of the table and picked up the serving spoon. "I've eaten. Who wants stew?"

CHAPTER 6

IN the span of two days, Dorothy said good-bye to all of her team except Faith, who flew back and forth into Occupied France, delivering and collecting people, dropping supplies, and performing aerial reconnaissance. Over the course of several weeks, the team of seven women had grown exceptionally close, and now the estate, though busy as ever with mission control and training recruits, felt a bit empty and lonely.

Fortunately, Dorothy always worked during Temperance's scheduled broadcast times, and often other times as well, fearing she'd end up missing an emergency broadcast. As soon as Temperance would realize she had "Charity" on the other end of the line, the two women fell into the habit of shorthand they'd created while working together. It added another impenetrable layer to the already tight code, because the shorthand remained in Temperance's head instead of in a code book somewhere.

She received missives or information on supply drops from command then drafted them to Temperance, who then delivered them to Prudence, who acted as a courier with the commander on the ground. In return, Prudence gave Temperance information, and Temperance relayed it to Dorothy, who delivered it to the War Office. Back and forth they went, all the while planning the largest prison breakout of the war to date.

While other sections in occupied Europe had multiple radio operators, in Area 3 of France, Temperance operated alone. Without her, London had no eyes on the ground and the Resistance had no eyes in Command. The radio operator she replaced had broken under the interrogation of the Nazis and revealed the known locations of other wireless operators in the network. Until another operator finished her training, Temperance remained the only one in her network.

Dorothy had started working closely with another woman a week before, training her for the field. But, it would take weeks to train her enough to actively work undercover in France. In the meantime, Temperance remained their only voice.

Dorothy also received brief missives from Command that she encoded into the private code only she and Tom shared. He sent information to her, letters she never even saw unless he had a private message for her, and she sent information back to him. Information like what to do with the special Red Cross packages he received within the rations of supplies.

She knew, from the work she did while encoding the letters, that the packages contained tools and items needed for the escape plan. But, she couldn't bear the thought of thinking about it too much. She'd worked out the variables over and over again and the math kept revealing the same terrifying truth: the odds of a successful escape attempt always came up very low. Even with all the outside help her Thomas, Sir Percy, and their fellow POWs received, the possibility remained mathematically certain that it couldn't happen. But, as he'd assured her a couple of times now, he felt it his duty to attempt escape. Especially while in France, an area where friends and sympathizers on the ground could help hide or aid them and prevent recapture.

While she worked and coordinated and sent missives, she prayed, begging God to keep him safe and shielded under His protective hand. It was a lot to ask, she knew. Every wife in the world, on whatever side of this war they happened to find themselves, likely prayed the same prayer to God. But, Dorothy kept it up in earnest, as a constant mantra in her head, pleading with God to protect her husband from whatever horrors a Nazi prison commander could give, and to protect her children from bombing by German planes.

⁣⁣⁣⁣

DOROTHY sat back in her chair and watched the newest recruit try to decode a message coming in through a horribly static-filled line. She had her own earphones on one ear, but off of the other so that she could hear the instructors across the room grumble together. She briefly wondered if at some point early in her training she'd made them frown in exasperation herself.

Three days had passed since she'd last heard from Temperance. She tried not to let that worry her. Operators on the ground couldn't always keep scheduled transmissions. But, Dorothy found herself spending more and more time like this, with the headphones on, even during off hours, just waiting. It neared four in the afternoon, and she'd started working at ten the night before.

The signal in her ear surprised her. It wasn't a scheduled time or day for anything to come from Temperance. She immediately put both of the headphones on and turned her body away from the rest of the room so that nothing would distract her from the sounds in her ears.

While she wrote the code, she knew what it said without even having to pull out the key to start deciphering it. Her heart started beating in fear, and she felt sweat bead her upper lip.

As abruptly as the signal started, it stopped. While Dorothy waited for it to resume, she carefully and intently deciphered the message, making sure she didn't make any mistakes.

TEMPERANCE COMPROMISED. NEED IMMED

Nothing more. She stood, with the headphones still on. "Martin!"

Her old instructor's face lost its amusement over the new recruit as he translated the tone of panic in her voice and the look on her face. He rushed to her and she held out the message with a shaking hand.

"How long since you heard from her?"

"It's just been a tick."

"Give it ten more minutes. I'll have a runner rush this to admin while you're waiting."

She waited five minutes, then five more that passed like hours. She wrote Temperance back, telling her she didn't get the entire message and to retransmit. Still nothing.

"Anything?" A crowd had formed around her now, and she didn't even know who had asked. She shook her head abruptly as she watched Charlene rush into the room.

"Anything else?"

"No, ma'am," Dorothy said, slipping one earphone off of her ear. "Not a peep."

Charlene pursed her lips and turned toward Martin. "Get with the radio station and encrypt a message for Praetorian. Ensure he knows Temperance has been compromised. Tell him to gen up some way to get Hope into that prison so she can transfer information." She whirled back around. "Come with me, Dorothy. We need to get a message in a letter out today and it must pass the most stringent scrutiny."

Dorothy kept up with Charlene's pace, rushing out of the building and across the grounds. She was one step behind her through the doorway of the mansion, and followed her through the massive hallway, down some back stairs, and into what appeared to be the wine cellar.

Tables and desks filled the room. A haze of smoke hovered about a foot above the heads of everyone. Dorothy recognized the rank of General on the shoulder boards of one of the many uniformed men, but did not recognize the man himself. Charlene took her into a back corner and asked her to sit at a small desk. She left, but returned almost immediately with a piece of paper and a sharpened pencil.

"I need you to write to Tom," Charlene said. She pulled a chair out from under a nearby table and sat across from the desk. "He has to know that any information he receives from Temperance after today is not really from her, and he needs to keep an eye and ear out for her at the prison."

Confused, Dorothy shook her head. "Tom knows Temperance?"

"Likely not. But as you know, Praetorian and Tom have been planning the prison break of 110 British soldiers from a Nazi prison."

She waited. "And now?"

"And now, it's likely Temperance is in that same prison. I need to confirm it through Hope." She tapped the paper in front of Dorothy. "Meantime, compose a note to Tom. Tell him we know Temperance was arrested and the date. Ask him to immediately confirm whether she's in his prison. We'll get it out today and hopefully into his hands within the next two days."

Dorothy frowned. "How?"

With a knowing smile, Charlene stood. "We have our resources." She straightened her jacket and turned on her heel. "I need Faith. Someone get me her location immediately."

As she walked away, Dorothy looked down at the blank paper in front of her and picked up the pencil. She carefully started drafting a letter to her husband.

Chapter Seven

THE atmosphere around Dorothy felt very tense. Already on edge, the suspicion of Temperance's capture added a heightened stress level to the group with which she worked. She could barely sleep, had no appetite to eat, and forced herself not to sit in the wireless room and wait for a signal that she knew in her heart would never come.

Two mornings after they received Temperance's last missive, Faith found her in the canteen, a cold cup of tea long forgotten in front of her.

"I wish they would let me fly over there, get information, and fly back here."

"You don't speak French," Dorothy said with half a smile. "You'd stand out like a sore thumb with your American accent and your pants."

"That's probably why Charlene keeps saying no." Faith pulled a worn Bible out of her jacket pocket and set it on the table in front of her. "I keep asking, though."

"What do you think they're planning?"

Faith stared at her for a long time, serious and contemplating. Finally, she said, "I don't think I have the security clearance that would allow me to hazard a guess, and neither do you."

A little half laugh escaped Dorothy's lips. "Well, I'm sure when something happens, we'll eventually find out."

"No doubt." She flipped the Bible open to a page marked with a red and blue ribbon. Dorothy could read the word, "Romans" upside down. Faith cleared her throat and read in a slow, southern American drawl, "Rejoicing in hope; patient in tribulation; continuing constant in prayer."

She shut the Bible and reached forward, taking Dorothy's hand. "I'm not going to pretend to understand. I don't have a husband. I don't have children. And I never even knew what friendship meant until I met y'all. I grew up isolated and alone in a house with no sisters, just brothers all old enough to be my father. I was raised by a man old enough to be my grandfather who only knew how to show his love by spending money. But one thing I do know, I know the Bible, and I know the people in it. This book is filled with tribulation and suffering that you and I could never even fathom, and through it all – through all that human suffering – is the grace and presence of God Almighty."

Dorothy felt heat flush her cheeks. She squeezed Faith's hand. "Thank you, my friend. I needed to be reminded of that."

Faith grinned. "I know." She gestured at the cup in front of the other woman. "How can you drink that stuff?"

"Well, I suppose you can know this. I'm a British housewife. It's what I do." She pushed the cup and saucer away from her. "But not cold like that."

"How about a nice cuppa joe?" Faith grinned and stood, slipping her Bible back into her jacket pocket. "My treat, even."

"Only with tons of sugar and gallons of milk."

Faith made a face and shuddered. "Ugh. That kind of defeats the point, doesn't it?"

With a laugh, Dorothy stood and picked up her dishes. "Kind of. How about we get a coffee to go? I have a shift starting in twenty minutes, and I want to go breathe some fresh air first."

"Sounds grand," Faith said, heading to the counter. "I'll meet you outside."

8 8 8 8

THREE days later, Charlene summoned Dorothy during the middle of her shift. As Dorothy sat across from her, she felt nervous anticipation at the sight of an open letter on the blotter. She could recognize Tom's handwriting.

"I want to tell you that, of course, this is entirely in confidence," Charlene said. "I don't even want you saying anything to Faith. I will tell her what I can when I can."

Dorothy nodded. "Understood."

"We received a letter from your husband today. First off, Temperance is in his prison. Hope saw her then made contact with Tom."

It fascinated her, this movement of information even when it shouldn't or couldn't possibly move. "How on earth did she manage that?"

Charlene smiled. "You and I both know our Hope has special powers of persuasion."

Despite the obvious seriousness of the coming conversation, Dorothy laughed as she shook her head. "I'm so happy she's on our side."

"Exactly." The small smile Charlene gave made Dorothy relax slightly. "We're hoping and praying that Temperance has and will continue to withstand interrogation. This letter is three days old. A lot can happen in that time."

In an attempt to stay calm and focused, Dorothy spread her fingers on her knee and stared at her wedding ring. "What now?"

"Arrangements are already underway. An attempt to rescue Temperance will be made during the already planned escape of the prisoners. We simply have to move our timeline up. She will be weak, though, and need immediate medical care. Mercy will be on hand to assess and will travel with her if need be. However, we'd prefer not to have Mercy break her cover if at all possible."

Dorothy examined the clues in Charlene's face. A tightening of the mouth, an extra swallow indicating nerves that were not normally present, shifting of the eyes. Even people could become puzzles to be solved. "You didn't bring me here to tell me about Temperance. What else is there?"

Charlene took a deep breath and slowly released it. "If all goes well, Tom will be part of the group escaping. As will your friend, Sir Percy."

She felt her heart flutter. Could it be that he might possibly be home soon? "Oh? When?"

Charlene looked at her intently. "I dare not say." She stood abruptly. "Not a word. I'm telling you out of pure courtesy and this is most secret." She walked around her desk and leaned against the front of it. "Pray. Spend the next week in prayer for this mission. There is much at stake."

Sharp knuckles wrapped on her door, and Charlene straightened. "Enter!" When her clerk came into the room with a stack of papers in his hand, Dorothy knew she was dismissed.

Dorothy left the office feeling excited, anticipating the coming week. To have Tom home! Heart fluttering, she suppressed a silly grin. As she went back to her duty station, she realized the constant litany of prayer in her head had changed. Success for the mission and safety for her friends had been added, and the prayer was made with as much fervor as the prayers for her husband and children.

8 8 8 8

CHAPTER 8

Chapter Eight

FOR the next week, the anticipation of the coming mission consumed her. Dorothy didn't know all the specific details, but she could feel the air around the facility change as the hours ticked by and the days raced past.

She and Faith could not discuss it. Charlene stressed two major rules for their group. First, share nothing personal. Occasionally things slipped out – like Faith's American heritage or Temperance's brother or Mercy's training as a surgeon, or her own husband's status as a prisoner of war. But, those facts amounted to the collective of what they knew about each other.

The second rule: don't talk about any missions. Ever. So, while Dorothy knew Faith's hours increased as she practiced and planned for a mission, she dared not ask her after any details, even though she'd love to know them.

One night before her next shift, she sat in the staff lounge against the arm of a sofa reading the newspaper someone had left behind. The room had been the main house's library and still had massive floor-to-ceiling books available for the staff to borrow. Lounges, couches, and chairs around the room gave them a space to have a semblance of relaxation. She'd spent the last hour writing letters to each of her children and enclosing a recent photograph of herself in each one. She longed to see them, to kiss them and hug them and tuck them into their beds at night. She promised herself when this mission was over, whatever the outcome, she'd go to her parents' house and stay with them while they waited for the war to end. She couldn't stand being separated from them any longer. The department could find someone else to write letters to her husband on her behalf, if need be.

When the door opened, she looked up, surprised to see Faith come storming into the room.

"The nerve of that air-dale," she spat as she threw herself down on the sofa next to Dorothy.

"Sorry. Whose nerve?" Dorothy asked with a smile, knowing the answer.

"That so-called pilot."

"Which one? There are so many."

Faith gritted her teeth. "You know the one. Captain Green." She hit the cushion next to her. "Him."

Dorothy nodded. "Yes. Him."

Faith whipped her head around and glared at her friend. "Are you making fun of me?"

"Not in the least." With a giggle, she reached out and took Faith's hand. "What did he do tonight?"

"He dared to condescend to me."

"As he very often does."

"He suggested," she said, running her fingers through her short curls, "that I wasn't strong enough to pilot the Avro Anson. As if I'd have any desire to get that flying brick off the ground in the first place. Like to take a few turns around his pretty Spitfire with the Diamond, I would."

Dorothy frowned, privately thinking it very unlikely that Captain Reginald Greene would dare suggest that Faith was weak in any way, considering the high regard in which he so obviously held the young woman. "Is that actually what he said?"

"Well," she sighed, slipping her hands into her pockets and leaning her head back against the couch cushion, "I think what he actually said was that I wasn't 'man enough' to fly it."

"Right. That sounds more like him," Dorothy said with a grin.

"It's not funny, you know," Faith said with very little heat.

Dorothy cleared her throat. "He is a terribly handsome man, is he not? Dishy."

Faith raised an eyebrow. "What's that got to do with anything?"

Dorothy raised her eyebrow right back at the young American. "That sounded very much like a yes."

Faith grinned and confessed. "He's a looker. But I am so tired of that attitude."

"He's just having a go at you. Winding you up."

"I feel pretty tightly wound," Faith admitted.

"Keep out-flying him. Eventually, he'll be your biggest fan."

Faith rolled her head against the back of the couch until she was looking at Dorothy. "I don't think so. I think he's one of those guys who does all right in the air and he's bad at just about everything on the ground. I know you think he likes me or something, but you couldn't be more wrong."

With a knowing smile, Dorothy picked her paper back up. "Of course, love."

As Faith growled at her and surged to her feet, Dorothy hid behind the paper and tried not to giggle out loud.

♟ ♟ ♟ ♟

BEFORE heading to the staff dining hall at the sound of the dinner bell, Dorothy looked around for Faith but did not see her. When she arrived at what the soldiers on the estate universally referred to as the Grub Tent, it surprised her to see so few people eating.

As she moved through the line and filled her tray with a root vegetable soup and hearty bread, she wondered about the emptiness of the room. She sat down, blessed her meal, and looked up, surprised to see Reginald Greene sitting across from her. She had not heard his approach.

"Captain," Dorothy greeted, placing her napkin in her lap. "Something I can help you with?"

He had a long, lean body and a classically handsome face. His straight brown hair brushed against his forehead, and his intensely green eyes swirled with worry. "She's gone."

As her stomach fell, she felt her hands go into fists in her napkin. "Gone where?"

"To France."

Dorothy nodded. "Right." He didn't say anything else so she boldly added. "You fancy her."

His cheeks colored and he slowly grinned. "I held the fact that she's a barmy Yank against her until I saw her fly. She's twice as good as anyone I've ever seen when she's flying her bespoke NA-16. That's a decent kite, that one."

Dorothy shook her head. "More than just the flying, I suspect."

Green harrumphed. "I fancy her a bit. Though I dislike that vile brew she favors over a decent cuppa. I shall cling to that I think."

Dorothy said, "I think she fancies you a bit as well. She just needs to convince herself."

He nodded and the color in his cheek turned a bit brighter. "I'm headed out in a tick. She's flying that slow, noisy beast of an Avro. She'll need cover."

"Why aren't you already with her?"

"I'm due to meet the convoy about halfway over the pond. Getting there wasn't the concern; it's getting them back here safely." He stood abruptly. "Any-road, I know you share my faith and I've seen you pray, so I wanted you should be aware. Pray for us both if you can."

Without another word, he turned on his heel and left the dining room. Now Dorothy understood the lack of personnel. They were all on duty, working for the rescue.

She tried to eat, but suddenly had no appetite. Instead, she wandered outside into the night and looked up at the sky. When Tom had first left, she used to sit in her little garden and stare up at the stars, knowing he would be doing the same thing if he had the opportunity. She did it every night, just in case he was too, just in case they were sharing that moment staring at the same moon.

Once news of his capture reached her, she didn't do it so often because it always made her think of him in a cold cell, closed off from the outside world, unable to see the stars he loved so much.

Tonight she looked up at the moon and stars again and thought of all of the years they'd been married and all of the dozens and dozens of times they'd taken a quilt outside and just lay back and looked up at the sky, at the magnificence of God's creation. She thought of all of the talks they'd shared under the stars – the embraces. She couldn't help but think of the love of the stars she and Tom had given to their children and of little Tommy and his saving every shilling he could get his hands on so that he could buy a telescope.

She wandered to the air field at the far end of the estate. She took off her wool jacket and folded it up to use as a head rest, then lay on the ground and watched the stars, letting the vastness of the night sky comfort her as it reminded her of the magnificence of its Creator. No words escaped her lips. Instead, she let her heart do the talking. As the hours faded away, she watched the night sky change and start to lighten, gradually obscuring the light from the countless heavenly bodies.

It occurred to her that she'd lain there for hours and hours. She needed to go bathe, brush the grass out of her hair, and change her clothes. She had to report for duty at seven and by the faint light in the sky, it was nearly six already. As she stood up she brushed off the seat of her skirt. She walked toward the hangar area and saw several people run out of the command center. They stared up at the sky behind her, and she could hear the buzz of excited conversation.

Faintly, very faintly, she heard the first distant sound of an engine sputter ominously.

She spun, looking at the very pale blue eastern sky. She wondered if she had perhaps imagined the sound, but then she heard it again. After her months of living in the city during the bombing of London, she recognized the distinctive bass roar of German aircraft engines. As her eyes strained on the horizon, desperately seeking, she finally saw it.

A *Luftwaffe* Junkers JU-52 appeared on the horizon, escorted on either wing by nearly new Submarine Spitfire Mk IIs that had been brought down from Bronwich just the prior month. Dorothy watched the big plane dip suddenly, wobble like a flying egg, then even out. The closer it got, the more detail she could see and she started to make out the flames coming from one of the engines in the right wing and the massive amounts of black smoke pouring out from behind it.

The nose dipped again, and the heavy beast almost shuddered as it leveled off. Dorothy held her breath as the wings seesawed in the sky and wondered, panicked, why British fighters were escorting a Nazi transport plane.

Unless....

While she watched, the right wing caught on fire and the propeller stopped spinning. Heart in her throat, Dorothy held her breath as the plane began a very early nose dive toward earth. The black *Swastika* outlined in white on the tail, and the straight armed *Balkenkreuz* on the side, stood out sharply against the green and gray of the aircraft's fuselage.

Faith must be flying it. She must have Temperance on board. Hope began to blossom in the deepest places of her heart, maybe even her Tom was on board!

Despite the danger in doing so, Dorothy started sprinting toward the landing strip. She saw movement beside her and heard shouts. She glanced over to see an ambulance and fire truck racing each other, passing her. As the plane barreled toward the ground, Dorothy pumped her arms and ran faster.

The End

Inspired by Real Events

WHILE the story of the special team of operators I named *The Virtues* is entirely fictional, set in a fictional town, and comprised of fictional characters who form a fictional military division, every single one of these fictional heavenly heroines was inspired by a real World War II heroine and their story was inspired by real events.

While every effort has been made to remain true to actual history, two of the real events of significance that are fictionalized in the story of Charity are the *Blitzkrieg*, also sometimes referred to as the Battle of Britain, and the British Ministry of Health Evacuation Scheme, which was the program to relocate the children of England to the countryside for the duration.

On the first of July in 1940, the freshly bloodied Luftwaffe capitalized on successful bombing raids against Poland and Holland, dropping the first bombs on England. The bombing would escalate into the *Blitzkrieg*, and between 7 September 1940 and 21 May 1941 there were almost daily (or nightly) major aerial raids on 16 British cities. The attacks resulted in more than 100 tonnes of high explosives being dropped on mostly civilian targets in England.

The *Luftwaffe* bombed Great Britain for 57 consecutive nights starting on 7 September 1940. Destroying or damaging more than one million London houses and killing more than 40,000 civilians. On the single night of 14 November 1940, Hitler sent 515 bombers against Britain in what was later called the Coventry raid. The destruction and the death toll was shocking.

Citizens had five minutes to get to shelters once the air raid sirens sounded. Many Londoners who had lost their homes to the relentless bombing simply moved into the underground subway tubes.

Courageous Londoners hunkered down every night, dusted off every morning, and picked up the pieces every day. Neighbors and families banded together. Neighborhoods organized into clearing teams. Blackout wardens comforted the living and counted the dead.

When war with Nazi Germany became imminent in the late 1930s, Great Britain began a huge effort to evacuate its children to rural areas of the country. The Ministry of Health was charged by King George VI with organizing an evacuation of as many children as possible from the urban centers to safer locales. Some children were sent to the United States, Australia, or Canada. The goal was to move them away from potential bombing targets such as London and urban centers near military production sites.

The Ministry of Health devised the Child Evacuation Scheme which was largely managed by volunteers. Although evacuation was never made mandatory, many parents put their children on the next scheduled train and sent them to parts unknown in the care of the British State simply to save them from the ravages of war.

After the first bombs fell, sending one's children to safety was widely viewed as the responsible thing to do. Countless parents who sent their children away from the cities saved their children's lives. At the end of the war, estimates suggest that more than 230,000 British children had been orphaned.

Every day hundreds of children wearing paper identification tags sewn to their clothing made their way, mostly by rail, to safe countryside locations. Some were fortunate enough to stay with relatives but most ended up staying with complete strangers in towns they had never before visited.

The worry and concern for their children served as a constant distraction and source of heartbreak to city dwellers who had lost nearly everything and often feared for their lives as the Nazi bombs continued to relentlessly fall overhead.

Sadly, many children were placed into group homes in the countryside or involuntarily evacuated to Australia when space got too tight to manage. Many of these children would never be reunited with their living parents at the conclusion of the war.

During World War II, the Germans remodeled a 400-year-old building called Colditz Castle (*Schloss Colditz*), a Renaissance castle located in the town of Colditz near Leipzig, Dresden, and Chemnitz in the state of Saxony in Germany. It overlooked the Mulde River and had 7-foot thick outside walls. The interior of the 6-story structure contained a maze of concealed staircases, hidden passageways, and hundreds of rooms.

Schloss Colditz aka Colditz Castle circa 1939

When they completed the work to turn the building into a prison, the Germans renamed it *Oflag IV C* (*Sonderlager IV C*) and claimed that escape would be impossible. It became the holding place for highly important prisoners and those that habitually tried to escape from other prisons.

On November 7, 1940, six British officers who had tried to escape from another prison camp arrived, including Rupert Barry. My towering and strong fictional character, Tom, is based on stalwart and faithful Rupert.

By Christmas, Colditz Castle held 200 prisoners – the maximum it could hold. By February 1941, another 200 French prisoners had arrived, doubling the maximum occupancy rate. By July, the Nazis held 500 POWs there.

Two of the British officers, Captain P. R. Reid and Captain Rupert Barry, worked together to create a code that Barry then wrote in a letter to his wife, Dodo, upon whom the fictional Dotty, code-named Charity, is based. The real life heroine, Dodo Barry, was a highly intelligent woman who could solve the complicated *Times of London* crossword puzzle in mere minutes. Captain Rupert Barry doted upon his beloved wife and, what's more, he deeply appreciated and respected her keen mind. He felt more than confident in his wife's abilities to crack the code they devised.

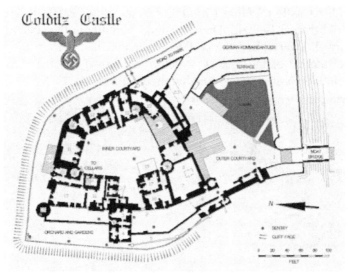

Floor plan of Castle Colditz once converted to Oflag IV C.

The address being written at an angle trailing up toward the stamp in the fictional story of Charity is a fiction based on numerous such factual occurrences throughout history. Soldiers during the American War Between the States would do this, hiding secret love messages beneath the postage stamps. Many spies used the same method during the First World War. During the Second World War, spies on all sides would hide microdots beneath postage stamps. The method of hiding keys and codes "under the rug" of a postage stamp became so popular, that a key to a cipher code was even hidden beneath a postage stamp in a famous Agatha Christie story.

In real life, upon receiving the letter, Dodo at first thought that conditions as a German POW had broken her dear husband's mind. He wrote about relatives they didn't have and referred to places they'd never visited. Then she realized that he'd written the letter in code and she spent the day deciphering the letter using nothing but her very own wits.

Decoded, it read:

> Go to the War Office, ask them to send forged Swedish diplomatic papers for Reid, Howe, Allan, Lockwood, Elliott, Wardle, Milne, and self."

The next morning, Dodo went to the War Office. The officer at the desk would not let her into the building. While she stood in front of the clerk's desk arguing with him, another officer walked by and she pleaded with him to help her. As if by providence, the officer happened to be assigned to military intelligence, a military branch with ties to MI-9.

The officer, whose name is lost to history, realized Dodo was onto something. He started working with her and had her write back to her husband and tell him, without code, that his elderly "Aunt Christine" was deeply saddened by her nephew's capture and would write him shortly.

Under that guise, and using the same code the prisoners had created, and Dodo had deciphered, the War Office sent him a coded letter that said:

> The War Office considered the use of
> Swedish diplomatic papers to be too
> dangerous.

Angry, disappointed, and frustrated with the news, instead of writing "Aunt Christine" back, Barry wrote Dodo back. Once she received his second encoded letter, she took it back to her contact at the War Office.

The deciphered message read:

> We will consider the danger and not the
> War Office. Would you please expedite
> the request?

The War Office never sent the papers. However, these first "Dodo" letters had opened up a line of communication between the War Office,

MI-9, and the POWs being held at Colditz Castle.

Of absolute primary importance, they needed to establish a better code.

Letter from Colditz sent home to Scotland by POW Captain Julius Morris Green. A dentist before the war, Green was captured fighting the Nazis at Dunkirk in 1940. Green sent more than 40 coded letters home once the letters sent to Dodo bore fruit.

To anyone who spoke English, the simply encoded letters would have read as a little bit odd or disjointed. The Nazi censors often only had a rudimentary grasp of the English language, so they were able to slip by unnoticed. However, four letters in this rudimentary code was pushing their luck. Eventually, they felt the Nazis would catch on and have insight into their plans.

Under the direction of her intelligence officer, Dodo wrote a letter to Rupert explaining that an International Red Cross package would arrive with further instructions. Along with some clothing, one package contained six handkerchiefs with different colored borders. Coded instructions in Dodo's letter directed Barry to place the green bordered handkerchief in hot water and stir for several minutes. Soon, a more elaborate code appeared in hidden ink on the handkerchief. Barry memorized the code then destroyed the material. Over time, she shared the code with his fellow prisoners who also memorized it.

The very tall Rupert Barry (second from the left) along with 5 former POWs pictured here outside Castle Colditz after the war.

With well coded letters and hidden supplies contained in Red Cross packages, the MI-9 office (escape and evasion service) supplied the prisoners in Colditz with money, identification documents, radios, tools, train schedules, border crossing policies and routines, clothing, and even weapons.

The war effort was greatly aided by critical intelligence sent home from the prisoners. One such prisoner, a skilled dentist, was often called upon to treat German soldiers and officers as well as his fellow prisoners. He sent letters back home to Scotland and the ones that began "Dear Dad" often contained crucial information pertaining to troop movements inside Germany.

With the aid of the secreted supplies and intelligence MI-9 could provide via this now secure communication channel, 130 prisoners escaped from Colditz Castle – either successfully or unsuccessfully – over a 5 year period.

Of those 130 escaped prisoners, 32 of them escaped successfully. In all, 12 Frenchmen, 11 Britons, 7 Dutch, and 1 Polish prisoner of war made it all the way home, a feat that came to be known as a *Home Run*. This number of prisoners of war escaping and making it all the way back home is unequaled in modern warfare. Among these successful escapees was Captain P. R. Reid who had helped Rupert Barry pen that very first letter to his wife, Dodo.

Because of Dodo, also the name of a now extinct bird, the Colditz Castle escapees came to be known as the "Birdmen of Colditz" and their escapes and attempted escapes have been the subject of many books, films, and even a BBC television series. Very few photographs of Dodo or her husband survive today.

Selected for the cover of this book is the incredible Yolande Betbeze (ne Fox) who may be most well known for her association with baseball great Joe Dimaggio, her marriage to movie tycoon Matthew Fox until his death, her activism in the 1960s, and for taking the Miss America crown in 1950. While not exactly a British housewife with "island blood," the publisher felt that this woman's indomitable spirit strongly represented the fictional character of Charity.

Excerpt from her official Miss America bio: "*Always courageous and sometimes controversial, Yolande has always been ahead of her time, tackling tough issues and making a stand before the issues at hand were fashionable.*"

Born in 1929 to William and Ethel of Mobile, Alabama, Yolande was raised in a strict Catholic family with Basque origins and was educated in a convent school. In 1950 shortly after her twentieth birthday, Betbeze traveled to Atlantic City, New Jersey, to compete in the Miss America pageant. Beyond her beauty and her operatic musical talent, Yolande handily took top honors for her scholarship, values, and leadership.

After winning the competition, she made no secret of her reluctance to don what she considered a very immodest swimsuit (tame by modern standards) and her refusal caused Catalina swimwear to withdraw their sponsorship from the pageant. To this day, the Miss America Organization claims that her actions were pivotal in directing the Miss America Pageant toward recognizing intellect, values, and leadership abilities, rather than focusing on beauty alone. From then on the Miss America pageant concentrated more on scholarship than beauty. Since there was no Miss America in 1950, Betbeze became the reigning Miss America in 1951.

After her year as Miss America, Yolande served as an ambassador to postwar Paris, France and was active in both the NAACP and CORE (Congress of Racial Equality) upon her return to the United States. She never lost her love for opera, even appearing with the Mobile Opera Guild (the Mobile Opera today), and helped found an off-Broadway theater.

♙ ♙ ♙ ♙

SUGGESTED questions for a discussion group surrounding *Charity's Code*, part 3 of the *Virtues and Valor* series.

While the characters and situations in the *Virtues and Valor* series are fictional, I pray that these extended parables can help readers come to a better understanding of truth. Please prayerfully consider the questions that follow, consult scripture, and pray upon your conclusions. May the Lord of the universe richly bless you.

Dorothy Ewing believes God gifted her with special skills to be utilized during the war.

> 1. Do you believe that God prepared Dorothy from birth for her place in the war.

> 2. The Bible tells us that every one of us has a special gift. Do you know what your gift is?

> 3. How do you use that gift for God's kingdom?

In the spirit of patriotism, Dorothy sends her children away from the danger in London but remains behind to work first at Bletchley Place then to be part of the Valor team.

4. As a mother in a time of war, with such tragedy and destruction all around, do you think she did the right thing in being separated from her children?

5. Thinking of the belief mentioned above in question 1, do you think this helped drive her to stay separated from her children?

"Grace" and Dorothy have a conversation about the attitude the men have about their work for the Valor team, and in Dorothy's chosen profession of engineering.

6. Do you think that the women in that time period were more heroric because they worked against the social norms – or –

7. – do you believe that the special circumstances of such a horrific war helped change the standard mindset at the time?

A Parcel for Prudence

HALLEE BRIDGEMAN

Virtues And Valor Series

A Parcel for Prudence

the Virtues and Valor Series part 4

a Novella by

HALLEE BRIDGEMAN

Published by

Olivia Kimbrell Press™

Olivia Kimbrell Press™

Library Cataloging Data
U. S. Library of Congress Control Number: 2014953678

Bridgeman, Hallee (Hallee A. Bridgeman) 1972-
  A Parcel for Prudence, Virtues and Valor series part 4/ Hallee Bridgeman
    102 p. 23cm x 15cm (9in x 6 in.)
      Summary: A PARCEL FOR PRUDENCE is part 4 of the Virtues and Valor series.

      ISBN: 978-1-939603-49-4 (ebook)

1. Christian fiction 2. World War II 3. war stories 4. spies 5. historical fiction 6. espionage

PS3568.B7534 T941 2014
[Fic.] 813.6 (DDC 23)

For those women who fought beside the men...

THIS series is dedicated to the amazing women who have worked, planned, strategized, served, led, and fought alongside men throughout human history. This novella is specifically dedicated to Cécile Pearl Witherington. To read more about this true heroine, read the Inspired by Real Events   section at the end of Prudence's story.

I, wisdom, dwell with prudence,

And find out knowledge and discretion.

Proverbs 8:12 (NKJV)

PROLOGUE

Prologue

Haysworth Estate, Great Britain: 1938

BRIGHT sunlight flooded into the room. Muriel buried her head under the pillow, but the chipper voice of Jane, her new lady's maid, kept her from sinking back into sleep.

"Good morning, m'lady," Jane singsonged. "Busy day today. His Lordship has requested that I wake you and ensure you are all set to go."

His Lordship? Why would her father-in-law summon her so early? Muriel pushed herself into a sitting position as Jane set the tray of hot chocolate and toast in front of her. She smiled at the pink rose in the small vase on the tray, knowing that her husband picked it during his morning stroll through the rose gardens. He always sent a different color for the day of the week. Pink meant that today was a beautiful Wednesday morning here on the country estate of the Earl of Bostwich.

"Get me ready for what or where, exactly?" she asked as she poured a cup of steaming chocolate.

"Your father, His Grace, is arriving on the ten o'clock train. His Lordship has asked that you be there to meet the train, m'lady."

Excitement made her heart beat a little faster. "Papa's coming?" She lifted aside the tray and pushed herself out of the bed. "Is mama with him?"

"I'm sure I don't know, m'lady." She went to the wardrobe and threw it open. "Now, what shall you wear today?"

Thirty minutes later, adorned in blue silk dress with white polka-dots, she glided down the grand staircase into the massive marbled foyer. She had tucked her gloves into the white leather purse that hung from her wrist. A uniformed maid, carrying a stack of sheets, rushed past her with a mumbled, "'Mornin', m'lady."

"There she is, all bright-eyed and bushy-tailed!" She smiled around the pins as her husband, Joseph, second son of the Earl of Bostwich, stepped out of the library. His brown striped suit made him look positively dashing, and she felt her heart grow as she fell in love with him all over again. She couldn't imagine how God had blessed her so abundantly as to have given her Joseph to love.

Muriel grinned and slipped the hat pins out of her mouth just in the nick of time. Joseph reached her and swung her into his arms. He kissed her, rather inappropriately considering the number of staff who might spy the public display, full on the mouth. "How's my beautiful lady?"

"Excited to hear that daddy's coming," she answered, stepping back from him to fasten the hat more securely. "What a surprise. Do you know if mama is coming too?"

"How else could she celebrate your birthday, but to come in person?"

Slapping her hands to her cheeks, she laughed, "It is my birthday! How could I have forgotten?"

"Well," her husband said with a gleam in his eye as he slipped his arm around her waist, "you've been in that honeymoon glow. Your mind's still a bit foggy with bliss."

Gasping with laughter, she slapped his chest with the glove she'd just pulled out of her purse. "You hush. And by the by, I, in no way, think my tail is bushy."

Joseph simply smiled and waggled his eyebrows. He looked poised to tease her further, but the words remained unsaid.

"There you are m'dear," the Earl announced, stepping into the foyer while sparing a glance at his pocket watch. He slipped an unlit cigar between his teeth as he returned the watch to the pocket of his ample waist coat. "Tut tut. Mustn't be late picking up the duke, must we?"

"Heavens, no. Daddy would never stand for that." She felt giddy with happiness. Her husband's eyes burned with a mischievous twinkle and she wondered what on earth might be occupying his thoughts. He hadn't even turned to spare a glimpse for his father. His eyes remained entirely on her. She asked him, "Are you staying here, darling?"

"What? And lose the opportunity to spend the next hour in the company of the most beautiful girl on this island? Perish the thought." He held out his arm, and she slipped her hand over his biceps with a smile on her face.

The Earl nodded his approval. "The car should be around front shortly. I assume my youngest son would prefer to rattle around in that obscenely fast sports car with you?"

Joseph finally looked in his father's direction. "Come now, father. That isn't even in question. In fact, I shall go and bring it round right away." With that he was off to the stables which now served as home for two fully equipped Lagonda 1930 2-liter Weymann saloons and Joseph's favored 1934 4.5-liter M45 Sports Tourer.

Muriel detected the Earl's tolerant grin as Joseph raced from the room. The Earl removed his unlit cigar and his voice lowered as he said, "Kindly inform your father, the duke, and your lady mother that we look forward to their company with great anticipation. And do enjoy the drive. It is a perfectly lovely day."

"I'm sure I will. And thank you."

The sports car's rather noisy raucous engine preceded the high pitched sound of the horn blast by mere seconds, and Muriel decided to add a scarf to secure her hat even further. She knew there would be no way to convince her husband to put the top up on a sunny day like this.

The End

Chapter One

PRUDENCE – a) careful good judgment that allows someone to avoid danger or risks: skill in the use of resources: ability to govern and discipline oneself by the use of reason, sagacity, or shrewdness. b) historically referred to as *auriga virtutum* (the charioteer of the heavenly virtues); guides the other virtues as one of the "cardinal" virtues.

THE bright light shown directly into Muriel Tolson's eyes and the heat of the bulb thoroughly exhausted her. She could barely see through the glare to the shadowed figures sitting at the table in front of her, so she quit trying and looked away. She found a spot on the far wall on which to focus her vision and attempted to find relief from the glare. She tried to ignore the fact that she sat in this room full of men, wearing nothing but her cotton slip. Her face burned with heat, but the rest of her body reacted to the chill. The stone floor felt ice cold against her bare feet, and only the heat from the light kept her from shivering in the otherwise chilly room.

"Let's go over this once again," her interrogator suggested in French thickened with a strong German accent. "How long have you known the Englishman who uses the code name Praetorian?"

Muriel sighed and closed her eyes, seeking a brief relief from the harsh lights. In perfectly unaccented French, she answered, "I've already told you, *Monsieur*. I don't know any Englishman."

He pounded the table with his fist, causing her to jump and open her eyes. "Lies!"

"No," she said, "I swear. I don't know anyone English."

"You were seen speaking to him outside of the train station in Montoire. Witnesses identified you."

Mind reeling, she tried desperately to give a good enough answer to end this ordeal. "In Montoire? The train station in Montoire? I did speak to a man there. He approached me. But the man was French, not English."

"This man, he gave you a package."

"No! No! He asked to see the newspaper I carried with me. But he gave it back to me!"

"Yes, he did. He also passed you a map of our prison in Valeurville, did he not?"

The glare of the lamp weakened her resolve. Her throat felt so dry that she thought she might gag if she tried to swallow again. Her lips cracked and her tongue felt like sandpaper in her mouth. "I had nothing to do with that. I didn't even know what it was! *Monsieur*, please. Please, *Monsieur*. I beg of you. I don't know how that got into my paper. I don't know this man."

"We know you are lying. Witnesses saw you trade newspapers with him. You were going to give the map to someone else. Who? Praetorian? Where is your drop point? Who is your controller?"

A pulsating headache thumped behind her eye. "I don't know what you're talking about," she whispered.

"Speak up!" His harsh voice, with its guttural German accent, sent fear coursing through her veins.

"I don't know what you're talking about, *Monsieur*," she repeated, a bit louder this time. "My name is Murielle St. Pierre. I moved here from Creuzier-le-Vieux two months ago. I teach piano

"Silence. We know that is not your name. You think we are fools! We also know that you have never even been to Creuzier-le-Vieux. I will hear no more lies, *Fräulein*. In fact, I want you to see if you can tell when I am speaking the truth. If I promised you that the next time you lie to me, you will regret it for the rest of your life, can you tell if this is true? Am I lying to you or will I keep my promise? Which do you think?"

"*Monsieur*, I beg you. I'm Murielle St. Pierre

"Stand up!"

Eyes darting back and forth, knowing others waited in the shadows, Muriel stood on shaking legs. Without warning, angry hands grabbed her arms from behind, strong hands that dragged her out of the light and into the dark corner. Her eyes, still dazzled from the glare of the light, couldn't make out what awaited her there, so when a foot kicked her knees out from beneath her, forcing her hard onto her knees on the ground in front of the wooden tub, she had no time to react to the hands against the back of her head, forcing her face under the ice cold water.

The initial reflexive reaction she experienced was to take in a deep breath from the shock of the cold. She very nearly did. Her mouth had flown open in surprise. When the icy water flooded back against her dehydrated throat, she partially regained her senses and did not inhale. Instead, she held her breath.

Her lungs began to burn. Her pulse beat against her tightly shut eyelids. She tried to struggle, but the strong hands painfully gripping her shoulders and forearms forced her even deeper beneath the icy cold water. She felt her legs going weak and wondered if they would let her die. Finally, a fist ripped her head back above the water by her hair and she gasped for breath.

"We can continue this until you are ready to speak the truth, *Fräulein*," the man behind her hissed. "I have all the time in the world."

She barely had time to react before the strong hands forced her head back under the water. This time she accidentally breathed in and the pain of the water entering her airway caused her to scream into the water.

Hands grabbed her hair forcefully and pulled her face from the water. Bits of ice floated on the surface. "How long have you known the Englishman code-named Praetorian?"

"I don't know any Englishman."

"Where is your drop point? Who is your controller?"

He repeated the questions. Over and over again. She didn't know how many times she went under the water, only to come back up again to offer her denials. She started to feel herself long to give in, to tell them what she knew so that they would stop the interrogation. Anything to get the angry hands off of her.

"What are you doing with the map? What are the plans?"

"I don't know what map!"

Several more rounds of questions and she felt her resistance starting to slip. Maybe she should just give in. What if she did?

The skin on her face no longer tingled, but rather felt completely numb. Her body felt weak, as if she had no strength left in her limbs Above the surface of the water, her ears were filled with her interrogator's rough voice.

Below the surface, she could hear muffled sounds of – was it laughter? Were they enjoying her plight? After several more minutes, Muriel entered a trance like state and she wondered if she were close to death.

When her captors pulled her up, they stood her on her feet and held her upright. Her antagonist swung the light to shine into her eyes again as she stood on weak knees, icy cold water dripping down her body, soaking her thin cotton shift.

"How long have you known Praetorian? Where is your drop point? Who is your controller? You will answer!"

Her voice sounded weak even to her own ears as she spoke through shivering, blued lips. "I don't know what you are asking me. I don't know."

She felt herself beginning to pass out until a leather gloved hand slapped her full across her numbed face. "You will learn very soon that your lies are useless," the man announced. "You think we don't know exactly who you are? You are Muriel Tolson. You are a British spy and your code name is Prudence. I assure you, we can keep you alive and in pain for a very long time or you can die quickly and with dignity before a firing squad. The choice is yours."

Muriel heard her pulse roaring in her ears. Her lips moved but made no sound. He leaned closer, close enough that she could smell his spicy, nauseating cologne. He hissed, "Speak up, *Fräulein.*"

She spit against his cheek.

The man stood straight and retrieved a handkerchief. He wiped the spittle from his face and then screamed, "Tell me what you know! Tell me now!"

A gloved fist punched her hard and fast just under the rib cage, a jab intended to paralyze her diaphragm, the very instant before they plunged her beneath the freezing water once more.

Several more rounds of questions and she felt her resistance starting to slip. Before she could give in and admit everything, the hands released her.

She gripped the side of the wooden tub, shudders running through her body, coughing and gagging until spots swam in front of her eyes.

"I think that's enough for now," the man said, this time in English, all traces of the German accent gone. "Remarkable job, Prudence. Brilliant." He addressed her by her code name only, despite the fact that he had used her real name in the interrogation.

Weary, she forced herself to stand on trembling legs, but stumbled and slapped a hand against the wall to right herself. A woman immediately arrived at her side and wrapped her in a warm woolen blanket. Unwilling to give in to the weakness inside of her, she did not collapse against the woman in a sobbing heap. Instead, she nodded her thanks and gripped the scratchy blanket close beneath her chin. "Thank you," she said in a whisper, her throat raw from gagging and coughing.

Barely able to move, she forced her legs to work as she followed the three men and the solitary woman from the basement room and up a staircase into a cozy study where her commander, Major Charlotte Radden, stood, concern etching lines into her face.

"Well, Prudence. After that ordeal, I'm sure you could use a nice cup of tea," Charlotte offered.

Muriel studied the woman, her vision still a little spotty. "*Ce serait parfait.*" That would be perfect, she mumbled, not even realizing she still spoke in French. "Especially if by 'tea' you mean brandy."

Major Radden raised a single eyebrow, but said not a word as she silently retrieved a flask from a desk drawer.

"Prudence, you have proven to be one of our top recruits," Lieutenant Colonel Donald Hendricks said, all traces of the German interrogator gone. "I confess I was one of those who objected to our bringing women on board for this type of work. Messy and risky, after all. All manner of ghastly things the Jerrys could do to a girl, after all. But it's you and a few others in your class who are making me rethink my original opinion. I've seen men break in half the time we spent with you."

"I appreciate that, sir," Muriel said, perching on the edge of the couch. Water ran down her temple from her soaked hair and a shudder suddenly wracked her so hard that she was a bit surprised her body didn't rip apart.

Major Radden kept her features perfectly expressionless, but observed, "A bit hard on the lass, were you?"

"On the contrary," Colonel Henry Walker huffed. "We did nothing like the kinds of things Jerry is likely to enjoy with a female operative."

None of the British officers needed to speak in any more detail. Everyone knew the stakes, and everyone realized that there were things evil men could do that were far worse than simple interrogation or torture, perhaps even worse than death.

"I am so thankful to be given this opportunity," Muriel interjected, forcing her voice to sound steady and calm. Charlene handed her a tea cup that smelled strongly of the cinnamon fragrance of aged brandy. As Muriel reached for it, she saw the uncontrollable tremor in her fingers. She hoped that if Charlene noticed it as well, she wouldn't think any less of her.

"Before we go further, however," Colonel Walker said from the other side of the room, "we must ensure this is something you truly want to do. You'll be in one of the most dangerous positions we have in the field, acting as courier between our contact in France, his team, and the wireless operator in your sector. You'll have access to critical information, codes, money, and, worse than that, you'll be one of the only people who knows who many of the other players are and their whereabouts. Items and correspondence you will be carrying along with the knowledge contained in your noggin can make or break our movement on the ground. I'm afraid once you are there, it will already be far too late to change your mind."

Muriel nodded and reflected. She thought back to the day months before, during her husband's last day home. The sun had shown brightly on the rolling hills of his parents' estate, and they'd walked hand-in-hand down the lane as they used to do when they first started courting.

"My love, I want to speak to you from the heart. The truth is I want you to do more than just roll bandages for the women's auxiliary. Your talents are wasted there," Joseph Tolson had said. "You are brilliant and talented. This war is too close to home. The Jerrys are just too big of a threat. We need every able body, male or female, fighting. I'm convinced it's the only way we are going to get through this."

Muriel had stopped in the lane and let him pull her into his arms. She rested her cheek against his uniformed chest and tried not to think about what would come next – about the good-bye waiting for them at the train station. "Joseph, darling, what can I possibly do?"

He put his hands on her shoulders and forced her to look up at him. "Listen to me, darling. There are few women in this world who are as capable as you. Go to London and find someone to talk to. Tell them you're fluent in French and German. You and I both know they're desperate for help so that they can relieve the men to go fight." He ran a finger through her blond curls. "They'll quit seeing the beautiful face and start seeing that beautiful brain soon enough."

She felt tears in her eyes. "You say that now, on this safe estate with the sun shining down on us. But would you say it while I'm hiding in a shelter during a bombing?"

He cupped her chin with his strong hand. "God gifted you, my love. You and I both know He does that for a reason. Go and find a way to help. The more who pitch in, the more poor slobs like me get to come home safe and sound when this awful war is finally over. Promise me, now."

Bringing herself back to the present, back into the sitting room, her shoulders and neck still throbbing from the torture of them forcibly dunking her head under water over and over again, with her face aching from the slap, her side throbbing from the punch, and a blinding headache overcoming almost every other sense, she lifted her chin and said very clearly and very plainly so that she could not be misunderstood, "I will not change my mind. I am ready."

"That's good," Charlene said. The major rose and walked around her desk. She sat on the settee across from her and opened a file folder. "Very good. Because your counterpart in what we call 'Area 3', was shot while fleeing a German guard who had stopped to question him."

Muriel's stomach turned to ice. Outwardly, she maintained a perfect calm disposition. "How soon can I leave?"

"Within a week. You need to heal, rest up from your ordeal tonight," Henry said. "Prepare yourself."

Muriel set the untouched brandy on the table in front of her and stood, clutching the blanket closed with her fist at her chest. "I understand. I shall be ready."

🎖🎖🎖🎖

CHAPTER 2

Outside of Milton Keynes, England: 1942

MURIEL heard a ruckus outside her window and sat straight up in bed, grabbing her alarm clock in the same movement. Apparently, in her exhaustion from the interrogation training the night before, she'd forgotten to wind it. With a huff, she threw the covers off and rushed to the window, trying to gauge the time. An audible groan escaped her lips when she saw a group of men and women in exercise regalia jog by. She should have been in that formation about twenty minutes ago.

Her core ached and her neck muscles hurt so badly that it made her entire spine groan. Her stomach rolled with nausea and every movement hurt. It made rushing through the room, grabbing a white T-shirt, a cotton skirt the color of ripe olives, and her leather running shoes so much harder to accomplish. She threw everything on as fast as she could and ran down the steps of her barracks room while trying to pull her hair up out of her face.

As she lifted her arms over her head, the pain in her muscles made her empty stomach roll. As a cold sweat broke out over her body, she stopped, breathless, and leaned against the outside of the building. With more concentrated movements, she lifted her arms again, ignoring the shooting pain and pulled her hair back with a ribbon. Once it was secure, she gently lowered her arms again, shook them at her sides, then took off at a fast run.

It took several minutes to catch up with her group, but once she did, everyone shifted a bit to make room for her, keeping the formation intact. They ran the normal Friday three-mile route, but within two miles, her energy completely diminished. It took every ounce of strength she had to stay with the group and not fall out. As soon as they reached the end, she fell to the ground, panting, sweat pouring down her face, nausea roiling in her stomach.

"Prudence, you did not need to be here this morning," Adam Harvey said over her. "Donald Hendrick gave you a pass this morning."

"He didn't tell me," Muriel said, wishing her arms didn't feel so much like jelly so that she could cover her eyes from the bright morning sun.

"Bad on him," Adam said before putting his hands on his hips and turning away from her. "Two hours! Meet me at the edge of the wood at half ten."

Muriel closed her eyes and she felt someone lie next to her. She opened her right eye just enough to see who it was before closing them again, identifying her companion as the mysterious woman code-named Grace. She had jet black curls, dark brown eyes, and a strange accent that Muriel couldn't identify. She was dying to ask her where she came from and what brought her here to this earl's estate to be trained to go out as a spy in Occupied France, but, of course, she couldn't. That would break about six of the organization's rules.

Grace ran a finger over Muriel's upper arm, clearly tracing the bruise shaped like a man's hand, and spoke quietly. "Was it awful?"

Tears poured out of her eyes before she even knew they'd formed. "I can't tell you how bad it was. I don't know if I can do this, even though I've assured them I can."

Grace sat up and crossed her feet at her ankles, then leaned back on her hands. To any observer, she appeared calm, at ease. But Muriel could see the intensity of her dark eyes. She spoke in flawless French, as she often did, because she had a difficult time speaking in English. "I can read people," she said with intensity. "And you are absolutely the strongest woman I know. If anyone can do this, it's you."

Gracefully, she rolled to her feet and held her hand out. "Come on. You need some eggs in you. The protein will help those muscles."

᠐᠐᠐᠐

THEY found their friends in the dining hall, cardboard cups of tea in front of them. Mercy, the surgeon turned nurse intelligence agent, had her ginger curls strategically pinned under her nurse's cap. She glanced up and saw them coming, then smiled and waved.

Next to her sat Hope, known by the world as Virginia Benoit, a tall, beautiful, chocolate skinned woman from Louisiana. She was a very popular singer in France and had escaped the day before the Germans rolled into Paris. While the intelligence community fooled the public into thinking she was currently back in the United States, she'd come to the camp to learn how to conspire, communicate, and send messages through underground channels. She would perform in enemy territory and act as eyes and ears on the ground to collect intel on German troop movements and positions.

Across from Mercy, the pilot, Faith, dumped another spoonful of sugar into her tea. An American, she much preferred coffee over the traditional English drink, but she often remarked that beggars couldn't be choosers. Because most male pilots were engaged in the war elsewhere, her flying skills made her an unimagined asset to the intelligence community.

To Mercy's left sat the red haired woman code-named Charity. She had a book of word puzzles next to her elbow, and Muriel could see the tip of a pencil sticking out of the top. Charity was a mastermind with puzzles and was being trained as a wireless operator and a code-breaker. Muriel knew Charity's husband was a prisoner of war, but she didn't know any of the details.

On the other side of Charity, Muriel's good friend, Temperance, sat, ignoring the tea in front of her while she worked on sewing a collar onto a man's dress shirt. Temperance admitted one day last month that she'd been on the training grounds with her brother, Edward, but that she knew he'd already been sent out somewhere. She knew she shouldn't tell them that much information, but she didn't give anyone his codename or describe him, and all she wanted was for her friends to pray for him.

That summed up the personal information she knew about her friends. It was safer that way, she knew, because if any of them were caught in France by the Nazis, they couldn't risk information about each other coming out in interrogation. So, they asked no questions, received no answers, and kept each other safe that way.

Muriel knew that they guessed that she was of noble birth, but they did not know that she was the third daughter of a duke. They also didn't know that her husband was the son of an earl, and that his family's estate, her home, very nearly rivaled the one on which they trained.

When their leader, Major Charlene Radden, interviewed each woman who came into the organization, she assigned them to their groups. Part of the interview process involved questions of religious beliefs. Muriel knew that her open and abiding faith in God is what placed her on the Virtues Team. She remained ever thankful to God that Charlene placed her here. She did not know how she could have survived the last several months of training, coupled with constantly worrying about Joseph's unit in North Africa, without having these sisters in Christ to rely upon.

Over the course of several months, the team on which she'd been placed had grown very close. They worked well together, they prayed together, and they held an almost daily Bible study together.

"Hello, ladies," Grace said, sliding onto the bench next to Hope. "How was today?"

"I'm learning nursing," Mercy grimaced. "Do you know how many years of school I endured to become a surgeon? Now I know all about balancing a full chamber pot."

Her Scottish accent rolled the 'r' in the word chamber. Muriel patted her on the back as she pulled out a chair to sit at the head of the table near Faith and Mercy. "The sacrifices we must make for the war effort, eh?"

"Indeed."

"Was it terribly frightening last night?" Hope asked, her dark eyes open wide with interest.

"About halfway through, I forgot it was a test. My mind switched and I felt like it was real." Muriel shuddered. "I honestly don't ever want to do that again."

"I remember from my training last week. I'm so afraid of that," Temperance almost whispered. "I don't think I would handle interrogation well."

"You remember your training," Grace said as she leaned back in her chair. "You will be surprised at how much this training will come back to you."

Faith raised an eyebrow. "I would ask if that's the voice of experience," she said, then dramatically looked over her shoulder. "But, you know, rules."

Charity snorted, then laughed. "Rules, rules everywhere."

Grace closed her mouth, mimed locking it and tossing the key over her shoulder, causing the other women to burst out laughing. She looked at her watch. "I have a class. Let's all go to the pub tonight." A murmur of assent washed through the group.

MURIEL placed the last dress in the leather suitcase and ran her hands over it to smooth it out. She'd never packed her own bag before, and didn't think she'd done nearly as good of a job as her maid Jane would have done.

After snapping the suitcase shut, she picked up the box of letters she had received from Joseph over the last several months and set it on top of the leather case. All afternoon, she'd read them over and over again, knowing that this would be the last time she'd read a letter from her darling husband until she returned to English soil. Charlene would store the box for her until her return.

She walked over to the small desk near the foot of her bed and picked up the letter she had written to Joseph that afternoon. She could tell him very little, so she'd simply said that he would be very proud of her courage and initiative, and that it would be a long while before she could write again. She'd closed the letter with "au revoir", thinking that he would piece together the clues and realize she'd gone into France. With a quiet giggle, she wondered if he knew that she wasn't safe in some facility like Bletchley Place but actually going into enemy territory. Knowing her husband, loving her husband the way she did, she thought maybe he knew exactly what she'd end up doing and knew she would be capable of doing it.

His confidence in her gave her the strength she needed. Her desire to make him proud had her sealing the envelope to give to Charlene to mail and picking up her suitcase.

She walked across the campus to the hangar on the edge of the airfield. When she walked in, she saw Faith standing next to an airplane, talking to a man in a pilot's uniform. She grinned and waved when she saw Muriel, who nodded her head in return because her hands were full. Standing near the plane, Temperance spoke to Charlene, who looked up and saw her. "Ah, there she is now. I suppose I shall not have to dispatch the troops to hunt her down after all."

Charlene approached and took the box of letters and the letter to Joseph from her and looked her in the eyes.

"You ready, Prudence?"

"As ever," she said with a smile.

"Very good." She gestured to a large wooden table near the wall. "Please place your cases on this table, ladies. We want to make sure that nothing in there would accidentally give you away."

After Charlene inspected clothing labels and soap brands, she gave a final briefing and bid them farewell. Temperance and Prudence boarded the plane.

During the flight, she found she could not engage Temperance in conversation. She kept getting lost in thoughts, thinking about life on the estate before the war, of her disappointment month after month with no pregnancy in sight, of her adoring husband who managed his father's business in his older brother's stead while he served in government in London, of her mother-in-law and her love of French pastries. Her mind flew through the three years since her wedding day, and she thought wistfully of the joy she faced each waking morning until the moment Joseph had put on that uniform. Her world darkened a bit that day.

It almost felt like minutes instead of hours of flight as they landed in a dark field then walked through the French countryside for several kilometers with a band of rather intimidating French countrymen. Finally she stood in the yard of a farmhouse looking up at the man code-named Praetorian. She almost stopped walking when she recognized him as Mr. Quentin Hughes, her husband's friend from Oxford. She'd met him at a reunion last year. During university, her husband and several friends formed a rowdy group of men called *The Second Sons Club, No Titles Here* that met annually to reminisce over the days at Oxford.

He was 28, the same age as her Joseph, and she wondered how he managed to be here now doing this instead of wearing the uniform of a proper British officer.

He looked at Muriel and Temperance with serious, tired gray eyes. She wondered if he recognized her as well. His face gave nothing away. "Names?"

Temperance answered for them. "I'm Temperance and that's Prudence over there."

He nodded. "Wireless?"

"That's me."

With his chin, he gestured at Prudence. "You?"

"Courier." She set her suitcase on the porch and shook her hand, working out the cramp that came from carrying the case for the last thirteen kilometers. "You?"

"Praetorian." With a sharp gesture he pointed to the door. "I have coffee and some eggs. I can make some tea if you prefer." He opened the door and they preceded him inside. Muriel looked curiously around the simple cottage. The furniture looked handmade, and the rugs worn thin. Praetorian led the way into the kitchen, where a coffee pot sat on top of a wood burning stove. Muriel noticed a very noticeable limp in his stride. She thought that might have something to do with his position here instead of in uniform in some company command somewhere. Pointing at the table, he said to them, "Sit. Rest a moment."

To the men who had brought them from the air field, he said, "Find any truffles?"

The tallest man nodded. "Three. You need anything?"

Praetorian shook his head. "I got a shipment lined up. Thank you. Your help is more than generous."

"Happy to help, Praetorian. Get us a message if you need anything else." The tall man tipped his hat toward the women. "Good luck, girls."

As they left, he set two metal mugs on the table and poured each of them some coffee. In English, he said, "I am relieved to see replacements come in. We're in the process of planning a massive operation, and without communication with London, I didn't if know we'd still be able to pull it off."

"Will I stay here?" Muriel asked.

"You will. I'll sleep in the barn. You will take messages from me and leave them at the church in town. They will look for them in the hymnal closest to the aisle in the second row. Temperance will retrieve the messages and leave any she has for me from London." He opened a cupboard and removed a heel of bread. "Rationing is tight. I apologize for the scarcity of food, but as I said, I have some eggs."

"No need to apologize," Muriel said as she tore a small piece off of the heel of the bread and offered some to Temperance. She took a small bite of the bread and took a sip of coffee to help soften the hard heel in her mouth.

"Where will I stay?" Marie asked.

Muriel listened to Praetorian and Temperance talk about the details of her cover with half an ear. Now that she was here, she wondered what it would be like. She hoped that Praetorian didn't recognize her. She had come to rely on the anonymity that she'd never had in her life. From birth, her social status and title preceded anything else about her. The liberty she'd found in these months of training under a code name had given her a freedom she never even knew she longed for.

Temperance stood to leave and Muriel put her arms around her. "Be safe. I hope to see you again."

When she was gone, Muriel looked at Praetorian. "What's next?"

He studied her face before he said, "Does Joseph know what you're doing? Does he know the danger you're going to face every day?"

So much for anonymity. "It was his idea."

His gray eyes grew serious. "Then he's a fool. Or he's ignorant. Ignorant fools are the worst."

Muriel gasped. "How dare you?"

With an almost loathing glare, he snatched up Temperance's cup. "If you'd lost as many couriers as I, you'd understand how I dare. This work is a death sentence, pure and simple. Now I'm responsible for the wife of one of my dearest friends."

"Suppose I told you this was my idea."

His serious expression didn't waiver. "Then I would have to say that was rather an imprudent decision on your part, your codename not withstanding. Let me be very frank with you. They're always found out. Jerry always catches them. It's only through sheer luck that I, myself, have managed to keep from discovery."

Muriel lifted her chin. "Or God's grace."

With a snort of laughter, he said, "God forsook from France when the Nazi devils moved in. Make no mistake, *Prudence*. You've arrived in hell."

"With that kind of attitude, it's small wonder you're so miserable and defeated." She took another bite of her bread.

"Rather like Joseph, aren't you, my lady? All that unwavering faith."

With a smile, Muriel took a sip of coffee to wash down the bread. "I can only hope to aspire to my husband's level of faith."

8 8 8 8

CHAPTER 3

North of Valeurville, Occupied France: 1941

MURIEL reached for the coffee pot on the stove, but yanked her hand away quickly, shaking it to ward off the burning heat that came from touching the hot handle.

"Sorry there's no kitchen staff this morning but there's a war on after all. First time making coffee with your own two hands?"

At the sound of Praetorian's voice, she jumped and spun around. He'd left the cottage after their exchange yesterday and never returned. Unsure of what to do, Muriel had spent the day fasting and praying and preparing for what lay ahead. She felt good today, centered, energized.

"I had a lesson at the camp," she replied. "I just forgot to get the towel for the handle."

His mocking look made her want to grit her teeth. "They taught you how to make coffee?" With a snort, he used a towel to lift the coffee pot. He poured himself a cup but did not offer one to her. "Rather odd training for a school of espionage."

"Perhaps, but they recognized I knew nothing and would have to pass as a simple French girl. So, I had classes in all sorts of the day-to-day mundane."

He stared at her for a long time before speaking. "Interesting."

With a forced polite smile, she replied, "Indeed."

"Tell me. Did you receive training in dusting, darning socks, or washing underclothes? If so, I may have a few chores for you before handing you your field assignment."

"I can barely wait to inform Joseph that you asked me to launder your soiled undergarments."

Praetorian frowned. "I pray you live that long."

Muriel took a deep, calming breath. "I fully intend to reunite with my husband the moment this awful war is over."

For the first time since she had seen him again, his gray eyes softened. "What's your cover?"

"Piano instructor." She poured herself a cup of coffee and dished the eggs she had scrambled onto her plate before taking a seat at the table across from him. "I'm to pick up my schedule of students from a café by the waterfront."

"I know that café. You'll use it as a drop point fairly often for now. The Germans leave it alone because they believe the owner is a collaborator. In fact, he feeds them tidbits we hand him from time to time. The staff is in the dark. It will be good to start taking meals there several times a week so that you're seen as a regular patron."

She took a bite of eggs and washed them down with coffee before speaking again. The coffee tasted bitter and somewhat stale and made her frown. "What will day-to-day look like?"

"We have various points of contact around the town. Right now it will be busy because we have a major operation in the planning. A go-between with the Resistance movement and our organization is a man who goes by the name Abiel. He will have someone meet you at the café where you're to retrieve your schedule. You will be our interpreter, as it were."

Fear of the unknown swirled in her chest, dampening her enthusiasm and watering down her confidence. "How will he know to meet me?"

"He will have gotten a message yesterday from the same men who led you here." Praetorian stood. "The only message I have for you to give him is that everything is back in place to set the plan back into motion. He will likely not be there himself, but whomever he sends, he'll trust implicitly. Whatever he says to do, wherever he says to go, listen to him. Few people are more capable on the ground."

Muriel went to the sink to wash her dishes. "If you'll provide me with a map to the café, I'll go and get my things sorted."

⚜ ⚜ ⚜ ⚜

A fly buzzed against the window, batting it over and over again. A clock ticked, every movement of the second hand reverberating the air around Muriel. She worked quickly and methodically, installing the listening device in the baby grand piano that sat in the drawing room of the house currently occupied by General Altenhofen. With the rush of adrenaline that heightened every sense she had, she listened for the possibility of anyone coming into the room while she attached the device to the inside of the frame of the piano.

The device looked incredibly small to her, measuring perhaps ten inches by six inches by six inches. Manufactured by the RCA company in America, it was remarkably similar to the devices used to record the conversations of the German POWs at Trent Park, though much smaller. Instead of a metal casing, it had a plain wooden casing which helped it hide inside the piano. It had only one switch, used to power it on, and no useless lights or dials. It relied upon two 88A pressure microphones and a battery powered VHF radio transmitter. She would have to figure some way to change out the battery if they needed to use the device again beyond the next week or so.

She heard a footstep, then a rustle of clothes, and quickly slipped the screwdriver into her pocket and slid onto the piano bench. Just as the maid opened the door, she ran her fingers over the keys. As the maid came into the room, she looked up and smiled. "Isn't this a beautiful instrument?" She said it with complete adoration. "I would love to have one like this one day."

The maid did not reply. Instead, she said, "The General will be home soon. It is best if you are gone before he arrives."

"Won't he want me to discuss what I did?"

"He does not care what you did. We are preparing for the star Virginia Benoit to come visit. He only cares that his home is prepared in time and would not appreciate any details bothering him."

"Very well," Muriel said, bemused at the way this maid treated her. Her mother taught her to run her own household with grace and kindness. Clearly, that wasn't the case here. She packed her tool kit and the maid handed her an envelope with her fee inside in reichsmarks. "If there are any problems or concerns, contact me and I will come directly."

She followed the maid through the large house and out the kitchen door. Once outside in the garden, she retrieved her bicycle and pedaled to the pharmacy two blocks away.

When she stepped into the tiny shop, the bell above the door jingled. Two older women stood in the back corner, looking at a display of Epsom salts.

"Good day," she said to the gentleman who emerged from the back room. "The sun is so bright out there." She administered the code phrase with natural ease. "I was wondering if you had any zinc oxide."

"We should get some in a shipment tomorrow," the man said with a smile, confirming that he'd received the message. "Shall I save some for you?"

"That would be lovely. Good day."

She knew that in the back of the shop, the receiver for the bug she'd just planted lay hidden inside of a radio. While the General held the reception for Virginia Benoit in his home tonight, they would be able to hear most of the conversations that happened anywhere near the piano.

From what Muriel understood, Hope had been given specific questions to ask to draw information out of one of the colonels who would attend the party. She would love to go to that party herself and hug Hope as hard as she could. She missed her team members with a passion, and felt a little bit lonely despite the constant daily interaction with so many people.

Early the next morning, she stood again in the pharmacy. "Good day. I was wondering if you received that shipment with the zinc oxide."

"Sorry, miss, won't be till the 6th. Check back around 9:30."

"Very well. Thank you!" She rushed back to the farm house, almost ignoring the dawning of such a brilliant day. Even with the presence of the Nazis, the birds still sang, the crickets still chirped, and the sun still warmed the skin. But, all of that got placed in the back of her mind while the mission consumed almost all of her thoughts.

She parked her bike in the shed behind the house and entered through the kitchen door. She found Praetorian at the table with a stranger. As she shut the door behind her, she saw the stranger slip a gun off of his lap and into his pocket. He'd clearly been prepared to shoot whomever came through that door. She was glad that he didn't shoot before seeing her.

"This is Abiel," Praetorian said abruptly.

She had delivered and received countless messages from the elusive Abiel, but had never actually met him until now. As she slipped her jacket off of her shoulders, she smiled. "Hello. It's nice to finally put a face to a name."

He had brown curly hair and dark green eyes. He looked like a fun loving boy next door, except that lines tightened around his mouth and no light shone from his eyes. Instead of returning her greeting, he asked, "Do we have a date?"

"He said the 6th at 9:30."

Praetorian nodded. "Anything else happening on the sixth?"

Abiel closed his eyes as he thought. Then he opened them again and said, "There's a reception at the docks. I am certain the officials arriving on this train plan to attend the reception." He stood. "I'll get busy with Matthew and Grace."

"Grace is here?" Muriel asked before thinking. The men both stared at her silently. "Sorry."

Praetorian turned back to Abiel. "Are we sure on the details?"

Abiel nodded as he slipped his hat onto his head. "The pharmacist wouldn't have given the date otherwise. That train will have cars full of new soldiers, including interrogators and torture experts. Not to mention the car that will be filled with high ranking prison officials."

Muriel, interested in the conversation, even though she barely understood what they were talking about, poured herself a cup of coffee and sat in the chair Abiel had vacated.

"So we'll blow it up?" Praetorian asked it so nonchalantly that Muriel nearly choked on her drink. At least she kept her dignity by not spewing coffee all over the table.

"We'll blow the bridge just as the train crosses it. That ought to do quite a bit of damage. We'd already planned on blowing the bridge to stop the supplies coming in for the prison camp. But, the intelligence of this train makes for an opportunity we don't want to miss."

"Absolutely." Praetorian held out his hand and Abiel shook it. "Godspeed, brother. We'll wait for news of the destruction of the train."

"Oh, you won't miss it when it happens." For the first time since Muriel came into the room, Abiel smiled. "I'll get the bomb makers to you post haste."

As soon as he left, Praetorian turned to her. "Get a message out to HQ. Let them know the date and time."

Muriel looked at her watch. "Temperance is due to transmit at thirteen hundred today. I have a scheduled drop for her prior to that. I'll leave in an hour."

He nodded. "I'll think if there's anything else I need to say before you go." He stared at her for a moment. "If they find that bug, they'll know you planted it."

Muriel lifted her chin. "They won't know it's there if we're not listening constantly. Listening at only special times should help prevent detection. Also, it's very short range. The odds of the Germans intercepting the transmission are rather low unless the interception team is in the same room."

He put his hand on the door. "Give me ten minutes and I'll have a message to you."

She smiled. "Marvelous."

As soon as he was gone, she closed her eyes and took a deep breath. Refocused, she pushed away from the table and grabbed an apple out of the bowl on the table.

CHAPTER 4

❧ ❧ ❧ ❧

Valeurville, Occupied France: 1942

MURIEL walked into the restaurant near the lumber yard. Men, old and young, filled the place for the noon lunch hour. She shouldered her way through the crowd to the counter. After she slid onto a stool, she reached into her bag and with a fluid movement, carefully and clandestinely attached an envelope to the underside of the counter. When she finished, she pulled a compact out of her bag and inspected her appearance in the mirror – the signal to the person watching that the envelope was ready.

Without ordering, she slid out of the stool and didn't look back to see who took her spot and collected the envelope of money.

She never feared the information she carried. The coded messages appeared innocent enough if one didn't know the code. But, she always feared getting caught with so much money on her person. Even if the Gestapo didn't immediately arrest her for interrogation, it would make the local German police suspicious of her and force them to watch her more closely. That would hurt her mission.

For nearly eight weeks now, having assumed the guise of a piano instructor, she'd carried money, information, and occasionally people, to various locations throughout her sector of Occupied France. The longer she performed this job, the more rebels and operatives she came in contact with, and the more dangerous her job became.

Nazi interrogators had been trained by experts, brought in as observers to Stalin's Red Army while they interrogated "dissidents" imprisoned in the Gulags of Ukraine. Under Nazi interrogation, most people would break before they died. They would name names and reveal information – anything to end the torture. She had come to accept the only possible outcomes of her work here. The Gestapo or the Nazis might capture her, in which case she could swallow her cyanide capsule and die quickly or else face endless torture that would certainly end in her own slow and painful death. If not that, then someone she had met during the course of her work might be captured and coerced into giving her up. Best option, this terrible war would finally end and she would return home, hopefully to her loving husband. Without the gift of prophecy, she had no way of knowing which would happen.

The longer she did this job, the less she remembered of her old life. Would she ever see the estate again? Would she ever wake up to the smell of hot chocolate and buttered toast carried in by a maid? Could she ever go back to living that life?

Until she walked through the gates of the training grounds, she had lived her entire life in households run silently and smoothly by well trained staff members who lived and breathed to make her life one of leisure and luxury. She didn't know how to drive a car. She didn't even know how to saddle a horse. She had no idea the process by which one could convert a wheat field and a cow into buttered bread.

Now, she washed her own laundry, cooked for herself, and let the wealthy and affluent Nazi loving collaborators in the surrounding towns treat her like a piece of the carpet to walk on because she performed a service for the students. Her mother would never have allowed anyone to speak to her staff the way some of these people spoke to her. The differences in how she lived now and how she once lived fascinated her. Occasionally, as she scrubbed clothes or reattached missing buttons, she wondered how poor Joseph fared in the conditions of deprivation and exposure he faced on the battlefields of Northern Africa.

She pushed through the throng at the entrance of the restaurant and stepped out into the street. As she straightened her skirt, she checked for oncoming traffic before crossing to the other side, pausing to let a large Opel *Blitz* truck rumble past. Out of the corner of her eye, she spotted a man in a German *Wehrmacht* uniform toss down a cigarette butt and follow her.

Senses heightened, she walked a bit faster. She could hear his footsteps behind her as she ducked down an alley, skirting trash bins and empty boxes. Not until she reached the end did she realize she'd entered a dead end. When she turned to go back to the street, the German soldier stood in her way.

"Well, well, well," he said in German, looking over his shoulder toward the street. "Look what I found."

Thanks to her governess *Frau* Heilbronner, she could speak German as fluently as this man in front of her. She waged an internal debate and decided to keep that information to herself. Instead, she spoke in French. "Good day, *Monsieur*."

As she tried to move past him, he grabbed her arm. "Oh, no you don't. We need to have us a little fun first," he said, pushing her against the brick wall. "I know all about you French girls."

Should she scream? She examined his face. His eyes looked puffy, his breath smelled like cheap wine. He was just a drunk, bored man who had something other than duty on his mind.

"*S'il vous plaît*," she whispered simply because he would expect it, looking around for a weapon to use. Maybe that trash bin lid. It was metal. It might buy her some time.

"Oh, I'll please you," he sneered, grabbing her chin in his hand and roughly turning her face. "Over and over again."

Without letting any indication of her intention cross her face, she very sharply brought her knee up. The drunk soldier gasped and stumbled backward, giving Muriel a chance to grab the trash bin lid and use all of her might to hit him over the head with it. He roared and clutched his temple where the lid had come in contact with his skull and he stumbled. His feet caught up in themselves and he tripped, falling backward, arms flailing, face trapped in a look of confused horror.

He landed head first against a pallet of boxes, the back of his head striking the corner of the wooden pallet. The impact of his head against the wood made a sickening cracking sound. There he remained, motionless, his eyes staring straight ahead as a pool of blood slowly formed beneath his hair.

Muriel closed her eyes and took a deep breath, then raised a shaking hand to her neck. She felt nauseated, but she needed to get out of this alley before more soldiers came looking for their friend.

She rushed toward the street entrance and, as she approached, she heard footsteps. Panicked, she backed up against the wall. If only she had some form of weapon! Why hadn't she thought to search him for his gun?

The slight figure who entered the alley wasn't dressed as a soldier. A couple more steps and Muriel gasped out loud. Grace!

"What are you doing here?"

"I was with Abiel when he came to collect the money," Grace said in perfect and unaccented French. She brushed a dark curl out of her eyes. "I watched the Nazi pig following you."

Muriel noticed the gun in Grace's hand, pressed against her thigh. "He tried to assault me, but I fought him off."

"Fought him off? Where is the swine?" Grace spat.

Muriel raised an eyebrow, curious at the vehemence in Grace's voice. "Dead, I think. Or dying. Over there."

Grace looked suitably impressed before she dashed to the end of the alley and inspected the soldier. Seconds later, she was back at Muriel's side.

"You killed him. Good work."

Muriel didn't know how to reply to the accolades so instead she asked, "Is he anyone of consequence?"

Grace shook her head. "Never seen him. He's an *Unteroffizier*. A junior sergeant. Probably he was with the new work detail that just arrived last night. Came from the coast from the look of his uniform."

"What do we do now?"

Grace looked at her as if she were insane. "Go. Get out of here before you're found out."

"What about you?"

Grace laughed. It didn't sound like a joyful sound. "I am a ghost to these clumsy pigs. They still don't see me." She put a hand on Muriel's shoulder. "God be with you, my friend."

"And also with you," Muriel recited. She walked quickly to the mouth of the alley and looked both ways down the street. Certain she wouldn't be seen, she slipped out of the alley and started walking, very casually, intentionally looking unhurried. As she approached the bus stop, the bus arrived and she climbed aboard. The bus was angled just right so she could look through the back window toward the alley entrance without drawing attention to herself. Seeing no one entering the alley, she felt a little relief.

The bus rumbled away as she took her seat. Muriel put a shaking hand against her stomach and closed her eyes, willing the reaction to pass.

Who was this man she had, albeit inadvertently, killed? Did he have a wife? Were his children now half orphaned? Who would receive the letter from the German sergeant's commander?

What had she done? What was she doing here? Behind her closed eyelids, she started to see colored spots as she felt the cold pinprick of panicked sweat break out over her body. The roaring in her ears battled with the sound of the bus engine.

She could not break down. That would surely be the end of her life here. Whoever he was, whatever his story, the fact remained that if she hadn't defended herself, there is no telling what he would have done to her. They were at war. At war, men died.

Deep calming breaths, a very deliberate prayer, and whispering the words to her favorite hymn helped her gradually feel better.

As the bus approached her stop, she stayed put. Instead, she silently prayed and remained on the bus until it stopped on the other side of town. She got off of the bus and walked to a nearby shop.

$$\text{\textbf{\&} \textbf{\&} \textbf{\&} \textbf{\&}}$$

"WHERE have you been? You should have been back hours ago," Praetorian hissed from the front yard of the farm house.

Muriel slipped off of the bike. "There was an incident."

"What kind of incident?" He stalked toward her. She saw movement out of the corner of her eye and looked toward the house, counting two men on the porch and a third in the house, looking out the window.

"It's sorted out. Who's here?"

"The bomb builders."

"We're still on schedule then?"

"Bridge goes up on the sixth. The prison is after."

She looked at the man on the porch again, then at Praetorian. "I need to talk to you."

His eyes, always serious, darkened. "So talk."

"I was assaulted by a German soldier, a sergeant, in an alley by the restaurant. He was drunk and clumsy and killed himself by hitting his head on a wooden pallet."

In her memory, she reviewed the moments in the alley with the drunken Nazi sergeant. Could she have done anything differently? Could she have suggested they go find a café or a hotel? Anything, just enough to get him out of the alley alive?

She knew that war meant taking the lives of the enemy combatants. Still, she never imagined she would personally have to take a life. Did this man have a wife or children back in Germany? Certainly he had parents or others who loved him and cared about him. Had she sent him to eternal damnation by the simple act of knocking him off balance?

For several seconds, he looked at her with narrowed eyes. "Were you seen?"

Despite her care, had she been seen leaving the alley? Was she being followed, watched even now? Had she led the enemy to Praetorian's doorstep?

She shook her head. "I don't think so."

"You don't think so? That does not fill me with confidence, Prudence."

"I'm as certain as I can be. Grace came to the rescue."

He nodded and his face somewhat relaxed. "Then she'll take care of it." He gestured to the house. "They will stay in the barn. Once they construct the devices, we'll find a way to get them out of the area. Two of them are wanted men. Every second here is risky."

"Isn't there some other place they can work?"

"Not that I can think of. They can't risk being in town. If they go anywhere outdoors, they may be discovered."

"Understood." She held up the paper bag. "I'm going to go darken my hair in case someone did see me go into or come out of the alley. A blonde is going to stand out more than a brunette."

"Will coloring your hair make your current patrons suspicious? The ones who know you as a blonde?"

"I rather think not." She supposed she would have to set her hair on fire to draw their notice.

He pulled a pocket watch out of his trousers. "Will it take long?"

"Shouldn't. Why?"

"I need you to deliver a message to Temperance and you're already late."

"I'll just be a tick."

She didn't speak to the bomb makers on the front porch, and they didn't speak to her. One man took off his round glasses and polished them with a dirty rag while the other one went back to writing something in the notebook in front of him. He had a bandaged hand that he cradled against his chest while he wrote. She silently nodded a hello.

After the incident with the soldier in the alley, she suddenly felt very exposed and isolated. What had she been thinking, playing cat and mouse, alone out here in the middle of the wilderness with a houseful of violent men?

Out of the blue, she wanted to go home. But not the home of now, with her Joseph gone – the home of two years ago, before the darkness.

She went through a mental self-tongue-lashing, reminding herself that these men were on her side, that Praetorian was actually a family friend, and that everyone here had a job to do. She went into the house and greeted the man who sat on the floor near the settee cleaning a pistol.

"Good afternoon," she said, slipping her hat off her head.

"Afternoon," he said gruffly, wiping the barrel with an oily rag. He had dark, curly hair and brown eyes. "I'm Matthew. You're Prudent."

"I am that," she laughed, "but I'm called Prudence."

"Prudence, right." He stood as he smiled a very charming smile. "Your French is very good. Pleasure to finally meet you, Prudence."

"And you. I don't think Praetorian admires many men as much as you."

"That's kind, but we have all been gifted in many ways by God for this work, don't you think? Take Praetorian, for example. How many men could lead such a revolution from the kitchen table of a farm house he rarely leaves? He's a brilliant leader who knows everything that's happening all the time. I'm thankful he's here."

"If you're trying to get a raise, keep talking," Praetorian said, limping into the room.

Matthew chuckled and slapped Praetorian hard on the shoulder. "No need for a raise. This job comes with perks found in no other line of work."

Muriel excused herself and ducked into the small bathroom. There she made quick work of the ink she'd bought to dye her hair, using rubber gloves so that she didn't stain her hands.

Careful not to go too dark, she managed to turn her hair a nice rich chestnut. Hopefully there wouldn't be an issue with the blonde picture on her identification. Women everywhere dyed their hair, so it wouldn't be an unusual thing.

She rinsed her hair several times to make sure no ink remained, then carefully towel dried it. The water dripping from the ends of her hair looked clear, so she went ahead and put her shirt back on then left the bathroom.

She encountered no one on her way to her bedroom. After she shut and locked the door, she half stumbled to the bed, where she fell to her knees and rested her elbows on the bed and began to pray, tears streaming out of her eyes and soaking the quilt on the bed.

Unwilling to face fear, she pushed it deep down inside and prayed a simple prayer of thanksgiving for the protection God had granted her that afternoon, for protection over Grace, and for wisdom for going forward from this moment. Finally, she prayed for God's forgiveness if she had been the cause of taking an innocent life and she prayed God's comfort for any loved ones the sergeant's death had left behind in this world.

Once she said, "Amen," she decided to go ahead and change clothes. She donned a black dress and pulled her hair back into a severe bun. With the dark hair, she looked strange in the mirror, but she didn't have time to stare at her reflection. She had a message to deliver.

ᕼ ᕼ ᕼ ᕼ

CHAPTER 5

Chapter Five

Valeurville, Occupied France: 1941

"YOU need a date."

Muriel paused and slipped the palm-sized camera out of her bag. She'd just come from the home currently occupied by a Nazi Colonel and had taken several photographs of documents in his desk while she tuned his piano. She pulled the film out of the camera and put it into the envelope she'd left lying on her bed. She looked at Praetorian, who leaned against her bedroom door frame, and raised her eyes.

"I beg your pardon?"

"A date. You need a date. You know. Like a boyfriend. There's a reception tomorrow night near the bridge we're blowing up. I need you to get inside the reception and secure Grace and Matthew invitations to it."

"I thought that was all taken care of."

"It was, until the bloated woman hostessing the *soirée* decided it would be more impressively formal and haughty if invitations had to be received at the door and guests were announced. Apparently, she is sparing no expense to show how she enjoys licking the jackboots of our current overlords."

He hadn't bothered to mask the irritation in his voice. Grace and Matthew had a plan in place to blow the bridge with the oncoming train in the middle of it. The party had something to do with their escape from detection, but that's about all Muriel knew.

"Praetorian, I cannot imagine how I will secure a date. Perhaps you already guessed that I'm married."

His eyes darkened. "No, actually, you're not, *Mademoiselle* Murielle St. Pierre. You've never been married, in fact. And it's best you remember that." He pushed away from the door frame. "You've spent weeks going to the café several times a week. You attracted one of them before. With the Nazi traffic in and out of that place, I'm certain you can smile pretty at one of them and secure a date for the big event."

He turned to go. "Make sure it's an officer, someone ranked *Hauptmann* or higher. No enlisted and no junior officers. I want to ensure it's someone who actually has access to the party."

How was she supposed to do that?

Hot tears came out of nowhere and stung her eyes. Grace had the skills to do something like this, not her. She transported money and information. Sometimes, she snuck around in someone's home, but never so much person-to-person contact as going on a date with a Nazi officer!

Sitting in her room crying wouldn't fix it. She needed help. She went to the mirror and ran a comb through her dark hair. She still didn't immediately recognize herself in the mirror. She longed for the day she could let her dyed hair grow back out and be a blonde again. As she set the comb down, she picked up a tube of lipstick and darkened her lips a daring, ruby red.

Making sure that the camera and film were out of her purse, she slung it over her arm and walked through the house. Praetorian sat in the armchair in the sitting room, a notepad and pencil in front of him. He glanced up at her. She asked, "Anything from town?"

With a raised eyebrow, he stared straight through her. She thought maybe he would be able to tell that she very nearly had surrendered to a crying jag. Finally, he shook his head. "No."

Without another word, she retrieved her bike from the barn and pedaled back to town. She left her bike at the bus station and took the bus to the docks. She strolled into a café she knew about but had never patronized and felt enormous relief at immediately seeing Grace at the counter.

Grace wore the uniform all the waitresses wore. Muriel knew she worked there as a cover. She also knew that she was to come here only in the event of an emergency.

Muriel sat at a table and picked up a menu. Within seconds, Grace stood next to her with a pencil in hand. "Would you like the special?"

Muriel scanned the room quickly. It looked as if they would be able to speak privately. "I need a date," she murmured.

Grace's eyes grew wider. "For tomorrow?"

After giving a curt nod of her head, she said, "You'll need invitations. I need to get in to get them."

"The brie is an excellent choice, *Mademoiselle*. Would you like some wine as well?" She asked in a normal tone.

"Just water. Thanks."

"One hour, out back," Grace whispered and went back to the counter to pour her some water.

§ § § §

"YOU'RE the piano instructor, are you not?" The *Wehrmacht* major with the ruddy skin around his cheekbones asked as he laid a meaty arm over her shoulder. "Play us a tune!"

Muriel laughed and ducked out from under his arm. Around her, his group cheered her on. "Okay," she laughed, "just one song."

She glanced at the clock on the mantle as she slid onto the stool. She still had forty minutes, but had not yet managed to secure an invitation. Her date had placed his in his coat pocket upon arrival. She just needed access to his coat.

She started playing a traditional German drinking song, *Trinklied* by Verdi, which her nanny had taught her years before. She accented the sharps, making it a very happy, uplifting song, a song meant to be sung by a jovial crowd standing around a piano at a party. The ploy worked, and soon half of the room sang the lyrics.

Thirty minutes later, she slipped off of the piano stool and handed the keys over to someone else. While the majority of the group stood around the piano and sang songs, she slipped out of the main hall and to the coat room.

The same teenaged girl who had taken their coats still stood behind the counter looking bored and rapidly tapping her fingers on the counter.

"Have you been here all night? This whole time?" Muriel asked in a friendly, conspiratorial tone.

"Yes."

"Are you thirsty? I could bring you something." Muriel guessed she was maybe thirteen.

The girl looked up at Muriel, her eyes betraying a different need. "No, but they won't even give me a minute for the bathroom," the girl replied, her voice pleading.

"Oh. Of course! I can watch things here for a minute if you want."

The young girl's eyes lit up. "That would be great." She ducked out from under the counter. "I'll be very quick."

"Take your time. I have nowhere to be."

As the girl dashed off, Muriel slipped into the coat room and ran her hand in and out of coat pockets until she felt a thick envelope. She pulled it out and smiled. Perfect.

As soon as the girl rushed back, uttering a sincere *"Merci!"*, Muriel walked casually outside and onto the back porch. Two floors up, it looked out onto the river. In the moonlight, she could see the shrubs and rocks below. She walked all the way to the corner of the porch and dropped the invitation to the ground below.

"Was machst du, Fräulein?" The friendly question came from right behind her.

What am I doing, indeed? Heart pounding, Muriel slowly spun around and faced her date, painting on as sincere a smile at seeing him as she could muster. In perfect French, she declared, "I love your German language. It sounds so vibrant. What did you just say? Say it again!"

His expression didn't change. In thickly accented French, he said, "I asked what you are doing."

Her smile felt shaky, but she forced herself to relax. "Oh. I was just getting some fresh air. It had gotten just a bit close in there with all you big, strong soldiers singing like that."

He narrowed his eyes and walked toward her, then looked down at the ground. She looked too, but saw no white invitation standing out on the dark ground below. Then she looked back at him, forcing her expression to one of inquisitiveness.

"What were you looking at?" he demanded.

"Just how far down it is." She giggled and put a hand to her heart. "I get vertigo with heights. It makes me all warm and tingly." She slipped her arm inside of his and steered him around. "Is anyone dancing yet, *Herr* Major? I'd love to dance. Wouldn't you?"

He swung her onto the dance floor and moved with astonishing grace for a man of his bulk, especially with the amount of alcohol he had consumed. She laughed and danced and twirled and watched the clock. When she heard the distant sound of a train whistle she felt the smile freeze on her face and her neck tense up. From across the room, she saw Grace and Matthew enter. Grace looked perfectly made up in a shimmering red dress, her hair pulled back and pinned with a glittering clip. She had a calm, relaxed look on her face as she smiled at her date. Matthew wore a tuxedo with a red rose on the lapel. They did not look at her as they gracefully moved onto the dance floor and started dancing the waltz.

Without warning, the explosion ripped through the room. Glass from the windows facing the river blew through the crowd. A giant pillar of bright orange fire lit up the room from somewhere outside. Muriel could feel the heat. After a heartbeat of stunned silence, the room erupted with commotion. Women screamed, men yelled. The band immediately stopped playing and everyone scurried.

Muriel watched as Grace covered her head with both hands and wailed. Matthew put an arm around her shoulder and gently guided her off of the dance floor, warning her to be careful of the glass littering the floor. Her own date had abandoned her, so she picked her way around the broken glass and the debris that had blown in with the windows. She bumped into a Nazi Colonel, an *Oberst*, who stood white as a sheet, staring toward the river. A woman Muriel identified as *Madame* Bardes gripped his arm with both of her hands and cried, black streaks of makeup ridden tears streaming down her face. The absurd hat with large purple plumes lay askew, though still on her head, one of the feathers falling over her eye.

"What was that? What was that?" she wailed.

Muriel put a hand to her heart. "I have no idea. I think I just lost ten years, though."

The colonel seemed to regain his surroundings. "Uh, this way, ladies," he said in German before correcting himself to French. "Please, this way." He led the two women off the dance floor and out into the corridor. He handed *Madame* Bardes a handkerchief from his pocket. "I must leave you. Where is your husband?"

The older woman sniffed and sniffled into the handkerchief before saying, "Of course, *Herr Oberst*. Go to your duties. My husband will be along soon. We will be just fine." Now that she no longer gripped the colonel's arm, her hands were free to right her hat. As she straightened it, she looked Muriel up and down and asked in a haughty voice. "Who are you?"

Muriel smiled her sweetest smile and thought about how this woman would react if she answered, "Muriel Tolson, daughter of the Duke of

Braynard, wife to the son of the Earl of Bostwich." Instead she answered, "I'm Murielle St. Pierre, *Madame*. I'm here with Major Grün."

The woman looked at the tips of Muriel's simple leather shoes that badly needed a good shining up, then sniffed her nose and turned her back. Unconcerned, Muriel turned and rushed out of the building along with a wave of party goers. She couldn't have been more than twenty feet behind Grace and Matthew, but as she exited with the crowd she made every effort to stay far away from them. As they stepped out of the building and into the chaos of the night, Muriel stopped and looked at the river.

In the light of the moon, she could see the ragged edge of the remaining pillar of the railroad bridge left standing on this side of the river. Military vehicles, motorbikes, and uniformed men carrying their weapons raced all around. An ambulance passed so close to Muriel that her dress shifted aside in the wake of its breeze.

Trying to stay inconspicuous, she walked several kilometers to where she had parked her bike. Next time she enjoyed such a clandestine evening, she would make sure her own private transportation waited much closer to the center of action!

Hours later, she walked into the kitchen of the farmhouse. There, Matthew and Praetorian sat, smiling. As soon as she shut the door behind her, Grace came into the room and straight to her, hugging her close.

"Beautiful job, Prudence," Grace said as she stepped back. "We almost got seen. When that swine looked over the railing, Matthew was crouching right beneath him!"

"That was crazy," Muriel said, readying the kettle to make tea. "I was worried he'd look and see the white envelope."

"He would have if I hadn't grabbed it. The bright moon was not our friend tonight." Matthew pushed his chair back and stood.

"The timing wasn't up to us, or else we never would have done it tonight. It might as well be daylight out there," Praetorian said, looking out the window. He turned his attention to Muriel. "Anyone suspect anything?"

She shook her head. "I'm certain not."

"Try to stay away from that side of town for a while."

She poured tea into the pot and thought about everything that could have gone wrong tonight, but remembered everything that had gone right.

Chapter Six

MURIEL slid into the pew next to the agent code-named Temperance. When her friend jumped and looked at her, she smiled.

"Hi," she whispered. "Thought I'd come in person this time."

"You gave me a fright," Temperance whispered back. "I thought we'd been compromised somehow."

Muriel looked behind her. The only person in the church was a single old woman several rows back, her head bowed in prayer. She gestured with her head and they left the church.

As she inspected her friend, she noted the lines of strain around her eyes and mouth. The constant stress of Nazi *Schutzstaffel* triangulating her position every time she sent a broadcast had clearly left its mark on Temperance. "How are things at the farm?" her friend asked.

Muriel smiled. "If you can't tell by the missives, it's been very... engaging."

Temperance looked around, then pulled out a compact mirror, apparently checking her appearance, but to Muriel's trained eyes, clearly making sure they still spoke in private. "Indeed. I even witnessed some of the after effects," she said. Muriel guessed she referenced the blowing up of the bridge. "Well, will it slow down after the big operation next month?"

"I'm sure that will just pave the way for another, and another. It would be nice to see an end to this war very soon."

With a gesture toward Muriel, she said, "The dark hair is kind of a change."

"It's been a month and I am still not fully used to it. Every time I look in the mirror, I have a bit of a shock."

They walked deeper into the town and stopped at the park in the town square. Temperance gestured to a bench. "I can't bear to be indoors. Let's sit here."

After the long bike ride and then walk she had to get here, Muriel gratefully sat. "Have you been keeping busy making dresses?"

"More than I care to, that's for sure," Temperance said with a smile. "But, the business is good. You hear a lot while bent over someone and pinning their skirt. It's funny how they think you don't have ears because you're in service of some sort."

Remembering her own life prior to this one, Muriel nodded in understanding. "I know. It's how they're raised." She habitually ran a thumb over her third finger, remembering her favorite dressmaker from what felt like a lifetime ago. "So, you know who all the unhappy wives are?"

"Exactly. And how they're seeking out happiness." Temperance looked over Muriel's shoulder and groaned. "Oh, no. Here he comes."

"He, who?" Muriel looked behind her and saw a German officer coming their way. Her heart rate increased and she felt the sting of sweat on her forehead, but she kept her face casual.

"No! Don't look!" Temperance leaned forward and whispered, "A German officer has taken a shine to me."

As soon as she realized what Temperance meant, she gasped and reached for her hand. "Oh no, Temperance. That's awful."

Against her will, the image of the dead Nazi sergeant flashed through her memory. She quickly swallowed back rising bile and tried to look unaffected by the images flashing through her mind.

"Tell me about it," Temperance said through gritted teeth, but smiled at the young officer's approach. "Hello, *Oberleutnant* Schäfer. How are you on this beautiful autumn day?"

"*Fräulein* Perrin," the young blond man greeted. He looked at Muriel. "Who is your friend?"

Deciding on a strategy, Muriel giggled and held out a hand. "I'm Murielle St. Pierre, *Oberleutnant*." She emphasized his rank as if promoting him to General. Then she looked at Temperance and stage whispered, "He really *is* handsome, Marie. You weren't exaggerating."

Marie gasped. "Murielle!"

The young officer's ears turned a bit red. "I am pleased to hear you think that of me, *Fräulein*." One of the men in the group of soldiers near a truck across the street barked in their direction. "I must go. We have to go arrest a farmer who has been helping the resistance. I hope to see you again soon. I am still waiting on your answer! I only hope you don't make me wait much longer, *Fräulein*."

He held his hat against his head as he trotted back to the group. Temperance looked at her with a frown. "What was that about?"

"Survival, my friend. He had to believe we were talking about something girlish." Very seriously, she said, "What answer is he seeking?"

"He wants to take me to see Hope perform. I guess she's going to be here in a few days." She pursed her lips. "It would be so amazing to see her. I've only heard rumors of her performances."

"But at what risk?" Muriel asked. What if Hope saw her and gave it away? What if she gave Hope away? Did the young Nazi *Oberleutnant* suspect?

"I know. There are times I have to remind myself that we have a mission and are at war. I get so caught up in dress patterns and such." Suddenly, she put a hand to her forehead. "Oh, my goodness. He's going to go arrest Marcel Bernard!"

Muriel knew that Marcel Bernard was a farmer who occasionally allowed Temperance to transmit wireless messages from his farm. Her mouth went dry. "Why do you think that?"

"Because the last time I was on his farm, it took so long to hear back from London. But, with the operation about to go down, I couldn't stop transmitting. I had to have a reply. I bet they were able to triangulate the signal enough to narrow it down to the vicinity of his farm."

Muriel looked around them, expecting knowing eyes and squadrons of soldiers. "Will he give you up?"

"No." Her voice came out in a whisper. "But his wife will."

Run! her mind screamed. Danger bells rang in her head.

Muriel abruptly stood and brushed at her skirt. "We may need to pull you out if you've been compromised. Let me go check with Praetorian and I'll leave you a message at the church." Her eyes darted all around. "Talking in public was dangerous for both of us. I'm sorry I risked it."

"I'm sorry too."

"Go. Hurry. I will be praying for you!"

❦ ❦ ❦ ❦

MURIEL slipped the missive inside the front cover of the hymnal. She kept her head covered with the black lace shawl and bowed her head for several minutes in case anyone saw her enter the church or someone came in while she was there. As soon as she felt like she'd been there long enough to have it be believed, she shifted the shawl off of her head and left the church.

For three days she and Praetorian had debated about Temperance's position. When the time came for the next scheduled message, the decision to send her back to England came easy. It was too much of a risk, and the farmer and his wife would eventually confess to her use of their farm in order to save their own lives.

She folded the shawl and put it in the bag on the back of her bike, then took care of several more scheduled drops and pickups before she went house to house and conducted four different piano lessons. By the time she pedaled out of the town and along the lane to take her back to the farm house, the sun had started to set. As she entered the yard, she saw a vehicle there that she did not recognize. Taking a quick mental inventory of what was in her bag, she determined it was safe to go ahead and go on into the house.

She found Praetorian at the table with Grace, Abiel, and Matthew. "Grace!" She said as her friend stood. The two women hugged tightly. "Why are you risking coming here?"

"We only have a few moments," she said in her accent-free French. "But we had to come. Temperance has been arrested."

Muriel gasped. "Oh, good Lord," she said, pulling out one of the chairs and sliding into it. "When?"

"Three hours ago." Abiel frowned. "The landlady of the boarding house sent me a message through our channels."

"What can we do?"

Grace answered. "The information she has in her head is of the utmost importance to Hitler. With it, the Nazis can decode missives and gain access to our plans. We must rescue her. The other option is not acceptable."

Muriel knew the other option would be to kill her. Rescue her or kill her. That would be the orders given to those who were part of the team. "You talk as if you're trying to convince me. Isn't rescue an option?"

Abiel shrugged. "The prison is on the second and third floors of a virtual fortress. But, we can move up our plan for the mass breakout of the prison. The problem is, they're going to have her centralized, and that will make it nearly impossible to get in and get her out. The original plan was to blow an outer wall out and have the prisoners we're after escape. We'll actually have to go in to get her."

Grace nodded. "If we had a few days we could properly plan it."

"We have no choice but to take a few days. If we go in there unprepared, we won't succeed." Praetorian leaned back in his chair. "How much time do you need?"

"Enough time to get a message to London to get Faith here to fly her out," Grace said. "There is no way we would be able to keep her in France. They would comb every inch of this land until they found her. Every minute she isn't out of the country would be a danger to the entire operation."

"How can we get a message to Faith?"

Praetorian lifted an eyebrow. "The old fashioned way." At Muriel's questioning look, he said, "There's a prisoner at the jail who is in communication with England via coded letters. We'll get a message to him and set plans in motion."

Muriel looked at Grace and they shared a common thought: Charity's husband. While she stayed in England receiving wireless communications and decoding German transmissions, she also communicated in code with her prisoner husband.

Grace stood. "Hope is in town. She should be able to gain access to the prison."

"How?" Muriel frowned.

Grace gave a rare smile. "She has her methods." She pulled a watch out of her pocket and looked at the face. "I will go see her."

"No," Abiel said, standing with her. "I will. You need to get with your bomb builders and see what else they need to push our plans forward."

Praetorian stood and shook Abiel's hand. "Give daily updates on a rotating basis with all of your points of contact. Prudence will start at the butcher tomorrow at thirteen hundred and then go in order from there. Don't come back here."

He turned to Grace. "What did you do with the body of the German soldier?"

With a stoic expression, Grace replied, "Which one?"

Praetorian lifted his eyebrow. "The one who attacked Prudence."

For a moment, Grace frowned as she thought. Then she smiled and said, "Oh. Him. I dumped a bottle of wine around him and left him there for someone to think he'd fallen on his own accord."

Praetorian nodded. "Very good."

♟ ♟ ♟ ♟

Chapter Seven

MURIEL pushed the door to the fish market open. She stood in line behind a large woman with a loud pink hat angled on her head. It took several minutes until it was her turn to order, and she felt impatient every second that went by. Finally, it was her turn.

"One halibut fillet, please, and make sure it's fresh," she said, using the code phrase.

"I have some fresh in the back. I'll get one for you," the clerk behind the counter said. Within minutes, he returned with a wrapped package and set it on the scale. He gave her the total, and when she handed him the money, she made sure that the note she'd tucked inside the bills couldn't be seen.

She left the shop and walked several blocks before opening the package. Next to the filet was a note - "2 weeks" was all it said.

She ripped the note into little pieces, then started walking down the street, slowly letting the tiny pieces go.

Before Temperance's arrest, she went to the little church on the corner regularly. So as not to break routine, in case the Gestapo had started watching her, she stopped at the little church to pray. She covered her head with the black prayer shawl and this time truly sought out her Heavenly Father.

She stayed in the church for about ten minutes, then left and very casually walked to the baker's home, where a meeting would take place in his basement.

THE lamp on the folded out card table illuminated the thin haze of smoke suspended above the map. Muriel thought it almost looked like a halo over the lit portion of the otherwise dark basement. Everyone huddled around the table, looking at the map and the sketches that Abiel had spread out.

"These are the sketches Hope made from everything she could see when she was inside the prison. She was extremely helpful and really insightful as to what information would be useful to us," Abiel said with a touch of unusual warmth in his voice.

"Radio broadcast this morning confirmed that England received the letter from Captain Ewing. We have another letter on the way with the date we plan to move." Grace placed a piece of paper on the table. "While Hope performs, we'll get inside the prison and place strategic bombs around. Between her keeping such a portion of the staff outdoors, and a series of explosions inside, the confusion should buy us a few precious seconds."

The man known as Remi asked around a lit cigarette, "How do we know her condition right now?"

"When the leaders in Paris were briefed on these plans, they gave us information from a confidential source as to her location within the prison and her status. Three days ago, she had not yet given any information. She's very ill. The thought is pneumonia, and she was hurt pretty badly her first few days there."

"Can she walk?" Grace asked.

"Unknown."

"So we need to plan to carry her if we must," Abiel said.

"That's going to seriously compromise this prison break," Remi opined. "We might just want to exercise our other option."

Grace and Abiel spoke in unison, "No."

Grace continued, "Temperance is small. Carrying her won't slow a grown man down. What about these other prisoners? This was the original plan, no?"

"We're going to break out the entire cell," Matthew said. "We'll have you, Prudence, over here," he spoke as he pointed to the map, "with their clothing and identification. This breakout has been moved up by two weeks, but we should be good. When Faith lands at twenty-one-hundred, she'll load Temperance and any of the other prisoners who will fit on the plane. The rest will have to find a way to either get to Switzerland or Spain or blend in with the local population until they can escape the country."

Abiel turned to Muriel. "Every prisoner knows his number. Every packet of clothes has a number attached to it. It's important that each man gets his own packet, because in the pocket of the jacket is the identification that was made for that man."

Muriel nodded. 'Understood. What if there isn't a packet for a man?"

"Then he doesn't belong there." He stared at her. "You understand?"

He was talking about restraining him, or immobilizing him, or something more permanent. Muriel felt her mouth dry as she once again heard the sickening sound of the German sergeant's head hit the pallet in her memory, as she saw the life fade out of his open eyes. She gave none of her thoughts away and simply nodded.

"Good. We'll have a truck of hay. Under the hay will be the clothing."

"What about Temperance?"

Grace answered. "Thanks to Hope we know where she is inside. I will go in with Abiel. We'll carry her out. Remi has a man who'll have a car here," she said, pointing to the map, "a block away from the prison. We'll drive straight to the field where Faith will land."

"Timing is crucial," Remi added. "They're going to be gunning hard for us. That plane cannot sit there forever. If we aren't there when we're supposed to be, the pilot has orders to take off."

Grace looked at her watch. "Let's go over this again. I also want a driver to take me to the field where the plane will land from the pickup point so that I know exactly how long the drive is and what the road is like."

"My driver knows the way," Remi said.

Grace lifted an eyebrow. "I don't care what your driver knows. Get me a car. Understood?"

Remi shrugged, which Muriel assumed was French for agreement. She looked at the map. "You should put me in the opposite direction of the airfield. At this point, everyone is going in the same direction."

"I know," Abiel said, "but there's nothing we can do about it. The original plan has the prisoners going here, and there's no way to get word to them to change it."

That made sense. "Okay. Let's go over this again. Is it possible to see one of the packets of clothing so that I know what they're supposed to be getting?"

They went over the plans again and again, studying maps, discussing details, discussing contingencies. By the time they concluded the meeting,

Muriel's head swam with vital information she had to relay to Praetorian.

She felt confidence in their plan. If everyone moved at the rate in which they were supposed to move, then all should turn out well.

8 8 8 8

Chapter Eight

HIDING behind the spokes of the donkey cart, Muriel watched a German soldier drive by on a *Zundapp* KS750 motorcycle with a helmeted German *Kapitän* in the *Steib* sidecar as it trundled by. Under a thin layer of hay, one hundred and ten packets of clothing and false identification lay hidden. Once it went by, she stood and walked to the road, then looked back at her hiding spot. In the edge of the wood, with just a thin sliver of a moon, she could not see the cart.

Going deeper into the tree line, she used her shuttered flashlight to check her watch. At any moment, the explosions would start going off. They would set off a chain reaction that would break over one hundred men out of the prison and hopefully mean rescue for Temperance.

"About forty-five seconds," said the woman who'd introduced herself as Reine.

"Let's pray they're on schedule." Muriel wished she was close enough to the airfield to hear Faith's airplane coming in.

Charity had communicated with her husband via their department for months, relaying the plans and instructions for breaking the men out of the prison. Every single detail had been gone over and determined. Until they had to move the date up by two weeks. That seriously compromised every intricate detail.

She checked her watch again, straining to hear any kind of activity. Just as the second hand hit the twelve, she saw the flash of light in the distance, then heard the loud rumble, felt it under her feet. One, two, three, four bombs going off in sequence.

She could hear gunfire – rapid, constant, too much gunfire. Cars raced by on the road, heading toward the prison in town, but she felt secure in their location inside the edge of the woods. Ten minutes later, she started to pray as she watched a tall male figure dart toward her. He wore a prison uniform and smiled as he spoke with a British accent, "Prisoner number twenty-three."

Remembering her system of organization, she dug through the hay to the stack of twenties and pulled out number twenty-three. "Here you go. Godspeed you," she said in English.

"Appreciate that." He ripped open the package and put the jacket over his prison shirt. "You're Prudence, then?"

She felt her eyebrows knotting. "Yes. That's right."

The man nodded. "I have a message for you from the dark haired woman," he said as he fastened the jacket.

"What did she need?"

"She said to tell you to have pity at the rendezvous."

"What? Have pity on who or what?"

He shook his head. "That's not it. Have mercy at the rendezvous. Said you'd understand."

Have Mercy at the rendezvous? Her heart leapt into her throat. This man had just informed her that the doctor code-named Mercy, operating here undercover as a Red Cross nurse, must join them at the airfield. What had gone wrong? Who was hurt?

She clamped down on her thoughts. "Thank you. Go, now. Find a place to hide." She looked up and saw another five prisoners coming toward them. "I have to go," she said to Reine. "Can you handle this?"

"Go? What are you saying? We've been planning this operation for weeks!"

"I know. I just got a message from Grace. Things have changed. Can you handle this or not?"

"Grace?" The indignant look left the woman's face. "Go do what Grace needs. She wouldn't ask if it wasn't vital to the mission. I can handle this."

"If I can come back, I will." She wrapped a cloak around her and took off running, thankful for the miles and miles she'd had to run while training. She ducked in between buildings and raced through alleys until she came to the hospital.

She knew Mercy. There's no way that woman would have heard gunfire and explosions and not immediately reported in to the hospital's emergency department.

8 8 8 8

WHEN Muriel entered the hospital, she stepped into organized chaos. She moved through the throng of uniformed soldiers, nurses, and doctors until she saw the rare flash of red hair under a nurse's cap. When she finally caught up with Mercy, she was shocked to find her rubbing the arm of Virginia Benoit, code-named Hope, who lay on a cot in the corner of a room with a bloodied white bandage pressed against her dark forehead. Muriel rushed into the room.

"Are you okay?" she asked Hope.

Hope recognized her immediately, even despite the dyed hair, and her smile brightened the room. "Oh, it's you! Oh, honey, it's so good to see you."

Muriel met Mercy's eyes and caught the look of stark concern. "Virginia!" Breaking protocol, she called the woman by her real name, thinking it best should they somehow be overheard. "Are you all right?"

"No need to fuss. I'm just dandy." She pushed herself up and put a woozy hand to her head. "Or not."

"She was very near to the explosion. She got quite a lot of the aftershock. I don't think there's any internal bleeding, but her head is badly concussed." Mercy patted her hand and then it apparently occurred to her that the agent code-named Prudence should in no way be here in the midst of this chaos. Not under any circumstances. She turned to Muriel and demanded, "What's the matter?"

"Grace needs you."

Mercy's eyes widened. "I'll need my bag."

"I'm coming with you," Hope said. "There's a pair of dead Nazis in my dressing room. I have to leave now. They'll certainly be looking for me soon if they aren't already."

"Can you get up?" Muriel asked.

Mercy held up a halting hand. "Her head injury could be very serious. Short of exploratory surgery, there's no way to tell without a few days of strict bed rest and observation."

Hope spoke up. "No time for any of that. I'll either be just fine or I won't. I know for sure if I lay in this hospital, they'll arrest me and I know I won't be fine then. Let's have faith and leave it in God's good hands. I could use some help, though." Muriel held her hand and Hope pushed herself to her feet rather unsteadily.

"This is impossible. We have a long way to go on foot."

Mercy looked at her. "Can you get us a car?"

"Maybe."

Hope turned to Mercy. "Go get your bag and head out front. Prudence, see if you can scare us up a car. I'll make my way out there. If I get outside in time, take me with you. If not, go help Grace. I'll make do."

Muriel rushed outside to the parking lot. Dozens of German vehicles filled the lot. Swallowing hard, she ran past the six wheeled Daimler-Benz G4 Staff Car and up to the less conspicuous Mercedes Benz 170V four-door *Tourenwagen* furthest away and close to the street. A quick look inside confirmed that the keys hung from the ignition on a steel lanyard secured to the steering wheel. This was a measure taken by the motor pool so that the keys were not lost. It helped Muriel considerably because she didn't feel certain she could quickly hot wire the car. She had only attended one afternoon class on how to do it, and she had no tools close at hand.

Looking all around to make sure she was unobserved, she slipped into the driver's seat, pressed in the clutch, and started the engine. It started smoothly so she put it in gear and drove to the entrance of the nurses' barracks next door to the hospital. She was surprised that when she pressed the clutch, her legs felt a bit shaky and wobbly. She took a deep breath. No time for nerves right now.

Mercy rushed down the steps toward her, black bag in hand, and hopped into the Mercedes. Looking anxiously back at the entrance of the hospital, Muriel saw Hope stumble out, gripping the handrail for support. She pressed hard on the accelerator and then skidded to a stop next to Hope. Mercy jumped out and helped her into the back seat. As soon as the door closed again, Muriel accelerated out of the parking lot as fast as she could without raising suspicion.

"What was happening back there?" Mercy asked over the sound of the engine.

"Temperance was arrested two weeks ago. This was her rescue."

Mercy's lips tightened. Unconsciously reverting to English, thick with her Scottish brogue, she said, "Aye. I saw her about a week ago. She's very sick. I told them she needed to be in hospital, but was told it was absolutely out of the question. I did what I could for her there, which wasn't much." She looked in her bag. "I'm relieved to hear she's alive. I think I'll be able to stabilize her." She turned in her seat and peered into the back seat. "What happened in your dressing room?"

Hope sat slumped back against the headrest with her eyes closed. At Mercy's question, she opened them and very stoically said, "A few members of Hitler's SS objected to the tone of my skin."

Muriel didn't recognize a single word Mercy mumbled, but the tone made it clear that they weren't nice words. She bit back a smile and concentrated on driving the awkward vehicle.

She hadn't driven since her driving lessons at the training camp. At first, shifting gears came a bit choppy, but she soon smoothed it out. She knew there would be roadblocks set up on the main roads leading out of the town, but she hoped that the back roads she took would remain clear, at least for now. After five miles she reckoned this was the furthest she had ever driven a car in her lifetime.

She'd traversed these very same back roads by bike or on foot for months, dashing from one clandestine meeting to another. Some roads she went down were little more than rutted dirt lanes, but she encountered no other traffic.

Ten minutes later, they pulled up to the field where Faith should have landed five minutes ago, except the field stood empty. No airplane in sight.

"Well, then. What now?" Mercy asked.

"Now I suggest we take time to pray."

៕ ៕ ៕ ៕

THREE minutes later, Muriel heard an airplane's engines, but could see no lights in the sky. It almost surprised her when a huge shadow with three propellers landed roughly and loudly on the darkened air strip. What kind of courage did it take for a pilot to attempt such a landing using only moonlight to guide the aircraft to the earth? Muriel thought she saw a *Balkenkreuz* on the corrugated side of the airplane, but convinced herself that the darkness and the silvery moonlight must just be playing tricks with her eyes. After all, why would a plane with a Nazi symbol emblazoned on it be landing in their secret airfield?

The plane taxied to the end of the field, then turned completely around and stopped with the propellers feathered and the engines set to idle, clearly ready to take off again as soon as possible. Just as Muriel was about to put the car in gear and drive to the plane, she heard the sound of a car engine.

A wooden paneled Ariès Berline tore onto the airfield and sped toward the parked plane. Muriel accelerated and drove fast across the field, right behind the other vehicle.

The shadowy upper body of someone in the back seat of the car in front of them emerged from the window and fired a pistol in their direction. The windshield between her and Mercy cracked into a spiderweb of glass as a large caliber bullet passed between them and then out through the cloth convertible roof.

"Prudence!" Mercy screamed, ducking. "Duck, Hope!"

"Quack," Hope giggled as she slid down onto the floorboard of the back seat.

Muriel didn't say a word as she slammed on the brakes, then veered quickly, attempting to put the other car between them and the passenger shooting at them. She didn't have a lot of driving experience, and over corrected, causing the rear end to fishtail.

With a prayer, she straightened out and then accelerated to pull up alongside the slower, older, and heavier car. They reached the plane at the same time and skidded to a halt. Muriel pulled the car to the left in an attempt to get it under control just as the other driver did the same. The front bumper of the Ariès came to rest against the rear bumper of the Mercedes she drove.

The door to the plane opened as Abiel leaped out of the driver's side of the Ariès and rushed their car with his pistol drawn. As soon as he saw Muriel, he pivoted and went back to his car, but he did not holster the pistol. He opened the back door and bent inside the car. When he emerged once more, he carried Temperance in his arms.

The relief she felt at seeing her friend freed from the prison was short lived as Grace leapt from the car and yelled, "Go!" She snatched a Sten submachine-gun out of the front seat and ran away from the plane. "I'll cover for you!"

Muriel and Mercy dashed out of their car. She ran around to the passenger door to help Mercy guide Hope from the car. She could hear more car engines and the sound of gunfire. The unmistakable sound of German 9 millimeter return fire came to their ears as Abiel climbed the steps of the airplane carrying Temperance.

From the trees, three escaped prisoners ran toward the plane. "Hurry!" The copilot yelled, rushing down the steps with a Sten machine-gun in his hand.

Pausing at the base of the stairs, Muriel put her hands on Mercy's and Hope's shoulders. "Be safe. I will be praying."

Abiel rushed out of the plane, ducking out of the way of the prisoners coming on board, and saw Hope. "What happened?" He asked, coming to a complete stop in front of her.

"Someone blew a building up right next to me," she said with a giggle. Abiel put his arm around her shoulders and turned toward the door of the plane. "One minute I was singing, and the next thing I know it all came crashing down on my head."

"You need to get out of here," he said gently. Hope reached up and clutched his hand.

"Please stay with me, Edward," she said urgently.

Edward? Could Abiel be Temperance's brother? Muriel drew in a quick breath. No wonder saving her was so important to him. And Grace must have known!

"Get her on the plane! Stay with her!" She yelled over the gunshots and the drowning roar of the plane's engine. "Faith can bring you back later!"

The sudden crack of gunfire from the nearby treeline took everyone by surprise. Grace was the first to react. She dove behind the hood of the Ariès Berline, using the iron engine block for cover. She studied the treeline in the darkness. As the gunfire sporadically came at them, she sought out the muzzle flashes which would become the targets for her returned fire. Moments later, the copilot joined her.

Muriel turned, dashing back to the vehicle she'd stolen. She intended to turn the headlights on and point them in the direction of the nearby woods, hopefully dazzling their aggressors or even making them visible. After three steps, she felt a sharp, ripping pain in her right shoulder and suddenly her legs gave out from under her. Mercy cried her name just as her knees hit the earth. As she fell forward, her world went black.

The End

INSPIRED BY REAL EVENTS

Inspired by Real Events

WHILE the story of the special team of operators I named *The Virtues* is entirely fictional, set in a fictional town, and comprised of fictional characters who form a fictional military division, every single one of these fictional heavenly heroines was inspired by a real World War II heroine and their stories were inspired by real events.

The woman depicted on the cover of this book is a thus far unidentified former French resistance operative who, shortly after the liberation of Paris and at the request of a war correspondent, demonstrated the means by which she photographed key Nazi targets using a mini-camera hidden inside her purse. There are thousands of stories of fearless women who worked to defeat Nazi Germany while behind enemy lines.

I made every effort to remain true to actual history in my fictionalized story of Prudence which is based upon the truly inspiring real life heroine, Cécile Pearl Cornioley (ne: Witherington).

Born in Paris, June 24, 1914 into a very troubled family, her father drank heavily and her mother barely spoke French, so her mother looked to Pearl to handle a lot of the family's business. This bleak childhood toughened Pearl into a strong woman, willing to fight for anything in life. Pearl didn't start attending school until age 13, and then went to a bilingual school where she studied entirely in French in the morning and in English in the afternoon.

Once she left school, she worked in the British Embassy in Paris. Her father had died and her embassy job provided the only means of financial support for her family. What complicated her life was that shortly after leaving school, Pearl had fallen in love.

Henri Cornioley had started courting Pearl in 1933, and she eventually accepted his proposal of marriage. Once engaged, they struggled to obtain the blessings of their families, but neither of their families supported the union. Her mother didn't want to lose her only means of financial support while Henri's father didn't want his son saddled with Pearl's financially dependent family.

Pearl worked at the Embassy for 7 years all the way up until the war started. Henri had been called into French military service in 1939. As fate would have it, Henri was taken prisoner by the Germans in 1940. Miraculously, he later escaped from a prisoner of war camp and made his way back to Pearl.

When the Germans invaded France, Pearl and her family fled to Normandy. Her family was British, but despite promises from the British Embassy where she had toiled for seven long years, they received no help in getting transportation to Great Britain. In the winter of 1940, they found out that the Nazis had begun to arrest British citizens and they, again, fled Paris. They had a harrowing journey, many times on foot, from Paris to Spain to Gibraltar to Scotland then at long last to London, arriving on July 14, 1941. Pearl's two sisters joined the Women's Auxiliary Air Force while she worked for two years for the director of Allied Air Forces and Foreign Liaison.

Ultimately, Pearl joined the Special Operations Executive (SOE) and trained as a courier. She specifically asked to be attached to the "Stationer network" which was run by an old school friend. Their mission: harass the enemy, exhaust them, impede them by destroying communications and transportation lines, stop munitions production, and anything else they could do to hurt the enemy's mission.

On September 22, 1943, Pearl parachuted into Occupied France and assumed the identity of a French national named Pauline and the codename, *Wrestler*. In wireless transmissions back to England, she was "Marie." She was not yet 30 years old. There, she worked as a courier for Maurice Southgate. She often traveled by train, and as a way to disguise her intent, carried with her "pro-Nazi" French magazines. Henri's father owned a cosmetics company named Isabelle Lancray, and Pearl had paperwork that provided a cover story of a cosmetic saleswoman to help explain why she traveled so much.

One of her team's secret missions was to recruit and train smaller teams all throughout France so that on D-Day, the Allies would have help everywhere. They organized over 1500 members. This drew attention and the Gestapo arrested Maurice on May 1, 1944. On May 2, Pearl and her team arrived at an estate in Indre. They had supplies parachuted in and accomplished two more missions in that month. On July 11, 1944, three German garrisons (about 2,000 men) surrounded and attacked the estate. During the battle, Pearl lost 24 men.

She ran from the house and hid in a wheat field, crawling on her hands and knees while Germans shot at her. She hid in the field until 10:30 that night. Then she hid in a house while the Germans searched farms, estates, and houses, killing some people, arresting a few, terrorizing others. They burned down houses and barns and searched for Pearl's team, whom they called "terrorists". This became known as the Battle of Les Souches, which was a small part of a larger battle in which 32 French patriots lost their lives.

After losing her that night, the Germans put a ƒ1,000,000 price on her head.

Pearl reorganized after Les Souches, and Henri, who had returned to France and reunited with her after his harrowing escape from the Nazi run prisoner of war camp, became her second in command. They lived in the woods, organizing the flood of volunteers who suddenly foresaw a positive outcome in the war after the successful D-Day invasion. Their constant acts of sabotage often prevented German troops and munitions from reaching the Normandy coast. They also provided the RAF with intelligence that led to the bombing of a German train carrying 60 tankers of gasoline. This raid seriously handicapped the German army.

Pearl rose to command more than 3,000 underground fighters who killed more than 1,000 Nazi troops and injured countless more. In September 1944, France was finally liberated. Pearl and Henri presided over the surrender of more than 18,000 German troops.

Within months, the couple returned to London where they finally, at long last, married thus ending their protracted eleven year engagement. They went on to have one daughter, Claire.

After the war, Pearl was nominated for an MBE, Member of the Most Excellent Order of the British Empire. However, there are two categories of the MBE: the military and the civil. Pearl had been nominated for the civil award, which she rejected with an icy note that stated, "There was nothing remotely 'civil' about what I did."

Though she had completed airborne training and became one of only a handful of women to jump into enemy territory during the war, she was never awarded her parachutist badge, a fact she felt was a grave injustice for her entire life. In September 1946, Great Britain finally awarded her the military MBE. Much more recently, she was also awarded the CBE, the order of Chivalry known as the Commander of the Most Excellent Order of the British Empire, and the French *Ordre national de la Légion d'honneur* or the National Order of the Legion of Honour.

Henri died in 1999. Pearl died in 2008 at the age of 93.

❦ ❦ ❦ ❦

SUGGESTED questions for a discussion group surrounding *A Parcel for Prudence*, part 4 of the *Virtues and Valor* series.

While the characters and situations in the *Virtues and Valor* series are fictional, I pray that these extended parables can help readers come to a better understanding of truth. Please prayerfully consider the questions that follow, consult scripture, and pray upon your conclusions. May the Lord of the universe richly bless you.

The fictional character, Muriel Tolson grew up in the lap of luxury. She had servants, personal maids, and was addressed since birth as "Lady Muriel" because her father was a duke. After several months in Occupied France, she wondered if she could possibly return to her old way of life.

    1. How much emphasis do you think our society places on status and wealth?

    2. The Bible tells us that the *love* of money is the root of evil. Do you think that the status of homes and estates and cars and such opens the door in our hearts for covetousness, greed, etc.?

    3. Do you think it's possible to maintain a faith filled life while living in the lap of luxury?

§ § § §

Muriel endures a rather harsh interrogation by her superiors in preparation for her assignment in Nazi Occupied France.

4. How do you think that prepared her for the duties she would perform?

5. Do you think that such harsh training was too much?

§ § § §

Muriel is attacked by a German soldier and accidentally kills him in the struggle that follows.

6. Do you think she was wrong in her actions in defending herself?

7. Do you think that, due to the soldier's clearly inebriated state, she should have found a different means of protection?

8. Do you believe that Muriel sinned in any way during the struggle and the death of the soldier?

§ § § §

Muriel said that she strives to be as faith-filled as her husband.

9. How do you think that the horrors of war have affected her faith?

10. Do you think that the concept of a group of sisters in Christ banded together by a love of God could be strong enough to withstand the horrors of war?

§ § § §

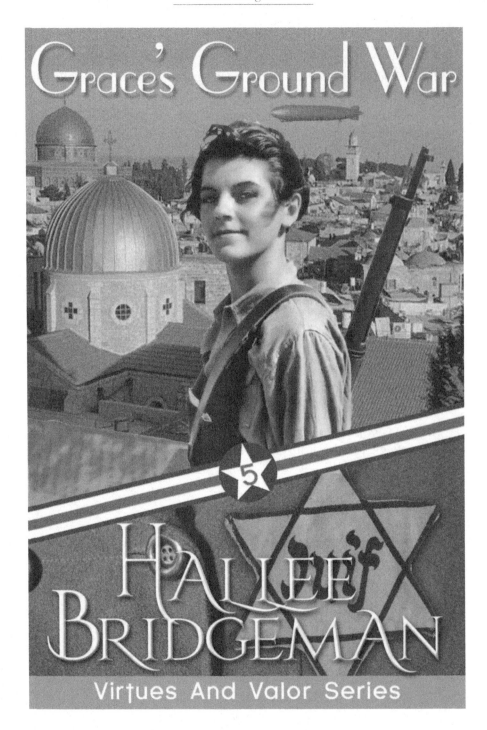

Grace's Ground War

the Virtues and Valor Series part 5

a Novella by

HALLEE BRIDGEMAN

Published by

Olivia Kimbrell Press™

Library Cataloging Data
U. S. Library of Congress Control Number: 2014953681

Bridgeman, Hallee (Hallee A. Bridgeman) 1972-
  Grace's Ground War, Virtues and Valor series part 5/ Hallee Bridgeman
    100 p. 23cm x 15cm (9in x 6 in.)

Summary: Ruth "Grace" Aubertin carries out asymmetric warfare in Occupied France.

   ISBN: 978-1-939603-49-4 (ebook)

1. Christian fiction 2. World War II 3. war stories 4. spies 5. historical fiction 6. espionage

PS3568.B7534 T494 2015
[Fic.] 813.6 (DDC 23)

For All the Rebels...

THIS novella is specifically dedicated to Nancy Grace Wake. To read more about her real story, read the Inspired by Real Events section at the end of Grace's story.

Let us therefore come boldly to the throne of grace, that we may obtain mercy and find grace to help in time of need.

Hebrews 4:16(NKJV)

GRACE –the free and unmerited favor of God, as manifested in the salvation of sinners and the bestowal of blessings. The love and mercy given to us by God because God desires us to have it, not because of anything we have done to earn it.

Hebron, British Palestine: 1929

RUTH Aubertin stood next to her father as he surveyed the remains of their house of worship. The walls still stood, but the burned roof left the interior exposed to sky and allowed the sun to shine down on the burned shell. Ruth bitterly stared at it. The fires had been set by the Arabs who had attacked four days ago. Ruth and her family had hidden in the police station until the attacks ended.

Her uncle Yoseph, looking all around, put a hand on her father's shoulder. "It is not safe. We must leave."

"My family and I will not be staying in Jerusalem with you," Andre said to his wife's brother. "We will go back to France."

Yoseph raised an eyebrow. "I thought you feared the return of the Germans."

"They will return. You and I both know it's unstoppable. But I can train my children with more freedom in the wilderness of France than I can here, where the Arabs would stoop to such atrocities as this."

"But –"

Andre put his hand on his brother-in-law's shoulder. "I know the children are all you have left of your sister. But, this world is groaning, and war is coming. My children need to be ready. Their mother will not have died in vain shielding them from the Germans."

Ruth had heard stories of her mother hiding her and her brothers in the root cellar while German soldiers invaded their home, but at one, she'd been too young to remember. Matthew would not speak of it and John often would cry very angry, very silent tears when he thought of it.

"Your children are Jewish. That will not be as widely accepted in Europe as it was ten years ago."

Andre nodded. "No more than also being Christ followers is accepted here. We are never going to be accepted, my children and I. But *Yah* has had us here until now, and He would have me prepare them for what He would have them to do there."

"I fear that you won't find what you're looking for there," Yoseph said. "Rebekah is not in France. You won't find her there."

Andre slowly shook his head. "My brother, I am seeking nothing. I am simply following right now."

Yoseph called for Ruth's brothers and cousins and, carefully stepping over rubble and debris, the group departed. Ruth thought of the days spent hiding in the police station, seeing the flames outside the windows, and hearing the fighting in the streets. She couldn't completely comprehend what she'd experienced.

Yoseph's wife, Breine, met them outside, carrying baby Doran in her arms. "Yoseph," she said, "I just talked to Erela. They found Aharan. He's dead."

Ruth gasped as her uncle and father wailed in grief. Her mother's youngest brother had died in the attack by the Arabs. So many in their little village had been slaughtered. She felt anger unlike anything she had ever felt before well up in her chest.

Hot tears stung her eyes as the bright sun beat down on her black hair. The attack had come swiftly, and for three days, men, women, and children were killed at the hands of the *jihadists*. Why? Because they were Jewish, and since as far back as the Caliphate of the seventh century, the two groups had hated each other.

Of course, Ruth had nothing to do with that history. Nor did her uncle. He just made the creamiest goat's milk cheese that anyone had ever tasted. His little shop was renowned throughout British Palestine. And now he was dead, leaving behind his wife and six children. What would they do now?

All the Jews in her village had to leave. The British authorities had arrived to remove the surviving Jews from their homes. They would all go to Jerusalem.

Ruth wanted to stay. She wanted to hide and train and fight back. The indignation rose up in her chest until she thought it would smother her, until she felt like she couldn't take another breath. A buzz sounded in her ears and the sun grew brighter until the world had a white haze to it. Her chest moved rapidly as she fought to breathe.

Her father's strong hand on her shoulder steadied her, quieted the buzzing, loosened the tightness in her chest. He looked down at her, his one good brown eye mirroring her emotions. "Wait," he gently urged, "your time is not now. Patience."

A woman in a British military uniform approached, looking starched and pressed in her wool despite the pressing heat of the day. Ruth thought she was absolutely beautiful with her blonde hair and pale skin.

"Colonel Aubertin?" the woman inquired, looking directly at Ruth's father then glancing at his three children.

"Charlie? Is that you?" her father asked, disbelieving.

The woman nodded. "Sir!"

Her father frowned. "No need for all that. How's your father, then? Still gadding about?"

The woman shook her head. "Dead, I'm afraid."

Andre's frown deepened. "That's rather sudden. I recently shared correspondence with him."

"Quite. Though I'm told he felt no pain. I take it this is your brood?"

At Andre's nod, she knelt and held out her hand. "Hello. I am Captain Charlene Radden. I've been sent here to assist you and your family in relocating." The children each shook her hand in turn. When she held her right hand out toward her father, Andre shifted his body and took her right hand with his good left hand. His bum right arm hung loosely at his side.

"I fear you've arrived a bit late, Captain. As you can see, I have no need of you. I have my wife's entire family to look after."

"Yes, sir. We've accounted for that. I have lorries at the ready. I am very sorry to hear of your losses." She gestured toward the large trucks rumbling into the synagogue yard.

Ruth slipped her slim hand into her father's strong one. Rather than relinquish the grip, he pulled Ruth with him as he and Charlene stepped away from the other members of the family. "My children and I are going to go to France, not Jerusalem."

Charlene looked down at Ruth and met her steady gaze. "Very well. I'll see to it transport is arranged." Ruth understood the English language, but had a hard time speaking it. It occurred to her that a British officer was not present for every family. Just why had this woman shown up and called her father "Colonel" and how did he know her as "Charlie" she wondered?

"Papa?" She asked, looking up at him while she held his hand. "Must we leave?" She spoke in French, as was her father's rule whenever someone who was not Jewish was present within earshot.

Before her father could speak, Charlene answered, also in French. "You must because it's no longer safe here. We clearly can't protect you should you remain."

Ruth raised her chin. "My papa can protect us."

The blonde woman gave a single nod. "Indeed, he can. But he would do better on his own soil, would he not?"

Andre squeezed Ruth's hand. "The enemy you'll be fighting won't be here in your home, *tochter*. That enemy will be in my home. You must train in France so that you know the lay of the land."

Charlene raised an eyebrow. "Of what do you speak, Colonel?"

"Germany will rise again, like a sleeping dog. I will train my children and they will learn how to survive and how to fight."

"Do you really think that likely in our lifetime? Their economy just crashed, you know."

"One day, we'll meet again and speak of it and you'll tell me how it was good that I prepared my children rather than remaining complacent."

Ruth watched Charlene's face intently. The woman did not dismiss her father. Instead, her lips tightened and she nodded as if agreeing with him.

§ § § §

Banks of Garonne River near Toulouse, France: 1940

RUTH stood next to Matthew beneath the quince tree as their brother John hammered a fresh wooden cross into the ground not far from a much older one. Their father, Andre Aubertin, had shown signs of an illness in his lungs for several months now, but would not allow them to seek treatment for him. Despite his Christian upbringing, he feared someone might learn of his wife's Jewish heritage, of his children's Jewish upbringing, and of their blood relatives living in Jerusalem even now.

At the turn of the century, the war weary man had made his way to Hebron, seeking out the family of his very best friend. In foxholes and crouching behind sandbags, he had heard his friend describe them all dozens of times. He felt obliged to find them and tell them of the man's courage under fire during the Battle of Peking. Andre wanted to tell them how he had died while saving the lives of seven others, himself included. No one dreamed he would fall in love with the sister of the fallen hero. No one dreamed her family would embrace him. No one could have imagined he would lead them to Christ while embracing their heritage and living as one of them in their ancestral home.

British by birth, but French by blood, Andre had taken his bride, Rebekah, and their baby boy, John, to France and had farmed in the countryside there until the beginning of the Great War. He had left his wife and three children at their farm and returned to his homeland to once again don the uniform of a British officer. While he fought the Germans in Arras, three German deserters attacked his home. Rebekah had seen them coming and hidden the three children in the root cellar. She was able to fend off the men and kill one of them, but the two survivors overpowered her. They had killed her the next morning.

Weeks later, Andre returned home, the right side of his body practically useless after an explosion that shredded the very horse out from under him. He arrived to find his ten-year-old son, John, minding the family farm and his wife's grave beneath the quince tree.

He took his grieving family and returned to Hebron, where they welcomed the children, and once more embraced Andre as their own. For nearly ten years he had lived in the ancestral home of the Jewish Patriarchs and trained his children to become well-honed soldiers. After the Battle of Hebron, they had returned once again to the farm in France to continue training.

The four of them had escaped the Nazi occupation of northern France, but just barely. For the last several months, they'd made their home in an abandoned hunting cabin while they continued to train, even though they could not possibly be more ready for their tasks at hand. Ruth and her brothers had simply been waiting for their father to leave this fallen world and enter through the gates of Heaven before initiating their plans.

Matthew broke the silence. "I'm glad we brought him here. It is right that he is next to mother. I think it was worth the risk coming to German territory to bury him."

His siblings didn't disagree with him.

"Papa was the strongest man I have ever known," John said as he set aside his hammer and pulled his hat off of his head to uncover his jet black hair. "I so admired and looked up to his faith, his courage, and his commitment to *Yah*."

Matthew removed his hat as well. "We should pray," he said, then spoke in Hebrew while he thanked God for protection and provision and asked for wisdom and courage. When he finished, he looked at Ruth. "Would you like to speak?"

She nodded and felt, for the first time since that day in Hebron, hot tears sting her eyes. "We have been preparing for this since before my second birthday. We won't fail Papa or God." She held her hands out and her brothers each took one. "He was right about the future of Europe, and that gives me confidence to know that *YHWH* is with us." Taking a deep breath, she said, "Victory."

Her brothers echoed the word, then Matthew spoke. "It's time to go to London. I'm sure Captain Radden has been anticipating our arrival since Dunkirk."

§ § § §

Chapter One

London, England: 1941

RUTH sat in a hard wooden chair with a brother on each side of her. Major Charlene Radden sat across from them at a large wooden desk, still clearly trying to digest it all.

"So, Aubbie – I beg your pardon. So your father said God told him that the Germans would be back and that you had to train?" she asked, seeking clarification.

Ruth briefly wondered what kind of relationship Charlene had shared with her father to address him as Aubbie in death instead of Colonel Aubertin as she had done in life. Likely, she would never understand the camaraderie. Her father couldn't tell her and Charlene likely wouldn't.

"Yes," Matthew replied. "Ever since the end of the Great War. Ruthie here teethed on wooden guns so she'd be familiar with the shape of them."

Charlene pursed her lips. "I see. And what do you think of that?"

Ruth raised an eyebrow. She had a lot to say and English would prove difficult, so instead she proudly answered in French. "I think we're sitting in this room, in a building with a bunker under it, while we listen with half an ear for air raid sirens, because the Germans are back. They're back and more dangerous than the last time."

She sat forward, feeling urgency like never before. "We are the most highly trained soldiers you will find, my brothers and I. We can cipher and decipher. We speak English, French, Hebrew, and German. We have an internal code between us that no one could crack. We are proficient in hand-to-hand combat, tactical driving, and any weapon from a simple blade or bow-and-arrow to any high powered explosive you want to give us."

John spoke. "Matthew can stay at your base and teach. We know that you're training spies. Ruth will go back into France, under your program, and work for you. I can enter your officer ranks and lead men in combat."

Charlene sighed. "Your father –"

"–was one of the most highly decorated officers in the Great War," Matthew interjected. "He fought for the British Empire with a skill and determination that can only come from *Yah*, from Jehovah God. He was a prophet who foretold of this conflict. From the moment the Holy Spirit revealed this truth to him, my father spent every moment of the rest of his life preparing the highly trained soldiers you see before you."

Charlene held Ruth's gaze as she had a decade earlier. "Why come to me?"

Ruth answered. "Because standing in front of our destroyed synagogue in Hebron, you looked our father in the eye when he told you about his vision, and you believed him."

Charlene smiled. "Too right. I remember feeling absolutely terrified after that conversation." She pushed back from her desk and stood. "I am delighted you're here. John, please come with me. I'm going to take you to General Franklin. He'll take over from here and get you sorted."

As they went to the door, she looked at Ruth and Matthew. "Feel free to help yourselves to more tea. I'll be back for you both very soon. I think I have the perfect program for Ruth."

☻ ☻ ☻ ☻

Outside of Milton Keynes, England: 1942

THE roar of the aircraft engines drowned out nearly every thought in Ruth Aubertin's head. The endless clamor deafened her until she genuinely feared for her ability to hear anything ever again. The cold seeped through the loose fitting uniform she wore and her fingers fumbled as she bound her ankles with ribbon.

The British forces had limited fuel, limited resources, and limited aircraft for training missions. The first 4 and up to 6 parachute training jumps were made from customized barrage balloons. Only the final "graduation" jump involved an actual airplane. Ruth's next jump from an airplane would be into enemy territory.

After four uneventful jumps from Barrage Balloons, Ruth had climbed on board this Avro Anson 652 with a cocky skip to her step that she almost immediately regretted. The training balloons had large gray wicker gondolas mocked up to simulate the Avro's cargo areas with bright painted lines and taped off lanes of approach. Other than a light breeze, the ride up in a balloon was completely silent, serene, even peaceful.

By contrast, once the heavy, noisy, smelly, all metal aircraft clawed its way free from the cradle of the earth, it felt as if her stomach had fallen out. She had never before flown in an airplane. To be heard over the powerful engines meant that the jump master had to scream in everyone's faces, nose to nose, at the top of his lungs. Everyone had to exaggerate their motions, pantomiming, using large, slow gestures as if playing a silly game of underwater charades. What she suddenly realized, despite nearly a month of airborne training, was that she was deathly afraid of flying.

After the horrible events during that bloody August in Hebron, her family had fled the ancient burial place of the patriarchs and traveled by truck to Tel Aviv. From there, they embarked on a ship to Barcelona, Spain. Then by bus, truck, and foot to their home in the wilds of central France. The first time Ruth had ever risen above an altitude of 3 stories had been in the training balloons.

Now, aboard this incredibly loud and apparently unsteady aircraft, this woman who had trained from birth to fight as a warrior, to face any situation with confidence and courage, realized that the emotion clawing at her far exceeded normal and perfectly healthy anxiety. She realized that the stark fear she felt bordered on panicked terror.

Ruth spared a glance at the man strapped in beside her, the agent code-named Augustine. Augustine knew her only by her code name as well; Grace. He made it sound like a curse each time he pronounced it. Next to him sat the agent code-named Scorpion, who appeared to be enjoying a nap. How was that man sleeping through the insane tilting, the occasional shuddering, and the unbelievable noise?

Augustine turned his head and stared back at her, his expression blank and somehow still mildly mocking, as if daring her to fail. He'd acted as her most vocal adversary, objecting to having her train with the men in the group. Most of the time, Ruth ignored him. Today, she worried he could read through her stoic expression and see the terror etched painfully into her heart.

Whispering a Hebrew prayer meant to focus her mind and calm her nerves, she watched the jump master open the door. She thought the sound of the engines was loud before. Now with the final barrier removed, her ears actually started to ache. The cargo bay suddenly filled with an acrid smell like burning kerosene as the exhaust from the nearby engine permeated the space.

Despite her previous thought that she'd left her stomach on the ground somewhere on the runway, she felt it fall again and a sick feeling of nausea rose up her throat. Might she get airsick? How humiliating would that be?

Then Ruth Aubertin, the SOE operative in training code-named Grace, came to the realization she most dreaded since the engines first fired up. She realized she couldn't do this.

Panic increased her heart rate. Adrenaline caused her skin to grow cold and her blood pressure to spike. She would freeze up in the door. She would cause the entire stick to miss their timed exit. She would have to leave the program in shame.

She saw little spots dance at the corners of her eyes. She tried to reason with herself, but she lost the internal argument. In the name of Jehovah God, she wouldn't have the strength of will to go out that door.

She watched the hand signals and knew that she had to move forward and crouch in a fetal position in front of the door. Gripping her static line by a four inch bite held tightly in her left fist, she slid that lifeline along the steel anchor-line cable that ran the length of the cabin floor. Slowly, inexorably, she approached the small door, thankful she had to fall to the ground since she didn't think her legs would continue to support her.

"God, help me. Just help me get out of this airplane. Please, Father!" Ruth mumbled a prayer.

She assumed the position and, at the not so gentle tap on her shoulder by the jump master, she closed her eyes, drew upon every ounce of strength she could muster, and rolled out of the door into the empty sky. The airplane's tail section vertical stabilizer whizzed by her face, close enough to touch had she felt so inclined. More than one trainee had sustained an injury by colliding with the Avro's tail section.

The jerk of the static line twisted her like a cheap yo-yo at the end of its string until the cotton webbing in the deployment bag separated from her silk circle, staying with the aircraft she had just abandoned. The shock of the flat circular canopy opening jarred the breath out of her body. Though her chin remained tucked tightly into her chest, the opening shock snapped her helmeted head forward and her chin punched against her sternum hard enough to bruise. Instantly, she looked up and grabbed the risers as high as she could reach while she watched the canopy of the parachute fill completely with air. She felt incredibly grateful that her suspension lines had not twisted and her risers had good separation all the way up to the skirt. Relinquishing the risers, Ruth snatched at her reserve parachute with both hands.

A parachute malfunction, a streamer, a cigarette roll, a Mae West, a blown gore, more than three broken suspension lines, or a ripped panel could mean that Ruth would have to immediately deploy her reserve parachute if she intended to live through the next few minutes. She kept her fingers tight on the stainless steel ring at her belly while she counted to four and inspected the gigantic umbrella overhead.

Her main parachute deployed into a nearly perfect circle, the leading edge folding and furling slightly in the gentle breeze. She relaxed her grip and uttered a quick prayer of thanks.

Almost immediately, the quiet engulfed her. This was the sensation she remembered from the Barrage Balloon training. For the first time since that dreadful machine left the ground, Ruth felt herself calming down. Parachutes, she could handle. Giant metal coffins with incredibly loud airplane engines, apparently not.

Taking the next few seconds to refocus herself and fight down the panic that had threatened to overwhelm her, Ruth fixed her eyes on the landscape below and took several calming breaths.

The stick had departed the aircraft at about two thousand feet above the ground. While it felt like she would just peacefully glide to the earth, the fact was that she was only in the air for about three minutes. One moment, it felt like she could float forever, the next, her brain registered the distance to the ground and her rate of descent and it felt like the ground suddenly rushed up to meet her. To avoid letting the feeling overwhelm her, Ruth clamped her jaw shut, fixed her eyes on the horizon, and concentrated on pushing her knees tightly together until impact.

When she felt the ground hit the balls of her feet, Ruth executed a passable parachute landing fall. They had rehearsed this hundreds of times, leaping from a three foot platform into a soggy sawdust pit. When the balls of her feet touched the ground, she relaxed and let her body fall to the right. Her calves rolled her onto her buttocks, then onto her shoulders. The maneuver allowed her small, light frame to absorb the brunt of the impact without injury, though she hit with such force that she ended up rolling over twice.

It took her a moment to catch her breath as the adrenaline rushed through her veins. The parachute began to catch air and tug on her. She quickly rolled onto her knees and released the left capewell while screaming "Riser!" just in case anyone was nearby. The whip-lashing riser buckle flung outward by her collapsing canopy could easily take out an unwary eye.

No longer worried about being dragged across the drop zone by her parachute, Ruth took her helmet off, annoyed at her shaking fingers and weak knees. She clawed at the ribbon binding her ankles until the knot surrendered and normal circulation began to restore the feeling in her toes. After the canopy fully collapsed, she loosened her harness and unstrapped the reserve parachute. She opened her kit bag, which she had worn tightly folded and tucked up inside her leg straps, and gathered the silk canopy into the roomy cotton duffel. Feeling calmer the longer she worked, she rolled it into an 'S' roll hand over forearm and packed it into her kit bag along with her reserve parachute and heavy steel parachutist helmet.

As soon as she finished, she dragged the bag behind her by one handle as she walked toward the recovery point. The bag weighed about ninety pounds. Since she barely breached one-twenty, carrying it would exhaust her, which she considered rather foolish. So, she dragged it until she spied Augustine and Scorpion. Then she heaved the bag over her shoulders and caught up with them, feeling her muscles burn with the exertion. As she drew closer, she noticed that Augustine had stripped down to his white linen T-shirt and trousers, which puzzled her.

"Hi guys," she greeted, straightening the cap on her black curls. "How was your jump?" No sooner had she asked then she noticed Augustine's limp. She also noticed that he dragged his kit bag on his uniform blouse, using the shirt like some sort of makeshift sled. "You okay, Auggie?"

He snarled at her, but did not reply. He had never pretended to like the fact that she was part of their class. She let his rudeness roll off of her shoulders, knowing that half of his issues stemmed from her besting him in the boxing ring.

Instead, she eyed Scorpion with a raised eyebrow. "Feet and knees together, the jump masters all said," he repeated with a half grin. "You'll break your legs, the jump masters said. Some of the more thick in this class apparently need object lessons."

"It's just sprained," Augustine asserted. "I'm sure of it."

Scorpion kept his tone completely droll. "Perhaps Grace can loan you her pretty ribbons and you can tie your ankles together like a girl when you jump into wherever it is you're going next. What do you say, old boy?"

Ruth smiled and reached for Augustine's kit bag. "Need help?"

Augustine stopped and she watched his pale face turn bright red. She had never seen a man's pallor change so completely in just a few heartbeats. "What have I ever done or said that would make you think that I'd want or need your help?"

"*Chacun à son goût.*" To each his own, she answered with a shrug, not realizing she'd switched to French. The language was so much easier for her than English. Apparently, Augustine was angry enough that he didn't realize he'd switched to French as well.

"I'll tell you what I need help with. This blouse here is going to have some mad grass and dirt stains on it when I get to the rally point. Why don't you be a good girl and handle that for me?"

She clucked her tongue. "Poor Augustine," she said, shifting the straps of her kit bag. "First, I beat you up in the boxing ring. Next, I jog my little self to the rally point while you limp behind me. I wonder, will you always come in second to me?"

She started off at a jog again and smiled as she looked over her shoulder, "*Au revoir, garçons.* I'll ask the truck to wait for you."

She moved as quickly as the heavy kit bag allowed and considered Augustine's childish attitude. What did he mean, be a good girl and take care of his shirt? She knew he meant it as an insult. She simply didn't understand what kind of insult he intended. Was he implying he wouldn't know how to get stains out of his own clothing? Wouldn't that make him inferior to her? She could get all kinds of stains, including blood, out of all kinds of fabric. Hopefully the man was a good spy. Otherwise, he might be utterly useless.

In her time here, Ruth had learned that she had to perform identical tasks better or faster than her male counterparts. Consequently, she didn't mind jogging all the way back to the rally point. She would admit to no one how exhausted her stomach and leg muscles felt after carrying that weight at a jog.

When she reached the tarmac of the recovery point, one of the jump masters lifted the bag from her shoulders as if it weighed no more than a cup of tea. "Well done, Grace. Good show running the length of the drop zone. Of course, this was your graduation jump so you could have walked, you know."

Ruth grinned, took a few deep, unencumbered breaths, and shrugged. "Felt like a run."

The jump master chuckled. "Well, it's a good day for a run whilst carrying half your weight. Don't forget to fill your canteen and don't forget to drink it all when you get back to barracks."

He tossed her kit bag into the back of the truck. Ruth climbed in next to it. She was the first one there. It made no sense because she'd been the first one out of the plane so she had landed furthest from the recovery point. She leaned against the kit bag and closed her eyes, idly wondering how much the silk parachute beneath her head might bring on the black market if she were actually inclined to try selling it.

When she first arrived at the training grounds to become a member of Britain's intelligence community, most of the men had treated her with condescension, not just because she was a woman, but because she was a foreign woman, a fact betrayed by her accented English. Over the last several weeks, as she had shown her mastery of weaponry, hand-to-hand combat, espionage, and basic survival skills, she had gained respect from about half the class, and contemptuous derision from the other half. She had gained no friends among her male counterparts. That had surprised her. Her brothers and father had always treated her with equality. She didn't understand the blatant sexism, or this culture that had obviously produced it. It took her some time to learn not to even bother trying to forge friendships with the male British operatives.

Regardless, she refused to let it matter to her. Her high skill level and her intended mission had her training with the men instead of the women, but she still bunked with the women, dined with them, and over the course of time had developed a very strong bond with the six other women on her special team – Major Charlene Radden's Heavenly Virtues.

Charlene had put together a team of women strong in faith and skill, an experiment that her superiors had condescended to allow her to undertake. The women prayed together, read their Bibles together, and encouraged each other. They neared the end of training now, and they would all soon serve together as well.

She wondered what the friends she had grown to know and love would think of her if they knew she came from a Jewish heritage, though she had long ago accepted Yeshua as Christ Messiah. She wondered if they knew that she kept her father's prayer shawl with its beautifully embroidered *phylacteries* in her room and used it to cover her head to pray in private. Would they still consider her a friend?

Thinking of the quality of women that comprised the Virtues team, she thought perhaps they would still love her and ignore cultural prejudice. Sometimes she wanted to tell them everything – about the massacre in Hebron that she'd witnessed as a young girl, about the loss of life and family, about living in the wild and training and training and training.

Of course, she could never say anything. They had to do their jobs as secretly as possible, and that meant no personal information shared between them. That way the Nazi pigs couldn't use them against each other in the event of capture.

Ruth checked her watch. They would head back for the graduation ceremony soon. Doubtless, the colonel would have some words of wisdom and inspiration to impart. Then, the Sergeant Major would inspect the ranks and hand each of the graduates a set of cloth parachutist wings that they were to sew onto the right shoulder of their dress uniforms.

She hoped she would have time for a quick cup of tea before meeting her friends at the pub. Her formative years, spent in near isolation with just her brothers and father, lent her a somewhat male-centric outlook on life. It surprised her how much she had grown to love the female interaction with her friends. She would relish it while she could. Soon Ruth would have to go to work – and do the job she'd trained for her entire life.

████

BACK at the camp, she jumped out of the truck and turned her gear in. Then she went into the barracks and climbed the stairs to her room. As she entered the spartan quarters, she stopped short when she saw her roommate, Charity.

No two roommates could be any more different. While Ruth was tall and lean, with dark hair cropped short and dark brown eyes, Charity was small, round, with bright red hair and beautifully smooth skin.

Charity wasn't like the other trainees. Most of them had focused training that would send them into the field. Charity would serve on the home front, at Intelligence headquarters. She had a masterful mind when it came to puzzles and patterns. Ruth was not supposed to know that her husband, a captain in the Royal Air Force, had been taken prisoner by the Germans months before. In his correspondence to her, he'd hidden an encrypted message. Charity broke the code and took it to the Intelligence Office. She attended the training to strengthen her code making and code breaking skills so that she and her husband could pass on helpful information.

Today, Charity sat on her bed, back against the wall, and stared at a paper in front of her. An envelope lay on the bed next to her.

"Is that a letter from your husband?" Ruth asked.

"Yes. A real letter this time. Not a work letter." A single tear rolled down her cheek. She tossed the letter on the bed and covered her face with her hands. "I'm so scared for him. I can't believe he's taken this on."

Ruth knelt next to the bed and took put her hand on her friend's knee. "He's doing what he has to. Just like you are."

"And you," Charity said. "How am I going to cope here once you're over in France? I worry enough about Tom. Now I need to add you and the others to my concern."

"Just add us to your prayers," Ruth said, smiling as she stood. A light tap-tap on the door preceded Temperance into the room.

"Got marching orders," she said, holding up an envelope. "I have to be in the hangar with Faith at twenty-one hundred. You should see the wireless they gave me. It is a beauty."

"So soon?" Charity asked, sitting straighter. "Why so soon?"

"They haven't heard from their other operator over there in a few weeks. They can only assume that he's been captured." Temperance was taller than Charity, but shorter than Ruth, with straight brown hair she wore cut to her chin. With big green eyes and full pouty lips, she turned the head of more than one man on their training base.

"You can only assume that he's a he," Ruth said with a smirk. Then she realized how that sounded. "Not that I'm making light of this," she said. She often forgot that the rest of the group hadn't spent their entire existence in training, that they had softer hearts than she often felt like she had.

"Of course not," Temperance said. She put a hand to her stomach. "I guess it's not too late to back out if I was considering it," she said.

Ruth looked at her watch. "Let's go find the other girls. We'll be together tonight, us seven, one last time."

"I think that's a novel idea. I'm going to need all the together I can get. After this, I'm going to be alone."

♛ ♛ ♛ ♛

THEY found their friends in the dining hall, cardboard cups of tea in front of them. The agent code-named Mercy, Scottish surgeon turned under-cover nurse intelligence operative, had her crimson curls strategically pinned back. She glanced up and saw them coming, then smiled and waved.

Across from Mercy, Prudence made notations in a leather-bound book. Her blonde hair swung unbound to her shoulders, brushing against the pink material of her dress. Her accent and mannerisms clearly indicated affluence and nobility. Despite being unable to talk about anything personal, she had admitted that her husband currently served in North Africa and Prudence had joined the intelligence community at his bidding.

Next to Prudence, Faith dumped two heaping spoonfuls of sugar into her tea. A native Texan, she much preferred coffee over the traditional English drink, but claimed the coffee in the canteen tasted like watered down tea, anyway. Faith was the youngest in the group, at just 19.

"Hello, ladies," Ruth greeted in heavily accented English while sliding onto the bench next to Prudence. "How was today?"

"I'm sure my suturing class had nothing on jumping from an airplane," Mercy observed, her voice thick with her Scottish brogue. "Never saw the point of jumping from a plane that can land. Of course, my medical degree didn't prevent them from sending me to suturing class, either."

"Did you end up teaching it?" Ruth asked.

"You rather know it." Mercy snickered. "I seriously believe that's why Clarence keeps sending me. He knows I'll end up teaching them something and they're not too proud to learn from a lass." She looked at Ruth and addressed her by her code name. "What about you, Grace? How did the jump go?"

"Let's just say I'm glad it's over," Ruth said. "The truth is I've never really felt such fear. Quite honestly, once I get to France, I don't intend to ever leave again if it means I have to get into another airplane."

"The thought of jumping out of a plane again does horrible things to my stomach," Temperance said. "Even though I've already done it twice."

Ruth shrugged. "It might have been easier if I'd known that I had a friend next to me, instead of Augustine with all of his constipated fury."

"I wish they'd let you train with us," Faith said in her iconic cowgirl drawl. "It ain't fair that you have to do it separate."

She hadn't had a female friend since she left Hebron, so she didn't understand Faith's pouty nature. But, she understood the words and thought she should address them. "Well, I'm more skilled than you. It would waste a great deal of my time."

Faith snickered, confusing Ruth even further. "The more I talk with you, the more I like you, Gracey. You sure you ain't from Texas?"

Prudence put an arm around her shoulder. "I, for one, am thrilled that you're the one who'll be working with us. It'll be nice to know you're the one who's covering our backs." Ruth knew Prudence was training to be a courier, one of the more dangerous jobs in their field. One of Ruth's tasks would be to protect Prudence from discovery, especially while carrying money or information.

"Where's Hope?" Temperance asked.

Faith raised an eyebrow, but did not speak. Ruth knew that meant she had left to begin her mission. "So it begins," Prudence said.

Ruth replied with a quote from a verse in Ecclesiastes. "Better is the end of a thing than the beginning." All of her life had served as the beginning. She felt anxious to start the end.

"You girls have trained so hard," Charity said. "I know that God will be with us."

Mercy looked down the table. "Do you think we'll all be together again?"

Ruth replied, "Maybe not on this side of glory."

Mercy took a deep breath. "I have loved every minute of the time we have spent together. What happens next is scary and unknown."

Prudence took a sip of her tea. "Temperance and I leave tonight. I for one am so very grateful for this chance. Let's do us proud out there."

Charity answered her. "God has equipped us for this time. I know that."

A murmur of assent washed across the table. Faith said, "He gifted us, then He opened doors. My hat's off to every one of y'all for walking through those doors." She lifted her cup in a toast. "We could have each found a dozen different excuses to sit back and observe this war from the sidelines, but we didn't. If nothing else, we are to be commended for that. Now, let's go kick some Nazi tail and make sure we all meet back again in our little pub when this is all done."

Those with cups raised them in agreement with her. Ruth looked at the clock on the wall and felt antsy, anticipatory. She wanted to be flying out with Temperance and Prudence now. Right now. But, she had to wait. She stood. "I have to go change out of these jump clothes. Early supper at the pub later?"

They set the time to meet for dinner, then Ruth left the dining hall. Impatient at the waiting game, she shoved her hands in her pockets and walked through the beautiful gardens of the estate that housed the training grounds. She paused at the stone fountain that sat in the center of the lawn and stared at the empty pool. Dried, brown leaves lined the bottom. She imagined that there was a time when this fountain spouted beautiful clear water into the air, welcoming guests arriving on the estate. How different life was now for the people who had lived normal lives until the start of the war. Now they had to deal with such disruption and uncertainty.

Ruth imagined that she and her brothers had it better than most. They'd known it would come and had simply waited. Now, it felt like their purpose for existence presented itself – and rather than the burden of a disrupted life, it was more like the culmination of everything for which they'd trained and waited.

She knew the time would come very quickly when Charlene would fire the proverbial starting gun. She was ready.

〈 〈 〈 〈

Chapter Three

"PRUDENCE and Temperance will be in their locations by now," Charlene announced, sliding a file folder across the desk toward Ruth. "You will parachute in tonight. Your flight leaves at twenty-three hundred hours."

Ruth flipped open the folder and found her identification. It listed her name as Lucienne Maitre. "I thought we wanted to keep first names to avoid slipping up?" They spoke in French, because it was easier and clearer for Ruth than English.

"We can't risk it. Ruth is not a common French name. It is, however, a common Jewish name. I'd rather something so simple not be the cause of compromising your cover."

Ruth felt anger burn deep and low in her stomach. She kept her voice even. "Major, to be clear, I am neither afraid of the Nazi swine, nor ashamed of my heritage."

Charlene sat back and raised a perfectly trimmed eyebrow. "Nor should you be. I'm thrilled you're on my team. But, I can't have you in a position to be quickly rounded up by the Gestapo and placed in a labor camp due to some ill-conceived ideas of what makes a perfect human being. You'd be absolutely no use to me in that case and you're one of the most valued members of my organization."

Ruth clenched her fist, but hid it on her lap. "You're right, of course," she said. "I'm not trying to be prideful."

"Let's get back to the business at hand," Charlene said. She reached forward and hit a button on her desk. Ruth could hear a loud buzz come from beyond the door behind her. Seconds later, the door opened and Matthew emerged. Ruth gasped in surprise and couldn't stop a smile before it emerged. She hadn't seen him or John in almost a year.

He looked a little leaner. He did not wear a standard military uniform, but rather a suit and tie. His shirt looked like it could use a press and his shoes a shine. Ruth imagined he must have changed clothes on the flight to the island.

"*Shalom*, Ruth," he greeted. She stood to greet him. He put his hands on her shoulders and kissed both of her cheeks. He continued in Hebrew. "It is so good to see you."

"And you," she said, this time allowing a smile. She switched to French. "I thought Charlene had eaten you up and spit you out."

"If only," he said, grinning at Charlene in reply.

Charlene snorted. "Matthew has been making arrangements in France. He just arrived back this morning."

"What are our plans?"

Matthew gestured to the two chairs in front of Charlene's desk and waited for Ruth to sit before taking the seat beside her. "The intelligence network on the ground is beginning the process to break 110 prisoners out of the jail in Valeurville. We have already placed one person inside the jail, but the identity of that one is highly classified and the operative will have no contact with anyone." Matthew hooked his foot on his knee and leaned back in the chair.

Charlene nodded and continued. "Mercy will go to work in the hospital that also provides care to the prisoners. She'll go with you tonight. Matthew, here, will take her to her contact and help establish her residency with the other nurses. Charity is communicating with her husband from inside, and Matthew has started sorting out the groundwork. They're in the process of building a POW camp. Our contact inside will let us know if the prisoners will be moved any time soon. But for now, it looks like they're keeping them there for a good bit of time."

Ruth opened the file folder again. "What is my cover?"

Charlene leaned back slightly. "You've been given a position as a waitress in a café. The owner is part of our network. You'll have to work at least three shifts a week, enough to have customers remember you. You'll monitor Prudence's movements and provide discreet protection. I don't even want her to know you're there. You'll assist Matthew in the planning and execution of the prison break and any other missions as they come up."

Ruth frowned. "Who else will be working with Matthew and me?"

Her brother answered. "There's already a network in place. I've been meeting with them for the last six months. They know you're coming."

"Matthew is second in command to Praetorian, who is currently in charge. If something happens to him, your brother is to take over the operations in area three."

Ruth turned to her brother. "What is your code name? What do I call you?"

Matthew shook his head. "We're fairly certain my code name was compromised three months ago. Just call me Matthew."

"Your actual name?"

"It's a common name."

With a nod, Ruth turned back to Charlene and shut the file folder. "I shall be ready to go tonight."

"This is a night jump," Matthew said. "Are you ready for that?"

Although her pulse fluttered at the thought of jumping out of a plane into utter darkness, Ruth replied, "Of course."

☗ ☗ ☗ ☗

RUTH sat next to Matthew and Mercy on the plane. No one spoke. From the pilot seat, Faith looked behind her at the small group and smiled, throwing them a thumb's up. Matthew responded before Ruth could.

"Y'all get ready to hop out!" Faith shouted, spinning a single finger above her head in a circular motion. "We're coming up on your stop on this here milk run."

Braking, Faith brought the airplane to nearly stall speed, holding her "low and slow" as she crossed the drop zone. Matthew unstrapped himself from the jump seat and hooked his static line to the anchor line cable. Mercy and Ruth followed his actions, hooking up as the copilot bounded out of his seat. He verified that all three of them had properly hooked their static lines to the steel anchor-line cable before he opened the door and stowed it in the rear of the plane.

Cool evening air billowed into the plane. The sharp smell of engine exhaust reminded her of the kerosene burning lamps they would light at night when she was just a girl. The noise inside the cabin became nearly unbearable.

Desperate to get out the metal beast, she willed Matthew to give the command to jump. Wanting to think of something other than the terror threatening to overwhelm all of her senses, she placed a hand on Mercy's shoulder and leaned forward to speak in her ear. "Godspeed, sister. I will be praying for you and our mission."

Mercy did not reply, but reached up and covered Ruth's hand with her chilled fingertips. At the go signal, Matthew scooted out the door. His static line slapped against the doorframe and the side of the aircraft a few times. A few seconds later, Mercy vanished in a similar manner. Ruth did not pause, though she desperately wanted to. Instead, she drew deeply from a well of courage and forced herself to exit the airplane.

The silence that surrounded her was almost shocking after the loud engines of the plane. She could still hear the engines as Faith brought the aircraft back up to speed for the short flight home, but the sound grew fainter and fainter very quickly. Her canopy fully deployed and all she could hear was the rushing of the wind in her ears. She could see nothing in the moonless night. Instead, she used her other senses to help her determine when the ground would rush up to meet her.

This flight hadn't been as bad as the other. Perhaps the simple knowledge that Faith piloted the airplane had kept the fear from overtaking every other sense. Or, perhaps the fact that she'd already jumped out of a plane and survived gave her mind experience that told her all would be well.

After executing a rough, but mostly proper parachute landing fall, she untied her ankles and rushed around, gathering her parachute and stuffing it into her kit bag. Her heart raced but she didn't feel panic. Whatever the outcome, she felt grateful that her arms weren't weak with fear as she gathered her parachute and stuffed the bright white silk in the tan kit bag.

Once she got her bearings, she rushed to the edge of the tree line and entered the woods. She had a different rendezvous point than Mercy and Matthew so she would have to travel alone. She'd memorized the map of the surrounding area, so, using the small luminous compass attached to the strap of her bag, she moved quickly, quietly, and efficiently through the woods.

Half a kilometer outside of town, she found the dirt path and followed it to a cabin on the edge of a stream. She crouched behind a bush and took out her flashlight, aiming it at the dark window by the door. She quickly turned the flashlight on, off, on, then off again and waited. Seconds later, someone inside the cabin returned the signal, and she left her crouched position and jogged to the door just as it opened and the lights inside the cabin came on.

"How was the flight?" Scorpion asked, taking her kit bag from her.

"Uneventful." She looked around the nearly empty cabin and saw the closed door on the other side of the room.

Scorpion nodded confirmation. "Clothes are in there."

Without speaking, she went into the small lavatory and stripped out of her jumpsuit and boots. On the back of the door hung a blue dress and cotton stockings, and in no time she buttoned the last button at the collar. She folded the jump suit and set it on top of the boots, taking her identification and money out of the inner pocket.

When she came out, Scorpion stood from the chair by the cold fireplace and tossed his cigarette butt into the hearth. He gestured at the suitcase by the door. "Some changes of clothes in there," he said. "You know where to go from here?"

"Yes." She picked up the suitcase and walked to the door.

Scorpion put his hand on the door but didn't open it. She looked up at him, puzzled. He said, "Godspeed, Grace."

She turned back toward the door, waiting for him to open it, but looked over her shoulder and gave him a half smile. "Victory," she replied.

Hauling the light bag, she cut west through the woods to the train station and waited for the train to arrive. After ten minutes, she walked down the road toward town as if she had just arrived. Should anyone challenge her as a single woman walking on the road, she had a train ticket stub from her supposed home town along with a letter of employment from the diner in her pocket.

Her eyes skimmed over the buildings as she entered the town. She saw the top of the jail almost immediately and then caught a glimpse of the hospital roof just down the hill. She followed the directions she had memorized and went the opposite direction, toward the docks. There she found the café where she would make her temporary home.

It was breakfast time when she opened the door. The smell of baking bread and brewing coffee tantalized her, making her empty stomach growl. Walking to the counter, she pulled the letter out of her pocket and smiled at the gray-haired woman in the stained apron. "*Bonjour*," she greeted, "I'm Lucienne Maitre. I start today, do I not?"

The huge smile she got in return told her that this woman was in the know. "Good morning," she said, "I'm Eileen. My husband and I run the café." She set the tray of dirty dishes on the counter and wiped her hands on a towel. "Come with me. I have a room for you upstairs. Have you eaten? No? You're in luck. We have eggs today."

Chapter Four

RUTH took a basket of salt shakers to the table next to the four-top table of German officers and sat with her back to them, listening intently to their hushed conversation spoken in German while she slowly refilled the salt. She caught occasional words: dignitaries, prison officials, general someone and colonel someone else. She wished she could hear every word, but they spoke so quietly it made it nearly impossible to make anything out.

"Waitress," the one immediately behind her demanded in French.

Unobserved, she closed her eyes, said a quick prayer for endurance, and released a slow breath. Then she stood and turned, smiling her most coy, flirtatious smile.

"Oui, monsieur?"

"Coffee," he demanded, holding up his cup.

"But of course, *monsieur*," Ruth answered. She rushed to the counter and returned with the pot of coffee, refilling each cup. She paused when she finished, her hand on the shoulder of the man closest to her. "Would you like anything else?"

She intentionally let the question hang in the air while she endured the supposedly knowing glances from the pig Nazis. The one across the table against the wall smiled. "Perhaps later?"

She giggled. "Perhaps."

When she returned to her work near them, she heard that the conversation had switched from whatever quiet conversation they had been having before to the quality of French girls here in Valeurville. Ruth kept her lip from curling in disgust as she finished her task and returned the salt shakers to their proper tables.

She glanced at the clock and noted that she had five minutes left in her shift before she had to prepare for a meeting with Matthew and Abiel. Just as she walked back behind the counter, the door opened and her replacement came into the café. She slipped her apron over her head and offered a casual wave of greeting as she left the dining room and rushed up the stairs to her room.

She missed the presence of Charity. In her months of training at the camp, she had grown accustomed to having a female roommate. Now she lived a life of solitude in her stark little room with the single bed, nightstand, and wooden chair.

She changed out of her waitress uniform and pulled on a simple linen dress. After she grabbed her hat and purse off the top of the wardrobe, she stopped by the mirror and took a moment to refresh her lipstick. Satisfied that she looked like any young French woman headed out for an afternoon of gaiety, she headed back down the stairs.

One of the German officers from the table inside waited near the back door. She'd halfway expected that. She slowed her walk to a casual stroll and batted her eyes. "Afternoon, *Herr Oberst*."

He leaned against the wall and casually lit a cigarette. "*Kapitan*," he corrected, though her apparently unintentional promotion clearly flattered him. "Hi." As he pulled the cigarette out of his mouth, he used the same hand to gesture behind him at the café. In appalling French, he asked, "Did you mean what you meant in there?"

It took her a moment to decipher what he intended to say. "Well," she said slowly, "I'm not sure what you mean."

"Would you like to go drink me?" His French was horrible. He closed his eyes and shook his head, his cheeks brightening to red. "Get a drink with me."

"I'd love to." A romantically involved captain might be useful. His demeanor suggested he would not be overly dangerous. She'd have to clear it with headquarters, though. "I can't immediately, though. Are you free at dinner tonight?"

She had overheard that he had a formation at eighteen hundred hours and wouldn't be free tonight, which made it safe to ask.

He shook his head. "No."

Ruth pouted her lip. "Too bad."

He took another puff on the cigarette. "I have mornings and lunch free."

She smiled and slipped her hat onto her head. "I'm off tomorrow. Would you like to join me for breakfast?"

With a grin, he straightened and tossed the half smoked butt onto the wet pavement. "*Ja.*" With a hand to his chest, he said, "I am Christof."

"Lucienne."

He actually clicked his heels together. "I will see you tomorrow morning, Lucienne."

When he turned to walk away, she made sure to go the opposite direction, crisscrossing through town before entering the hotel by the wharf. Casually, she strolled through the busy lobby, into the dining area, through the door to the kitchen, and down the basement stairs. She rapped her knuckles three times on the door at the base of the stairs, paused, and rapped two more times. Immediately, the door opened and she found herself face to face with the agent code-named Abiel.

He glared at her with his icy green eyes. "You're thirty minutes late."

"*Oui, je sais.*" She smiled as she pushed by him. "I can tell time, too." When she saw her brother was already there, she lifted her hand in a greeting. "*Shalom*, brother."

"*Shalom.*" He walked toward her, staring intently at her face, reading whatever was there. "What detained you?"

"A German captain with a schoolboy crush." She set her purse down and pulled a chair out from under the table. "I need permission to have breakfast with him in the morning."

Matthew cocked his head and raised an eyebrow while Abiel sat across from her. "Why?"

She shrugged. "He's harmless. And could prove useful. He and a group at the café were talking about people coming to visit. High ranking people. I tried to get the information, but they were speaking too quietly. So, he's clearly a viable intelligence asset."

"Name?" Abiel asked.

"Christof. The surname on the tag on his uniform said Kappel."

He nodded and made a notation in a notebook. "I'll get word to you in a few hours."

Ruth gestured at the map spread on the table. "What's this?"

"The new supply route for the prison camp." Matthew pointed to an area north of town. The map had no markings or notations on it in case it was captured or compromised. "This is a narrow road below the mountain ravine that edges this cliff. We're going to blow the side of the mountain and block the road."

"When?"

Abiel looked at his watch. "Car will be here in seven minutes." He gestured to a dressing screen behind him. "You can change back there."

She glanced at the clock and at him again. "In broad daylight?"

Matthew snorted, as if trying to contain a laugh. When she looked at him, he shrugged. "I'm sorry. I just said exactly the same thing."

Abiel tapped the map. "There's a massive delivery coming before dark. If we blow it now, we'll be able to stop it from coming for a very long time. Every delivery we hinder is time lost on the completion of the camp and more time for a thorough plan for the prison breakout."

It made sense, despite the danger with a daylight mission. "What's our cover?"

"Reine is driving. She's picked up a picnic and all of the accoutrements. We're just two couples, headed out to a romantic picnic in the countryside."

Ruth walked behind the screen and saw a pair of pants and a button down shirt. "If I'm on a picnic with my lover, should I wear slacks?"

"That can be your decision," Matthew said from the other side of the screen. "We have some pretty heavy terrain to maneuver. You can try it in a dress and those shoes, but you'll find it easier in the pants."

She mentally went through the pros and cons and finally settled on changing clothes. She'd add a fancy scarf for her hair, though, and freshen her lipstick. When she came from behind the screen, she carried her boots. "What kind of explosives are we using?"

"The section we're looking at is already pretty precarious. We don't need anything too fancy or too expensive." Matthew slid a photo across the table so that she could look at it while she tied her boot. "Simple TNT with a five minute fuse will be perfect. We'll dislodge this rock and this rock and the two should fall nicely and cause an avalanche."

Boots tied, Ruth reached for the picture and looked at it as closely as possible. "Anyone been on the ground to confirm?"

"Yes. Our bomb makers have been here for a week." Abiel pulled a revolver out of a box and opened the cylinder to check the rounds. He spun it once and clipped it shut, then tucked the pistol into his belt at his back. He put a hat on his head and smiled, the smile transforming his face into boy-next-door handsome. "Ready?"

When they met Reine, the beautiful blonde local girl laughed and hugged Matthew as if they were young, fresh lovers. Ruth kept her arm draped through Abiel's and giggled as he opened the back door of the car for her. The two girls slid into the back seat as Matthew took the driver's wheel. He carefully and casually drove out of town, toward the mountain pass. Once unobserved, the interior of the car stayed relatively sober and quiet.

About two kilometers from the target location, they pulled off the road and found a flowering tree. Reine spread out the picnic blanket beneath the shade of the tree while Abiel set out the picnic. Matthew loaded the backpack with the TNT and he and Ruth set out at a jog. About 100 meters from the cliff edge, they ducked down and walked the rest of the way.

Ruth left Matthew setting the charges while she climbed onto the rocks and surveyed the road below. She could see no sign of a lookout or enemy presence. Using binoculars, she checked all around, looking for any sign of human life. At Matthew's signal, she climbed down from the rocks. Just in case someone stopped them on the way back, he left the backpack there since they had no excuse for carrying it around empty.

They ran back to where Abiel and Reine waited. Just as they approached the picnic area, Ruth heard the explosion as the timed charge from the slow fuse detonated. She automatically ducked, even though they were far enough away that no debris could touch them. Gratefully, she took the canteen from Abiel and took a long swallow, feeling a trickle of sweat slide down her temple from the two kilometer run.

"Do you think the rocks blocked the road?" Reine asked.

"The munitions expert told me exactly where to place the charges. If he was right, then the road is well buried and blocked." Matthew took back the canteen from Ruth and drained it. "We can't check."

"No. We've done all we can, whether it worked or not." Abiel gestured at the picnic cloth on the ground. He and Reine had set out a partially consumed meal to give the appearance of all of them having spent some time in that spot. "Shall we pack it all up?"

Ruth grabbed a bunch of grapes and popped two into her mouth. "Give me just a moment. I'm starving."

Matthew tossed her a corner of cheese while he and Reine packed the concocted picnic. She sat on a rock near Abiel, who watched the nearby road with binoculars. "What's next on our dance card?"

He kept the binoculars to his eyes. "Every week we gain in hindering the building of that POW camp is another week we gain in preparation for the prison escape. At the moment, that is our primary concern."

"Are we on schedule?"

He lowered the lenses and looked at her with serious, tired eyes. "Yes." He went back to watching the road. "Go ahead and keep your date in the morning. I'll let you know if HQ wants it to continue."

Matthew spoke up as he shook the blanket out. "Need backup?"

Ruth snorted. "With *Kapitan* Christof Kappel? Hardly."

Matthew grinned and took the blanket to the car.

⋓⋓⋓⋓

RUTH sat in the passenger's seat of the car and watched Prudence walk down the sidewalk toward the busy café. She studied the people all around Prudence more than she watched the blonde spy. Did anyone stare at her too long? Did anyone signal anyone else? She knew that her friend carried a large amount of cash on her, cash to pay for a supply of explosives. She would certainly have a hard time explaining why she had so much money.

In the driver's seat, Matthew watched the men in the lumber yard to make sure no one there had any kind of reaction to Prudence's approach. "Looks all clear," he said.

Ruth nodded. "Same here." As Prudence entered the café, she spared a glance at her brother. "Have you heard talks of the labor camps?"

His lips thinned. "I heard they arrested thousands of Jews in Paris. Papa prepared us, but I don't know if even he understood the magnitude of the evil we face. There's a camp built outside of Krakow in Poland – Auschwitz they call it. The intelligence attached to the place is beyond belief. It's a death camp. The powers that be are denying it's even possible."

She felt an initial reaction of fear, much like she felt before getting on the airplane to come here. Ruth didn't know how to battle this fear and she didn't like it. She tried to distance herself and stay logical. "It's been systematic for years. It's possible. I don't know if people even understand the level of exploitation they've endured by the Nazis and their pig leader." She refocused her attention on the café just as Prudence exited. "Here she comes."

She paused on the sidewalk just as a large Opel Blitz truck rumbled past.

With her skirt still billowing from the wake left by the truck, she stepped into the street and crossed. She walked right by the car in which Ruth and Matthew sat waiting and watching, but if she saw them, she didn't let on. Matthew tapped Ruth's shoulder and nodded toward a German soldier just as he tossed down a cigarette and started following Prudence.

"I'll go," Ruth said, her hand on the door handle.

"Give her a minute." He looked beyond the man and scanned the crowd in front of the café. "I don't think he's working with anyone."

"She –"

"Is trained. Let her handle it until you know she can't."

Ruth sighed and sat back, keeping her hand on the door handle as Prudence ducked into an alley. The soldier's shoulder hit the corner of the brick wall as he turned to follow her.

"I don't think he's onto her. I think he's just drunk," Matthew observed. "And lonely."

"Looking for a good time with a pretty French girl," Ruth agreed through clenched teeth. She waited to a count of sixty before opening the car door. "It's been too long." As she slipped out of the car, she grabbed the pistol she kept stashed under the seat and pressed it against her thigh. She dashed toward the alley and paused, listening. Someone ran toward the entrance and suddenly stopped. Ruth waited one heartbeat, then two, then stepped into the alley and immediately spotted Prudence pressed up against the brick wall. A second later, she heard her gasp.

"What are you doing here?"

"I was with Abiel when he came to collect the money." Ruth looked beyond Prudence but couldn't see the Nazi anywhere. "I watched the Nazi pig following you."

Prudence put a shaking hand to her chest. "He tried to assault me, but I fought him off."

"Fought him off? Where is the swine?" The thought of the liberties these men thought they could take with the local population made Ruth's blood boil.

Prudence raised an eyebrow, clearly noticing the vehemence in Ruth's voice. "Dead, I think. Or dying. Over there."

Dead or dying? Impressed, Ruth rushed into the alley. She spotted his dirty boots first, then the rest of him. There, his head lying in a pool of blood, the filthy man lay staring blankly at the sky. She almost spit on him, but caught herself. Instead, she went back to Prudence. "You killed him. Good work."

She could see the shock settling into Prudence's face as the confirmation that she'd actually killed a man started to hit home. "Is he anyone of consequence?"

Now she would start thinking about who he might be, where he might come from, what kind of family he might have. Ruth could do nothing for her friend. This kind of battle had to be waged internally. She had found that killing another human being was remarkably easy. Dealing with the emotional consequence later was not at all easy. Every time she took a life, even the life of an enemy, she felt remorse. Ruth shook her head. "Never seen him. He's an *Unteroffizier*. A junior sergeant. He was probably with the new work detail that just arrived last night. Came from the coast from the look of his uniform."

Prudence put her hands on Ruth's arms. "What do we do now?"

Ruth scanned the street around them. "Go. Get out of here before you're found out."

"What about you?"

She laughed. She couldn't help herself. Having friends who cared for her warmed the anger that tried to freeze her heart. "I am a ghost to these clumsy pigs. They still don't see me." She put a hand on Prudence's shoulder, trying to offer her silent comfort. "God be with you, my friend."

"And also with you," Prudence recited with no emotion, as if by rote. Her face had paled so that even her lips looked white. But, she turned to leave and the second she stepped far enough out of the alley that Ruth knew Matthew would see her, she rushed back to the body. An inspection of the site revealed nothing that would indicate a struggle. She rushed back to the car just as she saw Prudence board a bus. Good.

"Do you have any wine in the trunk?" she asked.

Matthew nodded and got out of the car to open the trunk. "What happened?"

"She killed him. I need to fix the scene."

Matthew looked interested, but didn't seek any further details. "Need help?"

Ruth pulled a military pocket knife out of her pocket and opened the corkscrew. "I don't think so. Give me a few minutes and I'll meet you around the block."

She looked all around before rushing back into the alley. Arriving at the corpse, she opened the wine bottle, then wiped her fingerprints from it. She used his hands to grip it several different ways before dropping it next to the pallet and letting it break. She put a metal lid back on the proper garbage bin and double checked the area one more time. At first and second glance, it looked like a drunken accident. If this soldier was drunk this early in the day, hopefully he had a history of that kind of abuse that would make his superiors not question this incident too closely.

Casually and calmly, she strolled back to the car and slid into the passenger's seat. Looking all around, it did not appear that anyone even noticed her coming and going from the alley.

§ § § §

Chapter Five

THE prison break would be nearly unprecedented. Because of that, Praetorian wasn't comfortable not knowing what the German response would be like. Consequently, he planned the destruction of a major railway bridge that spanned the river on the north side of town, with the timing set precisely so that it would blow up just as a train full of dignitaries and prison officials crossed it.

For several months, Ruth had worked closely with Abiel, but it was nothing compared to the natural partnership she and Matthew had, born out of two decades of training together. So, the team decided the two of them would take on the bridge while Abiel monitored the response within the town, and Hope, performing for a large security force outside of town, monitored that response.

Information gathering by Hope, and also by Prudence, gave them the time the train would arrive – a time that showed up on no train schedules.

Final details set, plans already in motion, Ruth mechanically went through her waitressing routine the day before the big event was to happen while she continued to work details and timing out in her mind. As she wrote down the charge on the ticket in front of her, she casually looked up as the door opened. At first, she didn't recognize her because of the dark hair. But when she saw her face, she was shocked to realize that Prudence had just walked into the café.

She was only to come here in an emergency. As soon as she could make her way to her, Ruth stopped at her table.

"Would you like the special?"

Prudence scanned the room quickly. "I need a date," she murmured.

Ruth immediately understood the situation. "For tomorrow?"

After a curt nod confirmed, Prudence explained, "You'll need invitations. I need to get in to get them."

Invitations? Since when? Suddenly, the plan started to unravel. She had to process and work through it. "The brie is an excellent choice, *Mademoiselle*. Would you like some wine as well?"

"Just water. Thanks."

"One hour, out back," Ruth whispered and went back to the counter. She scanned the room and saw *Kapitan* Christof Kappel at his usual lunch table. She had spent weeks dating him regularly. He remained rather closed lipped for the most part, but occasionally let tiny gems of information spill. Ruth straightened her apron, grabbed the pot of coffee, and wandered over to him, plastering a huge smile on her face.

"Hello there, *Hauptmann*".

As usual, the tops of his cheeks turned red. "Hi."

"Do you still have duty tomorrow night?"

He ran a finger under his collar. "*Jawohl*. I could not get out of it."

Ruth let her lower lip pout out. "Pity. I'd cancel my date if it meant you could go."

"I wish you didn't have a date at all."

"Christof, this is the party of the month! Perhaps the year! Why would you want me to miss it? Do you really dislike me so?"

"I don't. I just –"

"You're just being mean and a bore."

She started to turn away, but he reached out and grabbed her wrist. "I'm sorry. I hope you have fun."

As she pulled her hand away, she smiled coyly. "I intend to." Then she lowered her voice to a conspiratorial whisper. "But I have a friend who needs a date. Do you know anyone who'd like a pretty girl on his arm?" She ran a finger over his shoulder. "I'd be most appreciative."

Kappel cleared his throat. "I, ah, I have a friend who asked if I could ask you for a date. Major Grün. He's a little older, though."

"Silly," Ruth said, giving him a playful slap on his shoulder as she straightened and picked up her pot of coffee. "She's not looking for marriage. Just a date to the soirée. I'll tell her to meet him there. Come by tomorrow morning and I'll tell you what she's wearing so he'll know to look for her."

"Lucienne –"

Halfway back to the counter, she turned and smiled. "Yes, Christof?"

"You'll owe me?"

She laughed and blew him a kiss, calling him a dozen vile names in her mind as she did so.

❦ ❦ ❦ ❦

THIRTY minutes before the train's scheduled arrival, Ruth climbed the trestles of the bridge and secured charges to the underside of the tracks while Matthew did the same thing to the legs of the track. While she worked, she both thanked God for the light of the full moon that made her job so much easier, and also cursed the light from the full moon that made her feel so much more exposed. She secured the device, set the timer, and quickly climbed back down to the ground.

Under the bridge, she unzipped her coveralls and stepped out of them, revealing an evening gown covered with red sequins. From inside her sleeves, she pulled out ballet slippers that matched the dress. She rolled her boots up inside the coveralls along with a clay brick and tossed the entire bundle into the water, sick at the thought of losing her good spare boots. The second bridge went up, the Germans would scour the entire area, searching for any kind of clue as to who set the bombs. She could not keep the boots.

Matthew met her at the base of the bridge and slipped his coveralls off. Underneath, he wore a slightly wrinkled tuxedo. After he tossed the coveralls into the water, he slipped a bow tie around his neck and quickly tied it.

Ruth walked all around him, inspecting him, then he did the same to her. When he slipped his hands in his pockets, he smiled and pulled out the sequined clip that she secured into her hair. From the base of the bridge, she collected the red rose she'd tossed there earlier that day and secured it to the lapel of his jacket.

"Ready?" he whispered.

She nodded and slipped an arm into his. The two strolled casually toward the lights of the offices of a shipping company mogul who was currently hosting a very extravagant black-tie affair. Several members of the Nazi party mingled inside wearing their dress uniforms while locals wore formal attire. They danced, sang, laughed, and sipped champagne. "Here's hoping Prudence comes through," Ruth said.

"Abiel has faith she will."

If they couldn't get an invitation into the party, they could potentially be arrested just for being in the vicinity of the explosion without any real reason to be there. Ruth knew Prudence would come through.

They crossed the lawn in front of the shipping company. On the floor above, Ruth could see the lights of the party. She felt very exposed as the bright moonlight reflected against the sequins of her dress. They walked quickly toward the corner of the building. Halfway across the lawn, they saw an envelope flutter down.

Seconds later, they heard the party sound grow louder as someone opened the door leading to the balcony. Matthew rushed forward. Ruth looked up and saw Prudence. Less than a second later, Ruth heard a man demand in German, "*Was machst du, Fräulein?*"

Ruth felt her heart skip as Prudence's eyes widened, then her face returned to normal as she smiled and turned. "I love your German language!" she exclaimed in French. "It sounds so vibrant. What did you just say? Say it again!"

The man repeated himself, this time in French. "I asked what you are doing."

Matthew snatched up the envelope and ducked beneath the balcony as Prudence said, "Oh. I was just getting some fresh air. It had gotten just a bit close in there with all you big, strong soldiers singing like that."

Ruth ducked into a shadow as the man looked over the railing. Matthew crouched directly under him, pressed against the wall of the building. He stared at the spot where the envelope had fallen, narrowed his eyes, said to Prudence, "What were you looking at?"

Ruth whispered a prayer for her sister. "Be quick on your feet, Prudence," she thought. "You trained for this."

"Just how far down it is." Prudence giggled and put a hand to her heart. "I get vertigo with heights. It makes me all warm and tingly." She slipped her arm inside of his and steered him around. "Is anyone dancing yet, *Herr* Major? I'd love to dance. Wouldn't you?"

They heard the boisterous sounds of the party flood the night again as the couple went back into the room. Matthew came out from under the balcony and grinned, holding the invitation up for her to see. They walked around the side of the building toward the front door. Once at the door, they handed the envelope to the bored soldier who stood guard. He barely glanced at the invitation before allowing them to enter.

She tightened her arm through Matthew's and laughed up at him as they passed the girl at the coat check counter. They entered the ballroom and immediately walked to the dance floor where Matthew swung her into his arms and they began dancing a waltz.

It disgusted Ruth to slip into the party, but she did it anyway. She'd suggested blowing this building up along with the bridge, but her team had talked her out of it. Grudgingly, she knew they were right. Too many innocent civilians attended the party – civilians like the teenaged coat check girl. To blow it would be wrong when the mission could be accomplished with just the bridge.

Just a few steps into the waltz, Ruth counted down to "zero" in her head. The wave of the explosion from the charges beneath the bridge ripped through the room. Even though she was expecting it, the noise and force of the blast still startled her. The windows blew out and threw glass and debris into the room as people started screaming and running in circles.

Knowing they needed to be seen by as many people as possible, Ruth put a hand to her chest. "What was that?" she yelled, allowing the sting of tears to come to her eyes.

Matthew put his arms around her shoulder. "No worries, darling. I'm sure they will figure it out. Come this way. Be careful now."

She started walking and shifting through the debris, trying to step carefully. Despite her caution, she felt something sharp go through her foot and she gasped and rose up onto her toes.

Her brother stopped and gripped the elbow of an elderly woman in a purple dress. "May I assist you?" While they were stopped, Ruth lifted her foot and pulled the chunk of glass out of her heel. She needed to flush the wound as soon as possible and make sure no other glass or foreign objects remained.

"No, thank you young man. My husband will see to me." She looked Ruth up and down. "Your head is bleeding," she said, brushing her own temple and lifting her chin to point to Ruth's.

Ruth lifted a hand and saw it come back smeared with blood. "Oh no!" She yelled in an exaggerated manner. "I'm bleeding!"

Matthew reached into his pocket and withdrew a white handkerchief. "There, there, darling. It will be okay. It won't even scar."

She held the handkerchief up to her temple and let tears stream out of her eyes. "I'm so scared. Is it an air raid? Why didn't sirens sound?"

"Let's get out of this building," her brother said, leading her through the panicked crowd. Out of the corner of her eye, she saw Prudence talking with a colonel and another woman, but she didn't stop in the flow of humans rushing out of the building.

In the parking lot, they went to the car they had parked there hours before and slid into it. As soon as they were secure inside the car with both doors shut, Ruth tossed the handkerchief onto the dash. "Next time," she said in Hebrew, "I need to remember to wear shoes with soles on them."

"Do you need Mercy?"

"Maybe. I need to see it in better light." She sat back in the seat watching a wave of cars clog up the shipping company's parking lot. Soldiers ran around in chaotic directions and she wondered how long it would take them to organize and set up checkpoints and roadblocks for the traffic leaving this area.

"I think we need to be seen by people at the hospital. I'll go ahead and take you." As they drove out of the parking lot, they watched the line of trucks heading their way. Matthew gestured toward them. "Not a huge response."

"No." Ruth narrowed her eyes. "I'll be curious to see what they pull from resources in other towns."

"I wonder if anyone on the train survived."

She looked over at the river and peered into the orange flames as they lit up the jagged edges of the only section of the bridge that remained standing. She knew the train lay in the bottom of the river. "Likely not." Later, in the privacy of her room she could think about the lives lost at her hands. Right now, she had to stay on task.

They pulled into the parking lot of the hospital. For show, Ruth held the bloody handkerchief to her forehead and let Matthew carry her into the busy emergency room filled with citizens in formal dress. He maneuvered his way through to the desk clerk, who looked very harried. "She needs a doctor," he yelled in a panicked voice.

"Sir, please calm down," the clerk said. She stood and handed him a piece of paper. "You will have to wait your turn."

"Everything okay, Alana?" Ruth recognized Mercy's Scottish brogue even before she saw her.

"Of course everything's not okay. Someone blew up the bridge!" The woman's eyes filled with tears and she sat back down. "And there are so many people needing medical help."

Mercy smiled at Matthew and Ruth. "How can I help you?"

"She stepped on a piece of glass. I told her that the slippers weren't suitable for going out, but she said they matched her dress."

"Of course they do," Mercy said gently, smiling into Ruth's eyes. "Let's just have a look."

"There's a dozen people in front of them," Alana said harshly.

"Well, now, I'm right here. No sense in pushing them out of my way, is there?" As she spoke, she carefully inspected Ruth's heel. "Looks like you don't need stitches. I can rinse it out for you."

"*Merci*," Ruth said, still in her brother's arms.

႘ ႘ ႘ ႘

Chapter Six

HOURS later they sat in the farmhouse across the table from Praetorian. He looked at the numbers on the paper in front of him that tallied the number of men the Nazis had deployed to the blast site.

"This is a pitiful response," he said, placing the papers, one at a time, into the wood stove. "*Der Führer* must be spread rather thin between here and his Atlantic wall. We are going to have an easy go of the prison break."

"We can't be sure. Maybe they'll beef up security now that this has happened." Matthew stood and paced to the other side of the room.

"Especially so soon after we blew the road." Ruth took a sip of the bitter coffee. "We may need to step back a bit and let them think the bridge was our final mission. We don't want them reinforcing while we're planning something so astronomical as freeing more than a hundred prisoners."

Praetorian sighed and rubbed the back of his neck. "It's still weeks away. We haven't finalized all of the identifications yet."

"I don't think we need to push the schedule up," Matthew clarified, "we just need to not plan any major damage between now and the breakout. Even if they beef up now, they may lower their guard by then."

Praetorian nodded. "Good point."

Ruth stood and limped to the sink to dump her coffee cup. She went into the bathroom and sat on the lip of the tub to look at her heel. She'd rinsed it twice, but she feared infection. It still looked okay. It just hurt now that the adrenaline had stopped raging through her body.

She heard the kitchen door open just as she stepped into the room and saw Prudence enter. "Beautiful job, Prudence," Ruth said. "We almost got seen. When that swine looked over the railing, Matthew was crouching right beneath him!"

"That was crazy," Prudence said. She grabbed the kettle off of the counter by the stove and filled it with water. "I was worried he'd look and see the white envelope."

Matthew pushed his chair back and stood. "He would have if I hadn't grabbed it. The bright moon was not our friend tonight."

"The timing wasn't up to us, or else we never would have done it tonight. It might as well be daylight out there," Praetorian said, looking out the window. He turned his attention to Prudence. "Anyone suspect anything?"

She shook her head. "I'm certain not."

"Try to stay away from that side of town for a while."

Matthew put his hand on the door. Ruth hugged Prudence and lifted her hand toward Praetorian. "You two be safe." She pointed at Prudence. "Don't go back out with that Major. He is a dangerous man."

Her friend shuddered and lifted a hand as if to ward her off. "No worries there."

"If you see him coming, try to go the other way." She glanced at Praetorian. "Next time, it would be good to have more than a day's notice."

His lips thinned. "Indeed it would."

Ruth hugged Prudence one more time and lifted a strand of her hair. "The dye job was probably a good idea," she said, "but you're much prettier as a blonde."

Prudence laughed. "Then maybe I'll stay brown the rest of the war. I'd rather stay nondescript."

8 8 8 8

RUTH sat straight up in her bed, heart pounding, ears roaring. It took a moment, but she gathered her bearings. She was in France, not Hebron. The Arab *jihadis* were not systematically destroying her city and killing her relatives. The current enemy preferred black *swastikas* instead of white robes.

The longer she stayed in France, the more the burning anger inside her grew. In England, no one spoke of the forced labor camps where the Nazis sent all the Jews and political prisoners. Here, everyone lived in fear. The camps were everywhere, and she knew through intelligence that the Germans had plans to build even more. The idea horrified her. What kind of people could do this to other human beings? What kind of thought process did it take to determine that an entire race of people could be systematically arrested, robbed, tortured, starved, and killed?

She knew she spanned two worlds. Being Jewish by birth and Christian by choice, Ruth had no real home among any people. Her observation of the annual feasts and her strict dietary laws confused Christians. Her embracing of Christ Jesus, Yeshua, as the Messiah confused Jews. She felt a kindred connection to Petros, commonly known as Peter, of the Bible. When she read his words and his actions in her study, she felt her heart swell with pride that he was the rock upon whom Christ built His church. In her mind, she claimed him as one of her kinsmen.

Unlike Peter, she was not bold in her faith. Here and now, she had to remain Jewish in secret, and more secular than devout with her Christianity. She could not proudly proclaim the Gospel, nor could she openly embrace her heritage. Instead, she worked both with her cover job at the café and with her secret assignment and she did as much as she humanly could to bring this war to an end.

She blew up roads, buildings, railway bridges, and supply boats. She danced with Nazi soldiers, begging ignorance to their harsh language, then listening to every word they said to each other. In recent weeks, on three separate occasions, she and the partner she happened to be with at the time came close to capture. Twice, she actually had to fight to free herself and eliminate the threat. As long as she lived, she would continue to fight.

She pushed herself out of bed. Today was a café day. Endless hours serving customers, more than half of whom would see her stripped and beaten in one of those camps if only they knew her true identity.

In no time she was dressed and downstairs, serving a croissant and a cup of coffee to a tired looking German lieutenant. She smiled and flirted like she did every shift, but in her imagination, she killed him three different ways with the fork sitting next to his elbow.

During the morning breakfast rush, Matthew came into the café. And after him, sitting at a different table, Abiel. Ruth felt her pulse start to race. Something had happened. To have all three of them in the same building in front of the public was absolutely out of protocol.

She couldn't get to Abiel fast enough to take his order. He gave nothing away. Frustrated, she served him and moved to Matthew.

As children, she and her brothers had developed their own code. They could speak about inane subjects, and someone listening would think nothing of the conversation. In their special code, he let her know the enemy had arrested Temperance.

For the briefest moment, she felt her hands grow cold, though outwardly she gave nothing away save a slightly raised eyebrow to signify that she got his message. In the same code, she told him when her shift would end. They would go see Praetorian.

Temperance had the wireless code in her head. The Germans would do everything in their power to get that code. Eventually, Temperance would break. Most humans did. The Nazis would torture her to death to get the information they required. Ruth had to rescue her.

While she worked, she developed half a dozen strategies. They'd been working on a massive breakout from that very prison. Most of the ground work had already been laid. She whispered a thousand prayers of thanksgiving for that fact. Whatever they decided to do could be done much more quickly because of the groundwork already in place.

As soon as her shift finished, she rushed upstairs and changed clothes, strapping a knife to her left calf and a single-shot pistol to her right. She pulled on a dress that had a hidden pocket sewn into the back, where she slipped her sheathed palm-sized knife. As she pulled a jacket on over the dress, she put a coil of rope in her pocket.

She ran a comb through her dark curls and freshened up her lipstick. Instead of dressy heels, she put on her flat leather shoes, which would allow her to run if she had to. What she wanted was her trousers and boots, but such clothing would cause her to stand out too much.

Going down the back stairs and out the back door, she slipped into the waiting car at the end of the alley. Matthew sat in the passenger's seat and Abiel drove. He normally chatted, but today his jaw remained clenched tight, the muscle near his molars occasionally ticking.

Ruth sat in the back seat and stared at his profile, seeing a resemblance there that she'd never seen before. Without needing him to confirm it, she knew he was Temperance's brother. How could Charlene do that? How could she place the two of them in the same district? She knew she and Matthew had been put together, but they'd spent their lives training and preparing for a time like this. Temperance and her brother had not.

"Any new news?" she asked.

Matthew looked over his shoulder at her. "We know nothing yet."

A shudder went through Ruth. The thought of what her friend likely endured at this moment... "God help her."

Abiel hit the steering wheel. "This wasn't supposed to happen. We had safeguards in place for her."

"We'll get her out," Matthew said, looking straight ahead.

"If she's alive," Abiel replied.

No one else spoke after that. They arrived at the farm house about twenty minutes later. Praetorian met them on the front porch. He watched them exit the vehicle and didn't say a word until they were walking up the stairs.

"This had better be worth all of you here at once," he cautioned.

"Temperance has been captured," Ruth said, brushing by him and opening the front door. "We need to make a plan."

They stood around the kitchen table and Praetorian pulled the pan of ashes out from under the stove. Using a small stick, Matthew quickly sketched the exterior of the prison.

"The original plan, as you know, was to blow out this wall. In the following chaos, the prisoners would escape, collect new clothing and identification, and hopefully most of them would make it to Switzerland or Spain." As he spoke, he squiggled through the line that marked the appropriate wall and made trails in the ash as if little ants escaped in the lines he drew.

"The problem," Abiel added, "is that she won't be anywhere near an outer wall. They're going to have her dead center in that cage where everyone going anywhere in that building is going to see her."

"We'll have to devise a plan to get to her in the cage," Ruth said with frown. "There has to be a way."

"We don't have the firepower to break through the German army. This building is well armed. There are soldiers everywhere." Matthew tapped the drawing of the building with his stick. "It's a centralized headquarters."

"Is there any way to get her moved?" Praetorian asked.

"Unknown." Abiel scrubbed his face with his hands. "Valor has been out of commission."

Ruth heard a footstep on the porch and held her hand up. Praetorian shook the tray so that all drawings disappeared and slid it back under the stove. Ruth slid into a chair and picked up a mug in front of her, not even knowing what was in it. Everybody in the room tensed up until Prudence walked in the door.

"Grace!" Prudence exclaimed as Ruth stood. A feeling of warmth flooded her. She never realized how much she missed her sisters until she saw one of them. The two women hugged tightly. "Why are you risking coming here?"

"We only have a few moments," Ruth replied, "but we had to come. Temperance has been arrested."

Prudence gasped. "Oh, good Lord," she prayed, pulling out one of the chairs and sliding into it. "When?"

"Three hours ago." Abiel frowned. "The landlady at the boarding house sent me a message through our channels."

"What can we do?" Prudence looked from Abiel to Ruth, who answered.

"The information she has in her head is of the utmost importance to the Germans. With it, they can decode missives and gain access to our plans. We must rescue her. The other option is not acceptable."

Ruth watched as Prudence's eyes widened, as the understanding that the 'other option' meant killing Temperance instead of rescuing her. "You talk as if you're trying to convince me. Isn't rescue an option?"

Abiel shrugged. "The jail is a fortress. But, we can move up our plan for the mass breakout of the prison. The problem is, they're going to have her centralized, and that will make it nearly impossible to get in and get her out. The original plan was to blow an outer wall out and have the prisoners we're after escape. We'll actually have to go in and get her."

Ruth nodded, her mind devising and rejecting plan after plan as she sat there. "If we had a few days we could properly plan it."

"We have no choice but to take a few days. If we go in there unprepared, we won't succeed." Praetorian leaned back in his chair. "How much time do you need?"

Considering the question, knowing the answer was of the utmost importance, Ruth replied, "Enough time to get a message to London to get Faith here to fly her out." She ran her fingers through her short hair. "There is no way we would be able to keep her in France. They would comb every inch of this land until they found her. Every minute she isn't out of the country would be a danger to the entire operation."

"How can we get a message to Faith?" Prudence asked.

Praetorian lifted an eyebrow. "The old fashioned way." At her questioning look, he clarified, "There's a prisoner at the jail who is in communication with England via coded letters. We'll get a message to him to pull the trigger and set our plans in motion."

Prudence darted a glance at Ruth and, as their eyes met, Ruth knew that she'd pieced together the information: Charity's husband. While she stayed in England receiving wireless communications and decoding German transmissions, she also communicated in code with her prisoner husband.

Ruth felt plans click into place in her mind as she stood. "Hope is in town. She should be able to gain access to the prison."

"How?" Prudence frowned.

Amused at the thought of their vivacious friend, she said, "She has her methods." She pulled a watch out of her pocket and looked at the face, calculating her day. "I will go see her."

"No," Abiel said, standing with her. "I will. You need to connect with your bomb builders and see what else they need in case we are able to push our plans forward."

Of course. Those details would be just as important as exactly when Faith could arrive. Charity's husband would write the letter. The radio announcer would give a coded transmission during the evening broadcast, telling them when and where Faith would arrive. But none of that would work if her bomb builders weren't ready to blow out the wall of the building.

Praetorian stood and shook Abiel's hand. "Give daily updates on a rotating basis with all of your points of contact. Prudence will start at the butcher tomorrow at thirteen hundred and then go in order from there. Don't come back here."

He turned to Ruth. "What did you do with the body of the German soldier?"

Still planning in her head, Ruth frowned, trying to figure out what he was talking about. Her life was full of handling German soldiers, and she'd had to deal with more than one body. "Which one?"

Praetorian lifted his eyebrow and looked almost amused. "The one who attacked Prudence."

When she realized the incident to which he referred, she smiled. That had been easy, with no unusual action required on her part, just a covering up of the fool's actions. "Oh. Him. I dumped a bottle of wine around him and left him there for someone to think he'd fallen on his own accord."

Praetorian nodded. "Very good."

"Be careful out there," Ruth said, walking out the door with her brother and partner. "If she breaks, there's no telling how much of our covers will be blown. I'll see you soon."

CHAPTER 7

Chapter Seven

RUTH sat on the folding chair and rubbed the back of her neck. In the center of the room, under the only light, a folding card table sat open with an open map on it. The dark permeated the rest of the basement room.

Everyone had already left except Abiel and Ruth. She looked at the man and saw the worry etched around his eyes and mouth. He had more of a stake here than the rest of them did.

"It's a solid plan," she said in an attempt to comfort him.

"I know it is. I planned it." He pushed the heels of his hands to his eyes and slumped his body down into his chair. "You know she's my sister, don't you?"

"I didn't know until the day we found out she was captured. Suddenly, I could see it in your face. I don't know how I missed it."

"You had no reason to see it." He lowered his hands and looked at her with red rimmed eyes. "I can't bear the thought of what she has endured. Mercy sent word about how sick she is. I can't –" His breath hitched and he paused. "This horrible war."

Ruth stood and walked to him, putting a hand on his shoulder. "I believe God has us here right now. We will prevail."

They heard footsteps on the stairs and Ruth stepped away from him and drew her gun from the holster on her thigh. She almost immediately reholstered it when she saw Matthew's boot.

"All's clear," he announced. He looked at Ruth. "Do you need a ride?"

"No. I can walk." She grabbed her coat and slipped her arms through the sleeves. With her chin, she gestured toward Abiel. In Hebrew, she said, "He could use an understanding ear."

Matthew nodded and grabbed a chair and moved it to sit next to Abiel while Ruth bounded up the stairs and entered the empty chemist's shop. She moved through the displays in the aisles, glanced out of each window as she passed it, and slipped out the unlocked back door.

The walk to the café took her less than 20 minutes. During that time, she went over the plan, and over it again and again, trying to find a hole. They had prepared for the prison breakout for months. Everything should be set in motion as soon as Hope took the stage to sing.

♙ ♙ ♙ ♙

"SHE isn't getting better," Mercy announced, looking around the busy hospital yard. Her cup of tea sat on the bench next to her, cooling in the afternoon breeze. She wore her nurse's uniform, complete with the blue and red cape and her Red Cross hat. "Despite everything I've done. I need to have her in a hospital or else she will surely die. Schäfer was supposed to arrange her move to the hospital yesterday, but –" she stopped speaking in the middle of her sentence and did not elaborate any further.

"Who is Schäfer?"

"The *Oberleutnant* who is over the prison. He escorts me to the prison to care for her."

Ruth narrowed her eyes. "Why?"

Mercy shrugged very gracefully and then, apparently choosing each word carefully, said, "I think it goes against orders to do it because it's always at odd hours. I think he has personal feelings for her." Her brogue rolled the r's. "I think he's a believer."

A bitter taste filled her mouth and she stopped herself from actually spitting it out. "I think he's a Nazi pig."

Mercy raised an eyebrow. "You do quite well masking your true feelings, you do." She smiled as she said it. "How's the foot?"

"Healed." picked up the waxed paper bundle and unwrapped her cheese sandwich, only interested in the plans for Temperance's rescue. "What kind of sick do I need to prepare for?" She took a bite of her sandwich as she watched a group of school girls enter the hospital.

"She has severe pneumonia. High fever, low oxygen levels, very weak. She has broken bones that aren't healing well, and I can't keep any food in her, not even broth, because of the medicine I'm trying to give her. It doesn't let you keep your supper down. So, to take the biscuit, she's also malnourished."

Ruth felt more anxiety at the tone of Mercy's voice than the words she said. "What do I need to do?"

"You need to carry her out and get her on a plane back to London. Take her to Doctor Mallory Knight at Winchmore Hill. He's a top pulmonary specialist. If anyone can save her life, he can."

Ruth took a deep breath and released it slowly. "What are the odds she'll survive the trip?"

Mercy's lips thinned. "I dare not guess. I only pray we can get it done quickly enough."

Her stomach knotted in terror of what she was about to suggest. "Should we just... ."

As red flushed Mercy's cheeks, she interrupted. "Absolutely not. You get her on that plane. God will put her in the palm of His hand. I believe He will. I have faith He will."

Ruth nodded. "Okay. Can you be available?"

Mercy casually looked around, clearly assessing whether anyone might overhear. "If you need me, you'll need to come find me. I'm on duty the same night, and it sounds like you're planning to fill my emergency room."

§ § § §

Chapter Eight

RUTH laughed drunkenly at the stupid joke the German sergeant had just told. "Funny and handsome," she cooed, laying a gloved hand lightly on his sleeve. She gently squeezed his biceps and allowed her eyes to flare as if deeply impressed. "I like that in a man."

His cheeks turned red and he ran a finger under his collar. "We should probably take our seats," he said in his broken and heavily accented French. "My friend is holding two seats close to the stage for us."

"I am so excited to see Virginia Benoit!" Ruth cozied up closer to the man's arm. "My friend's cousin saw her in Paris last year and simply loved her."

He led her to a row of folding chairs. Ruth's eyes skimmed over the men all around her, noting the ones who carried obvious firearms on their bodies. Stage lights lit up the area, casting weird shadows all around. As she flirted and chatted, she fought off a feeling of uncertainty at the plan. So many men had come to the concert. Weeks of thorough planning and now they would have to contend with a much larger military presence than what they had originally planned. She didn't know if the element of surprise would be enough to help them succeed at this point.

A man halfway down the third row waved at her companion and pointed to the empty seats next to him. "Here we are," he said, smiling.

Ruth patted her black curls. "Is there some place a lady could go... freshen up?"

"*Ja*, of course," he said, "I'll take you into the building."

"Oh, no need. Please stay with your friends and hold my spot. I don't want to end up having to sit on the ground if someone takes our seats. Just tell me where to go."

He looked around at the men near them and pointed toward the building. "Go right inside those doors down the hall to the second door on the left. If someone has a question, tell them you're with Sergeant Hammerlein."

She smiled and patted his cheek. "I'll be back before you miss me," she said, then turned away, not expecting him to follow her. As she approached the door, she spotted Abiel in his German uniform. She noticed a bruise under his left eye and a cut on his lip and wondered what kind of trouble he had encountered in the 24 hours since she'd last seen him. As soon as he noticed her approach, he bent and picked up a tote bag at his feet. He preceded her into the building by about 45 seconds.

On her way through the door, she ran into a captain who was exiting the building. "Pardon me," she said coyly, "someone told me the *toilettes* are this way?"

He gave her the same instructions Hammerlein had, and Ruth continued into the building. She encountered no one else in the empty halls and didn't see where Abiel had gone. Clearly, most of the staff had already made their way outside for the concert. When she entered the bathroom, she found the tote bag Abiel had set right inside the door. She opened it and right on top found her change of clothes.

In one move, she had her dress pulled off and kicked her shoes to the side. The dress should not be discovered before the charges blew. She slipped on the trousers and pulled a shirt over her head. It felt good to slip her boots onto her feet after teetering around in those ridiculous high heeled dress shoes. She slipped her arms through a shoulder holster and checked the pistols to make sure they were loaded. A knife went into a sheath at her back, and another into her boot.

Ruth stood on the commode and shifted the ceiling tile above her head. Once it was out of the way, she tossed the bag up into the ceiling, then pulled herself up after it.

Careful to keep her body weight on the ceiling beams, she pushed the bag in front of her and crawled through the space, using the map in her mind to find the right location. She carefully removed the bomb from inside the bag and secured it to the wall. With a pen light, she checked her watch and waited for the minute hand to hit the seven minute mark. At exactly that moment, she turned on the trigger and crawled away.

A few rooms away, she quietly and very carefully removed a ceiling tile and encountered an empty office. She lowered the bag to the desk below her, then crawled out of the ceiling. She did not bother putting the tile back in place. Soon, it would not matter.

Carefully opening the door, she saw a dark, empty hallway. She slung the strap of the bag over her body, left the office, and ran to the end of the hall to the back stairwell. Taking the steps two at a time, pausing at every turn to make sure she encountered no resistance, she went to the second floor.

Two floors below the prisoners, she raced to the end of the hall and turned the handle of the office door. Locked. Smoothly, she reached into her pocket and pulled out the lock pick tools she needed. Holding the penlight in her teeth, she knelt on one knee and worked the lock. Just as it released, she felt cold steel press against her ear.

"Who are you? The truth." the man asked in German as he dropped the dress she'd originally worn on the ground in front of her. The blue sequins looked especially out of place against the concrete floor.

She recognized the voice of Hammerlein. She'd picked him out of her regular customers from the café. Originally, she'd thought him simple and foolish. Clearly, she'd misjudged him. How had he found her? How had she been so overconfident as to not hear his approach?

Weighing her options, rejecting the idea of coy seduction in favor of swift surprise and overwhelming force, she shifted her grip on the lock picking tools so that they were both fisted in one hand. She drove her elbow as hard as she could up into his groin. As he bent in pain, she bounded to her feet and turned her entire body toward him, ready to kick or strike. Using the leverage of her upward momentum gained by the strength of her legs, she swung her arm up in an arch and drove the lock pick tools into his throat. As he fell to the ground, a look of complete shock on his face, she spat out in German, "*Ich bin Jude!*" I'm a Jew.

He opened and closed his mouth like a fish on dry land. His eyes registered disgust and surprise seconds before they rolled up in his skull and he went still. Ruth pushed open the office door, then grabbed Hammerlein's booted feet and dragged him just far enough through the opening to be able to shut the door.

She rushed to the far wall and pulled the bomb out of the bag. Once it was secured, she checked her time. Twenty seconds to go. Her date for the night had almost ruined her timing. As the second hand hit the twelve, she activated the bomb, then ran out of the office, leaving Hammerlein behind her.

She raced to the inner stairwell and rushed up the stairs to the third floor. She could hear Hope singing some ridiculous German song, their national anthem perhaps. Less than a minute later, Abiel joined her at the doorway, gun drawn. If all had gone according to plan, he should have set the bombs on the third floor and just under the floor of the fourth floor. He had blood spatter on the side of his face.

"Problems?" he asked.

"Nothing I couldn't handle. You?"

"Not anymore." He checked his watch and held up a hand, five fingers outstretched, indicating five minutes.

They remained crouched, guns drawn, and waited. At the thirty second mark, Ruth ducked her head and covered her ears with both hands, not wanting to temporarily lose her hearing.

The whole building shook with the force of the explosions that blew out the entire west wall. Before anyone would even be able to understand what was happening, Ruth and Abiel burst through the door.

Guns drawn, they shot their way through the skeleton crew of guards and made their way past the empty central cage to the hall that led to the individual cells. The odor hit Ruth the second they opened the heavy steel door. Fighting the impulse to gag against the smell of rotting human flesh, they looked for the keys that should have hung next to the door.

The hook was empty.

"We'll shoot the cell open," Ruth said.

"No need."

The sound of a man's voice startled her and she raised her gun, shocked to find a German *Oberlieutenant* cradling Temperance in his arms. He walked toward them, unperturbed by the fact that she kept her pistol trained on him. As he reached them, Abiel said, "You are blowing your cover."

"She is more important than my cover." Confused, Ruth realized they spoke in English.

"Who are you?" She looked from his concerned face to the flushed face of her friend. Temperance moaned and the officer shifted her slightly, cradling her closer to his chest.

"Who he is means nothing anymore," Abiel bit out. "He's foolish. Let me have her, Valor."

Ruth drew a breath in between her teeth. Valor? She had only heard rumors about him, about his daring lone-wolf acts and his deep intelligence cover. She could tell he didn't want to relinquish his hold on Temperance. The ragged look of helplessness on his face as he looked down at her friend made Ruth's heart twist in sympathy. Abiel took her from him and started running back toward the door.

"I did everything I could. She needs medicine. The nurse gave me some to slip to her, but it's just been in her water and I haven't been able to get her to drink any all day."

Ruth put her hand on his arm. "We will take care of her." She gestured to a chair next to the cage. "Sit. We need to give you cover."

He sat down and picked up the phone. "Tell her I'll find her," he said seconds before Ruth used the butt of her pistol and knocked him in the back of his head. Blood spattered onto the desk pad from the force of her blow, and she said a quick prayer that he would survive the head injury.

Ruth ran as fast as she could to catch up to Abiel. They encountered sporadic resistance, but nothing major, as was their hope. With most of the force outside at the time of the explosions, and the focus on the mass amount of men escaping out of the fourth floor on the opposite side of the building, they had a clear escape path.

Abiel handled Temperance's slight weight easily as they ran down three flights of stairs and out into the night. Matthew waited impatiently in a car just across the street at the corner of the building. He jumped out of the car and rushed toward them, raising a Sten submachinegun with a skeletonized folding stock to his shoulder. He fired two shots in quick succession, then a carefully aimed third shot. Clearly, he had just taken out a threat coming up behind them.

Abiel set Temperance in the back seat and slid into the driver's seat just as Ruth saw a prisoner run past. When Ruth dashed after the escapee, Matthew lowered his Sten and started walking backward toward the waiting car, his eyes peering into every shadow.

Ruth yelled. "You! Hey, you! Tell Prudence, 'Mercy at the airfield'," she instructed. "You understand?"

"Have mercy at the airfield," he repeated.

"Exactly like that. Very important."

He paused, looked at her, then saluted and ducked behind a parked vehicle as a spotlight shifted in their direction. Ruth rushed to the waiting car and slid into the back seat next to her friend.

Matthew shut the passenger door and Abiel punched the accelerator. Ruth put her hand on Temperance to keep her still. The heat from the woman's body burned through the cotton of her prison uniform and Ruth gasped. She'd never felt skin that hot before.

"Grace?" Temperance croaked.

"It's okay, Temperance. We have you. You'll be home soon."

CHAPTER 9

🎖 🎖 🎖 🎖

ABIEL drove the wooden paneled *Ariès Berline* through the streets of the town with the lights on and slowly enough to not arouse any undue attention. He clearly wanted to smash his foot down on the accelerator and barrel through the turns. Twice, they were followed by German vehicles. Twice he managed to lose them on the roads that he'd memorized and driven and walked over and over and over again.

They'd anticipated the areas where there would be roadblocks. They'd anticipated the response of the local forces. What they had not anticipated was the size of the group who would come to see Hope perform, nor the level of VIP status she would bring. The VIP's came with their own security forces, harder and more seasoned men than those in this obscure village in Occupied France. It was the wrench that they'd not anticipated thrown into the spokes of their plan.

The crackdown on the town came hard and fast. It forced Matthew onto back roads and what often counted for nothing more than ox trails. The car he'd chosen was small enough and strong enough to handle the trip. When they cleared the town, he extinguished the headlights and floored it. The back of the Ariès fishtailed. The tires spewed gravel. The occupants of the car found purchase whenever they could.

About half a mile from the field where Faith would land, Ruth yelled above the car engines, "We're already late. She has orders not to wait."

"She just landed," Matthew replied. "I saw the shadow of the plane cross over the moon."

Lights flashed and lit up the interior of the *Ariès*. Ruth looked behind them and yelled, "Three cars!"

Abiel downshifted and turned, spinning the wheel to maintain control while the rear end fishtailed. The field with the airstrip lay before them. As soon as they left the road, the ride grew considerably rougher as they bounced along the grassy field. Ruth peered through the rear window. "There's a Nazi staff car without lights behind us."

Matthew hung out the open window and fired a short burst from his Sten submachine gun at the other car. It veered and the rear-end fishtailed as he ducked back into the car. "I think it might be Temperance with Mercy. I think saw the white hat and red cross on her head."

Ruth felt a flutter of panic. "Did you hit one of them?"

"No idea. I was aiming for the driver."

From the driver's seat, Abiel said, "Plane looks German. Could explain why she's late."

Matthew spotted the distinctive straight-armed *Balkenkreuz* on the corrugated sides of the aircraft and exclaimed, "That's a Junkers!"

Abiel grinned. "I'd wager one of Hope's high ranking guests is going to be begging for a ride back to Berlin in the morning."

He skidded to a halt near the door of the airplane just as the car behind them, a Mercedes Benz 170V four-door *Tourenwagen*, slid to a stop and tapped their rear end with its front bumper.

Abiel hopped out of the front seat and rushed toward the other car with his Sten submachine gun at the ready. Ruth saw Prudence about the same time Abiel did, and he pivoted and came back to the car. Ruth helped him gather Temperance into his arms.

Ruth leapt from the back seat and yelled at Prudence, "Go!" She reached through the open passenger window and snatched Matthew's Sten submachine gun from the front seat. "I'll cover you!" She yelled as she ran away from the airplane and toward the oncoming vehicles.

Using Mercy's stolen car as cover, she bent on one knee and started firing short bursts. The sound of the plane's engine drowned out much of the sounds of the oncoming vehicles, but the full moon gave her sufficient light to fire.

She blew out one of the front tires of the lead vehicle, which caused the driver to lose control. As it spun, the vehicle behind it slammed into the side of it, causing a bottleneck into the entrance of the field. She felt a body next to her and barely looked as Matthew aimed and fired.

"You need to get on that plane. Your cover's blown," he yelled as he shot an approaching soldier.

He was right. She'd have to go back and let them establish a new cover for her. "I'll be back."

With a grin, he lifted his Sten. "I know. *Kol tuv*, sister," he said, telling her to be well.

"*Shalom*, brother," she replied.

"Peace is on the horizon," he agreed, then fired three rapid shots.

While he covered for her, Ruth ran to the plane. She could hear the bullets hitting the dirt behind her. When flaring pain ripped through her calf, she stumbled and cried out.

Abiel rushed toward her. "Grace!" he yelled.

She gritted her teeth, trying not to scream in agony. "It's nothing," she panted. "Just my leg."

"Well, you need your leg to run away from bullets," he said as he scooped her up.

It annoyed her beyond reason that he carried her onto the plane, but she had no choice. Before he even had the door shut, the plane started taxiing.

"Everybody aboard?" Faith yelled back from the pilot's seat. She looked like a small child sitting on a large throne.

"Go!" Abiel yelled.

"Hold your horses, Spanky. Everything up here's written in Kraut and I only took one semester." Faith licked her lips then eased back on the stick. The engine pitch changed and the airplane lurched forward. "And I did *nicht* so *gut* in that class if you catch my drift."

Ruth felt the plane pick up speed, felt the ruts and knocks of it rolling over the grassy field, then felt the slight sense of vertigo as it left the cradle of the earth and lifted into the air. Only then did she allow the pain to penetrate her vigilance. She panted in pain, barely containing the screams of agony she kept locked inside of her.

Trying to find something other than her calf on which to focus, she looked around the cargo area as Abiel ripped her pant leg. Mercy, hands covered in blood, inspected an unconscious Prudence's shoulder. Ruth wondered when Hope had boarded. She didn't remember seeing her on the airfield. Temperance lay flat on the floor of the aircraft, covered in a blanket. Three of the prisoners who had escaped sat on the deck beside her. Ruth recognized Charity's husband, Tom, and his friend, Sir Percy, from Charlene's intelligence briefing.

"What a fine lot," Ruth observed, hissing as Abiel probed her leg.

"Bullet snapped your tibia. Won't be jumping out of airplanes any time soon."

"Why are we on a Nazi airplane?" She could see the German warning signs over the door.

"Long story," the copilot said as he secured the door. He had a Sten submachine gun strapped across his back and wearily slipped it over his head. "Hang on. This isn't going to be a smooth flight. They know we're here. The Vichy aren't very good shots, but I am not overly fond of the prospect of flying what looks like a German bomber over Britain."

As he said that, the entire plane shook with the force of the exploding Archie. "If you can't strap in, grab onto something and hang on tight!" Faith yelled back.

Mercy finished applying a field dressing to Prudence's shoulder. "She needs stitches, but I'm not having a go at that while we're in the air with our friends trying to put us back on the ground so rapidly." She turned toward Ruth. "Now then, let's have a wee look at what kettle you've managed to get into."

"It's nothing," Ruth managed, but even her voice sounded weak to her own ears. She felt a blanket go over her shoulders, but didn't know who put it there. She could see Mercy's face, could read the concern and maybe even a touch of fear as she inspected the wound.

"Nuttin with you is ever really *nowt*, my friend," Mercy said.

The whole plane shook and Ruth felt a sense of weightlessness as it rapidly lost altitude. Overwhelming terror almost drowned out any sense of pain she might have felt. Until she tried to shift to sit up.

"Y'all hang on back there!" Faith yelled.

The copilot yelled, "Grab hold!"

Bits of jagged metal sprinkled the aircraft like sleet, hitting them from every angle. The shrapnel rained against the fuselage milliseconds before the exploding antiaircraft fire rocked the aircraft. The flashes of light that accompanied the explosions lit the inside of the JU-52 like lightning in a raging storm.

Ruth's stomach rolled and her peripheral vision darkened. She felt a clammy sweat break out on her skin. Whether it was a reaction to being in a flying metal coffin that was being bracketed on every side by antiaircraft fire or from the pain in her leg, she had no idea. Desperate for any source of comfort, she started praying out loud, in Hebrew.

Mercy leaned forward and put a hand on her shoulder. "Listen." Ruth stopped praying and tried to focus on her friend's face, but her eyes felt wobbly and her stomach rolled. "Grace, listen to me! This is bad. I can only temporarily set it. We have to wait until we land before I can work on your leg. Let me give you something for the pain."

"*Lo! Be'vakasha.*" At Mercy's confused look, she realized she still spoke in Hebrew. "No, please," she repeated. "Please. I have to stay awake. I can't stand the thought of going to sleep and never… ."

Mercy smiled in gentle understanding. "Okay. What can I do?"

Ruth took her hand in both of hers. "Save Temperance." Feeling a sense of desperation, she squeezed Mercy's hand. Her mission was the most important thing. "Save Temperance."

The airplane started to climb and the constant sounds of the antiaircraft fire stopped. Faith yelled back, "This ain't right. They stopped shooting, but we're pretty far from the coast."

The copilot yelled, "If you can manage, keep a look out the windows, lads and lasses! The only reason they'd stop shooting is if they sent up fighters to bring us down!"

Mercy looked behind her and motioned to the dashing looking man sitting on the deck. The escaped prisoner pushed himself onto his feet and made his way toward them. "What's yer name, *chiel?*"

Ruth noticed his dark hair and intelligent eyes. "Percy," he said.

"Right. Listen up, Percy. Sit next to my friend, Grace, here. She's in a wee bit more pain than she'll admit, even to herself. Try not to let her move around overly much." She pulled her hand from Ruth's grip. "Percy's going to sit with you. If you come to your senses, I'll give you that shot."

Ruth felt herself relax slightly. "Thank you."

"Hang on!" Faith yelled. "They're coming in low on our six."

Ruth heard the engines protest as the airplane banked into a hard right turn. She felt Percy take her hand and she closed her eyes, trying to beat back the consuming pain that radiated from her leg.

The entire aircraft suddenly fell out from beneath her and, had she not been well strapped in, Ruth felt certain she would have hit her head on the roof of the cabin. Her leg rose off the deck. When her boot slammed back to the blood slick deck, Ruth's vision blurred and faded to darkened pinpoints as she screamed in agony.

The End

INSPIRED BY REAL EVENTS

WHILE the story of the special team of operators I named The Virtues is entirely fictional, set in a fictional town, and comprised of fictional characters who form a fictional military division, every single one of my fictional heavenly heroines was inspired by a real World War II heroine, and each story was inspired by real events.

The girl on the cover of this book carrying the M1916 Spanish Mauser is a derivative image of the now iconic photograph of 17 year old Marina Ginestà. The original photograph was snapped on July 21, 1936 by Juan Guzman, who was born Hans Gutmann in Germany before moving to Spain. In the original photograph, Marina stands overlooking Barcelona from the rooftop of the Hotel Colón during the outset of the Spanish Civil War. At the time, she worked as a translator for a Soviet journalist of Pravda. She was a member of *Juventudes Socialistas Unificadas* (Socialist Youth), the youth organization mainly directed by *Partido Comunista de España* (PCE, Communist Party of Spain).

Despite her early involvement, Marina quickly realized she had been duped by the Stalinists and left the Soviet movement, joining up with the anti-Stalinist P.O.U.M – alongside such notables as George Orwell – and contributing as a militant soldier and journalist for several Republican media outlets in the struggle against Communism, Fascism, and Franco for the duration of the conflict.

Marina did not even know about the photo until 2006, although the image was printed, reprinted, and circulated everywhere and has become symbolic of the conflict and even of that time in history. Marina Ginestà died January 6, 2014 in Paris, at the age of 94.

The prologue of this book is set in Hebron immediately after the massacre that took place there in the late 1920s. While the Aubertins are fictional characters, the bloodshed there was all too real.

In August 1929, in an ominous prelude to the coming Nazi propaganda against the Jews in Europe, a radical Islamic faction of jihadists carrying out a fatwa against the Jews living in (then) British Palestine engaged in Taqiyya, which is to say they lied, deliberately deceived, and spread false rumors against the Jews. This organized campaign of deception spread throughout British Palestine with the intent of inciting violence against the Jewish population. The rumors claimed that Jews were massacring Arabs in Jerusalem and seizing control of Muslim holy places.

On August 24, 1929, the Hebron Massacre began. Hebron is a city south of Jerusalem and is Biblically the burial place of Abraham, Sarah, Isaac, Rebekah, Jacob, and Leah. After only 3 days, 67 Jews were killed, and many more were seriously injured or maimed. Homes and synagogues were pillaged and destroyed. Throughout British Palestine, 133 Jews and 110 Arabs were killed.

The British authorities relocated the 435 surviving Jews from Hebron to Jerusalem in an attempt to protect them. The massacres of the Jews in Hebron and in Safed led to the re-organization and development of the Jewish paramilitary organization, the Haganah, which later became the nucleus of the Israel Defense Forces.

The character of Ruth Aubertin, code-named Grace, was inspired by none other than "The White Mouse," better known as Nancy Grace Wake.

Nancy Grace Wake, aka: "The White Mouse"

An Australian by birth, Nancy left her native soil in her early twenties on a world tour, supporting herself with freelance journalism. She met Henri Fiocca, one of the wealthiest men in Marseille, France, at a party one evening and the two fell deeply and madly in love.

They married in 1939. Henri spoiled his beloved bride with a luxurious lifestyle she had never even imagined. When Henri prepared to go to war, Nancy said she wanted to go, too. He asked her what she could do, and she replied, "Drive an ambulance."

"But you can't drive," he'd reasoned.

"You must have me taught," she'd insisted.

Never one to deny her anything, he had one of the mechanics who worked for him teach her. She drove an ambulance back and forth from Belgium to Paris, transporting refugees, wounded soldiers, and civilians needing to escape the oncoming Nazi front. When Paris fell to the Germans, she knew she also had to leave or be arrested. She drove her truck until it broke down, then walked and hitchhiked the rest of the way back home to Marseille where her husband, a defeated French soldier from the front lines, met her.

With half of France under Hitler's boot heel, their area of Southern France fell under Vichy rule. However, the *Führer* could snatch it up at any time because the Vichy government collaborated with – and capitulated to – Berlin. While the Fioccas resumed what sense of a "normal" life they could manage, Nancy used their wealth to hoard as much canned food as possible, then started stockpiling black market soaps, cigarettes, and meat, all of which she generously shared with those in need.

Many British troops held as prisoners of war at Fort St. Jean had "parole" that allowed them to come into the town. Over time, Nancy and Henri became hosts to them. They fed them in their home, provided them with soap and cigarettes, and eventually with money. Their home became a planning center for the POWs at Fort St. Jean to escape back to Britain. Soon, she began traveling, delivering messages from the POWs to contacts in other towns. Eventually, she began making deliveries for the French Resistance as a trusted courier.

Because they lived across the street from the Vichy Commissaire, who had begun watching them closely, Nancy and Henri eventually rented a flat that they kept stocked with food where those planning illegal activities could meet.

In November 1942, the Germans marched into unoccupied France. By now, the Germans knew that a woman they assumed was a French (though

Nancy was not French) traveled and transported so much information, but they did not know her name so they dubbed her "The White Mouse."

One time, she and four men working with the Resistance rode a train. She carried a suitcase filled with a butchered black market pig. She ended up sharing a train compartment with a Gestapo agent who was actually on the train trying to capture "The White Mouse". She charmed him into carrying her suitcase for her, which breezed her through the customs checkpoint, and then made it safely away.

Eventually, she knew she had fallen under suspicion and that the Gestapo watched her. She and her husband made plans for her to return to Great Britain using the very underground she'd helped for years.

While making her escape, the Gestapo stopped her train and arrested everyone on board. *En route* to the prison, the trucks that transported the prisoners got stuck in traffic. Nancy and several others rushed out of the trucks and ran away. However, the arresting officers found her and took her to jail. There, she found out that the Gestapo in her own town denied knowing her existence, and the Gestapo in another town claimed her as a well-known prostitute. She then realized that they had framed her for blowing up a movie theater in another town. They spent days beating her and questioning her, trying to get her to admit to a crime she did not commit, or to admit to those who helped her. Enduring days of continual beatings, she said nothing.

Finally, the contact named O'Leary, who had planned to help get her out of France, arrived at the prison and used a ruse and false papers to secure her release. They tried to escape to Spain five times. On the sixth attempt, they had 10 escaped prisoners with them and, while they rode the train, a railway official came to their compartment and warned them that the Germans planned to stop the train ahead. As the train slowed, Nancy, O'Leary, and the prisoners jumped out the windows. Under heavy machine gun fire, Nancy ran through a field and up the side of a mountain, where she and the men who successfully escaped, hid for two days.

O'Leary went to meet a contact and got arrested. Nancy and the others disbanded, and she and a few of them made it to Nice, where Nancy hid in the home of an enemy of the Reich, Madame Sainson. She had sheltered many wanted men and women, and had teenaged children who also acted as couriers. Nancy stayed there for three weeks, until she could acquire new papers and travel to Perpignan, where she found one of O'Leary's contacts and convinced him to take her to Spain.

She and a group walked for three hours that night and at dawn, rode in the back of a coal truck. After going as far as the "lorry" could take them, they met up with two guides who marched them for 47 hours to Spain, walking across the mountains, through blizzards, and fighting hunger and thirst. No sooner had they arrived in Spain than she and her group of 6 were arrested. For three days they were given no food or water and endured miserable conditions in a cell with 17 other people. On the third day, the police took her out of the cell and shackled her to a chair and questioned her. She did not speak Spanish and did not answer any of their questions. They fed the bunch, then took them by bus to Gerona, where they were charged with illegal entry of the country. The judge was bribed £1,000 to let them free, and Nancy made it to Barcelona. Ten days later, she left for Great Britain.

After two months in London, it occurred to her that her husband would not be following her out of France, so she contacted Free French Headquarters and volunteered her services. Because she wasn't French, they didn't trust that she wasn't a British spy. In short order, she went to the British Special Operations Executive, or S.O.E.. After several weeks of training, she parachuted (wearing high heels!) back into France almost a year after the beginning of her escape. She worked as a liaison between London and the local maquis group headed by Captain Henri Tardivat in the Forest of Tronçais. She worked on securing arms and equipment that came in via parachute. She recruited members until the maquis groups grew into a formidable force of 7,500 strong. She also led attacks on German installations and the local Gestapo headquarters in Montluçon.

Nancy worked ruthlessly against the Nazis, at one point executing a female Nazi spy who the men in her unit did not have the "heart" to kill. Another time she killed a male sentry with her bare hands to keep him from sounding an alarm. During an interview in the 1990's, the interviewer asked Nancy about killing the sentry. She drew her finger across her throat in a slicing motion and said, "They'd taught this judo-chop stuff with the flat of the hand at SOE, and I practiced away at it. But this was the only time I used it – whack – and it killed him all right. I was really surprised."

At the end of the war, Nancy looked forward to being reunited with her beloved husband. It was only then that she discovered that the Gestapo had captured Henri and questioned him about Nancy's whereabouts. Through the days and nights of endless torture, Henri never betrayed her. He never gave her up. They eventually tortured him to death.

For her service and sacrifice, Nancy received the *George Medal*, the United States *Medal of Freedom*, the *Médaille de la Résistance*, and the *Croix de Guerre* three times. Nancy was also appointed a *Chevalier of the Legion of Honour* in 1970 and received a promotion to *Officer of the Legion of Honour* in 1988.

In February 2004, Nancy received the *Companion of the Order of Australia*. In April 2006, she was awarded the Royal New Zealand Returned and Services' Association's highest honor, the *RSA Badge in Gold*.

After the war, she worked for the Intelligence Department at the British Air Ministry attached to embassies in both Paris and Prague. She eventually became very active in Australian and British politics. In 1957, Nancy remarried, this time to a British RAF officer named John Forward. The couple lived in Australia until his death in 1997.

In 2001, Nancy returned to London, where she lived until her 98th year. Nancy Grace Wake died in August of 2011. The New York Times used her death to inspire the title and included her obituary in the book *The Socialite who Killed a Nazi with Her Bare Hands: And 144 Other Fascinating People who Died this Year.*

8 8 8 8

Reader's Guide

SUGGESTED questions for a discussion group surrounding *Grace's Ground War*, part 5 of the *Virtues and Valor* series.

While the characters and situations in the *Virtues and Valor* series are fictional, I pray that these extended parables can help readers come to a better understanding of truth. Please prayerfully consider the questions that follow, consult scripture, and pray upon your conclusions. May the Lord of the universe richly bless you.

Andre Aubertin believed that God had told him of the impending rise of the Nazi war machine and prepared his children to fight against them.

    1. Do you believe God speaks prophetic words to believers in the real world?

    2. How do you think you would react if God revealed such information about the future to you or a fellow believer whom you deeply trusted?

Ruth and her brothers are raised in an attitude of righteous indignation fueled by a desire to avenge the horrific death of their mother. Obviously, this kind of environment is not healthy, but the end result in their case is a trio of well trained soldiers who are driven by much more than civic duty.

3. Do you believe Ruth's disdain for the Nazis is sinful?

4. Could her thoughts and feelings about the Nazis come between her and God?

5. Do you think her Jewish heritage might have fueled her animosity toward members of the Third Reich?

Off and on the page, on more than one occasion, Ruth kills enemy soldiers seemingly without experiencing any remorse. The Bible instructs believers to forgive those who persecute us, pray for those who spitefully use us, love our enemies, and not to commit murder.

Yet, God Himself sent the angel of death to wipe out the entire army of Sennacherib (2 Kings 19:35; Isaiah 37:36; Psalm 76) and to take the lives of every first born son in all of Egypt regardless of age (Exodus 11:5; 12:29). God also directed armies into enemy camps and towns and instructed His people to utterly destroy every living thing (1 Samuel 15:2–3) and razed entire cities, like Jericho.

6. Does warfare call for different thoughts and actions on the part of believers than peacetime?

The Nazi war machine rolled over Europe with an agenda of genocide coupled with ruthless domination and extermination of opposition. Part of their model was to kill Jews, Christians, and political dissidents, and other groups including homosexuals, non-Arian minorities, the elderly, and even those with infirmaties or disablities. Fighting back with bloodshed was the only conceivable way to upset their power and loose their control.

7. Do you think the "ends" – the destruction of the Nazi state – justified the "means" – the killing of individuals?

Mission of Mercy

the Virtues and Valor Series part 6

a Novella by

HALLEE BRIDGEMAN

Published by

Olivia Kimbrell Press™

Olivia Kimbrell Press™

COPYRIGHT NOTICE

Library Cataloging Data
U. S. Library of Congress Control Number: 2014953682

Bridgeman, Hallee (Hallee A. Bridgeman) 1972-
  Mission of Mercy, Virtues and Valor series part 6/ Hallee Bridgeman
   100 p. 23cm x 15cm (9in x 6 in.)

Summary: Doctor Betty Grimes, code-named MERCY, works in Occupied France as a nurse, garnering information and secretly treating injured Resistance operatives.

   ISBN: 978-1-939603-50-0 (ebook)

1. Christian fiction 2. World War II 3. war stories 4. spies 5. historical fiction 6. espionage

PS3568.B7534 T500 2015
[Fic.] 813.6 (DDC 23)

For All the Nurses...

THIS novella is specifically dedicated to women like Marthe Cohn and Marguerite V. Clodfelter. To learn more about their real stories, read the *Inspired by Real Events* section at the end of Betty's story.

Oh, give thanks to the Lord, for He is good!
For His mercy *endures* forever.

Psalm 118:1 (NKJV)

Prologue

MERCY -the virtue of forgiveness in the face of wrongdoing, forgiving treatment of one who could justifiably be treated harshly. Mercy differs from clemency and amnesty. Clemency and amnesty renounce punishment while taking no stance on hatred. Mercy renounces hatred while taking no stance on punishment.

London: October: 1940

THE harsh bright light beat down on the back of Betty Grimes' head. She felt a trickle of sweat start at her temple and slide down her hairline, but she couldn't free her hands to wipe it away.

"Nurse," she ordered, and tilted her temple toward the nurse to her right. Behind her surgical mask, her strong Scottish brogue rolled the r in the word. "If you'd be so kind."

Before she could contaminate the patient's open abdomen on the table in front of her, the nurse quickly took a cotton cloth and dabbed at the beads of sweat on Betty's brow. Betty ignored her. She kept her eyes and hands completely involved with her surgical tasks. She moved efficiently and expediently while she clamped, snipped, and lifted the organ from the patient.

"Lovely work. Barely got it in time, didn't we?" Doctor Rudyard Barclay observed, examining the dark appendix Betty set onto the waiting tray.

"Aye. Another hour and it would likely have ruptured," Betty agreed. "That would have been a fine mess." She began the preparations to close the patient back up again.

So quietly that she nearly didn't hear him, he said, "Great catch, Bets. And fine work, besides." She smiled under her mask as much at the warmth and pride in his voice as his affectionate use of the pet name. She always felt a little giddy whenever her Rudy called her Bets.

She quietly answered, "Rudy, ya big *sook*."

Before he could speak again, sirens interrupted them. In a clear and loud voice, he demanded, "How much longer?"

"Five minutes, *mebbe*," Betty answered, stitching faster.

"Jerry may not spare us five minutes," Barclay announced. He looked at the nurse directly across from him. "Nurse Tatum, report to the bunker. Leave me two orderlies outside the room to help wheel our patient out after we close him up."

When the building shook from the shock of a nearby explosion, one of the nurses cried out. Betty looked up, halfway through stitching the incision. "Get *yerself* into the hallway. Tuck up under the stone archway clear of the windows. I'll finish up!"

"Doctor –" Nurse Tatum exclaimed, her eyes wide over her mask, "we can't leave you."

"You must," Barclay replied. "Get to safety until the all clear. Your patients need you more than we do. Besides, we'll be done in a jiffy."

The nurses left, all the while protesting leaving the two doctors. The door closed behind them and Betty spared Rudyard a glance.

"What can I do?" Barclay asked. Betty looked up and met his eyes again, feeling her pulse skitter with reaction to the intensity of his gaze. Telling him to leave would be useless, she knew. He wouldn't leave her side during a bombing attack any more than she'd leave his. She didn't have time to argue with him so she simply answered his question.

"Secure his IV then unlock the wheels on the table. Stay sterile if you can manage. We'll need to move him as soon as I finish the last stitch."

Doctor Barclay used the toe of his boot to unlock the wheels and unhooked the hanging glass bottle of saline and latex tubing with his left pinkie finger. Her nimble fingers moving as rapidly as possible, Betty finished the last of the sutures. Just as Barclay snipped the thread she held taut, and Betty proclaimed, "Bob's your uncle!" the whole room shook and the power went out. In the pitch black darkness, the smell of cordite filled the room.

Betty felt fine debris falling from the ceiling to land on her bare arms. She realized she had instinctively leaned over her patient, trying to keep the dust and grit from coming in contact with the freshly stitched wound. Barclay had leaned over as well, but his hands had covered the back of her head, protecting her.

"I've always admired your timing," Barclay observed before releasing her. Seconds later, the light of a small flashlight he'd had in his pocket filled the immediate area. "Let's get him into the hall until the lads fix the *lecky* in here."

Without stopping to remove her black rubber gloves or her stained surgical clothes, Betty rushed to the foot of the table and let Barclay guide them out of the room.

Hand held lanterns and flashlights sporadically illuminated sections of the darkened hallway with an eerie dim light. Betty pulled her mask down off of her face and slipped the gloves off before she touched Nurse Tatum's arm. "Can you tell me where to get a blanket for this patient?"

"There's fresh linens in the cupboard in recovery. I'll get it, Doctor."

"Cease that *haverin'*. Stay here in the *loaby* where it's safe. Just tell me where to go." Borrowing Barclay's flashlight, Betty made her way back through the surgical area and into the recovery room, where she found clean sheets and blankets. Grabbing as many stacks as she could handle, she turned to head back into the hallway.

The explosion, the solid wall of heat, the deafening noise that rolled over her like a wave – it all slammed into her entire body at once, singeing her hair and eyelashes. It knocked her clear off her feet and flung her backward across the room in the space of a single heartbeat. Her last sensation was a painful ringing in her ears, a terrifying numbness in her back, and fear of the dark as the flashlight rolled away from her. Something warm clouded her vision moments before a coppery taste filled her mouth. Before she lost consciousness, she realized it was blood. But whose? Her own? Then her eyes slid shut and the world vanished.

♀ ♀ ♀ ♀

WHEN Betty Grimes opened her eyes again, a blinding pain clamped down on her skull, overwhelming every other sense. She immediately closed her eyes and felt an involuntary hot tear escape the corner of her eye. With her stomach rolling in protest, she gradually opened her eyes again, recognizing the trauma ward in her own hospital. People milled about everywhere, and the noise of the crying, pleading, and screaming nearly overwhelmed her. The smell that assaulted her was a mixture of antiseptic and the sickening odor of scorched human skin.

Slowly, she pushed herself up onto her elbow. She still wore the bloodied surgical gown. Her hair had come down from its bun, though, and her long red braid brushed against her arm. Tendrils of escaping curls tickled the sides of her cheeks. She raised her hand to brush at them and winced when she came in contact with a painful bump just above the hairline over her left ear. She felt the weight of the bandage on her head without feeling the wound beneath. Had the shrapnel penetrated her *pate*?

"Nurse, you need to stay still." She didn't realize that the woman was speaking to her until she touched her shoulders and tried to gently press her back down onto the bed. "You have a nasty head injury."

"Doctor," Betty croaked, suddenly overwhelmingly thirsty.

"The doctors are very busy just now. One of them will see you just as soon as he can."

"Nay, ya' *dafty bairn*. I'm no' a nurse. I'm Doctor Grimes."

The nurse raised an eyebrow, as if finding the notion of the petite redheaded woman being a doctor impossible to fathom. In response she said, "Nevertheless. Down you go." After a pause, she added, "Doctor."

"Mah patient –" Betty began, her words beginning to slur, feeling her eyelids growing heavy again.

"– is no longer your immediate concern. You're the patient, now. So let's get you better first," the nurse said.

Betty struggled to remain conscious, struggled at an attempt to triage herself and the patients nearby. She struggled to ask this woman her name. Her struggle lasted only a few seconds before darkness reclaimed her.

Chapter One

Outside of Milton Keynes, England, 1940

BETTY opened her eyes and her puzzlement only increased. She found herself lying in an entirely unfamiliar room with a tall ceiling and elegant wallpaper. Beautiful oriental rugs lined the floor. The large and very comfortable bed sat next to a bright window. Sunlight bathed her legs and torso.

With a slight frown, she slowly and painfully turned her head, surprised to find her mother sitting in a rocking chair next to her, reading a leather bound Bible. She heard no sounds of pain or suffering. She smelled no hospital smells. None of her surroundings looked familiar.

"I'm dreamin' is it?" Betty asked, astonished at the weakness of her voice.

Immediately, her mother looked up from the book and smiled, relief flooding her green eyes. She set the Bible aside and smiled. "*Fille bien-aimée.*" She spoke in French, as she often did when it was just the two of them, calling Betty her adored daughter. "It is high time you woke again. I was beginning to wonder if you'd ever wake up."

"Mama?" she asked, also in French. "Where are we?"

"On an estate outside of Milton Keyes. They've established a care facility here for non-critical patients. Your father was just transferred here to take over as head of hospital operations. This is our room here, in the dowager cottage."

Her mother's answer only inspired additional questions. "What –?"

Her mother leaned forward and laid the back of her hand very gently on Betty's cheek. "I'm so happy you're alive. When we heard about the hospital –"

She remembered the bombing, the air raid sirens, the darkness. Denying a very clear memory, daring to hope, she asked, "Rudy?"

The single tear that slid down her mother's cheek told her everything she needed to know. Rudy – Doctor Rudyard Barclay – her soon-to-be husband – had not survived.

Sorrow flooded her chest, choking out anything she might say. All of the questions she had just seconds earlier evaporated like a morning mist. Hot tears streamed down her temples and into her hair. If her mother spoke, she couldn't hear her for the roaring in her ears. She ran her left thumb over her ring finger. She didn't even have her engagement ring because she'd taken it off to perform the surgery.

Praying that this was all some crazy dream brought on by a concussion, she closed her eyes again and willed herself to go back to sleep so that she could wake up and find her Rudy holding her hand.

8 8 8 8

BETTY sat at the table in the dining room, a cup of lukewarm tea in front of her. She'd managed to get dressed today. In the seven days since she'd arrived, she'd only forced herself out of bed twice. She walked the short distance to the hospital, a stone fortress that had once housed an earl's family back in the days of metal armor and damsels.

Now she felt exhausted and her head ached terribly. The stubborn weakness her body displayed disgusted and frustrated her. She felt betrayed by her very flesh. When a woman in a dark olive green uniform sat down directly across from her, she looked at her with curiosity.

"Doctor Grimes," the woman said, extending her hand, "Allow me to introduce myself. My name is Major Charlene Radden."

Betty reflexively took her hand. "Pleasure to meet you, Major," she replied automatically.

"The pleasure is all mine, I assure you. As a female officer in the British Services, it's always nice to meet a fellow pioneer of the fairer sex."

Betty slowly shook her head. "I'm no pioneer. Many, many women before me have forged the path I follow."

"I could say the same. However, you and I both know that's only half the battle."

With a shrug, Betty took a sip of her tepid tea and wished for the dozenth time she had fresh milk for it. "What can I do for you, Major Radden?"

"Charlene will do. And I appreciate your directness. With your permission, I'll also get right down to it." The older woman crossed her arms and leaned back in her chair. "I need you on my team."

"Beg pardon?"

"I am assembling a team of women, a group of extraordinary women such as yourself, who are extremely good at what they do. I feel we can complement each other in a way that can make a meaningful contribution to the war effort."

Curiosity piqued, Betty sat up straighter. "What kind of team?"

"Each of the ladies on this team are experts in their independent areas. They come from different backgrounds, even different nations. Married, single, mothers, wives... every last one dedicated to this team. Women with different strengths who can work together or separately, here at home or behind enemy lines, to help end this war." She took a quick glance around the room then leaned closer. "I think only a group of such extraordinary women can develop a sisterhood that will create a force to be reckoned with."

Betty felt her eyelids lowering. "Not sure I can be much help, Major."

She sat back again. "I believe you can. You see, I need a nurse."

"Well, then, my dear Major, you are certainly barking up the wrong tree." With a scowl, Betty took another sip. "I've never been a nurse. I'm a doctor."

"Yes. And a brilliant one, besides. However, I need a Red Cross nurse who can move through the enemy's territory without drawing too much attention to herself. But I also need a doctor who can secretly tend to wounds that otherwise might draw the attention of local and German authorities in Occupied France."

"France, is it?"

Charlene nodded exactly once and confirmed, "*Oui.*"

With a snort, Betty crumpled her empty paper cup in her hand. In perfect French, she responded, "A redheaded nurse in Nazi territory is going to draw attention, I'd wager."

Charlene continued in very quiet French as well. "Not if she doesn't try to be a doctor. They'll not even notice you, I assure you."

"The nurse's training is different. I wouldn't know where to start."

Charlene lifted an eyebrow. When she spoke again, it was with a very cultured English. "We'll train you. You'll know the ropes. And perhaps you can begin the process of healing your broken heart as you train."

"My heart? What do you know about my heart?"

Major Radden leaned forward, her expression absolutely serious. "I know he was a fine man who died far too young for no good reason. I know he loved you and wanted to marry you. And I know that your heart is broken and you are grieving that loss every waking minute. Have I got it right?"

Betty nodded. Grief threatened to strangle her. She didn't trust her voice so she just nodded. The Major reached across the table and lightly covered the back of her hand with her fingertips.

"I also know that there are many, many people who have lost loved ones in this conflict. Is it right to squander your God given gifts, or is it right to take back what was stolen so unfairly?"

Perhaps sensing she had said everything that mattered, Major Radden stood. Then she looked down at the younger woman and softly said, "Consider this. What would your Rudyard want you to do? Would he expect you to curl up and surrender? Turn a blind eye to the very enemy who killed him? Or would he expect you to put on a uniform and help prevent even more deaths?"

Betty swallowed a sob and shook her head. "That's not fair."

"There's a war on, Doctor Grimes. There's no time for fair just now." She glanced at her watch. "I don't leave for London for another week. Take that time and think about it." She gestured at the unopened Bible by Betty's elbow. "Pray about it. Let me know if you're interested. You can find me at the main house about a mile down the wooded path."

☷ ☷ ☷ ☷

Chapter Two

Outside of Milton Keynes, England, 1942

THE sound of footsteps came from beyond the door. Betty looked at the pretty pot of flowers her mother had set on the porch of the dowager cottage and smiled as the door opened. "Mama," she greeted, stepping forward and kissing her mother on the cheek.

"Betty! What a surprise! I wasn't expecting you until Sunday for dinner." She stepped aside and gestured into the parlor. "What are you doing here?"

"Is Papa home?"

"Aye," came the reply from near the fireplace in the parlor. Her father, a tall redheaded Scott with thick glasses and a trimmed beard, stood.

"Hello, Papa," she said, stepping into the room and meeting him for a hug.

"Is everything okay?" he asked.

Betty had spent the last several months training on the main part of the estate just a mile through the woods. Her father ran the hospital that had taken over the several centuries old stone fortress.

"I've come to tell you goodbye."

"Goodbye?" Her mother inquired, stopping in the process of pouring tea. "Is your training over then?"

Knowing the strict limitations on sharing any information, she simply said, "I —"

"Don't tell us *owt* what you can't, lass," her father said, sitting back in the chair.

"I shan't. I just wanted to come say good-bye and tell you I love you. I fear I won't be able to be in touch for the next little while." She perched on the couch next to her mother. "Thank you for letting me become a doctor. I know it took some sacrifice."

Her father, a well respected leader in the medical profession, waved a hand. "You sacrifice more than we will ever know. Your drive and dedication brought you this far. I know what you're doing will keep God by your side."

She felt tears sting her eyes. "That's why I'm here. I'd love it if you would pray for me before I must leave in the next few days."

"But of course!" Her mother said in her French-accented English. She placed a hand on Betty's shoulder and held the other out to her husband.

An hour later, Betty left the cottage and walked along the estate path back toward the training grounds. After twenty minutes, she entered the clearing near the airfield just in time to see Faith's distinctive North American Na-16 airplane, *Texas Diamond*, landing on the grassy field designated for that very purpose. Deciding to shed the heaviness she felt descending on her like a cloak, she started running and chased *Texas Diamond* while it taxied to the hangar.

Laughing, Faith climbed out of the plane. "Hey there, friend," she greeted, stripping off her helmet. Her thick Texas drawl set the young woman apart from every other pilot on the base even more than her sex. At just nineteen, Betty had already ascertained that Faith was the youngest woman on the base, though a few of the male soldiers posted here were at least as young if not younger. "Aren't you a sight for sore eyes?"

Betty hugged Faith, filling her nostrils with the comforting smell of mink oil from Faith's goatskin flight jacket. "Likewise." She gestured at the blackened window of the plane. "Practicing landing in the dark?"

"It's the strangest thing to be completely reliant on instruments. I keep thinking that any tiny bit of human error in calibrating those things will mean tragedy. But, you know, I probably wouldn't even feel it. I'd just be easing back on the flaps one second and standing there with my jaw hanging open asking Saint Peter what went wrong the next." Faith shuddered. "But, enough about that. What are we doing tonight? Painting the town red?"

"Tonight?"

"Yes! I heard Hope's leaving. It's the last time the seven of us can be together! Let's have dinner as a group in town. Heck, I'll even treat for some of that stuff you call pudding if you like."

Betty grinned. "I think that would be divine." She hooked an arm through Faith's. "Let's go find the girls."

They walked arm in arm and Faith jabbered, obviously burning off the adrenaline of her recent blind landing. "I know you say you're Scottish, but I'm not exactly sure why that justifies making pudding out of internal organs and such. Now if you want a real pudding. Tapioca. That's a good pudding. Or rice, even. Don't even get me started on banana."

❧❧❧❧

BY seven that night, Betty sat at the head of a table in the back room of the local pub with her six closest friends, empty plates and discarded glasses in front of them. The candles on the table had burned low.

To her right sat world famous singer and star of stage and screen, Virginia Benoit, code-named Hope. They all preposterously pretended they had no clue as to her actual identity. As the only other American on the team, Faith often teased Virginia that she kept meaning to get her a pair of glasses like Clark Kent, but Betty missed whatever American cultural reference the young woman was making by pointing out the flaw in Virginia's disguise.

Next to her was the exotic and fascinating woman code-named Grace. She spoke English with a heavy Hebrew accent, the same as some of the doctors she'd trained with in London, but perfect French. Betty wondered about her background and nationality and could not help but notice that she often reverted to French during long conversations.

Charity sat next to Grace. She was the brilliant minded code-breaker whose husband currently enjoyed the questionable hospitality of the Third Reich from a prison cell in Occupied France. He let no grass grow beneath his feet, even in captivity, and sent coded letters to the resistance movement through his wife.

Prudence sat across from Charity. She had her blonde hair pulled into a delicate twist and dabbed at the corners of her mouth like a woman raised in the lap of the aristocracy. Despite her obvious upper crust upbringing, she never, not once, acted better than the rest of them.

Prudence sat next to Temperance, who, despite rules against it, told the group that she and her brother had escaped from Vichy France and sought out their positions with this secret organization. She'd learned how to operate the wireless machine and transmit messages that would be received by Charity here in England.

Faith sat next to Temperance and to Betty's left. The young American pilot who, at first glance, looked like a very young teenager and not a young woman on the edge of her twenties. She was bold and often loud and a bit rough around the edges. But she was also rather observant and quite smart, with an unforgiving wit tempered only by a huge heart.

To the woman, the group had been hand-selected by Major Charlene Radden, and given specialized and individualized training. They were an experimental group. She reckoned that if she took seven women who shared a deep and abiding faith in God and placed them together on a team, they would grow closer and actually become one strong unit instead of a team of seven individuals. She felt that with them praying for each other and helping each other in love, they would be formidable, perhaps even unstoppable.

Somehow, Charlene had convinced the hierarchy of British command to approve her experiment. Starting tomorrow, they would be moved into play. Hope had a near perfect double performing in America on her behalf so that she could spend time here in England being trained how to create and write in invisible ink and how to transport what she'd written. Three days ago her double had boarded a ship bound for southern France via Casablanca. Hope would leave in two hours to rendezvous with the ship, then she would be the one to disembark in France.

Betty knew she had to leave in two days, but had no idea what the travel arrangements for the rest of the group were. She just knew that this would be the last time they would all be together.

"My friends," Hope said, rising to her feet and lifting her glass of lemonade. "This is our time. We have trained hard. We have prayed up. And now it's time to go out there and show Hitler how we can fight back." She extended her arm to the center of the table. Using Grace's favorite quote, she said, "To victory, my Virtues."

A round of "Victory!" erupted around the table.

Betty didn't know when she would see any of them again, but she had a feeling, knowing Charlene, that they would all be close together and working toward a common goal. She thought maybe Grace knew more than the rest of them, but that they each knew just enough to help them accomplish their individual missions.

Her primary role would be to provide medical attention to any of the resistance fighters who could not safely seek medical attention from official sources. She didn't want to think that she'd have to treat any of these women she called sister, but she felt thankful that if they did need medical care, she'd be there with them and was qualified to treat them.

After Hope sat back down, Betty stood. "I'd love it if we would all join hands and pray, one at a time. We know God is with us as we go into this battle. My prayer is that we stay focused and sharp and that we remember our training. I also pray that we all come back home safe and sound. Please, bow your heads."

8 8 8 8

CHAPTER 3

Chapter Three

"MERCY, this is Matthew. He is second in command on the ground where you're going." The tall, muscular man stood behind Charlene's desk, hands behind his back. He had jet black hair, a narrow face, and very keen, very hard dark eyes. He intrigued her for some reason that she could not explain.

"Hello, Matthew."

He nodded and launched into the mission without any kind of greeting or polite preamble. "Charlene says you can jump. Have you ever done it at night before?"

Betty tried to ignore the similarities in his accent and Grace's. Now she knew why she was so drawn to him. She studied his cheekbones and the shape of his eyes. Clearly, they were related in some way. By 'jump', Betty knew he meant out of an airplane while it was in flight. "I have only jumped out of balloons in the light of day so far. I have never graduated with an airplane jump and I have only jumped in daylight."

"Very good." He gave a sharp nod of his head. "We will take off tonight at twenty-three hundred."

He did not elaborate any further, so she pursued her curiosity. "So I'm to jump out of an airplane, then?"

"Yes. We risked a lot to land last night with Temperance and Prudence. To do so again so soon would be much risky." He closed his eyes in apparent impatience and shook his head, then switched to French, much like Grace often did. "Landing again is far too great a risk."

Also in French, Betty said, "I will have my medical bag with me. It will contain breakable items."

"The best we can do is to have the jump master and riggers secure your breakables as much as possible. We can drop your bag under a drogue parachute but we may never recover it if it lands in a pond or a treetop. If you would like for me to jump with the bag, I am happy to. I will have very little gear with me."

Knowing that no other options existed, Betty nodded. "Very well. What then?"

"The Red Cross is expecting Beatrice Renault on the ten-fifty-five train morning after next. We'll put you on a train in a neighboring village and the hospital staff will meet you at the station. Your papers have you arriving from Paris. You will house in the nurses' barracks and begin shifts at the hospital immediately."

Betty frowned. "If I'm in the nursing barracks, how will I treat wounded resistance workers?"

Matthew rubbed the back of his neck before he put his hands behind his back again. "Hopefully, we will never require your services. In case we do, we will have a facility. You'll be contacted and transported whenever needed. Coming to you would be too risky even if you lived alone."

Excitement at the thought of finally getting to work started to bloom inside her chest. "How would you like me to dress for the jump?"

Charlene answered, "Wear trousers and boots. Pack your uniform. You'll change after you land. If you're searched and questioned about the articles, make something up about tending gardens or some other rot."

She leaned forward and pushed a manila envelope toward her. "Here are your papers, cover story, and train tickets. There is a woman with a red braid and a nurse's uniform who is traveling from Paris to this village. You will meet in the women's sitting room with her and she will leave with Matthew. You will go on and be met by the nursing director." She tapped the envelope with her finger. "Any questions?"

Betty chuckled. Resuming her Scottish brogue, she admitted, "I'm sure I have a million, but I can't think of a single one just now. Head in the clouds, I reckon."

Charlene gifted her with a tiny smile. "You will have friends on the ground who can help you when you need it." She sat back in her chair and Betty knew she was being dismissed. "I will see you in the hangar at twenty-three hundred hours. Try to rest up before then if you can."

"Major, before I go there's words that need saying to ya." Betty stood and held her hand out to Charlene. "Thank ya for askin' me ta sign onto yer team. Thank ya for not bein' fair about it."

Charlene's smile was warm. She stood and took Betty's hand in her own. "Thank me when you come home safe."

§ § § §

BETTY rolled the rubber tubing up into a tight coil then placed it in its compartment in her housecall bag. At the jump master's instruction, she had removed anything breakable or fragile from the bag. The jump master and the riggers would carefully wrap each item as if it were a *Fabergé egg*, then secure all the breakables in a canvas kit bag filled largely with children's party balloons and inflated latex condoms. This bag, in turn, would be wrapped in three layers of wool fleece and straw. This contraption would then be attached to Matthew's harness on a twenty foot lowering line. He would lower it the moment his parachute got full. They all felt very optimistic that the majority of her supplies would survive.

"And what makes you think so?" she had asked.

"This is the same way we smuggle in cases of Scotch whiskey. Hardly ever lose a bottle," the rigger had replied.

She had given Matthew a disapproving stare, but he merely shrugged. "Any contraband has value. It can loosen tongues or grease palms. So can your morphine, by the way."

Betty had used the extra space in her medical bag to store more unbreakable supplies as well as her nurse uniform. The bag bulged in places it didn't normally bulge, but she felt like it might survive the jump.

She ran her fingers over the metal plate with Rudyard's initials engraved on it. Even as she wondered about the wisdom in taking such a precious treasure as his bag with her into a war zone, she knew she could never leave it behind. It was all she had left of him. She had never returned to London to collect any belongings and found out through correspondence with friends that the apartment building where she and Rudy had flats had been destroyed with a bomb.

She was so thankful that a doctor in the hospital had sent her Rudy's bag. Somewhere amidst bomb debris was the housecall bag he'd had designed for her, with what would be her married initials engraved on a silver plate very similar to this one. It would have been his wedding gift to her. Instead, she would use his bag. She would take his bag and go out and do her part to end this war, the very war which had taken him from her.

A sharp rap on her door pulled her out of what would certainly end in a feeling-sorry-for-herself crying jag. She shook her head, straightened her blouse, and opened the door.

"Hey there, Mercy. Ready to get this show on the road?" Faith asked in her robust American way.

Betty smiled. "Aye. Just you take care as I go out the door of that airplane. Keep her smooth and steady."

"This ain't my first rodeo." Faith grinned. "My part will be perfect. You going to be good with a night jump?"

"Haven't any other choice, have I?" She picked up Rudy's bag and gestured toward the door. "Best just get it done."

In the hall, Faith slipped her arm through Betty's. "It's been hard these past few nights getting rid of y'all. I don't know what me and Charity are going to do without the rest of you gals. Nothing against Charity, mind you. She's a good egg and we get on just fine. But you know, she misses her young 'uns and her fella something awful. I ain't much use to her in those departments. Still, we'll be praying for you with all that we have in us. Every single night."

Betty squeezed her arm as they walked out of the barracks. "I'm counting on that."

❦ ❦ ❦ ❦

CHAPTER 4

Chapter Four

BETTY rolled the parachute and stuffed it into her kit bag. She hauled the bag up over her shoulder, picked up her medical bag, and ran to the tree line. Within a minute, she heard Matthew come up behind her.

"Everything okay?" he asked, his voice low.

"Yes." She gestured to the bag at her feet. "What do I do with that?"

"I'll come back for it." He set his own bag next to it then stripped the fleece and straw off of the kit bag holding her breakables.

"How did it do?" Betty asked, concerned about the glass vials and bottles.

"I didn't hear anything break. I think the riggers knew what they were about." He hefted the bag, apparently deciding to leave the balloons intact until they arrived at their destination. It would probably help reduce their noise footprint not to have glass bottles and vials clinking together in the woods in the dead of night. "How did it do with you?"

Betty had never jumped with a lowering line load. She had to remember to lower the bag just after her parachute got full. In the dark of the moonless night, it had seemed like only a few seconds passed between the time when she lowered the housecall bag and the time her bound ankles hit the soft ground. She hefted the bag with Rudy's initials on it, showing him that it had survived the parachute jump.

Matthew nodded and said, "It's dark and I don't want to risk using a torch. Stay close."

Her stomach fluttered with nervousness at the thought of walking through the woods in the dark. She hated the dark. But, she must be brave right now.

They traveled through the woods for several kilometers until they came to a hunting cabin. She waited while Matthew inspected it, then stepped inside with him. He handed her the flashlight he'd held.

"We have another five kilometers to go," he said, "but there's no rush. We can sleep here tonight and go in the morning."

While she looked at the utterly bare single room cabin and wondered about sleeping on the floor, he walked over to the fireplace and knelt on the ground, reaching up in the chimney. After a firm tug, he withdrew a cloth package, streaked with black from the chimney. He set it on the ground and unwrapped it, revealing a loaf of bread, a hunk of cheese, a corked bottle, a candle, and two pistols. "That's a good lad," he said, almost to himself. He ripped off a chunk of the bread and held it out to Betty.

"Thenk ye," she said.

"*En français,*" he corrected.

She took the bread from him with a nod and bowed her head to thank God for the safety of the mission, for her medical supplies making the trip, and for the provision of food. Before she could pray, Matthew started praying out loud.

"*Baruch atah adonoi. Elo hainu melech haolam. Hamotzi lechem min haaretz.*" He paused, then repeated himself in French, apparently remembering his own scolding of seconds earlier. "We praise You, Eternal God, Sovereign of the universe, who causes bread to come forth from the earth...."

Not wanting to subtract from the beauty of his prayer, she simply said, "Amen." As she took a bite, he held out the bottle.

"It's water," he said. "There isn't a truly close source so I had some left here."

"I have my canteen," she replied, pulling it out of her bag. "But thank you." She took the cheese he offered and sat on her suitcase. "You're Hebrew."

He raised a dark eyebrow. "Few people can tell."

"I worked with several Jewish doctors in London." She took a sip of her water. "I recognized Grace's accent straight away." She studied him as she chewed, then swallowed and said, "She believes in Christ."

"She better." His grin did little to soften the hardness of his face. "We are Messianic believers, followers of Yeshua. We know He is Messiah."

Puzzled, she said, "You have just told me more in five minutes than she did in almost a year, and I consider her a very dear friend."

As he stood, he wrapped what was left of the bread. "My sister is very mission minded and will not be able to see or think of much else until this war is over. God has gifted her in a unique fashion. But, I am very pleased that she has formed the bond with your Virtues team. It is good for her to form friendships with women." He gestured to the door. "I am going to check the perimeter and locate the outhouse. Please take the opportunity of my absence to change into your nurse's uniform. I will not return without making some sign."

She changed into her uniform dress and woolen stockings quickly. She looked around the bare single room once more. She had never in her life slept under the same roof as a man who was not a blood relative. The thought of doing so unnerved her even more than jumping from an airplane in the dead of night. The very idea that she would even consent to strip down to her undergarments and change her entire wardrobe with a man she had known for bare hours just a wall away — and well-armed to boot — would have astonished her even as recently as a few months ago.

Using the clothes she'd changed out of as a pillow, she lay on the hard floor and closed her eyes, trying not to think about such things -- trying hard to just get on with the mission and do what needed to get done. Intending to just rest while she waited for him to return, she forced herself to relax. But, the stress of the night, the physical exertion, the worry and fear – all of it culminated into exhaustion. She barely realized when Matthew came back inside. She did not hear him move about, go through her things, or find the cape she would wear with her uniform. She didn't even feel him lay it over her.

When she woke, he sat with his back against a wall, head back, eyes closed, pistol in his lap. Her body ached from her surprise landing after last night's jump, followed by sleeping on the hard ground. She almost moaned out loud as she pushed herself to her feet. When she looked at Matthew again, he stood, slipping the pistol into his belt at his back. He looked a bit amused.

"Feeling it this morning?"

"Aye." She rubbed her lower back and wrapped the cloak around her shoulders.

"*En français*," he corrected automatically.

She shook her head. "*Oui*."

"You'll be sitting on a train, sipping a cup of tea soon enough," he said with a smile.

"I feel like you're laughing at me," she grimaced.

"Not at all." He snorted. "Well, not much. You're just very green. One day, you'll look at a new arrival and think the same as me."

"I'd like to see you handle a 24-hour shift in a London emergency room and laugh at me then."

"I imagine you're quite competent in your element." He wrapped up the cloth filled with supplies and hid the package back up in the chimney, keeping one of the pistols. "Ready?"

He carried the heavy canvas bag that had been packed with breakable medical supplies as well as what looked like a heavy pack. She carried Rudy's housecall bag and a canteen and didn't give the disparity in what weight they lugged a second thought, trusting in Matthew's judgment and experience.

The longer she walked, the more her muscles warmed up and loosened. It didn't take long until they stood on the outskirts of a small town. Matthew pointed to the rectangular building by the railroad tracks. "Station," he said. "I'll keep your doctor bag. A nurse wouldn't carry a medical doctor's housecall bag and it would stand out. Whenever we need you, the bag will be there."

She hesitated in handing it over. Matthew placed an understanding hand over hers where they gripped the handles. "I'll take good care of it. You have my word, Mercy."

Letting go of the bag felt like she'd just let go of the last thing that identified her. Suddenly all traces of Doctor Beatrice "Betty" Grimes vanished and she was Red Cross Nurse Beatrice Renault.

She blinked back the inappropriate tears and nodded. "I'll appreciate it if you would. It is very dear to me."

He left the bags behind and they walked down the road to the train station. Soon, they sat in the little restaurant, enjoying bitter coffee and sweet scones. They made inane small talk about Paris and a recent movie — anything to look and sound normal. When the train pulled into the station, Betty started to stand, but Matthew put a hand over hers.

"*Yah* be with you, Mercy," Matthew said so quietly that she barely heard him. "It has been an honor to travel with you."

She gave half a smile, suddenly realizing how alone she would be. "Thank you for your help and your courtesy."

He nodded and sat back. She went into the women's restroom and waited. Very soon after, a redheaded woman of her approximate build came into the room with her.

"Be ye therefore merciful, as your Father also is merciful," Betty said, using the key Bible verse from the book of Luke to identify herself.

"The Lord is good to all: and his tender mercies are over all his works," the woman replied from the book of Psalms. At Betty's answering smile, she gave the seat and compartment number on the train. "You've been alone this whole time, so no worries about continuing any conversations."

Betty recognized the Irish in her accent. "It's a good thing, too, isn't it then? We barely speak the same language."

The other woman grinned. "Suitcase is above the seat. Only one there. Has a brown handle. Godspeed to you."

"And to you."

The woman left the restroom and Betty waited another minute before going out herself. As she walked through the busy station, she saw her counterpart seated at the table with Matthew, having as casual of a conversation as they'd had mere minutes before. She walked out the door and climbed onto the train, finding her seat. She looked through her purse, making sure she had the proper paperwork and identification.

Three stops later, she stepped off the train, carrying the suitcase she'd found above the seat, and walked up to a large, older woman wearing a uniform identical to hers. "Name?" she inquired.

Betty nodded. "Beatrice Renault."

The woman looked at her paperwork and raised an eyebrow. "You're from Scotland?"

"Not for many years. I have lived in Paris for the last ten years."

"Your French is perfect," the woman replied in English.

"Aye. 'Tis my *mère's* native tongue."

The woman smiled and held out her hand. "Leslie Gay," she said by way of introduction. "I'll be your immediate supervisor. Come then, let's get you settled into your room. Your first shift begins at seven tonight."

Thankful she'd slept most of the night, Betty followed Leslie to the waiting car.

WITHIN two weeks of taking on the nursing job, Betty had a new and profound respect for the work nurses did every day, twelve hours a day. In her mind, she wondered how much the medical industry would shift if doctors were required to work as nurses at some point in their training.

Now, several months into the job, she longed to be a doctor again. The limitations placed on nurses and the assumption that they didn't know anything about patient care angered her. The longer she worked under cover, the more she penned a book in her mind to try to help educate doctors about the nursing world.

Thankfully, the Resistance gave her many opportunities to keep her surgical skills fresh. Right now, she stitched a badly cut hand while sitting at the kitchen table of a local baker. The man held onto his own wrist and kept his gaze averted while Betty worked. He did not speak to her, nor she to him. When she'd first arrived, he'd loudly, and more than likely drunkenly, judging by the smell of him, protested a woman sewing his hand. So, Betty left. Out in the alley behind the baker's shop, it took Matthew twenty minutes to convince her to go back inside.

"It's my policy never to treat patients who have an objection to my sex," she'd stated emphatically.

Matthew had looked all around, then pulled her back into the baker's shop. They hadn't gone back upstairs to where the patient sat, but instead stood by the door. He'd spoken to her in urgent tones, putting both hands on her shoulders. "I don't like him myself. He's a *meshuggener*." At her raised eyebrow, he'd smiled and said, "A crazy man. He's a senseless person."

"Aye, that he is. Best of luck."

"Listen. You have to be crazy to do what he does. Understand?"

"Enlighten me," she'd said in English, then bit her lip and repeated it in French. "Tell me why he's so important. Otherwise, I refuse to force him to endure my treatment."

"We need him," Matthew had said, his dark eyes intense in the dim light. "He is a master bomb builder, and I'm setting the bombs in two days. The timing fuses on them are critical. It could mean the difference between life and death for me." When she didn't relent, he had added, "and Grace."

Betty had closed her eyes and let out a deep sigh. "Fine," she'd reluctantly consented, "but I'm not giving him any narcotics. He can handle his own pain management. I believe he's fairly well anesthetized at the moment anyway."

He'd given her a rare smile and squeezed her shoulders before releasing her. "Thank you."

When she snipped the last thread, she put her supplies back in the bag. "Keep it clean," she tersely instructed. He did not reply. Betty shrugged and washed her hands at the kitchen sink. When she turned back around, Matthew stood in the kitchen and her patient had his head resting on his bent arms on top of the table, snoring.

"Looks like he calmed right down for you," he teased.

"He never said another word to me." Betty slipped her cloak around her neck. "Can you drive me back?"

"Of course." He slapped the bomb maker on the shoulder and spoke to him in English. "Go, rest. I will see you in the morning." He retrieved his hat off the coat hook from beside the door to the stairwell leading down to the bakery. "Ready?"

� � � �

CHAPTER 5

BETTY smiled at nurse Ginette as she sat on the hard wooden chair in the barracks' lounge. "I tell you, I can't tell if my feet hurt worse than my back or not."

Ginette pulled a compact out of her bag and inspected her hair. "Long shift?"

"Aye." Betty closed her eyes and leaned her head against the bare wood wall. She wanted a bath. And maybe tea. The only way she'd get a bath in this building filled with women would be to wait until the middle of the night. She longed for her flat back in London and the clawfoot marble tub she'd had delivered about a month before the war started. That flat no longer existed, of course.

"I go on at half past," Ginette said. "I hope it's not a slow night."

She felt the wood under her head rumble about a millisecond before she heard the explosion. Instantly and utterly against her will, her mind carried her back to the London hospital, the bombs, the heat, the noise, Rudyard. Her heart started pounding and she felt her muscles tense.

"What in the world?" Ginette exclaimed.

Coming back to the present, Betty pushed herself to her feet, no longer feeling the ache of tired muscles. "Something's happened. Let's get next door. I have a feeling they're going to be needing our help."

Thankful she hadn't already changed out of her uniform, she rushed out the front door and over to the hospital. Toward the river, she could see the orange glow of flames.

"What is it? What's happened?" Alana, the night clerk, met her at the door.

"I'm not sure. Something over by the river."

"Is it an air raid?"

The black haired woman gripped her hands together so hard that Betty wondered what damage she did to her own digits. "I never heard anything. No sirens or planes. Did you?"

"No! No!"

Betty put her hands on her shoulders. "Listen, it sounded pretty bad. We need to get ready for patients."

Ginette spoke from beside her. "Should I go round up the other girls?"

Betty nodded. "I think that would be best. Don't you?"

"Easier to send them home than wish they was here," she said with a smile and rushed out of the building.

"I'll help triage," Betty offered, turning to Alana. "We'll send critical patients into that area. Ambulatory patients can wait in these chairs. How about we get some cots ready?"

Keeping the staff busy, subtly and calmly taking charge, Betty kept everyone from panicking over the thought that another bomb could go off at any minute. As the first patients arrived, the staff forgot their fear and let their training take over.

She triaged dozens of patients, several of whom wore black tie clothes. They mainly suffered from cuts and bruises brought about as a result of attending a party next to where the railway bridge had been blown up. Very few survivors had suffered major injuries, which left the hospital filled with impatient, scared, traumatized people.

While she tried to help calm down a woman wearing a ridiculous purple feathered hat, she saw Matthew walking through the door carrying Grace. As she approached, Alana handed Matthew a piece of paper.

"Sir, please calm down," Alana said. "You will have to wait your turn."

"Everything okay, Alana?" She watched Grace's head turn toward her. Her friend did not act like she recognized her at all. Betty assessed her color and thought she looked good.

"Of course everything's not okay. Someone blew up the bridge!" Alana's eyes filled with tears and she sat back down. "And there are so many people needing medical help."

Betty smiled at Matthew and Grace. "How can I help you?"

"She stepped on a piece of glass. I told her that the slippers weren't suitable for going out, but she said they matched her dress." She heard a panic in his voice that didn't match the calm keenness in his eyes.

"Of course they do," Betty said gently, smiling into Grace's eyes. "Let's just have a look."

"There's a dozen people in front of them," Alana said harshly.

Alana's voice sounded like she was panicking again. As soon as the traffic thinned out, Betty intended to send her to the lounge to have a long cup of tea. "Well, now, I'm right here. No sense in pushing them out of my way, is there?" As she spoke, she carefully inspected Grace's heel. "Looks like you don't need stitches. I can rinse it out for you."

"*Merci,*" Grace said, still held in her brother's arms.

Betty led the way to a curtained area near a sink. She gestured to a chair. "Our resources are a bit low at the moment. I don't have any beds."

"No need," Grace said as Matthew set her in the chair. Betty filled a basin with water and pulled a chair up across from Grace, lifting her foot into her lap.

"Good cut," she remarked quietly, flushing the wound.

"Glass went right through my shoes," Grace said, clearly annoyed.

Betty looked up and winked at her friend, but did not speak. The curtained area only offered the illusion of privacy.

"The important thing is if they looked good." Betty grinned.

"Exactly!" Grace agreed, out of character for the warrior Betty personally knew.

"I'm not seeing any glass. But, if it doesn't start to feel better in a couple of days, you might want to come back." She slipped out from under Grace's foot and gingerly set it on the chair she'd just occupied. She grabbed a bandage and returned. "I'll wrap it. Keep it as clean as you can. I know it's in a bad spot."

She reached for her friend's hand and they just held hands for several seconds, silently communicating friendship and trust. Then Betty stood again. "You might want to carry her out. It's rather chaotic out there, and I wouldn't want to risk someone stepping on her foot."

Matthew nodded and scooped Grace up again. Betty took the opportunity to come closer to her and inspect the cut at her hairline. "Just superficial," she said with a smile, stepping back. "Wash it with soap and warm water."

"Thank you, nurse," Grace said.

"Be careful out there," Betty murmured, watching the two of them leave.

❦ ❦ ❦ ❦

BETTY lay in her bed and stared at the moon through the single window. Her body ached with exhaustion, but her mind could not shut off.

Rudyard felt so far away right now. She could barely picture his face in her memory. Nothing in her life was the same as it had been when he played an active part of her daily life. They'd worked together, worshipped together, played together, taken meals together. They had planned their future together. She had put off their wedding so that his brother, currently tending to patients in an African mobile hospital unit, could attend. Now she wished she'd given in to Rudy's urgings and married him privately, saving a larger public ceremony for their families after the war.

She didn't have anything normal to use to cling to, to remind her of life with him. Instead, she lived in this strange place, patching up bomb makers' hands, then caring for patients of railroad bombings. She tried hard not to think of the Nazi soldiers and the Gestapo agents who occasionally dropped by the hospital expressly to scrutinize the medical staff.

With a sigh, she rolled over onto her side and stared at the wall, listening to her roommate Ginette's steady breathing. She longed to see the end of this war so that she could go back to her life and give herself time to mourn Rudyard properly.

The hand on her shoulder startled her so abruptly that she gasped as she sat up. The spy, Abiel, put a finger to his lips, warning her to be silent. Then he held up two fingers, signaling that she had two minutes to make her way outside. He left her room as silently as he'd entered, and Betty threw her sheets and covers back and rushed out of the bed.

She dressed in a simple cotton dress, grabbed a sweater and a ribbon for her hair, and rushed outside to meet him. He waited for her in an idling car down the block from the barracks. When she got into the passenger's seat, she noticed Rudy's housecall bag in the back seat. "What happened?"

"Gunshot." Betty surmised that was as much as he was willing to share. In every encounter with this particular operative, he exemplified the notion of taciturn. She wondered if his terse manner of speech was natural for him or a learned behavior as a result of his chosen vocation.

Abiel drove normally, perhaps even slowly, through the nearly empty streets. Any vehicle on the road this close to curfew was bound to draw attention so he certainly couldn't race through the streets. Even so, she could feel the intensity and impatience almost radiating from him. After several minutes of driving he turned onto a lane located in between two fenced fields. He turned the car's barrage blacked out headlights all the way off and drove along the rutted lane to a farm house. Instead of parking next to the house, he parked next to the barn.

"In there." Abiel indicated before bounding out of the car and racing to the barn.

Betty opened her own car door and reached behind her to get the medical bag. By the time she caught up with him, Abiel was already inside the large barn. He took her past the stalls and to a tack room in the back.

"Praetorian, this is Mercy," he said in English. It was the first time she had ever heard him speak English and she wondered why he had switched from French.

The man called Praetorian filled the doorway with broad shoulders topping a lean, muscular frame. His jaw clenched and tensed as he stared at Betty in the dim light. Also speaking in English, he said, "I'm Praetorian. I've heard some things about you from the others. Please, this way."

Several lanterns lit up the inside of the tack room. Betty gasped when she saw the man on the cot. He wore a black turtle neck and black pants. A neatly pressed German officer's uniform sporting several medals was hanging on a hook above the bed. The man gripped his abdomen with both hands, breathing shallowly and rapidly, sweat leaving his skin shiny with a sheen that reflected even in the dim light.

Suddenly the English made sense. "A prisoner, then?"

Praetorian shook his head sharply. "No. He's on our side. Can you help?"

Betty set her surprise aside. Time to sort all this out later. She rushed forward, observing the dirty bed upon which the patient had been placed. "Right, then. Let's have us a *wee keek*. I'll be needin' clean blankets. Right away," she ordered. She heard the sound of footsteps running away, but did not look to see who did her bidding. She took the patient's hand and gently lifted it from his abdomen to examine the wound. "More light!"

A lantern appeared behind her shoulder and she assessed the wound. It would require all of her skill for this man to live through the night. She placed his hand back over the wound and applied some pressure to slow the bleeding. She then looked up at his face, noting that he was studying her expression as well. "I don't speak German. You speak French?"

He answered in English, his voice laced with the throbbing agony he endured. "English. English is easier." His words carried an unmistakable American accent, a sort of purified combination of Hope's syrupy Cajun lilt and Faith's Texan drawl.

In her comfortable Scottish brogue, Betty asked, "What do I call you, lad?"

"Call him Valor," Praetorian instructed from behind her and still in English. Betty recognized an upper crust British inflection to Praetorian's speech, much like that of Prudence. "He needs to be patched up and back at his duty station tomorrow or else things are likely to go very, very badly for our little operation here."

She lifted Valor's shirt. It was difficult to make out details due to the volume of blood and the dim lighting.

"I can't stay here," the man panted. She looked into his eyes and saw nothing but determination and strength in spite of the near mortal pain he suffered.

"Well, Valor, I'm afraid that's not necessarily up to me at the moment." She prodded the entrance wound. "I'm not seeing where the bullet came out. That means you're holding onto it somewhere. Stubborn, really. I'm going to have to cut on you a bit."

"Do what you need to."

"Right this moment, you probably think you can't hurt much worse. Sadly, you're mistaken. I c'n give ya something if you like."

"Can it wait?" Praetorian asked. "He needs to talk." He walked to the foot of the bed and spoke to her patient. "Tell me what you learned."

While Betty inspected the wound, she listened with half an ear to the conversation pertaining to intelligence the American-German-French spy here had gathered at a briefing.

"How compromised is your cover?"

Betty dug into her bag as Valor shook his head. "Not at all. They never saw me." He held up his bloody hands. "But they know they hit me."

On a crate by the cot, she spread out a white cloth and laid out a syringe, medication, scalpel, and other tools atop the cloth, placing them in as careful of an order as she would in the most advanced hospital in London. As she worked, under her breath and almost subconsciously, Betty recited a liturgy from the Scottish *Book of Common Prayer* that she always recited before surgery.

"Almighty and immortal God, giver of life and health: We beseech Thee to hear our prayers for Thy servant Valor, for whom we implore Thy mercy, that by Thy blessing upon him and upon those who minister to him of Thy healing gifts, he may be restored, if it be Thy gracious will, to soundness of health, and give thanks to Thee through Christ our Lord. Amen."

When she finished setting out everything she might need, she announced, "That's all boys. You can talk in a few hours."

She administered the injection and his eyes fluttered closed within seconds. With light and expert fingers, she checked his pulse at his throat before she slipped on some black rubber gloves and looked at Praetorian. "I need hot water." He hesitated, his cold gray eyes narrowing at her command. "If you want to keep him from dying of infection, get me some clean hot water."

As he left, she picked up her scalpel and carefully made the first incision.

◆ ◆ ◆ ◆

"HE'LL be needing these pills every four hours," Betty said, handing a glass bottle to Praetorian, "for the pain."

"He has to be back at his assignment in a few hours."

Betty shook her head and washed her hands in the basin by the door. "You'll be lucky if he wakes sometime in the next few hours."

"What am I supposed to do?"

"I'm sure I don't know." She turned as she dried her hands on the thin cotton cloth. "My job is to keep them alive. Your job is to coordinate all the other needful things. Have I got it right?"

He sighed and rubbed his eyes. "Thanks for the clarification," he said sarcastically. "What do I need to do for him?"

"When he wakes, give him a pill and some water. No more than one pill every four hours. Try to get him to take some sort of broth or something. My shift ends at five today. If you can send someone to fetch me, I'll come check on him."

"I heard your prayer earlier."

Betty nodded. "You can always pray for him. Pray with him, for that matter. Prayer always helps. Never hurts."

His eyes searched hers, his expression very serious and a bit inscrutable. His stark gaze began to unnerve Betty until he finally said, "I'd like you to teach me that prayer, sometime. It sounded perfect for a number of situations I encounter."

His sincerity touched her. She said, "It's from the Scottish *Book of Common Prayer* first printed in the 1630s. I'd be glad to teach you when we have time."

He nodded. "I appreciate it. And thanks for everything you did. More important than you know."

She grinned ironically. "But you can't share any details."

He mirrored her grin. "Of course not."

Abiel suddenly filled the doorway. "It's nearly dawn. I'll take you back."

Praetorian stopped her as she started to leave. "Has anyone been suspicious of your late night comings and goings?"

Betty smiled as she shrugged into her sweater. "Nay. They all think I head out to see some secret lover. They giggle and point and whisper behind their hands and never dare ask me a thing."

His laugh startled her. She smiled in return and left the barn.

ꝕ ꝕ ꝕ ꝕ

CHAPTER 6

Chapter Six

BETTY laid her fingertips on Valor's wrist and stared at his chest, counting his breathing and his pulse at the same time. She made her notations on the notebook she kept next to his cot, and felt herself jump a little when she noticed his eyes open.

"How are ye feeling, then?" she asked, taking the opportunity to put a hand on his forehead.

"Like someone shot me in the gut."

"Aye. I hear that's an occupational hazard."

"Here I thought I'd just be dancing the tango at various Embassy formals."

"Might want to consider a safer vocation. Spy isn't suiting you at the moment."

He smiled and pushed himself to a sitting position, sweat breaking out on his forehead. He panted out, "Wow, that smarts, doll." His inflection sounded more like Faith than Hope, but with less of a drawl.

His medicine sat on an overturned crate next to the bed beside a canteen of water. She handed him a pill and said, "Your color is better. Pardon the direct question but when is the last time you urinated?"

He answered without embarrassment, anticipating her next question. "About an hour before you got here. I didn't see any blood. It looked pretty clear."

"Any pain?"

He nodded. "Oh, my, yes. Do you know how long I've been here?"

"A day and a half."

He quickly set the canteen down and threw the wool blanket off. "I have to go."

Betty stood and put both hands on his shoulders. "You aren't going anywhere." As she pressed against his shoulders, he finally relented and lay back down. "Praetorian's establishing your cover story as we speak. Right now, concentrate on getting better."

"How soon can I go back?"

She shook her head. "I wouldn't recommend extended periods on your feet for at least another two or three days. I'd feel better if you gave it a full week."

"Doctor… what do I call you?"

He paused and she smiled. "Mercy."

"That works. Doctor Mercy, I have to go back. You have no idea –"

She leaned close until her nose almost touched his. "This is what I know, Valor. You could hemorrhage and someone could notice. Or, you could go into shock or get septic. Then, you could die. Just how do you intend to help the cause if you're dead, then?"

He closed his eyes, clearly conceding her point. She stood. "Best thing you can do is try to get some broth in you. Get some rest under your belt. Let your body heal. And pray. I'll be back tomorrow."

His eyes opened. "You're a believer, Mercy?"

She nodded. "I am."

"Pray with me, Mercy." It wasn't a request. He held out his hands and she placed her palms in his. When she bowed her head, he prayed, "Lord Jesus, surely you have borne our infirmities and carried our diseases. You were stricken and afflicted. You were wounded for our transgressions, yet, your punishment made us whole, and by your stripes we are healed. May we share in your sufferings, and through them, become more like you. Amen."

"Amen," she agreed.

♉ ♉ ♉ ♉

BETTY gathered the tin cup from the crate next to Valor's bed. "It pleases me that you ate it all," she said with a smile.

"I'm actually feeling hungry."

"I'll try to get you some bread tomorrow. Don't want to move too quickly."

As she handed him a pain pill, Praetorian rushed into the room. "Temperance has been arrested."

Betty felt her heart skip in her chest as Valor immediately pushed himself to a sitting position. Despite gritting his teeth and attempting to stifle his pain, he moaned out loud as he shakily pushed himself to his feet. Trying to rid herself of fear for her friend and stick to the task at hand, she rushed toward him as he reached for his uniform, but instead rested his hand against the wall and closed his eyes.

"You can't go."

"He must." Praetorian lifted the uniform from the hook and unbuttoned the shirt. Valor slipped his arm into the sleeve, cold sweat pouring from his face.

"How established is my cover?" Valor panted.

"Good enough. *Generalleutnant* von Stülpnagel met with Durandal and the *Obuerlieutenant* he introduced as his son. We have travel documentation coming in daily, prepared for whatever papers we needed for you." While Valor buttoned his shirt, Praetorian reached into his pocket and pulled out papers and a train ticket. "Last night, Durandal had a doctor friendly to the Resistance sent to the hotel to treat his son who will report that he treated a terrible case of food poisoning. That will help explain your weakness." He slipped the papers into Valor's jacket pocket. "No one will question Hess and I doubt they'll question you."

Valor braced his hand back up against the wall and closed his eyes. After a few moments, he straightened and turned. "I think I need another one of those pain pills."

Betty shook her head. "That will only serve to make you unconscious and stop your liver from working. One every four hours is nearly too high a dose as it is."

"Just this once. I have to get through the next few hours without anyone suspecting anything."

"Fine," she spat, opening the bottle and handing him a pill. "I'll be at the hospital when they carry you in on a stretcher."

She stormed out of the barn and waited by Abiel's car. Temperance had been arrested! What must she be enduring right now? Betty wondered, desperately, if there was anything she could personally do to help her.

When Praetorian emerged a minute later, she warily watched him approach. "I understand that this is going against your better judgment as his doctor. However, and Valor agrees, Temperance's safety is of the utmost concern at this point. I'm sure you understand. She knows far too much."

She gestured at the barn with her chin, keeping her arms crossed. "Who is this American, then, who can do anything for Temperance?"

"He runs the prison." She gasped in surprise and he nodded. "He's been absent too long now. There's no telling the damage that's already been done."

She wondered if he meant damage to the mission or to Temperance. He went back into the barn, but called out to her within seconds. "Mercy!"

She rushed in and found Valor on the cot, passed out, blood soaking his shirt. "*Glaikit dunderheid's* ripped his sutures," she spat, unbuttoning his uniform blouse. "Make yourself useful. Go get me some clean hot water. No more *blether* about the lad resuming his duties, now."

As she looked at his wane complexion and the cold sweat soaking his hair, she could not help but feel desperate about his condition. He needed to get better so that he could go save her friend!

⁙⁙⁙⁙

BETTY let the hot water trickle over her hand and rinsed the harsh lye soap off of her chapped red skin for what had to be the thousandth time that morning. As she dried her hands, she rolled her head on her neck and closed her eyes, wondering if it would be right and proper for a good sit-down with a nice cup of tea before she passed out after the grueling twelve-hour shift she'd just endured.

"Nurse Renault!"

Having learned to answer to that summons, she turned her head and spied *Oberleutnant* Leopold Schäfer, also known to her as Valor, standing by the nursing station. She couldn't believe he stood there, dressed, conscious.

"Hello, *Oberleutnant*."

Rather than reply to her greeting, he looked behind him, then over her shoulder. "I have a prisoner who needs immediate medical care."

Knowing he meant Temperance, she determined that she would stay in character and not react to the intensity of his voice. "It sounds urgent. Maybe you should see if a doctor is available."

"I have checked. No doctors are available and I am afraid it cannot wait. You should know that your supervisor already informed me that you're finishing your shift now, so I already know you are available."

Deciding that the tea could wait, she straightened her cap on her head. "Very well," she said, "I'll just fetch my cape."

She rushed to the nurses' locker room and grabbed her blue cape with the red lining. As she fastened it under her neck, she pulled some supplies from the medical bag she had hidden in the back of her locker and stuffed them into her pockets.

She found *Oberleutnant* Schäfer waiting for her right outside the door. As soon as he saw her, he pivoted on his heel and marched through the halls of the hospital in a very precise and military fashion. Betty could not help but notice that anyone who happened to be in his path quickly moved.

Betty had to skip every few steps to keep up with his long strides. They crossed the road, moved down one block, turned right, and went one more block into the huge imposing building near the town square. She knew the first two floors comprised Nazi administrative offices and that the prison was on the upper two floors. Schäfer took her in through a side door that accessed the stairwell.

Away from the eyes of anyone else, he slowly took the stairs, pausing in between flights to lean against the wall and rest. "Are you going to make it?" she whispered at the third rest.

He nodded and took a deep breath. "I have no choice."

They stopped at the third floor. As they entered the main room directly off the stairwell, her eyes immediately went to the large cage in the center of the room. That cage was reserved for the prisoner undergoing the most rigorous interrogation. Large hoses connected to a cold water tank shot high pressure water into the cage, keeping the prisoner cold, wet, and miserable for days at a time, unable to rest or sleep, unable to feel any warmth. He would be taken in and out of the cage and intimidated or abused until he gave the information the Nazis sought. The entire time the prisoner was in the cage, the daily business of running the prison happened all around at the desks and the outer offices. There was no break from the watchful eyes of the prison staff, no privacy for any reason, and no hope for escape.

Today, the cage stood empty, but Betty could see the puddles of water pooled on the concrete floor. Freshly watered-down blood stains broke the white and black striped pattern on the thin mattress.

Schäfer led the way to a heavy metal door which he unlocked using a key he retrieved from his pocket. At the entrance to the door, he pulled a large metal key ring off of a hook, then led the way to the cell three doors down.

He unlocked the cell, then stepped back and let Betty precede him inside. She gasped when she saw the woman curled up on the thin mattress. Her wet hair covered her face, and her blood stained slip clung wetly to her body. Betty rushed forward and knelt next to the cot.

"Save her," Schäfer whispered desperately. "Please."

Betty wondered at the tone, at the look of desperation on his face.

"Perhaps you shouldn't let them treat a woman like a man," she snarled, pushing the patient's hair off of her face. Her stomach turned when she barely recognized Temperance. Her face was battered and beaten, one eye completely swollen shut, her nose obviously broken, her lip cracked and bleeding. Even in her sleep, she cradled a hand to her chest, and Betty could see the tip of one finger had started to turn purple.

"I agree," he replied. She could hear the fury in his voice.

With less emotion she said, "I need dry clothes for her. And scissors, if you can get them, to get this wet garment off of her." As she pried Temperance's hands apart, the woman whimpered in her sleep. "Do we know how long she has been like this?"

"Yes, we do. Forty-seven hours."

Betty whipped her head around to stare at him, feeling her eyes widen. She could not imagine the cruelty of people who would do such a thing to another human being. She suddenly understood his urgency to leave the barn and resume his normal duties. He had known, or at least suspected, that this might happen. The intensity of emotions in Schäfer's eyes took her breath away. As she turned back to Temperance, she pulled some gauze out of her pocket. "I'm going to need your help."

"I'll get the scissors."

Betty cut the slip off of Temperance and tried to move her as little as possible to get it out from under her. Her skin felt ice cold to the touch, and she wished she'd brought a thermometer with her. At her request, Schäfer brought a thick pair of socks that she slipped on Temperance's feet. With the slip off, and using the sheet on the cot to protect her modesty as much as she could, she examined her. She had two snapped ribs on her right side. Putting her ear to Temperance's chest, Betty listened but couldn't hear any obvious labored breathing or crackling.

Schäfer averted his eyes and helped sit Temperance up while Betty wrapped her ribs tightly. As soon as she could, she slipped a cotton sheath over her, then covered her with the blanket again.

She took two tongue depressors and laid them alongside the broken finger. As quickly as possible, she set and splinted the finger. After about thirty seconds, she breathed a deep sigh of relief when Temperance's nail bed colored up with restored circulation.

As gently as possible, she probed her cheekbone with the tips of her fingers. "Her orbital may be broken," she observed. "If it is, it's going to really give her grief. If it gets infected that close to the brain, she could die in hours."

Betty closed her eyes and held Temperance's hand in both of her own. "Almighty, ever-living God, maker of mankind, who doth correct those whom Thou doth love, and chastise every one whom Thou doth receive: We beseech Thee to have mercy upon this Thy servant visited with Thine hand; and to grant that she may take her sickness patiently, and recover her bodily health, and if it be Thy gracious will, whensoever her soul depart from the body, that it may be without spot presented unto Thee; through Christ our Lord. Amen."

Schäfer whispered, "Amen."

Betty stood and slipped her hands into her pockets. "Watch her closely for signs of sickness. If she was cold and wet for two full days, probably hungry too, then she is susceptible to all kinds of illness. Her injuries only make her weaker and more likely to come down with something fatal."

He gave a curt nod of his head.

"Come get me if you need anything for her. I would like to be the one who treats her, if it's possible."

She could see a muscle tic in his jaw. "I will find you if I need you," he agreed. His voice sounded far away.

Betty walked closer to him and stood toe-to-toe with him. "Can you protect her?"

The intense look in his eyes spoke more than his words. "I can only protect her to an extent before the risk becomes unacceptable. I have to tread very carefully."

Betty felt her Scottish blood war against her French blood. Her cheeks flushed and she bit out, "Then tread."

He appeared to understand what she meant as he nodded again.

"And you," she added, pointing her finger at him, "find a place to lie down before you fall down. You'll be no use to anyone if you're out of commission."

"This first," he said. He gingerly put a hand on his abdomen. "Though, I'll confess that I'm actually feeling better now that I'm up and moving about."

She narrowed her eyes. "You may be a very good spy and skilled in the art of deception, but I'm afraid I don't believe you."

His smile barely reached his eyes. "You're not the one who has to, Doctor."

Chapter Seven

BETTY sat on the edge of Temperance's cot. She watched as she took a sip of broth. "I know the jaw hurts," she murmured, "but you really should try to eat some of the bread."

"I'm so hungry, but it hurts worse than it did the first day."

Betty reached over and felt along her patient's jawline. "It's likely broken. We need to get you out of here and get you some real medical care."

"Sshh," Temperance said, looking toward the door. "He might hear you."

Betty looked at the door, too, and back at her friend. Her eye swollen completely shut and her face so puffy and bruised it amazed Betty that she could speak at all. "He seems very smitten with you. Can you trust him?"

She knew she could not break Schäfer's cover, in case someone else interrogated Temperance. But she wanted to relieve her worries slightly.

"There is no one I will trust but you until I'm out of here or entering heaven." She dipped a small piece of bread into the broth and put it in her mouth, sucking the broth out of the bread instead of chewing it. "He is nice to me because he needs to get information out of me." She stopped talking to cough, putting a hand to her ribs. "Oh, heavens, that hurts."

Betty didn't like the sound of the cough and pulled a stethoscope out of her pocket. "How long have you been coughing like this?"

"Since this morning." A tear slid down her cheek. "It hurts my ribs so bad that I try not to cough, and that makes it worse."

Betty listened, but the lungs sounded clear. "I don't hear anything. Is there any pain other than the ribs?"

Temperance sat silent for a few heartbeats then said, "I can't tell."

Betty nodded and put her stethoscope away. "Try to get the soaked bread down."

"Nurse Renault," Temperance whispered, careful to use Betty's cover name. She swallowed then took a deep breath. "Nurse Renault, do you think … do you believe…" She never finished the sentence. Instead she slowly hung her head.

After an uncomfortable silence, Betty prompted, "What is it? Marie, what is it?"

All of a sudden, Temperance blurted, "Would it be sinful to take my own life?" Slow, fat tears fell from her swollen eyes.

Betty felt her heart stop. She felt her held breath burning in her lungs. Then she felt an overwhelming sadness. She heard herself whispering, "I do. But it won't come to that. Have faith. Be strong and have faith."

What kind of intolerable pain and terror must Temperance be enduring every second to even allow such a thought to enter her mind? She placed a gentle hand on the woman's knee and said, "Eat. Eat while I pray for you."

Betty silently prayed and felt unwanted tears begin to fall from her own eyes. She had no idea how long she prayed, nor any notion how many times she petitioned God to comfort and heal her friend, before a tap on the door which preceded Schäfer's entrance interrupted.

Schäfer's eyes darted back and forth between them, then studied the plate of food, apparently calculating just how little Temperance had managed to consume. "It's time to go, Nurse Renault."

"Be strong, Marie. Have faith." Betty stood and lifted her hand from Temperance's knee. She turned to Schäfer. "May I check in on the other prisoners in this wing?"

"If you wish." He looked at Temperance. "Just leave the tray when you're done with it, *Fräulein* Perrin. I will be back by to collect it. Take your time."

BETTY ran behind *Oberleutnant* Schäfer, gripping her cloak to her throat. They dashed through the rain drenched cobblestone streets, around parked cars, and through alleyways. He ripped open the door to the stairwell and it slammed on the brick wall and bounced off. He was halfway up the first flight of stairs before Betty even started climbing. She couldn't believe how quickly and fluidly he moved just a week since having a bullet removed from his gut. The young man had the constitution of an ox.

At the third floor, he paused, hand on the doorknob, and waited for her to catch up with him. As soon as she hit the landing, he straightened his jacket, slipped his hat off the top of his head and secured it under his arm, then gave her a curt nod.

He pushed open the door and walked casually into the main area. In the center cage, a man wearing only a soaking pair of cotton underwear covered his face with his hands while guards drenched him with a hose. Despite the early morning hour, uniformed soldiers occupied most of the desks, busy at their typewriters or talking on telephones. A haze of cigarette smoke hung in the air above their desks. No one, save the guards administering the torture, even looked at the prisoner.

Schäfer led the way to the cell block where she'd patched Temperance up the week before. He unlocked the big door, held it open for her, then stepped through behind her, grabbing the large ring of keys off the hook by the door.

Without a word, he led the way to Temperance's cell. Before he had the door unlocked, Betty could already see that her friend was very sick. As soon as the door opened, she rushed in.

As she knelt by her bedside, she reached out and felt Temperance's forehead with the palm of her hand. She gasped when the level of heat registered. "How long?" She bit out.

"Since yesterday."

"Why didn't you come get me sooner?"

She looked over her shoulder and watched him rub the back of his neck with his hands. He rested a shoulder on the open cell door. "Need I remind you that I am an officer in Hitler's military. I'm not always permitted to seek medical attention for sick prisoners, Nurse. I convinced them that Marie is important and we'd rather she not die. But it took me the day to do it."

He sounded weary, but Betty could not focus on him. She could diagnose him without even examining him – pushing himself too hard too soon after major trauma followed by major surgery.

She turned back to Temperance, pulled a stethoscope out of her bag, and slipped the earpieces into her ears. Until she drowned out the sounds of the prison, she hadn't realized how loud it was there. She'd barely placed the chestpiece against Temperance's ribs when she immediately heard the rattle.

She had Schäfer help lift her friend into a sitting position and listened from behind on both sides, registering the level of heat emanating from her body as she touched her. Temperance never even opened her eyes. She took a thermometer out of her bag and checked her temperature.

Betty pulled a piece of paper and the stub of a pencil out of the pocket of her cloak and created a chart, writing:

`0512, tmp 104F, pulse 120, resp 32`

The respiratory rate was too high. She didn't like it. Betty stood and turned. Schäfer straightened and looked expectant, almost hopeful. "Double pneumonia. She needs to be in the hospital."

He shook his head. "That won't happen. What are our other options?"

"It has to happen. That is the only option." She did not raise her voice, but she felt the intensity of what she said increase so that he looked over his shoulder before putting a finger to his lips.

"They'll let her die first. It cost me much to bring you here today," he murmured in his American English. "What you have to do, has to be done here. Tell me what to do. I will do anything you ask."

Betty sighed and opened her bag, pulling out a bottle of Sulfapyridine in half-gram pills. "You need to get her to ingest two of these pills at a time," she instructed as she handed him the bottle. "These are going to make her very sick to her stomach and she will vomit them back up. The longer she has them inside of her before she expels them, the better. Give them to her every four hours."

She pulled a clean cloth out of a pocket in her cape. "Cleanliness is important. I'll get you some clean sheets to put on her mattress. Keep a cool rag on her forehead. Wash your hands constantly. Try to get some broth in her between giving her the pills."

He took the cloth from her when she handed it to him. "Is she going to live?"

Betty smoothed the hair back from Temperance's face. The heat scared her. "If she were in a hospital under an oxygen tent, I wouldn't be sure she'd pull through. In these conditions," she stood and sighed, running her hands over her face, "I don't know. It's in God's hands."

His lips thinned. "I will give her the medicine."

"Meet me here tomorrow morning at five. My shift at the hospital starts at seven. That should give me time to get her vitals and check on her after having at least two doses of the medication."

Chapter Eight

BETTY lay the newborn baby in his mother's arms and smiled at the young woman. "Do you have a name?"

"I'll name him after his papa," she said softly, kissing the forehead of the hour-old infant. The midwife had brought her here in distress and the doctor performed a cesarean. "Henri."

"That's a perfect, strong name." Betty smiled. "He looks like every Henri I've ever met. Where is his papa?"

Her breath hitched and her lips tightened into a thin line. "He died before we even knew I was expecting."

Betty put her hand on her shoulder. "God bless you, child." She straightened her blankets and made sure there was water in her glass. "If you need anything, let me know. Anything. Don't try to get out of bed."

She left the young widow in her room and walked down the hall. If she went now, she might be able to snatch a quick bite to eat. She knew the warm sun shone outside, simply because rays beamed through the windows in the patients' rooms. She suddenly realized she hadn't been able to enjoy that very much recently. She bought a croissant, chicken sandwich, and cup of tea from the canteen and carried it outside.

As she sat down, someone sat on the bench beside her, and in a very familiar sounding French, said, "I've been waiting out here for over an hour."

Betty gasped. "Grace! What are you doing here?"

She held up a sandwich wrapped in paper. "Having lunch with a total stranger on a park bench." She took a bite of her sandwich and wrapped it back up. "Yum."

Betty smiled and took a sip of her tea. "It is so good to lay eyes on you again."

"And you." Grace looked around. "You look well. Tired, but well. I hear Temperance has taken ill."

She nodded. "She's very ill indeed."

"I'd thought she had been given some medicine."

"I prescribed her some medication. But, she needs to be in a hospital, not a damp concrete prison cell. She isn't getting any better. Despite everything I've done. I need to have her in a hospital or else she will surely die. Schäfer was supposed to arrange her move to the hospital yesterday, but –" she stopped speaking in the middle of her sentence and did not elaborate any further. She could not tell Grace that Schäfer had been called away on vital Resistance business and had been detained, missing the window of opportunity to have Temperance moved.

"Who is Schäfer?"

"The *Oberleutnant* who is over the prison. He escorts me to the prison to care for her."

Grace narrowed her eyes. "Why?"

Betty shrugged and chose each word carefully, thinking about the way Schäfer looked after Temperance and the care he showed her. "I think it goes against orders to do it because it's always at odd hours. I think he has personal feelings for her." Her brogue rolled the r's. "I think he's a believer."

Grace's face screwed up like she'd taken a bite of something bitter. "I think he's a Nazi pig."

Betty raised an eyebrow. "You do quite well masking your true feelings, you do." She smiled as she said it, loving her friend's passion. "How's the foot?"

"Healed." The abrupt answer told Betty that Grace had no desire to talk about herself. Her friend unwrapped her sandwich again. "We're going for her this week. What kind of sick do we need to prepare for?" She took a bite of her sandwich and her eyes shifted to look over Betty's shoulder toward the hospital entrance.

Betty felt nervous excitement at the prospect of a prison break. She tried to imagine the plans that would have anyone break out of that fortress of a prison. She summed up Temperance's condition as succinctly as possible. "She has severe pneumonia. High fever, low oxygen levels, very weak. She has broken bones that aren't healing well, and I can't keep any food in her, not even broth, because of the medication I'm trying to give her. It doesn't let you keep your supper down. So, she's also malnourished, to take the biscuit."

Grace's eyes met hers again. Betty could hear the anxiety in her voice. "What do I need to do?"

Betty wanted to reach out and grip her hand and convey the importance of what she would say next. "You need to carry her out and get her on a plane back to London. Take her to Doctor Mallory Knight at Winchmore Hill. He's a top pulmonary specialist. If anyone can save her life, he can."

Grace took a deep breath and released it slowly. "What are the odds she'll survive the trip?"

Betty felt her heart freeze in her chest, knowing how dire the situation was. "I dare not guess. I only pray we can get it done quickly enough."

Grace's normally unreadable face paled. "Should we just...."

Temper surged through her chest at the prospect of what Grace almost said. "Absolutely not. You get her on that plane. God will put her in the palm of His hand. I believe He will. I have faith He will."

Grace nodded. "Okay. Can you be available?"

Would she be available? It would break her cover. In a split second she weighed the danger and came to a decision. "If you need me, you'll need to come find me. I'm on duty the same night, and it sounds like you're planning to fill my emergency room."

Grace rewrapped her sandwich and stood. "Thursday," she whispered.

Betty nodded. "I'll be ready. Please get a message to Matthew or Abiel to bring me my bag. I should have it on hand. I have a place I can hide it for a short time."

ᵁ ᵁ ᵁ ᵁ

BETTY looked down at Temperance. Her lips displayed a bluish tinge and her breathing appeared much more labored. She no longer even needed the stethoscope to hear the rattle in her chest. "We don't have any more time," she said, picking up her friend's limp, hot hand.

Schäfer lowered his voice to barely a whisper. "Tonight."

"I pray we make it that long." She put a hand on Temperance's forehead and closed her eyes as she felt Schäfer lay his hand on her shoulder. Instead of one of the liturgical prayers she often preferred, Betty chose to pray from her heart. She whispered so softly that she doubted even Schäfer could hear what she said. "Father God, Jehova Rapha, You are a healing God. Please heal Temperance's lungs. Get her on that plane, God, so that she can get back to England and get the medical care she needs. Amen."

The spy in the Nazi uniform signified his agreement with her prayer by his confirming whisper of, "Amen."

She raised her head and looked over her shoulder. "It's in His hands now."

A muscle ticked in his jaw. "It has always been." He looked at his watch. "You must go."

"Aye." She stood and straightened her cape. "God be with you, Schäfer."

"And also with you."

⚜ ⚜ ⚜ ⚜

CHAPTER 9

Chapter Nine

BETTY sat in a chair on the porch of the nurses' barracks and watched car after car drive by, heading to the prison. Nurse Ginette walked out onto the porch and paused to look at her reflection in the window, straightening her hat and dabbing at the lipstick at the corner of her lips.

"Who's the lucky man?" Betty asked with a smile.

The young nurse turned and moved to sit in the chair next to Betty. "I wouldn't normally go out with a German soldier," she whispered, looking over her shoulder, "but we're going to see Virginia Benoit! Can you believe it? I'll sit next to a German to do that."

Betty smiled. She loved Virginia Benoit, code-named Hope. She had laughed with her, cried with her, and prayed with her many, many times. "How exciting. I've heard amazing things about her show."

Perhaps feeling emboldened by the small talk, Nurse Ginette asked, "And what of you, Nurse Renault? No gentleman caller who can escort you to the concert?"

Betty said, "Even if there were such a person, I am on duty tonight."

"So is there such a person?" Ginette grinned a knowing grin and Betty turned to give her an impatient look. "Perhaps such a person with the initials of R. B.? A person who sends for you in the middle of the night and keeps you out until dawn?"

Trying to keep her features blank, trying not to let her eyes widen even a little bit, she casually observed, "That seems like a rather specific question."

"I saw the doctor's housecall bag. None of the doctors here have those initials. Who is this mystery man?"

Thankfully, a sharp whistle drew both the women's attention to the street. A young private waved toward Ginette, who waved back and stood. "I'll tell you all about the show later," she said with a giggle, then rushed down the wooden steps. Betty watched as she slipped her arm through the uniformed sleeve of the private and practically dragged him down the street toward the prison.

She felt the nervous jumble in her stomach tighten into a hard knot. Tonight it would happen. And she had been careless. "Please God," she prayed silently, "let it go smoothly."

She realized she should eat something. Only God knew what the night would bring. She went into the barracks and walked through the main room to the kitchen. It was well past time for a regular meal, but the administrator had snacks readily available for off times, in case a nurse's shift did not coincide with a regular meal schedule. She dug through the cupboard and found an apple and a cheese pie.

Sitting back down in her chair on the porch, she bit into the pie, watching as the street and the area around the hospital quieted down for the night. She spoke to nurses who came and went, some leaving for shifts in the hospital, some returning from an evening out. She had gained some friends during her months working here and had definitely learned a lot about what a nurse went through in a day. While she sat and enjoyed the abnormal silence and peace, she thought about training other doctors to work more closely with the nurses and create a stronger bond that was lacking from the norm right now.

As she considered a series of articles she'd write on the subject once this blasted war was over with, she felt a rumble. A second later, she heard the distant sound of an explosion, then three more rapidly following. Nervous energy made her heart palpitate as she stood and brushed the crumbs off of her cape.

Her supervisor, Leslie Gay, rushed out of the barracks and looked down the street before looking at her. She held the collar of a quilted robe closed against her neck. "What was that?"

"Sounded like an explosion. You think I should head over to the hospital just in case?"

"Yes. Yes. Go and be ready. I can hear gunshots, too." She looked down at her bed attire. "I'll be there in ten minutes."

Betty nodded. "I'll let them know you're coming."

"A lot of gunshots. We're so short staffed because of the blasted concert. I let so many of the girls go. I hate this war."

Betty put a hand on her arm and guided her toward the door, opening it and gently encouraging her to go inside. "I'm sure we'll be fine. It may end up being nothing after all. I'll meet you over there."

She rushed to the hospital and through the doors to the emergency room, finding the head clerk. "There's been some sort of an explosion," she said. "Mrs. Gay will be here momentarily, but wants the staff prepared."

Twenty minutes later, injured people swamped the facility. Betty fought the impulse to take over as doctor while she held the hand of the man screaming while the doctor examined his crushed leg. Even through the chaos, she heard the murmur of stardom as medics rushed in, carrying an unconscious Virginia Benoit on a stretcher. The doctor gave the man a shot, which almost immediately relaxed him, and Betty left his side to rush to Hope before another nurse could stake her claim.

The medic looked at her. "Got hit in the head when the wall was blown out. Real close to the concussion, too. That was perhaps half an hour ago. She hasn't regained consciousness."

Betty nodded and lifted Hope's eyelids one at a time, checking her pupils' responses to light. She appreciated the fact that they were even and reactive, though she didn't like the sluggishness of the response. Oh, what she would do to be at home in her own hospital! She took her stethoscope from the pocket of her uniform and listened to Hope's chest. Good heart sounds, good lungs.

As she cleaned the bloody cut on her forehead, she spoke to her. "Virginia, can you hear me?" she asked in French, knowing that Hope would respond to French as much as English. "Virginia, can you hear me?"

The beautiful dark skinned star moaned and shifted her head on the cot. Betty spoke again. "Virginia, I need you to try to open your eyes, now. You're in a hospital."

Her eyelids suddenly flew open, and Betty could see the confusion and fear in them seconds before she tried to lunge out of the bed. She pinned her down with her own body and spoke in soothing tones. "It's okay. There was an explosion at your concert."

"Mercy?" Hope asked.

She knew her friend was confused and disoriented, but she couldn't risk her blowing her cover. "Your head must be hurting terribly if you're begging for God's mercy. There, there. We'll get the doctor over here to fix you up as soon as he's free."

Her eyes cleared and she visibly started to calm down. Hope lay back down and said, "Thank you, nurse."

Betty handed her a folded cloth. "Press this up to your forehead to help stop some of the bleeding."

Hope's eyes welled with tears and she whispered, "I pray they're okay."

Betty gave her half a smile. "It's all we can do, I'm afraid."

"Are you okay?"

Betty turned at the shocked voice and saw Prudence. It took her a moment to recognize her because her hair was now a rich chestnut brown instead of blonde. She looked pale, out of breath, and a little frazzled.

Hope clearly recognized her immediately, even despite the dyed hair. She had also obviously lost what clarity she'd regained just moments before. "Oh, it's you! Oh, honey, it's so good to see you."

Prudence immediately looked at Betty, suddenly worried that Hope would give them away. Prudence stepped all the way into the area and spoke loudly, speaking as if she knew Hope personally and would call the super star by her first name. "Virginia! Are you all right?"

"No need to fuss. I'm just dandy." She pushed herself up and put a shaking hand to her head. "Or not."

"She was very near to the explosion. She got quite a lot of the aftershock. I don't think there's any internal bleeding, but her head is badly concussed." Betty patted her hand, then realized that Prudence stood in the room with them. Why would Prudence be here on the night of the big operation? Quietly, she asked, "What's the matter?"

Just as quietly, Prudence answered, "Grace needs you."

She felt her eyes widen. Temperance. "I'll need my bag."

"I'm coming with you," Hope said in a stage whisper. "There's a pair of dead Nazis in my dressing room. I have to leave now. They'll certainly be looking for me soon if they aren't already."

A pair of dead Nazis? Betty wanted to ask a dozen questions, but Prudence stepped forward to help and asked, "Can you get up?"

Knowing how dangerous it would be for her to move at all, she held up a halting hand. "Her head injury could be very serious. Short of exploratory surgery, there's no way to tell without a few days of strict bed rest and observation."

Hope spoke up. "No time for any of that. I'll either be just fine or I won't. I know for sure if I lay in this hospital, they'll arrest me, and I know I won't be fine then. Let's have faith and leave it in God's good hands. I could use some help, though."

Prudence took her by the hand and helped her as she shakily got to her feet. "This is impossible. We have a long way to go on foot."

Betty looked at her. "Can you get us a car?"

"Maybe."

Hope, clear again, said to her, "Go get your bag and head out front. Prudence, see if you can scare us up a car. I'll make my way out there. If I get outside in time, take me with you. If not, go help Grace. I'll make do."

Betty hesitated, but Hope already carefully walked toward the entrance of the hospital. So, she left her and pushed her way through the throngs of people in the hospital, through the front lobby, out the front doors. She ran to the barracks and burst into the building. Everyone who lived there was currently next door at the hospital and the place was empty. She took the stairs two at a time, ran into her room, and to her bed. The bed was a simple construction, with a thin mattress set on top of a box frame. Betty had been able to pry the wooden plywood off and hide her bag inside the hollow box under the mattress. How Ginette had seen it would have to remain a mystery.

As soon as she had the bag in hand, she grabbed her cape and ran back down the stairs. Just as she opened the door, Prudence pulled up in a Mercedes. Betty rushed down the steps and yanked open the door.

"There's Hope!" she said, sliding into the seat. Hope stumbled out of the hospital, gripping the handrail alongside the steps as if her life depended on it. Prudence drove forward and stopped to collect her. Betty hopped out of the car and opened the back door, then helped Hope into the car as quickly as she could manage. Prudence started driving again before she had the door fully shut.

"What was happening back there?" she asked.

"Temperance was arrested two weeks ago. This was her rescue."

Betty didn't mean that. She'd known tonight was the rescue, but she didn't know the plans. She felt her lips tighten and replied in English. "Aye. I saw her daily since about a week ago. She's very sick. I told them she needed to be in hospital, but was told it was absolutely out of the question. I did what I could for her there, which wasn't much." She looked in her bag, inventorying the supplies she'd collected over the last two days. She thought of how sick she was that morning. "I'm relieved to hear she's alive. I think I'll be able to stabilize her." She turned in her seat and peered into the back seat. "What happened in your dressing room?"

Hope sat slumped back against the headrest with her eyes closed. At Mercy's question, she opened them and very stoically said, "A few members of Hitler's SS objected to the tone of my skin."

She had just accused the Nazis of being just as thick as a brick. She couldn't believe that people would be so blindly ignorant as to think that skin pigmentation had anything to do with a person's value. It frustrated her and angered her. A mild Gaelic curse escaped Betty's lips before she could stop herself. *"Chomh tiubh le balla brÃce!"*

They rode in silence after that. Betty didn't want to distract Prudence from driving. Instead, she prayed silently and continually – they had so many balls in the air right now with Hope, Temperance, and the prison escape. So much could go wrong very quickly and this juggling act would end in disaster.

As they pulled into the edge of a large field, Prudence stopped. She looked all around, then gripped the steering wheel with both hands and tilted her head to the side to look up at the sky. Betty knew she sought a glimpse of Faith's airplane, which didn't appear to be anywhere near them.

"Well, then. What now?" Betty asked.

"Now I suggest we take time to pray."

Less than five minutes later, the dark shadow of a plane blocked the moonlight overhead, close enough that Betty felt like she could reach up and touch the underside of it. After it taxied to the end of the field and turned around, it stopped. Prudence put her hand on the gear shift and started to press down on the clutch. Before she released it, a wooden paneled Ariès Berline tore onto the airfield and rushed right past them, speeding toward the parked plane. Prudence accelerated and sped across the field, right behind the other vehicle.

Betty saw the upper body of someone in the back seat of the car in front of them emerge from the window and fire a gun in their direction. The windshield between her and Prudence cracked into a spiderweb of glass as a large caliber bullet passed between them and then out through the cloth convertible roof.

"Prudence!" Betty screamed, ducking. "Duck, Hope!"

"Quack," Hope giggled as she slid down onto the floorboard of the back seat. In a way, Betty wished she could be so oblivious to what was going on around them. Terror threatened to overwhelm her as she pressed herself against the seat and started praying out loud for their protection. All the while, she hung onto the door handle and braced her other hand against the dashboard in an attempt to keep from being thrown about by Prudence's defensive driving.

She nearly fell forward as Prudence slammed on the brakes. Betty sat up and watched as Abiel leaped out of the driver's side of the Ariès and rushed their car with his pistol drawn. She tried to scream his name but her voice froze in terror. He looked right at Prudence, though, and as soon as he did, he pivoted and went back to his car. He opened the back door and bent inside the car. When he emerged once more, he carried Temperance in his arms, still clutching the pistol in his hand.

As soon as she saw her patient, she reigned in the adrenaline and fear and pushed open the car door. She and Prudence helped Hope out of the back seat and rushed her as fast as they could toward the plane, passing a machine-gun toting Grace, who focused on the cars that rapidly approached them.

From the tree line, three escaped prisoners ran toward the plane, reaching it about the same time as they did. "Hurry!" The copilot yelled, rushing down the plane's steps with a Sten submachine-gun in his hand.

Pausing at the base of the stairs, Prudence put her hands on Betty's and Hope's shoulders. "Be safe. I will be praying."

Abiel rushed out of the plane, dodging around the prisoners who were starting to board, and looked right at Betty and Hope. He ran down the steps and stopped right in front of Hope. "What happened?"

"Someone blew a building up right next to me," she said with a giggle. Abiel put his arm around her shoulders and turned toward the plane door. "One minute I was singing, and the next thing I know it all came crashing down on my head."

"You need to get out of here," he said gently. Hope reached up and clutched his hand.

"Please stay with me, Edward," she said urgently.

Edward? How did Hope know Abiel well enough to call him by a Christian name?

"Get her on the plane! Stay with her!" Prudence yelled over the gunshots and the drowning roar of the plane's engine. "Faith can bring you back later!"

Betty urged Abiel and Hope on board. She had her hand on the handle to the staircase when she heard a crack of gunfire very close by. Grace dove behind the hood of the Ariès Berline, using the iron engine block as cover. She studied the tree line in the darkness. As the gunfire came at them sporadically, she sought out the muzzle flashes which would become the targets for her returned fire. Moments later, the copilot joined her.

Betty watched Prudence as she turned, dashing back to the vehicle she'd stolen. After only three steps, she fell to the earth. Betty cried her name and ran toward her, reaching her at the same time as the copilot.

"Get her on board," she ordered as he scooped her into his arms. "Let's get out of here before we lose anyone else." Remembering her bag, she reached into the car and lifted it out of the front floorboard then ran back to the plane.

Just as she started to climb the steps, she heard Grace cry out. Betty turned and saw her fall to the ground. Abiel, who had looked out the door at that moment, jumped from the plane and ran toward Grace. He scooped her into his arms and ran back to the plane, the ground exploding in little bursts of dirt as bullets tracked every step he took.

♒ ♒ ♒ ♒

BEFORE Abiel even had the door shut, the plane started taxiing.

"Everybody aboard?" Faith yelled back from the pilot's seat. Betty opened her bag and pulled out a roll of bandages and a stethoscope. She tucked a capped syringe with pain medication, a needle, and thread into her pocket.

"Go!" Abiel yelled.

"Hold your horses, Spanky. Everything up here's written in Kraut and I only took one semester." It suddenly occurred to Betty that they were in a German aircraft. The engine pitch changed and the airplane lurched forward. "And I did *nicht* so *gut* in that class if you catch my drift."

Betty glanced at Temperance, who lay unconscious on a pallet on the plane's floor. She couldn't do much for her right now, not until they got to a hospital. In the meantime, she moved carefully through the cabin of the plane. She nodded a greeting to the escaped prisoners. They didn't have any obvious injuries, so her first stop was the unconscious Prudence, who lay about a foot away from Temperance.

It looked like a good through-and-through bullet wound in her shoulder. She quickly cleaned the entrance wound, padded the area around the exit wound, and wound the bandage around her shoulder. As she worked, she focused on a conversation between Grace and the copilot.

"Why are we on a Nazi airplane?" Grace asked.

"Long story," the copilot said as he secured the door. He had a Sten submachine gun strapped across his back and wearily slipped it over his head. "Hang on. This isn't going to be a smooth flight. They know we're here. The Vichy aren't very good shots, but I am not overly fond of the prospect of flying what looks like a German bomber over Britain."

As he said that, the entire plane shook with the force of exploding anti-aircraft artillery, which pilots called Archie. "If you can't strap in, grab onto something and hang on tight!" Faith yelled back.

Betty finished applying the field dressing to Prudence's shoulder and made a notation of her vital signs. "She needs stitches, but I'm not having a go at that while we're in the air with our friends trying to put us back on the ground so rapidly." She turned toward Grace, who lay on the floor in a 'T' at Prudence's feet. "Now then, let's have a wee look at what kettle you've managed to get into."

"It's nothing," Grace managed in a very weak voice. Abiel slipped a blanket over her shoulder as Betty looked at the leg.

"Nuttin' with you is ever really *nowt*, my friend," she said absently, noting the splintered bone and blood loss. She knew, without any further inspection, that Grace would lose that leg. The pain she would be in as the shock wore off was going to be extreme. She reached into her pocket to pull out the syringe and give her some relief as the whole plane shook and rapidly lost altitude.

"Y'all hang on back there!" Faith yelled.

The copilot yelled, "Grab hold!"

Bits of jagged metal sprinkled the aircraft like sleet, hitting them from every angle. The shrapnel rained against the fuselage milliseconds before the concussion of exploding antiaircraft fire rocked the aircraft. The flashes of light that accompanied the explosions lit the inside of the JU-52 like lightning in a raging storm.

Grace's face lost all color and she started praying loudly in Hebrew. Betty put a hand on her shoulder. "Listen." Grace stopped praying and looked at Betty, but her eyes were glassy and she knew she probably didn't even see her. "Grace, listen to me! This is bad. I can only temporarily set it. We have to wait until we land before I can work on your leg. Let me give you something for the pain."

"*Lo! Be'vakasha.*" Her friend still spoke in Hebrew, but quickly corrected herself. "No, please," she panted in French. "Please. I have to stay awake. I can't stand the thought of going to sleep and never...."

Remembering how much Grace feared flying, she smiled in understanding. "Okay. What can I do?"

Grace gripped her hand with both of hers. "Save Temperance." She started to close her eyes, but said the words again, weaker, almost in a whisper. "Save Temperance."

The airplane started to climb and the constant sounds of the antiaircraft fire stopped. Faith yelled back, "This ain't right. They stopped shooting, but we're pretty far from the coast."

The copilot yelled, "If you can manage, keep a look out the windows, lads and lasses! The only reason they'd stop shooting is if they sent up fighters to bring us down!"

Betty looked behind her and motioned to the dashing looking man sitting on the deck. The escaped prisoner pushed himself onto his feet and made his way toward them. "What's yer name, *chiel*?"

"Percy," he said with a charming and debonair smile.

"Right. Listen up, Percy. Sit next to my friend, Grace, here. She's in a *wee* bit more pain than she'll admit, even to herself. Try not to let her move around overly much." She pulled her hand from Grace's grip. "Percy's going to sit with you. If you come to your senses, I'll give you that shot."

Grace licked her lips. "Thank you."

"Hang on!" Faith yelled. "They're coming in low on our six."

The aircraft fell out from under them and Betty lost her balance, falling to the deck. She started to roll toward Temperance, but caught herself with the strap of a seatbelt as she heard Grace scream in agony.

"Shutting out the lights now, folks. Don't want to give those fighters too clear of a target," Faith yelled a split second before the cabin went completely black.

Even as a small child, Betty hated the dark. She would cry and cry until her mother would come in and hold her until she fell asleep. In the dark of the cabin, she froze. The flashes of light from the oncoming explosions looked like lightning flashes in a storm. The sounds of the explosions, the dark, took her back to the surgery and the bomb that took her Rudy.

She stayed on her side, gripping that loose seatbelt, cold chills wracking her body, nausea swirling in her stomach, frozen in terror. Until she heard Grace scream.

Shaking her head to clear it, she used her pen light to navigate to her bag. She dug inside until she found the flashlight and turned it on with shaking fingers.

The sound of metal hitting metal as bullets peppered the fuselage of the airplane sounded like angry hail on a tin roof. Working herself to her hands and knees, she crawled over to Temperance. Abiel had pulled her into his arms and sat on the floor against a seat. Hope sat on the ground next to him, holding an airsickness bag, her normally dark face nearly gray and ashy in the dim light of the flashlight.

"Hope, are you okay?"

Her head wobbled a bit on her shoulders. "Not particularly," she said. "My vision is spotty and I keep getting sick." She put a shaking hand to the bloody bandage on her forehead. "But thank God I'm away from there, and by His grace, I'm safe." Tears filled her eyes and she whispered, "I was so scared."

"You have been incredible," Betty said, using the pen light to check her pupils, noting no improvement. Not that she expected any since they'd been dodging bullets. "I'm so proud to know you." She looked at Abiel. "Has she roused at all?"

"No. I don't even know if she's still breathing."

"Whooo wheee! Hang on!" Faith yelled.

Hope heaved into the bag as Betty secured herself in a seat next to one of the prisoners. "What's your name?" she asked.

"Me name's Tom." He was a large man with black hair. She recognized the lyrical Scottish brogue and felt comforted enough by his presence to turn off her flashlight.

"I'm Mercy," she said.

"Mercy, eh? So what do they call you then? Mercy the Nursey?"

How could she come so close to laughing in this predicament? Instead, she smiled and snorted as she used her flashlight to check on her patients.

She looked at Percy, who still held Grace's hand, despite the fact that the warrior woman appeared to be unconscious. Betty unhooked her seatbelt and fell to the ground next to Prudence as the plane tilted almost completely on its side.

Betty bit her tongue to keep from yelling caution to Faith. She knew the woman was flying to save their very lives and that the status of the patients back here couldn't be her first priority. But, Betty worried about the damage to Prudence's shoulder and Grace's leg what with so much rolling around in the sky.

As the plane righted itself again, Betty sat up just as a bullet shot through the floor of the plane right where her shoulder had been. She cried out as the cold night air came up through the hole in the floor and the sound of more bullets hitting the plane overwhelmed any other sound. Clearly, these bullets were a larger caliber than what had peppered them like hail just minutes before.

As the plane continued to rock back and forth, she started to crawl back to check on Grace and make sure her leg was still stable. Her hand slipped on a puddle of warm fluid. At first she thought it was hot engine oil, then the reality hit her. She shone the light down. Blood. Far too much blood. Shining her light all around, checking on escaped prisoners and patients, she tried to determine where it had come from. If one of those large caliber bullets had torn through a person, it would account for the volume of blood on the deck, but she didn't imagine that person could live to talk about it.

The End

INSPIRED BY REAL EVENTS

WHILE the story of the special team of operators I named The Virtues is entirely fictional, set in a fictional town, and comprised of fictional characters who form a fictional military division, every single one of my fictional heavenly heroines was inspired by a real World War II heroine and the story was inspired by real events.

There are dozens of documented cases of female physicians – working on both sides of the conflict – but there are very few *detailed* stories about any of them, and I found no detailed stories about any women who worked covertly as a physician. Likewise, while members of the International Red Cross performed near miraculous acts of heroism and suffered incredible personal sacrifice throughout the conflict, the organization was then and is now, completely nuetral. And finally, the very much not red headed nurse on the cover of this book never personally went to combat, but represents so many young women who surrendered their lives to a life of service, willingly answering the call to offer aid and comfort in a time of global war.

Like all of my characters, the fictional character, Doctor Beatrice "Betty" Grimes, is entirely made up. The half Scottish and half French redheaded surgeon who worked in a London hospital until a bombing during the Blitz, and who later becomes a spy pretending to be a Red Cross nurse who really works covertly as a doctor for the resistance does not represent a single historical woman. The thing that makes her unique in my mind is that, more than any of my other Virtues heroines, Betty represents an amalgam of many real people and not just a single individual.

While there were few details of physicians working covertly to defeat the Nazis from which I could draw to fill out my fictional character, there is one particularly brave woman who came to mind. What follows is only a summary of the amazing story of the incredibly courageous woman named Marthe Cohn.

Marthe was a Jewish woman from Alsace-Lorraine, France, near the border of Germany. Her family actually helped hide Jews who fled Germany until the German occupation of France. Her sister, father, and brother were arrested in 1942. Her father and brother survived.

At one point, her sister was offered her freedom, but insisted on staying a Nazi captive in order to help care for the interned Jewish children. Eventually, she ended up at the Auschwitz concentration camp in Poland and did not survive the war.

After the liberation of Paris in 1945, Marthe joined the French army. Because she had blonde hair and spoke fluent German, the French intelligence created falsified documents and a fictional identity for her – that of a German nurse.

Marthe made 13 unsuccessful attempts to cross the border into Germany, finally succeeding. During a speech given after the war, Marthe said, "I took my little suitcase and walked towards the German border guard. Then I raised my right arm and said, 'Heil Hitler' and showed him my papers. It worked, and I was in Germany."

Her job was to seek out information regarding the German retreat; specifically, information about the Siegfred Line, a 400-mile long German defense system. While covertly obtaining and funneling vital information to her contacts, Marthe treated German soldiers, including members of the *Schutzstaffel*, the dreaded Waffen SS.

As a spy, to gain the sympathy of her assets, she told the Nazis she was desperately trying to find her fictional fiancé, a German soldier listed as missing in combat. Gaining the confidence of the men she treated, she discovered that the retreating German army lay in wait for Allied troops in the Black Forest, and that the Siegfred Line had, in fact, been abandoned.

Because of the intelligence she provided, Allied troops broke through the Siegfred Line and successfully penetrated into the heart of Germany, eventually taking Berlin.

In 2000, Marthe received France's highest military honor, the *Medaille Militaire*. In 2002, the Los Angeles based Simon Wisenthal Center declared her a *Woman of Valor* for her service to the Allied forces. In 2006, just four years after its establishment, she received the *Medaille de Reconnaissance de la Nation* from the French government.

Cadet Nurse Marguerite V. Clodfelter (circa 1944)

Pictured on the cover of this book is the very not red headed Marguerite V. Clodfelter. Canadian born, Marguerite and her family lived in upstate New York when the war broke out. Both of her brothers were offered American citizenship if they accepted the American draft versus going back to Canada to join the Canadian armed forces, and they readily accepted. In 1944, Marguerite graduated from high school and immediately joined the newly formed Cadet Nurse Corps.

At the height of the war and with a nursing crisis in America, Marguerite fast-tracked through nursing school then worked as a nurse in the House of the Good Samaritan Hospital in Watertown, New York. At any time, she could have been deployed to Europe or the Pacific. As it turned out, she served with the Nurse Corps until the end of the war, providing a much needed service on the home front. During her service, she applied for and received her American Citizenship. She married Bob Clodfelter in 1947.

Visit the ***Betty H. Carter Women Veterans Historical Project*** online at http://libcdm1.uncg.edu/cdm/landingpage/collection/WVHP/ or write to the project at: UNCG Digital Collections, PO Box 26170, Greensboro NC 27402-6170.

While my fictional Betty Grimes goes under cover as a Red Cross Nurse, this is just my own artistic license. It is unlikely that Betty's disguise as a Red Cross nurse would allow her to carry out a mission of espionage – but doing so allowed me, perhaps selfishly, to honor that organization in my own small way. The International Red Cross has always protected its neutral stance so that it can have access to the local populace in disputed territories and so that fear of spying will not hinder the performance of any of its very important duties.

The horrors of the first World War ran the gamut, ranging from tooth edged bayonets in the trenches all the way to widespread use of chemical weapons. After the armistice, nations met in neutral Geneva with the intent of creating and ratifying a set of conventions that would govern how warfare could legally be conducted should hostilities resume. The International Red Cross was linked to these Geneva Conventions with respect to how captured personnel should be treated during war. For the countries who ratified the Geneva Conventions, this gave them access to prisoners of war and captured civilians.

In 1934, the International Red Cross had attempted to get all nations to agree to legal safeguards for civilians in any area where war had broken out. However, those in authority agreed to defer further talks of this until 1940. Consequently, when WWII broke out, many civilians had no safeguarded legal rights – civilians including Jews, Priests, the elderly, homosexuals, gypsies, etc., became civilian victims of the Nazi regime. The Red Cross never stopped trying to access those who were arrested, deported, or sent into forced labor, but met with little success.

The Red Cross really went into action in Greece. Before the war, Greece imported one third of its food supplies. When it was occupied in April 1941, what crops existed were destroyed in fighting. During the first year of occupation, it is estimated that up to 500 children per day died of malnourishment. In March 1942, the Red Cross sought and received permission from the occupying nations to bring in food. They brought in freighters of food, painted with large red crosses, and set up food kitchens. In two months, they produced over 500,000 basins of soup, pulling the populace away from the very brink of starvation.

During the war, the Red Cross established and staffed auxiliary hospitals where permitted. The personnel were neutral and treated anyone – regardless of sides taken in any conflict. In return, the hospitals were not deemed legitimate targets. The distinctive Red Cross emblem and blue and red nurse cape of the Red Cross nurse became a welcome vision to wounded men of every nationality.

Article 79 of the Geneva Convention allowed the Red Cross collect letters and forward them to prisoners of war. The letters had to be only 25

words long and could only contain family news. The letters went to headquarters in Geneva, and there forwarded to the locations of the prisoners. By 1945, they had facilitated 24 million letters.

During WWII, the Red Cross had their hands full in keeping up with German prisoners of war. In September 1939, the Germans captured 500,000 Polish soldiers in just 22 days. By 1940, 30,000 British troops were prisoner, along with thousands of French, Belgium, and Dutch troops. By the end of the war, it is documented that Germany had captured over 232,000 western prisoners of war.

The Red Cross sent trained medical staff into prisons to check on the living conditions, the quality of food, and the health of the prisoners. They also fielded complaints about treatment.

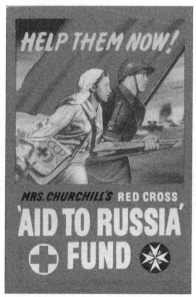

The first time the Red Cross had any kind of formal access to Russian POW's was in the last few weeks of the war as Nazi Germany crumbled.

The Red Cross could only operate in countries that allowed it to operate and who were part of the Geneva Convention. Since Russia had not signed the Geneva Convention, the many Russians who were taken as POW's did not receive Red Cross visits. The Germans kept the Russians in appalling conditions and were not required under any international laws to improve upon them. Over 3.2 million Soviets were taken prisoner by the Germans, and 2.8 million of them died due to the terrible conditions of imprisonment.

"The Red Cross, with its clubs for recreation, its coffee and doughnuts in the forward areas, its readiness to meet the needs of

the well and to help minister to the wounded... has often seemed to be the friendly hand of this nation, reaching across the sea to sustain its fighting men."
– Gen. Dwight Eisenhower, Address to Congress, June 18, 1945

The inhumane conditions prisoners endured at the hands of the Empire of Japan are now widely known though seldom discussed. Nearly all prisoners were starved, tortured, and humiliated. Female prisoners were routinely raped and beaten. Executions were commonplace and often involved stabbing, beating to death, or burning prisoners alive in order to conserve vital ammunition.

66 US Army nurses, 11 US Navy nurses, and a nurse-anesthetist were captured and imprisoned shortly after the Japanese invasion of the Philippines. These women became known as the "Angels of Bataan and Corregidor" and they were treated brutally by their Japanese captors until finally being liberated in 1945.

Ironically, Japan had signed the Geneva Conventions years before, but had never ratified them, so the land of the rising sun did not feel bound by any of the Conventions stipulations or terms. Japan hindered the Red Cross from doing any good at all, and instead accused workers of being spies. Japanese soldiers went so far as to arrest and summarily execute a Red Cross delegate and his wife on suspicion of espionage. They allowed no neutral ships into their harbors, which meant no food or aid parcels could be sent.

The Red Cross also attempted to help those in concentration camps, even though no official protection for civilians had been established. In 1943, they were allowed to send aid/food parcels to named prisoners in the camps, but they only had a few names. They sent the parcels, and receipts came back with dozens more names scribbled on them. By the time the war ended, the Red Cross has managed to compile a list of more than 105,000 names of people interred in concentration camps and was able to send out over 1 million parcels.

I imagine that the food and aid contained in those parcels meant the difference between life and death for many who received them. Near the end of the war, Red Cross delegates actually stayed in each of the camps as observers. This experience, and the sheer magnitude of the horrors they witnessed at places like Auschwitz and Bergen-Belsen, would haunt these men and women for the rest of their natural lives.

The agent I code-named Mercy represents so many actual historical women and is intended to honor them. So many that they would fill an entire set of books, I imagine. Even more, she represents many ideals that personally inspire me. May God bless you.

Let not <u>mercy</u> and truth forsake you;
Bind them around your neck,
Write them on the tablet of your heart,

Proverbs 3:3 (NKJV)

☗ ☗ ☗ ☗

SUGGESTED questions for a discussion group surrounding *Mission of Mercy*, part 6 of the *Virtues and Valor* series.

While the characters and situations in the *Virtues and Valor* series are fictional, I pray that these extended parables will help readers come to a better understanding of truth. Please prayerfully consider the questions that follow, consult scripture, and pray upon your conclusions. May the Lord of the universe richly bless you.

Betty Grimes often prays for her patients using a liturgy from the *Scottish Book of Common Prayer*.

1. Do you believe God hears prayers spoken by rote and repeated over and over again, provided they are sincere?

2. Do you think it detracts from faith in God's healing when a doctor prays for his or her patient prior to performing a procedure?

Many people today believe the miracles found in the Bible don't happen anymore. However, there are so many stories of healing through the power of prayer. Studies show that patients who have people praying for them actually heal faster and with more permanency than patients who do not have people praying for them.

    3. Do you believe in the power of healing through prayer?

    4. Do you believe God's healing can manifest slowly instead of instantaneously?

8 8 8 8

In Paul's letter to the Thessalonians, scripture informs believers to abstain from even the appearance of evil. However, Betty purposefully and intentionally misleads her coworkers so that they assume she is carrying on a love affair during the nights she stays out until dawn, while she is actually providing medical care to wounded Resistance fighters.

    5. Do you think that, given the circumstances, there are times when allowing an appearance of 'evil' to continue is beneficial enough to justify it?

8 8 8 8

As with most of the books in this series, the main character has to live a lie in order to survive and fulfill her duty. In the book of Genesis, Abraham orders his wife, Sarah, to inform others that she is his sister (Genesis 12:13 and 20:2) and Sarah maintains the deception in each case.

    6. Do you think that there are times when deceiving others or even telling lies is sanctioned as what we must do to overcome evil?

In one scene, Betty sews up the hand of a bomb maker. Later, she provides first aid to injured bomb victims.

7. Do you think this kind of dichotomy is healthy for the human heart, the human brain, and the immortal soul?

8. Do you think her actions ought to have been different in either case?

Flight of Faith

HALLEE
BRIDGEMAN

Virtues And Valor Series

Flight of Faith

the Virtues and Valor Series part 7

a Novella by

HALLEE
BRIDGEMAN

Published by

Olivia Kimbrell Press™

Olivia Kimbrell Press™

COPYRIGHT NOTICE

Library Cataloging Data
U. S. Library of Congress Control Number: 2014953683

Bridgeman, Hallee (Hallee A. Bridgeman) 1972-
  Flight of Faith, Virtues and Valor series part 7/Hallee Bridgeman
    106 p. 23cm x 15cm (9in x 6 in.)

Summary: Helen "Troy" Mulberry, code-named FAITH, flies secret missions between Britain and Occupied France at the outset of WWII.

      ISBN: 978-1-939603-51-7 (ebook)

1. Christian fiction 2. World War II 3. war stories 4. spies 5. historical fiction 6. espionage

PS3568.B7534 T941 2014
[Fic.] 813.6 (DDC 23)

FOR THOSE WOMEN WHO FOUGHT RIGHT BESIDE THE MEN...

THIS novella is specifically dedicated to Florene Miller Watson. To read more about this true heroine, read the "Inspired by Real Events" section at the end of Faith's story.

You see then that a man is justified by works, and not by faith only.

James 2:24 (NKJV)

NEAR LAMARR, CENTRAL TEXAS: 1941

HELEN Mulberry bit into a sweet roll as she read the newspaper article about the loss of pilots in the ongoing Battle of Britain. Absently licking the sugar from her fingers, she only half heard her sister-in-law, JoAnn. "Seriously, Helen, use a napkin. And get your feet off the chair!"

It took a lot of self control not to stick her tongue out at the woman. Instead, she kept reading and just straightened, pulling her feet off the dining chair next to her. JoAnn was the only member of the family who called her Helen. Everyone else called her Troy, a tongue-in-cheek acknowledgement of her utter lack of femininity and a play on Helen of Troy.

She sat at the end of a table that would seat 18, next to her father who sat at the head of the table, his eyes scrutinizing the financial section.

JoAnn huffed at her brother Dwight. "She acts like a 12-year-old boy instead of an eighteen-year-old woman. You should really do something."

Dwight, always her champion despite his wife's preference to the contrary, joked, "Actually, our 12-year-old son has much more dignity and grace. You really oughtn't compare him to Troy that'a way."

Behind the paper, Helen snickered. "Why do you think that's funny?" JoAnn inquired, popping the paper and breaking Helen's line of reading. "You'll never find a husband acting the way you do. You're so unladylike and crass. Wearing pants to the breakfast table!"

Helen threw down the paper and picked up her coffee cup, which the downstairs maid had just refilled, intentionally putting her elbows on the table just because JoAnn bristled every single time she did. Helen could not help but try and rile her sister-in-law once in a while. "Look-a here, JoAnn. First of all, I ain't looking for no husband," she said, blowing on her coffee to cool the brew. "'Sides, Daddy gets at least one sincere offer per week for my hand. So, were I looking, which I ain't, I'd have my pick of any one of those hundreds of gold diggers looking to marry into Daddy's wealth. Know what I mean?"

Her father peered over his paper. "Don't antagonize your brother's wife, Troy. No reason to make him suffer. And you know better than to say 'ain't.' You know I detest that."

To him, she did stick out her tongue, making him wink at her in return before he raised his paper back up.

"Every last one of you coddles that girl," JoAnn announced, tossing her napkin onto her untouched breakfast and surging to her feet. "If just one of you would say 'Boo' to her, she might just surprise you and actually start improving."

Knowing she'd pushed her long suffering sister-in-law to the edge, Helen waited until the older woman stormed out of the dining room before she looked at Dwight and said, "Boo!" before he could.

He did not laugh, but he smiled as he stood. "I'm fixin' to collect the boys from Nanny and head out to the field, Daddy. You free to come along? Check out that rig we talked about last night?"

No one thought it odd that a man of his age stilled referred to his father as "Daddy." Her father put down his paper and looked at his watch. "I have to head on into Dallas around noon, but I'm free right now."

Despite the luxury of the formal dining room, her father and brothers wore denim jeans and blue cotton shirts. They wore leather moccasins on their feet, which would come off at the back door. There, they would and very muddy and oily boots with steel toes before heading out to work.

Dwight left the room to retrieve Helen's nephews from their morning studies. Then he would head to the oil fields with them in tow. They would learn the family business in a very hands-on way this morning before reporting back to the tutor for afternoon studies. Her father and her brother both agreed that their education in the oil fields was just as important as the three R's in the classroom.

She looked at her brother, Eddie, who stared at his plate of cold eggs with an absent look on his face. She could see the ever present darkness starting to settle on him like a mantle and took a second to think of the best way to push it back. "Wanna take *Diamond* up after breakfast, Eddie?" He did not move, just sat perfectly still and stared. Helen glanced at her father, who frowned at his oldest son before he drained his coffee cup and left the room, pausing only to pat the top of her head.

Helen pushed her chair back and rushed around the table to pull out the seat next to her eldest brother. She flipped the chair around and straddled the chair back so that her arms crossed across the back and her legs were spread wide. The undisguised tomboyishness of this pose would have sent JoAnn into a fit. "Hey, Eddie," she said, nudging his shoulder. "Wanna go fly *Diamond* today?"

He looked at her with a blank stare, then shook his head. "What?"

"*Diamond*. Let's give her a breeze this morning. Just you and me."

"*Diamond*? Sure. Yeah, sure, Troy. Let me, ah –" He ran his hands through his prematurely silver hair.

Knowing him better than she knew any person on earth, she put a hand on his shoulder. "Why don't you go get your jacket and meet me in the hangar?"

He nodded, clarity finally returning to his eyes. "Absolutely. I'll see you out there in fifteen minutes."

Helen left the table and ran through the long dining room, out into the massive hall, and up the grand staircase. She went into her dressing room and found the wool lined lambskin leather jacket she'd tossed on the padded stool that sat in front of the hanging dresses that JoAnn insisted on stocking there with each fashion season.

Other than a famously unsuccessful debut three years ago, the only time Helen ever put on a dress was when she went to church. She exchanged her beloved denim dungarees for more feminine attire twice a week, forcing herself into a fashionable dress and those torture devices they considered shoes. When she came downstairs looking feminine and pretty, JoAnn would usually smile at her. That made pouring herself into what she considered "the contraption" worth it, because despite the constant bickering, she really did love her brother's wife.

Five minutes later, she slid open the hangar door. Her father's gift to her the Christmas of her 16th year, her beautiful North American Na-16, bright and shiny and silver, greeted her. She shone like a polished gemstone and so had been christened *Texas Diamond* almost immediately. On the side, near the cherry red nose, Eddie had painted a Texas flag in the shape of the state of Texas and added a huge diamond in the very center of it. She ran her fingers over the painting and thought about the hand that had so painstakingly painted it there.

Back in the Great War, Eddie had volunteered in front of America's involvement and flown in the Lafayette Escadrille, a mostly American unit which flew for France. He earned the title "Ace" during his fifth month in the air, and by the time the war ended, he had over 20 confirmed kills. In 1917, he transferred to the American 103rd Aero Squadron, joining his younger brother, Manny. Manny had trained with the squadron at Kelly Field not far from their Texas home before they set sail as a cohort to embattled France.

The two flew together for almost a year until a vicious dogfight over Montmédy, just one week before the Armistice was signed. Manny's Spad took one too many bullets and there was nothing Eddie could do except watch his brother's plane crash into the ground in a ball of flames. He knew Manny had followed him into combat, had hero-worshipped him for years while he flew missions for France, and likely never would have even been there had it not been for him. Eddie barely found a way to live with that knowledge.

Not long after Eddie's homecoming, their mother gave birth to Helen, a surprise pregnancy for the couple in their early 40's. The pregnancy was hard on their mother, and she was weak and worn out by the time Helen came into the world. Helen only knew her mother for a few hours. Her mother named her and held her close to her breast until she breathed her last breath.

Helen had dark hair and bright blue eyes, and could easily have passed for her older brother, Manny. Eddie latched onto her and, through her life, found a will to live. Instead of letting his mother's death be the final blow to break him, Eddie had become incredibly protective of his baby sister, during his lucid moments anyway.

But he suffered in that life. Memories of overflying the dead in the trenches at Verdun, of aerial battles, of dogfights that took the lives of almost all of his friends and his younger brother, played over and over in his memory. He once described the memories as cobwebs he could never clear out of the corners of his mind.

Their father buried himself in work to avoid grieving his wife and middle son. Dwight, the youngest son, went to college, and Helen was left to be raised by the suffering Eddie. He stopped learning the family business and spent his days flying all over Texas, teaching himself acrobatics, barnstorming, and reliving the fights where he saw so many friends perish in their burning flying coffins. He taught Helen to fly when she was barely tall enough to reach the pedals. Dwight came home from college with his beautiful, wealthy, east coast wife, who tried to tame the wild 6 year old with no success.

The older Eddie got, the deeper into his own tortured mind retreated. Nightmares plagued him, always worse near the anniversary of Manny's death. Eddie would abruptly stop talking in the middle of conversations or stop eating in the middle of meals and simply leave the room. He would go to his room and fall to his knees and pray for hours or days. About the only time Helen ever saw her eldest brother fully return to his good natured old self was when he was in the air. Flying in the clear blue skies under the Texas sun let Eddie leave his troubles on the ground. The problem was, every time Eddie landed, his troubles were still waiting right there for him.

Eventually, their roles reversed. It didn't happen right away. It happened a little at a time. Helen often felt like she was now the one raising Eddie, rather than the other way around. She desperately wanted to find a way to quiet his troubled mind, to soothe his troubled soul, but she didn't know how to do it. So she took him up into the air as often as their lives allowed.

ЦЦЦЦ

HELEN stood at the mantle and stared at the photograph of Eddie in his youth, wearing his leather flight jacket and a white silk scarf, looking dapper and happy. A deadly looking biplane crouched behind him and she could clearly see the squadron emblem of an Indian chief staring fiercely toward the nose the plane where the guns were situated. At her brother's feet lay a real live full grown lion, sprawling contentedly on the grass. Two lions served as the official mascots of the Escadrille and had freedom to roam the Aerodrome. She never knew whether to take Eddie seriously when he told her he couldn't remember if that particular lion was named Whiskey or Soda.

She turned and looked at her father, the man old enough to be her grandfather. He sat in his favorite chair, reading glasses perched on the very tip of his nose, while he read to the family from his worn leather Bible. Today he read from chapter 4 of the book of Judges. "And she said, I will surely go with thee: notwithstanding the journey that thou takest shall not be for thine honor; for the Lord shall sell Sisera into the hand of a woman. And Deborah arose, and went with Barak to Kedesh."

Helen broke the family rule and interrupted her father before he reached the end of the chapter. She knew she shouldn't, but her decision welled up in her chest until she felt like she would suffocate if she didn't get it out there.

"I'm going to England!"

The family stopped. Dwight's ten-year-old twins quit examining their checkerboard, her father set his Bible down in his lap with his index finger holding his place, Dwight's hand stilled, the Barlow knife stopping midstroke in the piece of wood he carved, JoAnn gasped and set her knitting down in her lap, and Eddie stopped staring off into space to look directly at her. Eddie's eyes looked ice cold and unusually alert and present for once.

"I beg your pardon?" Her father said, clearly disapproving of the interruption, but understanding the importance of what she said.

Eddie's voice sounded quiet, so quiet that Helen wondered if she was the only one who heard the slight edge of menace. "That ain't funny, Troy."

"I said I'm going. I'm leaving for England. In the morning."

JoAnn stood. "Don't be foolish. There's a war on. The seas aren't safe. I know you read about the Lusitania!"

"Well, good gracious! I ain't sailin' there." Helen swallowed and lifted her chin. "I'm flyin'. I'm flyin' *Texas Diamond* over and I'm gonna volunteer. Just like Eddie did. My exterior fuel tanks arrived this morning and Emilio installed them for me before dinner."

Eddie threw his glass into the fireplace as he stood. The shattering glass preceded the sound of hot coals protesting the introduction of his tea by loudly hissing and spitting. "No you will not. I'll be d – "

"Edward!" At his father's command he sat back down, and her father focused his attention back on Helen. "What are you talking about, Troy? If this is your idea of a joke, it's done. You're upsetting everyone, now."

"They're hurting for good pilots, Daddy. They have a program for Americans who want to help out. It's just a matter of time before we're in this war, anyway. You said so yourself."

Her sister-in-law's sharp laugh made everyone's head turn. "Despite your constant objection to the contrary, Helen, I will remind you that you are a lady. Ladies do not go off to fight in wars. It simply isn't done." JoAnn picked her knitting back up as if her words settled the matter for good.

"Well, gosh, JoAnn. Thanks for the reminder. Now I'd like to remind you of something. I am reliably informed that Deborah was also a person of the female persuasion. You remember? Deborah, who led the Israelites into war," Helen said. "Daddy just read that part in fact."

"You will not." Eddie stood again, more in control, no more risk of expletives leaving his mouth. "You have no idea what waits for you across that ocean. You have no concept of what it's like, of the hell that is combat. I will not let this war do to you what the last one did to Manny."

"Or to you?" Helen crossed her arms over her chest. "I wouldn't be allowed to fight. Y'all know that. They only use men for combat missions. But I could sure free up a man and handle all kinds of non-combat flying. Supply runs. Ferry runs. Medical evacuations. Messenger runs. Humanitarian missions. All kinds of things."

"You're too young, Troy," her father said. "You're only nineteen."

"Right. I'm nineteen. Which means I don't need your permission. But I would appreciate your blessing." She walked over to where her father sat and knelt on the floor next to his chair. "If I can free up a man to go help destroy the Third Reich, then shouldn't I try?"

He put a wrinkled hand on her chestnut colored hair. She thought perhaps his fingers trembled a bit. "My only and beloved daughter, good men don't send their daughters to war."

"Daddy, you're an incredibly good man. You're the very finest of all the fine men I know. But I feel God calling me." She stood and looked at her family. She tapped her chest. "Do you understand that? I almost hear it like a voice yelling in my ear. I have to go. I don't know why, but there's something waiting for me in England." She shoved her hands in her pockets. "I'm going to go pack and then go to bed. I love y'all, but this is something I simply must do."

"Helen! Don't." Eddie stood in the center of the room, fists balled, tears streaming out of his eyes. "Please. Please, don't. I beg you. Don't do this."

She went to him and put her arms around him. For a moment he stood completely still, his muscles so tight he felt like a hot steel oil derrick, then his arms wrapped around her so forcefully that she thought he might bruise a rib or two. "I have to, Eddie. Just like you had to. I know you'll understand after I get there."

♯ ♯ ♯ ♯

CHAPTER 1

FAITH - allegiance to duty or a person: loyalty: fidelity to one's promises or sincerity of intentions: belief and trust in and loyalty to God: firm belief in something: complete trust: something that is believed, especially with strong conviction.

HELEN popped the canopy on *Diamond* and pushed herself out of the cockpit. As her boots landed on the ground, she saw the two men rushing toward her, one of them with a gun drawn from the holster on his belt. She weakly raised her hands. "I have a letter of permission," she declared before they even came to a stop.

The man in the officer's uniform looked her up and down, intense green eyes taking in her leather jacket, pants, and boots. He inspected her with a methodical eye for detail, taking in her apparent age, weight, and state of alertness along with her very American accent. He waved a hand at the gun toting man next to him. "I suspect you can safely put that away, Chezwick."

The trip here had taken Helen from Texas to New York to Newfoundland to Greenland to Iceland and finally here. The trip had taken seven days. Exhaustion overrode every cell in her body, and Helen didn't know how much energy she had left from which to pull reserves, especially standing here with her hands in the air. "Let's have a looksie at your letter, then, shall we?" he demanded.

"I have to get it out of my jacket pocket," she warned, her voice hoarse with exhaustion. "Don't let Skippy here get an itchy trigger finger." The officer simply raised an eyebrow and extended his hand. She retrieved the letter from her inside pocket and handed it over to him.

After he skimmed it, he looked at her again. "This says H. 'Troy' Mulberry. There are a number of rather obvious observations that lead me to state that you don't strike me as a Troy, exactly."

She loved his accent. She didn't think he'd appreciate hearing it at this point, but she honestly thought she could listen to him talk all day. "Well, shucks, Admiral. We just met. Give it some time to grow on ya."

He didn't look amused. She slowly lowered her hands and shoved them into her pockets. "Everyone who knows me calls me Troy. Not my fault people assume that means I'm an *hombre* instead of a *señorita*." Helen slumped down onto the wing of her Na-16. "I've been flying for half a fortnight. Think I could catch forty winks somewhere, Admiral?"

He looked at *Texas Diamond*, dusty and dirty, and back at her. "Where did you fly out of, Miss Mulberry?"

"Lamarr, Texas." At his blank look, she elaborated. "Lamarr. Like Hedy Lamarr, the actress. Town's near Athens." He still didn't reply, so she added, "In America. Texas is part of America. For the time bein'."

"Yes. It may astonish you to learn that I know where Texas is." He looked at the nose of *Diamond* again. "You're telling me that you, *you*, flew from Texas to here?"

"All by my lonesome unless I got a mouse in my pocket."

He hesitated, then finally asked, "How old are you?"

She grinned. "Old enough to know it's rude to ask a lady how old she is. You must not yet have achieved the same level of maturity, Admiral."

His cheeks began to redden slightly. "Right you are. I beg your pardon, Miss Mulberry. You'll need to stay here for the time being while I run your letter up to HQ and see if we can get you sorted out."

Done. She was d-o-n-e. Had she been a man, he would have already had a hot meal and a cup of coffee in her hand. She hopped down and stepped toward him. The man next to him lifted his sidearm again. With a sideways glare, she warned, "Back off, Skippy. I ain't no Kraut."

When the toe of her boot hit the officer's spit-polished black leather boot, she said, "Look'a here, mister. I'm already as sorted as I'm gonna get. I'm hungry. I'm tired. I have permission to be here. That's sorted. See? If your problem is with my age or my sex, the fact is no one ever asked me about my plumbing when I filled out all those dozens of papers to get that permission. The subject just never seemed to come up. And as far as my age, I bet I got a year or two on Skippy, here. Way I see it, any problems along those lines are your own personal oversight. You can sort them out on your time, not mine. Now, if you'll direct me to where I can get some grub first and some shut eye second, I'll be much obliged."

He stared at her for several heartbeats before stepping backward and gesturing with his hand. "Right this way, Miss."

She couldn't help but notice that the guy with the gun took up the rear. As if she had the energy to do anything other than stumble along behind Captain Green Eyes.

⚜ ⚜ ⚜ ⚜

HELEN waited in the uncomfortable chair set just outside an office door. The office was in a mansion that rivaled her Texas home in size. Paintings of aristocrats in all manner of period dress and powder white wigs lined the long hallway, and a seamless Oriental rug ran the length of the hall. She liked the rug. She thought the portraits looked downright silly.

Her neck ached, her eyes burned, and her stomach growled painfully. She could hear the voices of the man and a woman through the door, but she could not understand their words. Just before she gave in and closed her eyes, the door opened.

"Please, come in, Miss Mulberry," the blonde woman said.

Helen warily rose to her feet and stumbled in behind the woman, who gestured to the tea service set up at a small table by the window. "Please, help yourself."

Helen couldn't stand tea. Her sister-in-law JoAnn had spent the better part of a decade trying to get her to drink tea instead of coffee or her favored chicory coffee from Louisiana. She had eventually thrown her hands up in frustration and given up about two years ago. Still, the little sandwiches next to the cups sure looked good, so she stuffed one in her mouth and picked up two more, not even caring how unladylike it looked.

The officer with the emerald eyes cleared his throat and with a cheek full of cucumbers and cheese, Helen raised an eyebrow. "Miss Mulberry, my name is Captain Reginald Green. I am the squadron commander of the pilots stationed here."

Helen swallowed half of what she had in her mouth before saying,

"Pleased ta meet ya."

The older woman stepped forward. "I am Major Charlene Radden. I command the women on the base."

This time she swallowed all the way. "It's a pleasure, Major. Green Eyes here made it out like there weren't no women around."

"That is not –"

"Captain Green, thank you for bringing Miss Mulberry to me."

Clearly, he understood her words to be a dismissal. "Ma'rm," he acknowledged with a sharp click of his boot heels and the tiniest of bows. He turned and left the office without another word.

Charlene pulled out a chair and sat near the little table, pouring herself a cup of tea. Helen slowly made her way to the seat across from her and sat down.

"I am impressed by what you went through to get here. Very clever to use a man's name on the application," she said as she added cream to her cup.

Helen shrugged. "It's my name. I'm Troy, to everyone who knows me. Like, Helen of Troy?"

"Indeed. I would hardly turn down a thousand ships right now if you happened to bring them along as well."

"I only had so much room in the cockpit."

"More's the pity." The Major took a sip of her tea and smiled as she set the cup in the saucer. She rather wistfully said, "I miss sugar."

Helen sat up straighter and reached into her inner jacket pocket, pulling out a little paper packet. She unwrapped it and handed Charlene a wilted green leaf.

"And what is this?"

As she wrapped the packet back up, she said, "Crush it a little and put it in your tea. It's perfect with chicory coffee, but I reckon it'll do with that just as well." Major Radden raised a perfectly groomed eyebrow but did as Helen instructed. When she took a sip, her eyes widened. Helen smiled. "Emilio, one of the foremen at one of daddy's rigs, is from a place called Paraguay. He grows this stuff in his little garden. They call it *ka'a he'ê*." She patted her jacket pocket. "He knows my sweet tooth and your rationing here, so he packed some to take along with me. Lighter than sugar. Sweeter, too, you ask me."

"Fascinating." She took another sip and closed her eyes as if savoring the sweet flavor. "I cannot thank you enough. That's just splendid." When she opened her eyes, her expression became business-like again. "So, Troy, why are you here?"

Helen huffed out a breath and slumped back in her chair. "My big brother Eddie flew for the Lafayette Escadrille."

"Eddie?" Charlene set her cup down and folded her manicured fingers together. "Your brother is Edward Mulberry the Flying Ace? Have I got it right?"

Helen perked up. "One and the same. You know my brother?"

"I had the privilege to meet him one time, but it was a lifetime ago." She cocked her head to the side. "You had another brother in the Great War, as I recall."

"Manny. He went down at Montmédy." She took another bite of sandwich, but swallowed before she spoke again. "That was before I was born, of course."

"Is Eddie well?"

Helen felt her neck tense up a little bit. "Well enough, I reckon."

Charlene nodded, apparently understanding the unstated facts of that answer. "Did Eddie teach you to fly?"

"Oh, heck yeah. He taught me to fly, do acrobatics, all sorts of stuff. I've been in the cockpit with him since I could walk."

Charlene raised an eyebrow. "Knowing certain things is my job, Troy. It's the very reason they pay me, in fact. And knowing things, as I tend to do, I can't imagine that your brother Eddie gave you his blessing to be here."

Helen lifted her chin. "Didn't need anyone's blessing. *Diamond*'s my plane. I'm 19, old enough to come on my own. He ain't speaking to me right now, but that's up to him and I can't let it affect whether I follow God's call or not."

"God's call? So, I'm to understand you're a woman of faith, then?"

"Faith is the most important thing in my life, Major."

"Flying faith," Charlene mused, then stood and went to her desk, picking up a file folder and walking back to the table. She opened the folder and skimmed the contents, then closed it again. "I just might have a position for you."

Adrenaline pushed back the tired. Helen stood, too. "Oh, Major Radden,

I'll do anything you need me to, so long as it involves flying. Whatever you need me to do. Ferrying, transporting, mechanics –"

"There may be some of that. Honestly, though, I have something rather different in mind. Something rather unique. I've been looking for a skilled pilot to join a rather special unit, an all woman team, in fact. After our short talk, I believe that pilot is very likely you."

Chapter Two

HELEN sat with her back against the flat tire of an Avro Ansen that sported about fifteen enormous looking bullet holes. She watched a similar plane make a rough landing on the airstrip in front of her and cringed at the sound of the tires hitting the runway. She almost felt sorry for the plane.

When a man-shaped shadow blocked the sunlight, she almost knew without looking that Captain Reginald Green stood next to her. With an inward sigh, she shielded her eyes with her hand and glanced up at him. "Hiya Captain Green Eyes."

His answering frown gave all the evidence of how much he appreciated her nickname for him. "Good morning, Miss Mulberry. Feeling rested?"

"You have quite an operation here under your command. But you might need to give some of your pilots a brush up on landing procedures."

"A brush up?" He pressed his lips together and released an audible sigh. "Major Radden has tasked me to take you into the air and see what you can do. Your airplane was refueled and cleaned while you slept for the last day. We've also taken the liberty of performing some basic maintenance. If it concerns you, her fluids looked quite clear and her points were clear of carbon. If you'd like to accompany me, we can get this over with."

Helen pushed herself to her feet. "Get this over with, Cap? You sound like you're going to your funeral."

He looked her up and down, much like he had done when she first landed. "Not today, though I have been to my fair share in recent months. I have also had the privilege of writing numerous letters of condolence to loved ones of men formerly under my command."

He pointed to the aircraft she had used as her backrest. "The young pilot of that very aircraft might pull through. If not, I will most assuredly be going to a funeral or writing yet another letter."

Helen met his glare, trying to appear unaffected, and offered, "Don't mind me, Cap. I'm new around here."

"Honestly, Miss, I don't know exactly who you are that you should warrant the special attention of the Major, but it is only out of due respect for her that I am speaking to you at all. So, if you'll kindly dispense with the American female jibber-jabbering, I'm to evaluate your skill level."

She mimicked his eye movement, from the top of his blue cap to his shiny black toes. "You mean you're not afraid to go into the air with little ole me?"

He closed his eyes in impatience. "Miss Mulberry –"

With a snicker, she waved her hand at him. "I'd love to take you flying, maybe show you a thing or two. But, I don't want to until I get those three extra fuel tanks off of *Diamond*. She's clumsy as a pig on a marble floor on take-off and flies like a pregnant cow with them on there, even empty. Found that out over the Straits. And I just bet you'll hold that against me."

His patient toothless smile spoke of the very edge of his impatience. "As much as I appreciate your litany of farm animal references, I feel it is fortunate for you that our chief mechanic had them removed already. They are being stored in Area 10 for your use on your return trip. Back to Lamarr, Texas." With a pointed look at his watch he continued, "Near Athens. In America. It may astonish you to learn that I have many other duties and responsibilities that are waiting on completion of this chore so if you'd be so kind as to please accompany me."

Excitement fluttered in her chest and made her fingertips itch to grip the yoke of her *Texas Diamond*. "Well, yee-haw," she said mildly. "After you, Cap. Hey! You got a stick of Beeman's?"

"I beg your pardon?"

"Chewing gum, Green Eyes. For luck."

He looked down at her hand, which she held out, extending a pack of Beeman's Brand chewing gum toward him. He looked back at her with an expression that made her want to belly laugh. "I have found that I have very little need of luck, Miss Mulberry. Perhaps you'd do well to chew my stick as well."

With a knowing little grin, Helen shrugged. "Suit yourself." She popped a stick of the Pepsin gum into her mouth. The medicinal ingredient in the chewing gum would help fight motion sickness during what she intended to be the most agile and gravity defying display of flight in her lifetime.

THIRTY minutes later, Helen performed loops and rolls, free falls, skimmed the tops of trees, flew straight up to the clouds, pulled a negative G from a flat spin, and felt joy well up inside of her as she wiggled her wings at a passing Hawker Tornado. When they finally landed, she plunked softly onto the tarmac in a perfect three point descent. She taxied to her hangar and pulled the helmet off her head before she laughed with pure joy, happy to be back in the pilot's seat and unencumbered with the heavy fuel tanks.

Captain Green somewhat gingerly climbed out of the seat behind her and made his way unsteadily to the ground. "Your gills are looking as green as your eyes, there, Cap. I thought you were some kind of hotshot pilot."

"Wherever did you learn to fly like that?" he asked in absolute amazement.

Helen smiled. "My brother Eddie taught me. I'm still just a novice compared to him."

Green pulled his helmet off. "Mulberry? Eddie Mulberry? Are you claiming that your brother is the Edward Mulberry? You're just winding me up, now."

Maybe she should have just written "Edward Mulberry's baby sister" on any application that asked for her name. "Why, yes sir, Captain, sir. Yes, he is. Do you know my brother?"

"No, but my father did, back in the Great War. Edward Mulberry saved my father's life one time over Verdun."

"So your daddy was probably Neville 'Ever' Green, then."

"He detests being called 'Ever'."

Helen shrugged. "Maybe so. But the name Neville Green kind of begs for it if you ask me... Greeeen Eeeeyes."

The corner of his mouth twitched. She saw it. "Miss Mulberry, I feel after your check flight we can be less formal. Henceforth, you have my permission to address me by my first name."

"Reginald?" She thought she remembered it correctly, but he shook his head.

"Captain," he corrected. "Commander will do in a pinch. I will also respond to 'sir.' Am I understood?"

"Well hush my mouth, Lord Green. I reckon you best get used to callin' me Faith, then, since that's gonna be my code name sure as day."

He shook his head again. "Very well, then, Faith it is. So, Faith. Do not ever, under any circumstances, address me as Lord Green. I am not a British Lord, nor a Scottish land owner. Titles mean something on this side of the pond."

She put a hand on his upper arm and squeezed, only mildly surprised to find his biceps were as hard as steel beneath his flight suit. "Thanks for the advice, Captain, sir. Much obliged."

He gestured toward the main house, which held the administrative offices. "Shall we go find Major Radden? I would like to speak to her about your God given talents as well as your well honed skills in the air."

"Well honed, now, eh?" She grinned and walked next to him. "Keep those compliments coming, Captain Green Eyes. Sure as shootin' I'll never tire of hearin' 'em. If you run dry just take it from the top again, like a rotation. I'll humor you like you're bein' original. Hey, you sure you're up to the walk? Look a little sea-sick, still. Little wobbly."

"Could I trouble you for a stick of that chewing gum, perhaps?"

Helen smiled a very sweet yet slightly mischievous grin and held out the pack of Beeman's.

🎖🎖🎖🎖

HELEN folded her arms on the table and rested her head on them. The waitress set a bowl in front of her, but she didn't even lift her head.

"Something amiss, Faith?" The redheaded Scottish agent that Helen knew only as Mercy asked, addressing her by her shiny new code name.

"This cold, damp weather," Helen said, her voice scratchy. "I can't get used to it. Makes my head ache and my nose run."

"Well, that's certainly not right. Your nose definitely should not run. Your nose should smell. Your feet ought to do all the running." Mercy sat down next to her. Helen loved the way the letter R rolled off this woman's tongue."Let me take a wee *keek, rùnag.*"

Warily, Helen raised her head and turned toward Mercy, trusting that *keeks* and *rùnags* were nothing to be feared. The red-haired doctor reached out and felt her neck, pressed under her eyes, felt her forehead. "You've a wee fever, you do," she announced. "It's off to bed with ya. No flying tomorrow, at least."

The idea of not flying tomorrow didn't even phase Helen, which told her she might really need to go to bed. "I'm on the roster. Have to fly. Shortage of pilots and all."

"Nay, lass. Ya hafta get well afore ya end up with pneumonia." She raised her hand at the waitress who was walking into the back room of the pub, carrying a tray of bread. "Dina, be a dear and bring the lass here a spot of tea. She's a bit under the weather so Irish it up a dram." Mercy held her finger and thumb apart by perhaps half an inch to demonstrate the size of the shot of Scotch Whiskey she desired.

Helen coughed and her chest burned. "I don't drink spirits, Mercy."

"*Anno.* I dinna wish to get ya intoxicated, lass. It's medicinal. A wee sip will relax your blood vessels and reduce the swelling in your throat and sinuses. Might help you get a good night's sleep as well, like as not, which will aid in a more rapid recovery." Mercy smiled at the waitress and handed Helen the cup she took from her. "Here you go, love. Hold your nose if you must but drink every last drop you shall. Doctor's orders."

Grace walked into the room as Helen took a sip of the nasty concoction and shuddered. "Ugh. How do people drink this? Tastes just like airplane fuel smells."

"What is the matter with your voice?" Grace asked in heavily accented English while easing herself into the chair across from her.

"I'm feelin' poorly. Mercy grounded me and now she's doctorin' me." Feeling silly and embarrassed, she felt tears come to her eyes. "I want to go back to my room."

"I'll walk with you," Temperance offered.

Mercy shook a finger. "Every drop, first. Then off for a *kip*. Ah mean it, now. Get ta sippin'."

Helen held her breath and downed the vile tea – which she hated – mixed with the even more vile whiskey – which she had never even tasted before – in three quick gulps. She set the tea cup down and gasped. "Okay, now that's just nasty, y'all. I kid you not."

"You'll thank me come the morn," Mercy promised.

Helen rose unsteadily to her feet. Temperance stood as well. "Let's go. I'm worn out tonight."

Helen wrapped the scarf Charity had knitted for her around her neck, pulled the matching wool cap over her ears, and bundled into her coat. She waved good-night to the rest of the Virtues team, sailing from the pub on a wave of her friends wishing her to feel better. As she and Temperance stepped outside and into the drizzly, damp night, she shoved her hands into her coat pockets.

"This weather is awful," she croaked out.

Temperance smiled. With barely a trace of her French accent, she said, "I don't mind the winters. It means spring will be marvelous."

"I don't mind it getting cold and wet. I just wish it wasn't all the time." She shuddered, feeling worse every second. She looked at Temperance's profile. "What's wrong?"

As they walked, her friend turned her head and looked at her. "How can you tell?"

"Because you're my friend."

Temperance shrugged. "My brother is gone. Now I feel all alone. And, I'm more than a little nervous about what comes next."

Helen pulled her hand out of her pocket and looped her arm through Temperance's. "Few people understand the bond of siblings more than I," she said, "but let me tell you something I have learned these recent months. You are not alone. You have me and those five other women sittin' back there in that pub. What happens with one of us will happen with all of us. We're all in this together."

Temperance smiled. "Thank you for reminding me."

Helen covered her mouth with her scarf and coughed until she had to stop walking and bend over to catch her breath. Temperance put a hand on her shoulder and waited with her. When she finally straightened, her friend said, "You really must take care. I had pneumonia when I was a teenager. It's awful stuff. Made me terribly ill for a very long time."

Helen nodded. "I just need to get back to my room and get to bed. I've never been more thankful to have Mercy as my roommate. At least I know if I take a turn, she'll be right there."

❡ ❡ ❡ ❡

CHAPTER 3

Chapter Three

"WELCOME back, Faith," Charlene greeted when Helen walked into the otherwise empty briefing room. "Good to see you back on your feet."

Helen opened her notebook to a blank page. "It's good to be out of that bed. I was goin' stir crazy in there. But I'm right as the mail this morning."

For three days she'd coughed and hacked and sniffled and napped her way through the day. Last night was the first good night's sleep she'd had in a week, and this morning she barely had any lingering symptoms. It helped that the sun shone and the temperature had warmed up about 20 degrees.

Charlene eyed her skeptically. "Are you ready to fly?"

"Absolutely." Since taking the assignment as the Virtue code-named Faith, Helen had flown forty-one missions. So far, she had made fifteen runs of personnel and supplies to and from Occupied France. Sometimes, the Nazis on the ground saw her coming or going and tried to blow her out of the sky. Other times, the flight went so smooth and by the numbers that Helen almost felt like she should wake up from a dream.

"And you've been medically cleared to fly?" Charlene looked even more skeptical and Helen knew that she could only answer truthfully. Because, usually, Charlene already knew the answer.

Fortunately, she had been cleared just hours before. Helen slapped her knee. "Fit as a fiddle and fixin' to fight."

Helen could see Charlene work through the answer in her mind. When she concluded that the response had been in the affirmative, she nodded.

"Very well, then." Charlene rattled of a series of coordinates. "I trust you are well and sorted because this mission is one that I can only entrust to someone of your skill and particular instinct. You understand that this mission is classified Most Secret?"

Helen felt her pulse speed up a bit. "Delivery or retrieval? Or a bit of both?"

"Both, I suppose. You're picking up a single passenger and delivering him to a specific location. He will be waiting for you at precisely at twenty-three fifteen. If you wait one second longer than five minutes, take off again immediately. We'll try a different location and time the following night."

Helen nodded as she wrote. The notebook would stay here. She never flew with it, so there was no risk in it ending up in the enemy's hands. But, she discovered during her training that she remembered things better when she wrote them down. "Where am I dropping him?"

"Actually, this passenger isn't supercargo. He's precious cargo. He's what is Most Secret. Faith, you may not discuss this mission with anyone. And, I do mean anyone at all. You understand?"

Helen nodded. "Completely."

Charlene pursed her lips. "Right. You'll come here, pull into hangar seventeen, and shut down the plane engines. When all the hangar doors are shut, let him out. He'll conduct his meetings in the hangar and you'll take back off well before sunrise. He'll parachute back in. Can't risk landing."

Helen raised her eyebrow. Rather difficult to parachute from *Diamond*. Not impossible, just problematic. "What am I flyin'?"

Charlene grinned. "The blacked out Avro will do nicely."

"Both legs in the Avro or just the return leg?"

"Your aircraft, while a lovely machine, is a tad too shiny for a covert night operation."

"Gotcha." Helen paused, pencil poised, and looked at the major. "Copilot?"

Charlene nodded her head. "Already in the hangar going through the preflight checks."

Helen sat back and closed her notebook. "If my right seat is already in the hangar, then I take it that there Sten on the rack behind you is for me." It wasn't a question.

"As is the extra ammunition and your standard kit for France. You'll also have your pistol, of course."

"Right."

"And this cyanide capsule."

"Oh." The excitement she felt a moment earlier began to take a turn. "Anything else I should know?"

Charlene gave the smallest of smiles. "Only that your cargo will likely be wearing a German *Wehrmacht* officer's uniform. Try not to shoot at him before the challenge and password are exchanged."

After several seconds, Helen finally nodded. "I see." When it was clear that there would be no elaboration, she added, "And what is my Most Secret precious cargo's name?"

"Call him Valor."

☷ ☷ ☷ ☷

HELEN strolled into the hangar and headed to her assigned aircraft. This particular Avro was painted flat black especially for performing night missions. Helen stopped short when she saw Captain Reginald Green standing next to the aircraft. Irritation at his presence bristled the nerves in her neck, making them tighten almost painfully.

"Well, good evening, Cap. To what do I owe the pleasure?"

"The Major didn't brief you? I'm acting as your copilot tonight, Faith."

Helen raised an eyebrow as she unlocked the door. "Well, no. The Major said I'd be flying with one of the best pilots on the base. Naturally, I assumed she didn't mean the Squadron Commander."

His lip twitched again at her double meaning. She could swear he nearly chuckled. "This is a need to know only operation. Most Secret and all that."

She boarded the plane and he followed her. Need to know only? She'd done some pretty secretive things with First Lieutenant Harold Curtis sitting next to her in the copilot's seat. She couldn't imagine what Captain Green meant.

Rather than ask a dozen questions, she grabbed the preflight checklist and began working through it. "You do realize I've already checked."

She nodded. "I do. And you realize I haven't."

"Quite right. Carry on."

She halfway expected him to take the lead, but he let her finish and assisted when called upon.

"Seniority should be the rule," she said as she started the engines. "Technically, you should be in the left seat, don't you think?"

"No argument. But, I have thousands more hours of logged flight time than you. Won't hurt for you to take the lead."

She could tell he wasn't saying everything he could, but she had a timeline to meet. Feeling strangely self-conscious, Helen taxied to the runway, waited for the go ahead from the tower, and took to the skies. The next several hours of sitting next to Captain Green loomed in front of her and she sighed almost audibly as she ascended to cruising altitude.

She activated the landing gear controls and listened to the seemingly endless whine as the struts and wheels took their sweet time slowly and painfully retracting. "Ya' know what? This is a decent plane, but I can't stand the landing gear. I mean, we might as well leave the wheels down, for goodness sakes."

"Used to."

"What?"

He looked at her. "We used to. You have a hydraulic system. The first Avros off the line had a little crank and the pilot had to turn it not less than 140 complete turns to raise or lower the landing gear. We used to just leave the wheels down for short hops. Thankfully, a small engineering firm in Bronwich solved that problem so all you do is pull that lever."

"You have to be joking."

"Likely. I'm well known the world over for my comic sense of humor." He added wryly, "Care to make altitude, Faith? Any time in the next few hours would be acceptable."

Helen reached forward, twisted the throttle locks, and kept an eye on the altimeter. As they reached the Channel it started holding steady and she started reciting some Shakespeare that came back to her from a long ago tutoring session. "And gentlemen in England now-a-bed; shall think themselves accurs'd they were not here, and hold their manhoods *cheap* whiles any speaks; that fought with us upon Saint Crispin's day."

Captain Green confirmed, "*Henry the Fifth, Act 4, Scene 3.*" After a moment, he added, "We few, we happy few, we band of brothers; For he today that sheds his blood with me, shall be my brother."

They flew in silence for another minute before Green abruptly said, "There's been a tremendous amount of bloodshed since Poland."

They flew in silent darkness for about another minute before he said,

"You know, Shakespeare never would have let you near his stage. Women were not permitted to be actors in his day. Besides which, your rather atrocious accent would have put him completely off his beam, I'd wager."

So, it was going to be that kind of night, was it? Helen sat back in her chair and scanned the empty sky. "So, Cap'n Green Eyes, why don't you fly combat missions? You seem like the type to step up for King and country and dash into the breach, rattling your saber."

He whipped his head around to look at her. She took her eyes off of the night blackened window and almost gasped at the intensity in his eyes. He stared at her for several seconds before he looked forward again. "As it happens, I've already done my part. I was shot down during the early days of the Battle of Britain. Something inside my left eye was torn loose. Lost most of my peripheral vision. I can still fly perfectly well, but the RAF doesn't feel I'm suited for a seat in a Spitfire any longer. Leastwise not in combat. Relegated to training men more fit than I to do that which must be done. I received word that Bronwich is sending down some special order two seaters just for me, in fact."

Helen hadn't ever even suspected Green was an injured war hero. She suddenly realized that he took the right seat because of the vision deficit in his left eye, brought on by his combat injury. He could scan the right side well enough but had to turn his head to look full at her. The insult she had seen flicker in his expression at her callous words earlier made her feel deep shame. Very quietly, she said, "I'm sorry if I sounded flippant."

"Miss Mulberry... Faith... you very often sound flippant. You're practically a walking caricature of what young ladies oughtn't do or say. I'd like to think I've grown somewhat immune to your nature." He gestured to the world outside the window and changed the subject. "Looks clear. Hopefully that means they don't know we're coming."

"Unless they just want to get us there so they can capture us and our plane."

He smiled. "Well, then. My advice would be to remember the Alamo." His clipped British accent made that all too familiar saying sound odd. After a brief pause, he astonished her even further by saying, "My father often speaks of your brother, you know. As often as he ever speaks of anything that happened back then, any road."

Thoughts of her family back home made her heart ache. She had not spent a single night away from them until the day she left for England. Knowing some sort of a reply was required, she said, "Eddie almost never talks about the war."

"No? Not even to his favorite flying sister?"

"Only sister." She shrugged, as unladylike as the movement may be. "My brother Dwight told me that before Eddie left for the war, he was vibrant and jolly and gay." She thought of his silver hair and absent stares and the amber liquid he consumed nearly every night. "Now he's a shell. Losing our brother Manny in that dogfight actually broke him. He is but a cracked shell of a man, now. I can't see he'll ever get over it."

When she looked at Green again, she caught him staring at her intently. "I am dreadfully sorry to hear that," he said, "but I cannot imagine what he must be going through with you here, doing this."

"He's suffering. That much is for sure. But, I have to go where God calls me. And He definitely called me to England." Not liking the seriousness of the conversation, she reached out and punched him lightly in the shoulder. "Who knows, Captain Green Eyes. Maybe the Man upstairs wanted me to meet you. Ever think about that one?"

"I suppose it's only right that I should inform you I have received no such instruction from on high as yet," the captain murmured.

She reached into her pocket and pulled out a slim white packet. "Would you like a stick of Beeman's?"

She could just barely see his thin smile in the dark. "Thank you. I would very much like a stick since you evidently have access to an endless supply."

❚❚❚❚

THEY flew in a surprisingly comfortable silence the rest of the way. Helen wanted to talk to him, but she didn't want to irritate him and break whatever truce they'd achieved tonight.

She followed the coordinates and found the field. Someone had lit flares on either end of the field and she used those as a guide. Green kept his hands inches from the controls, ready to take over, but remained absolutely silent and allowed her to get them to the ground. Once she taxied to the end of the field, she turned the plane and let the engine idle. "According to my orders, he has five minutes and then we leave. No exceptions."

"Those were the orders as I understood them as well." He unstrapped himself from the seat and went to the door, unlocking and opening it. Instead of sitting back down, he crouched near the open door, a vicious looking Sten submachine gun resting on his thigh.

He must have heard something over the airplane's twin 350 horsepower Armstrong Siddeley Cheetah engines, because he suddenly sat up straighter and pointed the muzzle of his deadly gun toward the door.

"Your faith should not stand in the wisdom of men, but in the power of God." Their contact spoke in English. His voice was a deep baritone and very American, as if he hailed from Northern California or the Pacific Northwest.

Recovering from her shock that an American wore a Nazi uniform and quoted Scripture, Helen held up her hand. "That's my challenge verse." She spoke toward the open door and threw a thumbs up.

Green lowered the muzzle and said, "Welcome aboard, Valor."

Their precious cargo ducked into the plane, holding both hands above his head, his German military medals gleaming in the moonlight. "I'm alone," he confirmed.

Captain Green secured the Sten behind his seat and shook Valor's hand as Helen taxied the plane. "Strap in, Valor. We never know when your mates know if we're coming or going, but they certainly let us know in due time and in very unsubtle ways."

Valor glanced toward the front of the aircraft, making out that he was in the presence of a female. With a raised eyebrow, he asked Green, "New driver?"

Green nodded. "Hap got reassigned, the sot. Avengers, I hear. Lucky stiff. That's Faith."

Valor said nothing else, just strapped in, shut his eyes, and apparently fell asleep within seconds. Helen had seen many men do that in her months of flying. It continued to amaze her, even though she understood the psychology behind it. Men were very odd creatures. She knew because she grew up surrounded by them.

They encountered no resistance on the flight back over the Channel. In no time, Helen taxied the plane into the hangar. The two guards who had stood outside and guided her into the hangar shut the door behind them, but remained outside. Helen killed the engines and pulled her headset off of her ears. "End of the line, folks. Put your token in the turnstile on your way out."

Valor glanced at her, recognizing an American accent and the attempt at American humor, then walked toward the cockpit and knelt behind the two seats. "I recognize that accent," he said with a smile. "Sooner or Longhorn?"

Always happy to hear an American voice, Helen smiled. "Lamarr Longhorn every day of my life."

"Ah. Lamarr. About an hour from Dallas over by Athens."

Color her properly surprised and impressed. "That's exactly right."

"Sure is different around here, isn't it?"

She raised an eyebrow. "You ain't from Texas, cowboy."

"Oregon."

"I reckon Oregon would feel as much like a foreign country as England does. Probably rains more here, though."

He laughed as he stood as tall as he could in the small confines of the Avro. "My part of the state is possibly the only place on earth that rains more than on this island. But the coffee is pretty good and we don't eat beans for breakfast."

Helen sat straighter in her chair. "Exactly what is that all about, anyway? What I wouldn't give for some cheese grits and corned beef hash next to an egg over easy."

He gestured to the door. "I'll let myself out. Nice meeting you, Faith."

"I'll see you again here in a second. I'm your ride home, Adolf."

He grinned, but she could tell by the look in his eyes that he didn't find that particular jab very funny. Helen watched from the window as the far door opened and Charlene Radden and two uniformed men came into the hangar. Valor walked right up to her and the two hugged. When they released each other, Charlene framed his face with her hands and spoke to him with a very warm and sincere smile on her face.

"Well, well," Helen murmured, "exactly who is he to her, I wonder?"

"I can assure you," Captain Green said, "it is none of our concern."

Helen nodded. "Goes without sayin'. Still, we have definitely fallen down the rabbit hole on this mission. Things just get curiouser and curiouser."

CHAPTER 4

Chapter Four

HELEN sat across from Prudence in the empty dining hall and stared at the checkerboard.

"I say," Prudence said as she jumped four of Helen's checkers in a row, "this game is so invigorating. Why have I never played it before?"

"Dare I guess that you did more entertaining things with your evening than checkers?" Helen teased. "You know, formal balls, elegant dining, all that jazz."

"Faith," Prudence laughed, "life has not been one continuous string of formal balls."

"I remember my first and last," Helen said, crowning Prudence's checker. "It was what my sister-in-law called an abject failure. You woulda thought that the end of the world had actually come and gone the way she acted. All I could think about was getting those torture devices she called shoes off of my feet."

Prudence leaned forward and whispered, "My coming out was a failure, too. It was pouring down rain and the line to the palace was forever long. When it was finally my turn to get out of the car, the footman hit me with the umbrella and my nose started bleeding."

Laughter bubbled up inside of Helen's chest. She so enjoyed listening to the bits and pieces of Prudence's life. "What happened?"

"Oh, mother ushered me into a side water closet and her cousin found us a spare dress. Somehow, the day was saved, but just barely."

By the time she finished speaking, Helen could hear the wistfulness in her voice. "Are you okay? We don't need to talk about this."

She smiled and waved her hand. "I'm just missing home. I don't think –"

Before she could finish her thought, the door to the canteen opened and a man in gray coveralls walked in carrying a wooden crate. "Oy? One o' you birds go by Faith?"

Curious, she lifted her hand. "I'm Faith."

"Right. Look'a here. Me sergeant says ta me 'bring this down ta the bird named Faith in the canteen,' he says. Said you tol' him how you was 'spectin' it."

'Spectin' it? What – "Oh! Expecting it! Yes. Thank you." She stood up excitedly and rushed toward him. "I checked to see if it had arrived this morning. Yes! Please, set it here."

She patted the top of the table with a giggle. "Thank you! And please give your sergeant my thanks, as well."

"Wiff pleasure, Miss. Any road, you birds have yasefs a fine day, now, won ways or anuva."

He set the wooden box on the table and left the room with a jaunty step. Prudence, who had remained silent during the entire exchange, watched the soldier march out of the canteen. The expression on her face puzzled Helen. The woman looked pleased and amused and somehow simultaneously displeased and puzzled. "What is it, Pru?"

Prudence met Helen's eyes and, with a somewhat bemused expression, confessed, "I do believe that's the very first time in my entire life I've ever been referred to as a bird."

Faith giggled. "Not me. For obvious reasons."

Prudence nodded. "Pilot. Right. I think the word has a slightly different connotation in this environment."

With a promise to be right back, Helen rushed to the kitchen and found one of the cooks. "Do you have a crowbar like you use to open crates that I could borrow?"

"Aye," the man said, gesturing toward the storage room, "in there. Be sure you bring it back, now, lass. An' watch out you don't go hurtin' yasef."

When she went back into the dining hall, she saw Prudence inspecting the crate. "I suspect you are up to something likely rather fun and rather American. Do tell. What's the big surprise?" she asked with a smile.

Helen smiled back conspiratorially and used the borrowed crowbar to pull the nails from the top of the crate. "America isn't under any kind of rationing yet, so I had my sister-in-law run a little errand for me when she went to Dallas a while back."

She dug through the packed in sawdust and withdrew a large metal tin. Prudence peered over her shoulder as she opened the lid and exposed the white granules of pure refined cane sugar.

"Is that real sugar?" Prudence gasped.

"Sweet, sweet sugar," Helen confirmed.

"Cane sugar? Not beet sugar? There's enough there for biscuits and tea for months!" Prudence exclaimed.

Helen carefully put the lid back on the tin and reached back into the crate, pulling out glass sugar dispensers – one for every table in the canteen – each carefully wrapped in cardboard and paper. JoAnn had gone through a lot of trouble and organizing for this, and she felt true love and respect for her. She would have to make sure that came through in her reply letter.

"I had somethin' else in mind. Help me fill these dispensers and we'll get them set out on the tables before lunch."

"You intend to share?" Prudence asked, wonder in her voice as she helped unpack four more tins of sugar. She stared at the sugar tins as if beholding King Solomon's mines.

"Of course. Why in the world would I hoard such a luxury? If you had lots of extra something and it wasn't much to you, wouldn't you share it with those in need who had none?" Helen unscrewed the metal lid from one of the glass containers and carefully poured sugar into it until it was full to the brim, then she screwed the lid back on.

Prudence didn't answer the question. Instead, she said, "You have a generous heart, Faith. I rather admire that."

Uncomfortable at the praise, Helen shrugged. "It ain't costing me a cent. My brother's wife did all the work with the packing and the shipping. I reckon she'd be mighty upset if I wasn't generous with her hard labor."

"Nevertheless." Prudence carefully filled her assigned container, jealously guarding every grain. "I wonder what would happen if I tried to sneak this with me on whatever mission they eventually set me on."

"I think they check your bags before you leave for a reason," Helen said with a smile, having flown many agents away from this camp. Their commander always went through suitcases and bags before departure. She held a freshly opened tin up to her nose and inhaled, breathing in the sweet smell, feeling transported back to the massive kitchen in her Texas home. "My nanny used to scold me about how much sugar I ate. She'd find me sneaking sweet rolls or even Daddy's sugar cubes."

Prudence laughed. "My serving maid never could understand why I needed three spoonfuls in my tea. She would always make such funny faces whenever I took a sip of it."

Feeling like she spoke to someone who might understand, Helen looked around then whispered conspiratorially. "Our cook used to keep a plate of sugar sprinkled doughnuts in a secret cupboard in our kitchen for me. I don't think anyone ever caught me. I'd hide my plate in the airplane hangar and sneak out to eat them."

Her friend's laughter rang through the room. "Hilarious. I fear I was much older before I ever really had much to do with the kitchen staff. In our households, things are rather separated. Not like in America. Americans are so much more egalitarian. It seems to almost be one large family."

Thinking of the army of workers Cookie and her huge staff fed three meals a day, Helen shrugged. "There is definitely a line of separation, but I don't think it's quite the chasm you're used to. It's all those titles. Dukes and countesses and princes and such. Lots of bowing and scraping."

"America is very young. We're an old nation. It's what we know. It's been like this for thousands of years." Prudence screwed the lid on a full container. "Our entire society is structured around it."

With a lifted eyebrow, Helen asked, "And what are you then?"

"Beg pardon?"

"Oh, no. Pardon me. I'll rephrase. What are you then, my lady?"

She watched as Prudence's cheeks reddened. "What am I? Indeed. Well, I'm a field agent specially trained in espionage and intelligence gathering."

"Right. But you're not a bird." Helen grinned.

Prudence grinned in return. "Not as far as I know."

Helen nodded and checked the crate. "I guess that's all the tins and dispensers. Won't people be surprised?"

"I do hope no one filches one."

"I think people will be generous. Better for everyone to have just a little bit than for one person to hog the whole stash." She swept loose sawdust off of the table and back into the crate. "I'll go get a letter written to my sister-in-law and thank her profusely for the sugar. Hopefully, if I do it good and proper, she'll send us some more."

"I have a letter to write as well." Prudence stood and brushed the skirt of her olive green uniform. "I need to find a way to say what I want to say."

Helen understood the seriousness of her tone, so she put the crate down and sat on the table in front of Prudence. "What do you want to say?"

She huffed out a breath and put her hands behind her back. "Do you think God prepared us for this before we even came here?"

"Prudence, I absolutely do believe that." She slapped her knee. "I absolutely believe it. Think of the various skills and gifts we each have. How else could you explain it? That we're just some random grouping of people who happened to all have highly honed skills? Come on. Of course He prepared us!"

"Which means He prepared our hearts as well." She brought her hands forward and laced her fingers. "Somehow, I have to put that into words on a written page in the form of a letter." She picked up the crate. "But first, let's get this contraband stashed away before looters come and pilfer it!"

She could tell her friend intentionally tried to lighten the mood, so she jumped off the table and slipped her arm through hers. "I think I have a good hiding spot for it. Provided Charlene can keep a secret. She strikes me as a lady who keeps lots of secrets. She give you that impression? And speaking of birds, I bet she's been called a tough old bird a time or two. Not that she's *that* old."

♙ ♙ ♙ ♙

HELEN walked into what used to be the library of the manor home. For now it served as a staff lounge. Floor-to-ceiling bookshelves lined the massive room, and leather couches, chairs, and sofas provided sitting areas all around. Helen couldn't imagine that so many books had been printed in history, much less that any one person could actually own them all. She had spent a lot of time simply browsing the spines of the books, reading titles, occasionally pulling out one that specifically had to do with flying, planes, travel, or maps.

As she ran her fingers over the spine of a leather book with what looked like a title in French words, Hope dashed into the room, waving a newspaper. "Oh, there you are!" she exclaimed.

Helen turned around. "Here I am." She smiled. "I've been sleeping today. Had a late flight last night."

Hope held up a newspaper. "JAPAN DECLARES WAR ON BRITAIN AND AMERICA," the headline read.

"What?" She snatched the paper from Hope's hand and skimmed the story, reading about the attack on a naval base called Pearl Harbor, the thousands dead, and America's quick response to Japan.

Heart pounding, eyes wide, she looked up at Hope. "Good heavens."

"I guess the official involvement eventually had to happen."

"But to attack us? To provoke us? On a Sunday? Why?"

"You assume it was to provoke and not to cripple," Charlene said, coming into the room. "Look at the destruction. Any advantage the U.S. Navy might have had in the Pacific is now effectively removed. The doorway to China, Burma, the Philippines, eventually, New Zealand and Australia – all of it – is now thrown wide open."

Grace rushed into the room, carrying a newspaper, but stopped when she saw the one in Helen's hand. "You've heard, then?"

"Yes! I'm at a loss for words!"

"Well, that is certainly rare." Charlene smiled. Mercy and Temperance strolled in arm in arm, laughing, but stopped when they saw the group there.

"What's happened, then? Something amiss?" Mercy demanded. She disengaged herself from Temperance and accepted the newspaper from Grace. "Good Lord above," she exclaimed, "is this real?"

Charity ran in, headphones around her neck. "I was in the radio room when I heard that –" she stopped short and saw the papers in Mercy and Helen's hands. "You know, then."

"Aye." Mercy held up the paper. "America may be joining us shortly. There's more than a few who will say it's well past time."

Helen raised an eyebrow. "There's more than a few who were here regardless, even if you don't count yours truly sittin' right here in the middle of y'all. I'm also pretty sure the 125 souls lost on the *Reuben James* in October would disagree with the notion that we've been sittin' on the sidelines."

"Indeed, lass. I'm not taking anything away from that. I'm just preparing you for what the talk around here will surely be. Especially for you, who has to interact with all of those pilots."

"But America declaring war on Japan isn't going to bring them here," Charity said.

"It's all the same Axis. It's only a matter of time," Charlene answered. "I give it a week."

Would America be invaded? Would her family have to suffer through the *Blitz* like London families did? What would happen to the coastal communities? Surely those were the most vulnerable. She suddenly felt very thankful that the state of Texas was so massive and prayed that her inland home would secure her family.

Charity's tone lost all emotion. "Big country. Lots of industry. Large population. Major metropolises. But can they support a war on two fronts? I need more data."

"Will that change what we're doing here?" Helen asked, leaving Charity to her puzzles.

Charlene raised an eyebrow. "Is there any reason it should?"

With a shrug, Helen answered, "Don't know. That's why I asked. When America entered the Great War, my brother left the French Air Force and joined an American unit. I know my job here and I'm good at it. I'd hate to be sent elsewhere."

"You aren't exactly a member of the military, though, are you?" Charlene patted her on the shoulder. "You are a special team. You stay with me until you or I say otherwise." She smiled and gestured toward Charity. "Now, back to work with you," she said as she turned toward Helen, "and to the hangar with you. This news hasn't changed what we're doing here, and there's still a job of work to be done."

$$\begin{matrix} \text{Ö} & \text{Ö} & \text{Ö} & \text{Ö} \end{matrix}$$

CHAPTER 5

Chapter Five

"WHAT do you think you were about up there?" Captain Green bellowed.

Helen ducked under the nose of the blackened Avro Anson and stood toe to toe with a red-faced Captain Green. Irritation at the dressing down in front of the ground crew bristled up and down her spine. It caused her to mouth off, which she immediately regretted and had a feeling she would regret. "You mean besides outflying the rest of your men?"

"The rest of my men did not break protocol."

"Break protocol?" With exaggerated movements, she tapped her chin with her finger, then her eyes widened and she held that finger up. "Oh! You mean with the lights? Gee, Cap, I was just sayin' howdy."

"Sayin' howdy?" he sputtered. He closed his eyes, as if praying for patience, then opened them and glared at her, his vivid green eyes staring her down and putting her into place much more quickly than any angry words he could speak. They almost shone in the night with their intensity and she knew she had crossed a line. "Faith, the second those lights came on, the aggressor had you in his sights and fired. You're officially dead. Consider that for the next three days if you can. You're grounded."

A huff of indignation escaped from deep within her chest. She had simply flashed her plane's exterior lights off and on one time after the exercise concluded. It was almost a victory flash more than anything. "Three days? You can't do that!"

"Oh, but I assure you that I absolutely can. In fact, I already have. It's done. Take protocol seriously, like those *men* you're up there flying with, and we shall never have to have this conversation again."

Helen glared at him, swallowing angry words as they formed on her tongue, before she turned on her heel and marched away from him, off of the airfield and over to the main campus of the training grounds. Ground her? No one grounded her. She was Helen Mulberry, daughter to – she paused outside of the canteen.

Where had this sudden pride come from? Captain Green had every right and every obligation to ground her. She'd flashed the lights at him in a mocking display of superiority, and he flat well knew it. She deserved to be grounded. It didn't take the sting of what happened away, but at least she accepted it.

"Faith!" She turned and saw a uniformed lieutenant waving her down. "Major Radden wanted to see you as soon as you landed. I tried to get word at the airfield, but they said you already left."

She nodded. She supposed she'd get it now. Contrite, almost dragging her feet, she headed to the main house, which used to be an earl's home and now housed the headquarters of this little faction of the British military intelligence agency. She wondered, really, how much of the war was actually affected from inside those stone walls – certainly more than she could ever conceptualize.

$$\text{\small 8 8 8 8}$$

HELEN walked into the front hall and up the grand staircase, down a long hallway, and stopped at Charlene's door, giving it a quick rap with her knuckles. At Charlene's bidding, she entered the office, surprised to see a man with slicked back black hair wearing a dark gray suit and a silk forest green vest. She thought he looked much like the English bulldog her nephews had.

"Ah, Faith, wonderful. Please meet *Monsieur* Benson Dubois."

"Howdy," Faith greeted while extending her right hand for a shake. "It's a pleasure."

He spoke to her in French, and Faith looked to Charlene for a translation. "He says it's an honor to meet you. Please, sit." She looked at Benson and spoke to him in French.

He nodded and stepped out of the office with an, "*Au revoir.*"

Helen perched on the edge of one of the two chairs in front of Charlene's desk, wanting to get this over with. "If this is about tonight –"

Charlene raised an eyebrow. "To what might you be referring?"

With a smile, Faith relaxed. Slightly. "Nothing, Major. Nothing you should worry about. No reason nagging you about every little thing. How can I help you?"

"The long and short of it, Faith, is that the situation in France has gone from somewhat intolerable to set on sixes and sevens. We've been training for months, and now the time has come to deploy the Virtues team into their assigned locales so that we can get things sorted."

A feeling of dread worked into her heart. She loved her sisters in Christ as much as she loved anyone on this earth. The thought of flying them into the heart of the enemy's nest filled her with trepidation. But, she couldn't express that to Charlene. "I'm sure they're ready to get to work," she said softly.

"Indeed." She shifted a sheet of paper toward her. "Here are the coordinates to drop Hope. She must not be seen by the local population. I cannot stress that enough."

"Right. Where to, then?"

"Casablanca."

Faith couldn't help but smile. "In Africa?"

"Yes. Northern Africa. You will fly tomorrow night and refuel there. The refueling will have to be done manually using a hand operated pump. It will take several hours. Try to rest while that's going on and then try your hardest to return just as soon as possible. If you must land short from fatigue, make for Portugal."

"Okay. Anything else?"

"Yes. This stays here as I have not yet briefed everyone. No morning training for the next three days. I need you sleeping during the day so you can fly at night. You're flying tomorrow and the next night, too. Meet me in the situation room tomorrow at 1600 for your briefing. Then, you'll be allowed to take up the blackened Avro and do one more test run on instruments only."

She stood. "I'll be ready to go. But, ma'am, I'm... that is, Captain Green, he...."

"You're grounded." Charlene finished the sentence for her.

"Yes, ma'am."

"For three days."

For some reason, this didn't surprise her. She visibly relaxed. "Right."

"I'm aware, Faith. There is very little that goes on here of which I remain unaware and absolutely nothing concerning any of the women placed in my charge goes without me being informed."

"I flashed my lights during training."

"Yes. I realize that. I am puzzled as to the why of it. You flashed your lights to what end?"

Faith felt genuine embarrassment making her cheeks feel hot. "I guess I was just full of myself. I'd just literally flown circles around all the fellas. They kind of give me a hard time on the ground, but they got nothing on me in the air."

Charlene's lip twitched in annoyance. "Your grounding from Captain Green will begin the first of next week. He has kindly granted you permission to fly these missions only because you're flying the Virtues." Helen felt her ears burn with shame. Understanding she was dismissed, she crossed the room and put her hand on the door knob when Charlene stopped her.

"Faith?" Her commander very firmly said, "Just so this doesn't go unsaid, I'd very much rather you extend me the courtesy of never doing something so childish and foolhardy again. You're a grown woman, after all, besides being a blood relative to honest to goodness war heroes. You have nothing to prove. To anyone. In the air or on the ground. Have I made myself clear?"

"Yes, ma'am. It won't happen again," Helen said, and scooted out of the room before Charlene changed her mind about letting her fly today.

8 8 8 8

Chapter Six

HELEN sat next to Mercy and Temperance at a table in the back room of their favorite pub. She looked around the table at the six women with whom she had trained, laughed, prayed, cried, and grown so close to that she actually felt like they were sisters.

She'd grown up in a male dominated household that, for the last twenty or so years, had been in a constant state of mourning. The loss of his son and wife sent her father into a tailspin of work from which he never recovered. Helen's brother Dwight focused on his wife and children, leaving her to be raised by Eddie – a wreck of a human being. Her sister-in-law, JoAnn, thought of Helen as a problem, an unruly child needing to be fixed and disciplined, who required constant correction in everything she said and did.

Here at this table, she had found a family who loved her, who saw nothing wrong with her, who accepted her and admired her for her strengths, who promised to uphold her in her times of weakness.

How could she fly them out, one at a time, into danger and peril? How could she bring herself to hit that green light and let them know when they could hook up the static lines of their parachutes and jump out of the airplane into enemy territory? How could she land and allow that door to open and watch them disembark her aircraft and embark onto a path that led to a most uncertain future?

As she thought about it, she realized that she absolutely had the strength to do that – because of Eddie and Manny. They were the reason why she must do this. Despite Captain Green's opinion to the contrary, she certainly could outfly any man on this base, and in doing so, in sending these women into the positions for which they had spent the better part of a year training, they might help bring about a quicker end to this war. The longer the war went on, the more likely brothers like Manny would die and brothers like

Eddie would cease to live lives of joy.

God brought them all together at this time. She had deep and abiding faith in that very notion. Each one of the women at this table had exceptional skills, honed to near perfection, that would help them in the difficult and dangerous work ahead. Why would God have given Charity and Temperance such minds for puzzles and code or Prudence such instinctive reactions to situations? Why would He have gifted Grace with the strength and agility of a warrior and Hope with the power of seduction and persuasion? Couple all of that with Mercy's surgical skills and her own flying skills, and what God had created decades before the mere mortals on earth even knew they needed it, was a finely tuned team. They came together as if made for each other, in love and trust, and one which could work as a single solid unit.

It filled her heart and took her breath away – that God would choose her, *her*, to be a part of this monumental moment – that He would have her, *little Helen from Lamarr,* begin flying these amazing and gifted women to their assignments so they could begin their work.

She pulled herself out of her own reverie as Hope stood to her feet and said, "My friends, this is our time. We have trained hard. We have prayed up. And now it's time to go out there and show Hitler how we can fight back." She extended her arm to the center of the table. Repeating what Grace often said, she added, "To victory, my Virtues."

A round of "Victory!" erupted around the table.

After Hope sat back down, Mercy stood at the head of the table. "I'd love it if we would all join hands and pray, one at a time." She held out her hands. Faith took Mercy's hand with her right and reached out to Temperance with her left hand. Everyone at the table joined hands. "We know God is with us as we go into this battle. My prayer is that we stay focused and sharp and that we remember our training. I also pray that we all come back home safe and sound. Please, bow your heads."

While Mercy prayed out loud, Helen prayed quietly to herself. She prayed for strength while flying, for quick reflexes, and smart thinking. She prayed that she would always give her all for the team, even if that all meant everything. And, she prayed for her brother back home, for his sanity, and for his forgiveness.

❦ ❦ ❦ ❦

"WE aren't going to make it!" Helen yelled as she struggled with the controls.

"Just lost the left engine," her copilot, Harold Curtis, announced, looking past Helen to the burning wing. Less than a second later, the entire plane shuddered as another antiaircraft burst exploded right next to them, causing them to rapidly lose altitude.

"You need to find me a place to set this baby down or else we're going to be in a heap of trouble," she managed to say as she stood and used the weight of her body to try to control the yoke. Some part of her brain told her that right now she ought to feel absolute terror, but she didn't have time for that. Maybe later, when this was over, she would take time and react to the fact that she was crash landing into enemy territory, into a country in which she did not speak the language.

"Another kilometer north and we'll be at an old field we used to use for delivery drop-offs," he yelled, pointing out the window. "You better strap back in," he said, "we're going in too fast."

"I can't shed any speed. The rudder feels like a crowbar!" Inspiration hit and she lowered the landing gear – at least she hoped it lowered. The dying airplane and the nearby antiaircraft fire had deafened her and she couldn't even hear the hydraulics. It either did or didn't. Whatever happened, they were landing. If the gear had gone down, she would shed about 30 knots of airspeed from the drag.

She sat back and Harold reached around her, grabbing her harness and strapping her in. She followed his directions to the field, fighting with the yoke as if it were a branding calf.

Without any meaningful altitude control, the aircraft hit the ground hard. As graceful as the aircraft might be in the air, she was proportionally ungainly on the ground. The nose of the airplane dug into the dirt and Helen and Harold were thrown forward against their harnesses.

About two seconds after they came to a complete stop, they both had their harnesses unhooked and Harold had the door open. They each gripped their flight kits and Harold snatched up the Sten submachine gun and extra ammunition. Helen opened her kit and retrieved her Enfield No. 2 .38 caliber pistol, securing the lanyard to her wrist as she had been trained, and they exited the aircraft. The pistol, though fairly light, felt as heavy as a bowling ball in her small hand after fighting with the controls for so long.

They dashed for the tree line with as much speed as they could muster. The burning aircraft lit up the field behind them like a bonfire, exposing them as completely as a search light, casting long shadows in their path.

Once deep inside the trees, Harold pulled out his compass. "You okay?"

"Nothing broken, but my wrists are throbbing. I got some pretty nice bruises from the straps, but nothing a few aspirin and a trip to San Juan won't fix."

"Bruised, you say?" Harold murmured, his tone droll. He had been tossed against his harness like a scarecrow on a hayride. He let the Sten hang by its strap against his side and held the compass as far from the metal weapon as he could while still making out the face. He figured his directionality and pointed west. "Run. That way, about three kilometers. There's an airfield where Jerry stores planes requiring mechanical work. It's our best chance in the time we have."

Helen followed him, running behind him as fast as she could. They had thirty minutes to get an airplane to a specific set of coordinates in order to pick up the rescued Temperance and maybe some high level escaped prisoners. No way would she fail Temperance by not being present at those coordinates with an aircraft. No one was going to quibble about where the airplane had been manufactured.

Legs pumping, arms pumping, she ducked branches, jumped over logs, and darted across roads. Ten minutes later, out of breath, sweat pouring from her pores, they stopped at the edge of an airstrip and crouched next to the fence.

"Uh, that doesn't look like a mechanic shop to me, Harry," Helen said. Trimotor Junkers JU-52s filled the taxiway, perfectly lined up like little soldiers in formation. "That's a lot of VIP power." She recognized the planes and the markings on them. These planes were assigned to high-ranking officers in every branch of the Nazi *Wehrmacht*. "What are they all doing here?"

"I wonder if it's about Hope," Harold said. "Can you fly a Jerry bird?" He gestured toward the *Luftwaffe* Junkers JU-52 closest to their present location. The *Balkenkreuz* on the fuselage and the *Swastika* on the vertical stabilizer gave her a little shiver.

"Can I fly it? It's a plane, ain't it?" She stood and started moving along the fence line. Harold followed her, holding the submachine gun steady and at the ready. "Never met a plane I couldn't fly yet." She silently prayed she wasn't about to.

Harold checked his watch. "We have to get airborne. If we don't –"

"I know." The darkness both helped and hindered them. They had absolutely no way to determine the amount of security there was for this airfield on the outskirts of the town. But they had no choice. Do or die.

"Let's go." She slipped the lanyard of her pistol off of her wrist and tucked the pistol into her flight jacket. Then she lifted up the bottom of the chain link fence. "Roll under, then lift it up for me."

☫ ☫ ☫ ☫

ON the other side of the fence, they sprinted toward the Junkers farthest down the line, closest to the runway, furthest from the lights on the field.

"*Halt!*"

Helen considered ignoring the command, but before her rational brain could fully comprehend that instinct, Harold grabbed her arm and the two of them stopped running.

"*Halt, oder ich schießen!*"

From her single semester of German tutoring, the context, and the tone, she figured she had just been informed that if she didn't stop she would be shot dead. She heard the unmistakable sound of a Mouser bolt cocking and realized she had best tread carefully. Slowly, without turning around, she raised her hands above her head.

"*Was machst du, hier?*"

Helen looked over at Harold, who gripped the submachine gun with both hands, keeping it out of sight in front of him. His eyes moved rapidly as he calculated their chances. His fingers gripped the firearm tightly. Sweat broke out on his upper lip and his jaw set tight.

"Hey Harry?" Faith breathed and he met her eyes. "Remember the Alamo."

With that, Faith slowly turned around, carefully keeping her hands above her head in plain sight. She saw only two men, a tall, lean man and a shorter man with a crooked hat. The shorter man trained a Mouser rifle on the center of Harry's back. The taller man appeared to have a Parabellum Pistol just like those the boys in Britain called a Luger, pointed directly at her. The 9 millimeter barrel looked like the mouth of a train tunnel at the moment.

"*Was machst du, hier, Fraulein? Beantworte die Fragen!*" The shorter man yelled.

"*Nicht Sprechen sie Deutsch!*" she proclaimed with the same thick Texas accent that had often sent her German tutor into a private rage.

The man smiled. It was not a happy expression. Sarcastically, he mixed German and French to ask, "*Ja? Est-ce vrai? Qu'est-ce que vous faites ici?*"

She closed her eyes and sighed. "Maybe stick with Kraut. I pretty much don't speak French, either, Jerry," she answered through her teeth.

"That's because you're from Lamarr, Texas," the tall one said in perfect and very American English. She squinted in the dark and gasped. Valor!

He spoke in rapid German to the other man with him, then gestured toward them. As the sergeant stepped forward, Valor shifted his pistol, aimed carefully, and shot the man at the base of his skull. The two rapid shots sent a blinding glare to Helen's shocked eyes as her ears rang with the deafening sound of shots fired in such close proximity. Helen gasped and covered her mouth with her hands. Harold spun around, simultaneously raising his Sten. Helen's arm shot out and pushed the muzzle down toward the ground. "No! Not him."

Valor took a few steps and knelt down, his pistol trained on the German sergeant. He needlessly laid his fingers along the sergeant's neck, verifying that the man was indeed dead. With a nod, he holstered his pistol.

When his eyes finally met hers, he said, "Faith. I take it you were the one flying that rather noisy ball of fire that crashed a few kilometers away a bit earlier this evening?"

"What are you doing here?" she demanded.

"Looking for you, of course. I'm glad I found you."

Harold interjected, "I feel like a bit of a third wheel, Faith. Care to make introductions?"

"Harry, this is Valor. You never met him and you won't speak of ever meeting him. Assuming we live to talk about it."

Harold nodded. "In that case, couldn't be happier to make your acquaintance."

Valor nodded. "Likewise, I'm sure."

Helen gestured toward the corpse of the sergeant lying face down in the grass. "I'm just curious. So, you know, what in the world?"

Valor looked at her. "He disobeyed my direct orders, arrested Temperance, and beat her to within an inch of her life. I would have had him shot already if I hadn't been given direct orders to the contrary."

"Did you have to kill him?"

"I doubt he would have refrained from killing you, even if I had asked nicely."

She froze. She couldn't fathom the necessities of war. It ran counter to everything her Christian worldview proclaimed. Taking a deep cleansing breath, she returned to the matter at hand. "I'm sorry. You don't owe me an explanation." She knew Harold was staring at her in the dark. "Valor, we need that plane," she said as she pointed.

"I know. And now you're free to take it."

She raised an eyebrow. "Well, gosh. You gonna sign a hand receipt, too? Maybe assign us a steward for an inflight meal?"

"Take it, but don't get caught." He did not smile in return. "I recognize that plane. It belongs to an SS Colonel who isn't here to enjoy a concert. I have to go and see to Hope."

"How will you explain this?"

He smirked. "You killed the sergeant who I sent to investigate the crash. His incompetence allowed you to steal an aircraft. I was never here."

She stepped forward and put a hand on his arm. "And you? How will you deal with this?"

"I'll deal with it in God's good time, Faith." His expression looked hard, cold. "Godspeed, Faith. I pray we'll meet again."

"Not like this," she said as she lifted her hand before she and Harold jogged to the trimotor plane. Harold opened the door and the two of them slipped inside. They moved through the cabin and up to the cockpit. Helen slipped into the pilot's seat and looked around.

"Everything's written in German," she said. For the first time, she allowed a little bit of anxiety to reach her conscious mind.

"The devil you say! In a *Luftwaffe* Junkers JU-52? How dare those cheeky Nazis write everything in German in a German aircraft," Harold replied.

"Wow, Lieutenant, that's mighty insightful. And helpful besides." It actually was helpful. It pulled her away from the despair that had started to clutch at her. She huffed out a breath and closed her eyes, willing herself to reflexively reach for the proper controls. She reached forward to where she thought the ignition should be and pressed the button. So far so good.

"You'd better suss this out quickly. I don't think we'll have a lot of time to disappear before they realize we're taking their airplane for a joyride," Harold said, trying to peer through the windows.

"Yeah, yeah. Keep a grip on your suspenders, Gabby, I know." She pushed forward on the throttle and sent the plane taxiing faster than it probably ever had before, pulling up maybe a little too early. She wanted to get up and be gone before they could scramble a fighter after them.

"A grip on my suspenders? Are you telling me to keep my shirt on?"

The airplane lifted from the earth. The landing gear brushed the treetops at the end of the airfield. She reached out to the logical place for landing gear controls and flipped the switch she found there. Behind her, below each of the wing mounted engines, she heard a silken whine and felt a very gentle shock as the struts and wheels tucked themselves in. "See that? That's German engineering. That's how landing gear's supposed to work. The boys at Avro could take a few notes."

Chapter Seven

HELEN headed in the opposite direction of the landing field, just to make sure they had the all clear. For fifteen minutes, she pretty much circled the town. From the air, she watched as a building exploded and burst into flames. "That looks like our cue," she said, turning back toward the rendezvous point.

"We're going to be late," Harold said, looking at the map in his hand, then at his watch.

"No rush. I have a feeling they'll be waiting on us," Helen replied. She found the coordinates of the field, but no one had set flares or fires. She circled back around and started praying out loud. "God, I know You're here. I know You hear me. Please give us a hand and help us land this Kraut beast."

She flipped the switch to deploy the landing gear, a bit surprised at how quickly and easily it deployed, almost cheering when she heard the strut motors engage and started having to overcorrect for the drag. With a prayer and a petition, she brought the plane to the ground, standing on the brakes, praying that she didn't crash into a mess of trees. No one observing the plane on the outside would be able to tell the inner turmoil she faced as she taxied to the end of the field and turned the plane around.

"Here they come, and I think they got company," she cried, seeing several cars racing toward them.

"Be ready to take off," Harold said as he unstrapped and snatched up the Sten. He opened the door and she could hear the gunshots over the plane's motors.

Helen pushed herself out of her seat and rushed to the back, finding blankets to use as a pallet for Temperance. As she made the bed, a man climbed on board, carrying her unconscious friend. "Lay her right there, son. We'll get her home."

He gently lay her down and Helen knelt next to her, brushing her hair out of her face. Her skin felt shockingly hot.

The man paused on his way out the door. "Who'd you steal the plane from?"

"According to my source, an SS Colonel. I have a feeling things are going to get very exciting around here in the next little while. Best get on out of here. I'm fixin' to take off."

With a nod, he rushed outside. As Helen passed the door to get back into the pilot's seat, she heard Prudence yell, "Get her on the plane! Stay with her!"

Get who on the plane? Seconds later, the same man guided Hope on board, his arms around her, almost cradling her to him as he helped her sit down. Helen saw the bloody bandage against her forehead.

"Hope?" She asked, turning to go back there.

"Get us out of here," the man said. "I don't know how much longer they'll be able to hold them back." He sat down in one of the jump seats and strapped Hope in next to him.

Several escaped prisoners bounded on board. "Welcome aboard, gentlemen. Please have your tickets ready for the steward to punch," Helen said while preparing to taxi. The sounds of the gunshots outside overrode the sound of the powerful plane engines. "Come on, Harold, I'm going to leave you!"

She probably wouldn't, and he probably didn't hear her, but it felt better to say something instead of just sitting here waiting, looking out the window at the cars pouring onto the field. The man sitting with Hope left her strapped in and looked out the plane door, then rushed back outside.

"Hey!" she yelled at his back. "Where are you going?" Harold carried an unconscious Prudence on board. "Is she okay?"

He lay her on the ground at Temperance's feet. "She got shot in the shoulder."

Seconds later, the man who had carried Temperance on board now carried Grace, who clutched a very nasty looking, bloody leg. Right behind her, Mercy dashed up the stairs, clutching her black medical bag.

She did a quick tally in her head. "Everybody aboard?"

"Go!" the man yelled.

"Hold your horses, Spanky. Everything up here's written in Kraut and I only took one semester." She licked her lips then eased back on the stick. The engine pitch changed and the airplane lurched forward. "And I did *nicht* so *gut* in that class if you catch my drift."

She taxied toward the oncoming vehicles and saw the sparks flash from the nose of the plane as bullets ricocheted off the metal shell. "Please God," she whispered, "give me speed."

"Why are we on a Nazi airplane?" Grace asked from behind her.

"Long story," Harold explained as he secured the door. "Hang on. This isn't going to be a smooth flight. They know we're here. The Vichy aren't very good shots, but I am not overly fond of the prospect of flying what looks like a German bomber over Britain."

Harold strapped in next to her, placing the Sten between their seats. She looked over at him as she pulled up on the stick and the beast of a Nazi plane found air. It took no time for the Germans on the ground to start firing Archie in their general vicinity. She gripped the yoke as the entire plane shook with the force of exploding antiaircraft artillery. "If you can't strap in, grab onto something and hang on tight!" Helen yelled back.

⁜ ⁜ ⁜ ⁜

CLIMBING as quickly as she possibly could, Helen tried to get out of artillery range. She had already experienced the kind of damage those things could do to a plane tonight. She had no desire to crash land in German territory with this load of precious cargo.

Suddenly, the world around them erupted as dozens of air bursts buffeted the plane. "Y'all hang on back there!" she yelled. She had never experienced such an onslaught before and used every ounce of skill she possessed to keep the plane in the air.

Harold yelled, "Grab hold!"

Bits of deadly jagged metal sprinkled the aircraft like sleet, hitting them from every angle. Shrapnel rained against the fuselage just milliseconds before exploding antiaircraft fire rocked the aircraft. The flashes of light that accompanied each explosion lit the inside of the JU-52 like lightning in a raging storm.

Without warning, the plane started losing altitude. "No way," Helen said, gripping the control wheel with both hands. She fought and won, her wrists throbbing in agony, bringing the aircraft back under control and heading back up to gain more altitude again.

Suddenly, the antiaircraft fire ceased. No more explosions tried to knock them from the sky.

"Not good," Harold murmured, looking out the window. "There's no way this beast can outfly fighters."

"I'm going to keep climbing. Maybe they won't see us," she said quietly. Then, because the plane was filled with intelligent, strong people, she yelled back to the cabin, "This ain't right. They stopped shooting, but we're pretty far from the coast."

Harold added in a voice intended to carry above the sound of the engines, "If you can manage, keep a look out the windows, lads and lasses! The only reason they'd stop shooting is if they sent up fighters to bring us down!"

Out of the corner of her eye, she saw a tracer. Twisting in her seat, she looked as far behind the plane as she could and saw a glimpse of something bright yellow in the moonlight. "Hang on!" she yelled. "They're coming in low on our six."

From behind her, she heard a woman scream in agony. A part of her brain wanted to stop and find out who was hurt and why, but she couldn't worry about that now. Instead, she flipped the switches she thought would turn out the cabin lights. "Shutting out the lights now, folks. Don't want to give those fighters too clear of a target."

The first few switches didn't extinguish the lights. But the third try did. "Whooo wheee! Hang on!" she yelled, excited to have accomplished the task.

She turned the plane almost sideways in an attempt to keep from getting shot at by the Messerschmitt that tailed her like a hound dog on a scent. The Junkers handled somewhat like an overloaded truck on an icy road. The wings had what the designers called *Doppelflügel*, or "double wing" trailing edge control surfaces instead of having the control surfaces built into the actual wings. Herexhausted wrists screamed in agony as she tried to turn it. Honestly, she'd never flown a more difficult plane, with or without combat conditions.

Knowing that some of her passengers couldn't hold on, she righted the plane when she thought it was safe again. From behind her, she heard the "Ping! Ping! Ping!" of rounds penetrating through the corrugated duralumin metal skin of the cabin.

She turned again, dodging more bullets as she saw tracers go by, and pulled up to gain even more altitude, trading speed for height, hoping that a cloud cover might miraculously appear to hide them. While she climbed, Harold unstrapped and looked behind him. He pointed toward the passengers. "You're Tom Ewing," he said. Helen gasped and wished she could look behind her to see which one was Charity's husband!

"Aye," the man answered.

"You were a fighter. Think you can man that MG 15?" Helen took a quick look over her shoulder when she heard that and saw the gun mounted behind the copilot's seat.

"Bob's your uncle. Not sure how much longer I can sit back here doing *nawt*."

"Great! Look in that boot and see if there are belts of rounds. Let's see what we can do to get these Krauts off our tail."

Tom grinned as he opened the lid to the ammunition store, "Well, in fairness, it is their airplane." Helen heard Tom speak again. "There's probably another gun by the fuselage."

Another man, whom Helen could not see, replied, "I'll go look."

She heard Mercy say, "Here, take my torch."

A few moments later, the incredibly loud sound of an MG15 machine gun filled the cabin, and not long after, the smell of cordite overwhelmed Helen's nostrils. About a minute later, she heard a similar sound from below. Dozens of spent brass cartridges as long as pencils and as wide as her thumb began to roll around on the cabin floor.

Giddy with relief at the ability to fight back, she climbed back up into what sparse clouds existed and rolled her neck on her shoulders. She could feel the muscles tensing up and had a feeling that tomorrow it would be very hard to move after that crash and the physical exertion of keeping the plane in the air.

"Gotcha ya sausage eatin' so-and-so!" Tom proclaimed. Helen looked behind her. "Aye, there's your wee parachute. Hope you land in a pile a' cow manure!"

"That's it, Ace! See any more?"

"Not as of yet. Honestly, I'm astonished I was able to shoot him down. I've been out of commission for a while."

"You're a natural," Helen encouraged as she checked her coordinates. Almost to the coast. Out of nowhere, she saw sparks come out of the left wing and a light on the dash started flashing.

Harold tapped the gauge next to it. He shined his flashlight onto the label next to the light. *"Flugbenzin,"* he said. "What is *Flugbenzin*? I think *benzin* is Jerry for petrol."

Next to the light, a gauge started moving, not too quickly, but much quicker than it had up until now. Helen felt a sinking feeling in the pit of her stomach that no amount of Beeman's was going to help. Harold yelled behind him. "Can anyone read in German?"

One of the prisoners pushed himself forward and leaned in between the two seats. "I have some German." He had black hair and a black mustache. "Sir Percy Montrose at your service."

Helen pulled a stick of Beeman's out of her breast pocket, quickly unwrapped it, and popped it into her mouth. Couldn't hurt. As soon as her hands gripped the wheel again, she dove low, rolling the plane almost on its side, trading altitude for speed this time. "Charmed, I'm sure," she said around the mouth full of gum as she righted the plane. She could hear the gun in the fuselage firing at whatever target was beneath them. "What's *Flugbenzin*?"

"Flugbenzin? Why, that would be airplane fuel."

Helen looked at Harold. "Airplane fuel, he says."

"Wonderful," Harold replied. He looked at Sir Percy. "Thank you for your help, sir. Do you mind sitting close in case we need you to translate again?"

"Absolutely not, chap. Happy to help."

"So, Faith, where would you like to pull in and refuel? I hope you brought *Reichsmarks*," Harold offered helpfully.

Helen searched the skies, looking for their Messerschmitt friends. "How long?" She asked Harold.

He shrugged. "Who can say? I don't know how big the tanks are. I know that we can probably get across the pond. If not, we can at least make for friendly waters and hope for rescue after a splash landing."

Sir Montrose studied his fingernails. "And me without my bathing suit."

Helen assessed her options. Things could be worse. She could be out of fuel completely. Or someone could be dead. "All right. Okay. We're okay. And besides, I'm so looking forward to hitting British skies with that gigantic Swastika painted on our tail. I bet the sun will just start rising about then, too. THERE you are!" She tilted the plane to the right as a Messerschmitt with bright yellow markings screamed past. The pilot flew beyond her eyesight, blending in with the night sky. "I bet he's coming back around. Aw, nuts!" she cried when she saw the first tracer round from his nose gun.

She pushed against the wheel and dropped altitude while increasing speed, trying to get him out from in front of her so that Tom could get a clear shot. Seven minutes dragged on like hours as she dodged, dove, rose, turned, tilted, and took too many bullets to count.

Exhausted, she wondered how much further they had to go. She glanced at the coordinates and tried to do the math, when suddenly, she saw two more fighters headed in their direction.

"Those are our lads," she said to Harold, "but they don't know that we're friendly."

"Can you get that radio onto the open frequency?"

Howard grabbed the handset but immediately tossed it back down. "It's shot."

"Shot? When did that happen?"

"Must have been one of those bullets that German chap so rudely shot into us back there," he surmised.

Tom yelled from his position at the gun, "Submarine Spitfire Mark Twos! British! Two seaters!" He yelled even louder, presumably to the person on the fuselage gun. "Friendlies. Keep your eyes peeled, Abiel!"

Spitfires? And two seater trainers at that? She'd bet a month's wages that Captain Green Eyes himself piloted one of those Spitfires. From her German language lessons she picked out a few words and recognized the switch labeled *Außenbeleuchtung*. She fought an internal debate with herself as she dove to avoid the gunfire from the Messerschmitt that suddenly appeared behind her. As she straightened out, she put her fingers on the switch.

"Faith? Does that word mean what I think it means?" Harold asked.

"Only if you think it means exterior lights!"

"You remember what happened last time you did that, right?" Harold said, eyeing her fingers.

"Yeah." She flicked the lights on, off, on, then off again. "Ole Cap was mighty put out with me. I reckon he'll remember it, too."

"If he's out there."

"He's out there." She grinned. "Have faith, Harry."

Within seconds, the Spitfires had lined up in protective order around her. One of them broke off to engage an enemy aircraft, but the other one held its position on her left wing.

"I almost feel like I can take a deep breath now," Helen said, sitting back against her seat for just a moment. "What a ride."

"We're not home yet," Harold said, tapping the gauge with his finger. "And at the rate our *Flugbenzin* is depleting, we'll be rather fortunate to get there."

"At least we're over the water now. Won't be any more Krauts coming at us."

The sun began to rise, lighting the sky as Helen saw the British coast. Now that she could see out the windows, she checked her status. She could see the black smoke pouring out of the right wing and made out the flicker of flames eating up the fuel that slowly leaked out. She looked at the gauge and saw that the needle was hovering dangerously close to the red line. As she watched, the engine sputtered and the propeller stopped moving entirely. She feathered the propeller. Without the propeller to actually fan down and inhibit the flame somewhat, the fire flared up, consuming fuel at a frightening rate.

"Fire," Harold said just as the plane began to lose altitude. "In case you didn't actually feel the heat on your skin. Say! Anyone bring any marshmallows?"

Helen looked over just in time to see the right wing catch on fire and the propeller stop moving entirely. She could see the airfield in the distance.

"We're almost home, Brunhilda," she said to the plane, christening her. "You got us this far, girl. Let's hear the fat lady sing, now. Get us all the way there."

The control wheel shuddered under her hands just as the propeller on the left wing stopped moving. "Well, that's that. We're coming in hard, folks. Strap in, grab an injured to hang onto, and say your prayers!"

"I'm not seeing a brass band," Harold replied, lowering the flaps even further.

"They probably want it to be a surprise," Helen replied, popping her gum. She saw Harold's finger hover over the controls for the landing gear. "Hit it."

He activated the landing gear, but nothing happened.

"Do it again."

Nothing.

Harold cocked an eyebrow at her. "Well, then. So much for German engineering."

No. They didn't get this far to die now. She wouldn't let that happen. "Crash landing, friends! Brace yourselves!"

She looked over at Harold as the control wheel shook and shuddered under her aching hands. "I have no doubt we're going to feel this in the morning."

"Isn't one crash landing per day enough for you?"

"Sure, Harry. It's a new day. Look, the sun's rising."

She started to lose altitude a little too soon and strained against the wheel to keep the nose up. The ground rushed toward her and as it finally met the metal bottom of the plane, the entire aircraft bounced up and crashed back down again, throwing her and everyone else forward. She closed her eyes and cried out, "Please help us, God!"

The plane skidded along the grass and turned sideways. The burning right wing hit the ground and sheared off, making a horrible screeching metal sound and spraying burning fuel in their wake like a flame thrower. Someone in the back cried out, either in pain or fear, and finally they came to a complete stop.

Helen put shaking hands up to her face and realized that tears streamed out of her eyes. As she unstrapped her buckle, she saw trucks pull up outside of the plane and then men hopped out, dragging a fire hose over and hurriedly dousing the burning wing.

Harold unstrapped and stared at her. "Well, Faith, you've gotten us home. Now, there's something I must tell you."

"What's that, Harry?"

"Don't take this personally, but I never want to fly with you again." His eyes captured hers and she knew he was deadly serious. "Ever."

Helen nodded. "Likewise. And Harry? You really aren't funny."

Harry grinned. "Yes, I am. But that's beside the point. Shall we?"

He climbed into the back to open the door. Helen crawled between the two seats and paused by Tom. She held out her hand. "Good shooting back there, cowboy. It's been an honor to have you on my team."

"That was some incredible flying," he replied, squeezing her hand with his warm, strong grip. "And I'll fly with you any time, lass. Count on it."

Chapter Eight

THE cabin was a wreck. Literally. It was cluttered with supplies and blankets scattered everywhere. Blood pooled on the floor and spent shell casings littered the floor, making walking through the cabin risky. She could actually see daylight coming through far too many bullet holes in the fuselage.

Helen heard the fire teams outside yelling to one another as they extinguished the flames. Shouts and yells and bellowed orders somehow sounded far away and distant to her exhausted ears, though if she looked through any one of the jagged tears in the fuselage she could probably see the people working to get them safely out of the downed airplane. The first person she stopped next to on her way toward the rear exit was Grace, who lay on a pallet with her bloodied leg stretched out in front of her. Helen reached out and touched her shoulder and Grace's eyes flew open. "We're on the ground," she announced with a smile. "You can relax."

"God is good," Grace whispered as the door flew open and a medic climbed on board.

Helen smiled. "All the time." She worked her way past Grace and saw the man Tom had called Abiel, who sat in a jump seat with Temperance in his lap. He held Hope's hand.

"What happened to your head, Hope?"

She put a shaking hand to the bloodied bandage on her head. "I was pretty near the building when they blew it up. I got hit with a big chunk of debris. Brick or something." She reached out and touched Temperance's hand. "Her fever is so high."

"I need to get Marie – Temperance – to a hospital," Abiel said. "If you can help clear me a path, I'll carry her myself."

Helen looked behind her and saw Sir Percy Montrose helping the medic carry Grace out on a stretcher. "Should be clear now."

He looked at Hope. "Can you walk?"

"I'll be right behind you. Never fear." She wore an exquisite sparkling red gown that looked entirely out of place in this smoke filled shattered airplane. Hope smiled at Helen then reached out and hugged her. "You're sure a sight for sore eyes, my American sister."

"Likewise." Squeezing Hope, she let go and saw Mercy kneeling on the ground next to Prudence. She crawled over to her, covering her hands and the legs of her flight suit with blood and soot in the process, and felt deep surprise upon seeing tears streaming from Mercy's eyes.

Hope spoke. "What's wrong, Sugar?"

"I couldn't save her," she confessed, her Scottish accent so thick that Helen had a hard time understanding her words. "A bullet designed to bring down an entire plane went right through her chest."

Couldn't save her? She glanced at Prudence's very pale face, saw her eyes staring blankly skyward, saw her slack-jawed expression. Sticky blood soaked the front of her dress and pooled on the floor around her. This was not the woman who had teased her while helping her fill sugar dispensers in the canteen. That woman had been full of life, full of joy, overflowing with love for her husband, at peace with the knowledge of her loving God. Grief welled up inside Helen's chest and kept any sound from escaping her throat.

"What?" Hope cried. "Oh no! No! No!" She knelt on that bloody floor and framed Prudence's lifeless face with her hands, sparkly rings looking completely out of place in the environment of the wrecked plane.

Helen felt a sob escape her chest and she grabbed Mercy, hugging her to her. This wasn't possible. The corpse strapped into the jump seat looked small and pale and fragile, so very fragile. That had not been the incredibly strong woman Helen had known in life. How could it be? "I'm so sorry. I should have flown better," she cried.

Mercy pulled away and gripped her shoulders. "You pull yourself together this second. You didn't do a thing wrong. You, in all your brilliance, saved us. You hear me, lass? Now, I'll hear no more talk of this."

Helen pushed away and scrambled to her feet. Blood stained the front of her uniform. Prudence's blood. She saw lights dance in front of her eyes and felt nausea swirl up in her gut. The smell of the smoke and the blood and the fuel all started to overwhelm her senses. She had to get out of that plane.

She scrambled away, tripping and stumbling, slipping on spent bullet casings and blood, until she escaped through the open doorway and out into the bright British sunshine.

She saw Charity buried in the arms of Tom Ewing, crying and laughing at the same time. She saw Grace getting loaded into an ambulance alongside Temperance. Next to a truck, Sir Percy Montrose shook an unfamiliar uniformed major's hand. Her ears buzzed and her head swam and she turned in a circle, putting her bloody hands up to her temples as she felt a sob start deep within her chest and try to rip itself out of her body.

Suddenly, strong arms came around her. She brought her arms up to push him away. A baritone British voice demanded, "Are you hurt? Are you bleeding? Where are you hit?"

Reginald Green. As soon as she realized it was him, she put her arms around him and her entire body shook. "It's not my blood," Helen gasped.

His arms encircled her, one around her shoulders and the other cradling her head, his fingers in her hair. His voice fell on her ears, low and comforting, "I didn't think you'd make it." Silent sobs shook her body. "What's all this, then? Here, now. You're safe, now. Stiff upper lip and all that."

Stiff upper lip. So British, and so very, very male. He smelled like machine oil and leather and aftershave, reminding her oddly of home. She burst out in a near hysterical laugh that instantly turned into a wrenching sob. Then the sob she'd tried to contain since seeing Prudence's corpse escaped in an almost inhuman wail. Captain Green didn't say another word; he just held her even when she felt her legs grow weak enough to collapse out from beneath her. After a time, she just sobbed quietly, soaking his shirt with her tears.

"Happy to have you back, Faith," Charlene said from beside them. She could feel Green's reluctance to release her, but eventually his arms loosened and she took a step back.

"She's dead," Helen said.

"Who?" Charlene looked toward the ambulance. "Temperance?"

Her breath hiccupped and fresh tears streamed from her eyes. "Prudence." She gestured to the plane as Mercy and Hope emerged. Mercy's nurse uniform and her hands were covered in blood. "It's my fault, Major."

"Oh?" Charlene stared at her coldly. "Did you kill her?"

"What? Why, of course not."

"Precisely." Charlene raised an eyebrow. "Excuse me for a moment,"

Charlene said, and Helen watched as she marched over to Mercy and Hope. Hope's arm came around Mercy's shoulders as the red-haired doctor very stoically spoke to their commander.

Staring at Mercy covered in Prudence's blood, Helen felt shock start to vibrate at the edges of her brain like a headache and heard a buzzing sound in her ears. Was she about to faint?

She looked at Captain Green and saw he wore his flight suit. "I thought that was you up there," she said hoarsely. "Sorry about flashing the lights. I know I promised never to do it again."

"*Bampot*," he whispered. "You brilliant *bampot*."

What? It didn't sound mean but it also sort of sounded mean. Before she could even comprehend what he said, much less what she could say back to him, Charlene walked briskly back to them.

"That was some rather amazing flying you did, Faith. I honestly don't think I've ever seen a plane shot up so completely actually stay in the air, much less make it back over the Channel and safely land. Good show." She looked at Captain Green. "See that she gets a hot meal and perhaps something warm to drink. I think we can wait on her report until she's had a moment to collect herself."

"Ma'rm." He gently put an arm over her shoulder and steered her away from the wreckage of the plane.

♫ ♫ ♫ ♫

TWENTY minutes later Helen stared at a plate of eggs and toast. Captain Green upended a container of sugar into a cup of the canteen's weak coffee and tapped the bottom of it. "Last of your gift I fear," he confirmed. "The lads saved this bit for you. Perhaps the post will deliver another package. Perhaps not, now that America is gearing up to join in the fray."

Sugar? Who in the world cared about sugar right now? Prudence – Helen took a shaky breath. "If I'd flown better, or maybe faster, then maybe –"

Green reached out and took her hand. "Look at me," he demanded.

She shook her head and stared down at where his hand gripped hers.

"Helen Mulberry, I order you to look me in the eye."

Reluctantly, she met his piercing green eyes and felt fresh tears well up in hers. "Don't –"

"No. You will hear me out. You've spent your entire life taking care of your brother because the idea that he was somehow responsible for your other brother's death broke him. The horrors of war do strange things to a person's mind. We aren't designed to experience such horror and it twists itself up inside our soul and haunts us for the rest of our days."

He leaned back a bit and cocked his head, perhaps looking at her more closely with his good eye. "Prudence knew going into this that what she was doing was risky and life threatening. She knew and she never backed down. She died saving Temperance. You would have died saving her, too, given the chance. The fact that a bullet fired by a *Luftwaffe* fighter pilot went through the fuselage of your stolen plane while you did the best you could to get your team to safety, and the fact that said bullet killed someone, takes nothing away from you or what you did."

Her body shuddered with her indrawn breath. "I don't know what to do now."

He squeezed her hand. "Quite simple, really. First, eat those eggs and drink that atrociously sweet coffee. Then pray, on your knees and with all you have inside of you. Then sleep for at least a day. Then deliver your full report. Take any jibes from higher headquarters over crashing your plane behind enemy lines on the chin. And finally, and most importantly, get back into the pilot's seat and fly the next mission."

He let go of her hand and gestured to her fork. "Let's begin, shall we? Eat."

Her wrists and fingers hurt from the exertion of the past 36 hours. Her hand shook so badly that the eggs fell off the fork twice before she could get a bite to her mouth. Only when she chewed and swallowed the first bite did he outwardly relax and lean back in his chair.

"Why are you doing this?" she whispered. "You don't even like me. You could send me home with a good riddance right now and I wouldn't blink and you'd finally get what you wanted ever since I landed here all those months ago."

"I don't even like you? Helen, are you mad?" He drummed three fingers on the table rhythmically. "I'm doing this because I love you, you insufferable *barmy* Yank. It's high time you paid attention to that fact."

Her fork clattered to the plate as it fell out of her hand. "What?"

He smiled, his face relaxing and his eyes shining. "Eat, Helen. Nourish your body. Pray, nourish your soul. Then sleep. Rest. We can talk when you're not overwhelmed." He looked over her shoulder and lifted a hand. "Here are your friends." He stood and stared down at her. "I'll see you tomorrow and take your report."

As he walked away, Hope, Mercy, and Charity sat down next to her and across from her. "You are quite amazing, Faith," Mercy said, hugging her. "I know we made it because of your flying."

Charity reached across the table and took her hand. "Thank you for bringing me my Tom home to me. I'd love to hear about how you ended up in a German plane, though."

Hope ran a hand down Helen's hair in a very maternal way. "You did wonderfully, child." She gestured at her plate. "I'm going to get myself something to eat. Then we need to go visit Grace."

"Aye. I have to operate on her. They're prepping her now," Mercy said. Her face looked dark, as if she knew something she couldn't bring herself to tell the others yet. "I'll meet you all at the hospital. My father knows you're coming." She stood and put her hands on Helen and Hope's backs. "It is so good to see you lasses. I have missed you so very much."

Helen reached up to cover Mercy's hand with her own but her fingers felt numb and painful. Mercy gently took her hand and raised it slightly to take a closer look. Then she stepped to the side and lifted her other hand. "Faith, make a fist for me."

She tried but the best she could manage without searing pain was to touch her thumbs with her fingertips. Her hands shook.

Mercy frowned. "You've fractured your wrists, lass. Both of them."

Helen stared at the dark bruises that had begun to form on the inside of her wrists. She had held onto the controls with a death grip through two crash landings in the past few hours. No wonder she felt so exhausted and buffeted. She dared not even guess when her wrist bones had cracked. "Doesn't hurt too much."

Mercy said, "Not yet. Get to medical soon as ya finish that drink and that meal. You lasses, help her eat if she needs it. Just like a baby if need be."

As Mercy marched away, Helen felt some of the tightness squeezing her heart loosen a little bit. Charity made to pick up her cup but Helen shook her head. "It's okay. I can manage." She picked up her cup and took a sip of the coffee, then even squeezed Charity's hand before releasing her and carefully picking up her fork again.

Haysworth Estate, Great Britain: 1946

THE sun shone brightly on the sprawling lush lawns of the Earl of Bostwich's land. Tuxedo clad waiters carried silver trays of drinks and hors-d'oeuvres. Women wore beautiful summer dresses and wide brimmed hats and men wore morning suits and brightly polished shoes. Huge open tents housed tables and chairs, providing a shaded place for people to sit and eat out of the sun.

Mrs. Helen and Major Reginald Green walked arm in arm into the tent that held the head table. She wore black chiffon slacks and a white blouse with a belt cinching her waist. Reginald had never complained about his bride's aversion to dresses and skirts, though she had perhaps wisely consented to JoAnn's insistence that she get married in a dress.

Beside her, Reginald Green wore his uniform with very few medals on his chest. However, his sleeve bore a wound stripe that spoke volumes. Though he did his level best to keep it secret, his eyesight had grown progressively worse. Finally, he could no longer hide his inability to see from his left eye and the RAF had grounded him for good. He had taken an assignment in Bronwich as military liaison where, ironically, his family manufactured parts for aircraft; landing gear and control systems, mostly. Helen had come to understand that while her husband was an excellent pilot, his real genius lay in the field of engineering.

Helen suddenly noticed Virginia, who she had only ever formally addressed as Hope, standing right inside the tent. After recognition dawned, Virginia hugged her tightly.

"I have missed you," the famous singer said. She wore a blue skirt suit and a hat that looked like it was made from peacock feathers. It was difficult to tell exactly where her well managed curls ended and the hat began. "Look at you all married and glowing." She hugged Reginald, too. "Major Green, handsome and dapper in your uniform, as always."

"Mrs. Gilbert," Reginald greeted curtly, smiling to disguise his very British discomfort at the famous woman's familiarity and physical contact.

Virginia smiled. "Edward and I haven't gotten married yet, but I do like the sound of that. Virginia Gilbert. That sounds very charming."

Reginald said, "You are always a charmer, Miss Benoit."

"God gave us all gifts, Major." Her face lit up. "There's Grace! I didn't think she'd make it!"

Helen spun and smiled as Ruth Aubertin, the agent formerly code-named Grace, walked fluidly toward them. She couldn't believe how gracefully the woman moved with her prosthetic leg, but it shouldn't have surprised her. She had watched her, six short months after her surgery, jump out of an airplane with her artificial leg strapped to her kit bag. Today, she wore a red and white checkered dress that perfectly complimented her dark hair. The men Helen now knew as her brothers walked in on either side of her.

"Grace!" Helen greeted out of long habit, rushing toward her and hugging her. "I didn't think you'd be back in the country."

"Helen, my American angel of the air. I suppose I can go back to being called Ruth now," the Jewish woman said in her very thick accent. The way she pronounced Helen's name had a strongly French influence, as if the H was silent. "We came especially for this."

"Will you go back to France, then?"

Her brother Matthew replied, "You know we cannot be too specific about where we might end up. Suffice to say there is a great deal of work we must do elsewhere to ensure justice for our people, though we hope to return to France again one day."

Reginald replied, "I don't think justice can ever be served for the atrocities committed against the Jews."

John agreed. "I think the true justice must come from God." He smiled. "But we can find moderate satisfaction in the work we can do here in this world. We can act as the sword of Gideon, perhaps."

Just then, Charity, also known as Dorothy Ewing, rushed into the tent holding her Tom's hand. Like Reginald, Tom wore his uniform. Unlike Reginald, his chest practically dripped with medals. "Isn't this place grand?"

she gushed. "I'll confess I spent our first eight months piecing you ladies together. Grace stayed a mystery, but I had Prudence pegged as living in a place just like this."

She hugged the ladies as Tom shook the men's hands.

"Major Green? How's the eye?" Tom's baritone voice somehow filled the air around them all.

"Still blind, I'm afraid. Don't see it getting better in this lifetime."

"Shame, that. No eye patch?"

"Not until I'm prepared to capture the Spanish Main and repel boarders."

"Makes it easy to turn a blind eye from time to time I suppose."

"Just so. How are the children?"

Tom grinned. "Loud and proud and somewhere on the estate just now. Likely put them to work polishing silverware. They're handy that way, what? Should see about getting some of your own. I happen to know what brings on the condition. Might even be convinced to share the secret with you if the price is right."

Reginald grinned at the former Prisoner of War's coarse humor. "Thanks ever so much, but I expect a number of little Greens will be along directly."

Tom nodded exactly once. "Good man. And good show landing yourself a Yank. Turnabout is certainly fair play after all."

The number of British women who had succumbed to the charms of the American soldiers stationed in Great Britain prior to the Normandy invasion was simply shocking. The number of broken marriages that resulted was still a sore spot in many British households.

Green grinned. "Did what I could to even the score. Just my luck Helen consented to marry a one eyed pilot who can't fly."

Meanwhile, Dorothy proclaimed, "It's amazing to see you all."

"Where are the children?" Virginia asked.

"A rather stern faced butler gathered them up and escorted them to a nanny who has all the children gathered somewhere." She looked at Helen. "And how's married life now that you've landed one of England's finest *Tommies*? Still glowing, I see."

Helen smiled. "It's everything I dreamed it would be now that the war is no longer occupying all of our free time."

"Have you decided you're staying in England or will you go back to America?"

When Helen looked to her husband, Reginald answered. "My father's company designs and builds airplanes. We've spent a lot of time talking with our families and feel that our place is in England. Helen's father never imagined she would have any station in his oil business, so now she actually feels as if she's come home."

Helen added, "My brother Eddie is coming here, too. He's going to work with the test pilots."

"Speaking of Edwards, here's mine," Virginia announced with an enormous smile. Temperance, who they now all knew as Marie Gilbert, and her brother Edward, whom most knew as Abiel, joined the group. Virginia slipped her arm through her fiance's as Helen threw her arms around Marie and hugged her tightly.

"I haven't seen you since you got off my plane and they carted you off to London," she said, tears filling her eyes. "Oh, it is so good to see you."

"It took so long to get well. I was in hospital for weeks and weeks. When they released me, I decided not to return to France. They sent me to Bletchley and I've worked there for the last few years."

Dr. Betty Grimes, formerly known as Mercy, walked into the tent unescorted. She wore a blue dress with a green collar and belt with a green hat jauntily perched atop her mess of curls. "Here are my bonnie Virtues," she hailed, hugging each one of them in turn. "I almost didn't get away. I had a patient take a turn early this morning."

"How is that book on nursing coming?" Helen asked.

"I finished it last week. There's a publisher claiming they're wanting a wee peek, but Charlene is having people go through it first." She put a finger to her lips. "Loose lips and all that rot. Mustn't accidently spill the beans."

"Indeed. One mustn't," Charlene agreed. "I'd hate to arrest you after all of the work you did."

The women turned as one and greeted their former commander. "Colonel Radden!"

Virginia laughed and Charlene cracked a smile. "Your secrets are safe with us, fearless leader," she promised.

"Please, just Charlene, today. We needn't be so formal considering the occasion. I'm all but out anyway and all's well. I've had enough and the good Lord knows they've had quite enough of me."

Prudence's husband, Joseph Tolson, approached the group, accompanied by a man about his age who walked with a very pronounced limp. When

Marie looked at him, she gasped. Matthew went to him immediately and shook his hand then hugged him. Joseph spoke, "Ladies, gentlemen, may I present Master Quentin Hughes? He was my best friend at Oxford." Joseph, who had already met everyone, took the opportunity to introduce Quentin to each member of the group.

"Praetorian," Mercy whispered, hugging him, "good to see you made it out of there alive."

"Just Quentin, Doctor, if you please. No more code names." Shadows loomed in the edges of his eyes. Helen recognized the look on his face as it very much resembled her brother Eddie's eyes. "I have to be honest and say I've hit some rough patches. I've still not fully adapted to life at home."

Joseph slapped him on the back. "Quentin has discovered a very serious knack with horses. Father brought him here for the season to see what he can do with our stables. We're considering breeding some racers."

"I bet it's very soothing to work with them," Helen offered. "My brother Edward always found flying settled him after he came home from France in '21."

Quentin looked at her. "They're big gentle beasts who don't kill each other for political reasons." He gestured with his chin. "Looks as if His Grace and the Lady, the parents of the departed, have finally arrived. Probably time for you to get this show started, Joe."

Joseph sighed and muttered, "Well, strike up the band."

On the far side of the tent, Helen watched a tall thin man with sandy blond hair, who she assumed was Prudence's father the Duke of something-or-other, walk toward Joseph's father, the Earl of Bostwich. There was a woman walking along beside the duke with a hand draped over his arm. If she were 20 years younger, the woman on his arm could have passed for Prudence's twin.

A uniformed butler quietly called everyone to their seats. Helen sat with Virginia on her right and Reginald on her left. She had grown used to sitting next to her husband this way while she drove them from place to place on the entirely wrong side of the road. He claimed he wanted to have his good eye toward her just as much as possible. Looking down the table she could see each of the other Virtues sitting with their guest. Charlene took the head of the table.

As they ate lunch, the group talked, laughed, and caught up. With the exception of Marie, they had all been together at Helen and Reginald's wedding just a few months earlier. Today they came together for a very different reason – to celebrate the life of someone who was loved by everyone there.

On cue, Charlene stood and took the podium at the front of the tent. She looked beautiful and poised in her uniform. Someone tapped a glass, and the crystal tone rang through the space, quieting everyone. Charlene pulled a folded piece of paper out of her jacket and inclined her head toward the head table.

"Your Graces, Lord and Lady Bostwick, Mr. Tolson, ladies and gentlemen, dear friends, thank you for inviting me here today to speak on behalf of your wife and daughter, Lady Muriel Tolson. Lady Muriel was a an indispensable member of my team. And while the Secrets Act would prevent me from ever being able to give you specifics, I will say that if not for her, so many lives would have been lost. She was adored by her team and respected by everyone who worked with her.

"Our team was comprised of many different nations and ethnicities, but the one thing that held us together was a faith in God that came before anything else. I know that we succeeded because of the bond that held us together through God.

"After completion of training, I had Muriel write a letter to her husband, Mr. Tolson, in the event that a day such as this might come. This gives a person an opportunity to say the things that she might have wished to say. Mr. Tolson has asked me to read you her letter."

Charlene cleared her throat and opened the folded letter that she had set on the podium. "My darling Joseph, I believe that God prepared me from the womb for this job. I wish I could tell you about it. Every moment I'm here, training with my colleagues and my team, it is affirmed that for this reason I was put on this earth. I have often felt like our farewell at the train station was truly our last, but I tried not to dwell on that thought too much because I feared perhaps I was being too morbid.

"I believe God put me here. I believe He gave me the skills needed to be really effective in what I'm doing, and I believe that He knew I would not be coming home. I'm sure that's why we never had children and why my love for you was so consuming in the short years we enjoyed marriage together on this earth.

"I wish I could tell you how much this team means to me, but I am so limited in what I can say. Temperance is so clever and fun. She and I have become good friends. Faith is very American and witty. She always makes me laugh and wish I could see her in her own element. Hope is someone whom you would recognize and envy my close friendship. She is so gracious in her love and her wisdom. Charity is the most logical person I have ever met and mother-hens us all. She knitted that scarf I sent you for Christmas. I hope it kept you warm. Grace is a fascinating woman whom I strive to emulate in strength and dignity. I want this war over so I can ask her a million questions and truly come to know this sister in Christ. Mercy is brilliant. When this war is over, I want you and my father to use my trust fund to create a scholarship for female medical students in her name, if the rules allow her name to be given to you.

"Major Radden —" Charlene paused and took a shaky breath. She continued, "saw each of us and our worth and through what could only be the guidance of the Holy Spirit, put us together and let us shine. We are a strong team, my dear, and my prayer is that we save lives and help bring this awful war to an end.

"I would give my life for any member of this team without hesitation, and know they would do the same for me.

"Thank you for loving me and encouraging me to do something more than what a proper wife ought to do in times of war. Thank you for believing in me. It is through your love for me that I found the courage to do this and what has sustained me through even the darkest parts of training."

Charlene put the paper down and added, "Lady Muriel will never be forgotten by anyone here. She was a lovely woman with a strong spirit that was never compromised in even the darkest of places.

"Our nation, our world, honors the sacrifice this family made in giving us Lady Muriel. We mourn with you and pray your family will be comforted in knowing just how valuable her part was, and what a vital part she played in the work we did."

She sat back down at the head of the table amid thunderous applause. Helen clapped and cried and clapped and found that the thought of Muriel's death didn't rip her heart apart anymore. The pain was sadder, deeper than it used to be, and she wondered if that was part of the healing process.

Long after the tent emptied of family, friends, and relatives, the Virtues team sat at their table, almost reluctant to part ways again. But, they all knew the time would eventually come when they would have to leave. Finally, Ruth stood and put her hand on Betty's shoulder. "I must go. My brothers and I —" she looked up and stopped speaking, her mouth falling open in shock.

Charlene followed her line of sight and stood, rushing toward the man who had come into the tent. He hugged Charlene, his face shadowed by the sun behind him, and she hooked her arm through his, bringing him fully to the table.

"I say!" Matthew said, standing and shaking his hand.

Betty gasped. "Valor!"

The tall blond man smiled. Charlene said, "Ladies, everyone, I'd like you to meet Leopold Schäfer." She paused and smiled. "Leo is my son."

Marie stood so suddenly that her chair fell over behind her. She put a hand to her heart. "What –?"

He walked forward and took her hand. "Marie. It is so good to see you again. I cannot tell you how pleased I am to see you and to see you looking so well."

The End

INSPIRED BY REAL EVENTS

Inspired by Real Events

WHILE the story of the special team of operators I named The Virtues is entirely fictional, set in a fictional town, and comprised of fictional characters who form a fictional military division, every single one of my fictional heavenly heroines was inspired by a real World War II heroine and the story was inspired by real events.

My fictional little town of Lamarr, Texas was inspired by none other than actress and inventor, Hedy Lamarr. Born in Austria as *Hedwig Eva Maria Kiesler* on November 9, 1914, Hedy died in her Florida home at the age of 85 on January 19, 2000. In 1933, Hedy had fled from her abusive husband and secretly moved to Paris, France. There, she soon met American film mogul, Louis B. Mayer. In no time, Hedy Lamarr became known the world over as the world's most beautiful woman and played alongside MGM's most famous leading men from Spencer Tracy to Clark Gable. What few people know is that Hedy was also a brilliant – or perhaps genius – mathematician.

Hedy, along with composer George Antheil, co-invented the technology for spread spectrum and frequency hopping communications. This became important to America's military during World War II and was used in everything from controlling torpedoes to helping guide bombers onto their targets. Her invention is still used today in such modern technologies as Wi-Fi and Bluetooth. Hedy Lamarr was posthumously inducted into the National Inventors Hall of Fame in 2014.

While researching the incredible women during World War II to write this series of books, I often experienced the difficult task of choosing between this or that remarkable story of one incredible woman or another equally incredible account to help inspire my heroines. However, in the case of my fictional character, young Helen Mulberry (later Green), my inspiration was very clear.

The heroic then 22 year old woman on the cover of this book photographed at Love Field, Texas in 1943 is the incredible Florene Miller (later Watson). Florene Miller was born on December 7, 1920. She turned 21 on the day the Japanese bombed Pearl Harbor. When writing my Virtues' stories, I very purposefully shied away from too much mention of specific historical events surrounding the war. I had no desire to tred on true history and sought only to create a world with my characters doing their things in the fictional towns I crafted. However, I did have a very significant scene in this book that pertained to the bombing of Pearl Harbor. In a way, that was my little nod to Florene.

Like my fictional Helen, the real-life Florene was a Texan, born in San Angelo. At 8-years-old, she took her first airpline ride in a WWI era Barnstormer's open-cockpit biplane and fell in love with flying. While she was in her sophomore year at Baylor University, her father purchased the family a Luscombe airplane. Much like my fictional character Ruth Aubertin in *Grace's Ground War*, the real life Florene's father believed his country would soon go to war with Germany and he wanted his children to be trained aviators in the war effort.

The Luscombe enabled Florene to spend numerous hours flying and studying aircraft engines, navigation, meteorology, and flight rules and regulations. At 19, she graduated from flight school. In a few short months Florene became a commercial pilot, obtained flight and ground school instructor ratings. Before her 21st birthday, she would be teaching men (including her future husband, Chris Watson) how to fly in the War Training Program in Odessa, Texas.

In 1939, after Germany invaded Poland, female pilot Jacqueline Cochran wrote to the first lady, Eleanor Roosevelt, regarding using women pilots in the armed forces. Shortly thereafter, female pilot Nancy Harkness Love wrote a similar letter to the people in charge of the Ferrying Division of the Armed Air Forces. Early in the European war, the United States wasn't quite ready to utilize women as pilots for military planes. However, by September 1942 – 9 months after the Pearl Harbor attack – they started shifting that idea.

An increased demand brought on by male pilots heading out of the country to fight in the war left a shortage of experienced pilots in the United States. The leaders of the Air Transport Command contacted Nancy Harkness Love, and hired her to recruit qualified women pilots.

As I mentioned, December 7, 1941, the day the Japanese attacked Pearl

Harbor, was Florene's 21st birthday. After Pearl Harbor attack, both Florene and her brother had volunteered for the Army Air Corps. To qualify as Army pilots, men were required to have 250 hours of flying time, a commercial license, and a horse power rating. On the other hand, women were required to have a minumum of 500 hours.

A call was put out for 50 women who had logged over 500 hours of flying to help ferry aircraft, cargo, and troops. Only 25 women in the entire country met the criteria, though the women who qualified at the time averaged 1,100 hours each.

Florene was one of those 25 women who qualified, and she became a member of the Women's Auxiliary Ferrying Squadron (WAFS) and, a very short time later, its first Commanding Officer. These women flew 8 months delivering airplanes nationally before any of the 1,074 other women pilots graduated from Jackie Cochran's flight training school.

Then, on September 14, 1942, General Henry "Hap" Arnold, Commanding General of the Army Air Forces, approved a program that would train qualified female pilots to serve as ferry pilots. The program was placed under the direction of Jacqueline Cochran, and named the Army Air Forces Women's Flying Training Detatchment (WFTD).

On August 5, 1943, the WAFS and the WFTD merged and became re-designated as the Women Airforce Service Pilots (WASPs). Jacqueline Cochran was appointed the Director and Nancy Harkness Love was named WASP Executive with the ATC Ferrying Division. Florene, the fomer Commanding Officer of the WAFS, became the first Commanding Officer of the WASPs stationed at Love Field, Dallas, Texas.

Although the WASP held officer status, they were classified as civilians, ineligible for government life insurance, military funerals, burial expenses, and other G.I. benefits. More than three decades elapsed before the first honorable discharge was awarded to a WASP.

By the end of the war, Florene had flown every type of plane that the Air Corps used including: Aeronea, Waco, Taylorcraft, Piper Cub, BT-13, PT-17, PT-19, AT-6, AT-9, AT-10, AT-11, AT-17, A-20, A-26, P-38, P-39, P-40, P-47, P-51, SB2C, C-47(DC-3), B-17, B-24, B-25, Lockheed P-38F Lightning and her favorite, the North American P-51D Mustang. In 1944, Florene was chosen to be a test pilot in a secret program to develop radar equipment for planes.

After the war, Florene and Chris Watson married, and she earned her BA then MBA. Her husband worked for Phillips Petroleum, and she taught college for 30 years.

The image used on the cover of this book was also selected by the US Department of Defense for its official WASP website:
http://www.defense.gov/home/features/2010/0310_wasp/

Among her many honors and distinctions are:

- Membership in the Distinguished Flying Corps in the Kritser Aviation and Space Museum, Amarillo, TX

- Induction into theNinety-Nines International Forest of Friendship, Atichison, Kansas (Amelia Earhart's home) for exceptional contributions to aviation

- First woman inductee into the Panhandle Veterans Hall of Fame

- Distinguished Veteran honoree at the Air Force Military Ball in Dallas, TX

- National Medal of Honor from The Daughters of the American Revolution

- Designation as an "Eagle" 4 separate times at the Air Force's annual Gathering of Eagles celebration

- National Air Force Association's Lifetime Achievement Award

- Induction into the Texas Aviation Hall of Fame

- The renaming of the airport in her hometown of Big Lake, TX the Florene Miller Watson Airport

- The Congressional Gold Medal, the highest award the United States Congress can present to a civilian.

Florene had extensive Bible training and spent ten years as the National Chaplain of the WASP. She was active in her church and community affairs in Borger, Texas near Amarillo.

I'm sad to say Florene died on February 4, 2014 at the age of 93, just 13 months before this book published. I've read numerous articles and interviews about this incredible woman. In everything I've read about her, this stood out to me:

"During the years, I have been asked to give many, many WAFS-WASP WWII presentations ... been inducted into several prestigious 'Hall of Fame' type honors, and been featured in newspapers, books and magazine articles - but the bottom line for me is - 'What does my Lord think of me!'"
– Florene Miller Watson

But those who wait on the Lord
Shall renew their strength;
They shall mount up with wings like eagles,
They shall run and not be weary,
They shall walk and not faint.
Isaiah 40:31 (NKJV)

Reader's Guide

SUGGESTED questions for a discussion group surrounding *A* Flight of Faith, part 7 of the *Virtues and Valor* series.

While the characters and situations in the *Virtues and Valor* series are fictional, I pray that these extended parables can help readers come to a better understanding of truth. Please prayerfully consider the questions that follow, consult scripture, and pray upon your conclusions. May the Lord of the universe richly bless you.

Helen's brother suffered terrible surivor's guilt in the wake of his brother's death. The guilt, combined with what was referred to at the time as "battle fatigue" broke his mind so that he became a shell of the person he was before the war. The United States and many other countries have been at war for over a decade at the time of the publishing of this book, and our nations are full of men and women who have suffereed great loss and trauma.

1. Do you have a veteran in your life who has suffered due to experiences in war?

2. The apostle Paul trained himself to say "Brothers, I do not consider that I have made it my own. But one thing I do: *forgetting what lies behind* and straining forward to what lies ahead, I press on toward the goal for the prize of the upward call of God in Christ Jesus (Philippians 3:13-14). Do you think that it is possible to truly forget what lies behind?

3. When Helen realized she had lost a team member, she felt herself drowning in feelings that might have broken her mind much like her brother, but Captain Green helped her regain some balance and he suggested that she fervently pray to overcome the feelings. Do you think that God will help ease our troubled minds and souls when we fervently seek Him?

♬ ♬ ♬ ♬

Helen Mulberry is an unusual woman for her decade. She doesn't like dresses or parties, and she prefers to be in pants, especially in her airplane.

4. The prejudice she experiences seems to be something she expects and doesn't resent as much as she just deals with it. What do you find in your life that may not be "right" that you just deal with and ignore?

5. How much do you think that the love and acceptance Helen had growing up with her father and brothers helped establish her confidence in performing so well in what was at the time almost predominately a "man's field"?

♬ ♬ ♬ ♬

Leopold Schafer shot the sergeant when the man turned his back without hesitation. In so doing he secured the success of the mission as best he could without completely blowing his cover, and he certainly saved the lives of Helen and her co-pilot Harold.

6. We have addressed the issue of lying for the sake of keeping the cover of the spies in previous books in this series; now, we're discussing almost a "justified" murder of the man who preemptively arrested Marie Gilbert, codenamed TEMPERANCE, and beat her nearly to death. Do you believe that the killing of this man was

justifiable?

7. Do you believe that God sees a difference between the lying and killing?

8. Do you believe Leopold Schafer *was* justified in the killing of the sergeant in the middle of this war zone in a "kill or be killed" scenario? If not, was there something else he could have done instead?

🎖🎖🎖🎖

Helen's faith that God would help her in the battle in the air and then in the landing of the plane full of wounded people sustained her to the point that she was able to fly with what were clearly broken wrists.

9. Do you believe that in such a scenario, God is ready and willing to answer our prayers?

10. Can you imagine yourself in some kind of extreme circumstances and then see yourself praying and trusting God to see you through?

Valor's Vigil

the Virtues and Valor Series part 8

a Novella by

HALLEE BRIDGEMAN

Published by

Olivia Kimbrell Press™

Olivia Kimbrell Press™

COPYRIGHT NOTICE

Library Cataloging Data

U. S. Library of Congress Control Number: 2015916441

Bridgeman, Hallee (Hallee A. Bridgeman) 1972-
  Valor's Vigil, Virtues and Valor series part 8/Hallee Bridgeman
xx p. 23cm x 15cm (9in x 6 in.)
  Summary: Can the American spy posing as a German officer protect her without risking his cover, or will he place his own life in danger to keep her safe?

        ISBN: 978-1-68190-022-3 (ebook)

1. Christian fiction 2. World War II 3. war stories 4. spies 5. historical fiction 6. espionage

PS3568.B7534 T941 2015
[Fic.] 813.6 (DDC 23)

DEDICATION

For All the Fred Mayers...

THIS novella is dedicated to the amazing men of valor such as German *Wehrmacht Oberleutnant* Werner Karl von Haeften pictured on the cover of this book and American Army Sergeant Friedreich "Fred" Mayer. Please read the "Inspired by Real Events" section in the back of this story to learn more about these amazing men.

> *And the Angel of the Lord appeared to [Gideon], and said to him, "The Lord is with you, you mighty man of valor!"*
>
> *Judges 6:12 (NKJV)*

London, England: 1915

CHARLENE Radden ran her hands down the sides of her long skirt and straightened her jacket. Once she ascertained that her clothing was in order, she felt her head to ensure that all of her blonde hair remained contained in the braids she had twisted into an elaborate bun on at the back of her head. Certain she would pass the most stringent of inspections, she rapped her knuckles on the thick wooden door in front of her.

At his bidding to enter, she opened the door and stepped into the large room. Sunlight poured in through the tall windows that faced the lavish gardens of the General's country estate. His large desk sat off to one side, with full bookshelves standing ready like sentries on either side of it. The walls held hunting trophies, elk and fox sharing space with lion heads and elephant tusks. Leather couches formed a sitting area around a bear skinned rug.

"You wanted to see me, father?" Charlene asked. Right away her father and the three other men in the room took to their feet, standing in deference to her sex.

She recognized Colonel Stuart from her father's dinner parties. He was tall and thin with salt-and-pepper hair and always had a peppermint in his mouth. It only slightly covered the stench of his preferred imported cigars. First Lieutenant Young served as her father's clerk. She had yet to care much for the man. He seemed arrogant in the extreme. Knowing the general, he must do good work or else he wouldn't have lasted six full months in this house. He had an air of male superiority that often made her neck bristle in annoyance. The third man she had never seen before. He was perhaps younger than Lieutenant Young, tall, broad shouldered, with blond hair and a well-groomed and waxed blond handlebar mustache. He wore an expensive civilian tailored suit and common dusty brown riding boots.

"Charlie, come in," her father said as he courteously ground out his cigar in the crystal ash tray to his right. None of the other men were smoking when she entered. "Thank you for joining us." He gestured toward the couches, so she followed his direction and took a seat in the indicated armchair. As soon as she sat, the men in the room joined her, filling the small area. It felt as if they all stared at her expectantly, and her mind raced to think if there was some task she was supposed to have accomplished.

Charlene had not expected to see this many men in the room when she had received her father's summons. She also felt some astonishment that he used his familiar pet name for her in the presence of these men, especially in front of the stranger before even introductions had been offered. She made bold to interject. "I don't mean to intrude. I can come back after you've finished your business if you like."

"Well, there's the rub, Charlie. You are my business today." With that, he stopped speaking and his forehead furrowed. Her father, a large and imposing man who walked with confidence among those whom he considered his inferiors, appeared at a loss for words for the first time in her life. He cleared his throat and actually ran a finger under his collar. Colonel Stuart intervened for him. "Miss Radden, we are here to offer you a very unique opportunity, though it does come with a bit of risk."

Considering the household in which she'd grown up, the times spent in Africa, Hong Kong, and several countries in Europe, she could not imagine what she might consider unique. "Indeed?"

Her father found his voice. "We've been working for the past several months on a Most Secret mission."

He paused and did not continue, so she encouraged him. "Most Secret?"

Colonel Stuart picked up. "Miss Radden, I'd like you to meet Captain Karl Schäfer."

Captain? He didn't look older than her own twenty years of age. "Very pleased to meet you, Captain," she replied automatically. The man looked tired and a bit gaunt, as if he had recently felt ill or else travelled a significant distance.

The room fell silent again so Captain Schäfer spoke with a shockingly American accent. "What they're trying to say to you, Miss, is that we have established a position wherein I will be able to embed myself deep in the Kaiser's military headquarters. I have accepted a staff position and am ordered to report in one week's time."

She couldn't help but notice the very slight German hard consonants in an otherwise very American accent. She grinned a bit at the puzzle this man presented. "Well done, sir. May I ask what that might have to do with me?"

Colonel Stuart cleared his throat, actually making a harrumph sound that filled the air around him with a smell of strong tobacco and peppermint. "Captain Schäfer's cover is well established and cannot be compromised. He will travel by balloon to a village outside of Frankfürt in the middle of the night of the twelfth and jump out of the balloon by parachute practically into Wilhelm's back yard. Once there, he will collect the cart full of belongings that has been packed as if he was leaving a country home and travel to the capital. He has a new flat, a new job, and new duties all waiting on him there."

He stopped speaking. Charlene waited and finally raised an eyebrow in inquiry. "I find this information extremely interesting, gentlemen. I must ask again, what all this has to do with me?"

Schäfer spoke again, this time in flawless German such as might be overheard in the halls of the *Bundesrat*. "The woman assigned to be my wife is ill. Her condition is very grave. The timing of this operation is vital. To come directly to the point, I need a new wife. Your father, the General, has volunteered you ... pending your consent of course."

A proper young lady would feel horror at the prospect. She knew that and tried to stamp down the surge of excitement that suddenly flooded her chest. She prayed her dash of powder masked the color she knew rushed to her cheeks. Also in German, she replied, "I beg your pardon? Don't you have any other trained women to do this kind of work?"

"Charlie," Her father cautioned in the same language, "Everyone here is not as fluent as you and young *Kapitän* Schäfer."

Schäfer clicked his heels before reverting to English. "My apologies, sir. Gentlemen. I was simply explaining the situation to Young Miss Radden. I confess, I also wanted to verify her fluency."

Her father nodded, obviously appreciating this young man's keen mind. Also in English, he said, "Very well. Charlie, we don't have another woman whose nanny taught her to speak German like a native as you do. Nor do we have a woman so fluent in German who has already successfully jumped from a balloon with a parachute as you have done – against my rather vocal objections at the time if memory serves," her father replied.

"Father, you know I have only jumped the once, and only for a lark. Never in the dead of night into enemy territory."

"Nevertheless," Lieutenant Young concluded. Charlene bristled at the very sound of the young man's voice.

"Charlie," her father said, reaching out and touching her knee with his large hand, "you and I both know you can do this. An opportunity won't present itself like this again. You're entire life, you've longed to be my son instead of daughter so that you could answer the call for King and Country. Well, old girl, here is your chance."

Schäfer added, "Our mission is of the utmost importance. Without you, I'm sure it will not succeed. I would be honored if you would consent to be my wife, Miss Radden." He paused and his cheeks reddened. "There's a vicar waiting to do the honors."

8 8 8 8

CHARLENE stood next to the fireplace and studied the tribal masks that graced the mantle. The weight of the gold brocade dressed dress combined with the elaborate beadwork in the ruby colored shawl pulled down on her shoulders, making it an effort to stand up straight. She ran her fingers over the beaded design covering her chest. She'd fallen in love with the dress in Egypt and had bought it and arranged for it to be packaged and shipped to her home in England. There, the housekeeper had stored it for a future wedding.

As she contemplated what she was about to do, she heard the door open behind her. The dress rustled and crinkled as she moved, the long skirts swaying against her legs.

Somehow, she had expected Karl Schäfer to enter the room. He now wore his Canadian military uniform, and she noticed that his boots no longer carried the dust of a long travel - rather, they gleamed with a high shine. As he approached, she could smell the aftershave he'd used after the bath she'd had drawn for him.

"Miss Radden," Karl said when he stopped, bowing slightly, "I cannot commend you enough for your courage and patriotism."

Charlene raised an eyebrow at the fact that he spoke in German, clearly, he still tested her skills. "Captain Schäfer, while I appreciate your sentiments, I confess that I'm standing here trying to work up the nerve to go forth and follow through."

He held out a hand and reflexively she placed hers in his. He guided her to the settee, and, despite the weight of the layers of her dress, she gracefully sat down. He pushed an armchair toward her and sat, his knees nearly touching hers. "Entering enemy territory is bad enough, I'm sure. But you have the added burden of marrying a stranger."

"What about you, then?" she inquired.

"Me?" He rubbed his smoothly shaven chin. "I trained for a month with my partner who has now taken ill. We grew rather fond of each other and determined that a marriage wouldn't be much of a burden."

Despite the circumstances and proper ladylike decorum, she couldn't help but bark out a laugh. "A burden?" Relaxing slightly, she settled back against the cushion. "Captain Schäfer, I believe the Word of God commands husbands to love their wives. What do you intend to do about that?"

He sighed heavily and stared at her, his blue eyes serious. "Miss Radden, my service to God comes before anything else. I wouldn't be here were it not for His voice. I never imagined this. I'd always fancied finding a sweetheart, falling in love, and starting a family. Always thought I'd name my first son Leopold."

"Leopold; meaning bold, courageous."

"Just so." He caught her gaze and held it. "How did you know that?"

"I'd always hoped to name my first son Leopold." For the first time since she had met him, the young Captain looked surprised. With a small smile and a faint flush in her cheeks, Charlene admitted, "Even girls raised by generals in the wilds of Africa dream of their wedding, their prince, and their one day children, Captain."

"I find that astonishing," he confessed. "Clearly this is confirmation from God, wouldn't you think?"

Hearing him speak of such devotion to their Maker helped her relax further. "What would you consider this marriage? A show? A convenience?" Using his own words, she raised an eyebrow. "A burden?"

As he smiled, the sides of his mustache raised. "It will be something that I take with the greatest of seriousness. You will be my wife. 'Husbands love your wives,' does not carry a prerequisite to 'first meet then fall in love with'. It is a simple command." He leaned forward and his urgency reflected in his eyes. "I need you, Miss Radden. I cannot do this without you. After speaking with you, I believe that we will make a terrific team. But you must go into this all the way, because our very lives will be in danger the entire time. You will have to trust me and let me lead you in the field and together we will complete this mission."

As they stared at each other, she could hear the clock ticking behind her. Finally, she said, "I will marry you, Captain Schäfer, with a few conditions."

It was his turn to raise an eyebrow. "Very well."

"Number one, you will understand that while I have no formal training, my father has taught me various skills, and I am a quick study. I need you to commit to training me and let me partner with you in this endeavor. Do not assume that because I am the weaker sex, I am in any way weak."

Karl nodded stiffly. "Absolutely. Understood."

Feeling a little flutter of nervousness, she continued. "And while this is a marriage of convenience and such, I'm not comfortable standing in front of a vicar, God, and my father and repeating vows I do not mean. So, please understand that I will respect you as my husband in all things. Scripture commands wives to respect their husbands, after all. It does not carry a prerequisite of making him earn that respect. It is a simple command to respect."

The corner of his mouth eased up into a pleased grin as she echoed his earlier sentiment. She continued, "Once we are bound in a state of holy matrimony, please know that out of that respect for my husband, anything I ever say to you will always be the truth, and I would like to have the same assurance."

Leaning forward, he took her hand. "Miss Radden, I could not agree with you more." He lifted her hand to his mouth and brushed his lips across the gloved knuckle. "You have my solemn word."

He released her hand and stood. His cheeks had taken on some color and he reached back to squeeze the muscles at the base of his skull. Her closed his eyes momentarily and then he took a deep breath and blew it all out at once. When he dropped his hand and opened his eyes, he offered in North American accented English, "Right. Now that's settled. Let's get married, shall we?"

ᛸᛸᛸᛸ

CHAPTER 1

Chapter One

VALOR – strength of mind or spirit that enables a person to encounter danger with firmness: personal courage. From the Medieval Latin *valor*, from the Latin *valere*: to be of worth, be strong; worth, worthiness, bravery.

Airfield near Milton Keynes, England, 1942

TWENTY-FOUR year old Leopold Schäfer jerked awake when he felt the wheels touch down on the runway. It took him a second to orient himself to his surroundings and to remember that he had fallen asleep aboard a blacked-out Avro on a covert late-night flight from Occupied France to Great Britain. The female pilot and her male counterpart had retrieved him from a field about ten kilometers from his duty station. He straightened the tie on his German *Wehrmacht* officer's uniform and checked that his appearance was in order.

"End of the line, folks. Put your token in the turnstile on your way out."

Leo, code-named Valor, glanced at the female pilot once more, recognizing an American accent and the attempt at American humor. He unhooked the seat belt and ducked as he walked up to the cockpit. He knelt between the two seats, in between the pilot code-named Faith and her copilot code-named Eagle Eye. "I recognize that accent," he said with a smile, pinpointing the area of Texas, home of his best friend. "Sooner or

Longhorn?"

Faith smiled. "Lamarr Longhorn every day of my life."

"Ah. Lamarr. About an hour from Dallas over by Athens."

She pursed her lips, clearly impressed. "That's exactly right."

"Sure is different around here, isn't it?"

With a raised eyebrow she said, "You ain't from Texas, cowboy."

He immediately thought of the snow-topped Mount Hood of his home. "Oregon."

"I reckon Oregon would feel as much like a foreign country as England does. Probably rains more here, though."

He laughed as he stood as tall as he could in the small confines of the Avro. "My part of the state is possibly the only place on earth that rains more than this island. But the coffee is pretty good and we don't eat beans for breakfast."

Faith sat straighter in her chair. "Exactly what is that all about, anyway? What I wouldn't give for some cheese grits and corned beef hash next to an egg over easy."

He gestured to the door. "I'll let myself out. Nice meeting you, Faith."

"I'll see you again here in a second. I'm your ride home, Adolf."

He grinned because he knew she only joked, but it still rubbed him a little in the wrong way to be compared to the *Führer*. Knowing she was just trying to be friendly, he made an effort not to bristle and exited the airplane just as the far door opened. He saw his mother, Charlene, enter the hangar escorted by two armed men.

With a genuine smile, she walked up to him. She framed his face with her hands and said, "It is so good to lay eyes on you again."

"Likewise, mother."

"Valor, this is Lieutenant Colonel Donald Hendricks and Colonel Henry Walker."

"Sir," Leo greeted, shaking Colonel Hendricks' hand and repeating the greeting with Colonel Walker. "It's a pleasure to meet you both."

"You're doing adequate work across the channel, my boy," Colonel Walker said. "Heard you're getting a permanent assignment."

"Yes. Valeurville. There's a prison there that they've assigned me to."

Colonel Hendricks nodded. "Fine strategic location."

"Unfortunately, it will mean that this is likely my last trip. I can't risk it anymore."

"We know," Charlene said. "Come over here and have a seat. I have the dossiers of the team that will be headed your way soon."

"Is this your Virtues team?"

His mother smiled. "It is."

Colonel Walker added, "We are cautiously optimistic about the results the team will bring. I'm starting to suspect your mother might just know what she's about."

Knowing how much Walker admired his mother, he knew he spoke with excessive British understatement. "I'd vouch for her, sir."

He walked across the hangar to the table with a stack of several file folders. As he sat, he opened the first file and saw the very familiar face of Virginia Benoit.

"I'm still a bit starstruck by this one," he admitted. "I'm kind of glad I don't have to pretend she's not THE Virginia Benoit."

Virginia was perhaps the most famous female performer in Europe. She also happened to be an American Negro, which in the wake of athlete Jesse Owens' multiple Olympic medal winning performance a few short years ago in Berlin, only helped to increase her fame and notoriety. Her voice had been compared to that of a songbird.

"Training Hope has been a dream," his mother admitted, using the star's code name. She set a paper cup of tea at his elbow. "Meeting her was, I confess, somewhat surreal. I only hope you get an opportunity to meet her. Could be a bit of a bodge considering you are supposedly an Aryan and presumably a racist of the highest order."

He took a sip of his tea and looked at her in surprise as sweetness flooded his mouth. "Are you running black market sugar now?"

She laughed and sat next to him, automatically straightening her uniform jacket. Even in an aircraft hangar that smelled of fuel and metal, she still maintained a perfect appearance. "Your pilot, Faith, brought me an entire packet of leaves called *ka'a he'ê* from her home in Texas. They sweeten the tea." She took a sip from her own cup. "She even managed to get the wood to make a raised bed and is growing the seeds she brought. She is everyone's best friend right now."

Leo laughed and opened the next file folder. A woman with short black curls, a hard face, and mean eyes stared back at him. He recognized the shape of her face without even looking at her name. "Isn't this Matthew Aubertin's sister?"

"Indeed." Charlene tapped the file with a manicured fingernail. "Grace. One of our strongest assets. She would be in the field already if she didn't need to learn some restraint and control."

"We've not had much contact, but what I've seen of her brother has impressed me greatly." His eyes skimmed the details. "Isn't there another brother?"

"He's teaching at the officer training corps now," Colonel Hendricks said. "What he knows about warfare tactics could fill volumes of books."

A rather plump and grinning red head smiled at him from the next file. Charlene interjected, "Charity. Her husband's in the Valeurville jail. Brilliant crypto analyst. She has a natural talent."

He looked at her name. Ewing. The tall Scott with the large black mustache came to mind. "He's a clever one as well. Has no idea who I am, of course, but we enjoy a bit of a back and forth whenever I'm near his cell."

The woman in the next picture looked rather unremarkable. Nothing stood out to him about her. But as he read the details of her file his eyebrow raised. "Evidently we're so in need of recruits we are looking to the daughters of dukes?"

"She came to us," Colonel Walker said. "It took a letter from her father-in-law before anyone would allow her to even put on running shoes. I'll admit I was against it, but quite frankly, everything I've seen has impressed me."

From what he knew of British upper crust society, Leo couldn't imagine. "And is she getting life lessons on how to tie the laces on those running shoes and such?"

Charlene snorted despite herself. "You are your father's son, did you know that?"

With a grin, he leaned forward and quickly kissed his mother's cheek. "I'll take that compliment."

"Indeed." She gestured at the file. "Prudence. Clever girl. Good instincts. I'd enter the field with her by my side in a heartbeat."

Knowing high praise when he heard it, he allowed himself to be impressed. "I look forward to seeing her in action."

Wild curly hair greeted him with the next picture. He read about the surgeon from London. "Mercy," he said, reading her code name out loud. "She suffering any ill effects from the bombing she survived?"

"Thankfully, none so far. We put her near some ordinance during training and she didn't bat an eye," Colonel Hendricks said. "Doc thinks she might have an issue with the dark, but she won't admit it. She's fighting us on the nurse ruse. Finds it insulting."

"The sacrifices we must make," Leo said under his breath. "Think she'll make a good nurse?"

"Yes," Charlene said emphatically. "I do."

He opened another file folder. This girl's brown eyes looked so sad. He wanted to find her and assure her it would all be okay. His eyes skimmed the name. Marie Perrin.

"She's our wireless," Charlene said.

She was? Knowing how hard the Germans searched for a wireless operator and what they did to any they managed to catch, his eyes widened and he swallowed a protest. "She looks very young." And frightened and fragile. What was the government thinking, putting this girl at great risk?

"Temperance. She's just a year younger than you."

"Brilliant girl," Colonel Walker added. "Given another few months, she could have written her own code. I've never seen the like."

He stared at her photo some more before he skimmed her information. "Edward's sister? I have to admit, he's been invaluable in building and training the Resistance in the Valeurville area."

"It's personal to him. Our intelligence tells us that their father died in custody."

He looked back at the sad eyes of her photo. "Do they know?"

"No."

He looked at his mother with a raised eyebrow but Colonel Hendricks replied, "We've not yet heard an official report. Until it's confirmed, we've nothing to say."

"Quite." Reluctantly, he closed the file and opened the next to find the pilot Faith.

"I knew her brother," Charlene said. "Met him at the end of the last war. Broken man. Strong spirit. He trained her. She can outfly nearly any pilot I've seen."

Knowing how closely the Germans watched the coastal sky from Hitler's Atlantic wall, Leo closed the file and looked at his mother. "She'll need to." He checked his watch. "I have about two hours before I need to return."

"Plenty of time before the end of the war," Colonel Walker said, putting another stack of files in front of him. "Let's go over some more details, shall we?"

8 8 8 8

Valeurville, Occupied France, 1942

LEO shifted the gears of the *Kübelwagen* and slowed the vehicle to go around the curve on the country road. As he drove with the top down, he enjoyed the warm French spring air versus the recent bitter Munich winter he'd endured. The breeze gently brushed his face as he drove made him miss his 1938 Opel Admiral convertible -- the college graduation present from his parents. Nothing about the boxy *Kübelwagen* handled like his sleek Opel, and he looked forward to getting behind her wheel again one day.

Pulling his mind from the nostalgia of his home in Oregon, he brought himself to the present day. Rumor had it, his commander planned to promote *Oberleutnant* Beck to *Kapitän* and transfer him to the prisoner of war camp currently under construction several miles from town. With Leo's recent rise to *Oberleutnant*, he knew he would receive orders to take over Beck's position as officer in charge of the prisoners in the Valeurville prison. In that position, he could help facilitate the passing of information from headquarters to the housed prisoners, ensuring the planned escape happened more smoothly. Everything he did, though, had to be completely above board and appear harmless, or else his cover would be jeopardized. If his cover became jeopardized, so would his father's.

As he rounded another corner, he saw a woman riding a bicycle. Even from this distance and from behind her, he recognized Marie, aka Temperance. He remembered from a briefing long ago that a farmer in this area was friendly to the Resistance. She likely had just used his farm to send a wireless message -- which meant that she probably carried her wireless machine in the basket strapped to the back of her bike.

He'd met her face-to-face once before, when he'd rigged his uniform pants to lose a button right before his promotion ceremony. It gave him access to her room -- she couldn't very well sew a button on his pants while he still wore them, unlike a uniform coat -- and he was able to inspect her living quarters and make sure nothing appeared out of order to a watchful eye. It had struck him then, as it did now, how drawn he'd felt to her since seeing her photograph in her dossier months ago in a hangar in Britain.

He had two choices. He could drive right by her. Or, he could give her a training opportunity. Let her speak to a German officer and work on traveling with such contraband on her person without giving anything away.

He slowly pulled alongside her. "Excuse me, *Fräulein!*"

She jumped and the front tire of her bike wobbled a bit as she recovered from her surprise. When she stopped the bike and put both feet on the ground, she covered her heart with her hand and smiled at him. "You startled me, *Oberleutnant.*"

Leo killed the engine and set the parking brake before hopping out of his car. He jogged over to her. "I am so sorry to startle you, *Fräulein* Perrin."

She smoothly raised an eyebrow. He found himself impressed and intrigued by the lack of fear she exhibited. "How do you know my name, *Oberleutnant?*"

He smiled as he searched his mind for a reason he would know her name. "I made an inquiry of your landlady. She was generous to give me your name."

She looked around before looking directly at him again. He wondered how long she would do this job before her brown eyes lost all their warmth and turned hard and cold. "Well, it's nice to see you again, *Oberleutnant,*" she said, clearly wanting to dismiss him. "Did you make it to your ceremony on time last week?"

Giving in to the irrational desire to have some form of contact with her, he held his hand out, hoping she would take it. As she placed her hand in his, he noticed how small her hands were compared to his, and felt the slight tremor that belied her calm expression. "Yes, thanks to you." He smiled, wishing she felt at ease with him. "You are very beautiful, *Fräulein* Perrin."

Why had he said that? Immediately, her face flooded with color and she started to pull her hand away. "*Oberleutnant* Schäfer, I hardly think that is appropriate."

Giving her a break, knowing she had no idea of his true identity, he released her hand and bowed stiffly. "You are correct, *Fräulein.* I apologize."

She gave him a slight nod but her eyes widened and an appalled look crossed her face. "Thank you. I hope you don't –"

He cut off her panicked apology. "Of course not. I should have kept that thought to myself even though it is a fact."

She lowered her eyes as her cheeks gained a bright red tinge. He cleared his throat, seizing the moment, knowing his superiors, and especially his mother, would not approve of the direction he planned to take the conversation. "I have been searching for you, *Fräulein.*"

As she looked up at him, the color started to leave her face. "You've been searching for me?"

"Yes. I want to ask you. Would you like to go see a show with me?"

She frowned and raised an eyebrow. "A show?"

"Yes. In a few weeks, Virginia Benoit will be here to perform for our *Oberst*, our Colonel. *Herr Oberst* is her biggest fan and we are all invited to see the show … to lift the morale of the troops, you see. Tell me, *Fräulein,* do you know Virginia Benoit?"

He had a feeling she would not appreciate it knowing that he tested her. He watched as she swallowed and clearly tried to think of a reply. "Of course I have heard of her."

"She is from America, like me," he proclaimed, as if giving her information she didn't already know.

Her eyebrows furrowed. "American? Why are you here in France, then?"

He gestured in the air. "The call of the Fatherland I'm afraid. My father insisted I return a few years ago."

With wide eyes, she let that digest. "Do you know Virginia Benoit?"

"No." He chuckled, thinking of America's vast size. "America is enormous. She's from a state called Louisiana in the deep south near the Gulf Coast. I'm from Oregon a few thousand kilometers away on the north of the Pacific Coast. Also, I understand the lady is a Negro. Perhaps you've heard that Negros and Aryans hardly ever socialize in America. Still, it will be nice to hear an American accent again, I think."

He hated acting like a racist. He personally believed that man originated from one person - Adam - and that race had nothing to do with a person's character. However, while undercover in this Nazi uniform, he must do nothing to rouse suspicion. Even if that generated the look of disgust that crossed her face.

She did recover very quickly, though. "I imagine you must feel very homesick at times, *Oberleutnant*."

"I am homesick." Now, that was the truth. He ached for his Oregon home. Putting a hand to his heart, he said sincerely, "It would do me a great deal of good to attend the performance with the most beautiful woman in the village on my arm."

"*Oberleutnant* Schäfer, I don't think –"

He held up a hand to halt her speech. "Please, don't say no, *Fräulein*. At least let me have a little hope by telling me you'll consider the offer. Besides, I still owe you for sewing on my button."

He watched her war with herself over whether she should accept his invitation until she pressed her lips together and finally nodded. "Very well, *Oberleutnant*. As you say, I will think about it."

With a cocked eyebrow he said, "You give me your word?"

After perhaps a half second hesitation, she nodded. "You have my word."

He clicked his heels again. "*Wunderbar*! I will seek you out in two days' time to learn your final decision." He leaned closer and whispered as if conspiring with her. She smelled of sunshine and lavender and he felt his heart rate increase with the closer proximity. His body's reaction made him curious. Surely he could think of a thousand better places and even more times that would be better suited to be consumed with attraction for this woman. "I hope you say yes."

To convey his sincerity, he took her hand and kissed the back of her knuckles. He felt the muscles under his fingers flex, but she did not actually pull her hand away. Deciding to release her from the torture of talking to him any longer, he smiled and said, "I look forward to speaking with you again, *Fräulein* Perrin."

"Good day, *Oberleutnant* Schäfer."

He climbed back into his *Kübelwagen* and started the engine. Without looking back at her, he headed on his way. As he drove, he frowned, thinking about the inappropriate timing of his pursuit for her attention. What had possessed him to do that? Yes, she was beautiful. Yes, he felt like he could talk to her for hours. But honestly, couldn't he have waited until this war ended?

Frustrated with himself, he clumsily ground the gears as he went around a corner. Maybe he could come up with a way to gracefully back out of his invitation. Especially before his mother or father caught wind of it.

ᵁ ᵁ ᵁ ᵁ

LEO clenched his jaw in frustration as he stared at the captain in front of him. His mind whirled with options, discarding each one of them. While he considered and rejected strategies, he maintained the conversation so as not to arouse any kind of suspicion. "Sir, I don't understand why you want me to come with you. I'm not on any sort of arrest team."

"*Herr Oberst* Müller asked me to have you be part of the arrest himself," Captain Neumann explained with a bored nod. "I'm to make sure you have as many duties as possible and experience as many different jobs as possible. Arresting this farmer won't take too much time out of your busy day, I'm sure."

He had worked hard for this level of respect and recognition. This kind of attention did not easily come to officers of American birth in the ranks, for obvious reasons. The prejudice and mistrust had only intensified since America's declaration of war on Germany. Clearly Müller had orders to groom him for something more than running one of his prisons in an obscure French village. He couldn't say or do anything to interfere with that now.

He inclined his head. "I appreciate the opportunity to be a part of your team, *Kapitän*. What would you like me to do?"

Neumann waved a hand in the general direction of his office door. "The team is assembling in the square. I will see you there."

Leo clicked his heels and came to attention then lifted his hand in salute to the *Führer* and the *Kapitän*. At the answering salute of his superior, Leo left the room and rushed down the hall to his own desk. What to do? How to warn Marie Perrin?

Neumann's electronic transmission surveillance team had triangulated Marie's last transmission to a farm on the outskirts of town. The Resistance had been warned that while the farmer was friendly to them, the wife was selfish and self-serving. That rather dashed any hopes for a positive outcome after their inevitable interrogation.

He knew Marie usually stored her wireless machine in her room at the boarding house. If he could warn her about the impending arrest, she would have time to hide her equipment. Without her equipment, she might just stand a chance to prevent arrest and remove suspicion, especially if he worked at keeping things in her favor.

Unfortunately, due to the nature of his job, he had to be above reproach and suspicion. Once they made the arrest, he would have no reason to leave the prison for several hours. He could not risk anyone seeing him speak to her after the farmer gave her up. And the farmer would give her up. Not many men would be able to withstand the interrogation of Sergeant Marco Hans. The sadistic man had trained with the *Schutzstaffel* in the Ukraine in 1939. He would extract any information he wanted, and he would enjoy every moment of the experience.

Frowning to himself, he pondered, discarded, considered, and rejected many ideas to get word to Marie in time to save her, but he finally came to the conclusion that he could do nothing. At this point, it would be up to God to intervene. This mission had so much on the line and he could not risk it to save the beautiful spy code-named Temperance, who smelled of lavender and sunshine and made his heart race.

Since it could only be up to God, he decided to say a quick prayer. Ducking behind a filing cabinet, away from prying eyes, he bowed his head and quickly and quietly prayed, "Please, God, intervene."

Rushing to his desk, he snatched up his sidearm and a helmet and slowly walked out of the prison. He didn't like the feeling of helplessness. Putting his hand on the door, he took a deep breath, shook it off and put on an air of excited anticipation, as would be expected of him, then rushed out of the building. Squinting in the bright sun, he saw the group of soldiers preparing to go arrest the farmer standing near two large trucks.

For weeks he had worked on establishing a reputation among these men, and they greeted him with warm respect. After greeting those he knew, he stood off to the side, not able to fraternize with the enlisted men in the group. But, he stood close enough to hear them talking about the two women who had walked into the square and sat on a bench. He looked up and saw Marie and the woman Murielle who went by the code name Prudence.

Thank you Father God, he thought to himself as he donned a smitten look and rushed toward the women.

He could see the look of dread cross Marie's face a split second before she smiled, but the warmth of her smile that didn't quite make it to her brown eyes. "Hello, *Oberleutnant* Schäfer. How are you on this beautiful autumn day?"

"*Fräulein* Perrin," he greeted in response. She wore her chestnut brown hair short, and the natural curls shined in the sunlight, giving them a hint of red. She wore a simple blue dress with a belt cinched at her thin waist, and lipstick the color of ripe apples. The more time he spent in her company, the more he liked her and wished she would give him a genuine smile. As long as he wore this uniform, however, he doubted that could happen. He glanced at Prudence, recognizing her from the briefing his mother had provided weeks earlier. "Who is your friend?"

Prudence giggled and held out a hand. "I'm Murielle St. Pierre, *Oberleutnant*." Her flirtation tactics were not lost on him. She emphasized his rank as if promoting him to General. Then she looked at Marie and stage whispered, "He really *is* handsome, Marie. You weren't exaggerating."

Marie gasped. "Murielle!"

Leo tried hard to imagine what it would be like to be young and innocent and attracted to the beautiful Marie Perrin, and to have her think him handsome. On cue, his face flooded with heat and he felt even the tips of his ears burn. "I am pleased to hear you think that of me, *Fräulein*."

One of the sergeants in the group of soldiers standing near the a truck across the street barked to him that they were loading up. If he had any opportunity at all to warn Marie that she needed to hide her wireless equipment, now was the only time - the only God arranged time. He quickly thought of what to say. "I must go. We have to go arrest a farmer who has been helping the resistance. I hope to see you again soon. I am still waiting on your answer! I only hope you don't make me wait much longer, *Fräulein*."

He held his hat against his head as he trotted back to the group, leaving the women on the bench behind, praying silently and fervently that they realized that the farmer was Marie's farmer and that she needed to get her gear stowed well away from her residence.

He rode in the passenger seat of the lead Opel *Blitz* truck, grateful for the thin cushion on which he sat. He felt some sympathy for the enlisted soldiers and noncommissioned officers riding on the wooden slats in the cargo area in back as the truck bounced ferociously on the rutted dirt road.

His neck tightened with tension as he rode toward the farm. He didn't relish the coming terror this team would unleash on this unsuspecting family. The longer they held out, though, the longer Marie had to hide her equipment and the longer he had to figure out what to do to help her. Maybe he could use some Resistance contacts to hide her until they could get her removed.

The size of the arrest detail intended to intimidate. The latest transmission had been triangulated to an area that could only be at this farm.

Four large trucks pulled up into the yard and twenty men got out, rifles drawn, and surrounded the farm yard. Leo walked to the front door and pounded on it with his fist. Seconds later, a very pale man opened the door. He was of medium build and probably fifty years old. Obviously scared, Leo could see the hate in his eyes.

"*Oui?*"

"Marcel Bernard?" Leo clarified.

"*Oui, je suis* Marcel Bernard." Leo could see the whites of the man's knuckles as he gripped the door.

Speaking in French, Leo announced, "You are under arrest for suspicion of aiding the resistance." Using force, he grabbed Marcel's arm and pulled him toward the closest truck.

A large thick woman with a faced flushed bright red came running from the house. "Marcel!" she screamed.

Leo gestured with his chin and a private grabbed her by the upper arms and pulled her along behind them.

"What is the meaning of this?" the wife, Armelle, demanded.

"You and your husband are under arrest for aiding the resistance," Leo answered as if this fact should be patently obvious. They reached the Opel *Blitz* truck and a private lowered the tailgate on the back. Leo watched as the Bernard's were loaded into the truck.

Marcel put his arm around his wife's shoulder and listened to her cry and blubber in terror. Leo turned away from them, feeling sympathy at their plight but reminding himself of the much, much bigger picture. He looked around the yard. "Search the barn. Arrest anyone else here."

The team ransacked the house, the barn, and the surrounding property searching for anything incriminating. An hour later, the Bernards separated in different cells, he went back to his own office that he shared with another *Oberleutnant*, only to find district manager *Kapitän* Neumann waiting there.

"Yes, sir?" Leo asked, coming to attention.

"I heard that the arrest went smoothly," Neumann said, crushing out a cigarette into a metal ashtray that hadn't been there when Leo left an hour ago.

"There were no issues."

"Very good," *Kapitän* Neumann said, as if mentally lining out the last item on a long to-do list. With a somewhat surprised look, he apparently noticed that Leo had come to a position of attention. Casually, he said, "At ease."

Leo allowed himself to relax his stance but he remained fully alert in the presence of this man. While the *Kapitän* appeared lackadaisical, nearly careless, Leo knew this to be a ruse. The man was a viper who conserved all his energy for the kill.

Neumann picked up a piece of paper from Leo's desk and handed it to him. "Your training here is complete, *Oberleutnant* Schäfer. Upon the orders of *Oberst* Müller, you are now officially in charge of the prisoners in this facility." He gestured vaguely above them, toward upper floors that housed the prisoners. "*Oberleutnant* Beck will be promoted tomorrow and is being assigned to the POW camp we are building. He speaks very highly of you and what you have learned thus far. I am assured that you are the right man for this job."

Neumann didn't sound personally convinced. Nevertheless, elation flooded Leo's chest. When the captain had started speaking, he feared that he would be reassigned to another location. Despite his inward thoughts, he kept a stoic expression on his face. "Thank you, sir."

"His office should be cleared and ready for you. His clerk is now your clerk and will assist you in settling in." He picked a file up from the top of the desk and looked at his watch. "I have to go to Berlin. I look forward to your report when I return. Good day, *Oberleutnant*."

Leo clicked his heels together and saluted. "*Sieg heil.*"

"*Ja, ja. Heil* Hitler," the captain answered emotionlessly, waving his hand in a returned salute that looked more like shooing a fly away from his meal as he walked out of the room.

♙ ♙ ♙ ♙

CHAPTER 2

Chapter Two

LEO made sure no one saw him as he carefully lowered his glass and poured the rich red wine through the wide crack in the restaurant's floorboard. As he raised his glass to his lips, he swallowed the last drop and slammed the glass on the table, laughing at the stupid joke the drunken man across from him had just told. Through the thick smoky room, he watched people come and go. Three tables down, his contact sat at a table, eating his evening meal.

Thirty minutes and three more glasses of dumped out wine, his contact took his glasses off and cleaned them with the linen handkerchief – the prearranged sign to follow him out of the building.

Leo surged to his feet, stumbling backward and tripping over his chair. He laughed so hard that he had to lean against the table for support. "I have a train to catch in a few hours, my friends. I must leave this party and go sleep at the station so that I don't miss it."

"Where are you off to, then?" Former *Oberleutnant,* now *Kapitän* Beck asked as he lit a cigarette.

He slipped his hand into his pocket and pulled out a folded telegram, waving it around. "Summoned to Paris to see *Generalleutnant* von Stülpnagel. I will see you soon, I am sure."

"I will drive you to the station," Lieutenant Hiegel said, moving as if to stand.

Leo snorted. "You have had twice as much to drink as I. I will be riding nowhere with you at the wheel. I'll walk, thank you."

The other men at the table laughed, then Hiegel laughed, too. Leo continued, "The night air will do me good. It should clear my head."

Beck's eyes narrowed, but he nodded. "Very well. Congratulations on the promotion. Must be nice to rub elbows with the likes of Stülpnagel."

"Thank you. Congratulations to you as well. And, no, it isn't really nice all the time." He sloppily raised his arm. "*Sieg heil*," he said, not mentioning "Hitler" by name, then stumbled as he turned, weaving through the crowded restaurant.

As he stepped outside, he put his hat on his head a bit crookedly and walked rather unsteadily until he could no longer see the lights of the restaurant. As soon as he thought himself in the clear, he darted down an alley and ran the three kilometers to the train station. His booted feet struck an odd noise on the damp cobblestones of the streets. He calculated he had about ten minutes before Beck showed up to check on him.

In the men's restroom, he found his contact with a folded newspaper. Before speaking, he checked every corner of the room to make sure they truly had it to themselves.

"Matthew," he said, holding out his hand. "It's good to see you still alive." He knew Matthew was a Jewish Christian whose father had been a hero in the Great War. Matthew, his brother, and his sister had trained in espionage and combat tactics since childhood. There were few men he trusted with his very life. Matthew was definitely one of them.

"Valor." He held up the paper, getting right to the point. "There's a meeting of the leaders of the Black Orchestra and Sector 4 Resistance leadership happening tomorrow night. We need you to help me handle security."

The Black Orchestra, or *Schwarze Kapelle*, was a secret group inside the German military who hated Hitler and what the insane man was doing to their country and their people. "You called me out at great risk to my cover to provide security for a meeting?" He took the paper from him. "Are your numbers so thin?"

"My numbers grow with every second of this occupation," Matthew replied, his face turning down into a frown, "but I need your eyes on the attendees. I need you to confirm the Germans attending are who they say they are."

Leo shook his head and looked at his watch. He had less than a minute left until he no longer felt comfortable continuing this exchange. "The Black Orchestra is secret in itself. I won't be able to confirm everyone."

"It will be enough, God willing." He gestured at the paper in Leo's hand.

"There's a cabin in the woods about eight kilometers northwest." Leo opened the newspaper and saw the map. "Memorize it. I can't give it to you."

"Of course."

"I'll have a list with me of those who are expected to attend."

He looked at the map closely, memorizing distances and key terrain. When he felt confident, he handed the paper back. "What time?"

"Twenty-three hundred."

"And my travel?"

"Here's your ticket." Leo took it from him. "Get off the train on the third stop. You'll have a double waiting in the latrine there. He'll check into your hotel in Paris and will return in two days."

They clasped hands. "I'll see you at twenty-three hundred."

Leo slipped out of the men's room into the still empty waiting area of the train station. He put his train ticket in the top of his jacket pocket and slipped down on the wooden bench until his legs stretched out in front of him. He leaned back, set his hat over his eyes, and feigned a drunken slumber.

As if on cue, seconds later, he saw *Kapitän* Beck enter the train station. He had felt the man's mistrust during the evening at the restaurant. What had he done to generate suspicion? Was it simply his American heritage? Or had he seen Leo dump some wine into the floor?

He had taken Beck's position at the prison. Perhaps Beck did not see his transfer to the prisoner of war camp as a promotion. Perhaps he saw Leo as a threat, someone trying to replace him. Whatever the case, he needed to tread cautiously around Beck until his permanent departure from Valeurville. He already had marks against him in the ranks due to his American upbringing. It would only take a whisper of suspicion to endanger his mission.

From under his uniform cap, Leo watched Beck's feet quietly cross the station. He entered the restroom and exited in just just a few seconds, leaving the building entirely a few moments later. Deciding to take advantage of the opportunity to rest, Leo closed his eyes for real this time and forced his body to relax enough to fall asleep. As he drifted off, the face of Marie Perrin flashed across his mind's eye. Had she gotten the equipment out of her room in time?

He felt frustration at the timing of this mission. From the prison, he could possibly stall any attention on Marie. He only prayed at the farmer wouldn't give her up. Maybe his loyalty to France would keep him from revealing any names or descriptions of the Resistance who used his farm.

He woke with a start as Sergeant Ernst Bauer rushed into the station. He stood several inches shorter than Leo, but had a large girth and a round face. Leo didn't think he'd ever met a more sadistic man. Recently, he sat next to his table in a café and listened to the man itemize in shocking detail all the things he had done to a 13-year-old Jewish girl the night before. "There you are, sir!" the Sergeant exclaimed.

As he stood, he glanced at the large clock near the tracks and saw he'd slept for about two hours. His train would be the first train of the day and would leave in under an hour. No one else was in the station yet.

"I'm headed to Paris, Sergeant. What do you need?"

"The farmer broke!" He held out a piece of paper. "We are awaiting your instructions, Oberleutnant."

Leo quickly skimmed the document. The foolish man had identified Marie by name. Biting back a curse, Leo wadded up the paper. "Listen to me carefully. I need you to heed my instructions." Clearly, this man was ready to gather the troops and storm the boarding house. "I do not want her touched. Do you understand me? There's a large contingency of resistance in this area of France, and I want her put under surveillance until I get back from Paris. Perhaps she will uncover this elusive leader of theirs."

"But, sir, interrogation can –"

"But?" He leaned in so close to the Sergeant's face that their noses almost touched. "You dare offer me insubordination, Sergeant? You question my orders?" He wondered if he could smell what little wine he'd actually consumed last night.

As color flushed his cheeks, the man came to attention. "No, sir."

"Very well. You have your orders." He held up the paper clutched in his fist. "Watch her carefully. I will be back in two days."

"*Javol, Oberleutnant!*" The Sergeant shot his arm out in a stiff salute. Leo hesitated just long enough to let the man see his irritation before returning the salute so the man could leave.

♗ ♗ ♗ ♗

LEO peered through the binoculars at the car pulling up to the cabin below. He lay sprawled on a flat rock about fifty meters above the cabin. To help camouflage himself, he wore a black turtleneck shirt, black pants, and a black skull cap. Next to him, Matthew peered over the iron sighs of an old bolt action .303 caliber Lee–Metford Mark II rifle someone had kept from the Great War. Leo wondered about the soundness of the ammunition. Matthew assured him the rounds were still good and the best he could find for long distance shooting.

"That's Jäger. He is Black Orchestra. I actually met him in London about three months ago." He shifted very slowly and glanced over at Matthew. "Not that he knows who I am, of course. Word is that he was planning to assassinate Hitler this year."

"Someone needs to kill that power mad ghoul before he devours the entire earth," Matthew muttered.

Still whispering, Leo said, "Unfortunately, his wife was killed in an Allied bombing raid against Lübeck and he missed his opportunity."

In the darkness, he felt Matthew tense. "Children, too?"

Leo understood the depths of this question. "I don't know. I doubt it, though. I think I would have heard."

Matthew quietly clicked his tongue several times as if bidding a pet to come sit in his lap. "Jäger is on our list. I don't understand where everyone else is. Wait –" Matthew lifted his head and looked toward the road. "Incoming."

They peered through their magnifying lenses and watched Jäger go into the cabin. Like the other two vehicles parked in the yard, the one approaching was not a military vehicle. The car pulled up next to Jäger's motorcycle. The man who emerged wore a dark blue suit and tie.

"Who are you then?" Matthew asked quietly. "You're not one of mine."

Leo watched and waited. "Come on, turn around," he whispered, willing the man to turn his face in their direction. He kept his head turned away while talking to the man seated in the driver's seat of his car. He finally got a good profile look at him and his pulse rate accelerated. "That's Heinrich."

He heard Matthew's sharp intake of breath. "Heinrich? How is he here?"

Heinrich did not enter the cabin, but waited by his door. "Careless talk costs lives," he whispered, mimicking a poster he'd seen in London.

Matthew muttered under his breath in Hebrew. Leo could read the tone and didn't need the exasperation to be translated. "Think he's a member of the Orchestra and you don't know about it?"

"Maybe," Leo replied, considering the heinous acts he knew had been credited to Heinrich. "If so, he's got a pretty solid cover."

Much to his surprise, the cabin door opened and Jäger waved Heinrich inside. The driver emerged from the vehicle and followed. Before closing the door to the cabin, the driver peered into every direction of the darkening landscape.

"Well now," Matthew said, peering back through his sniper scope. "That's rather interesting."

"Indeed." Leo sat back and contemplated what just happened. "This feels very bad."

"I concur."

His mind raced. "If Jäger brought Heinrich, then maybe Jäger's wife's death affected his level of patriotism for the true Germany."

"It's possible he switched alliances. Especially if an Allied bomb ended her life." Matthew peered down and squinted at his wrist, trying to make out the hands of his watch face in the darkness of the shadows where they hid. "I have a list of six Black Orchestra members attending. Jäger is the only one we've seen. We need to stop this meeting."

Leo slipped the binoculars over his head. "I'm going down."

"You can't. You may be spotted!"

"I need to see what's happening inside." He tugged on his ski cap and it opened to a full face mask called a balaclava. It completely covered his nose and mouth, revealing only his eyes. Retrieving his Luger Parabellum from his bag, he checked that a round was chambered then gripped it as he dashed down the hillside, hoping that the growing shadows from the setting sun would help cover him.

As he entered the yard of the cabin, he crouched behind Heinrich's Aries Berline. He waited, looking, listening. Seeing no other outdoor movement, he slipped around to the back of the cabin and approached the back window.

Through the open window, he heard the conversation between the men inside. He identified four distinct voices. They had only seen Jäger, Heinrich, and Heinrich's driver enter the cabin. The Resistance leaders were due to arrive in ten minutes.

"These are high level leaders," one man said. "When they are gone, it will temporarily cripple the resistance movement."

"I think we need more time. We could pretend to cooperate with them for the time being." Leo recognized Jäger's voice. "We would learn more about the movement and expose more members."

"You're soft in the heart, Colonel," another man said. "We agreed that this meeting would be an assassination. We have sustained too many strategic blows in this region of late. They're too organized and well supplied. They operate with military precision. Once we kill this group it will open inroads to start infiltrating their other units for the final blow."

Leo pulled a miniature camera out of his pocket. The camera would not operate very well in the dim light of the setting sun but he hoped it would be good enough to capture the speaker's face. Crouching beneath the window, he held the camera up and quickly snapped a photo. He lowered the camera and waited, holding his breath, listening to the men talk. He managed to take four more pictures before he thought it was too risky to try for a fifth.

He had left his bag atop the hill. He jammed the little camera into his trouser pocket. Praetorian and three other major leaders would arrive within minutes. Following the same path he took to come down, he dashed back up the hill and returned to Matthew's location.

"We need to stop this meeting," he said somewhat out of breath, mimicking Matthew's words from earlier.

"I know how." He put the scope of the rifle up to his eye again. "Watch the road. Let me know when the car is coming."

Less than a minute later, he heard the car engine. Then Leo spotted the grill of the car coming down the lane. They operated completely in the dark, without even blackout headlights, making the vehicle difficult to spot. "It's here."

Matthew fired the rifle into the house window, then quickly drew the bolt back and chambered another round. As he fired again, an officer ran from the cabin with his pistol drawn and Matthew shot him. The .303 round struck the man in his stomach and he crumpled to the ground. The oncoming car stopped, paused for a couple of seconds, then rapidly backed up in the direction it came, tires spinning, spewing dirt and gravel. The driver came to a small plateau and took a risk to turn the car 180 degrees to drive out forward. It was a maneuver only someone who knew this location well would have risked in the dim light of dusk with no headlights.

"That worked. They're gone," Leo said, crouching down to whisper to Matthew. "Good shooting."

"Here they come," Matthew replied while cycling the bolt on his rifle, sending another round into the chamber as three more men flooded out of the cabin door, guns drawn. Matthew carefully fired and another cabin window exploded. Immediately, all three guns pointed in their direction and fired.

"I think that's our cue," Leo observed while slinging his bag over his shoulder. He lifted his pistol and aimed then fired in the general direction of the group of men outside the cabin. The distance was too great for any real accuracy and his shots went wide. He merely intended to provide Matthew some covering fire as the man slung his sniper rifle over his shoulder. "Let's go."

Despite low crawling toward the cover of trees, they continued to receive fire. When Leo felt safe to stand, he moved to a crouch and instantaneously felt a searing pain rip through his stomach. He fell back to his knees and Matthew shot the uniformed soldier who had stepped out of the tree line. As the man fell, Matthew reached toward Leo and grabbed him by his arm.

"I got you, Valor."

If his arm hadn't been around him, Leo would have collapsed. The pain took his breath away and caused nausea to swirl in his gut. Inside the tree line, he paused and leaned against a huge pine. Matthew pushed his nose into his face. "No stopping. We have to go. Take deep breaths and try not to scream."

Shoring up whatever minuscule strength he had left in his limbs, he gripped his stomach with his hand and leaned into Matthew, who bore his weight and raced them through the woods.

After an agonizing and seemingly never ending kilometer, they reached Matthew's car. Leo climbed into the back seat and curled into a ball. For the next ten minutes, he gritted his teeth and tried desperately not to cry out in pain as Matthew drove the car out of the woods, over rutted fields, and through a stream before finally launching out onto a narrow paved road. The rear end of the car fishtailed as the tires fought for purchase on the pavement.

As the ride smoothed out, Leo found it harder and harder to keep his eyes open. While blood poured out of his wound and through his fingertips, he closed his eyes and let the darkness overtake him.

CHAPTER 3

Chapter Three

MATTHEW lay Leo down on a cot in the tack room of an 80 year old barn. "The worst is over. Doc's on the way," he assured, pressing a folded cloth against the wound. "Not long, now. I promise."

Leo could feel his body going into shock. He quaked and quivered and his breath sounded rapid and shallow to his own ears. His world coalesced into nothing more than a struggle to get enough oxygen into his lungs and suffer through the burning ball of pain searing through his gut. Light-headedness and the agony of the wound effectively obliterated the rest of the universe.

He had always assumed that shock helped remove pain, but that didn't appear to apply to this circumstance. Despite the pain, and despite his own personal dire circumstances, all he could think about was Marie and Sergeant Bauer.

Praetorian entered the room. "What is the meaning of this?"

Matthew gestured. "He was shot. I had to get him to a place Mercy could work on him safely."

"Is Mercy here?"

"Abiel's gone to fetch her. I have to leave him with you. He saw inside the cabin. You need to debrief him." Leo heard rustling behind him and the wood frame door squeak open then slam shut seconds later.

Praetorian leaned toward Leo. Leo stared into his eyes, finding signs of a man who had spent too long in such an intense position. Clearly, the man called Praetorian had seen too much of war in too short a time and the decisions he had to make that cost lives weighed heavily upon his heart.

"What do you know? What happened out there?"

"Before I tell you, you need to know that Temperance has been compromised."

"What?"

"The farmer broke," he whispered, attempting to focus as his vision grayed. "Get her out of there."

Praetorian nodded stiffly. "I'll handle it. Now, what happened tonight?" Before Leo could answer, Praetorian held up a hand and whispered, "I hear a car. Try not to make a sound."

Leo heard the door squeak again, but no answering slam as it shut. A few seconds later, he heard Praetorian's voice and that of a woman. He struggled, desperately, to maintain consciousness. He had to tell Praetorian what he heard. He had to give him something. What was it?

The camera! He took pictures of whoever was inside the cabin.

With quaking muscles that didn't seem to want to obey his brain's commands, he fumbled to unbutton the right cargo pocket of his trousers with blood soaked fingers, finally succeeding after the third attempt. At last, he put his hand in his right pocket and closed his fist around the miniature camera. He found he barely had the strength to pull his hand from his pocket as his body started to shudder. He felt like someone had covered him with an ice cold blanket.

When the door opened, a woman wearing a Red Cross nurse's uniform walked through the doorway, followed by Praetorian and Abiel. She looked at him and gasped.

"A prisoner, then?" she asked, her voice heavy with a Scottish brogue.

Praetorian answered her with a shake of his head. "No. He's on our side. Can you help?"

She stepped forward, concentration making her eyebrows furrow together in a single line. "Right, then. Let's have us a *wee keek*. I'll be needin' clean blankets. Right away," she ordered.

Leo watched Praetorian nod to Abiel, who left immediately. Where had Abiel come from? Leo's mind started to drift away. He must have driven the nurse here. But she's not a nurse. How did he know that? Who was she?

The woman knelt next to his cot and took one of the hands he clutched against his abdomen. "More light!" she demanded, and Praetorian held a lantern over her shoulder.

After inspecting his wound, she put his hand back on top of the bleeding wound and applied pressure. When he looked at her face again, she stared into his eyes. He recognized her face from her file but his mind was having a hard time connecting dots. "I don't speak German. You speak French?" She asked him in French.

He answered in English, speaking through the fog of pain, remembering the details of her file. "They said you spoke English. English is easier." He wanted to explain that the agony clouded his mind's ability to vocalize any other language. He could tell her that he actually had to mentally translate his thoughts into German or French most of the time, but he didn't have the energy.

Switching back to English, she said, "What do I call you, lad?"

"Call him Valor," Praetorian said from over her shoulder. "He needs to be patched up and back at his duty station tomorrow or else things are likely to go very, very badly for our little operation here."

All he could think about were *Kapitän* Beck's suspicions and Marie's name on that piece of paper. He had to leave. While Mercy lifted his shirt and pushed against the wound, he panted, "I can't stay here."

The side of her mouth lifted in a half-amused look. "Well, Valor, I'm afraid that's not necessarily up to me at the moment."

She prodded the wound on his stomach and shifted to feel underneath him. He felt his vision tunneled as if black blinders closed in from the sides. "I'm not seeing where the bullet came out. That means you're holding onto it somewhere. Stubborn, really. I'm going to have to cut on you a bit."

Nausea swirled in his stomach and his throat started to close with fear. "Do what you need to."

She gripped his bloody hand with her own. He found the strength in her grip comforting. "Right this moment, you probably think you can't hurt much worse. Sadly, you're mistaken. I c'n give ya something if you like."

"Can it wait?" Praetorian asked as he walked to the foot of the bed. "He needs to talk." Wait? Talk? Suddenly the mission came back into focus. "Tell me what you learned."

"It w-w-was a s-s-set-t-t-up," Leo stammered, tasting blood in his mouth. His fingers spasmed around the camera he clutched and he tried to open his hand, but his muscles would not obey his mind. "They w-w-wanted to lure you i-i-n and k-k-kill you. C-c-c-ripple the Res-is-stance."

"Who? Did you identify them?"

"Jäger. Heinrich." He closed his eyes and felt the world start to tilt when he remembered the mission. He opened his eyes again. "Two more. We never saw them go in."

"Matthew said you went down to the cabin. What did you see?"

"P-p-ictures," Leo whispered. His hand finally relinquished its grip and Praetorian saw the camera.

"Good lad," he said, taking it from his hand. "We'll get this developed and see what we discover." He frowned and leaned forward. "How compromised is your cover?"

Leo shook his head. "Not at all. They never saw me." As Mercy pushed his hands aside so she could cut open his shirt, he held up his hands, showing his bloody palms. "They know they hit me."

Mercy began praying out loud, a Scottish prayer that sounded as if from rote. Praetorian put a hand on Leo's booted foot. "Who knows of you?"

Leo knew Praetorian meant Black Orchestra. Many members knew of his existence in a vague sense, but had no idea exactly who the legendary Valor may be. "No one."

Mercy concluded her prayer, "Amen." She picked up a syringe. "That's all boys. You can talk in a few hours." He barely felt the needle prick into the vein of his forearm. The morphine burned a heated path up his arm toward his heart, feeling like hot venom as it worked through his bloodstream. When it reached his heart, he welcomed the relief as numbness and blackness wash over him.

♜ ♜ ♜ ♜

LEO'S mouth felt like someone had stuffed it with cotton. He struggled to open his eyes, and as his eyelids rose, he thought perhaps someone had glued sandpaper to the insides of them. All those sensations flew out the window, though, when the pain in his abdomen hit him. He actually groaned out loud despite his desire otherwise.

"So you're awake, then," Praetorian said from beside him. Leo opened his mouth, but he held up a hand. "No talking. Just take this pill." Praetorian grinned ironically. "I'm told you should sleep for a few more hours. I'm also reliably informed that we'll both regret it if we disregard the doctor's orders."

He had to get back to work. "I –" he thought he might try to shift upward in the bed, but the pain overwhelmed him and seared through his muscles, weakening them and causing a cold sweat to break out on his forehead.

"We're trying to establish a new cover now. Nothing you can do about anything. If the cover fails, we'll extract you. Take this pill. Mercy said it will help with the pain."

He swallowed the pill then greedily swallowed the water offered by Praetorian. Exhausted, he closed his eyes again. Thoughts of Marie Perrin's name on that sheet of paper plagued him until the dark void overtook him.

THE wounded spy sat up against the wall. It hurt, too much to sit like that, but he had to start getting stronger somehow. Mercy, doctor not nurse, had just prayed with him and left. She didn't appear to understand the urgency of his situation. Every single hour he spent here was an hour someone might spend questioning his absence, or questioning his identity.

He did not want his cover to fail and force them to extract him. His entire life had been spent in preparation for this time. His parents, Karl and Charlene Schäfer, had married the day they met, then parachuted into what was now Germany so that his father could take a position of espionage in the Kaiser's government.

In 1918, Charlene gave birth to Leo while under deep cover in Germany. Leo had just celebrated his first birthday when they left Germany. No one there ever suspected his father or mother of their true identities as spies for the British and Canadian governments. They had spent the entire war traveling throughout Europe, dispatching messages and intelligence, returning back to their home with no one the wiser. They had been brilliant at their jobs, highly decorated - though entirely in secret - and invaluable to their governments.

When his father, Karl, had resigned from the German bureaucratic position to move to America, the German government sent him away with honors. It was natural for the two operations agents to train their only child in the arts of their career, even while pursuing a relatively normal life on the coast of America's Pacific Northwest. Karl and Charlene both taught at the University of Oregon, Karl teaching business classes, and Charlene teaching accounting. Both were passionate followers of Christ and had a social life that revolved almost entirely around church and church friends. Charlene spent three months a year in England, continuing to work with intelligence agencies there in a reserve capacity.

In 1929, right after Leo's eleventh birthday, Charlene returned from her British military duty. He had overheard his parents talking about her experience in Hebron and shortly after, the two started training Leo with diligence. By his eighteenth birthday, he knew that he would be assigned a position in the German army. His mother returned to England under her maiden name to start the ground work to protect Britain from Germany's rising threat. After hiring a woman to live in their home and write letters on Charlene's behalf from Oregon, Karl and Leo returned to Germany.

Because of his service during the Great War, Karl was never suspected of treason. Instead, he received a warm welcome home, operating under the code name Durandal. Leo attended a *Kriegsschulen,* an officer training academy, in Munich, with the code name Valor. By the time the war truly began, Karl and Leo had well established covers and could arouse very little suspicion. Both knew if one were found out, the other would be in danger, and had prearranged ways to signal each other just in case.

He couldn't risk his position and his cover by his absence stretching any longer. He had to get to the point where he could pretend a state of fitness. Thirty-six hours had already passed. The longer he remained absent, the less weight his cover story could bear.

He heard booted steps on the wooden floor of the barn and slipped his hand under his sheet to grip the pistol he kept there. He relaxed only slightly when Praetorian came into the tack room.

"Good news. We just found out your father has been in Paris for the last three days. We have sources getting information to him about confirming a meeting with you. We'll get a letter from him as soon as we know how long you will be out of commission."

Leo closed his eyes in thanksgiving to God for His obvious protection. "That is excellent news."

"We had someone who looks enough like you check into his hotel in Paris yesterday evening." Praetorian handed him two photos. "About the other night. These are the only two pictures you took that had clear faces." Leo looked at them but did not immediately recognize the men. "Do you know them?"

He frowned. "Not at all. Any ideas?"

"You know nearly everything I know," Leo mused. "They're clearly leaders. Despite the civilian clothing, one was referred to as 'Colonel'."

"We'll get copies of the photos to London and see what Intelligence there knows. When you are back on your feet, keep an eye out for them. They're new to this region but they're likely military. "

"I will." His head began to spin as the pain pill he'd recently taken began to work. "Anything else?" His tongue felt heavy on the word "else".

"No. Sleep. Heal. Hopefully, Durandal can buy us some time."

"And Temperance?"

"We're getting a message to her to arrange extraction."

Feeling like he could relax a little, he nodded and closed his eyes.

MERCY held the spoon up to his lips. Despite the savory smell and taste of the broth, he felt more tired than hungry. "More?"

He shook his head, exhausted from the effort of eating. "Sorry. No more."

She smiled as she cleared the tin cup of clear broth from the table by the bed. "It pleases me that you ate at all."

Knowing it was a good sign, he weakly elaborated. "I'm actually feeling hungry."

Mercy stood. "I'll try to get you some bread tomorrow. Don' want to move too quickly." She took the glass bottle of pain pills from her pocket and fished one out for him. As she handed him a pain pill, Praetorian rushed into the room.

"Temperance has been arrested."

Adrenaline surged through his chest and without thinking, he pushed himself into a sitting position. Immediately, pain washed over him and he grit his teeth trying to block the moan that escaped. Limbs quaking, he somehow pushed himself into a standing position. He saw his pressed uniform hanging on a hook on the wall and started to reach for it, but had to brace his hand on the wall next to it to stay upright instead.

"You can't go," Mercy said with authority.

Before Leo could reply, Praetorian answered, "He must." Praetorian lifted the uniform from the hook and unbuttoned the shirt. Leo slipped his arm into the sleeve, cold sweat pouring from his face, his vision starting to go gray.

"How established is my cover?" he panted.

"Good enough. *Generalleutnant* von Stülpnagel met with Durandal and the man that Durandal introduced as his son, the *Obuerlieutenant* he introduced as his son. We have travel documentation coming in daily, prepared for whatever papers we needed for you."

While Leo listened, he forced his numb fingers to button his shirt.

Praetorian reached into his pocket and pulled out papers and a train ticket. "Last night, Durandal had a doctor friendly to the Resistance sent to the hotel to treat his son who will report that he treated a terrible case of food poisoning. That will help explain your weakness." He slipped the papers into the inside pocket of Leo's coat. "No one will question von Stülpnagel or Durandal and I doubt they'll question you."

Leo braced his hand on the wall again and felt his legs quaking. After a few moments, he straightened and turned toward Mercy. "I think I need another one of those pain pills."

She shook her head. "That will only serve to make you unconscious and destroy your liver. One every four hours is nearly too high a dose as it is."

He couldn't function with this pain. "Just this once. I have to get through the next few hours without anyone suspecting anything."

"Fine!" she spat, opening the bottle and handing him a pill. "I'll be at the hospital when they carry you in on a stretcher."

She stormed from the room while Leo swallowed the pill, his hand shaking so badly that water sloshed out of his glass.

"I'll be right back," Praetorian said as Leo pulled the uniform trousers off of the hanger.

He didn't know if he answered him or not. As he lowered himself to the cot to put on his trousers, he felt something like a ripping or tearing in his abdomen. With an almost detached curiosity, he watched as the front of his uniform shirt spread with blood seconds before the world grayed then went completely black.

8 8 8 8

LEO leaned against a wooden beam in the center of the barn. Mercy stood off to one side, arms folded across her chest, looking angry and defensive. The weakness in his legs coupled with the pain in his abdomen made his whole body quake as sweat poured down his face.

Every single twinge of pain only forced him to stand there longer as he thought about the torture Marie must certainly be suffering at the hands of the *Schutzstaffel* trained interrogator. Every second he spent in this barn, she spent in agony and fear.

Praetorian came through the side entrance, holding a piece of paper. "We've managed to give you appendicitis," he said without humor. "The doctor's surgical notes and duty recommendations are coming via courier in the morning."

"Did some poor sot have to endure an actual surgery?" Leo panted. Pinpricks of light danced in front of his eyes as his pain increased.

"Not at all. We have nurses friendly to the cause who will claim they took care of you. The cover is tight. I do not anticipate a problem."

"Then put him back to bed. He would need two full weeks of recovery after appendicitis surgery. If his cover is so tight, he can heal before leaving," Mercy demanded, stepping forward.

"No," Leo and Praetorian said together.

Praetorian continued, "Do you have any idea the kind of interrogation Temperance is enduring at this moment?"

Leo watched as her face paled. "I don't --"

"Despite the fact that she is a human being, a woman, who shouldn't have to be tortured for sadistic pleasure, putting that aside, let's remember everything Temperance knows." Praetorian made a wide sweeping gesture with his arm. "Let's start with the fact that she's been here, on this farm, in the presence of Prudence and three Frenchmen who lead a local team. Forgetting that, let's add her knowledge of the operatives in this area including you and me. Most importantly, let's consider all of the code in her head. What do you think will happen with everything we've managed to accomplish until this moment if she breaks?"

Leo interjected before Mercy could reply. "I will leave the second the cover papers are in my hand."

Praetorian nodded before rounding on Mercy once again. "Hear this, if Valor here can't get there in time to stop the interrogation, then Temperance becomes a liability."

Mercy's face flooded with color. "Are you saying --"

Praetorian gave Leo a look. "He's saying," Leo gasped, "she can't break. Period. My job is to ensure that she does not, one way or another."

Would he be able to insure it one way or another? If he couldn't stop the interrogation, he would have to kill her. That's what Praetorian meant. Could he? Knowing that the bigger picture, that the Allied presence in Occupied France far outweighed the life or death of a single woman, he knew he simply had to. Despite how it would make him feel later.

His priority at this point was to come up with a plan to make sure he didn't have to go to that extreme. What could he say or do to stop the interrogation of a suspected wireless operator? Something would have to come to him. Praying for God's omniscient wisdom, he turned, stumbling back to his room. While he wanted to stand longer, to force the strength back into his body, he couldn't risk falling. If he fell, he might reinjure himself and lose more time.

Mercy followed him. As he carefully lowered himself onto the cot, she hovered over him, pain pill and glass of water at the ready. "Valor --"

He held a hand up and she placed her hand in his. "Mercy, listen to me." His mouth felt stuffed with cotton and his voice sounded raspy. "Marie's well-being is my highest priority. I won't let --" Out of nowhere, nausea overwhelmed him. He reached for the bucket that sat next to the bed and thought the pain of his stomach muscles heaving might actually be the worst pain he'd ever endured.

Spent, he lay back on the pillow as Mercy put a cool cloth on his forehead. "Hush," she whispered when he tried to speak. "Save your strength."

U U U U

CHAPTER 4

Chapter Four

LEO lay his head back against the seat while Matthew, serving as a taxi driver, drove him from the train station. He met his eyes in the rear view mirror as he drove and spoke. "Perhaps she's withstood interrogation." The grim set of his mouth belied his true fears in the matter.

Clinging to fantasy would help no one at this point. The singer code-named Hope had confirmed the viciousness of her treatment over a day ago. "It's been nearly forty-eight hours. Hope confirmed Temperance's condition more than thirty hours ago. I know Sergeant Marco Hans. He was trained in interrogation tactics by the Soviets. I can't imagine she has held out." The thought of what that beautiful young woman likely had endured to this point nearly destroyed him. For two full days, he'd been helpless. He had spent that time imagining the terror inflicted on her based on the knowledge he had of interrogation methods they used at the prison.

The taxi came to a smooth stop in front of the prison. Shoring up what strength he could muster, he shakily got out of the car and made a show of paying Matthew for the taxi ride. The two men did not speak. Everything that could have been said had already been said.

As he started up the steps toward the front doors, *Kapitän* Richter came out of the building.

"Schäfer," he said, descending quickly. "I heard a report that you have been very ill." His eyes narrowed as he looked at Leo, clearly taking in the sweating face, the pale complexion, the shaky movements. "Are you certain you are well enough to return?"

"*Kapitän*," Leo replied, walking very slowly and gingerly to the top step, "I would like to come back to work for most of the day."

His suspicious air dissipated with each second spent in Leo's company. Clearly, he had not pretended to be sick in order to gain some additional days in Paris. "If you need to, go see the doctor."

"The doctor in Paris has assured me that I'll feel much stronger by the end of the week." He gestured toward the prison. "I have been gone from this brand new duty assignment for too long as it is. Have I missed anything important, *Herr Kapitän*?"

"Your clerk can brief you. I am late to a meeting with *Oberst* Müller at the site of the POW camp." As he started down the steps, he turned back. "*Kapitän* Neumann is due back in about an hour. Have your clerk send a driver to get him at the air strip in Field Six."

Leo saluted and went into the prison. It took him several minutes to walk up the stairs because he had to stop and lean against the stairwell wall every two or three steps. He finally made it to his floor.

In the center of the main room stood a large cage. In that cage, a very bruised and beaten Temperance crouched near the center of the floor, her arms wrapped around her legs. She rested her face on her knees, but he knew it was her. Water dripped down her face and back from matted hair. He could see the bruising on her shoulders and forehead and down her arms. Through the soaking wet, thin cotton slip, he could see her skin and the purpling bruise along her ribs. She did not look up and see him as he walked past her cage.

His clerk, Franz Kalb, rushed toward him as he went into his office. "*Oberleutnant* Schäfer! We weren't sure when to expect you back."

"As soon as the doctor released me to travel, I took the first train." He gestured beyond the office door toward the cage. "Who is that?" He shakily lowered himself into his seat.

"Sergeant Hans believes she is a wireless operator for the resistance." He set a stack of envelopes on his desk.

Leo raised an eyebrow. "Indeed. Was this intelligence gleaned from the farmer?"

"Yes, sir. He gave her name and where she lived. Sergeant Bauer arrested her two days ago."

He pursed his lips and nodded, rage swimming through his chest. He had specifically ordered Bauer not to arrest her, to keep her under surveillance. "Well done. I will go talk to Seargent Hans now."

"I know he was ready to see you whenever you got back."

"She's still in the cage. I assume that means she hasn't broken yet?"

He could see the look of discontent in his clerk's eyes as he looked at the cage and back at him. Clearly the young clerk didn't have much of a stomach for Marie's treatment. "Not to my knowledge. Not yet."

The way he answered made it clear that he felt she would certainly break. She would either break or she would die. Those were the only two possible outcomes.

"Very well." Exhibiting more agility than he actually felt, he pushed himself to his feet. "I'll be ready to tackle this work as soon as I hear a report from Hans."

Knowing that dismissed him, Kalb saluted and went back to his own desk. Leo looked at his watch and determined he could take another pain pill twenty minutes early.

‽ ‽ ‽ ‽

LEO stormed into the office of the head interrogator. "What is the meaning of this?" he spat out.

"Meaning of what, sir?" Sergeant Marco Hans asked warily.

"Is it not obvious you incompetent fool? What is the meaning of your treatment of the female prisoner?" Leo let his rage at Bauer flow through to Hans. He needed to make the man feel fear at the thought of his wrath. "The prisoner who was arrested without my orders and without my permission or foreknowledge."

"*Oberleutnant*, I am only doing my job," the older man said with disinterest. "What is it to you?" Leo knew that Hans had no respect for him due to his American citizenship, but, his usual disdain never came through with such insubordination.

"Where did you get your training, Sergeant? Let me guess. The gulags of our friends to the east?" Though the political landscape had recently changed, the Soviets had partnered with Germany for many years. Until very recently, Stalin had provided Hitler's Nazi party with safe ports for his U-boats, training, weapons, fuel, raw materials, and even rations. He waited for the Sergeant to offer a slight nod of confirmation before slamming his fist on the man's desk. "Idiot! That is not how you interrogate a French woman. You will get nothing from her using these tactics."

"What are you talking about?" The confusion on his face told Leo he truly didn't understand.

"You are treating her just like a male prisoner and your actions have cost us at least a week, if not two, of work for me. Have her removed to a private cell, and get her some dry clothes. See that her wounds are treated. Do it immediately."

"*Oberleutnant* Schäfer, I must protest. I personally trained with the *Schutzstaffel* in the Ukraine in 1939 and these tactics were very effective with the local women we interrogated there."

Reaching for patience, Leo explained, "Sergeant, when your SS friends beat and tortured a female villager to death without getting the information they needed, what did they do next?" He paused while the noncommissioned officer reflected. "What did they do, Sergeant? Did they simply take another woman into custody? How many women did they kill before they obtained the information they desired?"

The sergeant shrugged as if the lives of hundreds of helpless women meant so little to him.

"Fifty? A hundred? Let me speak plainly. Was it more than one? Because, Sergeant, we only have this single prisoner. Just the one. We do not have the luxury of every village in all of the Ukraine we can raid in the middle of the night. You understand?"

His logic started to make an impact because the Sergeant suddenly looked resentful, "Exactly what is your training, sir? How many interrogations did you perform in America, *Oberleutnant*? Who are you to tell me —"

Leo put his nose to the other man's and spoke very quietly and very firmly. "I assure you there are less desirable duty stations than France, Sergeant. Perhaps you would like to go back and visit some of your Soviet friends in Stalingrad? Who am I? I am your commanding officer, and if you don't follow my orders immediately, I can only assure you that you will regret it for the rest of your time in uniform."

The man came to sharp attention. "Yes, sir." He saluted and said, "*Heil* Hitler."

Leo casually returned the salute without even raising his hand above shoulder height. "*Sieg heil.*"

He left the man behind, feeling assured his orders would be followed exactly, and stormed through the halls of the prison offices. When he reached his own office, he was surprised to find *Kapitän* Neumann waiting behind his desk. He immediately came to attention, though the pain in his abdomen made him want to collapse in the chair currently occupied by his *Kapitän.*

"*Oberleutnant* Schäfer," the captain greeted, standing, "congratulations on the arrest."

"It was premature. We had her under surveillance and I did not know she was arrested until an hour ago."

The captain raised an eyebrow. "Do you need to be replaced as head of this facility?"

"Not at all, sir. I just need competent sergeants who don't act on their own accord without orders." And blatantly against orders, but he didn't add that. It would not do to let his commanding officer think he had no control over his enlisted men.

The captain froze and murmured, "Without orders?" The man began to pace around the office. Leo had not been told to stand at ease and thus had not moved from his position of attention. Therefore, he did not turn his head and visually track his commander as the captain paced around the room. Instead, he stared straight ahead, seething, hoping that Neumann would order him to have Sergeant Bauer arrested. He'd lock the cell himself.

"Why did your sergeant arrest her prematurely and without orders?" he asked, admiring a portrait print of his beloved *Führer* that hung on the wall.

"I had to go to Paris for a meeting. While I was gone, he acted. I think he wanted some glory. Instead, I think he's getting some prison time."

"Just have him beaten and be done with it." The captain waved a hand toward him then realized that the junior officer still stood in a stiff brace. Leo noted that his commander very carefully asked no questions about his Paris meeting. "At ease. What have you been able to glean from her so far? Anything?"

"Nothing. She's been beaten until she can't sit up by men twice her size. I suspect her jaw is broken. I don't know why they expected to get anything from her."

The captain met his eyes. "Did they violate the girl?"

Leo shrugged despite the fear that threatened to paralyze him at the thought. "I do not yet know, sir, but I think not."

"Does the girl have family?"

The question had plenty of depth. Did the girl have political connections? Would her rape while in custody prove an embarrassment? Is it possible they were mistaken about their quarry? Or could they arrest her family and use them as leverage?

"None here, sir. She is from the south of France originally."

The captain nodded then waved a hand. "If any of the men violated her, have them publically hanged. Best to set an example early on before the camp is built. Can't have any of the men sullying themselves with any of the filthy Jews we bring to the camp. We must keep the bloodlines pure for the glory of the Fatherland. If they think it's acceptable here with any female prisoner, they're going to continue to think it's acceptable there with those hairless apes."

With disgust coating his tongue, Leo nodded. "It will be done, sir. I'm not sure her interrogation can be salvaged."

The captain raised an eyebrow. "You have ideas of a different method?"

He thanked God for this unexpected opportunity. "Of course. She's a woman. Like all women she'll respond better to silk than to steel."

Neumann narrowed his eyes. "Rather American thinking. I suppose I should have expected no less."

Leo felt his cheeks burn, silently cursing his complexion that allowed the captain to see his visceral reaction even though he attempted to hide it from his expression. He was not embarrassed. Rage flooded his heart, causing the flush. "I cannot change where my father raised me, *Kapitän*. Besides, many great minds have come from America and been embraced by the likes of the *Führer* himself. Effinger, Pelley, Ezra Pound to name a few. Even now, Robert Henry Best is winning countless Americans to the great Nazi cause over the radio."

"Indeed." Neumann cocked his head and looked at Leo. He felt as if the commander studied him like a laboratory rat. "I read your file, *Oberleutnant*, as I do with every officer under my command. I know that William Dudley Pelley and the Friends of New Germany endorsed your commission and I know that none other than Rudolph Hess himself personally pinned on your rank. Very politically expedient, I'm sure. I am only observing that your thinking is very different than most European Aryans."

Leo wisely kept his mouth shut and wondered at the way that Neumann did not mention his father.

"I will give you three weeks to break her with your silky American kindness. Then, *Oberleutnant*, and I say this with all sincerity, *I* will make her talk using the steel."

The cold, dead look in the captain's eyes and the bored expression on his face reminded Leo of a viper watching a mouse. Men with even average intelligence would be well advised to find that look terrifying. Even so, three weeks was barely enough time to plan and execute a rescue. "Impossible. I need at least four weeks, sir. The girl has been beaten to within an inch of her life."

The captain retrieved his cap from the top of the desk. On his way out of the room, he stopped at Leo's shoulder. "Three. I have a schedule to keep."

"Understood sir." He clicked his heels together and saluted. "*Sieg heil.*"

"Yes, yes. *Heil* Hitler," the captain answered tiredly and without even raising his arm, he walked out of the room.

8 8 8 8

CHAPTER 5

Chapter Five

LEO balanced the food tray in one hand and unlocked the heavy cell door with the other. As he came in, Marie turned on her cot so that her feet touched the floor. He barely recognized her. One side of her face was so bruised and swollen she barely resembled a woman. She cradled her bandaged hand to her chest and stared at him, contempt and fear emanating from her one good eye.

After retrieving Mercy from the hospital so that she could tend to Marie's wounds, he had waited hours to approach her, fearing that if he appeared too eager, this opportunity to protect her would be taken from him. He carefully set the tray of broth, bread, and cheese on the cot and stood stiffly. He could feel his strength diminishing by the second.

"*Fräulein* Perrin, I must apologize for the treatment you've received here. I promise you that there will be no repeat of such treatment. You understand?"

Marie lifted the eyebrow of her good eye and picked up the cheese. "I beg your pardon?"

He wanted to reassure her that she was in the presence of a friend who would protect her at all costs. However, he did not have that option. Instead, he nodded stiffly. "This is my prison, but I was away. I did not even know they'd arrested you. Had I known —" He knelt next to her. As soon as his hand covered her bandaged one, he felt her stiffen. He ignored it and looked her in the eye, trying to silently convey his meaning. "If I had known I never would have allowed any of this to happen."

Her eye searched his face. Finally, she said, "I don't believe you."

Her courage was admirable. He smiled to help reassure her. "You don't?"

"No. I don't."

As per her training, she would assume he was nice to her only to get her to relax and reveal information to him. She would resist kindness. "Ah. Well, I shall simply avoid asking you any questions. Then maybe you'll start to trust my sincerity. I don't want to see you hurt, Marie." She had always intrigued him and he had felt inexplicably drawn to her the second he met her weeks ago. The longer he stayed in this room with her, the more that was true. "You will be safe here. My men are under orders not to come near you. Furthermore, I will personally provide for your care and see to your well-being."

"You?" She narrowed her eyes at him. Her mouth barely moved as she struggled to speak. "What do you get out of that?"

"Only the knowledge that a woman under my care isn't being tortured or in any other way … otherwise mistreated." He gracefully stood and ignored the pain in his stomach. If he didn't find a way to rest soon, he would likely collapse. "There is no right way to do the wrong thing. There are some things that are simply wrong even in a time of war."

He clicked his heels and stiffly nodded. "I pray that your injuries don't hurt you too much and that you heal quickly." The language choice of pray was intentional and to offer comfort to someone whom he knew to be deeply faithful. To further add to that comfort, he slipped his hand into the inside of his jacket and pulled out a small French translation of the King James Bible. "Please keep this hidden. I know it will bring you comfort, but if any guard sees it, they will take it and it may compromise me."

He was trusting her with his cover, possibly his very life, by giving her the Bible. If he thought he could get away with it, he would pray with her. Instead, he simply set the Bible on the cot next to her and said, "Good day, *Fräulein* Perrin."

8 8 8 8

LEO lay on his bed with his hands behind his head. He stared at the moonbeams shinging through his window, decorating the ornate ceiling of his room in the Valeurville Hotel. After time spent on his knees in prayer, he had climbed into bed, exhausted and in pain. The vision of Marie's beaten and bruised body, however, stole any immediate hope of sleep away from him.

On top of his duties that fell under the espionage umbrella, he had a prison to run that housed one hundred and twenty prisoners of war and dozens of high level political prisoners. With the *Führer* building a prisoner of war camp outside the town, he wondered what would happen to the prison. He expected it to be used to house more and more political prisoners. The longer the Nazi regime stayed in France, the more enemies it made, the more citizens would be arrested and interrogated.

Further down the road, he knew of another camp currently under construction. This one, he knew, would house political prisoners and Jews. Thankfully, he did not have to have a part in the construction of that facility.

With those two duties vying for his time, attention, and talents, he had, on his own accord, taken on the duty of protector, too. He could justify it with security – the longer he kept Marie safe, the longer the information contained in her mind would stay hidden from the enemy. But he knew it was more than a protection of information that drove him to keep her safe. He felt a very personal connection to her. While he stayed under cover, he did not have the freedom to explore the connection. But, he could protect her until Praetorian could get her out.

He could do absolutely nothing to aid in her escape, and he could provide no intelligence. Because he had stepped forward and risked his standing with Captain Neumann and his position in the prison in order to protect her, he had to be able to withstand the most vigorous scrutiny. What he wanted was to pick her up and carry her out of the prison, but he could do nothing.

Because of his conversation with Captain Neumann, he had the freedom to interact with her, provide her with medical care, and take care of her. While he was thankful for that, unfortunately, he could go no further. He could only pray for the team arranging her rescue.

He closed his eyes, feeling the buzz of the pain pill he'd taken thirty minutes ago finally kick in. As the pain faded from his abdomen, he willed his body to relax and rest, knowing that sleep would only help his body heal faster.

♙ ♙ ♙ ♙

"WHY are you giving me such attention?" Marie asked. It was the first thing she had said since he entered the cell that morning and her voice sounded hoarse. She kept her lips pressed tightly together and spoke quietly, as if pitching her voice to a puppet. Leo had visited her in the early morning hours every day for the last four days. They spent as many hours talking about inane subjects as they did political ones. He enjoyed her views on the political topics very much. "I can't imagine that your *Führer* would approve."

Leo bristled at the idea that anything about Adolf Hitler could be considered "his". He bit his tongue to keep from retorting with that fact and instead settled in more comfortably on the folding chair he'd brought into the cell with him. Every day, he felt stronger and in less pain. "My captain calls it my silky American kindness. I'll take that as a compliment and not change my ways."

She wrapped her arm around her middle and leaned forward to cough. He frowned, watching as she clearly struggled with the pain of coughing with broken ribs. He looked around the room, at the stone walls and concrete floor, and thought of the damp air in the centuries old building.

Before he could ask her about the cough, she looked up at him with a serious expression on the unbattered side of her face. "Why would you volunteer to come be part of a military that has such a disregard for human life? You could have joined the military in America and fought them. Instead, you chose to become one of them."

There were so many things he wanted to tell her. But he could not take the risk. Right now, she suffered no interrogation. But he didn't know what tomorrow would bring, and he couldn't guarantee that he would always be there to protect her. "I believe this is where God would have me." That was as close to the truth as he could get.

With a snarl she spat out, "God? You dare suggest God would have anything to do with the evil that is perpetrated by the Third Reich?"

He smiled. "You have no fear, do you?"

As soon as he said it, he regretted it, because her face fell. "I am afraid all the time," she admitted.

Despite the fact that she flinched away from him, he reached forward and took her unbandaged hand. "I so admire your courage. When this war is over –" he stopped and took a breath. "If nothing else, my presence saved your life. Have you not thought of that? You don't think that God works even in the midst of evil?"

"I wouldn't dare to pretend to know the mind of God or presume to know what God would or would not do. I can tell you that during my time in that cage, I struggled with the feeling that God had abandoned me entirely." She pulled her hand away to cough again, this time nearly doubling over. It took her a long time to straighten back up again. She leaned back against the stone wall. "I'm tired. Please go away."

He didn't like the sound of the cough. Maybe he should get Mercy. "Please try to eat what's on your tray. I will come back at the end of my shift."

"Your sergeant broke my jaw. It makes eating what's on my tray difficult." She lay on the cot and turned her back to him, clearly dismissing him.

He felt his hands ball into fists. His sergeant *had* broken her jaw. It made him want to beat the man all over again. Without another word, he turned and left the cell, leaving his folding chair behind. Perhaps she'd enjoy sitting on something other than the lone cot.

He went to his office. It was still early, and his clerk wouldn't arrive for another hour. On his desk sat letters that had arrived for the POW's. As part of his duties, he had to read them and keep track of pertinent information that may prove useful in the future, see if any secure information made it through the British sensors, and check that no contraband was smuggled in via the post.

As he skimmed the letters, he found one from Dorothy Ewing to her husband Tom. He knew Dorothy operated under the code name Charity and that this letter would be in response to the information that Marie was detained in this prison. As he read it, he marveled at how deeply the code was embedded. Nothing read out of place, nothing sounded wrong. He didn't personally know the code, but even knowing the code existed didn't make anything in the seemingly intimate letter of a wife to a husband out of place.

He made sure that the mail would be delivered to the prisoners immediately. Next, he drafted reports about the most recent detainees and the results of interrogation. As he typed, he tried to pretend he didn't know what would happen to those poor souls next. He knew he worked for a greater good, but a thousand times a day he wished that he could intervene. His father had tried to prepare him, intellectually and emotionally, but when his love for Christ reinforced his love for his fellow man, he suffered inside for what these innocent – and not so innocent – French citizens endured.

As he worked, the work force gradually shifted from the night crew to the day crew. When the clock on the corner of his desk read nine o'clock, he finished the last report, added it to the stack for his clerk to process, and went in search of *Kapitän* Richter. He found him at a table in the canteen, drinking a cup of coffee while he read a file.

Leo approached the table, came to attention, and saluted. "*Sieg heil!*"

The captain left him standing there a little longer than necessary before he looked at him over his glasses. "What is it, *Oberleutnant* Schäfer?"

"Sir, the prisoner Marie Perrin is ill. I would like permission to have a nurse from the hospital come and look at her."

"What do I care about a sick French woman, *Oberleutnant*? She is an enemy of the Reich. If she speaks, if she gives the information that Sergeant Hans seeks, then she can receive medical care." His voice sounded bored. "Use it as an incentive."

"Sir, if she truly is a wireless operator, we could intercept radio codes and analyze them using her knowledge. But if she dies before she speaks, then the information she has will be lost."

He closed the file and took off his glasses. "Then that will be one less prisoner to feed. You are dismissed, *Oberleutnant*."

It took great discipline to keep from grabbing the neck of the arrogant German and squeezing until – with a sigh, he turned on his heel and marched out of the canteen. The only option left was to ask Kapitän Neumann. Because he was the one who originally gave Leo permission to experiment with treating Marie with kindness, he could very easily counter Kapitän Richter's denial of medical care. But he wouldn't be back to the prison until tomorrow morning.

Worried about her, he went back to her cell. She still lay on her side, facing the wall, the way he'd left her hours before. Her food tray sat where he left it, still untouched.

"Marie?" He asked, approaching the cot.

She turned and looked at him, her eyes glassy and her face flushed. When she opened her mouth to speak, she coughed, curling into a ball from the obvious pain.

"I will get you Mercy, Marie."

Her eyes widened at the use of Mercy's code name. He smiled reassuringly. "Things aren't always as they seem, are they?" He put a hesitant hand on her shoulder. He could feel her skin burn through her dress. "Try to hang in there."

Chapter Six

LEO held Marie's frail frame as she retched up the medicine he'd given her about thirty minutes before. He could feel the heat from the fever radiating off her body. Mercy had said the medication would make her sick, but to try to keep it in her as long as possible. He didn't know if she had processed a single dose in the 24-hours since he'd started giving it to her.

He needed to get her to the hospital. *Kapitän* Richter had barely recovered any kind of civility toward him since he had gone over his head to Neumann to bring Mercy in. He knew that the answer would be a flat no if he requested transferring her to the hospital. He would wait until tonight when Neumann would be here.

Leo smoothed Marie's hair back from her face and placed a fresh damp cloth on her forehead. For the last two days, she had been incoherent. She occasionally opened her eyes, but she never spoke of anything that made sense. Once she'd called him Edward, and once Papa, but so far, it appeared that she no longer had any idea she was a prisoner in a Nazi prison cell. He prayed that she didn't start sharing mission related information in her delirium.

The medicine dispelled from her body, she started to relax and go into a deep sleep, broken only by coughing fits brought on by the pneumonia attacking both her lungs. When he knew she was settled, Leo put the medicine in his pocket and left the cell.

He contemplated removing her without permission, taking her to the hospital or even his hotel room. The hotel would certainly provide a cleaner, drier environment, but, he could not risk his position. The strategic foothold they currently enjoyed due to his military success could not be jeopardized. Leo had to remind himself of that almost every minute of every day. The mission had to come first.

He received the evening report from the lieutenant in charge of the night shift, then left the prison. His eyes burned with exhaustion brought on by sitting by Marie's bedside for most of the night. Deciding he would get a cup of coffee and some breakfast at the café on the corner, he crossed the street and started walking down the sidewalk. In his tired state, his steps almost faltered when he saw the sign in the café window announcing day-old bread for sale. That was one of his cues, a signal. He had to go to Bourges and meet with his father.

Instead of going into the café, he turned around and headed back to the hotel. He needed to pack some supplies, and he had to create a cover story before the eleven o'clock train left the station.

"SEEN your mother lately?" Karl Schäfer asked as he poured tea. The dishes from the shared late lunch still covered the table in his hotel suite. He would have them removed after their meeting. Instead of a military uniform, he wore a tailored suit and a white starched shirt.

"It's been a few months." Leo stretched his booted feet out and rested his head against the back of the settee. It felt good to speak English so freely. "Once I got the promotion, we felt the risk was too great. Now I get coded communiqués from time to time."

Karl sighed as he picked up his cup and settled back in the chair. "I miss her."

Leo smiled. "I know she misses you, too."

His father lifted his tea cup. "I can't imagine how she's handling her tea without sugar."

Thinking of the sweet leaves his mother had started putting in her tea, a gift from the Texan pilot, he smiled. "She has resources."

With a bark of a laugh, Karl replied, "I have no doubt!" His face sobered. "I'm quite ready for this war to be over and for our lives to be given back to us, to return to normal."

"Given back?" Leo straightened and met his father's gaze. "Your entire marriage has been fighting a war, preparing for the next one, and fighting that one. We don't have lives. We have missions. There is no normal for us Schäfers."

A smirk crossed Karl's lips. "Perhaps I'm ready for what normal could be."

On a sigh, Leo said, "Me, too." Would there ever be a normal life for him? Did he have a wife in his future? Children? A job that didn't require a uniform or deadly weapons? He rubbed his tired eyes. "What can I do for you, Father?"

"Virginia Benoit's upcoming concert is bringing in some big names. Many of the high ranks will be in one place for one night and they are all high value targets. We need to see what kind of strategies we can put together for eavesdropping and possible sabotage or assassination."

Leo shook his head. "We are going to be conducting the largest prison break in the history of this war. I imagine Praetorian's resources will be stretched thin."

"That is true for the time during the performance and after. Do you know if Colonel Müller is planning a reception of any sort?"

He pursed his lips as he considered what his father suggested. This would be an unprecedented opportunity. "I'll have my clerk make inquiries. If so, Praetorian would need to get some waitstaff and cooks on hand."

"Exactly what I was thinking." Karl leaned forward. "How are you feeling, lad?"

Without thinking, he put his hand on his stomach. "It doesn't hurt as badly as before, but my energy level is still very low."

"It's bound to be for a bit yet." He sat back again. "I heard about you and the girl. What is her status?"

"She's very ill. It looks grave. I fear we may not get her out alive." Saying it out loud tasted bad in his mouth. "I am trying to nurse her, but I have to use caution and not show her too much attention."

"Can't risk someone else doing it, eh?"

"No, sir. She is delirious in her fever now. She needs to be completely isolated." He looked at his watch. "I had hoped to speak to Captain Neumann about transferring her to hospital, but he would be gone by now."

Karl took a sip of his tea. "Thinking about it, it might be better to keep her where she is. Her rescue can be masked under the prison breakout and not get muddled by another location." He looked at his watch. "Right then, time to get you back to the station. Get some rest on the train if you can."

Knowing how formal they would have to be later, the men shared a long embrace. "I enjoyed having dinner with you, even if there were ulterior motives for the meeting."

Karl chuckled and slapped Leo on the shoulder affectionately. "All of this could have been done in five minutes. I enjoyed dinner with you, as well." He stared into Leo's eyes. "Get some sleep on the train. I mean it."

❖ ❖ ❖ ❖

FRANZ Kalb jumped to attention when Leo walked into the outer part of his office. Leo waved at him, granting him permission to return to his seat. "Did you hear back from *Oberst* Müller's people?"

"Yes, sir! There will be an open house reception starting at eighteen hundred hours to accommodate the officers as they arrive." Franz dug through the stack of papers on his desk and pulled one out. "Here is the name of the restaurant that will be providing the food and waitstaff."

Leo memorized the name of the company without taking the paper or even appearing to read it. "I don't need that. I just wanted to ensure we didn't need to assist with any details."

"His clerk knows I am available whenever he needs me." Franz handed Leo a stack of official communications. "The British captain upstairs is demanding a Red Cross visit. He is complaining again about using the prisoners for labor in building the POW camp."

Leo allowed himself to snarl with believable disgust. "Shall we wipe their bottoms for them, too?"

Franz laughed despite himself. "Shall I relay that to him, sir?"

"I'll go up there later today. I have to inspect the cells today anyway."

❖ ❖ ❖ ❖

CHAPTER 7

Chapter Seven

LEO walked Mercy from Marie's cell and through the prison. They had just prayed over the frail and fevered woman. He knew what Mercy wasn't saying – she needed medical care and she needed it last week. Even though the breakout of the prison would happen tonight, it wasn't soon enough. The only way she could survive at this point was through divine intervention from God Himself.

After walking Mercy out of the prison, he headed back to his office, stopping for a moment in the privacy of the stairwell. It just occurred to him that Marie's rescue would mean he would no longer have daily contact with her. He suddenly wished that didn't have to be the case. Where had these thoughts come from?

What would it be like, he wondered, to have met Marie outside of this terrible war? Would she have found him attractive? Would they have had an opportunity to get to know each other, fall in love perhaps?

Shaking his head, he mentally kicked himself. Too many events and duties competed in his life right now to afford him the luxury of thoughts like that! He clearly needed a good night's sleep and a reminder of the current situation.

Nevertheless, his heart and mind continued to war with each other as he went about the duties of his day, preparing for the arrival of many high ranking officers to their little corner of Occupied France. The stage construction outside the prison had finishing touches applied, chairs filled the yard, and the restaurant staff - hand-picked by Praetorian's team - arrived to serve those officers who came early enough to enjoy the open house style reception.

As afternoon gave way to evening, Leo could almost feel the tension in the air. He wondered if it came from the occupying Germans who felt nervous in the presence of such notable high ranking officers coming to the concert, or if it came from the prisoners who knew tonight would afford them an opportunity to make their escape.

"Sir," Franz said, interrupting his concentration on the schedule for tonight's events, "you wanted me to inform you when Virginia Benoit arrived. She is here, sir, and in the office *Herr Oberst* had converted to a dressing room for her."

Leo nodded and looked back at the paper in his hand, trying to look annoyed. "I'll go see to our ebony skinned guest in a few minutes. Thank you."

"Did you know her, sir? In America?"

Leo smiled. "Miss Benoit?" His clerk had an eager look on his face. Clearly, the young man had a touch of starstruck. "America is a very large country. Her home and my home were as far apart as Finland and Spain." At the widening of Franz's eyes, he knew the young German had very little concept of the size of the United States. Rather nostalgically, he added, "But it will be nice to speak English for a moment today, even if it is only with a Negro woman."

Franz cleared his throat as he looked at a notebook. "I confess it is difficult to think of you as an American."

"You don't think I look like Clark Gable, Franz?" Leo asked with a grin.

Franz very seriously answered, "Not at all. You look far more Aryan."

Leo considered the remark and realized his clerk meant it as a compliment. He intentionally preened and quietly said, "Thank you."

"Will you be attending the reception, *Oberleutnant*?"

Leo shook his head. "*Nein.* I will leave the elbow rubbing to the higher ranks." He looked at his watch. "Why don't you go take your evening meal early then enjoy the concert. I will see you bright and early tomorrow."

His clerk grinned. "*Danke, Oberleutnant!*"

As Franz left, Leo put his pen down and sat back in his chair. He felt restless. Knowing the plans in place and that the wheels had begun to turn made him want to *do* something. He pushed his chair back and surged to his feet. Maybe he would check on Marie one more time before she was no longer his responsibility.

He walked into the outer room. Every desk was empty. As Praetorian's team had hoped, the upcoming concert and the presence of the visiting dignitaries had distracted and drained the staff. It spoke well for possible success if things remained this predictable.

As he walked past the desk sergeant's duty station, the telephone rang. Just as Leo answered it, Sergeant Ernst Bauer marched into the room from the stairwell. "Yes?" Leo barked into the phone.

"This is headquarters. Artillery reports they shot down an enemy airplane a few kilometers from the airfield. Observers spotted no parachutes. Send someone out to inspect the wreckage and secure any enemy survivors."

An enemy airplane. This must be Faith – Marie's ticket home. Leo knew the situation but he also knew he had to play the game or suffer from suspicion. "Why are you calling the prison? Is this not the job for the Military Police or the Quick Reaction Force?"

"Your *Oberst* volunteered the prison garrison for this duty tonight in exchange for having his *schwarze* dog perform her concert. You have your orders?"

Clearly, the soldiers staffing headquarters tonight either wished they could attend the concert or were not fans of Miss Benoit's performances. "Give me the coordinates."

Leo hung up the telephone and looked at Sergeant Bauer. "We have a downed plane. Come with me. We need to check it out."

He could see the bristling in the sergeant's countenance as he would have to accompany the very *Oberleutnant* who'd had him beaten for arresting Marie against very explicit orders. But, like a good soldier, he went to the keybox near the stairwell door, secured a set of keys, and opened the door for his *Oberleutnant*.

In the *Kübelwagen*, Leo studied the map and worked out the coordinates while Sergeant Bauer drove. Within a few minutes, they found the wrecked Avro. A quick inspection revealed no one inside. Leo checked his watch by the light of the burning aircraft. The concert would begin within the hour. Now it appeared that the escapees would have no means of escape.

"There is an airfield just that way," the sergeant said, pointing west. "They may have been trying to bomb it."

"No bombs. This is either an empty bomber or a cargo plane. But, if they know about the airfield, they may try to steal an airplane to get back to England."

"The airfield is very secure, *Oberleutnant*. We can radio them to be on the lookout if you like."

Leo gave the man a droll look, as if witheringly disappointed by the noncommissioned officer's laziness. "We'd best check it out ourselves, just to be thorough."

Back in the *Kübelwagen*, Leo checked his watch again, willing the sergeant to drive faster. As they pulled up to the fence surrounding the airfield on the outskirts of Valeurville, he saw dozens of airplanes lined up like props in a child's soldier set. The number of aircraft far exceeded any he had ever seen in this airfield at one time. Each of the high ranking officers and dignitaries who had arrived for tonight's show had apparently arrived in his own airplane along with his staff.

"There," Leo said, pointing to the figures that dashed out of the tree line. "Be quiet and let's surprise them."

They entered through the gate and intercepted the duo as they sprinted toward the Junkers JU-52 farthest down the line, closest to the runway, furthest from the lights on the field.

Sergeant Bauer hastily raised his rifle and shouted. "*Halt!*"

Leo recognized the small frame of the pilot code-named Faith. The man running next to her reached out and grabbed her arm and the two of them stopped running.

"*Halt, oder ich schießen!*" Bauer barked, threatening to shoot them dead. Then the Sergeant hastily chambered a round in his Mouser rifle and the two prisoners raised their hands about their heads.

"*Was machst du, hier?*"

Leo watched with curiosity as Faith slowly turned her head to look at the man next to her, then whispered to him and slowly turned around, keeping her hands above her head. Leo drew his Luger Parabellum pistol from its holster and aimed it in her general direction, though his trigger finger lay alongside the trigger guard on the slide, far from the trigger itself.

The sight of a young woman apparently rattled Bauer. "*Was machst du, hier, Fraulein? Beantworte die Fragen!*" The sergeant yelled.

"*Nicht Sprechen sie Deutsch!*" Faith proclaimed, fascinatingly, with a Texas accent. He honestly didn't think he'd ever heard German spoken with a Texas drawl before.

Leo could see the sadism behind the smile on Sergeant Bauer's face.

Sarcastically, he mixed German and French to ask, "*Ja? Est-ce vrai? Qu'est-ce que vous faites ici?*"

Faith closed her eyes and sighed. "Maybe stick with Kraut. I pretty much don't speak French, either, Jerry," she answered through her teeth.

Leo tried not to smile, but it was hard. The young woman was feisty! He decided the time had come to intervene. In English, he drawled, "That's because you're from Lamarr, Texas."

Recognition dawned on Faith's face as she gasped. In German again, he said, "Arrest them and be done with it. I don't want to miss the show tonight."

As the man stepped forward with his rifle raised, Leo did not hesitate. He aimed his weapon at the back of the man's head. He kept the base of the man's skull perfectly in his gun sights, laid his finger carefully on the trigger, and fired two rapid shots. The man fell lifelessly to the ground as Faith's companion turned, aiming a Sten submachine gun right at him. Before he could react, duck, or fire back, Faith's hand shot out and grabbed the muzzle of the mean looking gun, pushing it down toward the ground.

"No! Not him," she yelled.

Leo knelt down and laid his fingers along the sergeant's neck, verifying that the man was indeed dead. With a nod, he slipped his pistol back into its holster.

When his eyes finally met hers, he drawled, "Faith. I take it you were the one flying that rather noisy ball of fire that crashed a few kilometers away a bit earlier this evening?"

"What are you doing here?" she demanded.

"Looking for you, of course. I'm glad I found you." He glanced up and his eyes ran across the tail of the Junkers in front of them. The SS Colonel who had come in that plane had not come to enjoy a concert by the famous American. No, he imagined he was here to arrest Miss Benoit because her skin looked something other than pearly white.

With a clipped British accent, Faith's companion interjected, "I feel like a bit of a third wheel, Faith. Care to make introductions?"

"Harry, this is Valor. You never met him and you won't speak of ever meeting him. Assuming we live to talk about it."

Harry nodded then offered a gloved hand. "In that case, couldn't be happier to make your acquaintance."

Leo smirked at the witticism in the midst of such a tense situation and nodded. He briefly gripped the man's hand and answered in English, "Likewise, I'm sure."

Faith gestured toward the corpse of the sergeant lying face down in the grass. "I'm just curious. So, you know, what in the world?"

Leo knew she was asking how he could just shoot a man in the back of the head. She had no idea about the sadism of this particular sergeant, of his joy in beating women and weaker men, of how he bragged about the things he did to defenseless Jewish teen girls in the town. She could not know the service Leo had just performed for the town in which he covertly served. Instead of explaining, he kept it simple. "He disobeyed my direct orders, arrested Temperance, and beat her to within an inch of her life. I would have had him shot already if I hadn't been given direct orders to the contrary."

"Did you have to kill him?"

Did he have to kill him? He tried to imagine any scenario that left the man alive and still accomplished the mission, but his imagination failed him. He was reminded of Ecclesiastes' assurance that there was, indeed, a time to kill. "I doubt he would have refrained from killing you, even if I had asked nicely."

The horror on her face was almost his undoing. She took a deep breath and said, "I'm sorry. You don't owe me an explanation." She pointed at the Junkers. "Valor, we need that plane."

"I know. And now you're free to take it."

She raised an eyebrow. "Well, gosh. You gonna sign a hand receipt, too? Maybe assign us a steward for an in-flight meal?"

"Take it, but don't get caught." He did not smile in return. He could almost hear time clicking away and he had to get back to the prison. "I recognize that plane. It belongs to an SS Colonel who isn't here to enjoy a concert. I have to go and see to Hope."

"How will you explain this?"

He smirked, thinking of the phone call to the prison. He had never identified himself on the phone, and as far as he knew, no one saw him leave with Sergeant Bauer. "You killed the sergeant whom I sent to investigate the crash. His incompetence allowed you to steal an aircraft. I was never here."

She stepped forward and put a hand on his arm. "And you? How will you deal with this?"

"I'll deal with it in God's good time, Faith." Right now, he had a mission. He could deal with his feelings on the matter of ending another human being's the life later, after he knew Marie was safely in the air, when he could find himself on his knees, a Bible in his hand. "Godspeed, Faith. I pray we'll meet again."

"Not like this," she said as she lifted her hand before she and Harry jogged to the trimotor airplane. Leo waited only long enough to see Harry open the door before he took off at a run. He could not take the vehicle in which they'd arrived because it would raise questions as to how Sergeant Bauer got to the air field. Resigned, he jogged into town and through the nearly empty streets.

Precious time passed before he knocked on Virginia Benoit's dressing room door.

"Yes?" she called loudly.

Pausing for just a moment, he used a handkerchief to wipe the sweat from his face and made sure his breathing slowed. After jogging nearly two miles in boots, he fought the demands of his still healing body to find a place to sit and rest. Prepared to face another human being, he opened the door and stepped into the office that had been converted to a temporary dressing room. The most famous performer in Europe stood and faced him. He could not help but be struck momentarily speechless by her beauty. She was tall and thin with chocolate colored skin and beautiful coffee colored eyes. Her sparkling red dress had a plunging neckline and hugged every curve of her body from her shoulders to the floor. She'd somehow fastened gemstones along her hairline and the light in the dressing room reflecting off them almost caused a glow around her face.

From the look of terror on her face to the rapid movement of her eyes, he knew something had happened here. "How may I help you, sir?"

He had thought to charm her, but needed her to shore herself up to get onto stage. "I am *Oberleutnant* Leopold Schäfer. This is my prison."

Virginia raised her eyebrows. "I was under the impression that this prison is Colonel Müller's responsibility."

"You are correct. *Herr Oberst* Müller is responsible for four prisons in this sector and I report to him. This prison is under my command." He stepped closer to her but did not shut the door behind him. She held her breath and her eyes dilated. "I did not know that your show had been moved up. When *Herr* General Schmid's men arrived yesterday to construct your stage, it was the first I had heard of your rescheduled performance. I do not like arrangements like this being made without my knowledge or consent."

Virginia licked her lips and spoke in a breathless voice. "I apologize. I do not have any experience in the politics of your military. I just have a General and a Colonel telling me when to be where."

He cocked his head and looked at her. "As do I," he said in English with a laugh.

"You're American. Where are you from?" she asked in perfect southern-accented English.

He raised both eyebrows. "Oregon."

Continuing in English, Virginia answered, "I'm from St. Louis by way of New Orleans."

"I know exactly who you are." As her face fell at his words, he gentled his voice slightly. "Even if I hadn't, I thought I heard a twang in your French."

"You heard no such thing." She shifted her long red skirts and sashayed across the room to the tea service that sat on a table by the couch. As she bent, he heard her gasp in pain and start to reach her hand toward her abdomen. Curious, he examined the room. In the corner from behind a dressing screen, he saw the tip of a black boot. Could that boot possibly be on the foot of an incapacitated German SS Colonel, owner of the aircraft currently commandeered by a pilot code-named Faith? "Would you care for some tea?"

"No, thank you." His gaze didn't leave the boot until he felt sure she observed his gaze. Then he turned a blank face back in her direction.

She lifted her cup. "I do hope you will enjoy the performance, even if you didn't get to approve it," she said with a flirtatious smile as she took a sip of her tea.

"I hope so, too," he replied. He could not risk anyone else coming into this room. Somehow, he had to start his cover story. "I confess I have been looking forward to meeting you. I will return in a moment." He clicked the heels of his highly shined jack boots and left the room, shutting the door behind him. In the hall, he found the young lieutenant who had been assigned to see to the needs of the famous singer.

"I will be escorting Miss Benoit to the stage. What time is she due to be on?"

"Five minutes, sir," the lieutenant replied, looking at his watch. "I was just on my way to give her the time."

"I'll handle it. Thank you, *Leutnant*."

Clearly dismissed, the younger man turned and Leo knocked sharply on the door of the room, then re-entered. He saw Virginia seated on the couch, her fist against her mouth, her eyes wide with fear.

She clearly forcibly relaxed then smiled at him. "No matter how big or small the venue, I always get a little jumpy right before a show."

Dryly, he replied, "I find that astonishing, Miss Benoit, given your credentials and years of experience."

Virginia took a deep breath and let out an exaggerated sigh. "It's true. Please don't let on. Underneath the glamorous gowns and the makeup, I'm still just a southern girl from small town America."

He stared at her and shook his head. "I would not be overly concerned about this crowd if I were you. The men are in such need of distraction after months of boredom, a monkey grinding a hand organ would surely entertain them at this point."

The look of pain that crossed her face made him regret his words. He so very much wanted to ask her about what happened before. Perhaps, one day, they could meet away from such a hostile environment. He looked around, trying to find clues.

"Have you seen me perform before?"

He shook his head. "I'm afraid not. But I am very much looking forward to it."

Virginia stood, placing herself between him and the dressing screen, clearly trying to block his view of the boot. "It's only a bit early. Would you escort me to the stage, sir? We could continue our conversation until it's time to perform."

"It will be my honor. And I hope it isn't forward of me to propose that we speak together more before you must depart, Miss Benoit. My English has suffered greatly in the last few months since my arrival."

She clearly attempted to dazzle him with a very practiced smile. "An opportunity to speak more with a handsome young officer in Hitler's mighty Army? What kind of red blooded woman could refuse such an offer?"

Chapter Eight

LEO rushed up the stairwell and through the door. He saw no other person. Sergeant Bauer should have been manning the desk. Instead, he lay lifeless on the ground near where a Junkers JU-52 had once been parked.

His hand trembled a bit as he pulled his hat from his head and unlocked his office door. The intellectual knowledge about what had happened, how it had happened, and the need for it to have happened in order to aid the greater good didn't detract from the fact that he'd taken a man's life. The image of the body falling, lifeless, started replaying itself in his mind over and over again.

He collapsed in his office chair and closed his eyes. Fatigue rippled through him. What he wouldn't give for just a single night in his bed in his own home.

Faintly, through the walls a few floors below him, he could hear Virginia Benoit singing. He shouldn't have been surprised that she began her concert with the German national anthem. The longer she sang, the louder the accompanying voices of those in the audience singing with her became. He looked at his watch and noted that he had about thirty seconds, so he moved to the doorway of his office, away from the outer wall. Nervous excitement sharpened his senses. He felt the rumble of the explosion and heard a loud blast followed by two more consecutive blasts. Without waiting for the concussion to stop, he raced into the area that housed the prisoners, grabbing the large key ring from the wall.

He could not risk the exposure that would come from letting the other secure prisoners out of their cells. But, he quietly unlocked Marie's door and went into her cell. She lay curled in a fetal position on her cot, her skin pale and gray, her breath shallow and uneven.

Using more familiarity with her than he'd ever shown before, he gently scooped her into his arms. She moaned and he cradled her to him, tucking her head under his chin, pressing his lips to her forehead. Her skin burned, scorching his lips. He didn't think he'd ever felt human skin so hot before. With his eyes closed, he gently held her and whispered a prayer over her.

"Please, God, get her to safety. Protect her and shield her. Let her live through this war." Without knowing he spoke the longing of his own heart, he added, "So I can find her after."

He heard the door to the stairwell open and stepped out of the cell and into the hall. There he saw the spy code-named Abiel and the young dark haired Jewish woman code-named Grace.

"We'll shoot the cell open," Grace said.

"No need," Leo replied. Grace raised her gun and trained it on him, a fierce look on her face. He knew without a doubt that had he not been holding Marie in his arms, she wouldn't have hesitated to pull the trigger. Yet, he felt no fear, all his attention focused on getting Marie away from the prison.

He walked toward them as Abiel very angrily said, "You are blowing your cover."

"She is more important than my cover." He meant it. When did she become more important than his cover? What did this mean?

Grace looked from his face to Marie's. "Who are you?" Knowing he needed to relinquish Marie to them, he hugged her a little tighter to his chest.

"Who he is means nothing anymore," Abiel bit out. "He's foolish. Let me have her, Valor."

Feeling his heart rip in two, he handed her over to his colleague, whom he knew to be Marie's brother. Looking at her face one more time, he willed her to open her eyes with clarity and see him. She did not. Abiel took her from him and turned, running back toward the door.

Desperate, he said to Grace, "I did everything I could. She needs medication. The nurse gave me some to slip to her, but it's just been in her water and I haven't been able to get her to drink any all day."

She put her hand on his arm in a clear attempt to comfort him. "We will take care of her." She gestured to a chair at a desk. "Sit. We need to give you cover."

He sat down and picked up the phone. "Tell her I'll find her," he said seconds before Grace used the butt of her pistol and knocked him across the back of his head. He barely felt the pain as his world went black.

§ § § §

THE pain in his head almost overwhelmed the nauseous feeling swirling in his stomach. What happened? His training had taught him to snap to situational awareness so he didn't risk giving anything away, even in a medical situation, but his memory remained foggy. No. Wait. Marie.

Grace had hit him in the back of the head. He could hear people milling about, could smell the disinfectant, could see the bright lights through his eyelids – he clearly was in the hospital.

Putting a hand to his head, he groaned and opened his eyes. He still wore his uniform. Had he revealed anything in his unconscious state? Perhaps murmuring in delirium? Did his cover remain tight? Would they recognize his gunshot as a gunshot and not appendix surgery? Wobbling a bit, he stumbled out of the room where he'd been lying on a cot.

"Sir!" a nurse called to him in German with a French accent, "you must get back in bed."

He smiled very charmingly at her as he gestured at the chaos all around. "There are so many who need that bed more than I. I assure you that I am fine."

"The doctor –"

"Will be thankful for one less head injury, I'm sure." He tried to walk straight as he walked through the mass of injured humans and out into the fresh air. Seconds later his feet gave out from under him and he collapsed to the ground as his world turned black again.

§ § § §

"I'M sure you know you have some explaining to do," *Kapitän* Neumann stood next to Leo's hospital bed, his hat tucked under his arm, his expression very serious. "Your prisoners of war escaped and we've only been able to recover thirty-seven of them."

Leo licked his dry lips, wishing he could have his conversation fully dressed and in uniform, not helplessly lying in a hospital bed in striped pajamas. "*Oberst* Müller is the one who arranged everything."

"Indeed. And *Herr* Müller is facing a tribunal as we speak." Leo couldn't help but notice the lack of military rank assigned to Müller. "It seems that his Negro performer has also disappeared. Two murdered members of the SS were found in her dressing room. Apparently, her talents didn't end at singing."

If Hope, Virginia, had escaped, maybe Marie got away, too. "What SS? Why was the SS in the lady's dressing room?"

Neumann pursed his lips. "We shall never know. I don't think that they appreciated her – talents – in the same way *Herr* Müller did."

Treading as carefully as he could, he asked, "If the prisoners of war escaped, why was I knocked out? I had no POW's on that floor."

He raised an eyebrow. "Didn't you hear? Your wireless operator also escaped. Somehow, her rescuers stole a German plane and flew it back over the channel." Neumann stepped forward. "The very same wireless operator you had spent so much time with, by the way."

"*Fräulein* Perrin escaped?"

"This concerns you?"

Leo frowned. "I am only surprised, *Kapitän. Fräulein* Perrin was on the very edge of death when I last checked in on her. Hardly worth the effort to rescue, I should think. Better simply to kill her if she were indeed a wireless operator."

"You think she was innocent?"

Leo gave Neumann a frank stare. "I confess it is a possibility. We have only the word of the farmer's wife. The woman was odious. She struck me as unreliable at best. Despite the wireless machine in *Fräulein* Perrin's quarters, she did not have a code book. I believe Bauer simply enjoys hurting helpless females and isn't above framing someone he may have taken a shine to. I do not trust his instincts regarding that prisoner." He intentionally spoke of Bauer in the present tense.

Neumann leaned forward very slightly. His baleful stare began to take a toll on Leo's calm. "You seem to have taken an unusual interest in that prisoner as well, *Oberleutnant* Schäfer. Why should I trust your instincts regarding her?"

Leo lowered his brows as if confused. "I merely tried to build a rapport with her so that I could glean information from her."

"Perhaps you were keeping her alive until her rescue could be accomplished."

"I think I see where this is going." Head pounding, heart rate accelerating, Leo forced his face to remain stoic and calm. "*Kapitän* Neumann, just because I was raised in America, I assure you that I won't be the scapegoat for failures on the part of others. Müller arranged the concert wth a Negro without my knowledge. He planned it while I was in Paris. I don't appreciate your implying that I would have anything to do with that. If you have questions about SS involvement and espionage, I assume you are free to ask him. And, *Kapitän*, if you have any concerns about my loyalty to the Reich, there are a number of high ranking officers with whom you can voice those concerns. I will be happy to arrange personal meetings if you wish, since most are good friends of my father. Thank you for visiting me while I am recovering from my injuries. My father will surely appreciate your concern. I'm sure you've already notified him of my current condition."

He closed his eyes, more fatigued than he liked. He rarely leveraged his father's high ranking position, but he felt weaker by the second and needed to end the interrogation. Several seconds went by before he heard Neumann walk out of his room.

☙☙☙☙

Six months later

LEO walked into the Berlin hotel lobby and spotted his father seated near the fire, reading a paper. He approached and Karl stood, folding the paper under his arm. "It's good to see you, my boy," he said in German.

Leo felt a wave of emotion wash over him at the familiar greeting. Six months had passed since the prison breakout. He had been removed as director of the prison and placed in an administrative position in Africa. His position gave him access to so much intelligence, but he had very little ability to disclose it. He had done what he could, but put in for a transfer to Berlin the first chance he could. He had no desire to serve the remainder of the war without a strategic foothold.

"Father," he said, fighting the sting of tears in his eyes, "I am so happy to be back on this continent."

Quietly, sincerely, Karl hugged him and replied in his ear, "The Americans are officially involved now. Keep praying."

"It's all I can do." He gestured toward the restaurant. "Shall we get something to eat?"

As the two men dined on eggs, cabbage, and potatoes, they talked like a German father and son would as they took a respite from the war. They discussed promotions and mutual acquaintances and the coming winter, never once giving any waiter or fellow diner a reason to think that something else might be discussed under the surface.

Later, in Karl's room, sitting next to the cold and dark fireplace, they discussed the real business at hand. As they talked, Leo stared into the empty hole as if he could see the cheery flames licking the logs in his father's hunting cabin high in the mountains of Oregon. "Is there any way you can get me back into France?" Leo took a sip of his now cold tea.

"Everything in France is shifted. Praetorian has been reassigned. Your mother's Virtues team is scattered about, no longer together. What could you do in France?"

"You act like my mission relied on the team from Britain. You and I both know my job was a lone-wolf kind of duty. I ended up embroiled in the prison escape, but I can go back to my original mission working covertly with the Black Orchestra and the Resistance."

Karl nodded. "I agree. I just needed you to understand that any possible familiar support is long removed. There's a position in France. It will be a valuable duty assignment."

"How so?"

His father stood and walked over to where he'd set his briefcase on the bed. He opened it, then opened a secret compartment within it and pulled out a file folder. "Remember the photos you took of the men inside that cabin the night you were wounded?"

How could he forget the night he'd been shot? "Of course. Yes."

"We've identified the officers in them." Leo took the offered folder and opened it. It contained two pages, each with one of his photos attached to it with a paper clip. "Colonel Fischer there is in need of a clerk and you're coming to him highly recommended." He sat back down and poured more tea into his cup. "You will infiltrate the organization that almost took down our resistance network and very nearly captured Praetorian in the process."

Leo smiled, feeling ready to get back to the work for which he'd trained most of his life. "I will not let you down."

"You, my son, never have." He lifted his cup. "May God go before you."

They sat in companionable silence for a while, each to their own thoughts, until Leo asked, "What are you doing when this is over?"

"Doing?"

"Where will you go? What will you do?"

Karl sat back and stared at his son. "I will go and get your mother and we will finally make a life together. Just the two of us for as long as God grants us life on this earth."

"She may not like leaving England."

Karl swallowed a sip and said, "I could not care much less where we live as long as it is together. But she has ties back in Oregon and I have family in British Columbia. We'll likely end up there, again."

After a few breaths, his father asked, "And what might your plans be, Leo? This war is winding down and our side is likely going to win despite Montgomery's best efforts to let Hitler win."

"That girl –" he didn't finish. His father's eyes sharpened.

"Temperance."

"I'd like to find her and ensure that she's okay."

His father laid a strong hand on Leo's shoulder and slowly squeezed then released him. "Then you must find her, son."

8 8 8 8

CHAPTER 9

Haysworth Estate, Great Britain: 1946

LEO nervously paced outside the tent where his mother and the remaining Virtues team had come to pay their respects to the family of Muriel Tolson, the Virtue code-named Prudence, who had died during the Valeurville Prison escape.

Somehow, his father had gotten word to his mother and his mother had made arrangements for him to join them today. He knew Marie Gilbert, whom he had known as Marie Perrin, sat just on the other side of the canvas wall from him. He wanted to reach through the material and hold her to him. But he reminded himself he must follow how she led with that, at least for now. Her brother, Edward, the agent previously code-named Abiel, had told him in very clear language of the emotional and spiritual trauma she'd endured along with her physical injuries.

What would seeing him do to her psychologically? Maybe this wasn't a good idea. Then again, if he never tried, he would never know.

Deciding he'd stalled long enough, and in doing so forced his mother to stall for him, he walked around the tent and came in through the open entrance. He could see dozens of empty tables and tuxedo clad waiters clearing the china and crystal from the luncheon. At the far end, he saw the table where the Virtues team and their companions dallied. As his eyes adjusted to the dim interior, he saw his mother cross the expanse toward him. When she reached him, she hugged him to her. "All will be well," she whispered, knowing as she had almost all along, his feelings for Marie.

She slipped her arm through his and turned to guide him fully into the tent and toward the table where all the Virtues sat. As soon as the sun behind him no longer shadowed his face, Matthew Aubertin stood and exclaimed, "I say!"

Leo grinned, shaking Matthew's hand. They had worked so closely and had developed an incredible bond of trust, both before the Valeurville escape and later in the war. It was so good to see him.

Doctor Betty Grimes, code-named Mercy, gasped. "Valor!" Leo smiled at her, wanting to spend some time with her to tell her how much he appreciated her risking her life to save his. However, he had other things on his mind right now and would look Doctor Grimes up another day. For now his attention was focused on the small beautiful woman wearing a brown dress and seated next to Virginia Benoit. She hadn't recognized him yet.

Charlene announced to the group, "Ladies, everyone, I'd like you to meet Leopold Schäfer." She paused and smiled. "Leo is my son."

As he watched recognition dawn in her eyes, Marie stood so suddenly that her chair fell over behind her. She put a hand to her heart. " What–"

He walked forward and took her hand. "Marie. It is so good to see you again. I cannot tell you how pleased I am to see you and to see you looking so well."

Marie's eyes shifted from him to Charlene and back to him, then she pulled her hand away and turned and looked directly at her brother. "Edward? Was I not clear?"

Leo felt his stomach sink. Marie had known he wanted to see her but had clearly told Edward that she didn't want to see him. How did he respond to that?

Before he could respond, Edward stood and put his arm over her shoulders. "You need to listen to him."

"You don't know what he was."

Charlene answered, "Leo was under deep cover in Valeurville."

She took a step back and met Leo's eyes. "You were in charge there. You let them --"

He didn't interrupt her because he thought she might need to voice some of the horrors she endured. However, she quit speaking and rubbed her arms as if experiencing a sudden chill. After waiting two or three seconds, he replied, "Actually, when you were arrested, I tried to get there to stop it all, but I was physically unable."

Betty interjected, "Aye, he's telling you the truth. He nearly bled to death trying to get to you."

Leo picked up Marie's chair and invited her to sit down. As he did, he saw his mother gesturing for the other people in the tent to silently leave. He looked directly at Edward, who appeared to hesitate before he put his hat on his head and walked out of the tent. Leo pulled a chair up and sat, his knees nearly brushing hers. "As soon as I was able to walk, I left. Mercy was quite angry with me and taught me a few choice words in Gaelic."

"Mercy?" Marie whispered as tears filled her eyes. "I remember now. You mentioned her when I was sick." She cleared her throat and her face lost a bit of the harsh panic he'd seen before. "Why didn't you say something to me?"

"I desperately wanted to. I wanted to reassure you so that you wouldn't be so afraid, but, I couldn't risk you revealing something in your delirium." The group had left them alone in the tent. Even the waiters had quit clearing the tables. "I wanted to help you escape and come back to Britain with you, but I was turned down. My position was too important for the war effort."

Marie gripped her fingers together so hard that her knuckles turned white. "I don't understand --"

Leo smiled. He had spent years behind enemy lines, seeing things, doing things, and living things that he relived in nightmares. He felt like half a human being right now, but for some reason he knew in his heart that Marie was his other half. He so wanted to be whole again.

However, his face was her memory of that prison cell. Perhaps talking to him out in the open air would help. "Can we walk? The gardens here are beautiful. I've spent the morning in them."

She followed him across the tent, but crossed her arms under her breasts as if to make clear that a touch from him would be unwelcome. He understood, all too well, the repercussions of emotions brought about by living in such intense conditions for so long. He thought he might do better to start at the beginning.

"Much like Ruth Aubertin and her brothers, I was raised for my wartime position. My parents entered a deep cover assignment in Germany in 1915, and I was born there in 1918. Even at the end of the war, their covers remained firmly established, so when the opportunity came again to infiltrate Hitler's government, we took it. I was placed in officer training, my father went back to Berlin, and we hired a woman to pose as my mother and write letters from Oregon, freeing my mother to operate incognito in London."

Marie so spoke quietly he almost didn't hear her. "It's so hard to tie you and Colonel Radden together. We hold her in such high esteem. She did so much for us." They stepped out into the sunlight and started walking toward the rose gardens. "Thinking about her as a wife and mother doesn't really fit in my mind."

Leo thought maybe he should reinforce his identity to her. "Her name is actually Charlene Schäfer. Like me. Radden was her maiden name used as a code name. We didn't want any hint of my father's ties to the British government getting back to Berlin and putting him, or me, at risk."

They walked in silence for a moment as they turned and walked along a row of rose bushes. Marie stopped and ran a finger over the petal of a yellow rose. "Did your father survive the war?"

"He did. He has spent several months testifying in trials and writing mountains of reports. We are looking forward to the true end so that we can all regain some semblance of normal life." He smiled and held his hands out, palms up, "Or maybe learn what it is to be normal. Our family has never had that. We've always been preparing." He looked at her face, lit by the bright sunlight, and watched the pain tighten her features. "Have you been able to discover what happened to your father?"

She shrugged and turned, walking slowly along the flowers. He fell in step beside her. "He was tried and found guilty of helping Jewish children escape. They intended to force him to name all those who helped, which was most of our village, but he refused to give any names. He died of a heart attack in his holding cell." Her accent thickened as she spoke and emotion clouded her words. Unexpectedly, she stopped and turned to face him. "I guess we are supposed to take comfort in the fact that he did not have to go to a concentration camp." A tear slipped out of her eye and slid down her cheek. "Did you know about the camps?"

He could hear the accusation in her voice. Images flashed through his mind – things he'd seen and could never unsee, events that had happened for which he'd had no control. "I knew about a lot of terrible things. I reported everything the second I could. We worked as fast as we could to end the war. Every second people like my father and me lived and worked among the enemy was a second in which we stood a chance at being caught and sent to one of those camps ourselves. Much like your family, it was a high risk we faced in helping others."

She did not reply to that, but her face softened. He continued with his story. "My mother briefed me on her team. I had full dossiers on each of you. I knew your name. I knew your brother Edward. I knew your father had been arrested and you escaped in the dead of night. I knew what you looked like. But none of that prepared me for the first time we met in your room."

She glanced up at him, surprise lighting her face. "Prepared you for what?"

"For the way I was inexorably drawn to you. I was there to make contact. But for some reason I wanted to scoop you up and hide you away in safety."

The smile that crossed her face was a little sad. "If only you had." They stopped at the end of the row of rose bushes. She gestured at a bench and sat down without speaking.

After several seconds he said, "Marie --"

She interrupted him. "You warned me, didn't you?"

He thought back through the years and realized her reference. "Yes. I knew we were going to arrest the farmer. You had to get your equipment out of your room at the boarding house."

After another long silence she spoke again, very quietly, "What did Mercy, I mean Betty, mean? How did you almost die?"

"Right after they arrested the farmer, I was on a mission with the Resistance. I was shot. Mercy patched me up and forced me to recuperate on a cot in a barn when the news came in that you'd been arrested. I got out of bed and she scolded me, told me how dangerous it was, but I couldn't let you --" He stopped, remembering her battered body. "My stitches ripped and I almost bled out. She had to do surgery again and give me some blood. It was three more days before I was able to get to you."

He told her about his conversation with Captain Neumann and how he became her caretaker. "I wanted to tell you who I was so that you wouldn't be so afraid. I was hoping the Bible I gave you would be clue enough."

They sat in silence for several moments before she spoke. "I have a hard time remembering a lot of the time I spent there. But I remember the conversations we had."

On a frustrated release of breath he said, "If I'd been stronger, I might have been more help to you. For days, though, I had to function like I was healthy and I was just hurt and exhausted."

She surprised them both by reaching out and putting a hand on his. "Thank you for protecting me."

He gently placed his hand on top of hers, sandwiching her hand between both of his. "Marie –" He closed his eyes and sighed. When he opened them again, he found her looking at their joined hands. "Can I show you something?"

She cleared her throat and licked her lips as she pulled her hand away. "Of course."

As he unfastened his watch from his left wrist, his hand fumbled a bit from nervousness. Within seconds, he had dismantled the back of the watch and handed her the backing, the inside facing up. When she saw it, she gasped.

"That's my photo. From my false identification papers!" Her eyes searched his as if trying to answer a question. "Why?"

"Marie, at some point in time between you sewing a button on my uniform pants and Edward taking your sick and broken body from my arms, I fell in love with you." He reached forward and took the watch backing from her fingers and began re-assembling the device. "I hid your picture in my watch because I could not be caught with it, but I didn't want to let go of that last piece of you. All through the rest of the war, I prayed for you daily. The last year has been the hardest because Edward was trying to make sure you were ready to see me before he would allow it."

Her eyes frantically searched his face. "In love with me?"

A small smile crossed his face. "Yes." He held his hand out and to his surprise, she placed hers in it. He stood, pulling her up with him. "I understand what kind of memories I inspire. And I know you've suffered these last few years. What you had to endure would have broken most men, and some things just never go away." He reached down and took her other hand, facing her fully. "But I would very much like permission to see you and spend time with you, in hopes that one day you might return my feelings."

He almost held his breath as she studied his face, clearly trying to process his words. When she looked away, looked down at their joined hands, he felt his heart start to crack. Finally, she looked up at him again. "I think, Leo, that I should like to give that a try."

The End

WHILE all of the characters in my *Virtues and Valor* series are fictional, each main character was inspired by a true heroine or hero in World War II. Along with the inspiration of the characters, all of the figures on the covers of the books are true heroes and heroines of that war.

On the cover of this book is a photograph of Werner Karl von Haeften. An attorney by trade, after receiving a debilitating injury on the front lines, Werner worked as adjutant to Colonel Claus von Stauffenberg. On July 20, 1944, Werner accompanied von Stauffenberg to the military high command of the *Wehrmacht* near Rastenburg, East Prussia. There, von Stauffenberg planted a suitcase bomb that should have killed Adolf Hitler -- who was saved by heavy wooden table leg between him and the bomb. Not knowing Hitler had survived, Claus and Werner returned to Berlin and attempted to launch a *coup d'état*, which failed. After a mock trial, Claus and Werner were ordered shot to death by firing squad that very night.

One witness claimed that Werner stepped in front of von Stauffenberg and took the first round of bullets intended for him in a final show of support for his commander. Later in the war, Werner's brother was also executed for his part in the attempted assassination of Hitler.

The inspiration for my fictional character Leopold Schäfer came from the remarkable story of courage and conviction of Medal of Honor recipient Fred Mayer.

Friedreich "Fred" Mayer was born to a Jewish family on October 28, 1921, in Freiburg im Breisgau, Baden, Germany. His father had served in the Imperial German Army during the First World War, and had received the Iron Cross Second Class for gallantry during the Battle of Verdun.

Despite the anti-Semitism in Europe in the mid-30's, Fred's father hoped that his distinguished military service would protect his family. However, the hatred grew and spread, and in 1938, he reluctantly moved his family to New York.

Shortly after the attack on Pearl Harbor, Fred enlisted in the United States Army. During a training exercise, he crossed the pretend enemy line and captured several officers, including a one-star general. The general accused him of breaking the rules, but Fred said, "War is not fair. The rules of war are to win."

Fred spoke fluent German, French, Spanish, and English. Because of his military training, his language skills, and his familiarity with the European culture, he was recruited by the Office of Strategic Services (OSS). One of his fellow students at OSS training was Hans Wynberg, who had emigrated from the Netherlands and was also a Jew whose parents and younger brother had been captured by the Nazis and sent to Auschwitz concentration camp in Poland from which they never returned.

On February 29, 1945, Fred, Hans, and Franz Weber, a former Austrian *Wehrmacht* officer, parachuted onto a frozen lake found between two mountain peaks. They jumped in the dark and landed on the ridge of a glacier with a 10,000 feet elevation. After walking down the mountain in waist-deep snow, their mission was to scout "the heavily fortified area of Austria's 'Alpine Redoubt' in 'Operation Greenup'."

Fred posed as a German Army officer and stayed in the officers' barracks in Innsbruck for several months. Hans served as his radio operator and transmitted the information collected by Fred. After several months, Fred changed his cover from German officer to French electrician who claimed to be fleeing from the advancing Soviet forces.

When the Gestapo arrested a black market racketeer, he gave Fred up as a spy. They arrested him and spent hours heinously torturing him trying to get the name and location of his radio operator. Fred would only speak French the entire interrogation and refused to give up Hans. Eventually, he admitted to being an American but insisted that he was working alone and still refused to identify his radio operator.

At the same location, another American spy named Hermann Matull was being interrogated. They showed him a photograph of Fred's beaten face and asked Hermann to identify him. Matull pretended Fred was a big shot in the American chain of command and that the advancing Americans would take retribution on any German who harmed him.

The local Nazi party leader, Franz Hofer, believed that German defeat was inevitable. He wanted to surrender to the Americans rather than the Soviets. He heard that Fred was a "big shot" in the American army and had him brought to him. He hosted a dinner party with Fred and the German ambassador to Mussolini's government in Italy, Rudolph Rahn, to discuss the German surrender. Rahn delivered a message to the OSS. His message read, "Fred Mayer reports he is in Gestapo hands but cabled 'Don't worry about me, I'm really not bad off'," Which amazed the OSS leaders because Fred was a Jew.

On May 3, 1945, the American 103rd Infantry Division approached Innsbruck. The intelligence officer of the division stopped an approaching car with the occupants waving a white banner made out of a bed sheet. Fred introduced himself as Lieutenant Mayer of the OSS, and explained that he had a German officer ready to surrender.

The German troops in Innsbruck surrendered to a mere sergeant -- a Jewish immigrant from Germany!

The United States Army awarded Fred the Legion of Merit and a Purple Heart. Due to the diligent work of West Virginia Secretary of State Natalie Tennant, on March 18, 2014, Fred Mayer received the Medal of Honor. At the time of this publication, Fred Mayer is still living and resides in West Virginia.

౹౹౹౹

SUGGESTED questions for a discussion group surrounding *Valor's Vigil*, part 8 of the *Virtues and Valor* series.

While the characters and situations in the *Virtues and Valor* series are fictional, I pray that these extended parables will help readers come to a better understanding of truth. Please prayerfully consider the questions that follow, consult scripture, and pray upon your conclusions. May the Lord of the universe richly bless you.

᥊᥊᥊᥊

Charlene and Karl agree to marry the day they met. In their conversation, they discuss the Biblical idea of marriage and love.

1. Do you think it's unreasonable to have such a conversation so soon after meeting?

It's made clear in the story that Karl and Charlene loved each other very much and had a high regard for each other.

2. Do you think that is due to some unnamed force of "nature" or "biology", or do you think they took their wedding vows seriously and chose to follow God's Biblical design for marriage, joining in a holy state of matrimony?

3. In this culture of easy divorce, broken families, single parenting, and counterfeit marriage, do you think that the devotion to a Biblical marriage can help stop the tide of the culture? Do you think that the Biblical model for marriage is something that can even realistically be applied today?

In his position, Leopold Schäfer has to terrorize local citizens, arrest them, and often oversee their interrogation.

4. Do you think that even though a "greater good" came into play, he should have done more to help the citizens of Valeurville?

5. What do you think it did to his heart and soul to be an officer serving in the enemy's armed forces?

While helping Faith and her copilot steal an enemy airplane, Leo shoots the Nazi noncommissioned officer with him "in the back," killing him. In so doing he secures the success of the mission without blowing his cover, and his actions certainly save Allied lives. In previous books in this series, we addressed the issues of theft and of lying for the sake of maintaining the cover of Allied spies. Now, we're discussing the intentional slaying of the sergeant who preemptively arrested TEMPERANCE, and beat her nearly to death.

6. Is killing ever justified? Do you believe that killing this man was equally justified as an act of war, just as the lying or theft under the guise of espionage?

7. Do you believe that God sees a difference between killing to accomplish a wartime goal and killing for personal

reasons?

8. Do you believe Leo *was* justified in the killing of the sergeant in the middle of this war zone in a "kill or be killed" scenario? If not, was there something else he could have done instead?

When Leo and Marie finally meet again after the end of the war, she initially reacted with anger over Leo's part in her ordeal.

9. Do you think that she is justified in her anger that he should have done something more to help her?

When Marie asks Leo if he knew about the concentration camps, it was with an implied tone that he should have done something more than he did.

10. Do you think that those who worked in secret to end the war should have risked their lives and covers to try to make changes, or do you think that it was better to maintain cover stories and continue in the art of espionage to help aid a more rapid end to the war?

British (and Scottish) words and phrases

a lot of bottle – (slang) fearless; a tremendous amount of courage

Anno – (Scottish) I know.

bairn – (Scottish) young child or babe; toddler

bampot – clumsy idiot. Typically used in an endearing or amusing way whenever some bumbling is witnessed; as when someone accidentally spills a drink, experiences a harmless trip in his or her step, or crash lands two airplanes in a single day. An American synonym might be *goofball*.

barmy – idiotic. Usually said in a good-natured way. Etymology is murky. The word may derive from the fact that there was once a psychiatric hospital in a place called *Barming*, near Maidstone in Kent, England. It may also have derived from an Old English word for yeast, "*barm*," intended to imply that the brain is fermenting. An American synonym might be *goofy*.

Belt up – (slang) stop talking; shut up

blether – (Scottish) babble; talking nonsense

bodge – (slang) Do a quick and dirty job of it. Make it look good for the next day or two and if it falls down after that - hey, well, we only bodged it!

cheeky – impudent or irreverent, typically used in an amusing or ironic way

chiel – Scottish for dear or darling

chin wag – (slang) to have a chat or to make small talk

Chomh tiubh le balla brÃce – (Gaelic) literally: *Thick as a brick*. Meaning, stupid or foolish.

codswollop – (slang) a load of nonsense; a bunch of baloney *daft* – (Scottish) silly

dear – (slang) something valuable, precious, or expensive

dunderheaded – (Scottish) foolish, thoughtless, idiotic

flat – an apartment

give us a bell – call me on the telephone

glaikit – (Scottish) foolish, daft

halesome – (Scottish) nutritious

haver – (Scottish) silly talk, talking nonsense (stap yer *haverin'*)

horses for courses – (cliché) an American might say, "To each his own" or "different strokes for different folks." It essentially means that different people have different roles in life.

jihadist – among Muslims, a *jihad* is a constant, sanctioned, and holy war against unbelievers similar to a *fatwa*. A *jihadist* or *jihadi* is a soldier or supplicant in such a war.

keek – (Scottish) to take a peek, to look at, to glimpse (*cf Dutch kijk*)

ken – (Scottish) know, understand. E.g.: *D'ya ken that 2 and 2 makes 4?*

kip – (Scottish) to sleep or to nap

loaby – (Scottish) hallway, lobby, passageway

lecky – (Scottish) electricity; often used in reference to bills (she didn't pay her *lecky* this month)

lorries – a *lorry* is the British word for a large, heavy motor vehicle for transporting goods or troops; Americans would say a truck.

magic –(Scottish) great, excellent, wonderful. Often used sarcastically.

Marm – (slang) Cockney slang version of "Ma'am" short for the more formal Madam from the French *Madame*

mebbe – (Scottish) maybe, perhaps, possibly

nowt – nothing (just as *owt* is anything) Also, *nuttin*.

nuttin – nothing. Also, *nowt*.

owt – anything (just as *nowt* is nothing)

pate – archaic for skull; usually refers to the hairline area of the head

Pip pip – (old slang) a popular and sweet way Britons said good-bye in the 1940s and 1950s. No longer used today.

Posh – The most expensive cabins used by the upper class on early voyages from England to India were Port side on the way Out and Starboard on the way Home. Posh means opulent, high class, or first class.

row – (rhymes with cow, not low) an argument, debate, altercation, or fight

rùnag – (Scottish Gaelic: Noun *f*) someone who is loved

seeing the elephant – (slang) As early as 1590, the English used the idiom to "see the lions." This referred to the Tower of London which is thought to have been one of the world's oldest zoos and in which the monarchs kept a menagerie of animals including several types of large cats. Travelers and visitors were ever hopeful for a glimpse of the animals, especially the lion, which was the living emblem of the king of England. Regardless of what side one took, the phrase was used by both the British and Continental armies during the American Revolution to describe the experience of combat. Thought to be a derivative phrase, "seeing the elephant" is an American idiom, very popular in the mid to late 19th century and very often repeated in literature describing experiences in the Mexican-American War, the Texas Santa Fe Expedition, the American Civil War, the 1849 Gold Rush, the Westward Expansion Trails and -- of course -- the first World War. Seeing the mythical elephant was an extremely popular way of expressing any overwhelmingly emotional experience, and especially the experience of combat. Sir Percy, a huge fan of the popular American film star Clark Gable – a well known firearms and hunting enthusiast in his own right – is likely the reason for Percy's use of the American phrase over the British phrase. After the war, Gable made a film centered around an elephant hunt.

set on sixes and sevens – British phrase meaning a state of complete confusion. The idiom likely came from a complicated dice game called "hazard" in which sixes and sevens were considered the riskiest numbers to shoot for (to "set on"), and those who tried for them were considered careless or confused. Similar American idioms might be "situation normal: all fouled up" often abbreviated to SNAFU, first uttered in 1942.

sook – (Scottish) big softie (ya wee sook)

Sten submachine-gun – also called the Sten gun, sputter gun, or grease gun, this British submachine gun was used extensively by British and Allied resistance forces throughout World War II and by other forces afterward. Due to it's light weight, shortened length, few parts, and relatively simple design, it was an ideal weapon for use by guerilla forces.

strop – (slang) to strop, to feel stroppy, or to get one's "strop on" means to sulk or have a "pity party"

suss – to figure out by acts of investigation, reasoning, deduction, logic, and intuition. To solve a puzzle or decipher.

swotting – to swot is to diligently study with a great deal of focus and concentration.

taking the biscuit – (slang) If something (or someone) really *takes the biscuit*, it means that person or thing wins, is the best, or comes out on top. An equivalent American term would be to say something (or someone) really "takes the cake."

throw a spanner in the works – (slang) A spanner is another word for a wrench. This is an expression meaning to wreck or ruin something by an act of intentional or unintended sabotage.

Tommies – (slang) also, Tom, Tommy or Thomas Atkins, meaning any common soldier in the British Army. It can be used as a term of reference, or as a form of address. The American equivelant is Joe, Joe Tentpeg, or G.I. Joe.

Trent Park – a posh POW installation exclusively reserved for high ranking Axis officers. The entire prison was bugged in every corner and about a third of the prisoners were British Intelligence officers in disguise.

wee – tiny or very small

Whinge – (slang) to whine. To be a whiner.

winding me up – (British) playing a prank or a practical joke; good natured teasing

French words and phrases

au revoir – literally, until we meet again. A salutation meaning good-bye or farewell.

bonjour – literally, good day. It is a greeting or salutation.

chacun à son goût – also, *à chacun son goût*. literally, "everyone to his taste." This popular French cliché implies the same as the English expression, *to each his own*.

Chic alors! – Literally "how chic" meaning excellent or wonderful. An expression of joyous approval.

en français – in French; as in *Parlez en français* or "Speak in French"

en route – either *on the way to* or *traveling from* somewhere.

Est-ce vrai? Qu'est-ce que vous faites ici? – Is that so? What are you doing here?

fille bien-aimée – daughter who is adored: beloved daughter

garçons – boys

je sais – I know.

Madame – a married woman

Mademoiselle – an unmarried woman

merci – thanks/thank you, often expressed as *merci beaucoup* or thanks a lot.

mère – mother

Monsieur – an honorific reserved for men, equivalent to mister or sir

naïveté – lack of experience, wisdom, or judgment; innocence or lack of sophistication.

Où avez-vous de deux venez? – here did you two come from?

Oui – Yes

Oui, je suis Marcel Bernard – Yes, I am Marcel Bernard

soirée – a party or reception held in the evening.

s'il vous plaît – literally, if you please, meaning please.

toilettes – lavatory, toilets, water closet.

Vous êtes Monsieur Marcel Bernard – You are Mr. Marcel Bernard

Hebrew and Yiddish words and phrases

Be'vakasha – please

Kol tuv – all the best

Lo! – No!

phylacteries – a small leather box containing Hebrew texts on vellum, worn by Jewish men at morning prayer as a reminder to keep the law.

Shalom – literally "peace", this is the Jewish greeting or salutation.

tochter – daughter

Yah – a shortened form of *YHVH* (Jehovah) or *YHWH* (Yahweh). This name occurs about 50 times in the Tanakh and is particularly stressed in Psalm 68:4. The name *YAH* is also found in the construct word "hallelu-*YAH*," which means "you [pl.] praise the LORD," as well as in many Biblical proper names (e.g., *Eliyahu*).

German words and phrases

Außenbeleuchtung – exterior light

Balkenkreuz – The straight-armed *Balkenkreuz* was the emblem of the World War II *Wehrmacht*. The design atop the wings of aircraft and vehicles varied slightly to the design used on the sides of the fuselage or vehicle and beneath the wings.

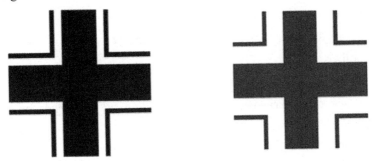

Upper wing (LEFT) and side and underwing (RIGHT) Balkenkreuz

Beantworte die Fragen – Answer the Question

Blitz – *Blitzkrieg* or "Lightning War." On the first of July in 1940, the freshly bloodied *Luftwaffe* capitalized on successful bombing raids against Poland and Holland, dropping the first bombs on England. The bombing would escalate into the *Blitzkrieg*, and between 7 September 1940 and 21 May 1941 there were almost daily (or nightly) major aerial raids conducted against 16 British cities. The attacks resulted in more than 100 tonnes of high explosives being dropped on mostly civilian targets in England.

Danke – Thanks (informal expression of gratitude)

Danke schön – Thank you (more formal)

Durchsuchen den raum – search this space (room)

Flugbenzin -- literally "flying fuel" meaning aircraft fuel

Fräu – a married woman

Fräulein – an unmarried woman

Führer – also *Fuehrer* (when the umlaut ü is not available) from *Führer und Reichskanzler* (meaning Chancellor) is the German title meaning leader or guide now most associated with Chancellor Adolf Hitler

Halt, oder ich schießen – Stop or else I will shoot.

Hauptmann — see *Kapitän*

Heil Hitler – The Nazi salute or Hitler salute was a gesture of greeting in Nazi Germany. Usually, the person offering the salute would say *"Heil Hitler!", "Heil, mein Führer!"*

Herr — an honorific reserved for men, equivalent to mister or sir

Ich bin Jude! – I am a Jew.

Ich danke Ihnen – I Thank YOU (very formal)

Ja – informal shortened version of the more formal *jawohl*, meaning yes or affirmative. *Ja* is informal similar to American "yeah"

Jawohl – formal word meaning yes or affirmative, often shortened to *Ja*.

Kapitän – company grade, a German Army Captain is equivalent to an O-3 and commands at the company level or serves on junior staff. Sometimes informally referred to as the *Hauptmann* or "top man" depending upon the military branch.

Leutnant – the lowest ranking commissioned officer in the German Army, equivalent to an O-1 the Second Lieutenant supervises enlisted ranks, technicians, and outranks cadets and ensigns. Often in charge of a platoon.

Mache schnell! Suche das Zimmer. Suche überall. – Make haste. Search the room. Search everything.

nicht sehr gut – meaning, not very good. Faith mixes this with English to say she did *"nicht* so *gut"* in her German Language class in school.

Nicht Sprechen sie Deutsch – I do not speak German

Oberleutnant – a senior or First Lieutenant, equivalent to an O-2, often in charge of the junior officers who were platoon leaders and sometimes company commanders.

Oberst – the Field grade German Army Colonel is equivalent to an O-6 and commands at the battalion or brigade level and serves on senior staff. This is one rank below General officer.

Reichsmarks – the official currency of Germany from 1924 until 20 June 1948 and also of Austria from 1938 to 1945

Schutzstaffel — translated to Protection Squadron or defense corps, abbreviated SS and occasionally referred to as the Waffen SS, the *Schutzstaffel* was a major paramilitary organization under Adolf Hitler and the Nazi Party throughout his rise to power and the rise and fall of the Third Reich. In the hierarchy of the Nazi party, they were known as the "super" Nazis, each having sworn an oath of eternal loyalty to the Third Reich and its ideals. They wore distinctive uniforms and insignia to visually separate them as the "elite" Nazi fighting force. Their uniform emblems included the

SS Totenkopf which was a skull and bones "Death's head" emblem worn on both the soft headgear as well as elsewhere on the dress uniform, the stylized "SS" that was made to resemble twin lightning bolts, and the red armband sporting a black Nazi *Swastika* on a circle of white.

Seig heil – a victory salute used originally by Nazis at political rallies

swastika – an ancient symbol in the form of an equal-armed cross with each arm continued at a right angle, used (in clockwise form) as the emblem of Hitler's Nazi Party.

Unteroffizier – historically (since the 17th century) a sergeant, it is both a specific military rank, *"Korporal"*, as well as a collective term for non-commissioned officers of the German military.

Was ist das? – What is this?

Was machst du – literally, "What are you making" meaning what are you doing.

Wehrmacht – literally "War Makers" this is the designation for the regular German Armed Forces and its branches: *Heer* (Army), *Luftwaffe* (Air Force), and *Kriegsmarine* (Navy).

Wunderbar – Wonderful

Spanish words and phrases

hombre – a man

señorita – an unmarried woman

Period Vehicles

Ariès Berline – The Ariès was a French automobile manufactured by La Société des Automobile Ariès in Asnières-sur-Seine which produced about 20,000 vehicles between 1910 and 1937. The Berline model was a four seat sedan with wood paneled sides and a jump seat.

1932 Ariès Berline

Avro Anson 652 – The Avro Anson was a British twin-engine, multi-role aircraft that served with the Royal Air Force, Fleet Air Arm, Royal Canadian Air Force, and numerous other air forces before, during, and after the Second World War. It was configured to support multiple roles from reconnaissance to transportation to close air support for combat operations.

Developed from the Avro 652 airliner, British pilots often *incorrectly* referred to the Avro Anson as the Avro Anson 652, just as US servicemen *incorrectly* referred to a GPW Light Duty Truck as a "Jeep".

British Avro Mk I aka "Avro Anson 652"

Daimler-Benz G4 Staff Car – also called the Heavy Personnel Staff Car, German three-axle six-wheeled vehicle produced by Daimler-Benz for the *Wehrmacht* between 1934 and 1939. The cars were designed as a seven-seat touring car, or closed saloon, and were mainly used by the upper echelons of the Nazi regime in parades and inspections as they were deemed too expensive for general Army use. This was the preferred vehicle of Adolf Hitler and his cabinet members when making public appearances.

Hermann Göring appearing in a Daimler-Benz G4 Staff Car

Junkers JU-52 – nicknamed Iron Annie and *Tante Ju* meaning "Aunt Ju," the 52 was a German trimotor transport/cargo aircraft manufactured between 1932 and 1945. The aircraft was visually distinctive in that it had a propeller on each wing and one on the nose but even more visually distinctive by the *Doppelflügel* or "double wing" trailing edge control surfaces behind the wings. The Ju-52 saw military service during the 1930s and 1940s, primarily flying with the *Luftwaffe* as a troop and cargo transport and briefly as a medium bomber.

Nazi Luftwaffe Junkers JU-52

Kübelwagen – (literally translated as "bucket car", for its resemblance to a metal bathtub on wheels) The Volkswagen *Kübelwagen* was a light military vehicle designed by Ferdinand Porsche himself and built by Volkswagen during World War II for the exclusive use of the Nazi military (both *Wehrmacht* and *Waffen-SS*). Based heavily on the Volkswagen Beetle it was considerably more boxy in appearance.

Nazi *Kübelwagen* made for use by the Nazi land forces

Lagonda 1930 2-liter Weymann saloon – Lagonda built only 250 of these custom luxury convertible vehicles between 1926 and 1930. Before the second world war they were mainly owned by royalty or the very wealthy.

Lagonda 1934 4.5-liter M45 Sports Tourer – Lagonda built only 260 of these custom convertible sportsters between 1932 and 1934. These were the status symbols of the upper class before the *Blitz*.

Mercedes-Benz 170V four-door *Tourenwagen* – First presented to the public in 1936, more than 75,000 of these front engined 4-cylinder models were manufactured in Stuttgart, Germany between 1936 and 1939 for use as the all-purpose staff car.

Messerschmitt Bf 109 – Often incorrectly called the Me 109, the Bf 109 (Bf for *Bayerische Flugzeugwerke*) was designed in 1934 as a high-speed, short range interceptor. The aircraft utilized the most advanced aerodynamics of the time and embodied advanced design such as its all-metal monocoque construction, a closed canopy, retractable landing gear, and a liquid-cooled, inverted-V12 aero engine.

During the *Blitzkrieg*, the Bf 109 was the only single-engined fighter operated by the *Luftwaffe* until the appearance of the superior Focke-Wulf Fw 190. The Bf 109 remained in production from 1937 through 1945 in many different variants and sub-variants with a total of 33,984 airframes produced.

Nazi Luftwaffe configuration of the Messerschmitt Bf 109

North American Na-16 — Originally developed in the early 1930s, the North American Aviation NA-16 was the first trainer aircraft built by North American Aviation, Inc. and was the beginning of a long line of closely related North American trainer aircraft that would eventually number more than 17,000 examples including the BT-9, NJ-1, Harvard I, NA-57, and SK-14 to name a few.

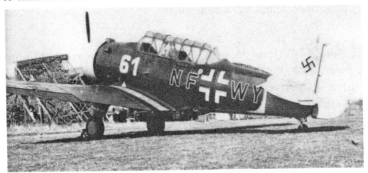

Nazi Luftwaffe pre-war configuration of the North American Na-57

This was a single engine three wheel aircraft with tandem seating in the most common configuration, although certain variants had up to four seats. It was widely used as a training aircraft by many countries, including the United States and Nazi Germany.

US Air Force post war configuration of the North American Na-16

Opel *Blitz* truck – Opel *Blitz* (German for "lightning") was the name given to various German light and middle-weight truck series built by the German Adam Opel AG automobile manufacturer between 1930 and 1975.

Spitfire – also called the Submarine Spitfire, one of the most formidable aircraft in history. had it's roots in a racing design which set records in 1929. Designed around a 12-cylinder liquid-cooled Rolls-Royce PV-12 engine (later dubbed the Merlin), the Spitfire first flew in March 1935. Due to its superb performance and flight characteristics, deliveries to operational Royal Air Force squadrons commenced in the summer of 1938.

British RAF configuration of the Submarine Spitfire

A more radical design than the Hawker Hurricane, the Spitfire had a stressed-skin aluminum structure and a graceful elliptical wing with a thin airfoil that, in combination with the Merlin's efficient two-stage supercharger, gave it exceptional performance at high altitudes. Faster than its formidable opponent the Bf 109 at altitudes above 15,000 feet and just as maneuverable, Spitfires were sent by preference to engage German fighters while the slower Hurricanes went for the bombers. In 1947 when production ceased, 20,334 Spitfires of all versions had been produced.

Rare Submarine Spitfire two-seater variant

Trippel SG-6 *Schwimkraftwagen* – Development of this amphibious vehicle began prior to 1939 at the Trippelwerke Hamburg Saar. Used by the Nazis in towns with ports and bodies of water, the vehicle mostly served as a land born light truck or troop transport.

Zundapp KS750 motorcycle (with or without sidecar) – Purpose built for the Nazi German military, the motorcycle had 10 speeds and topped out at 60mph. It was agile and able to handle very steep climbs and rough terrain with relative ease. It was often coupled with a *Steib* sidecar, the BW38 (*Beiwagen* 1938) and used extensively for courier runs and other missions to conserve fuel.

Zundapp KS750 motorcycle with *Steib* sidecar

CAST OF CHARACTERS

Part 1 Temperance's Trial:

MARIE GILBERT, codenamed TEMPERANCE, is recruited into an experimental all female cohort dubbed the Virtues, a collection of seven extraordinary women with highly specialized skills. Back in her home country of France, Marie clandestinely communicates vital intelligence directly back to Headquarters with a wireless radio, playing a deadly game of cat-and-mouse with the Nazis.

Part 2 Homeland's Hope:

Codenamed HOPE, famed performer VIRGINIA BENOIT performs for standing room only crowds in her adopted home of France. When the Nazis roll into Paris, she flees to Casablanca, taking the heart of an enemy General with her. She joins the Virtues team and uses her position, talent, and influence with the high ranking Axis officer to aid the Allied cause.

Part 3 Charity's Code:

DORTHY EWING, codenamed CHARITY, works on the home-front, receiving and sending messages to her team in France and coordinating a secret mission with her husband via coded letters. She intercepts a transmission alerting to her to a blown cover. The clock is ticking in a race to save a friend's life.

Part 4 A Parcel for Prudence:

Codenamed PRUDENCE, royal blooded MURIEL TOLSON speaks French like any native, allowing her to infiltrate Occupied France where she works as a courier; carrying messages, money, and sometimes people through the secret resistance network aiding the allies to accomplish very dangerous missions behind enemy lines.

Part 5 Grace's Ground War:

RUTH AUBERTIN, codenamed GRACE, is a highly trained multi-lingual soldier and expert with weapons, explosives, and hand-to-hand combat. Can her team pull off the mission of rescuing a compromised agent, or will too many variables crash together at the wrong time?

Part 6 Mission of Mercy:

Codenamed MERCY, Doctor BETTY GRIMES spends her days under cover as a Red Cross nurse in Occupied France and her nights providing medical care to injured members of the French Resistance. When Betty is sent to the local prison to see to a prisoner who has taken ill, her shock at treating a dear friend nearly blows her own cover. Betty needs to get her deathly ill patient well enough for the coming rescue operation to succeed.

Part 7 Flight of Faith:

Pilot HELEN MULBERRY, codenamed FAITH, flies between Britain and France transporting passengers, supplies, or performing reconnaissance. The Nazis guard their skies with vigor, and Helen learns to fly in combat, land in darkened fields with no lights, and how to evade the anti-aircraft fire. Shot down over France during the mission to rescue her fellow agent from the clutches of the Nazis, Helen must make her way through enemy territory with no language skills and somehow come through with a means to get her team back to Britain.

ABOUT THE AUTHOR

About the Author

HALLEE BRIDGEMAN is a best-selling Christian author who writes action-packed romantic suspense focusing on true to life characters facing real world problems.

An Army brat turned Floridian, Hallee finally settled in central Kentucky with her family so she could enjoy the beautiful changing seasons. She enjoys the roller-coaster ride thrills that life with a National Guard husband, a teenage daughter, and two elementary age sons delivers.

Her passion for cooking spurred her to launch a whole food, real food "Parody" cookbook series. In addition to nutritious, Biblically grounded recipes, readers will find that each cookbook also confronts some controversial aspect of secular pop culture.

Hallee loves coffee, campy action movies, and regular date nights with her husband. Above all else, she loves God with all her heart, soul, mind, and strength; has been redeemed by the blood of Christ; and relies on the presence of the Holy Spirit. She prays her work here on earth is a blessing to you and would love to hear from you.

Newsletter:	tinyurl.com/HalleeNews/
Author Site:	hallee.bridgemanfamily.com/
Homemaking:	www.halleethehomemaker.com/
Facebook:	www.facebook.com/pages/Hallee-Bridgeman/192799110825012
Twitter:	twitter.com/halleeb
Google+:	plus.google.com/105383805410764959843
Goodreads:	www.goodreads.com/author/show/5815249.Hallee_Bridgeman

PERSONAL NOTE

A Note from the Author...

I'M so glad that you chose to read all eight stories in the *Virtues and Valor* series. I pray that these stories blessed you.

I'd love to hear from you. Leave a comment online at Hallee Bridgeman, Novelist. Your feedback inspires me and keeps me writing.

http://hallee.bridgemanfamily.com

May God richly bless you,

HALLEE BRIDGEMAN

Find the latest information and connect with Hallee
at her website: http://hallee.bridgemanfamily.com/

FICTION BOOKS BY HALLEE

Virtues and Valor series:

Book 1: Temperance's Trial
Book 2: Homeland's Hope
Book 3: Charity's Code
Book 4: A Parcel for Prudence
Book 5: Grace's Ground War
Book 6: Mission of Mercy
Book 7: Fight of Faith
Book 7: Valor's Vigil

The Jewel Series:

Book 1: Sapphire Ice,
Book 1.5: Greater Than Rubies (novella inspired by The Jewel Series)
Book 2: Emerald Fire, book 2
Book 3: Topaz Heat, book 3
Christmas Diamond (Bonus novella inspired by Virtues and Valor Series)
Christmas Star Sapphire (novella inspired by The Jewel Series)

The Song of Suspense Series:

Book 1: A Melody for James
Book 2: An Aria for Nick
Book 3: A Carol for Kent
Book 4: A Harmony for Steve (Fall 2015)

PARODY COOKBOOKS BY HALLEE

Vol 1: Fifty Shades of Gravy, a Christian gets Saucy!
Vol 2: The Walking Bread, the Bread Will Rise
Vol 3: Iron Skillet Man, the Stark Truth about Pepper and Pots
Vol 4: Hallee Crockpotter & the Chamber of Sacred Ingredients (Fall 2015)

HALLEE ONLINE

BEFORE Hallee published great Christian fiction, she was a pretty famous blogger. Catch her online for great "whole food real food" recipes, helpful tips, and inspiration.

Hallee the Homemaker blog
www.halleethehomemaker.com/

Hallee Bridgeman, Novelist blog
www.bridgemanfamily.com/hallee/

NEWSLETTER

SIGN up for Hallee's monthly newsletter! Every newsletter recipient is automatically entered into a monthly giveaway! The real prize is you will never miss updates about upcoming releases, book signings, appearances, or other events.

Hallee News Letter
http://tinyurl.com/HalleeNews/

Made in the USA
Middletown, DE
29 November 2022

16263931R00331